Spawn of the Penitentiary

Spawn of the Penitentiary

by
Goron & Émile Gautier

translated, annotated and introduced by
Brian Stableford

A Black Coat Press Book

Thanks to Jean-Daniel Brèque.

English adaptation and introduction Copyright © 2013 by Brian Stableford.
Cover illustration Copyright © 2013 by Jean-Claude Claeys.

Visit our website at www.blackcoatpress.com

Introduction

Fleur de Bagne by Goron and Émile Gautier, here translated as *Spawn of the Penitentiary*, was originally published as a *feuilleton* serial in the Parisian newspaper *Le Journal* in 1901. It was reprinted the following year in book form by Ernest Flammarion as *Fleur de Bagne, roman contemporain*, in three volumes, each of which was given an individual title: *De Cayenne à la Place Vendôme, Pirates cosmopolites* and *Detectives et bandits scientifiques*. That version was reprinted in 1904, but the novel then dropped out of sight until Black Coat Press' French sister imprint, Rivière Blanche, produced a new edition edited by Jean-Daniel Brèque in 2012, each of the three volumes being augmented with a wealth of appendices relating their content to material from Goron's memoirs, Gautier's books and articles, and contemporary newspaper reports.

The original version of the novel followed up a long series of *feuilletons* published in *Le Journal* with Goron's signature, but the previous episodes had all been non-fictional, consisting of memoirs of his career in the police force, which had culminated in a seven-year stint as the head of the Sûreté from 1887-94. His full name was Marie-François Goron, but he only used his surname in his signature, because that seemed more befitting to his status as a policeman. He was not the first head of the Sûreté to write his memoirs, and was, in a sense, carrying forward a tradition originally begun half a century before by the fantasist Eugène Vidocq, whose almost-wholly-invented life story climaxed with an stint as the head of a special police unit, and which certainly contributed massively to the subsequent public image of the Sûreté, if it did not actually prompt the invention and shape the philosophy of the institution itself. All of Vidocq's works are, in essence, fiction, but he, too, went on from supposed memoirs to acknowledged novels—which were much less successful—and he, too, preferred to be known by his bare surname, as if he were a legendary figure (as, indeed, he became).

The first of Goron's *feuilletons*, which offered his memoirs in twelve parts, was reprinted in book form in four volumes, and proved so popular in both formats that the author must have been under considerable pressure to supply more—which he obligingly did, adding a further nine parts to his serial memoirs, subsequently reprinted in three further volumes. Eventually, however, he ran out of material that could be plausibly represented as autobiographical, so he took the natural next step, following time-honored tradition, and switched from narrativized accounts of "true crime" to crime fiction. Although that was a relatively short step, he evidently felt that some assistance was in order, and joined forces for the purpose of the new *feuilleton* with an old acquaintance who was now working as a scientific journalist, Émile Gautier. All his other novels were, however, written solo, including *Les Antres de Paris* [The Animal-Dens of Paris] (1901), whose publication while the *feuilleton* was running might imply that it had been written earlier.

Had they not known one another in youth in their native town of Rennes, Goron and Émile Gautier would have seen an odd pairing, as Gautier was famous—or, rather, notorious—for having been on the wrong side of the law in the 1880s while Goron was working as a policeman. The two had, in fact, followed very different career paths since their overlapping childhood, although they cannot have been close friends then, as Goron, born in 1847, was more than five years older than Gautier, born in 1853. The latter was only twelve years old when Goron embarked on a military career in 1865, serving in Martinique and Algeria before being caught up in the Franco-Prussian War of 1870.

Goron rose through the ranks, serving as a *sous-officier* (the equivalent of a "non-commissioned officer" in the British army) in the marine infantry before being promoted to lieutenant, and then to captain, when he was relegated to the reserves after the war. He then went into the wholesale wine business for some years in his native town of Rennes, when he presumably renewed his acquaintance with Gautier, but traveled to South America in 1879 with the intention of becoming a serious colonist in the Central American region of Formosa. The vicissitudes of tropical life, however, prompted his return to France at the end of 1880, where he joined the Parisian police and, once again, rose through the ranks of the organization to become the most important active policeman in Paris. When he resigned as head of the Sûreté, he set up a private detective agency, which still exists, but he probably made far more money from his writing. That career was cut short when he returned to active service in 1914, and, although he did not die until 1933, he did not return to writing after the Great War, living quietly in retirement.

While Goron was serving in the marine infantry, Gautier completed his education and qualified as a lawyer, but did not practice, embarking on a career as a journalist instead. Heavily influenced by the socialist journalist Jules Vallès, who had been one of the leading members of the Paris Commune, and had then fled the country, Gautier became intimately associated with the development in France of the political theory of Anarchism, and was one of that movement's principal orators. In that capacity, he was inevitably seen as dangerous by the authorities, and he was arrested in Lyon in 1883 along with Pyotr Kropotkin, who had succeeded Mikhail Bakunin as the principal theorist and most high-profile advocate of Anarchism. Gautier was tried alongside Kropotkin, although neither had committed any criminal offence, under the provisions of a law passed in the wake of the Paris Commune, which proscribed membership of certain political institutions.

Gautier and Kropotkin were convicted and sentenced to five years imprisonment, but the judgment was widely, and rightly, considered to be outrageous, and a campaign immediately began to have them released, which was ultimately successful. Kropotkin then went to England, but when Gautier was pardoned in 1885, he returned to Paris and resumed his journalistic career; he published four books in that year, including *Propos anarchistes* [Anarchist Doctrines], which might well have been written in prison, following an age-old tradition. He also drew on his unfortunate experience in his most extensive work, *Le Monde des prisons* [The World of Prisons] (1889), but the book for which he remains most famous today is one he had written earlier, *Le Darwinisme social* (1880), which certainly popularized, if it did not actually coin, the term "social Darwinism."

Although Gautier did not abandon his Anarchist convictions, he ceased active campaigning on behalf of the movement and devoted himself primarily to his endeavors as a scientific journalist. Pyotr Kropotkin had been a scientist of some note, primarily noted for his work as a zoologist, evolutionary theorist and geographer—he had initially been alienated from his aristocratic family because they considered his interest in science unbefitting, before he became involved with anarchist politics—and one of the most prominent French anarchists, Élisée Reclus, had been one of the nation's leading geographers and geologists: a vocation that was not unduly hampered when he was permanently banished from France in the wake of the Commune. The fact that he was unable join Kropotkin and Gautier in Lyon in 1883 saved Reclus from being in the dock alongside them, but he was, in a sense, with them in spirit.

Reclus was continually honored in his absence by French scientific organizations annoyed by his exile, and his name was defiantly attached to the masthead of several scientific periodicals, including Louis Figuier's *La Science Illustrée*, for which Gautier did a good deal of work, including a novella for the magazine's regular *roman scientifique* feature. Before taking a hand in *Fleur de Bagne*, Gautier had been the editor for nearly a decade of *La Science Française*, a clone of *La Science Illustrée*, which also ran a fictional *feuilleton* feature in the 1890s. Several other leading anarchists also dabbled in the writing of speculative fiction, most prominently Louise Michel—who planned a six-volume futuristic epic celebrating the triumph of Anarchism throughout and beyond the Earth, but only managed to publish versions of its first two episodes, *Les Microbes humains* (1887)[1] and *Le Monde nouveau* (1888)[2]—and Jules Lermina, author of the satirical anarchist utopia "Mystère-Ville" (1904-05)[3]. Gautier's association with this nexus of activity was undoubtedly one of the factors influencing Goron's recruitment of his assistance in writing his own ultra-contemporary novel.

---

[1] tr. as *The Human Microbes*, Black Coat Press, ISBN 978-1-61227-116-3.
[2] tr. as *The New World*, Black Coat Press, ISBN 978-1-61227-117-0.
[3] tr. as *Mysteryville*, Black Coat Press, ISBN 978-1-935558-27-9.

Goron's position in the police force would have prevented him from campaigning openly for the release of men duly sentenced by a court—even one in Lyon—but he presumably put in a good word for his friend in private, and might have helped to win Gautier his pardon. He would have been well aware of the fact that there was a considerable difference between anarchists who campaigned politically for radical social reorganization and those dedicated to "propaganda by action," who wanted to prompt that reorganization by campaigns of political assassination, and who were primarily responsible for the popular image of anarchists as bomb-throwers—an image retained in satirical cartoons for a hundred years after the fad had ended. It is unlikely that Goron actually had much sympathy for Gautier's anarchist ideals, but he was at least prepared to tolerate them, and *Fleur de Bagne* is a deeply ambivalent text in political terms, showing considerable sympathy not only for the ideals espoused by the anarchist scientist Sokoloff, whose character includes some deliberate echoes of Kropotkin, but also treating his more violently-inclined intellectual kin with a certain respect. The villain at the heart of the plot cruelly exploits his anarchist acquaintances, pretending loyalty to their cause while betraying them all along the line.

The ambivalence of the text is not restricted to its exceptional political complexion. In terms of its method and content, *Fleur de Bagne* is a curious hybrid of the old and the new. As a *feuilleton* serial, it is deliberately reminiscent in its form and method of such sprawling classics of the genre as Alexandre Dumas' *Le Comte de Monte Cristo* (1844-5; tr. as *The Count of Monte Cristo*) and Paul Féval's *Jean Diable* (1862)[4]. It is very long, and was clearly made up by the authors as they went along, with only the vaguest idea in mind as to how they might eventually get to the inevitable end-point of their story. It is virtually devoid of plot, wandering around as if completely lost, continually introducing improvisations to move the story along and sometimes forgetting all about them thereafter. Given that it has two authors, the impression it occasionally gives that the author of the current chapter has not read the previous one might be accurate, but such a lack of continuity and coherency is typical of *feuilleton* fiction, which cannot make heavy demands on readers in terms of what they can be expected to remember from previous episodes. What is important in such fiction is that what is happening on the present page should be graspable and, if possible, gripping, and it is hardly surprising that the latter requirement sometimes falters as the writers procrastinate desperately until they can think of something else to do next.

On the other hand, the novel does attempt to be authentically groundbreaking in its modernity, examining the potential impact of developing technologies on both criminal activity and police detective work. Like all significant pioneering works, it suffers somewhat in modern eyes from the fact that most of

---

[4] tr. as *John Devil*, Black Coat Press, ISBN 978-1-932983-15-9.

its innovations in that respect have become standardized and sophisticated, in both fiction and reality, so that contemporary readers are bound to find it primitive, and rather quaint, but that should not prevent our appreciation of the heroism of the endeavor. Ironically, the novel was perhaps a little too up-to-date for its own good, in that some of its imaginative innovations were so close to the horizon of practicability that they had been overtaken in the real world in less than a decade. Had the authors been slightly less scrupulous in that regard, the novel would have had a longer shelf-life, and might not have dropped out of sight so completely.

As an item of crime fiction, *Fleur de Bagne* is undoubtedly weak, because rather than in spite of Goron's long experience in the Sûreté. Over the last century, the inexorable progress of melodramatic inflation has made fictional detectives and the master criminals they pursue increasingly ingenious, reaching extremes of complexity and cleverness that are positively bizarre. Without the example of that heritage to draw on, Goron and Gautier had little or no idea of how a master criminal might go about planning nefarious schemes, or how a scientifically sophisticated detective might go about penetrating and unpicking those schemes. The reader is, therefore, constantly assured that Gaston Rozen is a criminal genius, but whenever any of his plans is revealed in detail, he inevitably seems to modern eyes to be a woeful incompetent, all his successes emerging from sheer blind luck—and exactly the same is true of Monsieur Cardec, the head of the Sûreté who must bring him to justice. Cardec is at least honest enough in this respect to declare explicitly that the god of the police is chance, and that there is, in fact, very little the police can do, in practical terms, to make sure that criminals get their moral comeuppance, except to wait patiently for someone to volunteer the necessary information. Goron knew that, even if his emblematic precursor Vidocq and all the latter's glamorous fictitious descendants did not—or, at least, refused to admit it.

As an eccentric specimen of the *roman scientifique*, too, *Fleur de Bagne* is bound to seem a trifle lacking nowadays, partly because its exceedingly laborious build-up leaves the greater part of that element of the story to the final third of the text, but mainly because the authors backed some wrong horses in races that were already under starter's orders. They should not be judged too harshly on those grounds, however, as such flaws illustrate the inevitable precariousness and awkwardness of the genre, and if one can accept that it is the thought that counts rather than the precise nature of the gift, then *Fleur de Bagne* is certainly a story with its speculative heart in the right place. Everything that it attempts to do was more successfully accomplished by later works, but the fact that it attempts so much is rather remarkable, and deserves due credit. The novel is a landmark work in more ways than one, and it still has a certain quality of fascination when read with an informed retrospective eye.

This translation has been taken from the version of the Ernest Flammarion edition reproduced on the Bibliothèque Nationale's website *gallica*, but I also had the Rivière Blanche edition edited by Jean-Daniel Brèque available for reference, and found its supplementary material and footnotes useful in compiling my own commentary.

Brian Stableford

Part One
FROM CAYENNE TO THE PLACE VENDÔME

I. Train 53

At 4:25 a.m. train no. 53, from Paris to Le Havre, had just gone through Holbec and Blait station at top speed, heading for Beuzeville. In a first-class compartment, a passenger, its only occupant, was lying on the cushions, profoundly asleep. As it was winter and glacially cold, he was buried under two thick blankets, with his cap pulled down over his eyes. Above him, an overcoat, hanging by a thread, was swaying back and forth.

At the door to his right, the one opening on to the trackside, a head appeared, wearing a braided cap. After a rapid glance inside, the man in the braided cap opened the door, without making any noise, and came into the compartment.

He considered the sleeper attentively.

"Perfect," he murmured.

That reflection was motivated by the combination of circumstances, which was fortunate for him. The traveler was occupying the last compartment in the carriage, and in order to ensure his privacy he had used his overcoat to block the little window that served to look from one compartment into the next.

At that moment, the sleeper moved. One of the blankets draped over his shoulders slipped down to his knees. He caught it with a mechanical gesture and wrapped himself in it tightly; then, ensconcing himself against the window, he became still again. Almost immediately, a sonorous snore preceded by a deep sigh attested that he had not really woken up.

The newcomer had immediately hidden, pressing himself tightly against the banquette, his face flattened against the fabric.

"Oof!" he murmured. "What a scare! I was afraid..."

Reassured by the passenger's regular and noisy breathing, he took a handkerchief out of his pocket and folded it into quarters; then, taking out a little bottle, he emptied its contests on to the cloth. A slight odor of garlic spread through the compartment.

A second later, the handkerchief was abruptly applied to the face of the sleeper, who, after a violent start, fell back on the banquette, his limbs extended and his head limp, with a dull croak.

The other took his arm and shook him violently. He did not move; one might have thought that he was dead.

"That's the ticket! The boss's drug has done the trick. It's better than their filthy chloroform."

He lowered the window slightly, in order to let in cold air from outside and disperse the insidiously troubling odor that was floating around him.

"No danger that the fellow will wake up just yet—but I mustn't go to sleep myself; that would be lousy way to finish, and that blessed drug is strong! Let's get on with it—the boss told me that the effect of ethyl bromide only lasts for ten minutes."

Taking off his thick overcoat, he took a short stick, a sort of club akin to the truncheons carried by London policemen or the guardians of the peace directing traffic at intersections. He leaned over, taking another close look at the passenger, who was in a coma, almost breathless, his features frozen in a spasmodic grimace.

"Blind and deaf," he said, with an evil smile, moving the felt cap to cover the eyes and ears with his fingertip. He won't suffer—won't even feel a thing. One has to be humane in this wicked world."

He stood up, moved back, lifted his club and delivered a mighty blow to the sleeper's head.

The unfortunate twitched, but did not cry out: a dull groan, and that was all.

"Ah," said the man, with a sigh of satisfaction. "I haven't lost the old knack..."

Without wasting any time, he removed the blankets from the man he had just killed. He unbuttoned his jacket, searched his pockets, and took out a wallet. By the light of the lamp he examined the wallet's contents. There were numerous documents and three hundred-franc bills.

The murderer reached out as if to take the bills, but changed his mind and pushed them back into the wallet's interior pocket.

"No stupidity!" he murmured. "That's forbidden...although it's a great pity to lose what one's only just picked up. Since those are the orders, though..."

Passing on to the papers, he examined them carefully without getting them out of order. He ended up discovering one that was tucked protectively into the other pocket, secured to the morocco leather by a pin. That had to be the one he was looking for, because he uttered a sigh of satisfaction. He stuffed it into his pocket, replaced the wallet in his victim's pocket, and set about buttoning up the jacket.

At that moment, however, a characteristic grinding sound made him shiver. The brakes had been applied. The train was arriving at a station and was about to stop. The murder made haste to lower the little mobile blind over the lamp, which plunged the compartment into darkness.

He was just in time; the train came to a standstill.

"Beuzeville-Bréauté! Five minutes halt!" shouted the crewman responsible for informing the passengers.

There was a moment of terrible anxiety. Five minutes, during which a passenger might board the train or a guard might glance through the window or open the door!

The murderer pressed himself into the corner, his left hand on the door to the corridor and his right armed with his terrible cudgel, ready to strike down anyone who showed himself and then flee into the dark night—but all remained calm, and after an interval that seemed to last for centuries, he heard the stationmaster's whistle giving the signal to depart.

The bandit straightened up again, filling his oppressed lungs with air.

As soon as the train moved off, he finished buttoning the dead man's jacket. Then he opened the door to the outside, grabbed the cadaver around the waist and, after swinging it around, hurled it on to the trackside.

Everyone on the train was asleep. No one heard the sound of the body's fall, covered as it was by the rattle of the carriages.

The man raised the blind again and inspected the cushion. Not a single drop of blood had stained it. Thanks to the thick cap on the head, none had leaked out.

With a sigh of relief, the murderer got down on to the footplate and, leaving the door open, moved along the carriage.

Just as no one had heard anything, no one saw him. In any case, the braided cap would not have attracted attention; he would have been taken for an inspector making his round.

Having arrived at an empty third-class compartment, he opened the door, went in, got rid of his stick and his cap, which he wrapped in a newspaper, and took a soft cap out of his overcoat pocket, which he put on. Then he lit a cigarette and waited for the journey to end,

At five past five, train 53 drew into Le Havre station. Only five or six people were waiting for the train at that excessively early hour. There were, in any case, only a few passengers.

The murderer leapt down briskly from his carriage, handed his ticket to the guard and disappeared into the shadows of the streets.

One by one, the travelers emerged and the waiting-room empted. Only one young woman, about twenty-five years old, still remained, gazing at the deserted track.

When the guard closed the door she went over to him. "This is the Paris train, isn't it, Monsieur?" he asked, in a strained voice.

"Yes, Madame."

"The one that left at ten past eleven?"

"Indeed. You were expecting someone by that train?"

"My husband. He sent me a telegram to say that he would take that train. I don't know what this means..."

"He'll have missed it. He'll arrive by the next train."

"You think so?"

"Of course! We see it all the time. It's nothing to get upset about."

And the guard, shrugging his shoulders, made as if to leave. The young woman held him back. "And there are other trains soon?"

"Certainly. The 61 arrives at seven forty. You'll find that your husband has taken it—unless he waited for the express, which will only get here at eleven. Come back in two hours, though; I'm sure he'll be on the 61—that's what people who miss the 53 do."

"Thank you, Monsieur; I'll wait."

Wrapping herself up in her mantle, garnished with wretched furs, the young woman went to sit down in a corner.

The wait was long and uncomfortable, interrupted by the arrival of two suburban trains, which, in her impatience, the young woman mistook for the Paris train.

Finally, the 61 was signaled. She hurried forward, gluing her face to the window of the waiting-room, examining all the passengers getting out of the carriages one by one.

Alas, the one for whom she as waiting did not appear.

On the other hand, the train brought bad news. A traveler had been found dead beside the track some distance from Beuzeville-Bréauté station, doubtless the victim of some accident.

"It's him!" cried the unfortunate woman, going pale.

People crowded around her. They tried to reason with her, even to persuade her otherwise...all in vain.

"It's him!" she said. "I'm sure it's him! I want to go and see!"

And no matter how hard they tried to stop her, she took the eight o'clock train to go to Beuzeville.

The public prosecutor, the examining magistrate and his clerk got off the train with her, having been alerted by the Company. Accompanied by a policeman in plain clothes, they were coming to make their investigation.

The poor woman was not mistaken. It was indeed her husband who lay there, bloody and disfigured, on a camp-bed in a room at the station. The papers found on the corpse had revealed his identity: Charles-Louis Lavardens, former non-commissioned officer in the third marine infantry regiment, now a commercial traveler.

The inquest concluded that it was an accident. In fact, no theft had been committed; the dead man still had his coin-purse, his wallet and his watch with a gold chain. The purse contained twelve francs in silver, the wallet three hundred-franc bills. A thief would not have left that behind.

Furthermore, the corpse did not bear a single wound that had apparently been produced by a weapon: a single blow to the head—produced, according to all the evidence, by the fall from a height on to the trackside—had caused the death. Having fallen outside the rails, the body had neither been dragged nor crushed by the subsequent trains.

Finally, before leaving, the magistrates had received the report from the senior guard on train 53. That report mentioned that, on arrival at Le Havre, the door of one compartment had been found open; in that compartment were two blankets, an overcoat and various trivial objects that testified to the presence of a passenger. That passenger had disappeared, without taking his luggage and blankets; the guard had revealed that fact to the policeman. It was just as the functionary was going to make enquiries that he had learned about the discovery of the body at Beuzeville-Bréauté.

The accident was easily reconstituted. For some reason, perhaps misled by the guard's call and thinking that he had arrived, the passenger had wanted to get off; opening the door, he had leaned out, had lost his balance when there was a jolt, and had fallen, head first...

That was the formal judgment of the physician who accompanied the magistrates in their legal inquest. It was, naturally, also the judgment of the station-master, whose only concern was to relieve the Company of any responsibility.

"But I tell you that he's been murdered!" cried Madame Lavardens, confronting them.

The doctor, a tall, thin old man, widened his eyes in alarm behind his gold-rimmed spectacles. No less amazed, the public prosecutor stared at the woman who was behaving so audaciously. He was struck by the character of her physiognomy. Of medium height, but with a good figure and poise, Madame Lavardens had the tanned complexion of a southerner, and the graceful oval face that gives Spanish and Pyrenean women an appearance that is both child-like and impertinent. Her mouth, contracted by pain, was small and red as a grenadine. Her eyes were shining beneath her tears like two black diamonds.

"He's been murdered, I tell you!" she repeated, violently. "And I know who murdered him!"

II. The Denunciation

The public prosecutor dew nearer to the unfortunate woman, whose face was wracked by pain, and said, with a softness imprinted with great compassion: "Calm down Madame. The work of the law is delicate, but it's necessary not to let despair lead you astray. Friend or relative of the deceased?"

"His wife, Monsieur."

The magistrate bowed. "Whatever our conviction is, Madame, it is our duty to hear you."

Oliva Ossona, Lavardens' widow, did not appear to hear what the prosecutor was saying. Prey to one of those violent crises that the strongest will cannot resist, she fell to her knees beside her husband's corpse, and in a hoarse voice, through her sobs, cried: "Oh, poor Charles! So good, so trusting...the wretch has killed you! It's over...finished..."

Deeply moved, the prosecutor hastened to follow the young woman. "Madame," he murmured, "you can't stay here. Come, I beg you..." And as Oliva looked at him with haggard eyes, grimly crouched over her husband's body, he added: "You mentioned murder. Come, Madame—we're ready to listen to you." He turned to the examining magistrate and the doctor. "We ought not to neglect any means of information in order to discover the truth—isn't that so, Messieurs?"

The doctor shrugged his shoulders and snorted skeptically. "The truth...an accident, of course! Perhaps a suicide..."

Madame Lavardens heard that. Quivering, she stood up in front of the physician. "Oh, no! No! That's a lie! He loved me too much for that—that's an insult to his memory..."

She had a handkerchief in her hand, which she passed over her face; a sigh escaped her lips...and, pulling herself together, overcoming her weakness, she said: "I'll go with you, Messieurs. I have a duty to fulfill in your regard. I want my beloved Charles to be avenged..."

The magistrates and the doctor went into the office that the station-master had obligingly lent them; the clerk accompanied them.

As soon as the door was closed, the prosecutor asked the young woman to sit down. "We're listening, Madame," he said. "Would you care to justify the suspicion you expressed just now?"

"Take notes, Jacquier," the magistrate ordered his clerk. The latter sat down at the station-master's desk, beside the plain clothes policeman—who, for his part, was compiling an official report.

Madame Lavardens wiped her tearful eyes and began: "My husband, the son of petty provincial shopkeepers, had naturally been intended by his parents

16

to be a great success in business. They wanted to make a ship-owner of him, one of those great merchants who has branches in all five continents.

"With that aim, they sent him to London when he left school, in order to learn English and familiarize himself with British commercial practices, which are said to be more practical than ours.

"In a French establishment in London, he met a man whose life is a veritable novel. That man, whose extraordinary life-story has been told in all the newspapers, was Gaston Rozen..."

At that name, the prosecutor and the examining magistrate started, and exchanged knowing glances.

"You've heard of him, haven't you?"

"Yes, Madame, but please continue."

"Gaston Rozen was himself placed by his family in a particular institution. Finding his plebeian name insufficiently chic, he called himself *de* Rozen. He lived the high life, like the son of the family to which he claimed to belong. He had his own hansom cab, went to grand theaters, socialized with rich people, or people who passed for such, gambled and had mistresses.

"Charles did not really become his friend; the difference in their lives was too great, but in the capacity of a compatriot, he often saw him, and his features remained engraved in his memory.

"In his twentieth year, Lavardens, who had just left England, met me in Biarritz, where I was a milliner. We fell in love—but his mother, already a widow, thinking that he was too young and that my status was too modest for him, refused her consent to our marriage. It was then that, although exempt from military service, he joined the third regiment of the marine infantry and was sent to a garrison in Guiana.

"There, the newspapers arrive in bundles, and late. Lavardens learned about the fantastic adventures of his former companion in London, concluded by a condemnation to hard labor. The newspapers announced his imminent arrival in the *bagne*.[5]

"By virtue of a residue of sympathy, he watched out for his arrival, recognized him, kept track of him and, insofar as the strictness of the rules permitted, tried to make his captivity more comfortable. Rozen seemed to be grateful to

---

[5] In translating the title of the novel I have rendered *bagne* as "penitentiary," but the term has no exact equivalent in English, so I have retained it here. French convicts sentenced to hard labor rather than mere confinement were sent to special establishments designed for that purpose, called *bagnes*; these were originally located in France—there was a notorious one in Toulon—but during the 19th century prison colonies were set up in far-flung locations like Guiana and New Caledonia, and became an integral part of the project of colonization, much as Botany Bay did in the English colonization of Australia.

him—but how can one know what was happening in the depths of that perverse soul?

"The four years of his military engagement went by. Returned to civilian life, Charles succeeded in overcoming his mother's resistance. We were married, and, taking advantage of his sojourn in Guiana and the knowledge he had acquired there, he left as the agent of a rubber manufacturer to make purchases in Venezuela, where he set up a branch office.

"His services were very satisfactory, and it was decided, on his return to France, that he would continue them—and he did in fact, undertake several voyages. It was during one of them that he learned about Rozen's escape."

"Pardon me, Madame," the examining magistrate interrupted. "I believe I understand that it's to Rozen that you're attributing your husband's death..."

"Yes, Monsieur!" exclaimed the widow. "And I'll tell you why!"

"I respect your grief," the magistrate went on, "but it's impossible to leave you in error any longer. The man you're accusing, who was certainly the most audacious of bandits, is no longer alive. He perished while trying to escape from Cayenne."

"People believe so...my husband believed it, like everyone else...but I'm sure, myself, that Rozen is alive."

"The Minister, however," the prosecutor declared, "has received official confirmation of his death."

"And what proof is there that it is not mistaken?"

The doctor made a sign to the examining magistrate, who shrugged his shoulders.

"Perhaps you think I'm mad," Madame Lavardens exclaimed. "You're wrong." In spite of all her efforts, she could not suppress an explosion of grief. "Oh, my God! They don't believe me!" Joining her hands in ardent prayer, she implored them: "Messieurs, I beg you, in the name of justice, in the name of truth...listen to me!"

"Speak, Madame," said the prosecutor, generously. Turning to his companions, he added, in a low voice: "Let her continue; it's a question of humanity."

The magistrate and the physician, visibly irritated, made no protest.

"First, I must bring you up to date with our current situation," Oliva went on. "My husband, in the position he occupied, made a good living for us both. We even had a few savings, which enabled us to decide, in order to avoid a long and painful separation, that I would accompany him on his next voyage to America—but we were struck by a bolt from the blue. The business my husband represented went bankrupt. My husband found himself out of work.

"He started looking for a new job, but it was difficult. He had lost all his connections. Then he got the idea of starting a company, not only to resume the exploitation of rubber, but also, and in particular, that of ironwood and mahogany, in which the forests out there are so rich. In his opinion, with an insignificant capital, one could make considerable profits within a few years."

"If one doesn't catch yellow fever," muttered the doctor.

"That was what most of the people he approached replied. Time passed. The little money we had was spent. I saw my poor Charles becoming desperate…I was afraid that he might go mad…every day he got more depressed.

"One day, he came back to the house and I saw—with great joy!—that he was smiling. He kissed me effusively. 'We're saved!' he told me—and when I questioned him, curious to know what had made him so happy, he went on: 'I ran into a friend of my youth, whom I would never have recognized if he hadn't told me who he was himself, so changed is he, physically and morally. Oh, I knew that, with regard to an intelligence like his, one should never despair…'

"I tried to find out who the individual was that Charles had met. 'I can't tell you that, my love…' And my husband, who had never had any secrets from me until then, evaded all my questions. 'You'll be astonished,' he said, finally, in the face of my persistence. 'You'll know in time…it's a man whom everyone believes to be dead…and he really is, in fact, for no one could suspect him of being the man who disappeared. Oh, if he's committed sins, he's redeemed them by means of his intelligence…he now has an important position…to name him would be to ruin him…and you wouldn't want me to betray him, when he came to me of his own accord, and enquired about my distress, and I left me with the promise that I'd be leaving for Venezuela within a week, with an investment of a hundred thousand francs, advanced without guarantees, with only my honesty as a pledge.'

"While Charles was saying all that to me, I was racking my brains, thinking back, seeking among the comrades that I knew him to have. 'Why trouble your mind, darling?' Charles went on, gaily. 'We're going to be happy. Tomorrow, I'll obtain a check for a hundred thousand francs from the Crédit Lyonnais.'"

Madame Lavardens paused momentarily. "I don't know why," she continued, "but one name came to mind obstinately. I stared at my husband. 'The man you met isn't the one whose adventures you told me about…that Rozen?' I saw Charles shiver. He got up to hide his embarrassment.

"'Oh, if it's him,' I cried, 'I'll die…he's afraid that you'll recognize him, that you'll denounce him…'

"'Go on—you're crazy,' Lavardens said.

"'Oh, my love, be careful—if it's a trap that's being set for you…'

"'Shut up! Don't question me anymore; I have nothing more to say to you but this: tomorrow, I'll have a hundred thousand francs, and we'll recover our fortunes. But I've sworn to keep my partnership secret—even to you, the confidante of my most intimate thoughts, I won't betray the secret.'

"I had to keep my suspicions and anxieties to myself. We left for Le Havre. For a wee, we've been staying at the Hotel Frascati, waiting. The steamer leaves today. Charles went to Paris to obtain the promised investment."

"Do you think the promise was serious, then? That your husband wasn't deluded by a vain hope?"

"This is the telegram I received yesterday evening," the young woman replied, simply, holding out a blue slip of paper to the magistrate, who read it aloud.

Madame Lavardens, Hotel Frascati, Le Havre.
Business concluded. Will arrive by seven forty-one train. Pack for departure.

Love, Charles.

"And my poor husband took that train!" cried Madame Lavardens, sobbing. "He was coming back to meet me, full of joy, to make the voyage that we hoped would make our fortune—but the bandit's generosity concealed a trap. He was murdered *en route* in order to get back the check given to him out of fear."

While she remained plunged in her grief, the three men conferred.

"It's curious, all the same," the prosecutor murmured, pensively.

"Yes, but is it really true?" murmured the examining magistrate, in a whisper.

"With a bandit like Gaston Rozen, anything is possible."

"Who says so? During and after the trial, fantastic rumors went around...the legends of Cartouche, Mandrin and Jack Sheppard all rolled into one."

"Then what the poor woman had told us..."

"Perhaps true, perhaps false. It would certainly be a great coup to recapture the bandit, if he really were still alive..."

"Fantasy!" said the doctor, stubbornly.

"It's certainly confused, vague. It doesn't give us any indication of the position held by the ghost. For lack of the name, that might give us a clue."

"Let's try," said the prosecutor, and asked: "Are you quite sure, Madame, that your husband didn't leave any piece of paper on which we might find Rozen's name?"

"Absolutely sure, unfortunately."

"But at least you know what the escapee is doing—what kind of position he holds?"

"Alas, no—nothing!"

"Not even the place where your husband met him?"

"Not even that."

"Hmm," said the magistrate. "As a trail, it's poor—and the telegram was sent from the Bourse; that doesn't tell us anything."

"Then you think...?" asked the prosecutor.

"I think," said the skeptical magistrate, "that we'd be wasting our time and intelligence looking for something. You don't even have any idea of Rozen's description?"

"The man Lavardens met bore no resemblance either to the Rozen of London, the Rozen of France or that of Cayenne. Go and make something of that!"

"It's vague, indeed," the physician sniggered, "and only Monsieur Bertillon, who has a theory of description,[6] would be anything to do anything with it, assuming that the theory isn't one of those hoaxes that people in Paris make up to make fun of provincials..." He shrugged his shoulders, and added: "Who nevertheless believe them."

"In that case," said the prosecutor, "your opinion, doctor..."

"It's not an opinion—I'm certain, absolutely certain, that this man wasn't murdered. The body has no other contusions than those necessarily resulting from his fall. There was no struggle. He fell from the carriage by accident, and that's the truth."

"He might have been pushed."

"I'd like to think so—but then, the door would have to have been open, and he would have had to have been in the right place."

"Indeed," observed the examining magistrate, "it's scarcely admissible otherwise."

"And another thing," the physician went on, implacably. "His money was found in the dead man's pockets; to get it, the murderer would have had to jump out of the carriage after him. Now that murderer, if there was a murderer, would have broken his arms or legs...not to mention that he'd have touched down half a kilometer from where he'd thrown the body. Get away! Fairy tales, all of it! Personally, I reconstitute the scene in a simpler fashion. The passenger hadn't closed the door properly. He leaned on it; the door gave way and he fell, head first. It's simple...elementary: child's play."

And as the two magistrates looked at him, still undecided, he old doctor exclaimed, violently: "Those are my conclusions, which I'm telling you in the name of science, in the name of my twenty years' experience, in the name of my conscience as a physician and an honest man! If you don't believe me, if you don't trust me, if you think me incapable or biased..."

---

[6] Alphonse Bertillon devised "Bertillonage," or anthropometry, in the 1880s, which pioneered the use of police "mug shots," accompanied by elaborate descriptions based on carefully-taken measurements. Goron must have known him, as the director of an "Anthropometric Service" set up by the Prefecture of Police during his tenure. Bertillon blotted his copybook in 1894 when he gave evidence against Alfred Dreyfus that assisted in his wrongful conviction, and his anthropometric methods of identification were soon overtaken and replaced by fingerprints, but they were a significant contribution to forensic science in their day.

"There, there, my dear doctor, don't get upset," said the prosecutor, clapping him on the shoulder amicably. "We don't doubt your observations, but our duty is to examine the affair in all its facets, and we're permitted to make enquiries."

"Make all the enquiries you wish. Get another expert if you want. I have no objection. We'll see whether he offers an opinion different from mine."

The magistrate thought it futile to continue the discussion with such a sensitive adversary.

"We give in," he said. "Jacquier, conclude your official report with the doctor's conclusions: a pure and simple accident."

"What, Monsieur!" cried the widow, bursting into sobs again. "After what I've just told you, you still think…"

"I am obliged to, Madame," said the prosecutor, gently. "All I can do is to assure you that if you can discover some serious evidence to support your allegation, I'll always be ready to listen to you. I make that a formal promise."

"Oh, thank you, Monsieur, thank you!" the widow cried. "and I'll succeed, be sure of it—for even if everyone in the world abandons me, even if I remain alone, without support, without resources, without food, I shall devote my entire life, all my strength, I swear, to discover the murderer and to avenge my poor husband's death!"

III. Rozen's Youth

"I believe we've taken the wisest course," said the magistrate, when the men had climbed back into the carriage to return to Le Havre. "To begin with, we've concluded in accordance with the excellent doctor's observations."

"Observations that are the expression of the truth, believe me!" the doctor put in.

"However," observed the prosecutor, "what the victim's wife told you..."

"The ramblings of an excited hysteric!" proclaimed the doctor, with asperity.

"Pooh!" said the examining magistrate, lightly. "Perhaps there's some truth in what she said...but, even if she had been able to give us more precise details, where would it have led us?"

"What!" exclaimed the prosecutor. "To recapturing Rozen, whose resurrection she affirms."

"Get away! We'd be tied up in red tape, making reports, running around...and who'd get the grapnel on Rozen? You? Me? Not at all. The magistrates in Paris, to whom all the glory would be attributed!"

"Perhaps you're right," said the prosecutor, "but one has to do one's duty, if even if one gets no benefit from it. Tell me, you who know Rozen's story in detail—is it as extraordinary as the legend claims?"

"Perhaps even more so. Anyway, I had the opportunity to get to know all the details when I was attached to the Court of the Seine, and if you'll lend me your ears for a few minutes, you can judge for yourself."

"Do tell, my dear friend. We have a good half-hour before we get to Le Havre; nothing makes a journey seem shorter than an interesting story...unless it would annoy the doctor?"

"Me!" exclaimed he latter. "Are you joking, Monsieur le Procureur? I am, on the contrary, very keen to hear the odyssey of the individual whose name has been ringing in my ears all morning. Narrate, my dear magistrate—I'm listening."

"In that case, Messieurs," said the examining magistrate, "I'll begin.

"First, you need to know that Gaston Rozen is the son of a Parisian *demi-mondaine* who was very well known there twenty-five years ago. Where did she come from? Was she French, German or Hungarian? No one really cared. She was pretty; that was sufficient. In fashionable society, she was known by the aristocratic name of Rosa de la Croix."[7]

---

[7] This is a deliberate echo (shortly to be re-emphasized) of the name attached to a symbolic figure associated with the "Rosicrucian manifestos" published in Germany in the early 17th century. Two essays advertizing a fictitious secret

"Rosa de la Croix!" the doctor interjected. "I've heard of her, of course…a superb creature, believe me! Was she married, then?"

"Naïve disciple of Aesculapius!" exclaimed the magistrate, laughing. "Do women need to be married to have children?"

"I didn't say…only…"

"The father," the examining magistrate continued, "was as well-known as Rosa de la Croix. He was one of those exotic characters whose origins and antecedents one never knows, and yet, thanks to their impudence, their glibness and their lies, hold the high ground on the boulevard, have the best seats at all the premières and their invitations to all ceremonies, judging all talents without appeal…"

"While waiting," the prosecutor put in, "for us to be called to judge them in our turn—which happens more frequently than those who admire and envy them think."

"It's the revenge of honest people," observed the physician.

"The flashy fellow in question," the narrator went on, "called himself Prince Hadil Ahmed. He was an Oriental of magnificent bearing, and, it must be admitted, truly handsome. It's to him that Gaston owed his simultaneously seductive and commanding gaze, which the poor woman whose husband has just died might have mentioned to you."

"This Rozen was only French by birth, then?" said the doctor.

"Absolutely. His father didn't acknowledge him. He was entered into the civil registry under the name of Rosenkrutz, son of an unknown father and Rose Kruz—but you can imagine what that combination of a hetaira and a knight of industry might produce. At a very young age, Gaston manifested the most perverse instincts, combined with the most consummate skill. At ten, in the school where he mother had placed him, he made skeleton keys to all his fellow pupils' desks, from which he stole chocolate and jam. At twelve he was expelled for stealing a watch."

"A nice start," said the procurator.

"It wasn't that he lacked money. His mother gave him as much as he wanted—but the boy had a passion for theft infused in his blood. At fifteen and a half, he did better. He forged his mother's signature in order to obtain gems from a jeweler, which he pawned, similarly fraudulently. At seventeen, he ran off with his mother's chambermaid and set her up, on credit, in an apartment,

---

society, "The Brotherhood of the Rose-Cross," were followed up by an allegorical story generally known in English translation as "The Alchemical Marriage of Christian Rosenkreutz," the acknowledged work of the utopian philosopher J. V. Andreae. Goron and Gautier obviously resisted the temptation to call their own novel "The Alchemical Marriage of Unchristian Rosenkreutz," but more echoes will eventually become evident, if only temporarily.

under the name of Rozen. He thought it more elegant to shorten his name, and that was, in any case, what his friends always called him."

"What a rogue!" exulted the doctor.

"At eighteen," the magistrate continued, "he was in debt to the tune of fifty thousand francs, and mocked his creditors by telling them that, as he was a minor, they had taken advantage of his youth to exploit him. It was then that his mother sent him to England."

"Where Lavardens knew him," said the prosecutor.

"According to what his wife told us, yes—but what she didn't tell us is that young Rozen, placed with a semi-commercial and semi-family firm, seduced a young woman and brought her back to Paris, after persuading her to take twenty thousand francs from her father's safe."

"He wasn't arrested?" asked the prosecutor, astonished.

"No, his mother, besotted with him and submissive to the ascendancy he had been able to assume over her, paid for 'her bandit son's ingenuousness.' She forgave him what she called his juvenile 'escapades,' convinced that he would settle down ne ay and marry some rich heiress, thanks to his good looks.

"It must be admitted that, at twenty-two, Gaston was very seductive. From his father he inherited the Assyrian type, the famous 'velvet eyes' and a rich, bushy ebony black beard, admirably well placed, which made his matt white complexion stand out. His golden voice, tender, attractive and persuasive, resonated musically in his listeners' ears. Highly intelligent, in addition to French, his native language, he spoke English, German, Spanish, Italian and Arabic fluently.

In England, he had led an open-air life, and had developed considerable strength in all kinds of physical exercise: swimming, riding, riding. He was expert with both pistol and sword; he could slice a bullet on a blade at twenty paces..."

"In brief, an accomplished gentleman," said the doctor.

"You could say so—for he was also a distinguished musician, improvising on the piano without the slightest hesitation and singing any opera piece at first glance, however difficult it seemed..."

"His mother's blind love is comprehensible, even excusable."

Attentive to the magistrate's story, the prosecutor and the judge had drawn nearer to the narrator. The story interested them—impassioned them, so to speak—and they forgot the tragic adventure of the unfortunate Lavardens.

The magistrate, carried away himself by Rozen's story, told them about the career of that evil genius in military service, the sufferings inflicted by discipline on a man avid for worldly pleasures, in whose hands the few louis sent by his mother melted like snow in the sun. He told them how, one day, tempted by the need to obtain money at any price, he had succeeded in forcing the company treasurer's safe, with such diabolical cunning that he had escaped suspicion for several days. Then, denounced by a jealous mistress, he had been arrested, tried and, in spite of the steps taken by his mother, sent to prison. In prison, submissive and simulating a profound repentance, he had gained the pity of military leaders, who contrived to have him included in a list of pardons signed by the President of the Republic on Bastille Day. Free, he returned to Paris, to his mother's great joy. It was then that he launched forth upon a series of thefts and frauds of unprecedented audacity...until the day when he fell into the talons of the law.

The train arrived in the station just as the magistrate reached the end of his story.

"A fine romance," snorted the physician. "Worthy of Rocambole... resurrection included!"

"Pardon me," said the judge, laughing, "but I didn't mention that. I'm convinced, on the contrary, that the bandit whose story I've told you really is dead. I read the report of the director of the penitentiary, furnishing the most complete details of the frightful death of the convict Rozen—and I'm sure that poor Madame Lavardens is mistaken."

"Of course," agreed the doctor. "And one must also admit that her husband lied to her. Isn't it possible that, coming back from Paris in despair, he committed suicide?"

"That's my opinion," said the examining magistrate.

"Nevertheless, whatever the result, I'd like to look at Rozen's story again."

"Do you want me to send you my newspaper clippings from that era, my dear prosecutor?"

"I have them, thanks."

"Very well," said the doctor, "go distract yourself, Monsieur le Procureur—but take as mathematical the explanation I've given you: Madame Lavardens is mad."

The three men separated on the station platform, after shaking hands.

As the men of law all headed for the exit, Oliva, having got out of a third-class compartment, went past them.

"Poor woman," murmured the prosecutor.

"Yes," riposted the examining magistrate, "but time's a great healer, you know. In a year's time, pretty as she is, Madame Lavardens will console herself with another husband."

After parting company with the examining magistrate and the doctor, the public prosecutor continued, in the silence of his study, to read the original story of Rozen, who appeared to him to be the modern bandit incarnate.

All the details that filled the newspapers scanned by the lawyer seemed to have emerge from the fecund imagination of a master novelist. He remained astonished by the ingenuity, the audacity and the science of life placed in the service of the young man whose appetites had been far from finding satisfaction in the meager wages of a bank clerk.

Rozen, as a bank employee in the midst of the manipulation of shares and money, a spectator of rapid profits and coups on the Bourse, had been a wolf introduced to a sheepfold!

His first concern had been, from the start, to ensure himself the reputation of a model employee. A quick learner, he had familiarized himself with the different branches of the business with a prodigious rapidity. He had an admirable understanding of all the complicated mechanisms of finance, and his superiors, filled with admiration for the beginner, who soon knew as much as they did, predicted a brilliant future for him—but Rozen envisaged the role reserved for him with scorn. A job as a division head or agent? A fine reward for his immeasurable ambition! That would not ensure him the life of a great lord that he wanted to lead. Then again, it would be necessary for him to wait, and he wanted to enjoy his pleasures as soon as possible, not to say immediately.

Surreptitiously, his entire intelligence was directed toward an imminent goal: bringing off some great coup that would permit him to have money—a lot of money!

One day, Rozen found the means to realize his dream, but he needed an accomplice. He had anticipated that, and chance, which often favors evildoers, had set a reliable accomplice next to him in the same bank: a man he had very rapidly been able to put at his mercy, profiting from his weaknesses.

In addition to their financial services, the Rumsel Brothers, Bankers, had installed a small office to which the innumerable requests for help addressed to them were sent. The director of that office was a young man of about thirty, who had entered the Rumsel Brothers employ at a very young age and to whom, as a reward for loyal service, his employers had given that independent and well-paid position. The head of charity had a small capital at his disposal, which the bankers replenished according to need.

The employee, very zealous and reliable until then, allowed himself to be drawn into gambling at racecourses, at first as an amateur, quite mildly—but then it had become a passion for him. His entire salary went into the bookmakers' pockets, and he lived wretchedly, bombarded with urgent debts and harassed by creditors, whom he was able to mollify from time to time with small payments funded by the rare wins returned by his bets—which were quickly swallowed up.

Rozen, on the lookout for any circumstances that might aid him in his plan, had an intuition that the needy fellow might be useful to him. He had befriended the head of charity and found the means to help him out when he had a run of bad luck. He had even suggested to him that he might make fictitious requests for aid, which would permit the gambler to take a little cash from his treasury to satisfy his passion.

One Saturday, when he left the office, the unfortunate, absolutely crazed by some mysterious tip that a bookmaker had given him, had carried away the five thousand francs remaining in his safe, and had gone to lose them on the course. On Monday, absolutely desperate, he confided his exploit to Rozen.

At that exact moment, the latter had glimpsed a coup that ought to bring in a great deal of money, and was planning the means of bringing it off. He wondered what he could do to interest his accomplice, without giving him too big a slice of the cake.

He welcomed the gambler with a singular smile, took him by the hand and said to him: "You're not going to get upset over such a small matter?"

"You don't know, then, that I no longer have anything in the safe—not a centime to give to the people who will come today. It's the end, I tell you; there's nothing left to do but kill myself."

Rozen shrugged. "Don't be silly, old chap. Come on, let's take care of the most urgent matter first. How much do you need today?"

"A thousand francs."

"Your office opens at noon. You'll have the thousand francs."

"But what about tomorrow?" the head of charity groaned, partially reassured by Rozen's offer. "The bosses might ask for my accounts!"

"Tomorrow," Rozen replied, "We'll have found something else, trust me. We'll discuss it this evening. You'll dine with me, won't you?"

At noon, Gaston brought the promised thousand francs to the cashier. He had obtained them from the maternal purse—not without difficulty, for his mother had finally grown weary of all the hand-outs, but as the thousand francs were absolutely necessary to succeed, Rozen, who had been treating her coldly for some time, had played a comedy of sentiment. He had wept, struck his breast with a tone of heart-rending repentance, accusing himself of being a coward and a wretch, of having neglected a mother who had made so many sacrifices for him—and his mother had consented yet again to open her purse.

That evening, in a small restaurant in Montmartre—Rozen had carefully chosen a place where no one knew him—the head of charity joined his friend, and they shut themselves up in a private room. Over dessert, when Gaston saw that his guest was primed, overexcited without being drunk, he leaned toward him and aid, seductively: "You still owe your safe four thousand francs. It's impossible to pay them back. Listen: I heard your name mentioned yesterday. The bosses have been alerted; they know that you were gambling on Sunday— they've even learned that you were laying big bets."

The other became livid. "I'm doomed!"

"Not if you do as I say." It was the first time that Rozen had addressed the head of charity as "*tu*." The latter did not notice, and more than he sensed the tone of command in which his perfidious interlocutor continued. "Listen: tomorrow you'll have fifty thousand francs. Buy an advance ticket to Le Havre, and the day after tomorrow, you'll be far away...on your way to New York. Over there, with fifty thousand francs, a determined man can get into the clear."

"My word," said the other, after having hesitated. "One theft added to another! It's all over now. Tell me, what do I have to do?"

"This is it: tomorrow, a man named Jacobsen will arrive in Paris from Amsterdam. He'll have a fortune on him."

"How do you know?"

"Yesterday evening, I was at the gem-dealer's café...you know where it is?"

"Yes."

"I overheard two diamond-merchants in conversation, and I know that Monsieur Jacobsen, from Amsterdam, is disembarking in Paris, carrying two hundred thousand francs' worth of fine stones in paper. You know—with a wallet in his pocket containing diamonds wrapped in paper."

"Yes, yes..."

"You'll take that wallet. You'll also take Jacobsen's letters of recommendation. He must be the representative of a rich foreign merchant..."

"But how shall I do that?"

Rozen shrugged his shoulders. "It's simple. Do you know what chloroform is? Yes? Well, you'll have some on you. You'll go to the hotel, you'll ask for Jacobsen..."

"They won't let me in."

"They will if you give them this card."

"The bosses' card?"

"What does it matter to you, as you'll be taking flight? You understand the rest of the operation. When Jacobsen's asleep, you take the diamonds, the papers, the lot, and you go in his stead to realize the two hundred thousand francs. I wait for you; we share it out...and you run away. Understand?"

"Yes."

The next day, the coup was brought off, exactly as Rozen had planned...

The lawyer read the relevant judiciary report with great attention. He rapidly scanned the pages dealing with the audacious theft.

Rozen had calmly returned to his office after the coup.

The Rumsels' card had been found in Jacobsen's room, and suspicion had naturally fallen on the head of charity, who had fled—and the rumors of racecourses that Rozen had cleverly spread around took off.

For some time, Rozen had lived the high life. That evening, he had transformed himself, and the employee became a rich foreigner, disembarked in Paris to have some fun. Then his accomplice had returned to France and had come to find him, to get another slice of the cake.

"I no longer have any, old chap."

"Nothing? Get away—if you don't give me twenty thousand francs tonight, I'll turn you in."

Rozen had not believed that, but the following day he was arrested at home.

At first he had denied it, but, having been confronted with his accomplice, unable to explain a sum of ten thousand francs found in his bedroom, and recognized by the owner of the restaurant in which he had dined with his accomplice, Rozen had played a clever comedy.

"If I stole," he said, "it wasn't for myself; it was to save a comrade in distress."

He appealed to his employers and to his mother, but no one answered his pleas. Then he changed tactics and admitted everything—but from that moment on, all his intelligence and cunning were directed to one sole objective: escape.

As soon as that idea was embedded in his brain, he studied the means of fooling the law, of evading public vengeance. He was the most submissive of accused persons, and replied abundantly to the questions of the examining magistrate charged with his case. On only one point did he remain intractable. Every time the magistrate asked him where the rest of the stolen money was, the young thief insisted that he had squandered it all, that nothing remained—and every day there were interminable discussions on that subject in the magistrate's study. In spite of all his efforts, all the traps he set in order to lead the guilty party to contradict himself and finally get the truth out of him, the magistrate was defeated.

With great gesture of despair, Rozen beat his breast, swore that he had spent the stolen money, and defended himself step by step, skillfully inventing an entire detailed account to prove what he was saying.

The magistrate, however, did not believe Rozen; he hoped that he would finally obtain the deserted confession by dint of patience, and the investigation dragged on. That was what the crook wanted. In the meantime, he looked for a means of recovering his liberty.

While he went through the corridors of the court, escorted by a municipal guard and kept in shackles, he observed the locations, memorizing another detail of the interior layout of the Palais at every visit.

One day, he said to the magistrate who was questioning him: "Monsieur le Juge, everything that I have old you thus far is false. I see that I was wrong to deny it for such a long time. It was childish. Yes, I hid a substantial part of the money from the diamonds. I put fifty thousand francs in a safe place, but I can't tell you where it is yet." And with a singular smile, he added: "Tomorrow or the day after, I'll show you my hiding place."

The magistrate, knowing for experience that one gains nothing by annoying an accused person, did not persist. He was already satisfied to have obtained the result that he had been seeking for some time. "All right," he replied. "As you please. I'll wait until tomorrow."

The following day, when the guard brought him into the examining magistrate's study, he simulated violent abdominal pains. He writhed, seemingly prey to atrocious agonies, and begged to be taken to the toilet.

Set on the top floor, beneath the eaves of the Palais, the examining magistrate's study was served by a long corridor that terminated in a cul-de-sac, with the privy.

Rozen had worked out his plan carefully. He had observed that the window lighting that little room had no bars and that it was situated directly above a ledge that ran all the way around the Palais.

As soon as he had gone in, he slid the interior bolt very quietly. The guard did not notice that detail. How could the soldier possibly have any fear?

After a quarter of an hour, the magistrate began to get anxious about his accused, and the clerk questioned the guard. The latter, who was also showing signs of impatience and thought that his prisoner was "taking his time," knocked on the privy door. But he knocked in vain; "all ears within were deaf."

The magistrate was alerted; no one thought of an escape.

"We'll have to fetch a locksmith," the magistrate declared. "The young man's doubtless been taken ill."

When the locksmith had opened the door, the soldier, seeing the window open and the room empty, uttered a formidable oath. "Good God! He's escaped!"

The clerk and the guard ran downstairs to raise the alarm, but Rozen could not be found.

The next day, moreover, the examining magistrate received a brief letter.

Monsieur le Juge and my dear sir,
In greatly regret having taken my leave of a man as amiable and indulgent as you, and I am sorry for having been obliged to use mean that are perhaps a trifle…risky to break off my relationship with you, but necessity makes the law. The fool was the guard, and perhaps you too, a little, my dear sir.
Hoping never to see you again, I salute you respectfully.
Vae victis!

Rozen,
guilty man in flight

P.S. I would be deeply sorry to have failed to keep a promise. I promised to tell you today where the rest of the sum realized by the stolen diamonds could be found. Here you are: that sum is presently in my wallet. Don't ask me to let you know my new address.

The magistrate charged with the Bréauté affair was becoming increasingly interested in the adventures of this veritable Rocambole. He forgot his own investigation while rereading the details of the young bandit's escape.

By following the gutter with which the ledge was equipped, the fugitive had reached a window left ajar to allow smoke to escape. He looked in; it was a kitchen, invaded by the smoke of a fire reluctant to catch hold. A young woman, doubtless a maid, red-faced with wrath, was striving to blow on the stubborn coals.

Rozen opened the window quietly, jumped nimbly down on to the kitchen floor, and, before the young maid had time to take account of what was happening, she was in a chair, bound and gagged with all the dusters that were hanging up in the kitchen.

"I beg your pardon," Rozen said, "but I did it as delicately as possible, didn't I, Mademoiselle?"

The young servant found nothing better to do in the excess of her terror, but faint, so he paid no further heed to her, and tried to get his bearings.

First, he cocked an ear; the apartment had no other occupant, for the time being, than the unconscious young woman trussed up like a sausage.

The fugitive went through one room, then another. It was a bedroom. Resting on the bed were an advocate's robe and wig. Why were they there? On examining them, Rozen perceived that the robe was a trifle fanciful, and that the wig was not entirely traditional in form. Beside the effects a little program had been laid, which gave him the key to the enigma. Inscribed on the card were the words: *Masked ball; fancy dress*. It was March, coming up to Shrove Tuesday, with the procession of celebrations. It was the costume of a woman looking for a husband, or the daughter of some functionary lodged in the Palais.

At hazard, Rozen put on the robe. While dressing, he thought that they must be looking for him everywhere by now, and that chance had served him admirably. Without that providential robe, he would have been forced to shut himself away in some deserted corner of the Palais and wait for nightfall in order to attempt a perilous exit.

Rapidly, he quit the apartment, went down a staircase, went along thirty-six corridors, and was soon in the animated hallways of the civil court, mingling with the host of solicitors, advocates and attorneys. In that hubbub he passed unnoticed; he was assumed to be a trainee.

He saw busy guardsmen running rapidly through the courtrooms looking at everyone's faces…except those of the men in robes.

One thing, however, was still tormenting him. How could he get out of the Palais? Advocates do not usually go out in their robes.

Once again, he appealed to his lucky star and continued walking, attentively.

At one moment, as he found himself behind two advocates, he heard one of them say: "It's scheduled for three o'clock, you know, my dear sir."

"The body's being taken to the mortuary?"

"Yes—meet outside the Palais."

Rozen was triumphant. *There's my way out*, he said to himself.

A few moments later, he was in the street, in the midst of a crowd of advocates, who, all in their robes, were going in a body to the funeral of a celebrate colleague. A file of carriages and fiacres was advancing slowly, picking people up. Rozen did not hesitate for a moment. He dived into a closed fiacre….

There, too, he had one inconvenience. What if other advocates—real ones—were to get in with him? He tried to get out of the queue.

The coachman could not do it.

Finally, they set off. Rozen was alone in his fiacre. Carriages had been furnished in abundance by the organizers.

On the way, the fugitive leaned out of the window. "Coachman…quickly…I've forgotten…oh, damn! Quickly…Boulevard Malesherbes, 255…we'll come back here afterwards. Good tip!"

The fiacre quit the file and gained speed rapidly. The promise of a tip usually has the gift of giving wings to trees. After a quarter of an hour, Rozen arrived at the home of his ex-mistress, who was already consoled for the misadventure he had occasioned her.

Madame was not at home. The domestic, recognizing the pseudo-advocate, uttered an exclamation: "Monsieur Ro…"

He put his hand over her mouth and growled, in an imperious, staccato voice: "Shut up—or you're dead!"

Shoving the poor woman, rendered mute by terror, ahead of him, he went in. Then he locked the door and put the key in his pocket. Having done that, without hesitation, he went straight to the bedroom, took a quilted chair, and, without worrying about leaving the footprints of his soles in the velvet fabric, climbed on to it in order to reach the top of the mirror-fronted wardrobe. From there, behind the fronton, under a thick layer of dust, he took a small packet, opened it rapidly and counted.

"Fifty thousand. That's good. It's all here."

The simplest hiding places are also the best, and when the agents of the law had searched the room, they had thought of everything except that.

In the bathroom he removed his advocate disguise, modified his hair and beard with a clever thrust of a comb, put on a black-rimmed pince-nez and grabbed his hat. Returning to the maid, who had taken refuge in the kitchen, trembling all over and not daring to call for help, he shot off a threat: "If you or your mistress talk about my visit, I'll have my revenge…"

And he left.

He headed for London by the evening train.

Sentenced in his absence, he had been condemned to twenty years of hard labor.

There had been no sighting of him for some time; then he reemerged successively in Berlin, Vienna, Budapest and various other capitals and spas, living as a great lord, never under the same name, amazing everyone with his luxury, conquering slightly mature but rich *demi-mondaines*, deceiving them all but never leaving them, dazed and confused, without having stolen their most beautiful plumage. The king of thieves, the prince of fraud, he won enormous sums gambling thanks to the complicity of waiters to whom he abandoned a share of his profits. It was impossible to catch him red-handed.

Finally, gripped by nostalgia for Paris, he returned there to spend the proceeds of a "nice touch" pulled off in Brussels.

One evening, at the exit from a theater, as he was in a hurry to hail a cab, he collided violently with a man going in the opposite direction.

Both slightly stunned, they were apologizing, when Rozen was suddenly unable to retain a muffled oath: it was the chief deputy of the Prefect of Police.

The functionary in question hesitated momentarily. His intuition told him that he had before him the bandit everyone had been seeking for a long time, whose photographic description was engraved in his memory—but that second of indecision saved Rozen.

Profiting from an eddy in the crowd that was emerging from the theater, hastening toward the cab-rank and the omnibus that was passing with a long squeal of its brakes, the wanted man had fled.

For a further interval he continued his life of pillage and debauchery, but the encounter with the functionary on the Parisian boulevard had brought him bad luck, and two months later, at a spa, he stupidly allowed himself to be caught in the arms of a high-class *horizontale* who had been captivated by his beautiful manners and whom he was in the process of conscientiously stripping bare.

He had tried hard to escape from the police, against whom he had put up a desperate resistance. He almost killed one of the men who had grabbed him—but he had rapidly been reduced to impotence.

Securely held this time, watched over with jealous care, he could not escape the assizes—and the judge, on reading the examining magistrate's report, could not help admiring the ingenuity, skill and energy the malefactor who, during the investigation, so long as he had the hope of escaping, remained proud, mocking, cynical and even brutal, but who had been humble and repentant before the jurors, swearing that fatality alone had dragged him into the gears of crime, and launching theatrical reproaches at the mother who had abandoned him. Had that piteous attitude, which had deceived the public, attracted a little pity from the judges? At any rate, he got away with fifteen years of hard labor, five years less than the sentence imposed in his absence.

Transported to Guiana, he attempted to escape again, but this time, he escaped permanently. There was proof that he had been killed during his flight from the bagne. A certificate of death, duly drawn up by the penitentiary administration, had given credence to it.

The lawyer wondered whether the bandit might not have deceived society again by passing himself off as dead; he was influenced in spite of himself by the affirmations of Madame Laverdens—but the official document was there, certifying that Rozen was no longer numbered among the living. And, like the physician, like all the experts and other magistrates, the prosecutor said to himself, shaking his head: "All fantasies. The poor woman is mistaken. There's no crime; it was an accident, that's absolutely certain."

A few days after the drama of Bréauté, the medical examiners in Rouen, to whom the autopsy of Lavardens' body had been entrusted, concluded, like the first doctor, that the death was accidental.

The corpse was returned to the widow, who rendered it the last rites.

For everyone, the matter was reduced to an accident—tragic, to be sure, but banal. It was filed away.

Except that Oliva persisted in declaring that her husband had been the victim of a murder, and at the cemetery, in bidding a final adieu to the man she had loved, she murmured through her sobs: "Charles, my beloved…everyone has abandoned me; I remain alone…there's no one but me to avenge you!"

IV. The Hôtel de Saint-Magloire

On the same evening as the accident at Beuzeville-Bréauté, the Baron de Saint-Magloire gave a dinner at his sumptuous house in the Champs-Élysées.

A few days previously, thirty important individuals, carefully selected from among the most influential in every category, had received a glossy card with gilded edges bearing an enigmatic invitation:

Monsieur le Baron de Saint-Magloire begs M. _____ to do him the honor of dinging at his home in his house in the Champs-Élysées (men only) on Thursday 22 February 189 , at eight o'clock.
Very important information: we shall be talking business.
R. S. V. P.

All those invited had accepted, with the exception of Notard, the great businessman, who was confined to bed by an inopportune attack of influenza.

At the appointed hour, everyone had gathered.

The large windows of the first floor, where the dining room and drawing room were located, appeared as brilliantly-lit rectangles cut out in the façade, from which broad beams of vivid light escaped, projected into the distance along the road.

In front of the house, along the sidewalks, superb carriages were lined up, with an uninterrupted racket of hooves striking the wooden pavement and harnesses shaken by the impatient horses.

In groups—one might say in classes—coachmen and footmen, as shiny and varnished as the harnesses of their horses and the panels of their carriages, awaited orders. Some were exchanging racing tips, others denigrating their masters. There was no wine-merchant's nearby where the gentlemen in question could devote themselves to the pleasures and excitements of a game of Zanzibar while sipping an *aperitif* or a *digestif,* according to circumstance. They had to pass the time somehow, and passed it at the expense of their masters. What could be more natural? That evening, of course, Amphitryon was bearing all the expenses of the whispered discussion; is it not necessary always to make sacrifices to the truth?

"Ah," said one lanky fellow, majestic in his chestnut livery, "It truly pains me to see Monsieur le Marquis, my master, compromising his name in this fashion in this Saint-Magloire's house."

"Baron de Saint-Magloire," a footman corrected.

"A Baron like you."

"Oh me...I couldn't care less."

"You couldn't care less—but if you did, you'd only have to take ten thousand bullets, go and find the pope and come back a Comte or a Baron. It's no more difficult than that..."

"Me, if I had ten thousand bullets, I'd rather buy a wine-merchant's. It brings in good money, when one has a little wife who understands business."

"I don't deny it—but do you think the title of Baron doesn't bring in anything to Saint-Magloire? If he only had his bank, he wouldn't have a hope of getting us into his house..."

"He might be content with political and financial types..."

"In that case, he'd only have to transport his drawing rooms to the Mazas. At present, there's no shortage of them there!"

A burst of laughter greeted this reply, put in by a newcomer.

"Hark at the anarcho! Always the same—sees nothing anywhere but thieves, scoundrels, swindlers, corruption..."

"You only have to read the newspapers. If you'd lost your savings in Panama, like me..."

"Oh no! You're not going to bore us to death again with your Panama. You had to be stupid to get mixed up in that, which promised you more butter than bread. I didn't trust..."

"Where do you invest your funds?"

"In Zanzi..." said another.

"Without security, of course."

"At the end of the day, you can say what you like," said a short coachman with a red face, whose long overcoat, trailing on the ground, made him look like a performing monkey. "You can mock. Even if this Saint-Magloire is a papal baron, even if his title's fake, his gold isn't. He's jolly rich, and generous..."

"Rich! There are some in the Place de Paris who appear so, by squandering other people's cash."

"Anyway, I couldn't care less. Whether he's a baron or not, rich or hard up, that doesn't stop him being a marvelous fellow, since the whole of high society comes running when he cheeps."

"Why aren't there any tarts this evening, then, in that factory?" a footman asked, all of a sudden.

"It's not his custom, though, as in Andalusia, to shun the sex. He always has three or four hags in dry dock, not to mention his legitimate, to whom I'd certainly have a few words to say, without bragging, between the sheets."

"That's true, though," said another. "Not a skirt in the place. Not like the other day, at the party he threw in honor of the Abyssinian ambassador, a bunch of dirty negroes. There were women showing some skin that night. Underdressed enough—beautiful gauzes, mind—to make your eyes pop out of your head. Today, there's only men. Why's that?"

"Well," said a third, sarcastically, "we're in the Champs-Élysées, a few steps away from the Rue de Surène!"

"No, no, you don't get it. It's probably because they're going to be talking finance, and on days when they talk finance, women have to be kept out. They have big mouths, women, and that inconveniences these fellows in their dirty tricks. It isn't the first time I've seen it."

One by one, the orders arrived, brought by the domestics from the house, and the coachmen and footman went away.

In their conversation, of which we have only recorded a few samples for the reader, there was a brutal expression of what everybody thought about the Baron de Saint-Magloire. No one really knew where the cosmopolitan banker came from, who had turned up in Paris one day, to throw one party after another, host one dinner after another. He seemed immensely rich, and that was sufficient to put a shutter over the widow of public curiosity.

The money the Baron spent in profusion gave him the keys to the city. No one asks to see the passport of a man who directs a business where millions are moved around with a shovel, and the Banque Saint-Magloire was one of those. It only dealt in colossal operations. So all of Paris, dazzled by the luxury and captivated by the noble banker's audacious and successful enterprises, competed for the honor of being among his guests. The magistracy, finance, the arts—the charmer had conquered them all. Even the nobility had fallen into step! The old aristocracy! The great names and the ancient escutcheons had come to bow down before the petty lordling whose title had no ancestry at all.

Money works miracles. It is the king. The value of a man is judged by the weight of the money that he disposes.

The dinner had been exceedingly merry. The Baron had an incomparable chef, famous throughout Europe, whom he had filched from the greatest gourmet among Archdukes by offering him a bridge of gold.

That evening, the chef had surpassed himself. Having the greatest love of and pride in his profession, he had been determined to show all those people, however blasé they might be about good food, that he was worthy of his reputation, and the ministerial salary that it brought in.

The menu was a marvel, the wines chosen with superior artistry, beyond all praise—so the faces were blooming; the threats of gout and dyspepsia scarcely brought an occasional frown-line to the odd forehead, or a crease of anxiety to the corner of the occasional tremulous lip.

Entirely given over to present enjoyment, the guests scarcely spared a thought for the promised "business," which must be serious, since it had deprived the lovers of flirtation of the pleasure of gladdening their eyes by admiring the Baron's beautiful arm-candy—the most beautiful arm-candy in Paris.

Besides which, Saint-Magloire kept his company in stitches. Over the champagne, he held forth.

Why, someone had asked him, had he not gone into Parliament, where the need for men like him was so keenly felt?

"No, Messieurs, I haven't gone near Parliament, because I think that everyone has his own role marked out down here. Business matters absorb me entirely. I don't have the right to steal a single minute of my life from ensuring the fate of the capital that workers of every rank confide to me.

"Finance is the key to universal happiness; it's by means of finance that universal peace can be established. The army? God knows how much I admire the fine feats of arms by which it has glorified our country. God knows how my heart beats when I proudly salute the tricolor of our beautiful France, floating above battalions as they pass by—but it must be said that the army's role is just about finished. The very exaggeration of the murderous machines at the disposal of peoples will make them increasingly hesitant from now on to settle difficulties by armed conflict. People understand that it's no longer necessary to cut one another's throats, and that all humankind ought to unite in a sublime effort of endeavor—and it's finance that will hold the most precious place in all the disarmed nations.

"I've had a dream—yes, a beautiful dream—and I hope, Messieurs, that I shall realize it...

"I'd need collaborators, but I'm convinced that there will be no lack of them...

"My dream is that of creating the financial solidarity that will assure the solidarity of all nations—and then, no more wars: peace; endeavor..."

Discreet applause greeted this little speech, delivered in a contained but vibrant voice. Everyone admired Saint-Magloire's genius.

The man would go a long way—upwards—and the most powerful people were paying self-interested court to him, convinced that, before long, the Baron would be the unique dispenser of everything, from the wings. His occult power would become immense. He would hold all the financial, industrial, commercial, political and even governmental mechanisms in his hands.

Scarcely had the applause died away, amid the hubbub of moving chairs, just as they were about to go into the smoking room, when a footman brought in an envelope on a silver tray.

Saint-Magloire's guests did not notice that the envelope trembled in the Baron's hands when he broke the seal and took out a card. The man was, in any case, always on his guard. He had time to collect himself, and he smiled as he read the sentence: *I need to talk to you.* The note was signed by a simple initial: *B*.

The footman who had brought it was waiting.

Saint-Magloire was anxious but did not want to let it show. He knew who the signatory of the note was, and he knew why the intruder, so familiar and so indiscreet, needed to talk to him at such a moment. But how could he leave his guests at the very moment when he was about to take them into his confidence?

Perhaps, once the coffee had been served, by virtue of the indulgent bliss produced by the first cigar, it would be permissible for him to absent himself for a few minutes. He had to, anyway, at any cost.

In pencil, on the card signed by B, he wrote: *Wait for me in the Place de l'Étoile at the corner of the Avenue du Bois. I'll be there shortly.*

"Fetch me an envelope," he ordered the servant.

While the latter was carrying out this instruction, the Baron, smiling and self-controlled, as if no anxiety were gnawing at him, resumed conversing with his guests.

"Where were we?" he said. "With business, one can never rest easy..."

"Business!" said someone. "My dear Baron, you must never get any sleep."

"You're exaggerating, Monsieur le Marquis."

"Not at all."

The domestic came back, carrying an envelope. Carefully, and unhurriedly, Saint-Magloire put the card inside.

"Give that to the person who's waiting."

"Yes, Monsieur le Baron."

The Marquis came closer to Saint-Magloire and leaned toward him. "Well, my dear chap, I'll wager that the business for which someone's writing to you won't bring much profit."

"Hmm! Perhaps, Marquis..."

"An affair of the heart?"

The Baron smiled enigmatically. That said what needed to be said, and dispensed with the need to reply.

"I knew it!" said the Marquis. "No one but a lover would dare to disturb people at such an hour, in the midst of his guests!"

A quarter of a hour later, the inquisitive individual, who was also an incorrigible gossip—as Saint-Magloire knew very well—was telling the tale in every corner of how the Amphitryon had yet another new intrigue with an adorable woman. Everyone was talking at the same time, though, and no one listened to him—and no one noticed Saint-Magloire's disappearance.

Without wasting an instant, the banker had gone up to his dressing-room. Without the aid of any domestic he had put a light traveling-coat over his evening suit, put on a felt hat and, by way of the service stairs, in order to avoid meeting anyone, he had gone out into the garden, and then into the Champs-Élysées.

Now that he was alone, Saint-Magloire gave free rein to his anxiety. The anguish that was clawing at him was visible in his face. He took large strides, in haste to know.

"Has he succeeded?" he murmured. "No...since, instead of the agreed telegram, he's come in person, at the risk of compromising me..."

In the Place de l'Étoile, a man was pacing back and forth. Short and thick-set, he was swinging his hips, with his hands in his pockets whistling. It was the mysterious correspondent. From time to time he stopped, looked toward the Avenue des Champ-Élysées and muttered: "Hurry up…is the boss going to leave me cooling my heels like this for much longer?" Then, while walking, he started a monologue in a low voice, as if to keep himself from getting bored: "He must have had a fit when he recognized my handwriting. A telegram! You're joking, old man. I'd have had to wait till tomorrow for the cash. That's no go…"

He finally perceived the Baron crossing the square, deserted at this late hour, and advanced to meet him, ceremoniously.

"M'sieu le Baron…!"

Brows furrowed and cheeks blanched, Saint-Magloire cut him off in a curt tone. "Enough jokes!"

"All right, old chap. After work, a little fun…it does no harm..."

"Well? The affair?"

"In the bag."

"Nothing to fear?"

"Not a hitch."

"You're sure no one saw you?"

"I said that the affair is in the bag. You can take my word for it..."

"Not so loud."

"Oh, at this hour…"

"It's always necessary to be prudent."

"You're right."

"You have the paper?"

"Of course. Here, Emperor..."

The man took a rectangular piece of paper from his wallet, which Saint-Magloire examined by the light of a gas-lamp.

"Good," he said. "I feel better now. Now, let me tell you that I'm displeased with you...."

"Impossible," the other replied, sarcastically. "I've done the job properly. That poor fellow, in the train out there…if he could tell you…do me justice…*bang*, one blow and it was done. Not a drop of blood in the carriage. Good stuff, your drug..."

The Baron smiled vaguely. "Yes," he murmured. "Ethyl bromide is a marvelous anesthetic."

"He didn't even say *oof*. Then, in no time, he was out the door on to the trackside. After I'd taken the money…of which you're so fond. Oh, it's true that a hundred thousand franc check signed Saint-Mag..."

"Shhh!" growled the Baron. "Shut up, Bastien."

The man he had called Bastien was not listening. "Of course, that would be inconvenient, found on the body. They would have come to ask you questions."

"That doesn't matter. Listen: I told you, if you succeeded, to send me a telegram. I gave you the agreed signal. You didn't obey. Why not?"

"Because I didn't want to. I wanted to see you..."

"That's imprudent. Henceforth, if you remain under my orders..."

"Your partner, you mean..."

"Partner, then..."

"Of course, a partner has some benefits, some kind of interest in a business."

"What are you complaining about?"

"Nothing...except, well...I'm broke. I was playing cards yesterday, and had a run of bad luck. Just now, I borrowed five francs from a mate—they had the same fate as my two hundred bullets last evening. That's the picture. I said to myself: Monsieur le Baron has guests tonight...I can go tap him. He must be in a hurry to sleep peacefully, old Ro..."

Saint-Magloire shook Bastien's arm violently—so violently that the latter could not retain a cry of "Ouch!"

"You must never pronounce the name that you just had on your lips."

"I'll watch out..."

"You'd pay for that stupidity with your life."

"It's well-known that you don't like talkative people."

"Why did you come to my house? I don't like imprudence..."

"I needed funds, damn it."

"Well, here's five hundred francs, to tide you over." The Baron took a banknote out of his pocket, which was swallowed up by Bastien's with vertiginous rapidity.

"*Au revoir*, Monsieur le Baron."

"And above all, be prudent!"

"I will..."

Saint-Magloire headed back to his house. "That's good...that Lavardens could have recognized me and denounced me. I had to forestall him—I couldn't let him go on living..."

A quarter of an hour after the scene that we have just related, Baron de Saint-Magloire arrived home, discarded his coat and felt hat, and, radiant, with more verve than ever, went back down to the smoking room.

V. The International Syndicate of Moroccan Gold Mines

Saint-Magloire's absence had lasted no more than twenty minutes.

What is twenty minutes for people who have just got up from a princely table, galvanized by the light and delicious intoxication of refined fare and the noblest vintages, killing time by savoring exquisite cigars, watered by expensive liqueurs? No one had noticed the Amphitryon's absence.

When the Baron came back into the smoking room, embalmed by the subtle perfume of Havanas, the conversations were so animated that no one heard the sound of his footsteps, muffled as they were by the thick carpet.

His eyes shining, his features relaxed, having made an abrupt effort of will to erase every trace of the violent emotion that had recently contracted them, whose last echoes he could still feel in the intimacy of his fibers, he paused briefly in the doorway, and embraced the brilliant crowd with a rapid glance in which there was both scorn and pride both suggestion and triumph.

There, he had a dozen of the most powerful financiers in Paris—those who are known as the kings of the marketplace—along with a choice selection of engineers, manufacturers and artists, two generals on active service and three in retirement, several princes of medicine, a member of the Institut and two newspaper editors: in sum, the epitome of that "All Paris" of the premières, which flatters itself, and not mistakenly, with comprising the movers and shakers of opinion, of distributing glory and discredit more-or-less arbitrarily, of making the rain and fine weather. To complete the collection, there were even had a dozen specimens of the old aristocracy, those gentlemen with the sonorous names and glittering pedigrees that are necessary to put on a good show on administrative boards whose prestige needs to be established in advance, and a whole gang of flashy foreigners sporting implausible decorations, dressed like fashionable engravings: Spaniards, Americans, Hungarians, and more than one red-sealed Turk; and, finally, the secretary of a prospective Minister, there to represent the government *in partibus*, of whom he was assumed to be the confidant and factotum in delicate and secret missions.

"And to think," Saint-Magloire muttered between his teeth, "that all these spear-carriers, all these puppets, are mine, ready to oblige me at the flick of a finger or the wink of an eye. Wealth, talent, science, art, intellect, luxury, the Bourse, the Press, the Army, Diplomacy—everything that shines, everything that has a ring to it, everything that weighs in the balance of history—I have in my hand, in the actualities and appearances of that flock of imbeciles, swindlers and poseurs, whom snobbery has made into my general staff. Oh, but I've come a long way...

"Life is strange. They're all here, the smartest of the smart, those with whom 'one mustn't trifle.' There's not one of them—not even Wilhems, who claims to know things by divinatory intuition at least twenty-four hours before they happen—who suspects that I've just disposed of an inconvenience. Has any of them even thought of wondering where I've been? It would be a sin not to put them in my pocket. Let's get on with it."

He advanced, at a supple feline tread, into the midst of the noisiest group. "Messieurs!" he cried. "Business is business! We're not here to amuse ourselves."

Those simple words, negligently uttered by that crystalline voice, simultaneously imperious and seductive—which no one, it was said, could resist—worked like a charm. Suddenly, all the stories of women, the parliamentary and worldly gossip, the lewd and spiteful anecdotes with which digestion had been soothed thus far, came to a stop.

Even Wilhems, the "best-informed journalist in Europe," interrupted a confused explanation, peppered with witty remarks, about the war in the Transvaal,[8] without frowning. What Saint-Magloire had said was more interesting. Obviously, he had not disturbed so many people for nothing. He was about to pull some stunning surprise out of his bag of tricks, from which everyone might make a profit.

A circle formed of men in suits, standing up, ears pricked. Only the oldest of the generals, an old man with a ruddy face quartered by countless intersecting wrinkles, underlined by a formidable white moustache reddened by the abuse of cigars remained half-slouched in a vast armchair, his gout, reawakened by the Chambertin, preventing him from standing up—but he was no less attentive; that was visible in the furrowing of his stubborn forehead.

With his back to the monumental fireplace, where enormous oak logs were aflame, with the thumb of his left hand in the armhole of his waistcoat and the other hand lifted in a fine gesture of bringing the room to order, sure of his effect, not a crease disturbing the immaculate whiteness of his short-front, the Baron resumed.

"Messieurs, I repeat, we're not here to amuse ourselves. I was obliged just now to slip away unceremoniously for a few moments. I offer you all my apologies, for it as an apparent lapse in my duty as a host. I say 'apparently,' not only to claim, as redemption for that incorrectness, the benefit of extenuating circumstances, but because it is, in fact, strictly accurate. If I was absent just now, it was with the sole objective of fortifying what have to tell you this evening. It was as much in your interests as mine, since we're marching in step. I have, in fact, a proposal to make to you: an admirable business opportunity, a colossal and prodigious opportunity; one of those opportunities that only come along once or twice in a century, and which revolutionize the world.

---

[8] The Boer war began in 1899, thus enabling this scene to be temporally located more accurately than the obscured date on the invitation.

"Very well! One of my engineers, having returned from a confidential mission that I had entrusted to him, has come hotfoot, without losing a minute—it's not two hours since he disembarked at the Gare de Lyon—to bring me a rich harvest of priceless information. You, Messieurs, will immediately have the pick up the crop.

"Will you forgive me, now, for having given you the slip?"

"No, no."

"Bravo! Bravo!"

"There's only one Saint-Magloire!"

"Let him speak."

The Baron smiled, bowed, lit a cigar, and continued. "You know, Messieurs—if you don't, permit me to tell you—that I once lived in Morocco. Not the bastard Morocco, the laughable Morocco, the comic opera Morocco, adapted to the usage of Thomas Cook tourists, of which one or two of you might have formed a superficial, but quite false, idea by making a stopover in Tangier, but the real Morocco, the inhospitable Morocco, wild and savage, the Morocco behind the caliphs. That Morocco, the only, true and terrible one, in which I lived for several years..."

"If all the countries where he lived for several years were laid end to end," murmured one of the journalists in his colleague's ear, "it would be necessary to go around the world at least three times, like Robert Planquette's hero[9]—and if he's isn't more than a hundred years old, my name's not..."

"Shut up, viper," replied the other, interested by the discourse. "What do his age, his odyssey and his stories matter, if he's going to make you a nice profit? You haven't, I imagine had any cause for complaint thus far about being in the fake centenarian's good books?"

"That's true."

"Well then, shut your mouth and open your pockets; I think it's going to rain money."

Saint-Magloire had divined and sensed rather than heard that conservation. His troubling, hypnotic gaze weighed upon the skeptic for a few seconds—who blew his nose loudly in embarrassment.

Then, slightly raising the volume of his golden voice, into which an occasional argot term put a hint of the street-urchin, adding a spice of roguish sonority, he went on.

"Yes, Messieurs, I knew Morocco as you know the département of the Seine, or as you, general, know southern Algeria. I traded wool with the Saharan caravans, with which I led a nomadic life under camel-skin tents, eating couscous, date paste and *chorba*. That was not, as you can imagine, in the capacity of

---

[9] The reference is to a song in Planquette's record-breaking operetta *Les Cloches de Corneville* (1878), "J'ai fait trois fois le tour du monde" [I've been around the world three times].

45

a European merchant, for, especially in those days, no *roumi* would have ventured into the depths of the Maghreb with impunity. It was as a Muslim, a faithful disciple of the Prophet. I had everything necessary to play the role."

"Everything?" the incorrigible journalist put in. "Including the last formality?"

"Exactly," the Baron replied. "I did not hesitate over that little formality. Business is business!"

Stifled laughter, swollen by equivocal jests, caused the shoulders of the audience to undulate. Only the Jewish bankers remained serious, nodding their heads with penetrative expressions.

Saint-Magloire closed his eyes briefly, and in an ecstatic tone, *mezza voce*, he added: "Oh, Morocco! The sand dunes with changing forms, which resemble the pepper lakes of Cayenne, and the stony Hamada…and the cold nights, beneath the velvet-blue awning of the sky, in which the stars, so bright that they seems close at hand, are as resplendent as a sprinkling of golden nails. When one has lived in that country, in spite of the dangers, the privations and the miseries, one retains a certain nostalgia for it. But I'm getting sentimental, I believe. Excuse me, Messieurs; one does not relive such a dream without emotion…

"What will doubtless make your heartbeats quicken is that the entire interior of Morocco is nothing but an immense chaplet of gold-bearing deposits, prodigiously rich, and that that mass of gold…"

At that point, Saint-Magloire paused, emphasizing his words, managing his effect like an expert actor. "And that that mass of gold is mine…which is to say, ours, since we shall work it together!"

A frisson of cupidity ran through the audience, too breathless to applaud.

"Yes, Messieurs, as I have the honor of telling you, from the southern face of the Moroccan Atlas to the foot of Mount Tesah, which is 3,500 meters in altitude, to the highest plateau of the Hagar, and perhaps beyond—personally I've never been beyond Mount Tassili, passing through Tafilet, Touat, Tarmentit and Sabat—there is gold that can be stirred with a spade. It's a fabulous Eldorado, compared with which California, the Transvaal and the Klondike are pitiful.

"I've known that for a long time, but my engineer—the man I've just left—has just brought me official proof that all my personal observations were still an underestimation, to an improbable degree.

"Well, I repeat, all that gold is ours, for, during my residence out there, I took advantage of my knowledge of the Arabic language, my conversion to Islam, my affiliation to the all-powerful sect of the Senussi, my friendly relations with the sheikhs and marabouts—to whom I had rendered services that the men of the tents never forget, and my collaborators in the Sultan's entourage. The exploitation of all that gold-bearing terrain has been conceded to me and my associates, to the exclusion of all others, for fifty years.

46

"All of that is legal, in conformity with Moroccan tradition, confirmed by the seal of the imperial and papal Sharif—proof against anything. There is no more to do but find the necessary capital and start work."

"But what will Spain say?" objected one timid fox-faced old man with discolored lips—one of those whose orders, issued on one stock exchange or another, drive prices up and down, which is to say, ruining or making the fortune of ten thousand families. "You know, my dear Baron, that Spain considers Morocco to be an extension of the peninsula, and will not take kindly to Frenchmen trampling on what it calls its historic rights. Beware of those diplomatic complications whose first effect, by sowing anxiety and panic, is to ruin the finest business deal."

"Come on, old chap," Saint-Magloire replied. "Do you take me for a child? My first thought was of Spain—that goes without saying—and I've done what's necessary. Spain is with us. I'm not only talking about Spanish financiers, so brilliantly represented here..."

The most olive-skinned of the foreigners, a lean fellow with a sparse beard, whose shirt-buttons were diamonds as big as hazelnuts, gleaming with a thousand iridescent fires, uttered a peremptory *yo lo créo.*

"...I'm talking about the Spanish government itself, whose assent we have."

The plenipotentiary minister and the chief of the cabinet nodded, after having exchanged a knowing glance.

"One does not undertake a project of this magnitude," Saint-Magloire continued, "without holding all the trumps in one's hand. The Spanish government is on side, the French government is on side. Even the English are on side—in the wings." Then, lowering his voice, he added: "Chamberlain is involved."[10]

The emotion was at its peak. The circle closed in around the orator; thirty hands reached toward him as if to a fetish.

"You're a man of genius!" cried Wilhems, appointing himself the interpreter of everyone's enthusiasm.

The other journalist outbid him, as if to beg pardon for his fit of skepticism and spite. "That man," he said, ought not to be called Saint-Magloire, but Midas, since everything he touches turns to gold."

The comment spread; it was a success.

Meanwhile, Saint-Magloire modest and teasing, made a sign indicating that he had not finished.

"The Sharif has given me," he went on, "the concession of all the gold-bearing lands of Southern Morocco, with the right to found towns there, to construct railways, to canalize the Oued-Draa and to create a large harbor at its mouth. In brief, it's a matter of nothing less than developing that admirable region, whose wealth is incalculable, and which will become the most prosperous

---

[10] The British statesman Joseph Chamberlain (1836-1914).

country in the world once we have introduced the benefits of civilization and the progress of science and industry.

"Such, Messieurs, is what I bring to the International Syndicate that is to be constituted, and which is already constituted, since you are here."

A thunder of cheers interrupted him, but he was in full flow. Raising his voice, whose stridency rose above the tumult, he had a flight of great eloquence—one of those "oral coups" than rouse crowds. And he spoke, in a warm, persuasive voice,

Morocco would be colonized. A Franco-Spanish consortium, with the moral and financial support of the biggest banks in England, Germany, America and Russia, was about to raise North-Western Africa from the barbarity in which it had sunk two centuries before.

Hypnotized by the sorcery of gold, many thousands of emigrants would flood from the four corners of the world, bringing with them the fever of labor that can transform a country in a matter of years. The marvels of the American Far-West, southern Africa and Alaska were about to be seen only three days from Marseilles. A new Algeria would be born, even more beautiful, even richer than the other, which would amply console France for the loss of Egypt, which could henceforth be conclusively abandoned, without any bitter resentment to the English, as compensation for their collaboration.

Spain too, refashioned and rejuvenated, would see the rebirth of the sumptuous era of the Vigo galleons.[11] In less than ten years, Morocco would be covered by railways, electric tramways, mining, industrial and agricultural operations. Cities more opulent and more beautiful than Melbourne, Dawson City, Sacramento or Johannesburg would emerge from the ground as if by magic; on the threshold of the desert, diverted toward their markets, freely open to international traffic, all the commercial currents of the Sahara would flow, from Adrar to Darfur: all the caravans bringing gum, ivory and precious essences.

The gold of the Atlas would pay for all of that.

What glory, and what profits, there would be for the initiators of that grandiose work, perhaps unprecedented in the history of the civilized world!

And the actor, completely given over to his current role, forgot what he had said a short while before in a quasi-sublime appeal for peace.

"Perhaps it will be necessary to fight," he continued, in his enthusiasm, "for the Muslim fanatics will not allow the accursed Christians to install themselves in their midst, overturning their traditions, their mores and their way of live, without resistance—and the Muslims of Morocco are both the bravest and most intransigent in all Islam. Blood will flow in rivers; but, as they say, one can't make an omelet without breaking eggs. Spain has not left all its soldiers in

---

[11] In 1702 a Franco-Spanish fleet escorting galleons loaded with American gold was attacked by the British and the Dutch in Vigo Bay, and most of the treasure sunk.

Cuba, and if France has finally decided to put together a colonial army, it's not to let it languish inactively, like a rusty implement."

Besides which, will a few judiciously placed millions, he, Saint-Magloire, would take responsibility for buying the neutrality, if not the active alliance, of the Sultan and the principal tribal chiefs. He knew how to do that.

"Remember, too," he added, "what there is to be founded, and what there is to be conquered. If Paris, in the words of Henri IV, is well worth a mass, what will Morocco not be worth, especially when it will be the fortune and the glory of the Fatherland?"

"Vive la France!" shouted the old general—and, standing up painfully on his stuff legs, he embraced the Baron.

Engineers and financiers then tried to raise a few objections, but they were as many pretexts for Saint-Magloire to shine more brightly. The diabolical man had an answer for everything. After an hour of taut argument, nothing was left in the shade—not even the smallest details of the future share-issue. He had won his cause.

When they separated, the plan of campaign was drawn up, the work shared out, and the eventual profits divided between the promoters. Naturally, Saint-Magloire had taken the lion's share without anyone raising a protest.

The International Syndicate of Moroccan Gold Mines—the greatest idea of the century—was virtually constituted.

VI. The Île Royale

Gradually, the house's drawing rooms emptied. It was getting late and a only few rare initiates, privileged individuals whom the Master admitted to his intimacy, remained with the Baron, awaiting for the windfall of another precious 'tip,' a clever dodge for the following day on the Bourse.

To see them grouped around him, timid and silent, one might have thought them a group of acolytes prostrated before a god. Was Monsieur de Saint-Magloire not a god for all those worshipers of the Golden Calf? Was every one of those indications not prophetic? The king of finance had never been mistaken in his anticipations. He guided the market as he wished, provoking rises or falls with a gesture, sowing ruin or fortune around him, in the temple of the stock exchange.

Never had Saint-Magloire had as much verve as that evening, and his intimates left him enthused, intoxicated by the fabulous dreams with which he had lulled them.

Left alone, the Baron, slightly fatigued by the soirée in which he had lavished himself, went back to his apartment. In his bedroom, his valet was awaiting his orders. He sent him away, wanting to be alone with his thoughts.

As soon as the domestic had gone, Saint-Magloire, sprawling in an armchair, took a carefully-folded piece of paper from his waistcoat pocket. He read it, with a satisfied expression. Then he got to his feet, applied the piece of paper to a candle flame, and threw the ashes into the fireplace.

"Well," he murmured, "I think that was a good day. No one will ever be able to suspect that Baron de Saint-Magloire had anything to do with the accident at Beuzeville-Bréauté. Well played, Baron: no longer a cloud on the horizon; the future is yours."

At that moment, his eyes glimpsed his image reflected in the mirror—a masterpiece of sculpture—and he smiled at himself. Then his gaze made a tour of the room, furnished with exquisite artistry. Never had he savored the joy of living, the pride of success and the satisfaction of all the luxury that surrounded him as much as at that moment.

A kind of blissful intoxication gripped him.

"Ha ha!" he sniggered. "Number 883 has definitely come a long way."

Lighting a Havana, he stretched himself out in the armchair again, distractedly following the blue smoke of the cigar, which was rising toward the ceiling in capricious spirals.

The Baron was daydreaming. It was an entire novel that unfolded before him, a series of prodigious adventures worthy of the pen of a Balzac, a Jules Verne and a Gaboriau all rolled into one. An interested spectator, he witnessed all the drama of that stormy and picturesque life, in which audacity and cunning had only been equaled by extraordinary luck.

First, the stage was set in a coastal town, Biarritz, where, having taken in countless dupes in various European capitals, the man he saw again in his reverie had boldly come to live on the spoils in company with a superb creature, conquered by his magician's eyes and his lordly manners.

At that moment, it seemed that the luck that had propelled the young man so far had decided to abandon him.

One day, as he was getting out of his landau, insouciant and cheerful, two agents of the Sûreté had arrested Gaston Rozen—for, as the reader has deduced, he was the adventurer in question.

Closely guarded, he was taken back to Paris, and no prisoner was ever subjected to more attentive surveillance. His previous audacious escape necessitated all the excessive precautions they took in his regard. Rozen understood that there was no hope of escaping punishment. He became humble and repentant, and threw all the responsibility for his sins on to the bad education he had received.

Parisians had flocked to the Assize Court to see the famous crook tried. No trial had ever drawn more notable men or elegant women to the courtroom, which was too small that day. The cream of all social and artistic celebrity was there—but that audience, fond of sensational cases, was disappointed by the piteous attitude and tearful tone of the handsome fellow whose near-legendary exploits had been all over the news.

Gaston sensing that he was doomed, had only one objective: to attenuate the inevitable sentence as much as possible. He wept, lamenting the abandonment of his relatives, so affectively that the judges did not go as far as the maximum in determining his sentence.

After the verdict, internment in the Île de Ré,[12] the departure with the cohort of convicts on a naval transport ship, the crossing in steerage, heaped pell-mell with a hundred wretches wedged like beasts of burden behind iron grilles, guarded by armed sentinels, the disembarkation in Cayenne!

All that passed before the eyes of the Baron de Saint-Magloire.

A glimmer of anger shone in his gaze; a frown creased his forehead.

Now he saw Rozen, the sprightly gentleman, the Don Juan of lovely *horizontales*, clad in the ignominious uniform, shaved and shorn, a lamentable rag lost in the gross troop of *bagnards*, ill-treated by the guards, looked at askance by his companions in infamy, who found him too much of a poseur to begin with. And every day, beneath the leaden sky, brutalized by the overseers, it was necessary to bend his back to the hard labor of the penitentiary. His hands

---

[12] An island off La Rochelle, used as a transit depot for convicts and exiles shipped off the New Caledonia and French Guiana.

once delicate and well-cared-for, were torn by crude tools; his complexion became earthen.

On arriving in Cayenne, Rozen had wondered where he would be interned. He had hoped at first to be left on the mainland, where the regime was less harsh and escape possible.

The penitentiary colony of Guiana comprise, in fact, several places of deportation: Cayenne, Kourou and the Îles du Salut. The latter are three in number: Île du Diable, Île Saint-Joseph and Île Royale. It is in the last two islands that the dangerous, the incorrigible, and those prisoners of recommended on their departure from the metropolis for special surveillance are interned. There, the regime is strict, the guards pitiless, and escape chimerical.

Rozen was taken to Île Royale and registered with the number 883.

The island is fairly large; it is there that the command post is located. A few single-story houses, gathered around a modest church, serve to lodge the commandant and guards; near those groups is the hospital, and further away, in a series of barracks, the bagnards' workshops and dormitories are established.

883 was somber and taciturn...a dull rage possessed him, at having lost the contest in which he had engaged against society.

Many a time, he wondered whether it might not be getter to get it over with, to throw himself into the sea, to give himself as fodder to the sharks that mounted guard along the coast, awaiting the prey that the hospital reserved for them. There is no burial on that island of expiation; cadavers are thrown into the sea.

Those suicidal ideas soon abandoned him; after a short while, Rozen was broken in to that new life; his flexible character had got the upper hand.

A clever actor, he played the role of submissive prisoner admirably, gradually gaining the confidence of his companions at the expense of a thousand small services he strove to render them.

The guards, for their part, noted him as disciplined number, and one day, the commandant, during a review, had encouraged 883 to persevere in that conduct, allowing him to glimpse, perhaps in two years, a relaxation of the iron regime under which he lived.

But when he was alone, and everyone around him was asleep, Rozen, his head in his hands and his gaze lost in a reverie, wept over his sins, bitterly regretting squandering so much ingenuity and talent only to end up miserably clad in a convict's uniform.

"Oh," he said to himself, with his fists clenched and his eyes sparkling with fury, "I shall have my revenge, and it will be spectacular! How, I shall I make use then of my education, audacity and the resources of my fecund intelligence! I made a false step, I slipped—so be it; but I shall get up again. I shall get out of here, and the lesson will have been useful. I was too young. Now...I want everything to fold beneath me. I want the most powerful men on earth to have to reckon with me.

"Yes, I shall flee this accursed island; I shall set foot in life again and I shall climb so high, so high, on a golden pedestal, that the greatest of men will wallow at my feet, imploring my protection.

"It's no longer just fortune and love that I need; I want that which contains everything: Power! I want to bend everyone and everything beneath my hand. I want to be a king, more than a king: the arbiter of the world!

"The honor of men and the virtue of women; Glory and Genius; I shall trample all of that underfoot when I have gold, enough gold to stifle everything that is great, everything that is generous; under my law, humankind will no longer be anything more than a host of marionettes, whose strings I shall hold.

"Rozen, poor imbecile libertine, ingenious crook, you're dead! It's another man that will emerge from the uniform of 883. Before that new conqueror, everyone will bow down; an incarnation of the demon, he will lead the infernal dance around the Golden Calf!

And before the convict's eyes, in the obscurity of the hut, Paris appeared: Paris, which he dreamed of setting in order; Paris, which he would inundate, if necessary, with blood and tears, to slake his thirst for domination...

Sometimes, after these dreams, these hallucinations, 883 reflected for a long time.

He told himself that submission and good conduct would get him from the islands to the mainland in two years, at the most—and he wanted to gain time, to get back as rapidly as possible into the struggle, initially to make, or rather to appropriate, sufficient capital to lay the foundations of the gigantic enterprise of which he had dreamed.

Escape from Île Royale? That was impractical. Escape, Rozen knew full well, was only possible from Maroni, the place to which exiles were sent, and convicts who were granted a gentler lot after a long enough stay, and a relative liberty. That, therefore, was where it was necessary for him to be transported.

From the day that idea came to him, 883 sought the means of realizing it.

He simulated an illness. He was taken to the hospital. There he strove, by means of a resigned attitude and an appearance of fervent piety, to gain the good graces of the sisters. They cared for him benevolently, but he soon understood that nothing could be expected in that direction. The mother superior commended him to the guards, but that was all.

Rozen despaired. There seemed to be no means of getting off Île Royale.

It was necessary, in order to attract the attention of the authorities, for an opportunity to present itself to accomplish some courageous deed or to advertise himself by means of one of those services that are generously rewarded while the person rendering them is scorned...it did not matter which. He was prepared for anything; for heroism as for cowardice. The essential thing was to get off the island. For that, he would risk anything, even his life.

He was resolved to play the game of two stakes—liberty or death—to the end.

VII. A False Brother

883 was visibly deteriorating.

The rage of knowing that he was there, a prisoner, constrained to the hard labor of the *bagne*, obliged to submit to contact with ignoble and stupid companions, was making Rozen feverish. And every evening, when he found himself alone in the hut, lying in his hammock, he closed his eyes, and his dream of grandeur and power ran its course.

Oh, to be free!

All his intelligence, and all the resources of his fecund imagination, were devoted to that end.

The craziest ideas passed through his head, but in that chaos of projects, none could be carried out, even at the cost of the most incredible audacity. There was not one chance in a thousand of getting away from Île Royale alive.

Fits of furious rage agitated the condemned man; he worked lazily, and when the voice of an overseer called him to order, the desire seized him to leap at the guard's throat, and to strangle him, in order to put an end to it—but Rozen did not take long to comprehend the inanity of resistance and indiscipline; that would militate against what he wanted: to be sent to Maroni in order to escape. So he persisted, in spite of his interior rebellions, in his original strategy: to be the most resigned and submissive of convicts.

The authorities held him up as a model.

Sensing that they were interested in him, the bandit made himself more and more docile, more and more humble, and played the comedy of repentance like a master. He deplored his guilty youth, promising, when his penalty was purged to become a perfect colonist in Guiana, since it was henceforth forbidden for him to live in the Metropolis. And when he spoke to the overseers, to the supervisors, to the nuns and to the doctors, his harmonious voice and penetrating charm, and his mobile eyes, nacreously moistened, gradually attracted sympathy.

The wretch would gladly have killed them all, however, if he could. What did human lives matter to him? He would have consented to vanquish his atavistic repugnance for murder and to wade through blood for hours on end, in order to reach open ground!

One evening, when he was plunged in his reverie, seeing himself in a magnificent town house overlooking a crowd of powerful individuals who had come running to pay court to him, the sound of a voice attracted his attention. It was more like a whisper. People spoke in whispers so as not to attract the attention of the guards.

At first, Rozen could not suppress a gesture of discontent. Someone was interrupting his dreams. He resented their having woken him up, brought him back to reality. With wide open eyes he gazed, desolately, at the row of hammocks suspended from the beams of the hut.

The bare framework seemed to him all the more lugubrious because he had just glimpsed marvelous drawing rooms, whose walls were decked with masterpieces, and whose gold sparkled in the light of electric bulbs.

But the muffled conversation was still going on. He pricked up his ears.

"Yes," said a voice, "that would be possible—but all the comrades would have to be in agreement."

"Of course," the other replied, "but that can't be done...we'd soon be stitched up, old man."

"And goodbye escape..."

Escape! That word got Rozen's attention. So he was not the only one thinking about it; close at hand, other convicts were rolling escape plans around their heads.

Oh, he could help them...pull their chestnuts out of the fire...

He listened more attentively still.

"Do you know how many anarchos there are here?" one of the speakers asked.

"Damn! One can count a good dozen."

"As many as there are overseers."

"One each..."

"We could kill the commandant."

"We could seize the boats."

"And sail the galley!"

"Yes, but the thing is that it all has to be arranged without the administration suspecting anything."

"Bah! We'll take our time—in order to be sure that there isn't a snitch among those we let in on the secret."

"Then, when we get back home...to Paris..."

"And blow up their Bourse—the bourgeoisie..."

"I think so...a firework to send their whole rotten society flying through the air, right down to the foundations."

Rozen got up quietly and slipped closer to the two talkers. "Blow up the Bourse?" he said. "Why?"

The two anarchists looked at the newcomer over the edges of their hammocks, menacingly. One raised his hand—the coarse, callused hand of a laborer, at the end of an athletic arm.

"Have no fear," murmured 883. "I'm a brother."

"A brother?"

"Yes—and the proof is that I can offer you the means for which you're searching. First, you need a leader."

"A leader!" growled one of the convicts. "Never..."

"Neither God nor Master," said the other.

"Let's say a guide, a pilot—someone who knows how to steer the boat—then. Listen to me anyway: you'll understand.

"Yes, you're right to want the end of the sybaritic bourgeoisie, which exploits the poverty of the laborer, which lives on his pain, which tramples his corpse when he dies on the job...yes, you're right; everyone should have an equal share in life's feast. Like you, I've struggled for the good cause, and that's why I'm here, like you. I took individual reprisals, and I was shopped—that's the way it is.

"Let me tell you, though, that we've all taken a false path. Our isolated attempts at propaganda by action have only ended in our being crushed by bourgeois so-called justice."

The two anarchists were listening to Rozen religiously. The latter paraphrased their doctrines in a soft voice, scarcely more perceptible than a breath of air.

"No," the charmer went on, "it's not necessary to blow up the Bourse; it's only necessary to take the place of those who are there, to administer society's progress to the advantage of the affiliated comrades. And for every member of the association we shall form, there'll be a fortune. Gold will have changed hands. Wealth to the workers! The guillotine for the bourgeoisie! We need to be the stronger, don't we? Without that, the social revolution will be held back.

"Now, in order to be the stronger, we need gold, because in bourgeois society, gold is the ultimate instrument, the supreme lever. If we want the revolution to triumph, the revolutionaries need to begin by taking over the treasure-chest. It's necessary to destroy the exploiters with their own weapons."

"You're right," replied one of the convicts.

"Yes, I am right, and I've brought you the collaboration of my intelligence and my arm. Trust me; I'll get you out of here. You need an agreement with the other companions; I can make that agreement. You know that I enjoy a relative liberty here..."

The eyes of the two bagnards fixed themselves on Rozen. "This liberty...you acquired it by...?"

Rozen did not let the speaker finish. "I acquired it at the price of my humiliation. Since bourgeois injustice threw me into this bagne, I've only had one aim: revenge; and one idea: revenge. Oh, I've submitted to the vile demands of these brutes who guard us, and for whom we're less than dogs. I've crawled, in order to be able to bite harder later. I've retracted my claws in order to tear more effectively when the moment came.

"And it's come. I sensed that just now when I heard you talking about your plans. Ah, companions, do you think that I haven't suffered, bending my spine beneath the tyranny of the overseers...?"

The other two were listening silently, lulled by Rozen's voice, captivated by his hypocritical eloquence.

"Well," the Levantine continued, "I've suffered because I wanted to serve the cause one day...and the favors I've been able to obtain by concealing my pride in the depths of my soul, stifling the revolt ready to spring forth from my entire being...I bless them, for they'll serve to set us free. And then we'll see what we can do for the triumph of anarchism. Do you want me?"

"Yes," the two companions replied, simultaneously.

"That's good—let me do what I can, and in a few days, we'll be ready. At a signal we'll all agree, we'll act..."

At that moment, a door opened at the far end of the hut.

"The round!" Rozen murmured. "Soon, comrades."

With the agility of a cat, he climbed back into his hammock.

The watchman passed by, projecting the rays of his lantern into every corner of the dormitory. He did not see anything abnormal.

Rozen could not get back to sleep. Oh, if the two anarchists to whom he had just spouted such beautiful theories had been able to divine what was going through his head, they would have been rapidly edified as to the goal pursued by the false brother.

At that moment, 883 was putting together a Machiavellian plan, whose execution would get him to Maroni...

On the one hand, he would excite the anarchist companions with whom he could communicate during the hours of labor. On the other, he would continue to be submissive and crawling in the presence of the guards and their superiors.

It was a serious revolt that he needed—a bloody one, even—not an insignificant mutiny, soon stifled. The commandant of Île Royale had to be convinced, when Rozen denounced the plot, that he and all his subordinates had escaped a massacre. And for the service rendered, but reason of the favorable notes he had already accumulated, 883 hoped that his classification would be changed, and he would be transferred to Saint-Laurent.

Meanwhile, in spite of his habitual self-control, the wretch shivered as he thought of the redoubtable double role he was about to play. On the one hand, he had to fear giving himself away to the anarchists, and on the other, he needed to lead the revolt with sufficient skill for none of the overseers to suspect the provocation too soon.

First, he thought about winning the confidence of all the companions whom propaganda by action had led to the bagne—and every day, in mysterious conversation, he approached one, and threw his subversive theories at him, lulling him with all his social utopias.

Gradually, all the companions came to regard him as the purest of their own, as the hope of the *idea*.

That first part of 883's program went marvelously, without a hitch or any alarm.

Now, Rozen said to himself, *I can make my move; when I betray these imbeciles, not one of them will dare to suspect me.*

The fact is that all the revolutionaries, unpolished and credulous individuals, were disposed to see the infamous scoundrel who would betray them as some kind of second Bakunin or Ravachol:[13] an initiator of a new era, a prophet, a demigod. Not one suspected the Machiavellian plan that he had cleverly drawn up to destroy them.

---

[13] Mikhail Bakunin (1814-1876) was the anarchist theorist whose ideas were the principal basis of the French anarchist manifesto drawn up in Paris in the 1880s, with whose drafting Gautier was marginally involved. Ravachol (François Koenigstein), guillotined in 1892, became the most famous anarchist terrorist in France, allegedly associated with three bomb attacks of his own and several ostensibly carried out to avenge him. He was merely imitating the exploits of the Russian nihilists who tried repeatedly to blow up Tsar Alexander II, and ultimately succeeded in 1881, but his example helped cement the image of anarchists as bomb-throwers.

VIII. Bastien, alias *Macaron*

Patiently, Rozen prepared the revolt.

One by one, he excited the fanaticism of the companions, demonstrating to them that the cost of liberty was forceful action.

When some of them, struck by the sentimentality that is more frequent among the primitive than one might suppose, hesitated at the thought of being obliged to kill the guards, poor men who were there to earn their bread—"also victims, in the final count, of a rotten society"—883 shrugged his shoulders.

"Killing guards...that's what stops them from behaving like ferocious beasts. How many comrades have been murdered by those bandits? Only yesterday, 775 was killed by a revolver-shot by Pegrini, who had been after him for a long time. Pegrini simply shot him in the back. He made a report saying that 775 had tried to escape. And *Amen!* 775 was thrown to the sharks. And Pegrini isn't the worst—he kills, without torturing! What? You'd take pity those dogs? No more hesitation, then. When you want to get into a property, do you hesitate to kill the guard-dogs? No. Well, these men are the guard-dogs of the bourgeoisie. Come on, comrades—no pity! Are you or are you not for social revolution?"

"Am I?" replied the anarchist, with a tear in his eye. "I am! For sure, then!"

"You'll move when I tell you?"

"Yes."

To hasten the adventure, Rozen had also propagated the idea of the revolt among the other convicts, Although not anarchists, a number of them, skillfully measured and chosen, were worse, having agreed to enter into the plot.

Everything was ready.

883 had found a precious auxiliary to help him in the affair: a beardless Parisian street-urchin, short but solidly-built. He was a cheery soul, but that did not prevent him from being more ferocious and hateful than the other companions. The bagnards of Île Royale submitted to the ascendancy of the little faubourgian, who amused them with his baroque repartee.

It must be admitted that Bastien—that was the anarchist' name—was quite capable of earning respect. Beneath an almost child-like appearance, he concealed an astonishing muscular strength, combined with the agility of an acrobat. By virtue of his glibness, strength and skill, did not Bastien, whose nickname was Macaron, have everything required to play the double role of the life and soul of the party and cut-throat?

Rozen had taken note of the short man, and before undertaking his propaganda with the other companions, he had first made an ally of him. The charmer had been able to capture Bastien's confidence to such an extent that the undisciplined, untamable fellow obeyed him blindly. Macaron, it must be said, was not very scrupulous by nature, and provided that Rozen's plans did not conflict with his own, everything was fine by him.

"Macaron," the Levantine had said to him, "would you like to be free?"

"I'll say!" Bastien replied.

"Then you've only to shut your eyes to everything you see me do. When the companions are in on the secret, and when they've all agreed to move, you won't leave my side. I need my lieutenant close at hand."

"Since I say so, that's the way it is!" But Bastien was wary. Was Rozen, by chance, meditating turning him in things went wrong at the critical moment? Not so fast, Lisette!

"Oh," said Rozen, with a strange smile, "don't be afraid that anyone will shirk the task."

Finally, the day fixed by the conspirators arrived, after long weeks of anxious expectation. That same evening, at a signal from Rozen, the rioters were to emerge from the dormitories *en masse*, kill the guards, take their weapons, and then march on the sleeping post, jumping the sentinels before they had time to cry out...

And when that was done, the entire island would fall into the hands of the convicts, who would start by cutting the submarine cable lining it to the mainland. The commandant, the sisters at the hospital and the menial workers would be taken prisoner without anyone being able to raise the alarm. The safe would be seized and its contents shared out; that would be traveling money. And it would be easy to arm the boats and escape…to reach British Guiana, where they would land on a deserted beach, for from any inhabited place—for it was necessary to beware of extradition.

Then, they would disperse. Everyone would go his own way, but they would rendezvous in Paris for the day of revenge, for the blessed day when they would make the dirty bourgeois pay for so much humiliation, suffering and misery. Hurrah for anarchy!

Rozen and Macaron had so enthused all their companions in chains that the wretches saw no difficulty in the accomplishment of the fabulous plan concocted by 883. They would "march in step, like one man," according to Bastien's expression. Those mostly-uneducated minds, habituated to soothing themselves with utopias, thought it entirely natural that such an enterprise could succeed. Better still, 883 had persuaded them that they would not be running any risk.

All day long, gliding prudently through the groups of convicts at work, Rozen and Bastien had given them the rallying cry for that night.

Everything went well; even the storm was a further but of luck for the rebels—one more trump in their hand. It would be easy, in those conditions, to avoid the vigilance of the sentinels.

The return to the dormitories took place as usual. After an hour, everyone seemed to be asleep. Suddenly, however, a soft whistle was heard. Men descended from the hammocks and crept silently toward the door. It yielded.

Outside, the storm was raging; rain was falling in torrents, as it does in the tropics.

"Courage, comrades!" said Bastien. "To the post!"

They had scarcely taken ten paces, however, when a loud voice ordered; "Halt!"

"Good God!" cried 883, shaking his fists. "We're surrounded!"

"Betrayed," said a companion.

"Betrayed!" howled Rozen. "God's thunder! He'll pay dearly, that one! Later... We're the stronger—forward!"

Roused by that invective, the anarchists bounded forward.

Rozen gripped Bastien's arm forcefully. "Lie down!" he said.

Macaron obeyed, instinctively. At that moment, a command rang out: "Fire!"

Shots crackled. Five men fell in the mob's ranks. The companions were seeing red now. Mad with fury, they continued the charge.

A second salvo felled another ten, and only a few remained standing, whom the guards and soldiers would soon capture.

Under cover of the disorder, Rozen dragged Bastien back to the hut. Woken up by the fusillade, the bagnards were on their feet, ready to join the riot.

"Too late," said Rozen. "We've been betrayed." His face expressed a profound despair.

"Who's the traitor, then?" Bastien asked Rozen.

"We'll find out one day," 883 replied "For the moment, Macaron, let me save you—follow me."

While their comrades were being taken to the cells of the command-post, the two leaders of the revolt went back into the hut and slid into their hammocks.

No one seemed to have budged.

The overseers—forewarned, as you have guessed, by Rozen—had let things develop until the psychological moment. That same morning, thanks to the bandit, everyone was alerted. The guards had been given *carte blanche*. They were not displeased to be able to take advantage of the revolt, under the pretext of "legitimate defense" to kill a few of the bagne's anarchists, seriously recommended in Paris to the vigilance of the administration. We have just seen how Rozen had acquitted his task and how the overseers had proceeded with a few "eliminations."

Now that 83 had rendered an important service to the colony, his transfer was only a matter of hours.

The first step had been taken on the road to liberty.

IX. Eléna Ruiz

At that moment, interrupting his retrospective dream, Baron de Saint-Magloire got up from his armchair. He threw away his extinct cigar and walked around the room nervously.

The ghosts of the men that Rozen had had shot down—that he had, so to speak, led to the slaughter with the aim of getting away from Île Royale—were passing before his eyes. He seemed to hear their voices crying, above the fusillade: "Traitor! Traitor!"

Then he shrugged his shoulders. Traitor? No...Rozen had had no choice. Corpses? Well, yes; 883 had strewn them in his path. He had to! One can't make omelets without breaking eggs. The triumph of conquerors is erected on human slaughterhouses, and the smoke of their glory mingles with the bitter vapor of the blood they have spilled.

Then again, the imbeciles had seen nothing. Those who had survived, and whom the governor had punished severely, had not said a word to direct the vindictiveness of the authorities to the man who had led them into the abyss. They had kept silent. And even Bastien had never suspected the role that Rozen had played; he had never suspected that if the boss had saved him, it was because he understood the necessity of subsequently having in hand a man capable of aiding him in dangerous tasks.

Oh, Rozen had calculated well. He was not the naïve little crook that the jury had sent to Cayenne. He was a cold man, resolved to march ahead at any cost, ready to kill anyone who might be an obstacle to his plans...

The walk around the room calmed the Baron's nerves. He lay down and went to sleep thinking about all the things he had to do the following day.

Let us leave Saint-Magloire plunged in slumber, and continue Rozen's story.

He did not have long to wait for the reward for what the authorities considered to be a meritorious action. He had arranged matters to permit the belief that he had caught wind of the anarchists' revolt; he had protected himself on both sides. On the one hand, the bagnards saw him as a brother, and on the other, the administration congratulated him for his courageous denunciation. The director of the penitentiary colony promoted 883 several degrees in the relaxation of the bagne's regime, having him brought to Cayenne and employing him in the administrative offices.

Bastien, alias Macaron, whom Rozen had identified as a valuable assistant in the discovered of the attempted revolt, had also benefited from administrative clemency—and Rozen had been clever enough to forestall the suspicions to which the benevolent measure in question could not fail to give rise in the mind of that disciple of Ravachol.

Bastien was a cunning Parisian *gamin*, sharp and quick-witted, but he had a gullible side, which Rozen was able to exploit admirably. In addition, it must be said, delighted with the stroke of luck and the considerable improvement in his situation, he did not try too hard to get to the bottom of things. He had a broad conscience; the relative wellbeing he enjoyed incited him to close his eyes. In brief, from then on, he was utterly devoted to Rozen, whose audacity—"balls," as he put it, in his faubourgian parlance—he admired, and in his new employment as a mechanic aboard the steam-launch that provided a service between the islands of Guiana, the memory of the companions who had died on Île Royale scarcely haunted him.

In two shakes of a dog's tail, just like that, Bastien thought. *Some cop it and others profit…and isn't "every man for himself" the anarchist motto? Only the individual counts. The rest is just the packaging; the shell around the snail.*

That was all the regret that he avowed for the companions mowed down by the bullets; and the fellow lived contentedly, still looking out for an opportunity to say goodbye to the colony and to attempt to make a fortune in the wake of 883—a man bound for the top!

Faithful to the line of conduct that he had traced, Rozen, increasingly docile and submissive, feigning sincere repentance for past sins and swearing to rehabilitate himself by hard work and a life of probity and devotion, gradually captured the full benevolence of the director.

Another circumstance also served the interests of the young bandit. In his leisure time, the director, an amateur scientist, worked hard. He was obsessed with electricity, and to satisfy his avid curiosity in that regard and keep up to date he collected all the scientific journals, French, German, English and American. An accomplished polyglot, Gaston rendered sterling service to the head of the penitentiary. He was the one who translated the majority of the articles that his master collected.

Gradually, the director forgot that he had a convict by his side; Rozen's perfect education contributed to that illusion—and three months after the riot, 883 enjoyed a relative freedom. He was a kind of secretary to the functionary, and except for the obligation to respond in the evening to the recall to the bagne, the Levantine might have thought himself completely reprieved.

The almost-bourgeois life of a petty clerk, however, did not make him forget his dreams of domination, his aspirations to luxury and a sumptuous existence…and while he worked, he studied the means of escape.

Escape from the Cayenne penitentiary is easy; the prisoners are numerous and the personnel few; it is only possible to perceive absence at the evening roll-call—but the majority of escapes are reduced, so to speak, to excursions, illicit absences of individuals avid for liberty. Without money, and without civilian clothing, they cannot get far; sick and starving, they return to the colony of their own accord, or are easily recaptured by the police.

Rozen had weighed up all the difficulties of such an enterprise, one by one. He knew that flight was impossible by way of French Guiana. Along the coast, he was aware of the perils of marigots,[14] the dire danger of vicious animals of every sort, from vipers, coral snakes and other reptiles whose bite causes almost immediate death to jaguars, perhaps a little less terrible in appearance than Asian tigers, but almost as ferocious and dangerous to travelers.

All that, 883 had taken into account; he was not unaware that two hundred kilometers of coast-line separated him from Dutch Guiana, the only territory via which escape was almost practicable. Oh, if he had only been able to get himself sent to Maroni or Saint-Laurent! There, he could have attempted to flee with some chance of success, but he would still have needed money to get away, to buy clothes and reach Venezuela…for if Dutch Guiana does not reserve for runaway convicts the perils we have just listed, it is not much more hospitable to them.

Without formality, by virtue of a tacit accord, with a view to purging their colony of dangerous inhabitants, of whom there is no lack in the bulk of the population, the Dutch authorities send escapees back to the French authorities—and as a protective measure, fugitives from the penitentiary are tracked and usually captured, in order to be sent back to the bagne, where they are subjected to closer surveillance and a more rigorous regime.

A convict without money is in no condition to escape searches, unless he follows the banks of the Maroni—in which case, he faces almost certain death in some marigot.

In spite of all these not-very-promising difficulties, Rozen lived in hope. He had faith in his lucky star. Besides which, he could wait…

Everything seemed to make him forget that he was only a convict, a mere number.

An idyll introduced a note of tenderness into his existence, and for a time, the socialite bagnard did not think so much about his escape plans.

His velvet eyes and innate elegance, which the penitentiary livery did not entirely conceal, his good manners and his seductive and musical voice, had charmed a woman…the convict was beloved.

The woman whose heart he had touched was named Eléna Ruiz. She was governess to the director's children.

Small but admirably formed, a brunette with blue eyes of an extraordinary brightness, Eléna was the perfect incarnation of the Spanish type, in all its seductive splendor.

Rozen had often encountered her in the director's house when he came to the office to report for work. It had seemed to him that she looked at him, curiously at first, and then with a particular expression in which admiration and pity

---

[14] A marigot is approximately equivalent to an American bayou: a shallow river-branch, more marsh than water-course.

were mingled: admiration for the man with the delicate and symmetrical features, the sparkling gaze, the lips that seemed to have been created for the voluptuousness of kisses; pity for the unfortunate condemned to the ignominy of the bagne.

With his intelligence and experience of women, the convict fully understood the advantage he might take of Eléna Ruiz. He sensed that she had a romantic nature, a soul ready for devotion, a heart that demanded no more than to beat faster and sacrifice itself...

Gradually, he contrived to render her a host of small services, to demonstrate his humility, full of respectful solicitude...

He dogged her heels, so to speak, when she took her master's children for a walk in the director's garden, on the lookout for an opportunity to talk to her, to use the methods of seduction on her with which nature had endowed him so abundantly.

The pretext he sought soon offered itself.

One of the director's little boys, while trying to launch a toy boat on the pond, accidentally fell in. Eléna, busy watching the youngest child, had not seen anything—but Rozen, who was passing, as if by chance, raced to rescue the imprudent child, who, thanks to his intervention, got away with a slight ducking.

Tremulous at the thought of the misfortune that the Levantine's presence had avoided, Eléna thanked him warmly.

"Mademoiselle," the young man said to her, fixing her with his ardent eyes, "I bless the small accident that has permitted me to hear a few words fall from your adorable lips—which are, for an unfortunate convict, like beneficent dew on a flower desiccated by the burning sun..."

The young woman blushed.

That pompous statement, spoken slowly, in a harmonious voice that gave the words a singular significance, troubled her.

When she did not reply, Rozen added, with a sad smile: "But since I have had the rare pleasure of being useful to you, permit me to complete the task. Run to the house to fetch a change of clothes for the child; I'll look after him. You can change him here; that way, you might perhaps avoid being reprimanded."

Eléna left swiftly, and soon returned. While she dressed the child, who had entirely recovered from his misadventure, 883 sat down beside her, contemplating her with a admirable feigned dolorous expression.

There was silence for a few seconds, interrupted by a profound sigh on Rozen's part. His lips pursed, as if to hold back a plaint on the brink of escape. He put his hands over his eyes and stood up.

"You're going! Let me tell you that I shall never forget the service you've just rendered me. But for you, the child would have drowned! I love him dearly, and, what's more, I would have got the blame."

He remained mute, hiding his face in his hands, as if he were ashamed. Then he put on a show of going away—but suddenly let himself fall on the far end of the bench on which the governess was sitting, seemingly prey to a violent crisis of despair.

"You're unhappy, aren't you?" asked the young woman, emotionally.

He nodded his head affirmatively, and drew closer to her, resolutely. "Yes, I'm unhappy…and you can't imagine how much I'm suffering at this moment. It seems to me that the ignoble livery I'm wearing is burning my body. Oh, Mademoiselle, if you only knew…"

In the blink of a eye, his fertile imagination had composed an entire romance for the circumstance.

It was by virtue of having wanted to save a friend from death, to avoid dishonor for him—a suicide—that his honor had doomed him, that a pitiless society had stamped him with the seal of infamy…

She listened, full of indulgence, taking pity on the unjust fate of the poor boy, punished so severely for having wanted to do a good deed. Eléna had a very vivid imagination, and submitted easily to the impression of the moment. She knew that the bagne has its martyrs, like the guillotine, and for her, now, the convict was a victim of fatality, a martyr to friendship. She held her hand out to him.

"Courage," she murmured. "One day, perhaps you'll be happy."

"Oh!" he said covering the slender and delicate hand he held in his own with kisses, feeling it tremble beneath his caresses. "You don't despise me…"

"You're suffering," Eléna replied, simply, "and I'd like to be able to console you…"

Rozen judged that things had gone far enough, this time.

"Monsieur le Directeur is waiting for me; I must go. Adieu, Mademoiselle. You've just given me the supreme hope. Thanks to you, the pariah can still believe in possible happiness…the happiness that he thought forever extinct for him."

Eléna raised her large sky-blue eyes toward him; her tint hand squeezed the bandit's nervously, and in a tone pierced by an indescribable emotion, she said: "Yes…hope…hope…"

When he had taken a few steps away from her he turned round and raised his fingertips to his lips.

The young woman did not appear to have seen that gesture, but she got up all a-quiver and, to hide her emotion, joined in the games of the young children whose guardian she was.

As he drew away, Rozen smiled in satisfaction. *Well*, he said to himself, *she'll bill and coo…it's all going well. She'll fall in love with me, and she'll provide the means for me to get away from this accursed land. It was women who ruined me; it's a woman who'll save me.*

From that day forward, love was born in Eléna's heart. Her romantic nature drove her into the charmer's arms; she loved him all the more because she knew that he was unhappy and thought that she could rehabilitate him—that, thanks to her, he would resume a place is society that he should never have lost.

Rozen measured out his relationship with the governess with infinite care. He was careful not to rush things, and showed himself to be sentimental, gradually exasperating the poor child's ardor by clever tactics, leading her progressively to become nothing but a passive instrument in his hands.

He had found a means to be with her frequently. Being very ingenious, he knew exactly how to amuse the children, and the latter, whose mother and father gave in to all their whims, imperiously demanded 883's presence at their recreations.

One day, while the children were playing with a little carriage that Rozen had made for them, Eléna, driven by a need to confide in him, told him her own life story. She had led a terribly dramatic existence.

Born in Santiago in Cuba, Eléna Ruiz was the daughter of a hacienda-owner executed by a Spanish firing squad for having tried to defend the liberty of his country.

After the first events that were to mark the bloody history of Cuba, Ruiz had taken his place among the leaders of the Insurrection. That was in 1868. Eléna had only just been born. Her childhood was spent in camps; she followed the Cuban insurgents, tracked like wild beasts along with their families, and she grew up amid gunshots, marches through the undergrowth, hasty flights to escape massacre. The first air she had breathed had been laden with the smoke of gunpowder and the bitter vapor of blood...

It was an entire epic that she brought back to life in simple sentences, with tears in her eyes at the memory of those no longer alive.

Rozen seemed compassionate, but the expression legible in his face was due more because of a idea that had just occurred to him. It was, however, necessary for him to play his role.

"You've been very unfortunate, Mademoiselle."

Eléna nodded her head, and the Levantine, his gaze charged with sadness—one of those gazes whose seductive power he knew—added: "Oh, I understand! Like me, you've been the victim of the injustice of fate."

Eléna paid no heed to the audacious comparison that Rozen was making. She only heard the sound of his voice...a warm, vibrant, passionate timbre that seemed to be a caress.

She continued her story, becoming increasingly excited as she approached the horrible drama of which she had been the heroine.

After the suppression of the first Cuban uprising, Ruiz, on whose head a price had been set by the Spaniards, only got away with great difficulty. With his wife and child he reached the open sea aboard a schooner commanded by an American smuggler. Having taken refuge in New York, utterly ruined, he knew the atrocious misery of days without food in the pitiless great city.

Exhausted by the scares she had experienced during the recently-concluded struggle, and by the annihilation of her husband's fortune and hopes, Madame Ruiz fell ill. Already grown up, Eléna remembered the suffering in the sordid attic where the sick woman was dying for want of the medicine that might perhaps have prolonged her life. The family's poverty had, however, been brought to the attention of a few rich inhabitants of New York. One of them, a major manufacturer, offered Ruiz a job as an accountant.

That was salvation. The hacienda-owner accepted, and the man who was used to giving orders, whose lungs were accustomed to the open air of mountains and savannas, rapidly knuckled down to the monotonous and debilitating work of bureaucracy.

Salvation had come too late, though. Madame Ruiz died. When she closed her eyes she had, at least, the final joy of knowing that those she was leaving behind were safe from starvation.

Gradually, Ruiz had become involved in business. He wanted to become rich, richer than he has been before being deprived by Spain. Hatred of the oppressor was still seething in his soul, and he dreamed of resuming the struggle in earnest some day. His understanding of business, his honesty, his rectitude were soon appreciated, and he became the confidant, the associate and the partner of his employer.

The latter, moreover, had a hidden agenda. Like many other Yankees, he applauded Ruiz' dream of a free Cuba: a Cuba open to American commerce, the pearl of the Antilles finally taking full effect. There was money to be made there on a large scale. America was on the side of the Cuban rebels, even at the price of a war with Spain.

In that environment, in which she heard nothing but talk of conspiracies, secret expeditions, filibusters, clandestine cargoes of arms and ammunition disembarked with difficulty on the coasts of the large island, Eléna quickly acquired a masculine energy. She too worked hard in order to help her father in the future conquest of her homeland's independence.

She was brought up entirely in the American fashion, learning English and French, excelling in all kind of sports. She was an accomplished gymnast and a powerful cyclist, and was also cited as a consummate horsewoman. She wielded an épée with a graceful impetuosity, and her skill with a pistol won the admiration of the regulars in the stands. Eléna abandoned herself ardently to all of that, because she wanted to become strong and valiant, in order to accompany her father if he embarked one day on a campaign against the aggressor.

A number of young Americans had paid court to her; she had refused all advances. Her heart was not free; it belonged to the fatherland.

Son, he exasperated Cubans rose up again. In order to set himself at the head of the insurrection, and to offer his blood and his fortune to the Republican cause, Ruiz abandoned everything. Eléna wanted to follow her father in the camps; she dreamed of fighting by his side, but Ruiz anticipated that the struggle would be atrocious, pitiless and merciless, and he refused to take Eléna with him. He left her in New York, with his partner.

The insurgent's daughter read the news of the insurrection's initial success in the newspapers, joyfully. Would the liberty of the pearl of the Antilles finally emerged from that new war?

Alas, no. The victories were only temporary. Ill-prepared and poorly armed, succumbing to the numbers of the queen's soldiers, the rebels were driven back and obliged to take refuge in the bush. There they had the advantage, but Cuba was still under the yoke.

Almost all the towns were in a state of siege. The prisons were overflowing, courts martial functioning at top speed, sending anyone linked to, or even suspected of being linked to the rebels to the gallows or the penal battalion...

Eléna had to pause; the painful memory of the sufferings endured by her compatriots overwhelmed her.

Rozen took her hand, and said, in an affectionate tone: "Eléna, Eléna, forget all that. The future will be better. You'll be happy..."

The young bandit knew that pompous assertions were necessary in order to console that exalted soul, and his Oriental temperament facilitated their impression. He spoke in his turn, issuing grandiose tirades about the solidarity of peoples. With Eléna, he acted as he had done with his anarchist companions.

The young woman resumed her story. She had arrived at the most tragic part.

One day, a telegram brought her terrible news. Wounded in a bloody battle, her father had fallen into the hands of the Spaniards. Eléna understood that, for the man she adored, it would mean summary execution, without appeal or remission. Ruiz, captured bearing arms, would be tried and, inevitably, shot.

Only one resource remained to save him: mercy.

Eléna left for Havana, and from there, without losing any time, went to the Spanish camp. Abandoning all her pride, having but one desire—that of snatching her father from the jaws of death, even if she had to submit to every humiliation, every shame—she threw herself at the feet of the Spanish general and, with her hands joined together and her great blue eyes bathed with tears humble and pleading, she begged the victor for clemency.

The general in command of Spain's forces was a kind of naturalized German *reiter*, a mercenary devoid of generosity. Cruel and brutal, he had been one of those whose tyranny had provoked the exasperation of the Cuban patriots.

The woman dragging herself at his feet was beautiful, and dolor added to her beauty. The general looked at her for a long time, and conceived a desire to possess that superb creature. She was an enemy, the daughter of an insurgent, but what point was there in being scrupulous? It was all-out war, after all—but he preferred cunning to violence.

"Get up, Senorita," he said, gallantly. "A queen's place is not at her subject's feet."

He took her hand, sat her down beside him and, alone with her, told her what passion she inspired in him. Oh, if she would love him, if she would grant him the divine moment of which he dreamed, he would not grant complete mercy to Ruiz, for that was impossible, but he would spare his life, and would then arrange to let him escape.

She too could leave with her father, and go back tranquilly to America,

At first she jibbed at the outrage. She had a desire to spit all of her hatred and scorn in the face of the infamous creature—but her father's life was in the monster's hands. It was up to her to save him, the adored father whom she would then lead out of peril, and would console him, leaving him in ignorance of the shameful step to which he owed his life and liberty.

The sacrifice was so great, however, that she could not resolve to make it. Not only did her modesty revolt, but she was disgusted by the thought of belonging to that bandit whose hands were stained with the blood of the unfortunate Cubans.

The general understood the young woman's hesitation. He took her hand, which she dared not withdraw from his, and said, in a paternal tone: "Senorita, I am better than my reputation; I would never owe the favor of a woman to violence...it is of your own free will that I desire you." And as Eléna, trembling with dread and indignation, did not push him away, he added: "I can defer Ruiz' execution until eight o'clock tomorrow morning. Tomorrow at eight o'clock, I shall come to you and...your father's fate will depend on the answer you give me. You are at home here, and you will be treated with all the respect due to you..."

He got up to take his leave of her.

She held him back. "General, I only implore one favor..."

"Speak, Senorita...until tomorrow, your desires are my orders."

"That my poor father remain in ignorance of my presence here!"

"Granted."

The next morning, when he came into the tent reserved for her, the general found his victim resolved. She had reflected, and had accepted the shame, the infamous measure...

She would pay with her honor for her father's life!

The general had agreed to let her leave first; then Senor Ruiz would be set free; she would find him at an agreed location outside the camp; thus, he would not know to what price he owed his salvation.

At Eléna's request, he signed a guarantee of safe conduct for her and for Ruiz. The young man tucked the precious document into her bosom.

The moment of sacrifice had come.

Eléna closed her eyes and abandoned herself...

Suddenly, gunshots rang out.

Ruiz' daughter shoved away the man who still held her in his arms. She had a sinister presentiment. She ran to the flap of the tent...and, her eyes widened by the horror of the spectacle she saw before her, she uttered a scream, the roar of a wounded tigress.

Her father was there, covered in blood, lying on the ground, struck by a dozen bullets.

"Imbeciles!" growled the general. "They've acted too soon!"

He tried to go out, but Eléna, transfigured, was standing before him. She had taken her revolver from her pocket and, taking aim at the wretch whose ignominy leapt to her eyes, she cried: "Monster! You shall die!"

Before the Spaniard had time the defend himself, the shot was fired. The bullet hit him full in the chest. He spun around and fell heavily, without uttering a groan.

At the sound of the shot, soldiers came running and captured the young woman.

Taken to the nearby fortress, she was locked up for several days, then brought before a court martial, which sentenced her to be executed by firing squad. But Eléna's beauty and filial devotion had inspired considerable pity in the Spanish officers, and they signed an appeal for mercy addressed to the Governor of Cuba.

Less cruel than the leader who had paid for his infamous conduct with his life, they hoped that the sentence would not be carried out.

That delay saved the young woman.

X. The Escape

At the tale of that tragic adventure, Roe could not help experiencing a tug at his heart. He took the governess's hand and squeezed it emotionally. "Poor child," he murmured.

At that moment, perhaps the convict was sincere. The dramatic tone that underlined Eléna's story, the young woman's anguished face, in which all the suffering she had endured, whose memory alone sufficed to revive her grief, was clearly legible, had made an impression on him.

For her part, the governess experienced an irresistible attraction to the handsome fellow who was commiserating with her, speaking to her softly, whose tender voice seemed to her to be a balm upon the wounds of her soul— and in that need for tenderness, which overwhelmed her entirely, she went frankly to the man who seemed to her to be good, worthy of love, because he too had suffered a great deal.

If the Cuban woman's sentiments were profound, however, Rozen's were entirely superficial.

Come on! he said to himself. *Am I going to let myself be taken in? A fling, yes, if she can be useful to me, Love—never in this life! It's fortune, power that I want...and this woman, if I loved her, would be an obstacle.*

"Oh, why am I not dead!" Eléna went on. "Why wasn't I shot right away? Why have I been obliged to lead, for such a long time, the miserable existence of those who have no hope...those who no longer have any support, any affection?"

"Don't say that, Mademoiselle. The future belongs to those who know how to hope. Don't look backwards any longer; throw a veil over that sad past of horror ad mourning!"

"What good is illusion? I know full well that a poor governess can no longer know joy. A servant I am, a servant I shall remain...forever."

He made no reply, but he enveloped her with an ardent gaze, under which Eléna felt disturbed. Her hand responded gently to the pressure of the young man's...and hey both remained thus, silently: Eléna rocked by a dream, her heart ready to overflow with tenderness, Rozen greatly enjoying the comedy of a timid love that dared not confess itself...

Then the governess resumed the story of her life.

In the fortress where she was a prisoner, awaiting the decision of the Governor-General of Cuba, two reporters from a large American newspaper were authorized to interview her. They had paid generously for the right to see the poor young woman, the victim of her devotion for her father.

One, whose name was Harris, was an American national; he was a tall, thin, phlegmatic fellow whose gestures were jerky. Without his face showing the slightest trace of emotion, he took down the young woman's replies to the questions his colleague asked her.

The latter, whose appearance testified to French ancestry, was named Lemoine. While very young, driven by a need for adventure, he had left Paris, after having concluded brilliant scientific studies, and had come to the New World in search of dangers to run and strong emotions to glean. The Cuban insurrection had excited him greatly, and he had left with Harris to report on it for one of the most important newspapers in the United States. The paper on whose behalf he was following the war had opened considerable credit for him. A small steamship was put at their disposal. All expenses were permissible to them, provided that their paper was the most extensively and most rapidly informed.

In the bloodiest battles, paying no heed to the bullets and ardent fevers that were decimating the ranks of people unused to the murderous climate, the two journalists had followed all the ups and downs of the struggle between the soldiers of Spain and the Cuban patriots. They had documented the phases of the war elaborately.

As soon as he had heard about the capture of the insurgent leader Ruiz, Lemoine had come running, accompanied by his impassive colleague. Both had heard about the drama that has cost the life of the Spanish general and was about to hurl a gracious child, a noble and beautiful girl, in front of the dozen rifles of a firing squad. A generous notion had immediately taken root in Lemoine's brain.

"We have to save that young woman, Harris," he said to his companion.

"Yes, I think so," said Harris. "We must."

"We'll abduct her."

"Yes."

"By force, if necessary."

"All right."

"With audacity, and a good revolver apiece, we ought to succeed."

"Very well..."

As a good Yankee, who liked his comforts, Harris had himself followed everywhere by a gigantic basket full of fine wines. As the hospitality of the fortress had been afforded to the two journalists, Harris has brought in his canteen—but he had taken care, on Lemoine's advice, to mix with the excellent products of the best vintage of France a certain quantity of narcotics—enough to procure sleep without causing death.

So, in the evening of their visit to the fort, the American had offered the garrison the bottles that filled his wicker basket. The soldiers and officers had drunk, glad to taste the juice of good French vines. They had clinked glasses merrily in honor of the journalists—but all of them, gripped by an invincible drowsiness, had fallen into a deep sleep, and Eléna, on the arm of the two reporters, had emerged from the fortress in the most natural fashion in the world.

"And that's it!" said Lemoine, as they went out of the gate of the fortress. "Simple!"

"Very ingenious!" agreed the American.

Ruiz' daughter did not know how to express her gratitude to her two saviors.

"No need, Mademoiselle; my colleague and I are abundantly recompensed by the superb article that we'll write on the subject—isn't that so, Harris?"

"All right!"

Lemoine and Harris had had horses made ready, and in a matter of hours they reached the coast, where the paper's yacht was waiting for them.

That escape was the high point of their reportage. They told themselves that they could go home, and they accompanied Eléna to New York—where, thanks to the Frenchman's subsidies, the young woman was able to live for some time, while he looked for a job for her.

Unfortunately, Lemoine, suddenly recalled to France by his mother's serious illness, was obliged to leave Eléna. Once again, destiny had been cruel.

However, the young man had not forgotten his protégée, whom he considered as a fiancée. He wrote to her, but the letters never reached poor Eléna, wandering the streets of the great American city, dying of hunger, reduced to the hospitality of night-shelters.

Harris had, in fact, abandoned her. For that practical man, the woman was nothing but a pretty little animal, very intelligent but burdensome. To save Eléna from poverty, he had thought of exhibiting her in music halls. He offered to serve as her Barnum, to give lectures on the Cuban insurrection. That prospect made the proud Cuban sick. She refused the American's grotesque offer pointblank, and the latter, shrugging his shoulders, disappeared without worrying about her any more.

"You're refusing a fortune, Miss. Very stupid on your part. I don't want to have anything more to do with you. Goodbye."

Just then, his paper had offered him a commission in Sudan, following the English expedition to Khartoum, and Harris set off phlegmatically, no longer giving a thought to the "silly little chick" who had refused his advantageous offer.

Alone henceforth—truly alone—Eléna had known poverty in its most atrocious form. She had appealed in vain to the bankers who had been friends and associates of her father. The latter, half-ruined by the failure of the Cuban insurrection, had fallen out with the island's patriots, who did not entirely trust them, not wanting to exchange one tyranny for another; they did not want to see the daughter of a rebel, and closed their doors to her.

One day, when she was wandering around the harbor, having decided to put a end to the martyr's existence that had been reserved for her, she fell into the arms of an old school-friend, a young woman with whom she had, so to speak, been brought up. The latter seized by pity at the sight of such distress, had obliged Ruiz's daughter to accept her hospitality. Although American, she had married a French civil servant, the director of penitentiary services in Guiana. She had come, without her husband, to send a few days in New York with her family.

She rescued Eléna, and absolutely insisted that she go with her to Cayenne—but the Cuban woman, too proud to live on someone else's handouts, had only consented on the condition that she became the children's governess.

"That is what my sad life had been," the young woman concluded, raising eyes veiled with tears to look at Rozen. "You see that I was right just now—it would have been better if I'd been shot. I wouldn't have the dolorous memory of a futile soiling...and now, it's all over, over and done with..."

Rozen interrupted her. "Mademoiselle Eléna, I too, before meeting you, was an unfortunate in despair, put in irons by a youthful error. I no longer dared to believe that happiness could exist for me...but today, I no longer think that. I have seen you, and my heart is beating more rapidly in my breast. I have recovered my love of life.

"I am telling myself that if you wanted to share my life, to be the companion of my labor, the good fairy that would transform my efforts into success, I would be capable of becoming someone, and I would return to you, in love, everything that you would give me in the strength and courage to live, to struggle, to recapture an honorable place in society..."

He talked for a long time, lending to his words the penetrating suggestion of a warm voice and an irresistible charm.

Eléna felt herself enveloped, caught in the net of that dangerous bird-catcher.

Rozen was such an accomplished actor that he had deceived people less credulous than that young woman, whose unhappiness had taken the edge off her innate perspicacity, and who was clinging to the supreme hope of being loved, of loving, of finally living happily...and freely!"

Rozen had conquered her completely.

Everything that he asked of her, she was ready to do...if she had to follow him to the ends of the earth, to run the worst dangers with him.

To escape from the bagne, she offered him her meager savings: a thousand francs, which she had amassed since she had been in the service of the director of the penitentiary.

Rosen, as can be imagined, accepted it with a joy that he went to great pains to conceal. With infinite artistry, he succeeded in persuading the young woman that it was necessary for him to leave on his own, that she could not risk confronting the perils of an escape through the marshes and forests of Guiana.

She resisted for a while, not wanting to be separated from the man she loved, fearful that he might be lost to her forever. She would prefer, she said, to die with him rather than to live alone in the distress into which his departure would plunge her. 883 was so clever, though, and so insidious, that she was defeated.

He told her his idea—a plan matured by reflection.

"Dear heart, you'll keep enough money to take the steamer from Cayenne to Colon. As soon as I reach that city, I'll let you know—no one opens your letters!—and you'll reply to me there. Then we'll go to San Francisco. I'll get work, and we'll be married. In the name of the love I have for you, in the name of the sympathy you have for me, accept. For you to leave with me would be perilous; I'd be bound to be captured—and you'd pay with our liberty for the generous aid you'd have given me. By doing as I ask, you'll ensure the success of my escape and the happiness of us both..."

He returned to the task several times over, developing his plan with a thousand details, which brought out its practicality and demonstrated the certainty of its success. She ended up yielding, and promised to give him eight hundred francs, keeping two hundred for herself in order to rejoin him in Colon.

But Gaston thought that he could not escape as long as he was in Cayenne. Even with money, flight through the forest was materially impossible. It was necessary to wait for an opportunity.

One soon presented itself.

The director, summoned to Saint-Laurent, where the exiles were established, took the convict-secretary with him.

Saint-Laurent! It was the open door to liberty.

His heart beat violently when the director told him the news. Finally, he was about to make the supreme effort, to put his foot in the stirrup in order to launch himself on a hectic race to conquer a fortune, and all the pleasures that it procures for its elect.

With Eléna, he played the comedy of love, heaping her with caresses and consoling her with regard to the separation by means of the mirage of a delightful future.

The governess tried in vain to be included in the trip. Quite often, in fact, the director took his family with him when he went away, but this time, it was a matter of going to hear the grievances of the discontented exiles on the spot; there might be a riot.

Already, for some time, the inmates of Saint-Laurent had been complaining about the poor quality of the canned food distributed to them, and he was afraid that they might start a petty revolution in the penitentiary if the authorities did not intervene, with benevolence but also with firmness, to calm the effervescence.

In those conditions, the director wanted to go to Saint-Laurent alone. He would only taken Rozen, his secretary, with him, with whom he expected to work throughout the trip. He was working on a problem in electricity, which probably preoccupied him more than the difficulties that had arisen between the exiles and their guards, and he needed his documents.

The departure was fixed for the next day, at nine o'clock in the morning.

When the director traveled he usually took passage on the naval corvette, the *Pourvoyeur*, or on a commercial schooner. This time, however, neither the corvette nor any schooner was available, and it was the service launch that had to take the chief of the penitentiary colony to Saint-Laurent.

They took the food and utensils necessary for a two-day trip.

Rozen, in an admirably-played love-scene, bid *au revoir* to the young woman who had invested all her confidence and all her dreams of future happiness in him, and collected the eight hundred francs that Eléna had promised him.

Eight hundred francs! A pittance! But thanks to that meager sum, it would be possible for him to take care of the immediate needs of the first three or four days of his flight.

The amorous woman, her heart swollen and her eyes full of tears, gave her beloved a long kiss, and, in a voice broken by emotion, said: "Soon, Gaston! I'll wait for a letter from you, and leave immediately for Colon. Wait for me there…I'll join you there."

"Yes, Adieu, my love…only the idea of seeing one another again, free, will give me the strength and courage to triumph over the difficulties and dangers that there will be…but don't worry; thanks to your generosity, for which I can never repay you, I shall triumph over all perils. Within three weeks, you'll receive a letter from Colon, saying: 'Come my beautiful fiancée, your lover's arms are reaching out to you!'"

And they separated, having embraced tightly.

Eléna stayed in her room, oppressed and anxious, her head full of dark thoughts…

The next day, at nine o'clock, the director and his secretary embarked on the steam-launch.

Next to the boat's little engine a man was crouched, casting a last glance over the machine, pouring oil on to the bearings. Rozen recognized Bastien, his accomplice from Île Royale. The two bagnards exchanged a knowing look, and while the director's back was turned, Rozen held his hand out to the anarchist. It held a little piece of paper, folded in four, of which Bastien rapidly took possession.

I'm off tomorrow; if you can escape, I'll meet you in Valencia in Venezuela. From there we'll set out to conquer the fortune of which I promise to give you a generous share. See you soon, and long live liberty!

Having read the note, Bastien darted a glance at Rozen. His features expressed joy, and he signaled to his comrade that he had understood.

When they disembarked at Saint-Laurent, 883 furtively shook the mechanic's hand and whispered: "Valencia—agreed, no?"

"For sure," said the other, mysteriously. "Don't worry—I'll be close behind you."

No one had overheard this brief exchange between the two accomplices. The handshake was noticed, but no one was surprised by that; everyone knew that it was thanks to the influence obtained over the director by Rozen that the Parisian street-arab had become a mechanic aboard the service launch.

For some time, Bastien had been thinking about the means of making sure of his escape. He too was in haste to bid farewell to the accursed land, and eventually to be free, by the side of the man with whom he might sail on the Pactolus.[15]

The launch on which he fulfilled the function of helmsman-mechanic, skillfully, made trips back and forth between the capital of Guiana and the various parts of the penitentiary.

Bastien had already learned that audacious convicts had been able to escape and reach the open sea, but where they had been recaptured before long because of their ignorance of marine matters. They had set out to sea—a grave error!—and without a compass they had doubtless followed a large semicircle that had brought them back into the vicinity of Île Royale, where they had come to a standstill. However, Bastien, alias Macaron, had studied the curious details of these attempts.

The launch is manned by a mechanic and a helmsman recruited from the convicts or exiles noted by the directorate for their exemplary conduct or having rendered some important service to the colony. It is the vessel that provides a daily postal and treasury service. Two armed overseers constitute a crew charged with ensuring the transportation of messages and money, but the shortage of personnel often obliges it to travel with only one overseer aboard.

When the launch docks in a harbor, the overseer, before going on to land in order to perform his duties, is obliged b the regulations to see that the fire in the boiler is damped down and that the job is properly done. He must also take away one of the essential components of the mechanism, either a flange from the cylinder or a cotter-pin from the piston-rod. In brief, he is not supposed to go ashore until the steam-launch is absolutely impossible to navigate.

Bastien had learned that the escapees, taking advantage of the negligence of an overseer who was content with a simulated damping down of the fire, had been able to get away, but an exemplary punishment inflicted on the guard had revived the ardor of their colleagues, and it was necessary not to count on any future negligence on their part.

Macaron was not to be put off by something so trivial. Patiently, in the workshop, he secretly constructed various spare parts one by one—"good luck charms," as mariners say—and waited until everything was in place to enable flight, planned down to the slightest detail. He knew now, thanks to the note that

---

[15] A legendary river that had the ability to turn anything dipped in it to gold.

78

he had just read, that Rozen would wait in Valencia. That was enough for him. A delay of a few more days could be endured without inconvenience.

For his part, Gaston did not waste any time. During the leisure time left to him by his work for the director he observed the surroundings. Right away, he noticed that the surveillance was not very active: one or two marine infantry posts that it would be easy to avoid. It was considered that the Dutch customs officers on the coast and the virgin forest on the far shore mounted a sufficiently good guard around the people that French society rejected as dangerous.

In the course of his investigations, an exile charged with the maintenance of the colony's boats attracted Rozen's particular attention. The man had exactly the same height and build as himself—and he did not wear a convict's uniform!

883 approached the boatman.

"Do you like it here, comrade?"

"Me? Oh, no!"

"Why do you stay here?"

"You're joking! Because I haven't any alternative."

"Get away! With a boat, it can't be difficult to get to the other side."

"No, old chap—but what's the point? The customs men or the blacks would turn up, and you're right back where you started, with privileges withdrawn. To get away you'd need money..."

"How much?"

"Well, five or six hundred bullets..."

"What if I said that I have them?"

"Well, that's different. You're a nabob, then?"

"A nabob, yet—will you help me?"

"I wouldn't refuse if I could go with you."

"Certainly."

"It'd need to be quick."

"This evening."

Listen, then...I'll be over there, upriver of the post, with a little dinghy. The tide's just right this evening. I'll half-fill the boat, to lie low in the water. It'll go up without being seen—I'll lie down on the benches."

"That's dangerous. And then?"

"There's no risk. I'll come alongside."

"You just have to be there, a kilometer upriver..."

"We'll empty the boat, and off we go, en route to Holland. Agreed?"

"Understood. For liberty, Comrade!"

"I hear you."

Rozen drew away.

If the boatman had been able to see the sinister smile that strayed over the lips of the director's secretary, he would have been frightened—but the exile probably did not have very fraternal intentions himself, for once his interlocutor had gone, he murmured:

"Six hundred bullets! Some drink! I've never seen so many..."

That same evening, 883 and the man in charge of Saint-Laurent's boats set foot on Dutch territory.

XI. De Profundis!

As soon as they had disembarked, Rozen and his companion hoisted the boat that had transported them on to the shore.

"Have to sink it," said the exile. "Otherwise it's like a handkerchief we've dropped behind us."

"You're right, Rozen said, "but it seems to me that we can't set off just yet. We need to wait for daylight."

"Wait! No, old chap. Do you want to rejoin your corps? In my opinion, the more kilometers there are between us and the bagne, the better our chances are of not being nabbed."

Rozen had no intention of doing anything else, but he appeared to cede to the observations of his fellow escaper. They both set about sinking the boat they had used. They filled it will large stones, then pushed it into the Maroni and, tugging violently on the mooring-rope, one end of which they had retained, they made the little boat spin—which, loaded to the brim, took on water and went under.

The two bagnards saw eddies of river-water swirling in the place where the boat had vanished. Then they raised their eyes to the other shore. The lights of Saint-Laurent were scintillating in the darkness.

"The director must be looking for me by now," Rozen sniggered.

"For sure—that's why we have to look lively. Oh, if only it were like the old days, when Dutch Guiana was a free country..."

"Get away!" said Gaston. "A country is always free when one can shift for oneself. Then again, one could get into trouble in the old days..."

"That's true, as the massacre of 188 proves," the boatman declared.

"You were already here when that happened?"

"Yes, I was here. Oh, colonist! Look, this is how it happened. You know that at times, in the bagne, it's as if there are epidemics of escape. The inmates take to their heels in droves..."

"I know. They cut bamboo, hide the sticks in bundles under the mangroves, and when they have enough, they make a raft...and do as we did, taking advantage of the tide."

"Fifty meters to cross. That's nothing—not to mention the sandbanks where they can push with a pole Most of the poor saps haven't a sou, and don't take long to get lost in the forest...where the snakes[16] swallow them before they

---

[16] The author inserts a footnote to say that the word he employs here—*couleuvre*, which usually refers to grass snakes—is used in Guiana to refer to "an enormous serpent, a sort of boa, which attains gigantic proportions." The

81

have time to die of hunger. The time I'm talking about, there were thirty runaways, all Arbicos...Arabs... That lot are rabid to take off, and they set off with their bodies covered with little packets of rice... in what you'd call scapulars. They plaster them back and front, and hold them with string."

Rozen shrugged his shoulders. "Nice supplies," he murmured. "And then?"

"Then, when they've crossed over—that's easy—they head north, invariably convinced that in a fortnight or so they'll have reached Algeria...that's their geography, poor saps. So, there were thirty of them, led by an educated man, a handsome fellow from a good Arab family, who'd been brought up in Algiers in the French fashion—which didn't prevent him ending up here. All roads lead to Rome."

"To Cayenne, you mean."

The man smiled vaguely. "You're a joker, you are!"

"You'll see, my friend—but you've left your Arbicos in the lurch."

"Right. They'd all succeeded in getting to the other side and they were going to find...thingy...whatsisname...damn it, I can't remember his name..."

"It doesn't matter."

"He was a chap who'd set up a trading-post near a Galibi village, doing deals with a few Indians who love along the river. From time to time, he received *tapouyes*...do you know what that is?"

"Of course—little merchant ships—schooners. Go on..."

In exchange for a little money, this chap allowed the escapees to take passage on his *tapouyes*; they were taken to Paramaribo, where they found work as laborers. But his time, when he saw the thirty lascars in question arriving at his post, who hadn't a penny, I have no need to tell you, he was scared.

"Then he shot off to Saint-Laurent, where he ran into the chief of the penitentiary. I don't know exactly what he said to him, but the end of the story will tell you. Back at his property, he negotiated with the bagnards. They accepted his proposals.

"The next day, at dawn, five or six Indian pirogues were to take them to Paramaribo..."

"By sea?"

"No—the Indians know the coastline, the creeks...those little bits of rivers that cross the marshes."

"Arroyos."

"If you like. The Indians know all that like the backs of their hands, and in a few days they got to the town."

"Good to know," Rozen said to himself.

"What are you thinking?" asked the exile.

---

notion that anacondas can swallow human beings is, of course, a common fantasy of popular fiction and travelers' tales.

"Nothing. Or, rather, if…I know the end of your story. They still talk about it at the penitentiary, and I'll tell you.

"The next day, as soon as the sun rose on a river as smooth as oil, as shiny as gold leaf in the first rays of sunlight that pierce the mist, the Arabs embarked. Quietly, the little fleet of pirogues quit the bank and went downstream. The escapees were singing, and that was marvelous, their rhythmic singing in the silence of the morning.

"Suddenly, four launches emerged from the mangroves of Saint-Laurent, manned by negro paddlers, each having three or four bagne-guards in the stern, armed to the teeth, and gave chase to the runaways.

"It was frightful. The blackguards who set up the coup knew what they were doing. They had taken blacks…and you know how they hate Arbis. The launches were fast! Nothing could be seen around them but white foam raised by the furious thrust of paddles. In the stern, sheltered by the grilles that separated them from the convicts, the guards were beating the rhythm…'Han! Han!' And the boats flew over the river like great white birds.

In the blink of a eye, the escapers were within pistol-range. Then the guards, standing up, started howling: 'Surrender! Surrender!'

"'No! No!' the Arabs replied. And the one who was their leader, the one you mentioned just now who was educated, stood up and shouted: 'It's an infamy! In foreign territory, we're free! You have no right to stop us. We're under the protection of the Dutch government.' And he held up a sheet of paper that the man with the tapouyes had given him.

"'To hell with that!' replied the guards. 'Surrender, or we shoot.'

"'Never!' cried the Arab. 'You're bandits!' He was standing in the stern of a pirogue, brandishing his fists at his pursuers. *Bang, bang!* Two gunshots, and the poor brute fell head-first into the water.

"At that moment, as if they were obeying an order, the Indian paddlers dived into the river, abandoning the pirogues.

"*Bang, bang, bang!* Revolvers fired from every direction, and the unfortunate Arabs in the pirogues took the shots. The waters of the Maroni ran red with blood.

"The launches reached the pirogues. Now it was butchery. Escapers had jumped into the water, and with the rage imparted by despair they were trying to cling on to the launches and turn them over. The guards fired from above, and smashed the gun-butts down in the hands gripping the edges of the boats.

"The blacks, glad to satisfy their rancor against the Arabs, greeted them with blows of the paddles on the head, and when they were stunned, they hoisted them into the boats and trampled them underfoot, bruised, bloody and half-dead.

"It didn't last long…

"Fifteen escapers were captured and shackled; the others, dead or mortally wounded, were carried by the current to feed the sharks out at sea…

"And that's how hospitality worked when Dutch territory as free!"

"You know my story better than I do," said the exile, surprised.

"Of course! Don't they still talk about it in the penitentiary?" As he finished the story himself, Rozen felt strongly oppressed. His present situation as an escaped convict, exposed to the greatest dangers, and his preoccupation with getting rid of his companion as soon as possible, put him in a state of nervous exasperation.

"Damn!" he said. "It would have been better not to talk about that. That story of brigands will stop us sleeping..."

"Bah!" said the boatman. "Dawn come early...we'll sleep better when we've found a Galibi village. There, with your cash, we'll be able to sort things out...but we'll have to trot all night."

They began to move along the bank of the Maroni.

At the place where they had landed the ground was rocky, the bank falling almost vertically into the Maroni, deep and calm, and as shiny as silver in the moonlight.

Rozen and his companion marched side by side, silent and attentive, resting from time to time.

Finally, they tried to get their bearings, to take account of how far they had come since setting off. All around them, however, the forest extended its impenetrable depths, with its trees more than fifty feet high, through the crowns of which no ray of sunlight ever filtered.

"Let's go on a bit further," said Rozen.

"Yes, but let's follow the bank."

Suddenly, an obstacle presented itself. It was necessary to cross a marsh, if they bore right, or go along a narrow goat-track that the rocks left free on the river's edge. It was obviously the latter path that they had to take; there was no point, since they had a safe road, risking getting trapped in putrid mud that as swarming with reptiles—but the path was only wide enough for one man.

"After you," said Rozen to the exile.

"No, you first," the other replied.

"You..."

"No."

"Oh, we're not in a drawing-room here—there's no need for manners."

"No, but I don't want to go first, because..."

The two men were standing some distance away from one another. The same thought had occurred to both of them: to take advantage of the path to get rid of their comrade.

The exile coveted the money that Rozen was carrying on him. Rozen wanted to obtain possession of the boatman's clothes. The latter was not wearing a convict's uniform, which would indicate an escaped convict to the vigilance of the Dutch customs officers and black militiamen avid for a reward.

Neither one of them had any need to explain himself for both of them to guess their reciprocal intentions. The insistence that each of them had put into not wanting to take the first step along the narrow path was a revelation.

"Because..." The bagne's boatman had said—and he had not completed his remark.

Rozen had understood, but 883 was not afraid. He was confident of his strength and agility, which playing sports had once developed in a remarkable fashion. It did not even displease him to be attacked by the bandit who was accompanying him. By virtue of a sort of capitulation with conscience, he told himself that the boatman's death would, after all, be a legitimate action, for which he need not have the slightest remorse.

Sure of himself as he was, however, Rozen tried to avoid a fight. It would be more convenient, once the man was on the path, to put his hands around his throat and strangle him from behind, without him being able to utter a cry.

A silence had followed the few words exchanged by the two escapers.

Rozen took a step toward the exile, and said, in an authoritative tone: "You go first!"

"No," growled the other.

"I want you to!"

"Of, you want it! Well, too bad! I'm in command here—and since I'm the master, I want your money."

Rozen went pale, and stepped back.

The boatman had a long knife in his hand, the blade of which shone in the wan moonlight.

"Your money!" he continued, marching toward his adversary, his arm raised, the point of the dagger threatening. "Your money, or I'll kill you!"

As the boatman advanced, Rozen retreated. He could have fled, but that would not serve his interests. He wanted the other man's clothes, and he was enraged by not being the stronger. The knife gave every advantage to the exile. Rozen had not anticipated that his fellow escaper might be armed.

Emboldened by the retreat of the man he intended to be his victim, the boatman continued advancing. "Your money, I say!"

"I don't have any," said 883. Knowing men well, he wanted to gain time by arguing.

"You don't have any? Then what you said to me back there, before leaving..."

"Was a lie."

A lie? The six hundred bullets..."

"Nothing."

"That's not true! You're lying. I want them."

"I tell you it was a lie, to encourage you to go with me."

"We'll see about that. Empty your pockets."

85

During this discussion, Rozen had arrived at the edge of a marigot. Backed into a corner, he could no longer gain ground. On one side was his enemy's blade, on the other, the deadly mud of the marsh. Suddenly, however, he uttered a cry of triumph. A large loose stone had just rolled under his foot.

There was a flash of inspiration in his fecund and resourceful mind. "Come and get your money!" he cried.

The other launched himself forward, sure of his action, the knife raised.

Rapid as the movement was, however, Rozen got in first. He bent down and seized the stone, which he hurled with all his might, with a vigor that desperation had multiplied tenfold.

It struck the boatman full in the chest. There was a dull thud, and a cry of pain. The man collapsed like a dead weight.

The Levantine bounded toward him, and tried to grab the knife.

The shock had not quite stunned the exile; he defended himself energetically, but in a hand-to-hand struggle he could not defeat an adversary like Rosen. The latter had a vice-like grip on the wrist of the arm that held the knife, and had gripped the man's throat with his other hand.

The boatman, at the limit of his strength, did not take long to drop the knife. Gaston grabbed the weapon and angrily, with a kind of crazed fury, fell upon the wretch. Eventually, he stood up, exhausted but satisfied.

He did not consider the act he had just committed to be a crime,

He set about stripping the clothes from the cadaver and, while he was still warm, he dressed the other as best he could in his trousers and his convict's smoke, marked near the collar with the regulation C. P., followed by the number 883. Then, with the aid of a large stone, he crushed the boatman's skull.

"Like that, no one will recognize you. The rats, the crabs and the ants will do the rest. Gaston Rozen the bagnard is dead. *De profundis!*"

XII. The Gold-Seekers

Selecting for preference the paths traced through the edge of the forest by the indigenes, Rozen had marched, living on roots and drinking the water that oozed from the feet of the trees, which he also found in the shoots of wild pineapples.

He had required a supernatural energy to resist the horrible fatigues of the trek through the forest, in the glaucous daylight, obscured by the thick foliage.

Twice, he had been lucky, after unintentionally coming back to the river bank, to escape the attention of Dutch customs men. The latter might not have believed his affirmations. Doubtless with great respect, but with the obstinacy of soldiers who only know how to follow orders, they would have taken Rozen to Paramaribo, where the authorities, alerted to an escape, would not have failed, after a investigation, to send the prisoner back to the bagne—and the prospect of falling back into the hands of the prison guards, of being sent back to Île Royale, of losing any hope of ever recovering his liberty, of leading the high life, of dominating men and taking his revenge on them, gave the refugee the strength to bear the tortures and privations of that frightful odyssey through the inextricable thickets, through which he could not clear a path without lacerating his hands and face.

He did not feel the horrible bites of the ticks, bugs and parasites of every sort that scarred his legs. Fever prevented him sleeping. In any case, sleep might have been fatal…he might have become torpid in the cold, damp night, and fallen. To fall would have meant death, and what a death!

He heard jaguars prowling around him, with muffled mewling sounds, sniffing hi fresh flesh.

Gradually, he had reached the state of only having one thought in his mind, a kind of obsession, such as record-breaking cyclists have in the middle of a race: to march, march on, march further, march incessantly, except to succumb at last to exhaustion and collapse like a inert mass.

Time dragged on terrible for the refugee. He began to hallucinate. Several times, he thought he was going mad. The ghost of the boatman loomed up in front of him, spectral and menacing, the body quivering…and the sinister apparition sniggered.

Cruel and ironic words buzzed in Rozen's ears. "It wasn't worth the trouble of knifing me. You won't get much further. You're going to die too. Farewell, dreams of fortune and grandeur Yes, yes, your carcass will go that way; like mine, it will be prey to the ants!"

And the unfortunate man felt his entire being shaken by dolorous frissons. His skull seemed ready to explode; cold sweat covered his body. His teeth chattered. But his natural vigor ended up getting the upper hand again, and the fit of fever passed; all his energy sand determination returned, and furiously, haunted by the desire to find a native village, he parted the undergrowth, insensible to the scratches that bloodied his flesh.

Finally, after several days, on the bank of the Maroni, to which he had unwittingly returned, he spotted the huts of an Indian tribe. Half-naked women and children fled as he approached, and the entire village was soon in uproar.

Rozen's heart was beating precipitately. His fate depended on the welcome the Indians gave him. On the one hand, he was glad to find shelter, a place to rest. He was hungry, he needed sleep and he was incapable of going any further. One more hour and his bruised, stiff legs would have given way beneath him. On the other, the indigenes might take him back to the penitentiary in order to claim the reward given to those who brought back a escaped prisoner.

That terror disturbed the fugitive, but he suppressed his anxiety and with a apparent calm, he made his way into the village.

It was a small agglomeration: half a dozen round wooden huts covered with foliage, grouped around a fairly large circular space, at the center of which stood a hut larger than the others.

Outside the door of that hut, which doubtless belong to the chief of the tribe, Rozen saw several men, into whose midst the women and children had run a little while before, shouting and waving their arms.

One of the men detached himself from the group and advanced toward the fugitive.

The Indians did not seem at all threatening. They had, in any case, noticed that the newcomer was unarmed. His weakened condition had not escaped them either.

Having arrived a few paces away from the white man, the black man stopped and made a sign instructing him to do the same.

Rozen obeyed.

"Who are you?" asked the indigene, expressing himself in bad English.

Rozen answered the question with a question: "First, can you tell me where I am?"

"In a Youdi tribe," the Indian replied.

"You're the village chief?"

"Yes...but who are you? Where have you come from?"

"An English traveler. I've come from Oyampi. On the way, my porters robbed me and I had to run away to escape death."

"Indian pirates," said he chief, with a hearty laugh that uncovered his white teeth. "You have no money?"

"That's right," said Rozen.

"How are you going to pay?"

In the blink of an eye, Rozen understood the situation; it was necessary at all costs to tempt the barbarian's cupidity. "Listen," he said. "You can see that I'm unarmed, hungry, exhausted by fever. There's no need to be afraid..."

The Indian shook his head. "We're powerful, never afraid."

"Good. Would you like to earn fifty piastres?"

"Speak. I'll see."

"Give my hospitality until tomorrow—and when day breaks, a pirogue and men to take me to Paramaribo. There you'll get the promised sum..."

"Who will give it to me?"

Rozen had not thought of that. He could not tell the savage that he had a relatively large sum on him; he was afraid of being robbed. He wondered momentarily how he could inspire trust in the Youdi chief."

"Do you know Paramaribo?"

"Yes. We sometimes go there via the creeks, to sell what we hunt, and cinchona bark."

"Good. If I don't keep my word you can take me to the governor of Paramaribo. He's my friend. He'll pay for me."

The India appeared to reflect. In truth, he was delighted with the windfall. It was exactly the time when he had to make his annual trip to the Dutch town, and Rozen's proposition assured him of an unexpected sum, which he would earn without difficult while going about his ordinary business.

"I accept," he said. "But if you're lying, beware my vengeance. Now, come. You're my guest. You'll be given something to eat. You can sleep in my hut. We'll make up a beverage against the fever."

The next day, Rozen, escorted by four vigorous fellows, took the road to Paramaribo—the road to freedom.

He was not at ease until the pirogue had set off into the network of channels that ran along the Dutch shore. There, he had no fear of falling into the path of a Dutch patrol; his escort gave him the appearance of a traveler on an excursion.

At Paramaribo he took the purse that Eléna had given him in Cayenne from his belt.

The chief's eyes sparkled with avarice at the sight of the gold coins.

Rozen looked at him, laughing. "You didn't know I was so rich."

"No," said the other, with a sigh of regret.

"Otherwise, you'd have done the same as my porters."

"No, no!"

"Anyway, here's fifty piastres. May the Devil protect you. Adieu!" And without any further explanation, Gaston drew away.

In the harbor of the Dutch city he spotted a clothing-merchant, to whom he recounted a long story, and from whom he bought new clothes.

The shopkeeper looked at him with a knowing expression. "You didn't need to go to all that trouble; I saw right away that you're French...escaped..." The fugitive suddenly went pale. "Don't worry about a thing. You're safe here."

Rozen knew that he had nothing to fear, but he could not help a thrill of fear on seeing that the merchant had seen through him. The man appeared to be a good sort. He asked him about the *tapouyes* and steamers that were about to leave the port, and learned that an American steamship was due to leave that evening for Valencia.

Everything was working out marvelously.

883 soon came to an arrangement with the captain to reserve a passage.

Luck seemed to be following him. As soon as he set foot in the Venezuelan city he was safe from apprehension, but he was anxious about the future nevertheless, being almost out of money. He wondered what he could do to vanquish the initial difficulties of his new life and await Bastien, on whose collaboration he had funded his great hopes for making war on society.

Pensively, he considered the possibility that things might not go in accordance with his dream, and that he might experience terrible days before realizing his hopes; he became discouraged now that he was free; a collapse of morale followed the expenditure of energy that he had made to get his far. He had never felt as depressed as he did at the moment when he became certain of not falling back into the hands of the French police.

He tried in vain to pull himself together; he was overwhelmed by a kind of spleen. He was ready to treat the conquest of his fortune as folly...

Was it the fever that rendered him thus—morose and crestfallen when he ought, by contrast, to be summoning up all the resources of his imagination, all the vigor of his muscles? He did not know...but he went straight ahead, mechanically, his head bowed.

One might have thought, on seeing him, that he was a drunkard trying to conceal is drunkenness, stiffening himself in order not to stumble.

In the three weeks since he had fled the penitentiary, in consequence of the privations and fatigue of his journey through the forest, his mind had lost some of its lucidity; a kind of numbness was paralyzing his limbs.

It required a fortunate accident to vanquish that torpor, which might have doomed him.

Suddenly, he bumped into a preoccupied man who was emerging from a business premises on the façade of which was legible, in large letters:

LAVARDENS
Raw rubber—Commission—Export

A double exclamation followed the collision.

"Rozen!"

"Lavardens!"

There was joy in the cry uttered by Rozen, amazement and even fear in the one that has escaped Lavardens.

Hazard had brought the two men together again. They had not spoken to one another since they had left London, where they had served their commercial apprenticeship together.

Lavardens had seen Rozen again, the previous year, in a convict's uniform, while he had been in Cayenne completing his military service as a non-commissioned officer in the marine infantry. He knew all about the Levantine's odyssey, his crimes, his sentence. In the bagne, he had not appeared to recognize him, out of pity of the man he had known rich and joyful, who was grieving in the livery of ignominy. To the extent that was possible, however, he had contributed to the easing of Rozen's plight. On leaving the regiment, Lavardens had married, and then had established himself as a rubber-merchant, founding a branch of his employer's business in Valencia. Every year, at harvest-time he came to supervise his purchases.

"Lavardens!" Rozen continued, offering his hand to the businessman. "What a pleasure it is to find you here."

The ex-NCO did not appear to see the rather compromising hand held out by his compatriot, whom destiny had thrown into his path.

"You!" he stammered. "But I thought you were dead!"

Gaston looked at his interlocutor with a strange smile, and a rapidly-extinguished glimmer in his eye. "Why did you think that?" he asked.

"Why, because last week, in Cayenne, I learned of your escape..."

"Ah! And?"

"And...the discovery of mangled human remains, half-devoured by rodents and insects. Only a few scraps of flesh remained on the bones, and only a few shreds of clothing escaped destruction by the insects, doubtless interrupted in their work by an ant-eater. One of those shreds, however, still bore the inscription C.P. 883. It was on that basis that your death-certificate was drawn up."

The trader saw a hint of anxiety in Gaston's eyes. "Don't worry," he added. "I won't betray you. Another man—an exile—left on the same day as you. He hasn't been found."

The fugitive smiled enigmatically. He did not give his interlocutor time to continue. "So Rozen no longer exists, officially," he declared. "So much the better. I'll be able to make a new skin, undertake what I've dreamed of doing...the conquest of the world...and you'll help me. Lavardens. Oh, forget the past, I beg you, forget those sins...due more to my deplorable education than evil instincts. Misfortune has corrected and matured me. I want to begin my life again.

"Come on, let's go into the posada. I want to tell you everything, and if you consent to give me the help I need, I'll make you rich."

While speaking, he drew Lavardens into a tavern, and when they were both at table in a small separate room, he told him about his sufferings. With a persuasive eloquence, he told him about his hopes, his plans for rehabilitation, his dreams of fortune and greatness.

The trader had listened to him, slightly intoxicated by the audacity of his interlocutor's vision, but retaining a certain definite preoccupation: that of ridding himself as soon as possible of a person that he feared deep down, knowing that he was capable of anything...except good.

"There!" said Rozen, concluding. "When I've acquired the necessary capital, by any means possible...I'll go back to Paris. There, in a short time, I'll become the arbiter of business, the *deus ex machina* of commercial life. But I lack an initial stake...oh, not much—enough to live fashionably for a month. Can you let me have a small advance?"

Thinking that he might get rid of Rozen permanently, Lavardens consented to give him what he wanted. "I have to leave of France tomorrow. Come to my branch in the morning—where you met me just now—and I'll give you a thousand francs."

"Lavardens, you won't have obliged an ingrate. I promise you that when my fortune's made, I won't forget the service you've rendered me..."

The trader simply said: "Until tomorrow"—and he separated from the convict hurriedly, glad to get out of it, in sum, so cheaply, by sacrificing a thousand francs to be rid of that embarrassing companion.

The next day, at the appointed hour, Rozen pocketed the sum promised by Lavardens, and the latter took the steamship to return to France, hoping never to see the convict again.

Thanks to that money, Rozen could live while waiting for Bastien.

Every day he went to the harbor, watching the ships arrive. After a month, he finally saw the Parisian disembark.

"Well, my old mate!" cried Macaron, joyfully. "You can see that I'm as good as my word. It hasn't been plain sailing—three days at sea with nothing to eat. I was grinding my teeth aboard that damned launch, but I was finally able to land on the English shore. There, I sold my boat—yes, my dear chap, an opportunity. You can see that I think of everything. And now, to work, eh? But first, I have to drink to glory."

In a café, Macaron told Rozen about his escape. It had taken him more than a fortnight to fabricate the spare parts necessary to the functioning of the launch. For a fortnight, he had patiently put coal aside in the rear bunker, in order to travel for a few hours and put himself beyond the range of pursuit. He told his companion about the distress he had suffered during the three days he had drifted in the open sea, without knowing where he was.

"Finally," he concluded, "here I am. That's the essential thing. Gold and pleasure for us, as they sing in *Faust*. For us...I suppose you have a plan, don't you? For we won't get far on our meager money. Suppose we head for the gold-deposits in the Contesté?"[17]

---

[17] The Contesté was a tract of land on the border between Guiana and Brazil that was claimed by both France and Brazil, eventually settled by an agreement signed in 1897, after the discovery of gold in 1894 lent the longstanding dispute a new urgency.

"I thought of that," said Rozen. "Tomorrow, we'll set off for Alemquer. That's a center where the gold-prospectors meet. We'll get hired!"

"All right. Forward forever, as the English say. Nuggets and chicks for us!"

"Yes," Rozen replied, his eyes shining and his lip trembling. "Infamous capital for us…and we'll have the world at our feet."

In the town of Alemquer they met a group of *regatos* departing for the Contesté. Regatos are traveling merchants who go into Indian territory and the goldfields, from tribe to tribe and from camp to camp, doing business. They take items of clothing, alcohol, wine, canned food, weapons, tools and glassware, and come back laden with precious wood and gold dust, sometimes even sizable nuggets.

Many of these merchants are Portuguese. Rozen, who knew that language well, was easily able to strike up a relationship with the travelers. He took the opportunity to buy two fine Winchester rifles for himself and Bastien, cartridges and a few provisions. Three days later, they were *en route* to the gold-fields.

During the month that the journey lasted they lived a nomadic life as best they could, hunting and fishing.

Having reached the deposits, they thanked their guides and hired themselves out to a crew of gold-prospectors.

The life of hard work under the leaden sun was not the one of which they dreamed, however. They were on the lookout for an opportunity to obtain a large haul of gold at a single stroke, without difficulty.

"There's too much hard work in this place," Macaron said. "We need to find a way of getting to balmier shores."

"Be patient," Rozen replied. "A consignment of gold has to leave here soon for Obidos."

"Silly name."

"It's a little town on the bank of the Amazon."

"Well, what of it? Will it get us any further forward to be there?"

The Levantine smiled. "Yes—I've got a plan. Gold-prospectors have one passion—gambling. When they're there, in the taverns, they risk everything on the green baize..."

"Cards! Oh, in that case..."

"Exactly. It's only a matter, for us, of raking in…from the winners."

"You think so?" Bastien said. "You know, your ideas aren't very..."

"I'll have whatever ideas I want…which you'll follow, if you have any intention of profiting from my fortune. You need to obey me blindly, understand?"

Gaston had said that in a tone that brooked no reply. His voice had become imperious. His gaze, suddenly harsh, weighed upon his acolyte.

The latter understood that he had a master in his companion: an audacious and resolute master, with whom he might go far. "Don't get bad-tempered, old chap," he said, soothingly. "Don't blow up. Go forward…I'll go along with your scheme…"

During their sojourn in the gold-field, they had collected a kilo of gold between them. They asked to go with the party that was about to leave for Obidos. The gold-prospectors agreed, hoping that the two novices would be easy prey for old bush-rangers. They did not know their guests.

After long days of wearying march, the little troop, comprising eight men in all, including Rozen and Bastien, finally arrived in Obidos, a small settlement mostly made up of Portuguese immigrants.

That same evening, the majority of the two Frenchmen's companions were dead drunk. All the gold gleaned by three months of relentless labor had become the property of one alone: a Maltese with powerful muscles; a kind of Hercules resistant to the fumes of alcohol. He could drink and keep drinking; it did not appear to have any effect.

All day, the escaped convicts had prudently kept apart, letting their companions gamble and drink to their hearts' content.

It was midnight. The Maltese, the bearer of a veritable fortune composed of ingots won or stolen from the others, had gone into a drinking den.

"Now's the moment to act," said Rozen. "The inn's deserted. We'll get the innkeeper drunk first…"

"Understood."

"Then, I'll offer the Maltese a game. You'll sit down to watch. You'll watch out for the most favorable moment, and…"

"A clean sweep," sniggered the anarchist. "I'll take care of it. And then?"

"Then you'll make yourself scarce. I'll play the indignant, and while you go left, I'll lead the other astray to the right."

"Not bad."

"You'll respond to my whistle—and when we're back together, we'll take off with the gold…"

"All right—there must be at least…"

"Ten kilos, at three thousand francs a kilo. That makes…"

"Thirty thousand bullets! A nice touch! It'll set us up. Agreed…"

They went into the *venda*. In a corner of the tavern's only room, the Maltese, slumped on at table in front of a bottle of *cachaça*, seemed to be asleep. He had set his revolver down close at hand.

Rozen went straight over to him and put a hand on his shoulder.

The Hercules started.

"Well, friend," said Rozen, looking the prospector in the eye. "Have you had any luck?"

"A little," growled the colossus.

"Would you do me the favor of playing a little game?"

"Yes, why not?"

"Waiter—cards!"

"Here," said the man thus summoned. "What'll you have?"

"Whatever you like. A glass of *paraty*."[18]

The game commenced.

Faithful to the program mapped out by Rozen, Bastien drew away from the players and sat down with the owner of the *venda*.

"Say, old chap," he said, in his faubourgian accent. "While they're playing, why don't we down a glass of *capilé*. I'll buy."

The innkeeper, already dulled by the libations he had made during the day, accepted. A former merchant seaman, he had travelled a great deal and knew several languages, including French, of which a shipmate had taught him a slang-laden variant. The innkeeper's comrade had been a son of Belleville.

After a few more or less banal exchanges, Bastien raised the subject of drink.

"People don't know how to drink hereabouts," he said.

"You're joking!"

"One Parisian can drink twenty of you under the table."

"That remains to be seen."

"It's obvious. Look—I bet that I'll have emptied my half-gallon of *laranghina*[19] before you. Loser pays the bill."

"I'll take the bet," said the man, looking Bastien up and down with an expression of pity."

"Go on, then!"

The innkeeper filled two large glasses with laranghina.

"Listen: one, two—and on three, hey presto! The first to put his empty glass on the table. Ready?"

Each of them took his glass in hand, and raised it to the level of his lips.

"One...two...three!" said Macaron.

And while his adversary conscientiously drank his enormous measure of alcohol, the Parisian tipped the contents of his glass on the floor and swiftly put it down on the table.

"I win!" he exclaimed.

"No! You...didn't...drink..."

The voice of the unfortunate innkeeper thickened. Fire burned his throat. His eyes became bloodshot.

"Did I say that we had to drink?" Bastien riposted, with a mocking expression. "I said 'emptied.' *Emptied*, understand?"

The other could no longer hear; he had stood up. His yes haggard, he raised his hand to his throat, as if to remove a weight that was choking him. Then his

---

[18] The text includes a note identifying *paraty* as alcohol made from sugar cane. *Cachaça* is similarly derived and was often used to sweeten *capilé,* derived from the syrup of the maidenhair fern.

[19] Again, the text adds a note defining this as alcohol derived from oranges.

arm beat the air, and he sat down again, thunderstruck, like an inert mass. The infernal beverage had done its work.

Still playing with the Maltese, Rozen had not missed a single one of his accomplice's movements. The Parisian looked at him and, pointing to the inn-keeper slumped in his chair, he smiled.

His expressive physiognomy seemed to be saying: "That's a job well done, eh?"

Suddenly, Gaston, stopping the prospector's arm, said: "Void hand—you cheated."

The Hercules stood up, white with wrath. "That's not true!"

"It is, I tell you—I don't want to be robbed."

"Robbed!" howled the Maltese, beside himself...and, seizing the revolver placed within arm's each, he aimed it at the man who had just insulted him.

The shot was fired.

The Levantine, with an abrupt side-step, avoided the bullet.

The Maltese took aim for a second time.

Rozen was doomed...when, all of a sudden, the colossus uttered a dull roar, dropped his weapon and collapsed on the floor, unconscious.

At the same time, a joyful exclamation went up behind him. "There you go!" And Gaston saw Bastien, perched on his legs in the attitude of a trained monkey calling out to a passer-by.

"He won't talk, eh? Always had a neat flick of the wrist, for slicing..."

In his fist, the Parisian was still clutching the knife with which he had struck Rozen's adversary. The thrust, delivered with astonishing accuracy, had been delivered to the middle of the nape, at the base of the skull.

The Maltese was on the ground. He had been killed instantly, like an ox in an abattoir, and in the same fashion.

"God's thunder!" grumbled Rozen. "That's a fine item you've put on our bill. This isn't the time to discuss it. Quickly, quickly, let's get the gold—and get out of here, if we have time."

"That's it...let's be off," said the incorrigible street-arab, merrily.

Rosen trembled, involuntarily. He was not afraid, but he had a horror of blood, and, since his flight from the bagne, this was the second corpse he had left in his wake.

"Let's go," Bastien grumbled, "Don't get on your high horse. One more or less doesn't count—we'll see plenty more. Get out, old chap, and at the gallop..."

"Bah!" Gaston concluded. "You're right..."

"Legitimate self defense. Your conscience can rest easy."

Carrying the Maltese's gold, they left the tavern. Outside, all was calm. No one in the town had stirred. The inhabitants, accustomed to brawls between prospectors, had been unmoved by the sound of the gunshot. They had heard—and seen—many others.

"Here's the land of my dreams," murmured Bastien. "No cops to disturb good men. Forward, sonny boy. You can be sure the chap won't tell anyone who hit him—it's more reliable than marking cards."

Rozen made no reply to his companion's jests. He went rapidly through the deserted streets. When they reach the last houses, he got his bearings. To his left he perceived, shiny in the moonlight, the vast river Amazon, its waters flowing majestically.

"Come on," he ordered, in an imperious tone. "We'll march until sunrise. We need to be far away by daybreak."

"You're right, Boss. Forward, backs bent! We'll carry our bags bravely. The gold weighs no more than a feather! We're rich, eh? Aren't we? Thirty thousand bullets."

Rozen shrugged his shoulders.

"Rich?" he said. "Not yet!"

XII. The Sertão

When the first glimmer of daylight emerged from the rising sun, Rozen and Bastien came to a halt, out of breath.

Where were they? How far had they traveled since leaving Obidos after murdering the Maltese?

Bastien wanted to go on along the river bank, heading upstream.

"That way," he said, "there's no risk of ending up back in the town."

Gaston stopped him. "Where do you expect to get to in that direction? It's a desert."

"A desert, with all that greenery!"

"Yes—virgin forest is even more terrible than burning sands. Listen; this is what we'll do. By now, the prospectors will have found their comrade's body, and as we're no longer there to console them, they're going to set out in search of the metal that we've been careful to carry away. We need to hide. We don't have strength enough to fight them."

"Good thinking."

"We'll take advantage of that to rest…we'll go over to the other side of the river: that's the beginning of the *sertão*, populated by ferocious animals."

"*Sertão?* Is that argot?"

"No, it's the local language. *Sertão*[20] means 'the forest.' The river is the *riacho*."

"*Riacho* or not, we'll have get out feet wet."

The watercourse was not deep; they had no difficult in crossing to the other side. Then they headed toward the forest by a path that Rozen had pointed out to his companion shortly before.

They were in the middle of a vast clearing.

"Nice!" said Bastien. "We can settle down…"

"Not before we've inspected the surroundings."

"Are you afraid of ticks?"

"No, giant ants—big winged ants."

"Damn it, you're a scholar, you are…"

"Not such a scholar as all that," Rozen said, disdainfully. "I've just read a lot of accounts of voyages, and remembered some useful details…"

"All the same, what a nasty place! I like Paris better."

"Don't worry, we'll get back there…but before anything else, we need capital."

"Yes, Milord!"

---

[20] Sertão actually means "back country." The term usually refers to an arid hilly region in north-eastern Brazil.

"Enough chat. You can sleep for three hours. I'll stand guard."

"My guardian angel," mocked the urchin. "Watch over Bibi, who's going to bye-byes."

And a few moments later, lying on the ground, carpeted with a thick layer of dry grass, Bastien was sleeping peacefully.

Rozen sat down beside him, rifle in hand. Around them stretched the endless *sertão*. As far as the eye could see through the trees, the ex-883 could not see a single hut or any other vestige of habitation.

The watch was easy. If an enemy appeared, he would be visible a long way off. Rozen was certain that no one could get to the place where they were except via the plain. Behind the clump of palm trees that sheltered him and his companion the terrain was marshy, strewn with pointed reds whose leaves cut like a sharpened saber.

From the direction, Rozen said to himself, *it's unthinkable that anyone could get close to us. The marsh is uncrossable, and anyone who ventures into it would sink into the mud and die.*

While gazing at the landscape, his eyes attentive to the slightest movement of the long grass, the Levantine reflected on what he ought to do.

"Thirty thousand francs," he murmured. "With that we could get back to Europe, to Paris—but for the two of us to go downriver to Macapa would be dangerous. Better to wait here for a few days. We'd have a chance of encountering a group of regatos, who would take us for travelers without our boats. We can pay. Tomorrow, when I've made certain that the prospectors aren't thinking of pursuing us, we'll go around the forest and set up camp in on the river's edge."

Suddenly, he interrupted himself.

Bastien was running toward him, pale and trembling.

"There! There!" he stammered.

The Levantine, endowed with an imperturbable self-possession, shook his acolyte.

"What's there?"

"Look!"

An animal was creeping through the tall grass, and the Parisian had just spotted its menacing maw, equipped with enormous fangs.

"A jaguar," Gaston murmured. "Come on, don't be scared. A rifle-bullet will take care of it."

As he got ready to fire, there was a noise a few paces away from him. A roar resounded. Another jaguar, larger than the first, whose shiner coat was more vigorously spotted, bounded forward.

"Damn it!" Rozen groaned. "A male. That one's yours, Bastien!"

Macaron, somewhat heartened by Gaston's self-assurance, shouldered his rifle.

With an astonishingly sure aim, the Levantine shot the first feline. Bastien's shot was almost confused with his own, but, whether because he did not have sufficient skill or because fear made him tremble, he missed the jaguar, which bounded toward him in a trice.

In the blink of an eye, Rozen took stock of the situation. To use the rifle would be dangerous; there was a risk of hitting the Parisian. With a rapid movement he pulled his machete from the sheath dangling from his belt, and leapt resolutely between the ferocious beast and Bastien, who had collapsed in fear.

The jaguar, surprised by the rapidity of the moment, stopped dead.

Crouched low on its paws, its open mouth offering a glimpse of its formidable jaws, the American tiger, its yellow coat dotted with ocellate patches, and its paws armed with sharp claws, would be a redoubtable adversary.

He did not have time to shoulder his gun. It was with the naked blade that he had to fight. Rozen, his eyes ardent and his lips drawn back, firm and resolute, clutched the hilt of his machete intently.

Behind him, Bastien lay face down, livid, trembling in every limb, his teeth chattering. He stammered: "Done! We're cooked! Poor chap!"

The scene played out with lightning rapidity.

The jaguar leapt at Rozen. The latter swayed back, and planted his blade in the tiger's throat as it passed by, with a bold and vigorous thrust.

The beast uttered a dull groan and fell, inert, on to Macaron's back, more dead than alive.

"Come on," said Gaston to his companion. "You can get up now...coward."

Reassured, the street-arab slowly recovered his composure.

"But for you, old chap, I'd have been well and truly..."

"One good turn deserves another. You saved me yesterday, I've saved you today. We're quits."

"Through life and death," the anarchist replied. "All the same, you know, I'd rather have two men before my blade than an animal like that before my shooter."

"You're not a hunter—you need hardening," Rozen concluded, simply, with a smile. "Unfortunately, that dagger-blow won't bring us thirty thousand francs, like the other..."

The night passed peacefully. Macaron was no longer fearful; he stood his watch calmly while Rozen slept, and the next day, at dawn, certain that they were not being pursued, they moved on.

Following the plan decided by the Levantine, they returned to the riverbank. The adventure of the tiger had given Gaston a considerable empire over the Parisian, who, utterly hypnotized, obeyed him henceforth as a dog obeys its master.

They walked for a week, camping under the stars, living on their hunting in the flat and marshy land, which was difficult to cross. Rozen, whose good humor was unrelenting, educated Bastien with regard to the country.

"Here," he told him, "we really only have two perils to fear, one of them major: hostile Indians, a race of nomadic thieves, true tigers, who kill for the pleasure of killing..."

"Oh, the savages!"

"They're also knows as wild Indians, as opposed to tame Indians, tribes that live in one location, exploiting the land, and don't attack travelers. The wild Indians are fearsome. That's why, when we camp, it's always necessary for one of us to keep his eyes open."

"Good thing. I have no desire to be bumped off by those fellows, you know. At any rate, you're scarcely comforting, and I won't deny that I prefer La Villette and the Place d'Italie."

These prospective dangers made Bastien shiver, but his companion's audacity reassured him. He trusted him, and that confidence was supported, in that rough character, by an absolute submission to his companion—his master.

A week after fleeing Obidos, the two escapees were far enough away to be beyond the range of pursuit.

"We'll set up camp," said Rozen, "and rest for a few days at the edge of the forest. A little behind the trees, we'll build a hut—a ranch-house."

"A house! I'm all for it."

"To work, then...we need to sleep under shelter tonight."

"For once, there's no refusing—but what about tools?"

"Our machetes: with them we can cut branches, lianas and foliage. That's all we need."

While they were searching the edge of the forest for long straight branches that might serve as stakes they made a strange discovery.

"A pick!" Bastien exclaimed, suddenly.

"A spade," replied Rozen, in his turn.

They searched more carefully beneath the thick foliage carpeting the ground and discovered human bones. They were both insensitive, but that funereal find in the wilderness made a deep impression on them.

"That's one in the eye!" groaned Macaron.

Rozen collected himself rapidly. "Why? With these tools our hut will soon be built."

There were more surprises to come. Suddenly, while digging in the ground in order to plant the stakes that would serve to support their cabin, which they wanted to raise two or three meters above the ground in order to be protected from insects, snakes and the dampness of the grass, Rozen stopped and uttered a joyful exclamation.

"Gold!"

"Gold?" repeated the anarchist, admiringly.

"Look," said Rozen. So saying, he picked up a handful of red-tinted soil, in the midst of which numerous flakes of the precious metal were scintillating. "Yes, gold...the earth is rich in it. And I wouldn't be surprised if we were able to reap a rich harvest: a fortune."

"Very good—but that's not all. We'd have to carry it away, to a town, to change the nuggets into money."

Rozen shrugged his shoulders. "Just do as I say."

"You're right. I'll follow you, eyes shut."

"This changes my plans," Rozen went on.

"Your plans?"

"Yes. My intention was to reach Macapa as soon as possible, but now...this changes things. We can reap a prodigious harvest in a matter of days; then we'll move our camp closer to the river, and when the first part of regatos comes along, we'll head for the mouth of the Amazon."

That find gave them an astonishing ardor. By nightfall they had built a small cabin two meters square, mounted on four poles and covered with branches, whose walls were made with earth plastered over wood.

"A palace," Bastien declared, glad finally to be able to sleep under cover.

They spent a pleasant night, and at dawn the next day they undertook an inspection of the terrain.

Rozen was not mistaken. They had fallen on an auriferous deposit of the first magnitude. Gold, scarcely mixed with an alluvial matrix, was visible in several places. Mere washing sufficed to collect the nuggets, and a little stream was flowing rapidly very close to the hillock on which they were standing.

"We've put our hands on the Pactolus, old chap," said Rozen, cheerfully.

"The Pactolus?"

"You don't need to know. In fact...yes, you do. It's a river that..."

But the lesson was cut short.

In the distance, in the long grass, which sparkled in the sunlight and through which the breeze caused waves like those of the sea to run over the vast plain, into the distance, Rozen, whose glance was as sure as if he has always lived the life of a pioneer, perceived two or three forms that seemed to be coming toward them rather rapidly. With a fearful expression, he grabbed his companion's wrist.

"Quickly, Bastien, quickly—to the hut. We might have to fight dearly for our gold—and our lives."

The warning gave Macaron wings. They went back to their cabin at a gallop and set about loading their rifles and filling the cartridge-cases in their belts. In a matter of moments, Rozen took stock of the situation.

They were going to have to sustain a siege.

The enemy was still some distance away—about a dozen men. He could make out their silhouettes clearly now.

"Wild Indians," he murmured.

102

Almost immediately, he shouldered his rifle. "The honor's mine," he said. He smiled. In that well-tempered being, all forms of struggle were a pleasure.

He was fully aware of the danger he was running at that moment, and was not in the least afraid. Bastien, somewhat battle-hardened and reinforced by his master's courage, also put on a brave face.

"We'll send them raisins that aren't from Agen..."

To the first rifle-shot fired by Gaston, a howl of agony replied.

"Touché!" Macaron sniggered. But his laughter was soon frozen. Fear chilled him. At all points of the plain, in a semicircle, twenty...thirty...forty Indians showed themselves, howling death-threats.

They would be able to shoot four or five—perhaps ten—but what then? They were scarcely two hundred meters away.

"We're done for," stammered the Parisian, whose teeth were chattering.

He had good reason to tremble. Within three or four minutes, at the most, the bandit Indians would be there...and it would be impossible to win the battle. It was death, with no mercy and no defense, so to speak.

"Oh, shit!" cried Bastien, who remain entirely faubourgian at heart. "I think, old man, that they're going to make us pay!"

But the former 883 made no reply. He was observing. Suddenly, he said to Macaron: "Come quickly—quickly! Right now!"

"You're mad. We'll die all the sooner."

"Go, I tell you. Look sharp!"

The order was given in an imperious tone, which brooked no reply.

Uncomprehendingly, Bastien obeyed. While he emerged from the "ranchhouse," carrying arms and ammunition—the only things that Rozen permitted him to take—the latter, bringing a tinder-box out of his bag, ignited pieces of tinder and scattered them around the cabin.

"Retreat, at the gallop!" he shouted.

They both ran away as fast as they could.

In the blink of an eye, the dry grass caught fire.

A cloud of smoke rose up, borne by the wind in the direction of the attackers. At the same time, an intense crackling rent the air.

Rozen had had an idea suggested to him by the memory of campaigns in the Sudan. He had learned that troops surrounded by excessively numerous enemies had got rid of them by this heroic means.

"Bravo! Bravo!" howled Bastien, enthused. "That's good thinking, Colonel!"

Rozen shrugged his shoulders disdainfully. "Come on, quickly! Or we'll be roasted too..."

The fire was, in fact spreading rapidly, but less violently in their direction, being driven toward the Indians by the wind. At a hectic run, they reached the edge of the forest. There, Rozen gave Bastien the signal to stop.

"Thanks to the dampness of the wood," he said, "we're safe here. Anyway, we're in luck—the wind's getting up."

The fire reached the forest. Thick swirls of smoke spiraled upwards, into which flames put occasional sinister red gleams. And above the crackling of the burning grass, they heard the howls of the Indians, who could not flee fast enough.

"Thunder! A clever ploy, which does you honor."

"Yes," Rosen replied, shaking his head sadly. That's true—for the moment; but we need to leave this place. Otherwise, in two days, we'll doubtless be attacked again…and the next time..."

"Get away—they'll all be grilled."

"But we'll have others on our necks—and they'll avenge their dead."

"Bah! We'll see about that…with you, I no longer fear anything!"

Gaston shook his head, and continued: "And all our efforts thus far would be in vain. We're almost ruined. We only have enough gold left to make two thousand francs. A speck, that's all. Furthermore, we only have enough cartridges for four days. If you find that a cheerful prospect..."

"Come on, Bro…shut it! There'll be time enough later to whine. In the meantime, I'm going to enjoy the performance." Agonized screams reached their retreat. "Can you hear the orchestra?"

As nimble as a squirrel, Bastien climbed a tree.

"Oh, mate, if you could see this! It's worth a look. Caramba! Hey—I can speak the local lingo. What a barbecue!"

Gradually, the screams died away.

The flames, finding no more fuel, stopped at the edge of the *riacho* that wound around the forest.

Not one Indian had escaped the scourge.

From his observatory, Bastien applauded his companion's stratagem. "Job done then, for sure!" he concluded. "That's that..."

A hoarse growl, coming from the wood, cut short the street-arab's joke.

Behind Rozen, mouth agape, an American lion—a puma, as it is known over there—was gliding through the foliage of the bushes.

Ordinarily, such lions do not attack humans, but this one, its fur half-singed, maddened by the fire that Gaston had lit, had become redoubtable.

The Levantine did not have time to turn to face the beast. It bounded toward him, and with a terrible thrust of its claw, ripped open his cheek. Rozen fell backwards, uttering a howl of agony.

Swift as an arrow, however, Bastien, to whom the danger his master was in gave courage, was at the foot of the tree. With a thrust of his machete he transfixed the animal.

At that moment, another enemy appeared—the mate of the first.

"God's thunder!" muttered the Parisian, cocking his rifle. The former Parisian gamin was transformed. A world of thoughts was whirling in his head.

The idea that he might be left alone, ignorant, in this place, caused him to shudder.

Rapidly, he took aim and fired.

The wild beast, struck between the eyes, made a prodigious leap, and fell at Bastien's feet, panting.

"Dispatched!" exclaimed the anarchist. "Now it's time to look after my comrade. Damn! One might think that he'd had his lot!"

After a few moments, though, the wounded man came to.

"Water! It's nothing, it's nothing!" stammered Macaron, overcome by emotion. "Hang on, old man—I'll get you some."

He ran to the stream and came back, having filled his flask with fresh water. He washed Rozen's wound.

It was not serious, but the Levantine's fine and symmetrical face was striped by three long scratches, which had opened the flesh of his cheeks all the way to the gums.

"That'll change your description," Macaron declared. "That's all right; a little higher and he'd have taken out your eyes."

"Yes," Gaston murmured, feebly. "I really thought I was finished..."

For two days, fever retained the two men on the edge of the forest, but Rozen's robust temperament soon reckoned with the illness. On the third say, he was fit enough to march, and they both set off for the bank of the Amazon.

They were devoid of hope now, though, having lost their provision of gold. All they had left was a little powder and bullets, for hunting.

Chance, the god of the desperate, came to their aid once again.

After two interminable days of waiting, during which they lived on a capybara—a river-hog—killed by Bastien, they were fortunate enough to be seen by traders coming down the Amazon.

Rozen told them that he and his companion were French explorers, robbed and abandoned by the Indian porters they had hired. The traders took them aboard their pirogues, and, a short while thereafter, Rozen and Bastien arrived in Macapa.

They still had a few gold nuggets on them, which they were able to sell, thanks to which they realized a couple of thousand francs.

That nest-egg permitted them to take passage aboard an American vessel, a kind of smuggler, headed for Buenos Aires. There, Gaston intended, with the resources at his disposal, to engage in a little commerce, and then buy some sheep. He hoped that before long, he might have made enough money to return to Paris.

XIV. The Land of the Tobas

When they disembarked on the quay in Buenos Aires, Rozen and Macaron had a sensation of pleasure. Both of them, as sons of the big city, were slightly nostalgic for large houses nicely aligned, squares and boulevards planted with trees. For a long time, they had been cut off from the spectacle of animated streets, and they experienced a veritable joy in mingling with the crowd of passers-by walking along the Calle Indepencia, by which they left the harbor.

Where were they going?

They did not now themselves.

They wandered at hazard, glad to be free, without too much anxiety for the morrow, resolved to reward themselves with a little enjoyment by means of the savings they had been able to accumulate.

While walking, Rozen, who had a prodigious memory, told his companion everything he knew about the city.

Founded in 1535, the Argentine capital owes its name, according to some historians, to the exclamation of one of the leaders of the first expeditions sent by Charles the Fifth to conquer the territory. On disembarking at the place where the city would be built, Don Sancho de Campo, the brother of the expedition' commander, Pedro de Mendoza, cried enthusiastically: *"Que Buenos aires hay acqui!"*—how good the air is here—and the nascent city was named Buenos Aires.

Others say that mariners from Cadiz, belonging for the most part to the congregation of *Nuestra Senora de los Buenos Aires*—Our Lady of the Kindly Winds—gave the place the name of their patron saint, Santa Maria de Buenos Aires, in gratitude for the success of their expedition.

Either way, the city rapidly became prosperous. Its population, which numbered 178,000 inhabitants in 1869, is now in excess of 800,000.

The two escaped convicts had seen in the harbor that recent work had rendered capable of receiving ships of the largest tonnage, and provided a series of docks whose extent covered four kilometers, whereas ships had previously been obliged to remain at sea,

Rozen pointed out to his companion the delicate and capricious architecture of the private houses of the elegant city occupying the north of Buenos Aires. He called his attention to the grandiose appearance of the public buildings, which were very numerous.

In addition to the governmental palace and the Treasury, the capital possesses a cathedral, a dozen theaters, twenty-five banks, a stock exchange, colleges of military studies, medicine and law, a library and interesting museums.

Not wanting to alarm his comrade, Rozen deliberately left out any mention of the entirely European organization of the Buenos Aires police, due in large part to the initiative of the distinguished Secretary General Mujica Farias, who had come to spend several months in Europe, particularly in Paris, especially to make a conscientious study of the functioning of the Prefecture of Police. Rozen avoided drawing Macaron's attention to the 3,561 *vigilantes* and the 250 agents of the Sûreté, as well as the *escuadron de seguridad*, which is not unlike our Parisian "sepoys."

He knew, in any case, that the little army in question had better things to do than occupy itself with two poor French refugees.

The newly-disembarked pair had gone through the city center and business quarter, and arrived in the southern part of the city, passing through the Plaza de la Vitoria and the Plaza Miserere.

Dusk was already falling. Gas-lamps and electric lights were being illuminated everywhere.

"Good!" exclaimed Bastien. "At least it's civilized here! One can see clearly even when there's no moon."

"I believe," said Rozen, without paying any heed to the exclamation of the Parisian admirer of well-lit streets, "that we can find somewhere to stay hereabouts."

The quarter in which they found themselves was formed entirely of wooden houses constructed on pilings, and was inhabited by a population that was, so to speak, exclusively maritime.

First they went into a restaurant, where they had a substantial meal.

Rozen told Bastien, who was delighted to tuck into a succulent beefsteak, that Buenos Aires is the city with the highest average consumption of meat per person in the world.

After having eaten well, they decided to spend the evening at the theater, but as they emerged from the restaurant, Bastien suddenly took Gaston's arm and said: "My God, that's lucky!"

"What?"

"You see that chap there?"

Macaron drew Gaston's attention to a man—a veritable colossus—heading in their direction, a short distance away. In the glare of an electric light, his bronzed masculine face stood out clearly. He had a black beard, curly hair and keen eyes—and his entire physiognomy gave an impression of placidity.

"Comrade Dulac," murmured Bastien.

The name Dulac was not unfamiliar to Rozen. He had often seen it printed in the Parisian newspapers in the era when the anarchists were causing the French bourgeoisie to tremble. He recalled a strange story told about the man, whom a bitter disappointment in love had thrown outside normal life and who had taken refuge in the ranks of "propagandists by action."

Dulac was a weakling, beneath his virile appearance. His athletic body housed a sentimental soul—the soul of a woman. That giant, of Breton origin, brought up by his mother, an inconsolable widow, had come to Paris and obtained work in journalism. Gaston recalled having seen him when he was the lover of Germane Reyval, a theater actress, a star for whom Dulac had committed follies, and who had left him one day for a professional gymnast and a banker. Ruined and despairing, the lover had held society responsible for his misfortune...and an anarchist was born.

He had committed himself to the cause and, led astray by the party leaders, with the help of his exasperated mysticism, he had not taken long to become one of the most fervent adepts of the new doctrine.

By now, Dulac had arrived in front of the two escaped convicts.

Bastien went to meet him, his hand held out. "Hello, Comrade Dulac."

The colossus, plunged into a reverie, started. He did not recognize the man who had spoken to him immediately.

"I need to refresh your memory," said the faubourgian, cheerfully. "Bastien...Macaron, if you prefer."

"Oh yes! I remember..."

"Of course! It's a pleasure to meet a mate, thousands of kilometers from home. And I have someone to introduce to you...a true friend: Gaston Rozen." To the Levantine, he said: "Comrade Henri Dulac. A brother. You were made for each other."

Dulac and Rozen shook hands.

"But we can't talk on the sidewalk," Macaron added. "Shall we step into a bistro?"

Not far away, the brilliantly-illuminated window of a café lit up the street. They went in.

Bastien brought Dulac up to date with their adventures. He told him about the anarchists' revolt, the escape from the bagne and the vicissitudes of their life since the escape. He omitted to mention the murder of the Maltese, of course, certain in advance that the exploit in question would cool any interest that Dulac might take in Rozen and him.

While Macaron narrated their triumphs with considerable verve Rozen studied the former journalist. Fixing his eyes on Dulac, the Levantine tried to divine the man's character. The gaze was keen, the face intelligent, but one sensed, in spite of Dulac's apparent strength, that he was irresolute, a malleable individual, easily-led.

The conversation gradually changed direction, and moved on to confidences. They discussed future plans on both sides.

Rozen spoke eloquently, with the warm and persuasive voice that enveloped his interlocutors and gripped them to the marrow. He made an entire romance of his youth, to his own advantage: he showed himself unjustly condemned for wanting to save the life of a friend, a brother worker—and Dulac listened trustingly to that fable, which had succeeded so well with Eléna in Cayenne, and was moved by it.

Macaron listened too, lulled by Gaston's musical voice.

Then Rozen told Dulac their dream: society tamed; wealth and power in the hands of a few companions, who would consent to follow him. He spoke at length, demonstrating that although the work would be difficult to begin with, happiness and glory would crown the efforts of his associates. Thanks to them, society, having been improved, would see the flowering of a new era. No more poverty, no more slavery, but free men, working for themselves and not for the financial oligarchy, workers no longer receiving humiliating wages but each taking a share of common fortune proportionate to his endeavor.

Dulac listened, utterly entranced by the revolutionary utopias beneath which Rozen concealed his avidity for lucre and his formidable appetite for domination.

"Ah!" he said, visibly emotional, when the Levantine had concluded his inflamed speeches. "What a pity that Sokoloff isn't here. He'd embrace you. With a man like you, we'd go far; we'd reconstruct the world."

"Sokoloff!" exclaimed Rozen. "You know where Sokoloff is?"

"He was here two months ago..."

"His collaboration would be invaluable to us," Gaston continued. "The profound science and genius of that apostle of the sacred cause would help us triumph over the initial difficulties...we need him to be one of us."

"Presently," Dulac replied, "He's in the Chaco, near the territory of Formosa."

"The Chaco?"

"Yes. He went out there with half a dozen companions to found an Arcadia—a country where there are neither masters nor servants."

A singular smile passed over the Levantine's lips, unseen by the other two. That was typical of Sokoloff, a generous intellectual, a man capable of any sacrifice for the victory of his idea, his insane dream: absolute equality in society. He remembered that the scientist had endeavored to make gold chemically. His research on argentaurum[21] had been particularly interesting. At all costs, he needed to recruit that strength, to have it at his disposal in order to undertake the conquest of Paris. Sokoloff had sought a method of making gold in order that the debased metal would lose its value and thus become accessible to everyone. Obvious madness!

---

[21] The term *argentaurum* was coined by Stephen Emmens, an American chemist who worked extensively on explosives before claiming that gold and silver were chemically related and that the former could be derived from the later, passing through the intermediate stage in question. Although he began selling gold that he had supposedly manufactured to the U.S. Mint in 1897, his claims to have produced gold from silver by means of a "force-engine" were not widely publicized until 1899, when a storm of controversy blew up. Emmens died shortly thereafter and his secret, if he really had one, died with him.

But if the seeker found argentaurum, Rozen wanted to be the first to exploit the discovery. His resolution was immediately made.

"I'll go in search of Sokoloff," he said, "and I'll bring him back here." Then he asked Dulac: "Why didn't you go with him?"

"I was ill when he left. I haven't recovered completely yet."

"All right. You stay here and wait for us. Tomorrow, I'll make preparations to go to the Chaco..."

"That's easy. A party of diamond-prospectors is leaving any day. They're looking for resolute men to go with them into Coroado territory."

"In the Brazilian Parana? I thought diamonds were only found in the Matto Grosso, north of Paraguay."

"A few mines have been discovered in Coroado territory. The diamonds are inferior to the others, but the mines can make a profit nevertheless—at the price of greater dangers, it's true. The men I'm talking about can take you as far as Corrientes. There, you'll be well on the way to the Chaco."

"Understood," said Rozen. "Tomorrow, we'll make our arrangements."

Of course, Bastien said to himself, thoughtfully. *Diamonds. I'm in!*

The three men left the café.

Dulac offered his two new friends hospitality, and the next day, following his indications, Gaston and Macaron sought employment with the small band of diamond prospectors. The leader of the party was a Paraguayan; thanks to his perfect knowledge of Spanish, Rozen was able to persuade him to take them on. He told him the banal and always plausible story of travelers gone astray and ruined, robbed by Indian porters, desirous of putting together a nest-egg by means of hard work.

"Caballero," he said, "my companion and I are sturdy and resolute, energetic and ready for anything. We'll be valuable auxiliaries for you."

The terms of employment were quickly discussed, and agreed by both sides.

Rozen and Bastien refrained from telling Dulac that their intention was to go to the mines. The Levantine had the idea of going there, but did not want to let Sokoloff's companion in on his plans. So far as Dulac was concerned, the two men's sole objective was a passage to Corrientes; there, they would make arrangements to go to the Chaco, in the vicinity of Formosa, where Sokoloff was.

The two escaped convicts reached the mine without incident, and to get into the good graces of their companions, they set about digging fervently for diamonds.

While he worked, Rozen told Macaron that the first diamonds had been discovered in Brazil in 1725, but that the stones were less esteemed than those from the Cape and India. He brought him rapidly up to date with the somewhat primitive method of mining.

The ground is dug up the earth thus removed in washed; the most delicate operation, and the most difficult challenge to the eyesight, consists of sorting out the stones that the washing separates from the matrix. Among the fragments of transparent quartz, known as *fujão*, it is necessary to recognize diamonds of various sizes.

Rozen, who was very ingenious, constructed a series of troughs in which the earth, washed repeatedly, was separated from the stones. Thanks to that still-rudimentary method, the harvest was more abundant than during previous expeditions. The miners were delighted with their new recruits.

Gaston was particularly friendly with one of them, a chatty Frenchman who was very glad to find someone interested in his story.

Although all his comrades knew him by the name of Pierre, his real name was Saint-Magloire, and he was entitled to wear the title of Baron. He had his family documents with him, in a fat leather wallet, which he carried religiously in his jacket pocket. Ruined by the Revolution, his grandfather had left his descendants nothing but those yellowing parchments. A fine thing, to be called the Baron de Saint-Magloire when one has no money!

Having tried various professions, Pierre's father had left Europe and come to settle in Venezuela, where he had married a creole—but Revolution, which had killed the grandfather, was also fatal to the emigrant. In the course of one of the crises that are so frequent in the petty Republics of South America, he had been killed, and his widow had consoled herself by marrying a Peruvian general, who had run away one day after having got his vile hands on the money left by the deceased. The general's wife had died of grief and Pierre, who was then twenty years old, had left that inhospitable land, with only his parchments for a patrimony, and landed in Argentinian territory, where he became a *gaucho*.

He too had no luck; the pueblo he had funded with a few others was devastated by the Tobas. His live had been saved thanks to the speed of his horse, but, disgusted with farm life, he had joined a company of diamond prospectors.

"And that," Pierre concluded, "is why the Baron de Saint-Magloire, who ought to be cutting a fine figure in Parisian high society, is merely a simple miner! But fortune has smiled on me; I have the hope of getting rich here in a few years, and then I'll resume in Paris the position to which my birth entitles me. I no longer have any relatives, it's true, but I'll found a new dynasty! I only ask one thing of you, my friend, which is—pure coquetry on my part, but I'm determined—that no one apart from you should know who I really am."

"Don't worry," Rozen replied with a strange smile. "No one will."

He had listened to the strange story with amiable indifference at first, but while the verbose individual talked, he reflected. The man was alone in the world! His family had left Paris long ago. If he disappeared, and someone else took his documents, who could dispute the right of that man to bear the same of Saint-Magloire?

And with the rapidity of decision that was characteristic of his audacious nature, the Levantine promised himself to take advantage of the windfall.

His companions in the mine were unaware of Pierre's origins; the latter had just told him that he was the only man in whom he had confided—and he had told him the reason, in addition to the coquetry to which he had initially made allusion. "I'm afraid that someone might steal my papers, you see. With you, a compatriot, it's different. Then again, there are sympathies that are spontaneous. As soon as I saw you, I felt a friendship toward you. You have my full confidence."

The gaucho's confidence was well placed!

One evening, Rozen said to Macaron: "Do you like the miner's life?"

"Not much. It takes too long to earn a crust."

"Well, old chap, tonight we'll bring of a coup that will make us both rich."

"I'm listening."

"The harvest of precious stones is locked in the bosses' safe..."

"Understood: it's a matter of getting in, killing them quietly, without them making a sound, then taking possession of the lovely stones, jumping into the saddle and sailing away. *En route*, nabobs!"

Cynical in planning the crime, as carefree and cheerful as if it were a pleasure-trip, Bastien started singing, parodying a song that as popular at the time.

Here come the nabo-bobs!
I'm with them all the way.

Rozen gripped his wrist violently. "This is no time for joking! We need to act. In half an hour, wait for me outside the bosses' hut; I'll meet you there."

"Understood, old man; I'll have my blade. Go in peace, Eustache, and do the good work!"

They separated—and while Bastien went back to his hut, Rozen went into Pierre's.

The former gaucho was not asleep. Wide awake, he was dreaming about the Parisian high life, already seeing himself as the Baron de Saint-Magloire, fêted and pampered by all, marrying a rich heiress. Oh, she would have diamonds, Madame de Saint-Magloire!

On seeing Gaston come in, he had difficulty standing up. "It's you, my dear friend. You interrupted my dream. No matter—I'll pick it up later. Since you've been so kind as to pay me a visit, may I offer you a glass of eau-de-vie?"

He went to fetch a bottle and two glasses from a plank set in a corner of the hut.

"It's good, my..."

He did not have time to finish. A knife-thrust between his shoulder-blades killed him instantly. He did not utter a groan.

Without losing a minute, Gaston opened the unfortunate man's jacket and took possession of the wallet containing the family papers. There was a glint of joy in his eyes. A diabolical smile passed over his lips. "Now," he murmured, "the bagnard Rozen is well and truly dead. Here's my identity papers. Long live the Baron de Saint-Magloire!" He glanced down at the corpse. "Poor sap!" he murmured—but, quickly dispelling that fit of pity, he added: "Bah! He'll be content, all the same. The Baron will cut a fine figure in society."

Prudently, he rejoined Bastien.

Faithful to the summons, the Parisian was lying down outside the bosses' hut.

"Let's go," Rozen ordered.

Stealthily, they approached the cabin. Slowly, holding his breath, Bastien tried to open the door.

"God's thunder!" he groaned. "It's bolted inside. Bah! There are only three of them! Should I force it?"

"Yes," growled the Levantine.

But the door was solid. The pressure put on it by Macaron had no other result than waking the diamonds' guardians. They leapt on their weapons, and the entire mine was soon on foot.

Rozen and Bastien only just had time to escape being shot by the miners. Fortunately for them, they had taken the precaution of saddling the horses, and, taking advantage of the disorder in the camp, in spite of the diamond prospectors' fusillade, they were able to get away. They did not stop riding until they were sure that they were out of reach.

Desolate at having lost such a good opportunity to enrich themselves, they remained bleakly mute, not daring to exchange the painful impressions that weighed upon them.

Bastien was the first to break the silence. "Well, Gaston, more bad luck, eh? The conquest of the world has certainly made a sticky start, I think."

Rozen did not reply. He was thinking.

It did not matter much to him that the theft of the diamonds had gone awry. He had something more precious than that: an identity that no one could challenge—but he did not think it necessary to let Bastien in on the secret.

"What are you thinking about?" Macaron went on. "The millions we've lost?"

"No," the Levantine grunted. "I think we'd better get to the Chaco as soon as possible..."

"To find Sokoloff!"

"Yes, and we'll go back to Europe as soon as possible."

"Good idea. The Old World! It's the only one, old chap."

In the exhaustion that had followed the furious race, thanks to which they had escaped death, they had not thought about tethering their horses. When they looked for them, in the early morning, the animals had disappeared.

"They've gone back to the mine," Rozen declared.

"Well, now we're in a proper pickle," the Parisian muttered. We'll have to content ourselves with train 11, low speed."

"Do you think it's funny?" growled Rozen, distressed by the loss of their mounts—but his depression did not last long.

They would find the anarchist scientist anyway, and would go back to Buenos Aires. After that, they would act. Sokoloff and Dulac had some money at their disposal. Now, he could be the Baron de Saint-Magloire whenever he wanted to be. It was necessary to struggle on; so be it—he would struggle.

For several days the adventurers wandered at random, marching by night and hiding by day, in order not to fall into the hands of the miners who might have set out to pursue them.

Eventually reassured, they walked for three weeks, living by hunting, sleeping under the stars, and arrived within the borders of Paraguay, some way south of the city of Asuncion.

Rozen whiled away the leisure time of the journey with a course in the history of the country they were about to reach. From a young age, the man seemed to have had a presentiment of the adventurous life for which he was destined and, neglecting the rest of his studies completely, had devoted himself exclusively to learning foreign languages, and had avidly read the history, arid and complex as it was, of South America. Thanks to his astonishing memory, he had retained the most important facts.

"You see, Bastien," he said, "although it's claimed that a happy country has no history, thus one has a terrible one. Since Vicente Yanez-Pinzon and Juan Dias de Solis discovered the River Plate at the beginning of the sixteenth century, wars have never ceased to stain the soil with blood.

"Solis, returning alone a little later, was massacred by the Charva Indians. It was Sebastian Cabot who was the first of sail up the Parana and then the River Paraguay, in whose vicinity we are now, and then the River Bermejo."

"Keep going," said the Parisian. "It's interesting." A significant yawn gave the lie to his words. But Rozen was in full flow; his memory was recovering a host of facts about the country.

"Cabot," he continued, without paying any heed to his listener's lack of attention, "encountered Diego Garcia, to whom Charles the Fifth had entrusted the navigation of the Rio de Solis. The new explorers waited five years for help from the Empire, in vain."

"Five years! A long time to be clicking their heels."

"Then Cabot when back to Spain. At Fort San Espiritu, which he had built, he left a hundred and seventy men commanded by Mino de Lara, but they had to evacuate the fort. The first serious conquest was undertaken by Pedro de Mendoza. He had nearly three thousand men under his command, and seventy horses."

"We don't even have one!" Macaron moaned. "And I'm exhausted."

They were obliged to stop. The heat was overwhelming. Large clouds were building up in the sky, presaging a storm. The Levantine continued his history lesson, while Bastien went to sleep; he talked about the early conquistadors.

"Ayolas, the founder of the city of Asuncion, and then Martinez de Isala, who crossed the Chaco with the aim of reaching Peru and was massacred by the Payagua Indians, just as the unfortunate Doctor Crevaux was to be, five hundred years later, by the Tobas..."

And the Levantine, carried away by his dream of the past, reviewed all the heroic struggles of Ayolas' successors. Successively, he cited Orthez de Vergara and Juan de Torres, and talked about the attempts at evangelization made by the Franciscans and Fathers of Mercy—attempts that left profound roots in the Indian tribes and were the origin of the semi-Catholic semi-pagan religion that one finds today among the indigenes of those regions.

The work of the Jesuits was fecund; several tribes were pacified, becoming less resistant to commerce with the white men. In the number of those precursors he did not neglect to cite Francisco Blanco, who had the good idea of merging the religion of Christ with those of the Indians. When the Jesuits, chased from their *Réductions*, where obliged to flee, in the 1830s, they took with them twelve thousand Guarani Indians, who settled with them in Missions in the territories of Uruguay and Parana.

And the bloody wars between the conquistadors and the original masters of the region multiplied. Revolutions succeeded revolutions...until the rise to power of Doctor Francis, who secured peace and developed agriculture and animal husbandry. On his death, a temporary junta was instituted by Duré and Ocampos...but power soon fell into the hands of Carlos Antonio Lopez, who was obliged to sustain a bitter conflict against the Argentine tyrant Rosas, who threatened the independence of Paraguay.

Bastien's sonorous snoring interrupted the historian's lecture in full flow. "Hey!" he said, striking the sleeper on the shoulder.

"What?" said the other.

"Is it worth the trouble of me trying to educate you?"

"Oh, all those names made my eyes blink."

"I'll never make anything of you."

"That depends. Not with your tedious histories, Colonel."

"I've nearly finished...I've just got to Francisco Solano Lopez, a general at nineteen."

"Like our Revolutionary generals?"

"Exactly! And he was obliged to battle hard. He was killed on the first of March 1870, on the banks of the Aquidaban, and establishing the borders of the belligerent countries required the arbitration of the United States. Their president, Hayes, attributed La Villa Occidental to Paraguay, and the east to the Grand Chaco—but that country, hitherto so powerful, lost a large part of its territory in subsequent treaties..."

115

At that moment, Rozen and Macaron were on the bank of a broad stream, the sinuous course of which made countless turnings in the marshy prairie. At intervals, a few small rocky hillocks broke the monotony of the landscape.

"While you're reciting our sermon, do you know what interests me?" said Macaron.

"No."

"Well, look at that…"

"What?"

"That odd-looking tree two hundred meters away…it looks like a big beet-root."

"It's a *palo borracho*—a drunken tree."[22]

"That's true; one might think that it were having difficulty standing up."

Rozen had an idea. "Are you tired of walking, Bastien?"

"For sure."

"We're going to make a canoe."

"You're joking."

"Not at all. Help me…"

They went over to the tree and set about felling it with their machetes. The task was relatively easy.

The tree in question is formed like an elongated egg, narrowed at the top and the bottom. Its bark is very hard and very thick, and he cottony pulp that forms the heart of the trunk does not have a very solid consistency.

They soon succeeded, in a matter of hours, in slicing the trunk lengthwise and hollowing it out by removing the soft fibrous substance.

The canoe was made; they tried it out. With the aid of poles, they went downstream to begin with, but were soon forced to stop, because mosquitoes were buzzing in thousands in the long grass.

There was, moreover, another reason to call a halt to their navigation project. The storm that had been threatening for some time burst. Rain fell in large drops.

They hoisted their light skiff on to the side of a hillock, and sought shelter.

Night fell, darkly.

A violent wind got up, flattening the grass and howling through the tree branches. Thousands of fireflies and grasshoppers were swirling in the air, carried away by the squall.

The storm passed overhead, accompanied by a veritable waterspout, devastating the countryside, which was soon no more than a lake from which a few rocks protruded.

Soaked to the skin, in spite of the shelter behind which they had taken cover, the adventurers shivered. The night seemed interminable.

---

[22] *Palo borracho* means "drunken stick." The reference is to *Ceiba speciosa*, more commonly known as the silk floss tree.

At daybreak, a calm succeeded the storm, but a liquid sheet extended around them as far as the eye could see. Fortunately, they had a boat. Otherwise, they would have been trapped.

The streams, swollen by abundant diluvian rain, typical of the tropics, had overflowed.

For twenty-four hours, Rozen and Bastien floated, steering somewhat at hazard, but trying to gain ground in a westward direction.

They killed a tinamou, a kind of fowl somewhat reminiscent of a pheasant; a capybara, a water-pig; and a peacock, a regal turkey.

"That's our provisions," said Bastien, "but we can't cook them on board."

At that moment they were in a reed-strewn marsh, through which it was difficult to steer their little oat, but he marsh was soon crossed and they were able to land on firm ground.

They held a discussion and decided to construct a small cabin in order to enjoy a few days' rest.

With branches and foliage that had soon erected a shelter; then they lit a fire, roasted the tinamou and a leg of the capybara, and ate a meal that Bastien declared to be succulent.

Two days later, when they were well rested, Rozen proposed that they set out on an excursion.

"We need to find out where we are," he declared.

"In Paraguay, of course."

"You're not telling me anything. Close to what town? Capilla? Vila-Rica? Angostino?"

"You don't intend to go into a town, old chap?"

"Certainly not. We might find our diamond-hunters there—they know the way and they might perhaps have had the notion of looking for us there, but we'll undertake a reconnaissance."

Macron agreed, gladly.

They left the cabin, carefully noting reference points in order to be able to find their way back, and set off across country.

They had scarcely gone a kilometer when they heard singing, modulated in a bizarre fashion.

"Indians!" Bastien exclaimed.

"If you like—but they're doubtless Guaranis, otherwise known as Paraguayans. There's a village to our right."

"Let's go back!"

"Too late—we've been spotted."

Men clad in calconcillos and ponchos, with large sombreros on their heads, were advancing toward the former convicts.

"*Hombre!*" called one of them.

Rozen, who knew the customs of the region, replied: "*Ave Maria.*"

They were soon surrounded by a dozen men, but they did not seem to be savages. Hey pointed to the village. "*Velorio, Guaranis,*" they said.

"What's that?" Macaron queried.

"Follow them," Gaston relied. "I'll explain on the way. A *velorio* is a funeral ceremony, which is generally held when a child is buried."

"Really? They sing?"

"Yes—the soul of the innocent is going to Heaven; they're rejoicing for the child's death."

"Well!"

"If you'd listened to me when I took the trouble to tell you the history of the region's conquest..."

"You're not going to start again?"

"No—I'll just tell you this: the *velorio* is a mixture of ceremonies of Catholic worship and the Indians' ancient religious practices. At the end of the sixteenth century, one of the conquistadors had the idea of confiding the job of civilizing the tribe to missionaries. I told you that the Franciscans and Fathers of Mercy did that with perfect science."

"Yes, I remember. Go on."

"Have you remembered that the Reverends Macela and Cataldino were the first to form *Réductions*?"

"*Réductions*?"

"Establishments, if you prefer. Gradually, the Guaranis fused, or rather hybridized, with the white invaders."

"Yes, yes—mercy! I don't like history."

They reached the town.

"Where are we?" Gaston asked one of the men they had met.

"Capilla, Señor."

Huts were arranged around a circular space. All the inhabitants were outside. A group in front of one of the habitations attracted the attention of Gaston and Macaron. A man and a woman were standing beside a crib garlanded with foliage and flowers. In the crib, a child with closed eyes, a face as pale as wax and discolored lips, was sleeping the eternal sleep.

Bastien had no time to think. As soon as the woman perceived the white men, she precipitated herself toward them, and said, with reverential urgency: "*Siente se seores, quiere usted tomar una copita de caña.*"

"*Mil gracias,*" Rozen replied. And he translated he woman's words for his companion: "She said: 'Sit down, sirs; will you take a glass of caña?' Caña is simply sugar-cane alcohol, something like the *tafia* of our colonies; all the rejoicings and mourning of these peoples end with a party for which caña provides the fuel."

Until nightfall, Bastien and Rozen watched the fête. Dancing, singing and prayers succeeded one another around the tiny corpse. By turns, there were cries of distress, farewells to the deceased, and then surges of joy, the regret of parting and the joy of believing in his election to Paradise, close to the Creator: a bizarre mixture, as Rozen had said, of paganism and the Catholic religion; a striking example of the enormous influence that the monks had exercised since 1591 on races in which tradition persisted.

The Guaranis heaped the two Frenchmen with respect. They were given *yerba maté*, or Jesuit tea, prepared in a small calabash or gourd in which the tea is pressed. A woman bearing a kettle of hot water made a tour of the assembly, pouring it into the gourds. The tea was drunk with a *bombilla*, a sort of metal pipe, ornamented to various extents, terminated by a spatulate nozzle. The consumers passed the recipient and the bombilla around.

Bastien's eyes widened at this spectacle, which was new to him. He could not, however, overcome a profound disgust on seeing all those people suck on the same bombilla.

When the woman with the kettle arrived in front of him, she asked him the question which is invariably addressed to a European: "*Amargo ô dulcé?*"— bitter or sweet. The Guaranis never sweeten the infusion of *yerba maté*, but they know that in Europe, tea is often taken with sugar, and they offer it to their guests out of politeness. And Bastien had to suck the bombilla.

His disgust for indigenous beverages was further accentuated, however, when he had tasted *chica*. Rozen explained to him, maliciously, that the liquor in question is manufactured in the evening of the previous day by the women, who chew maize, and when mastication and salivation has reduced it to a soft paste, spit it into an earthenware bowl in order to let it ferment.

After numerous libations, Bastien and Rozen were taken to the home of one of the most important Paraguayans, and, with their heads heavy and stomachs burned by the strong liquors, they went to sleep.

The next day, heaped with gifts of *galettas*—maize pancakes—and gourds of *caña*, they returned to their cabin. Not only had they received a benevolent welcome from the inhabitants of Capilla, but, thanks to their indications, they were able to continue their journey toward the Chaco. The Guaranis advised them to by-pass the villages and go to Asuncion, where they could renew their provisions and munitions. The headman of Capilla had also mentioned a white man, a German, who was exploiting *quebrancho colorado*, a kind of ironwood whose name means "ax-breaker." He suggested that they try to find that European.

The fugitives were, on the contrary, anxious to avoid agglomerations where they feared being questioned by Italian, German, English or French colonists who had settled there to plant crops and rear livestock. They left, therefore, refreshed and knowing where they were going, and two weeks later, without incident, they reached the Paraguay river, which they crossed with the aid of a new canoe made from a *palo borracho*.

They were well used by now to the nomadic life, but it weighed upon them; they were only sustained by the hope of finding Sokoloff and returning with him to Buenos Aires.

More than a month had gone by since they had left Capilla. They had not made any further contact, and, having crossed the river, finally reached the wilderness of the Chaco—but, unfortunately for them, not Formosa as yet.

Difficulties were about to emerge again.

Everything went well at first, but one morning, they had scarcely started walking when they fell unexpectedly into the midst of a band of Toba Indians. Surrounded by menacing warriors, Bastien was about to defend himself, but Rozen, stopping his companion from shouldering his weapon, said: "Wait. We need to talk, and find out who we're dealing with."

Then, addressing himself in Spanish to the man who seemed to be in command of the Indian band, he asked him who he was.

The chief, who knew a few words of the Iberian language, understood him very well.

"I am the cacique Carraja, chief of the Toba tribe. These are my warriors. And who are you and your companion?"

"We're Europeans—Frenchmen."

"Good, *Caballero*. I knew one of your compatriots, an eminent chief..."

While he was speaking, Bastien and Rozen observed Carraja, He was strangely dressed. His head disappeared into a bizarre hat, a kind of bonnet fabricates from the skin of a howler monkey. It was doubtless this headgear that had earned the cacique the name of Carraja, by which the singular quadrumane that howls by night, and whose lugubrious cries frighten those unused to them, is known in the Chaco.

The cacique had a near-naked body, but his shoulders were covered by a kind of mantle, half of which was made from deer-skin and the other from the skin of a jaguar. On his breast a silver epaulette was swinging, suspended from a string passed around his neck. Carraja was very fond of that ornament, which he owed to the generosity of the Frenchman to whom he had made allusion just now: a Breton who belonged to the marine infantry, who had come to explore the country a few years before.[23]

"Your epaulette isn't regulation," said Bastien, who thought himself perfectly safe, thanks to his rifle.

"Shut up," said Rozen. "This is no time for joking. You're lucky the man doesn't understand French."

And Gaston was absolutely right. Intelligent and accustomed to reading physiognomies, he divined that the India chief must be ferocious; his eyes were shining with avarice, and never quit the two Frenchmen's weapons.

"What are you doing in these parts?" asked Carraja.

_____

[23] Goron, perhaps?

"Lost travelers...."

"That's a lie. You've come to swell the number of *Christianos* who are making war on our tribes."

"No."

"No one calls Carraja a liar—understand! Carraja knows white men—rogues and murderers."

The man speaking thus had doubtless cut the throat of more than one unfortunate fellow whose confidence he had captured...

"Rozen tried to flatter the Indian. "Carraja, you are a great chief," he said, pompously, "And it would be futile and stupid bravado on our part to fight you and your valiant warriors."

"If you are peaceful travelers, what use are those weapons?"

"For hunting..."

"That's not true. They're long-range rifles, weapons of war, Your weapons make Carraja desirous. I want them. Give them to me."

"I have the greatest confidence in you—and to prove it to you...look..."

Rozen tried to take Macaron's weapons. "Hey!" the latter cried. "You've gone mad! You're crazy. Give away the toys? Never! If these fellows want bullets, I'll serve them up..."

But the Levantine, striking Bastien's wrist violently, wrenched away his carbine by force.

"Bloody idiot," he said. "If you killed one or two, where would that get us? They'd torture us afterwards."

The tone in which Gaston spoke was so imperious that the anarchist obeyed, and handed over his revolver as well as the rifle.

"There!" Rozen said to Carraja. "I'm ready to make you a gift of all this..."

Carraja's eyes lit up. "Good. Put it all at the foot of that tree. Your lives will be spared, and you will have the amity of Carraja."

Rozen did as he was asked.

Scarcely had he put the weapons in the designated place when the Indians surrounded him and Bastien. They were both tied up, loaded on to the chief's *recado*[24] and taken to the Toba camp, then thrown into the cacique's *tolderia*, or tent.

On the ground around the huts, Rozen had noticed human bones. He told Bastien that the funereal debris in question was that of victims of hemorrhagic fever, and that the Tobas abandoned everything when that terrible malady broke out in the tribe. Carraja and his men had returned to a camp that they or others had deserted years before.

"Well," growled Bastien, furious, "are you pleased with your idea of giving them our weapons?"

---

[24] The author includes a footnote defining a *recado* as a kind of saddle.

"Shut up," Rozen riposted. "Our lives will be spared—Carraja promised that; he'll keep his promise."

At that moment the chief came into the tent. "Christianos," he said, "you will be untied. You are Carraja's guests, and you will be, until another white man pays your ransom. I have promised to spare your lives, and I will keep my word. But if you attempt to escape I shall kill you."

Rozen smiled. "When one has the amity of a man like Carraja, one has no fear. We will have the ransom paid."

"This tent is yours."

"Thank you."

"You are free; you will be untied."

A few moments later, the two escaped convicts, prisoners of the Tobas, were sitting sadly by the tent.

Gaston was thinking. Bastien was no longer recriminating.

"After all," murmured Rozen. "We haven't had our throats cut; that's a win. Although Carraja is a ferocious chief, the gift of our weapons has put us in his god graces..."

"Maybe," moaned the Parisian, "but we're prisoners nonetheless...in perpetuity...and when they've waited long enough, they'll take away our appetite for bread."

"Between now and then, we'll find a means of escaping...the English way."

"Unless..."

"Go on—spit it out."

"Unless we pay them back in kind."

"What?" Rozen looked at his acolyte. He thought that Bastien had gone mad.

But no, the street-arab got up, his eyes bright, laughing out loud. "Aha! This time, Colonel, it's Bastien who'll save your bacon."

"How?"

"You'll see. One has one's little social talents. One will make use of them."

Dusk was falling. The sun had just disappeared over the horizon. A feeble red glow, which put something like the distant reflection of a fire beneath the crowns of the trees, in the undergrowth and the creepers, was the only mark of the summary twilight that separates the dazzle of daylight from the gloom of night in those climes, in the shade of the virgin forest, for a mere matter of minutes.

Abruptly, the glow was snuffed out, while an imposing and grandiose silence descended upon people and things. One might have thought that life, overwhelmed by the oppression of the diurnal heat, had suddenly become extinct. But it was soon to take its revenge.

Slyly and gradually, strange noises begin to crepitate here and there: first the croaking of batrachians, colossal frogs and giant toads, alternately as raucous as roars and as timid as plaints—an entire concert of metallic sonorities and crystalline notes, which mingles with a harmonious racket of insectile stridulations, the distress-calls of night-birds, the mysterious fluttering of fruit-bats, swinging invisibly on wings of dream, the creaking of branches quivering under the expanding coolness, and the sinister howling of red monkeys.

Then, as the darkness became thicker and more opaque, the sky, the woods and the earth itself light up with a thousand fires. Here, enormous *cocuyos*, flying through the air like brilliant meteors, describe the flaming curves of capricious spirals; there, glow-worms, miniature night-lights, clinging to mossy trunks, radiate a green-tinted splendor in all directions.

The damp soil, felted with organic debris in the process of decomposition, seems to be streaming with sparks; phosphorescent larvae crawl, run and fly in the grass under the dry leaves and rotting twigs, where myriads of similarly-luminous microscopic animalcules swarm. One might think that heaps of incandescent embers were collapsing everywhere.

Rozen and Macaron paid no heed of that enchantment, which was never unmoving, in spite of the strangeness of their situation; at every dusk, the Indians lit a circle of fire around the clearing, intended to keep snakes and wild animals away. In the meantime, the women came and went, busily occupied with preparations for the evening meal.

"They're more like ugly boys, these gingerbread tarts," Macaron murmured.

The fact is that the Toba women are not particularly seductive, with their coarse features, straight shiny black hair, and pendant lips bristling like pincushions with palm thorns. When one adds to that their red and blur tattoos, their limp and pendulous breasts that primitive silver and copper jewelry cannot embellish, and one can form an idea of the beauty of Carraja's female subjects. Only the young girls have slender, almost elegant figures capable of reminding one that one is in the presence of specimens of the fair sex.

The meal, to which the cacique invited the two Europeans to come and take part, was soon ready. That day, there was a veritable feast in the Indian camp, for the hunting had been fruitful and the menu was very varied. First to be served were large green lizards that had been exposed to hot coals for a few minutes to remove the scales.

That was a horror, but Rozen, who had no prejudices, even those of the stomach, and who was dying of hunger, did not hesitate to eat it, salt and *aji*—hot pepper—aiding him to overcome an instinctive and sufficiently justified repugnance. Moreover, that won him a smile—a grimace, rather—of sympathy from the savage audience, and a few appreciative grunts, with which the women joined in.

Among all the Indians of South America, from the Araucans of the Cordillera to the Roucouyenes of the Rio Branco, it is traditional to subject palefaces to the redoubtable proof of the indigenous cuisine. Only those who can brave it without vomiting—they are rare, but they exist—are judged worthy of esteem and amity. Rozen did not know that, but, guided by the subtlety of his instinct, he had bravely risked nausea as if he did. Nothing more was needed to earn him the immediate consideration of his hosts.

On the other hand, they looked askance at Bastien, who did not have the same courage.

"I've tried," he groaned, "but I can't. I'll spill my guts for sure if I swallow that. What vile grub! In truth, I prefer the beans of the Maroni."

He did no better with an armadillo cooked whole in its carapace. In vain, Rozen explained to him, while preaching by example, that armadillo is a delicacy served throughout South America on gourmet tables, and which the finest mouths do not disdain; the anarchist "did not want to know."

"You can call it a delicacy if you want," he replied, with shivers of disgust. "I'm not touching it."

"You shouldn't go traveling, then, my friend," Rozen replied. Completely composed, he was amused by his companion's discomfiture. "When one travels, one has to adapt to the habits of the locality. Why didn't you bring your cook with you?"

And, stretching out his hand, he carved off another piece of the bizarrely-perfumed pink flesh of the armadillo.

Macaron did not starve, though. He caught up on the *tapajo*—raw beef dried in the sun and cut into long strips. He also had his full share of maize pancakes, and especially the bitter and peppery eau-de-vie that was passed around in an earthenware bowl.

"Don't drink too much—it's treacherous," Rozen said to him from time to time, on seeing him bending his elbow enthusiastically. "Soon, we're going to need clear heads."

"Understood, Sonny," Bastien replied, without missing a mouthful of the atrocious liquor. Fortunately, he had a solid head.

When the bowls were finally empty and nothing any longer remained of the lizard and the armadillo than calcined scales, the sated Indians thought of dancing. Among all peoples, barbaric or civilized, there is no good party without music and dancing.

The preparations were soon made. The men sat in a circle, legs crossed, like tailors, smoking bitter and foul-smelling tobacco in bizarre pipes ornamented with multicolored fringes, with stems made from hollow reeds and stone bowls.

The young boys and girls, arranged behind one another in order of height in two parallel lines, began prancing on the spot, using their feet to beat time, initially to a slow rhythm, and then increasingly precipitately, ending up in a double farandole whose complicated figures and overlapping circles were not ungraceful.

At the same time, they all sang, in chorus, a monotonous and nasal chant, accompanied—to Bastien and Rozen's great surprise—but the fervent music of a barrel-organ. How had that instrument, so dear to European mendicants, found its way into the hands of these Indians? How did that orchestra in a box, able to play seven tunes, come to be there, recreating polkas and waltzes once fashionable in Paris found its way into the hands of the ferocious enemies of white men? Carraja had doubtless stolen it while looting an estancia during an expedition on the Paraguay—and since then, the music machine had been considered as a fetish and entrusted to the tribal elders.

When the organ fell silent, it was succeeded by the cacophony of an infernal band. Standing in the background, women formed a summary orchestra whose instruments were very simple: firstly, a hollow calabash containing a dozen small stones the size of buckshot, which was shaken in cadence; then a kind of two-string guitar with a fractured timbre; and finally, a drum with a single back whose skin was pierced the middle by a hole, through with a rod passed, the friction of which produced a raucous growl that awoke echoes in the distance.

From time to time, the band abruptly stopped playing to allow the dancers to get their breath back. Then, at a signal from the leader, uttering a shrill shriek, the charivari and the saraband began again, more urgently.

It was during one of those intermissions that Macaron thought it a good idea to go on stage. A few minutes before, lying in the grass next to Rozen, he had explained his plan in a low voice.

"That's an excellent idea, Bastien! I have one of my own, as you'll see. But go on—now's the time."

Bastien got up and, having thrown his jacket on the ground, took up a position, standing in his shirt sleeves, in the middle of the circle. Astonished, the Tobas looked at him with grim and suspicious eyes. The Parisian, however, who had recovered all his self-confidence, was not intimidated by such a small thing. He tightened his belt-buckle; then, having flexed his knees three or four times, as if to assure himself of the flexibility of his hamstrings, he made an abrupt and perilous backward somersault, shouting "hop!" at the top of his voice.

Among the innumerable professions that he had had occasion to exercise in the course of an adventurous existence, Bastien had once been a clown in a fairground circus, and he had thought, not implausibly, that his small talents might favorably impress the Redskins, just as they had amused the convicts in the bagne, and even the guards, more than once.

He had guessed correctly, for, in spite of their imperturbable composure, at the sight of that acrobatic feat, which would have made Europeans blasé with regard to gymnastic miracles smile, they could not hide their surprise, mingled with a commencement of admiration.

Those big children might well have had an extraordinary suppleness and agility, but they knew nothing about acrobatics, which is a civilized sport, and which they were not far from seeing as both a kind of sorcery and a mark of superior genius. Even the cacique, although he had more self-control than his companions and subjects, had sketched a gesture of alarm that had not escaped Rozen's lynx-sharp eyes.

"Well done!" he cried. "Keep going! They're biting!"

Bastien had no need of encouragement, though. He started walking on his hands, then turning cartwheels, and multiplying perilous somersaults, forwards, backwards and sideways, with a consummate ease worthy of the best artistes at the Folies-Bergère.

The Indians, who had never seen such a performance, were literally dazzled. Men, women, children and elders had risen to their feet, breathing heavily, their eyes gleaming and their bodies quivering with ill-suppressed enthusiasm; if they had known how to do it, they would have applauded—but when Bastien, tucking his legs over his shoulders, "making a frog," and stated rolling like a ball with vertiginous rapidity around a tree, the enthusiasm turned to delirium.

Carraja approached Rozen and put a hand on his shoulder. "That one is a great chief," he said, in a convinced tone in which sincere emption was detectable.

"*Yo lo creo*," Gaston relied, immediately understanding how to take full advantage of the situation. "Yes, he's a great chief."

"You are also a great chief."

"I too am a great chief. Watch, *hombre*, and you'll see what a great white chief can do."

Then randomly grabbing wooden bowls, knives, pipes—all the objects, heavy or light, that happened to be within arm's reach—he begins juggling.

As if petrified, the Tobas are holding their breath. Visibly, for those primitive and naïve imaginations, a juggler is not merely a great chief; if he is not the Great Spirit in person, or the Devil, he is not far off.

They have not, moreover, reached the end of their surprises yet, for the devil has more than one trick in his bag. Suddenly ceasing to juggle, he takes from his pocket one of those briquettes of Magnus pyrophoric iron that can be found in well-stocked bazaars almost everywhere.[25]

He has just remembered that in Buenos Aires, more out of curiosity than utilitarian concern, he acquired one of those little tubes, similar to painters' pigment-tubes, full of a pulverized mixture of aluminum and iron oxide reduced by hydrogen, which, thanks to its extreme division, catches fire spontaneously on contact with atmospheric oxygen.

[25] The physicist Heinrich Gustave Magnus publicized the properties of pyrophoric iron compounds, which catch fire spontaneously on exposure to oxygen, in 1825.

He removes the stopper with an earnest and inspired mime, and immediately, a firework escapes from his fingers—a rain of sparks that, adroitly directed, falls on a heap of dry and spongy wood that the Indians use instead of tinder, and sets it alight. Rozen leans over, blows on the nucleus, on to which he throws a handful of dry leaves, and hey presto!—a fire, which, as if by a miracle, at the gesture of the thaumaturge, ignites and bursts into flame, while a cavernous voice that one would swear is emerging from the tenebrous depths of the undergrowth, growls in hoarse and solemn Spanish: "Tremble, *hombres*, and bow down before the white man: he is the master of fire."

The Indians do not need to be told twice. With an instinctive movement, men, women and children throw themselves face down on the ground, clucking in terror. The cacique himself has provided the example—which extends as far as Bastien, who is staggered as he declares, in a whisper, with a frisson of intimate emotion: "Well, done, Colonel!"—which is, from him, the ultimate exclamation of enthusiasm.

Rozen is not astonished, however. Sure now of the effect of his double talent as a conjurer and ventriloquist, he carefully records his magic bottle and puts it back in his pocket.

Paralyzed by terror, The Indians continued to lie prone in the grass, not even daring to raise their heads. Only the cacique, perhaps conscious of his responsibility, dragged himself on his knees to the feet of the man he would henceforth consider as a redoubtable divinity, and extended his imploring hands toward him.

Rozen made a benevolent gesture. Seizing Carraja by the wrist, he brought him to his feet and shook him, in such a way as to make him understand not only his magnanimity and clemency, but also the vigor of his biceps. "We are friends," he said, in a soft voice, "if you will consent to obey me. Tell your companions that the master of fire does not mean them any harm. On the contrary; he will take them under his protection from now on. Come on—bring on the *chicha*, and let the party begin!"

Glad to get out of it so well, Carraja makes a sign to his wives, who hasten to fetch an enormous pitcher full of eau-de-vie, doubtless the produce, like the barrel-organ, of an expedition to the Argentine frontier. A calabash is filled, in which Rozen and Bastien take turns to wet their lips, and which is the passed from hand to hand.

An hour later, all the Indians were lying down in the clearing for a second time. This time, however, they were no longer afraid; it was drunkenness that had laid the out. Only the two white men, standing in the midst of that mock-massacre, had maintained the plenitude of their reason.

Rozen laughed silently; Macaron, more expansive and careless of his dignity as a freshly graduated god, sketched the steps of a cancan. They had good reason to rejoice, for their presence of mind and their know-how had not only saved their lives but had created an exceptionally advantageous situation for them, for which they could not have hoped. It was evident, in fact, that they would henceforth be the object of the Indians' devotion.

The Levantine had no reason to play the role he had just played for the Tobas any longer, however. He told himself that the Indians, once recovered from the stupor that his skill had caused, might see through the trickery. "They're dead drunk," he said to his companion. We have a few hours in hand. Let's take back our arms and ammunition, get astride the tribe's two best horses—and ride hard...

Bastien understood the prudence of the move, and obeyed without any thought of argument.

They galloped for several hours, only stopping when their exhausted mounts refused to go any further.

Dawn was breaking.

"Where are we?" Macaron asked. "We took to our heels blindly, without a compass."

"It doesn't matter," Rozen declared. "The most important thing is to put a respectable number of kilometers between us and our hosts."

They had stopped at the bottom of a hillock. Rozen made the ascent, leaving the Parisian to guard the horses. When he came down again, his face was radiant.

"Well?" Bastien queried. "Good news, I think?"

"Yes, we're lucky. A few hundred meters away over there I spotted a pueblo: huts that are certainly occupied by Europeans, on the bank of the Paraguay, which I could see further away."

"We need to get to the pueblo as quickly as possible."

"Of course—but we need to let our horses get a little rest."

"That's true, poor beasts—they certainly need it."

The ate a few provisions they had taken care to carry away when fleeing Carraja's tribe, drank a little water from a limpid spring they had discovered nearby, washed it all down with a finger of *chicha* similarly appropriated from the Tobas and, refreshed, took their horses by the bridle and headed for the habitations glimpsed by Rozen.

The pueblo they had seen was occupied by Europeans. It was a colony founded by two engineers who had come primarily to deal in wood. The factory employed about fifty men, of whom ten were white and the others Guarani Indians. The pueblo was admirably defended against possible attacks by marauders. All the men were armed and stood watch in shifts, especially at night, darkness being favorable to raids by Carraja's peers.

Rozen and Bastien received a cordial welcome from the factory owners, who were discreet enough not to ask the too many questions. They were lost white men, devoid of support. They were offered generous hospitality, without any enquiry as to their status.

Although the sojourn in the pueblo, not far from Asuncion, was very pleasant, Gaston had no intention of prolonging it. It was Sokoloff he wanted to find, and he did not want to waste precious time.

He asked his hosts a few questions. As soon as he mentioned Sokoloff they shrugged their shoulders.

"A madman," they said. "A brave man, who came from a long way away to found a new society, with neither servants nor masters. It didn't work. After a month, as it had no leader, and, in consequence, no discipline, everyone wanted to take charge. Sokoloff's companions fell into discord. They came to blows. There were dead and wounded. In brief, everyone pulled his own way, and the apostle of universal happiness was obliged to flee. We took him in here..."

"He's here!" Rozen exclaimed, joyfully.

"He was here for a fortnight, but he left for Buenos Aires. We put him aboard the *Formosa*, the little steamboat that maintains communication between our exploitation and the Argentine capital."

Sokoloff had returned to Buenos Aires!

Rozen and Bastien had only one objective thereafter—to get back there as soon as possible—and it was with genuine gratitude that they accepted a passage aboard the Formosa when, a few days later, the boat returned to pick up freight for Buenos Aires.

Bastien was delighted to leave a region where he had believed that he would leave his skin.

On the bridge of the steamboat, as it went downriver, Rozen gazed into the distance, pensively. He was thinking about the fruitful association of his adventurous genius with the Russian's science, and the world subjugated, tamed by the audacious coups of the Baron de Saint-Magloire.

On arrival in Buenos Aires, Rozen and Macaron immediately hastened to Dulac's home and brought him rapidly up to date with their peregrinations—omitting, of course, the incident at the diamond mine.

Then they arranged to meet the following day at Sokoloff's residence, the address of which the anarchist gave them. "I'll be there," the latter declared, "and I'll introduce you."

They took their leave of their friend and found a hotel.

Bastien, very happy to be "lying in a foot-bath," as he put it, slept blissfully and without a care until the next day—but the Levantine, in spite of his fatigue, hardly slept at all.

He was thinking, and preparing his plan of campaign. He sensed that his future depended on is interview with Sokoloff.

"Tomorrow," he murmured, "I'll take the first step on the road to fortune!"

XV. An Alliance

At the time fixed by Dulac, the two adventurers rang the bell at the gate of the elegant villa that Sokoloff occupied in the Paseo de San Pablo, in the center of the manufacturing district of Buenos Aires.

A negro introduced them into a small drawing room, where Dulac joined them shortly afterwards.

"Bonjour, comrades," the latter exclaimed, joyfully, at the sight of Rozen and Macaron. "Our friend is just taking care of a business matter with a merchant who has come for that express purpose from Montevideo. He'll be free in a quarter of an hour, and we can talk at our ease."

"Sokoloff is rich, then?" asked Macaron, dazzled by the comfortable furniture and elegant decoration of the drawing room.

"Comrade Sokoloff could be," Dulac replied, "for he makes a great deal of money, but in addition to the generous share that he gives to the workers in the factory whose direction he's resumed since his fruitless endeavor in Formosa, the expenses of revolutionary propaganda eat up most of his profits."

"Didn't you tell us," Rozen put in, "that when he landed in America three years ago, Sokoloff was without resources? By what prodigy has he been able to create such a considerable industrial establishment in such a short time?"

"It's quite simple," Dulac replied. "After living in Buenos Aires for a few weeks, Sokoloff, flat broke, succeeded in getting a job as a manual laborer in one of the machine-construction workshops of the Argentine Company, the gigantic chimneys of which you might have seen in the Calle dal Rio Grande.

"Hardly a week had gone by since the entry of that strange man into the company's factory than he submitted to the chief engineer a new model of electric regulator and a light accumulator, which were immediately adopted, and whose patents he sold for fifty thousand piastres.

"Sokoloff's adventure generated a lot of talk, and several local capitalists came to offer the Russia scientist the funds necessary for the exploitation of his industrial methods and inventions. He was offered nothing less that the foundation of a joint stock company—the Sokoloff Company Limited—with a capital that would not be limited for him, an enormous salary, almost equivalent to the Civil List of a king, and a substantial share package, not to mention a share in the profits, the right to work at his ease, etc.—such was his lot. On the other hand, everything new and original that he created would become, *ipso facto*, the property of the company.

"Sokoloff refused the offer, marvelous as it was; he's cantankerous and exceedingly jealous of his autonomy. He came to set up a modest machine-shop in the Paseo de San Pablo, and that workshop, in a few years, has been transformed into a factory employing no fewer than a hundred and fifty workers.

130

"I met Sokoloff in the offices of the chief engineer of the Argentine Company, where I had a modest job as a draughtsman. We quickly became the best of friends. So, when Sokoloff had the idea of setting up as a manufacturer of electrical apparatus, he wanted to bring me into his business, in spite of my destitution and almost complete ignorance of physics and mechanics, as a commercial agent, or rather as general secretary-and when he left recently for the Chaco in order to try to realize his dream—'free human beings in a country without conventions or prejudices'—he confided the management of his interests here to me.

"An incomparable chemist, a first-class technologist, much sought after in the high society of Buenos Aires, our friend could monopolize the manufacture of telegraph and telephone equipment, lighting installations and electric trams, and make an enormous fortune, but, as I've already told you, he only thinks of producing more and more inventions in order to procure the funds necessary for the propaganda of anarchist ideas, of which he is, in the opinion of the comrades of Europe and America, the most eminent representative."

Dulac was obliged to suspend the biography of the eccentric scientist. A tall man with a slightly flattened nose furnished with gold-rimmed spectacles, soft bright eyes and a long red beard, appeared on the threshold of the room. It was Sokoloff.

The three companions got to their feet and bowed to the newcomer.

"I've been looking forward to meeting you, my dear comrades," said the Russian, in a warm voice, advancing toward Rozen and Macaron, whose hands he shook effusively. "Dulac has told me about your adventures. I know that after giving the slip to the prison-guards of Île du Diable, you've run a thousand dangers, and that at the price of privations that prove in those who confront them a real courage and an uncommon endurance, you've arrived here...

"I know that you left to search for me in the territory of Formosa, the destination for which I departed in the hope of founding a new society." The scientist uttered a dolorous sight. "Alas, centuries of servitude have left too deep an impression on people; they're not yet ready to understand the beauty of our principles."

Then, dispelling the chagrin that was assailing his thoughts, he went on: "Anyway, here you are, back again safe and sound. You're safe here. That's the main thing, for the moment. Although all unfortunates have a right to my sympathy and my aid, those who share my faith are brothers to me—which tells you that my purse, my house and my influence are entirely at your disposal."

"We know," said Rozen, "that your generosity is only equaled by your genius."

Although the comrades had the habit of addressing one another in the familiar manner, the Levantine did not address the Russian savant as "*tu*," in order to mark a filial deference. He had his plan, and was acting accordingly. He wanted, by seeming more submissive, to obtain a complete ascendancy over this simple soul.

"Don't shower Citizen Sokoloff with compliments, which, I'm sure, he holds in repugnance," said Bastien, in a sharp tone that contrasted with the deference that he usually showed to Gaston. "We're pursued, unfortunate, without a sou; a comrade is giving us hospitality and sharing his purse with us. What could be more natural? Sokoloff knows his anarchist catechism, and, what is worth more to us and the revolutionary cause, he puts it into broad and honest application every day."

"Comrade Bastien is right," said the engineer approvingly. "Besides which, we haven't heard of one another for the first time today. The poor anarchist party isn't so very numerous, alas. We're bound to know one another, at least by reputation. It's true, he knows me well. I hate flattery and detest hypocrisy."

"Why don't we have lunch?" Dulac proposed.

"That's true," Sokoloff replied. "Let's eat first; we can talk afterwards."

Taking the lead, he headed toward the dining room. The newcomers sat down at the table.

"I never eat meat or drink wine," the Slav observed, "but don't think you're obliged by politeness to follow a regime that doesn't suit you; every temperament requires a particular nourishment. Eat and drink what you like; you're at home here."

"That's true anarchism!" exclaimed Macaron, vigorously attacking an appetizing mutton chop. "Comrade Sokoloff eats potato salad and washes it down with Adam's Ale, but he leaves the mates free to wrap themselves around a nice joint and drink to settle their thirst. Each to his own, no?"

"As in the Abbey of Thelema," added Rozen, placidly.

Sokoloff smiled indulgently. "*Do as thou wilt* is, in effect, the whole of anarchism."

By way of exception, at dessert, the Russian half-filed a glass with fine champagne, and clinked glasses with his friends, one by one. "To the triumph of anarchism!" he proclaimed, in a vibrant voice.

"Long live anarchism!" his companions repeated.

"Dulac only gave me a broad outline of your adventures," Sokoloff continued, addressing Rozen. "Would you be kind enough to give me a detailed account?"

"Gladly," the Levantine agreed.

In a calm voice, and in a precise and colorful language, the former convict constructed an entire romance to his advantage. First he explained how he had been converted to the principles of anarchism by some of his companions in the penitentiary of Île du Diable;[26] then, having painted a moving picture of the bar-

---

[26] It is not obvious why Île du Diable [Devil's Island] has been substituted for Île Royale here, although it is possible that Île Royale had only been used in the

baric treatment of political detainees by the prison-guards, he described the various ups and downs of the conspiracy whose promoter he had been, which the treason of a false brother had so tragically subverted. Then he told the story of their escape, and with perfect modesty, praising the courage of Comrade Bastien, he narrated all their adventures in South America."

Macaron interrupted him from time to time in order, he said, to set the record straight and render to Rozen all the credit that was due to him. That contest of generosity between the two colleagues made a favorable impression on the worthy and naïve Sokoloff—a man who, in spite of his science, had retained the credulity of a small child, and had tears in his eyes as he listened to the story carefully concocted by the Levantine, who knew how to give his voice a warm tone full of emotion.

"Let's forget the miseries and dangers of evil days," said Sokoloff, "and since fortunate hazard has brought us together, let us join forces, putting at the service of the revolutionary cause all the material resources and intellectual and moral means that we have at our disposal, and let's march to the conquest of liberty and equality, without fear and without weakness."

"Without weakness," Dulac sighed. "Comrades, don't imitate that madman Dulac, who has not yet been able to extirpate from his heart the unworthy woman who betrayed him." As the Russian made a gesture of protest, he added, forcefully: "But believe, my dear Sokoloff, that I am cured of my unfortunate passion, just as I am cured of my bourgeois egoism.

"Germaine loved me, and then, one day, out of pure caprice or desire for luxury, she abandoned me. I was unjust in heaping reproaches upon her and in wanting to impose upon her a love of which she was weary. She had given; she had taken away; that was her right.

"Every human being must be able to dispose of her person, her heart and hr flesh as she wishes: that is what I have learned from the same philosophy that you have taught me, and whose principles I strive to put into better practice every day—not always without difficulty, of course, nor without chagrin, which is stronger than I am!"

"Bah!" exclaimed Bastien, pouring himself another glass of fine champagne. "One lost, ten found! There's no shortage of women! Nice cognac, by the way—better than the Paraguayans' *caña*." Then, having clicked his tongue like a connoisseur, he continued in a more earnest tone: "That a bourgeois like Dulac, betrayed and ruined by a slut, should be converted to anarchism I can understand—but what I can't explain is that an aristo like Sokoloff, noble and rich, has voluntarily given up the nobility, the money, the honors and the whole shebang to adopt our principles. Not to mention what anarchism brings: in pris-

first place to spare Rozen and the reader the embarrassment of running into Captain Dreyfus.

on or in exile all the time, ruination—for he's had his share of poverty!—criticism, etc., etc. That, truly, surpasses my understanding."

"You know the principal facts of my life," Sokoloff replied, "but you don't know that Sokoloff the millionaire, the prince and the senior officer wasn't transformed into a terrorist and libertarian overnight.

"Naturally inclined to pity, with little attachment to money, I've always had what is conventionally known as a good heart; I suffered in seeing others suffer; people always found me ready to participate in what bourgeois terminology call charity and philanthropy—deceptions invented by human injustice in order to take the place of justice.

"I believed, naturally, that authority, the distinction and hierarchy of social classes, government and waged employment were as many social necessities, deriving from human nature and historical fatality—but encountering the dear and admirable creature who has played such an important role in my life modified my idea profoundly.

"Sonia Alexandrovna was, as you know, one of the leaders of the Nihilist party. She introduced me to revolutionary meetings in which ardent innovators exposed doctrines that I considered at first to be subversive or inane, but which I was soon to share. In Europe and America, the theories and propaganda of the Nihilists is widely misunderstood. Abused by the energy of the propaganda of revolutionary Slavs, doctrines were attributes to them that most of them would have repudiated.

"With the exception of a handful of terrorists of the libertarian school, the great majority of Nihilists were simple politicians, who believed naively in the sovereign virtue of political revolutions, whose ideals did not extend beyond universal suffrage and constitutional government, in the manner of Belgium or England. They did not even go as far as Republicanism! Then there were a few tender-hearted democrats and egalitarians, who were grieved and indignant to see people, especially Russian people, bowed down in brutality and ignorance.

"It was among the latter that those apostles were recruited of whom you have doubtless heard mention, who went to the poor districts of big cities or to even poorer villages lost in the country, to live the wretched, brutal and vulgar life of workers and peasants, whom they strove to prepare for emancipation, while working with their hands like comrades."

"All that's quite harmless," Dulac put in.

"You don't say?" Sokoloff riposted. "Harmless and futile, It requires a far more energetic leaven to make the revolutionary dough rise and change the face of the world. That didn't prevent the Russian government pricking up its ears. The slightest attempt to change the established order, even peacefully, and especially to stimulate the masses, whom they wanted, with good reason, to keep in the state of human dust, was considered as a crime against the fatherland. The police pursued the gentle socialists and impotent constitutionalists furiously, as if they were criminals. Siberia was populated by administratively exiled apostles, of whom no further word was heard.

"The situation was untenable. All those of us who could, sought to leave the country. I was one of them. As I was not too badly compromised, escape was relatively easy for me, but I left with rage in my heart, revolted by the atrocity of the persecution. Sonia, who was more ardent than me was already ripe for Nihilism. I didn't take long to raise myself to her level.

"It was, however, Mikhail Bakunin, a saint among saints, whom we met in Lugano, who determined our vocation by rallying us definitively to militant Anarchism."

Lulled by his reminiscences, Sokoloff was speaking slowly, his eyes lost in the distance, his voice sonorous and grave.

"We clearly understood the insufficiency of Platonic socialism, which could only appeal to purely material interests and made pacts with the enemy if necessary, when the ambition of its leaders—what leaders!—became overly impatient. We understood that social evil is not only in political oppression, in economic iniquities and in rivalries between races or classes, but also, and above all, in the absence of a moral doctrine.

"Now, only anarchism gives us that superior morality. It remains to discover how to bring it to triumph. There is only one means, and that is force. Force is the ultimate bedrock of progress. Nothing can be done without it.

"When we returned to Russia, tempered by contact with the international revolution, we had the souls of terrorists. You know the rest. Sonia was hanged...

"I was there, lost in the crowd, on an icy winter morning; when the executioner put the fatal cord around her neck, my eyes, blurred with tears, encountered her agonizing gaze, whose cold energy softened, and fixed on me in a poignant fashion..."

Sokoloff's voice died away in a sob. Macaron blew his nose noisily. Even Rozen—the impassive Rozen, the man with the heart of stone—felt deeply moved, and meticulously rolled breadcrumbs over the tablecloth to hide his emotion, which he judged unworthy of his systematic attitude of insensitivity. Dulac was weeping like a child.

Sokoloff shook his grey hair. "Come on," he said, "no weakness. The past is dead; we must only think about the future.

"If I have succeeded in escaping from Siberia, after having had a close brush with the gallows myself, my duty is to avenge the friends and brothers—and the adored sister—who were not as lucky as I was. And the best means of honoring and avenging their memory is to work for the triumph of the cause that was theirs, for which they suffered, and for which they died.

"I have acquired by sad experience the conclusive conviction that isolated attempts are futile. The anarchist community cannot live in the putrid atmosphere of authoritarian and bourgeois organization. Even in the Chaco, its poisonous breath paralyzes and corrupts the best intentions. Before sowing the good seed of anarchism, it is necessary to have prepared the ground by making a *tabula rasa* of the former society; it is necessary that the revolutionary tempest has swept everything away in a universal cataclysm.

"There seems to me to be no need to ask the survivors of the revolt in the penitentiary of Îles du Salut, the indomitable adventurers who have triumphed over the wilderness, whether they are ready to cooperate in that work of vengeance and justice. Come on! If I believed in God, I would say that he is the one who sent you, just at the psychological moment, to do the good work. But as Proudhon said: 'God has but one excuse—that he does not exist.'"

"Personally," said Bastien, "I'm in favor of the gun; propaganda by action, the bomb, the dagger, poison. Ravachol, Henry, Vaillant[27] and all the nihilists of Sokoloff's homeland who blew up the Winter Palace and squashed an emperor like a bug—they're men! They have blood, those lads. And the bourgeois have got the wind up in consequence. Make us dynamite, invent infernal machines, O Sokoloff, you who are half-sorcerer, and we'll blow everything up, sowing fire everywhere.

"Is that what the cataclysm will be? How do I know? I'm lost in your blessed scientific names—but where I'm not lost, is when it comes to handing out a beating. Rozen can tell you—he's seen me 'on the job.' Isn't it true, my old mate, that Macaron doesn't skimp on the task?"

"You're an excellent workman in terrorism," Rozen replied, "but permit me to say that we have better things to do, at least for the time being, than risk our necks in tragic adventures. While Sokoloff was talking, a plan of campaign occurred to me, that I want to set out before you."

"We're listening, comrade," said Sokoloff, seduced by his guest's lofty manners, the penetrating softness of his gaze and the indescribable charm of his voice.

The moment had come for the Levantine to put flesh on his ambitious projects.

"I don't construct theories," he said, "because philosophy isn't my strong suit. I'm a practical man myself and I only want to consider the eventual triumph of Anarchism, for the moment, as a practical problem to be resolved, as business to be transacted.

"Now, whoever wants the end wants the means.

"The means tried thus far by our comrades are not to be disdained, and I don't wish to speak ill of them. Riots, individual assassinations, propaganda by action and all that doubtless have much to recommend them. But what has that

---

[27] Émile Henry was a French anarchist guillotined in 1894 for detonating a bomb in a café at the Gare Saint-Lazare, shortly after Auguste Vaillant had been guillotined for a rather feeble bomb attack on the parliamentary Chambre, intended to avenge Ravachol.

done for anarchists, thus far? It has discredited them with the masses, of whom they have need, and whom they can't by-pass, since they're working on their behalf, and robbed them of a substantial number of their most energetic combatants.

"On that battleground, we'll always be beaten, and beaten all the more definitively the more heroism we display. It's a contest between an earthenware pot and an iron pot. We'll have all the world on our backs, slaves and masters alike, the exploited along with the exploiters."

"Only too true, alas," Sokoloff put in, "but..."

"I beg your pardon," Rozen continued, "but there are no buts. It's the simple truth. We need to change our weaponry. We need to begin by capturing the public powers."

"That's a bit stiff!" Bastien exclaimed. "You're a funny kind of anarcho. It's possibilism that you're skirting there, old chap! I heard that anthem at Epinettes, in an electoral hustings, before going away to wear away the sun with a pumice-stone. Public powers? Oo la la! That's been tried, damn it."

"Shut up," said Rozen, and let me finish. Yes, it's necessary to take over the public powers—except that there's only one public power, and that's money—the *galette*, as you faubourgian Parisians say. That's the sovereign instrument before which députés, senators, privy councilors, municipal councilors and ministers, great and small, not excepting princes, king, sultans and emperors, bow down.

"When one has capital, one is the master of the world, because with capital, one can crush resistance, buy consciences and intelligences, and sow peace and war—and the masses, enthused and dazzled, will cheer you and follow you.

"Anarchism will never triumph—never, you understand—while anarchists fail to comprehend the necessity of doing business, of moving gold by the spadeful, and imposing itself on human stupidity by means of the prestige and omnipotence of wealth.

"Did the Jesuits—whose cleverness you won't deny, my old Macaron—proceed differently? They began by being rich, and it's because they're rich that they lead humankind. Oh, if I had capital—speaking as a man who knows how to cook books—I'd soon create a force that no one would be able to resist; I'd soon be able, all the more easily because no one would know my hidden agenda, to create anarchy in the financial markets...which is to say, in everything: *everything!*"

Rozen had risen to his feet, emphasizing his eloquent tirade with authoritative gestures.

"Alas," he went on, "it's only a dream. Money attracts money. To make money, it's necessary to have some to start with. Woe to the poor! How can one do business when one hasn't a sou?

"My God, I know that Comrade Sokoloff has a certain fortune, although it must be badly dented by the adventure in Formosa. We too, when we've disposed of our diamonds, will have a small capital at our disposal—but what's a hundred thousand francs, two hundred thousand, even five hundred thousand, for the grand plan of which I'm dreaming—and which you comprehend, my dear Sokoloff; I can see it in your eyes! A drop in the ocean.

"It's a few million that we need, to get into the game, to do things properly and surely."

Pale with emotion, his eyes shining with enthusiasm, Sokoloff stood up and took Rozen's hands. "You shall have your millions to found your bank!" cried the Slav. "A few more months, and you can set to work. This diabolical strategy is not my line of country, because I have no understanding of finance, but I can see that you're right. There's no dynamite worth as much as that, cleverly managed. Patience! The future is ours—or, rather, it belong to Anarchism."

"You can supply me with millions?" said Rozen, feigning amazement.

"Sokoloff's gone mad!" Dulac murmured in Bastien's ear.

"I'm afraid so," the latter replied.

"You think I've lost my mind?" said Sokoloff. "Don't worry, my dear friends. I don't possess, at the present moment, the millions that I shall confide to Rozen, but I hope—what am I saying? I'm sure—that they'll be in my hands in a matter of months."

"Sokoloff is doubtless hoping for a inheritance from an Australian uncle?" joked Macaron.

"It's not a matter of inheritance," the Russian scientist replied, "but of an invention, abandoned a hundred times over and take up again a hundred times. I've found the secret of the transmutation of metals, sought in vain by the alchemists. I can make gold."

"In large quantities?" Rozen asked.

"As much as I please," the engineer replied.

"Might you not have been deceived by an unfounded theory and deceptive experiments?" Dulac suggested.

"I told you, and I repeat," Sokoloff declared firmly, "that I've discovered a mean of making gold. Listen to me!

"Like a number of contemporary chemists—I'm not talking about dreamers but proven scientists—I have the conviction that matter is *one* in its essence, and that the different substances whose appearance it assumes in order to manifest itself to our senses are only temporary, variable forms, which only differ from one another by virtue of the arrangement of their constitutive particles.

"Thus, if one could reduce a substance—a metal for example—to the primitive and fundamental state of matter, it would be possible, by virtue of that regression, to transform it into another metal.[28]

---

[28] The notion of the unity of matter goes back to the Classical idea of an element prior to the compromise that admitted four (or five) rather than one. The ideas that Sokoloff are expressing here—confusedly, for the argument is somewhat

"Well, after long and laborious research, I have succeeded in rendering silver previously reduced to dust into the condition of gold. Every kilogram of gold obtained presently costs me five hundred francs, which renders about two thousand francs profit, and I haven't given up hope of halving the cost of manufacture.

"Don't think that the metal I extract in this way from silver has only a mere external resemblance to gold. Once melted, the artificial gold possesses all the physical and chemical properties of gold extracted from mines or panned."

"I have the greatest confidence in your knowledge and inventive genius," Rozen objected, "but I can't believe in the discovery of a process that would make you the master of the world. Haven't you fallen into the error of the worthy man who claimed in 1842 to have manufactured authentic gold in Mexico by treating a mixture of silver and copper filings with nitric acid under the influence of sunlight?[29] When he returned to France he tried to repeat his experiments, but without success. He was unable to rediscover in Paris the conditions of temperature, electricity and magnetism apparently unique to the Mexican climate, and which he planned to replace with a special treatment, by means of an apparatus that was never actually constructed."

"I can see that you're up to date with the question," Sokoloff interrupted, "but I can only repeat to you that I've made gold with silver."

"Granted," Rozen continued, "But doesn't the gold extracted from silver ingots or coins come from those ingots and coins? Don't you know that American piastres, and especially piastres struck in mints near mines are made with aurified silver minerals? Since the Restoration, the pence struck for the occasion of the coronation of Queen Victoria have been much south after by jewelers for the gold they contain. In 1836, a French chemist named Poizat, learned that Russia was in the process of negotiating with the Rothschild bank for a loan of fifty millions. Poizat, who knew that some Russian silver money contained gold, went to see Baron Rothschild and suggested that he stipulate that the repayment of the loan be made in silver coins. Tsar Nicholas did not take care to refuse, and the famous bank realized an enormous profit from the deal—of which, it appears, the chemist Poizat had a considerable share."

"There are none so deaf as those who will not hear," said Sokoloff. "You all love me, I'm convinced, and you don't doubt my scientific competence, but

---

different from the argument Emmens employed in connection with argentaurum, which is also quoted later in the passage—might owe something to the contemporary notions of Gustave Le Bon, publicized some years after the appearance of the novel in *L'Évolution de la matière* (1905; tr. as *The Evolution of Matter*).

[29] The reference is obviously to Théodore Tiffereau, although the date is wrong; it was in 1845 that he was introduced to the theory that silver can "ripen" into gold by Mexican gold-diggers, and subsequently conducted experiments attempting to hasten the process chemically.

you dare not believe in an invention that will furnish you with the means to put flesh on an idea that you deem to be impossible to realize."

The scientist headed for the door, adding: A little patience, comrades. In a few minutes, I'll display to your incredulous eyes specimens of artificial gold that I've recently obtained."

"Has Sokoloff been afflicted with delusions of grandeur?" Rozen asked.

"Our friend is perfectly capable of having resolved the problem of manufacturing gold," Dulac replied. "He's probably the foremost chemist of the era."

"For me," said Macaron, "Comrade Sokoloff knows everything that can be known scientifically. Besides which, he never lies, and the moment that he told us that he'd discovered a means of making gold from silver, that was the case."

"I'll believe in the transmutation of silver into gold when I've examined the specimens that Sokoloff has promise to show us," Rozen retorted.

The doubt expressed by Gaston had no other purpose than driving Sokoloff to give him his unreserved collaboration.

The scientist reappeared and handed the adventurer a platinum ladle containing a dozen metallic nuggets as big as a weight, of a beautiful yellow color.

"To judge by the color, the weight and general appearance of these grains," said Rozen, rolling the pieces of metal fabricated by Sokoloff in his fingers, I have a kind of gold before my eyes—but is it really gold and not a clever counterfeit of the metal?"

"Artificial gold," Sokoloff replied, possesses all the qualities of native gold. It has the same color, density, durability and malleability, as well as the same chemical and spectroscopic properties."

"One more objection," said Gaston. "This will be the last. Isn't artificial gold destined to remain a laboratory curiosity, like the artificial diamonds obtained in microscopic fragments by Moissan by means of dissolving carbon in the bosom of a mass of cast iron in an electric furnace?"[30]

"Until today," Sokoloff replied, "I was only able to obtain artificial gold in small masses and after long and complicate operations—too long. Without going into the details of a manufacture into which I shall initiate you when the time comes, I can tell you right away that I treat silver reduced to a very fine powder with extreme cold.

"I've invented an apparatus that will permit the production of a temperature of 250° below zero, but I can't construct it in Buenos Aires. Only having defective refrigerant apparatus at my disposal, I've only been able to subject the

---

[30] The chemist Henri Moissan put forward the theory that diamonds could be manufactured by crystallizing carbon under pressure at very high temperatures in 1892; his experimental results were poor, but the electric-arc furnace he developed in order to carry out his investigation proved to be a useful instrument for many other purposes.

silver filings to temperatures insufficient to determine a new condensation of molecules dispersed by the grinding and its passage to the state of gold.

"That's the explanation for the small volume of the pieces of gold that you see. When I have an improved apparatus at my disposal, I'll be able to make gold very rapidly, and in masses of five or six kilos."

Rozen had to admit that Sokoloff did indeed seem to have solved the problem of the transmutation of metals. It was, therefore, possible to create the millions necessary to the realization of his dream.

"Since my projects please you," he said to Sokoloff, "and, on the other hand, you can only fabricate enough gold with the aid of apparatus impossible to manufacture or construct in Buenos Aires, we'll have to go Europe."

"This very day," Sokoloff said, I'll start arranging for the sale of my industrial equipment and the collection of the sums that are owed to me. Within a month, we can embark for London—for it's to London that it's necessary to go." There's a man named Dewar there with whom I can soon reach an understanding, and who will be the most valuable of collaborators. What do you say, comrades?"

"Your will is mine," Dulac replied.

"Do you think I'm a man to run away from a fight?" exclaimed Macaron. "I'll go wherever Sokoloff goes, be it to the ends of the earth, or to the Devil!"

"Agreed," said Rozen.

"Alliance concluded," Sokoloff replied.

"The above script approved," added Dulac, laughing.

"Death to the bourgeoisie! Long live the social revolution!"

"Long live the Great Silversmith of Anarchism!" proclaimed Macaron—who added, in a flippant voice: "Travelers for London or the Place de la Roquette[31] please take their seats!"

---

[31] Outside one of the prisons at La Roquette, where the guillotine was set up in Paris, when required, at the turn of the century.

XVI. The Chelsea Laboratory

"Yes, my dear friend, this time, we are all set and the game is conclusively won. Anarchism has its gold mine, richer and more valuable than the most famous deposits of the Transvaal and the Klondike, since it can never run out, and since I'm the master and can determine the dosage of its release as I please."

It was with these words, pronounced in a low voice but in an inspired tone, that Sokoloff greeted Rozen, one winter evening, in an isolated house at on the utmost outskirts of London, on the outer border of Chelsea.

Outside, there was one of those dirty and sinister London chills, in which one breathes mud mingled with semi-fluid soot and poorly-melted snow, such as is only seen on the banks of the Thames. A thick yellow fog, in the bosom of which the blinking of gaslights was scarcely distinguishable, weighed upon the city like an immense shroud.

Even though he had made the journey by cab, Rozen was shivering and his clothing, penetrated by the damp, gave off a cloud of vapor.

"But you're freezing, my poor friend!" Sokoloff cried. "Warm yourself first. We have plenty of time to chat. I only have good news to give you, and good news can wait. Hang up your overcoat and come close to the fire. You'll take a glass of cognac?"

"I won't say no," Rozen replied, stretching his hands toward the fireplace, where a large heap of coal was burning, "especially if it's your cognac from Buenos Aires."

"I never drink any other. 1815, old chap—the year of the battle of Waterloo. You know that I don't drink, but that fine old champagne, I confess, is my little sin. Liquor doesn't suffer mediocrity."

"Still the aristocrat, then?" jested the Levantine, cheered up by the heat, as he raised the glass that his host had poured for him to his lips.

"Absolutely. The word doesn't frighten me, if by aristocracy you mean a man who prefers the best of everything. I'm only an aristocrat and revolutionary because I want to put the best of everything at everyone's disposal."

"Yes, yes—the right to fine champagne. We know that. On that terrain, you can be sure that Bastien will follow you to the ends of the earth. But enough joking; we're not here to amuse ourselves. I got your telegram summoning me urgently an hour ago. I leapt into a cab, and here I am. It seems that you have good news to give me. So much the better! For, in truth, I was beginning to tear my hair out—we've been in this damnable country where the sun never shines for three months, waiting for you to furnish us with the means to go forward and start the great work."

"Rejoice, my dear friend—the moment has come! If I've asked you to come and see me on your own, it's because, in order to understand what I have to explain, it requires scientific knowledge that our comrades Bastien and Dulac are unfortunately deprived. Their education in that regard has been somewhat neglected, alas. It's sufficient for them to know he results; they'll take your word for it. Besides which, I'll bring them evident proof, visible and palpable, which will make their eyes pop. But to you, I owe the details. Listen."

"It's still the matter of the artificial gold?"

"You've guessed it. Until now, my experiments, which I'd already carried out back in America, had remained simple laboratory experiments; I'd resolved the problem theoretically, as you know, but in practice, I hadn't obtained anything serious-scarcely a few grains of gold, pinches of powder with no more value than that of a paradoxical curiosity. In brief, enough to issue a sensational communication to the Académie des Sciences or the Royal Society, but not enough to conquer the world and revolutionize finance and industry from top to bottom, as we have dreamed of doing."

"That's why I've been skeptical," Gaston put in. "Pure science, even when marked with the seal of genius, has no utility."

"How wrong you are! On the contrary—only pure science, which is disinterested in consequences and pursues no other objective than the discovery of truth for truth's sake, is fecund. It is what engenders the other, by opening the way for it and furnishing the instrument—and this is a further example.

"Theoretically, I repeat, I had solved the problem. I knew how to make gold from silver; I had still to industrialize the method. For that I required an element that I could not produce in my poor little laboratory with my two-sou tools..."

"Which was?"

"Extremely low temperatures—exorbitant cold two hundred and fifty degrees below zero."

"I remember you telling me that in Buenos Aires. But why? There, in truth, I lost the thread."

"We're getting to the nub of the problem. It's a little delicate, and I require all your attention and patience."

"I'm all ears."

"My dear friend, I must first go back to the principle itself—the directive idea that served me as a point of departure and guide. Can you tell me what matter is?"

"Matter? Matter...to tell the truth, you're embarrassing me slightly. I know perfectly well what matter is, but I can't see how to define it in an exact and complete fashion. Let's say that matter is the ensemble of all the simple bodies that we know—solids, liquids and gases—and of which everything that exists is made. Is that satisfactory?"

"Undoubtedly; it doesn't appear to be possible, in the present state of our knowledge, to give a better definition. Matter is the ensemble of all that exists; it is, in consequence, the name common to the sixty-some simple substances whose combination represents all that exists, since the smallest particle of what exists is necessarily composed of one or several of those simple substances. Is that understood?"

"Yes, of course. All that is as clear as crystal."

"It now remains to ascertain whether matter really is divided into the sixty-some simple substances of chemical nomenclature—which is to say, whether each of those sixty-some substances corresponds to an irreducible form of matter—or whether matter is traceable back to a single substance of some unknown sort: something homogeneous, essential and fundamental, which affects, according to the hazards of molecular combinations and exterior influences, a host of modes of being, metamorphoses and transformations.

"In the second hypothesis, the one I have adopted, matter would be, in its multiple appearances, like an actor, who is always the same man within his successive disguises. There would be one unique substance, everywhere and always the same, but capable of presenting itself in infinitely varied forms, in aspects or special states that are more or less fixed and durable—to which, given our provisional inability to know more and for linguistic convenience, we have assigned distinct labels: in effect, words with no other value than that of convention. Am I making myself sufficiently comprehensible?"

"Certainly. According to you, the diversity of simple substances is merely the manifestation of innumerable modifications, all superficial and stemming from undetermined causes, of a single unique substance, a single unique fabric, called matter."

"That's right."

"By that reckoning, then, between chlorine and iron, for example, phosphorus and arsenic, oxygen or nitrogen and mercury, there is no difference in nature, but differences of degree, as between amorphous sulfur and crystalline sulfur, ice and water, diamond and coal?"

"Gaston, you're an angel! There is no longer a difference in nature, but only differences of degree and appearance, between gold and silver. Gold and silver, in reality and fundamentally, are the same thing, because all simple substances, in reality and fundamentally, are the same thing.

"If gold and silver seemed different from one another, if all simple substances show themselves to us in different aspects and with incompatible properties, it's for external reasons: a little more or less heat, for example, a little more or less electricity, an oxidation more or less advanced, occult affinities…what do I know? But all of that is so many contingent and transitory appearances overlying an immutable foundation to which one ought to be able to return.

"In brief, one ought to be able to reconstitute the primal substance, truly initial and ultimate at the same time, the true pith, the universal embryo, the protoplasm of beings and things, the primordial weft of matter, of which various so-called distinct substance are merely superficial, ephemeral and interchangeable modalities, only different from one another by virtue of the style in which their elements—always and everywhere identical in themselves—are arranged."

"I've got it!" said Rozen. "In those conditions, if you're right, it ought to be possible to return any substance whatsoever to the primitive and fundamental substance that is the common basis of them all, and to metamorphose that substance into another—any whatsoever—by virtue of that regression."

"Yes, it is possible. It's scientifically and logically possible to change silver into gold; the ancient alchemists' transmutation of metals is no longer a utopia. It's merely a matter of knowing how to do it."

"And that's the snag!"

"It is, but I have the key to the enigma. Suppose that I take an ingot of silver and crush it in such a fashion as to reduce it to powder: an impalpable powder finer than the finest flour. If that pulverization is taken far enough, to the extreme limit, a sort of dissociation occurs—which is to say that the metal loses all its characteristic properties, including its individuality. It is no longer silver, but something unknown, having no name in any language: something anonymous, uniform, indeterminate; the very prototypical matter that I was talking about just now, and from which a chemist knowing his trade could produce, at whim, sulfur or carbon, iodine, hydrogen or zinc.

"Personally, I shall make it into gold! My intimate conviction is that, in the endless series of metamorphoses of matter, gold starts off being silver, which is nothing other than young gold. By artificially aging silver, as one artificially ages wine, I can make it into gold."

Rozen had risen to his feet, as excited by the Sokoloff's contagious tone of conviction as by the powerful logic of his argument. Feverishly chewing his cigar, he advanced toward the scientist, placed a hand on his shoulder and looked him in the eyes. "And you know how to age silver?" he demanded.

"Yes, I know how. It only requires an electric current of a determined intensity, a few drop of a reagent whose formula I shall give you, plus the collaboration of certain carefully—selected leavens—microbes if you prefer. In a matter of hours, the greenish precipitate resulting from the pulverization of silver is transformed into gold: a gold that returns a profit, at the lowest estimate, in the most disadvantageous working conditions, of no less than a hundred and fifty francs a kilogram."

"What's stopping you, then?"

"What *was* stopping me, to be more precise, for I've overcome the difficulty. Oh, a silly thing, nothing at all, as often happens when one grapples a new problem. I could only reduce the silver to impalpable powder by smashing it powerfully, beating it relentlessly."

"Couldn't you simply crush it in a powerful press—a hydraulic press, for example?"

"I thought of that right away, but the experiments were unfavorable. It requires, in fact, that the division of the metal to be extreme, regular and homogeneous. I repeat, there must be, so to speak, a dissociation, which can only be realized by prolonged hammering. Unfortunately, those mechanical shocks have one inconvenience: they raise the temperature of the metal filings, and from then on, one can obtain no further result."

"You need to surround the crucible with a sleeve of cold water."

"That's not sufficient. Even ordinary refrigerant mixtures are insufficient. I have been forced to have recourse to the formidable cooling that only liquefied gases can provide."

"Oh yes—liquefied air. You were already toying with that idea in Buenos Aires."

"Exactly: liquid air. I've been to see Professor Dewar,[32] probably the living man who had gone into these questions most deeply. I introduced myself to him as the representative of the American automobile company John Spencer and Sons. He showed me his apparatus and we chatted."

"You didn't tell him what you wanted to do?"

"Come on, friend—do you take me for an idiot? I'm neither a diplomat, nor a fancier, nor a businessman, but I've been a conspirator too long not to know the price of discretion. You can rest easy. Professor Dewar doesn't suspect anything; he thinks he's dealing with a specialist desirous of knowing whether it's possible to utilize the release of liquid air as a source of motive force and to apply the energy thus obtained to road traction—that's all.

"Anyway, after an hour of conversation, I knew as much as Dewar, perhaps more. According to the indications he gave me, I've bought a machine to manufacture liquid air, of the most recent and improved model. I've made a few modifications to its details myself with the aid of a skilled technologist who worked on the designs with me without knowing what it was for. Oh, it's a fine machine…come and see it!"

Sokoloff got up, took a key from his pocket, and opened a small door hidden behind a tapestry in a corner. Then, going ahead of Rozen, he showed him the way.

As the door opened it had activated a switch controlled by a spring above the lintel, with the result that the room into which the two men went was abruptly inundated by a flood of electric light. One could see there as easily as in broad daylight.

It was a rather large *fin-de-siècle* workshop, surrounded on all sides by frosted glass windows, with a glass floor, meticulously clean, without a speck of dust or a patch of oil, into which one could have come in an evening suit, waistcoat, cravat and white gloves, for everything there was done automatically.

---

[32] The Scottish physicist James Dewar (1842-1923) conducted extensive research into the liquefaction of gases, collecting liquid hydrogen for the first time in 1898 with a refrigeration machine constructed at the Royal Institution in London. He also invented the thermos flask.

There, on a solid wooden pedestal, stood a bizarre apparatus: a sort of bronze container surmounted by a cylinder in the form of a truncated column, connected by a double pipe to a powerful pump linked to a dynamo. The ensemble was decorated with an unexpected luxury of manometers, taps, valves and keys.

The Russian went straight to the electrical distribution panel and, with an assured gesture, flipped a switch.

Immediately, the dynamo started up, with a dull purr, occasionally interrupted by strange rumblings.

"The principle is quite simple," Sokoloff resumed. "It's the air itself that, by virtue of the cold produced by its expansion, operated its liquefaction—no need, as Dewar says, for an external refrigerant. I compress it in this pump, activated by the mains current at two hundred atmospheres. It then passes into this cylinder and descends along a serpentine at the base of which it expands at twenty atmospheres and then returns through a serpentine concentric with the first to the compression pump, releasing en route the cold produced by its expansion to new compressed air arriving via the inferior tube. I thus have at my disposal both maximum refrigeration and maximum pressure, with the result that by combining the effects, the air ends up reaching the critical point of liquidation by itself.

"See for yourself!"

Opening a tap, the scientist placed beneath it a small tin-plate pail wrapped in felt, into which the amazed Rozen saw a bluish liquid flowing like water, over which a white fog floated.

"Two hundred degrees below zero, my dear chap. At that astonishing temperature, which I might be able to reduce further still, it's as if matter goes crazy; it is something inert, passive, indeterminate, amorphous and plastic, no longer having any physical aptitudes, chemical affinities, vita force or anything, and with which one can do as one wishes. Watch!"

Sokoloff took an iron rod and plunged it into the magic liquid; then, having removed it, he crushed it effortlessly between two fingers, as if it were friable clay.

"Iron is no longer iron in the bosom of liquid air. Silver is no longer silver. It is deindividualized, ready to take on any form, to submit to any influence. It no longer warms up even under the action of mechanical labor, for at minus two hundred degrees, energies are suspended. It is no longer anything more that a kind of protoplasm that I can dress as I please.

"It pleases me to dress it as gold—and here is the result."

The chemist opened a drawer and placed in the hands of the astounded Rozen a superb ingot weighing hundreds of grams, having every appearance of native gold.

"Oh, your eyes might well widen—it's gold, or, at least, something exactly equivalent, from the monetary as well as the metallurgical viewpoint. It not only has the color, the weight, the density, the luster and the ring, but I defy the subtlest specialist to find therein, by chemical assay, spectral analysis or any other method, the slightest difference from the gold of placers. It's gold, I tell you!"

"It's true," Rozen replied. "I know it well, and I'm flabbergasted. But how were you able to make so much?"

"With my liquid air, of which I'm equipped to obtain sixty to eighty liters an hour, I can, in this laboratory, with one or two companions, deliver to the revolution between eight and ten kilos of gold a day. Can you take responsibility for changing the ingots into pounds sterling?"

"Of course," said Rozen, after a moment's hesitation. "Nothing simpler…but it will be necessary to recast these nuggets first; they don't have the external appearance of the nuggets one usually finds in natural deposits. That originality, although superficial, might arouse the attention of professional assayers. They're always on watch, those guard-dogs! I wonder if you're organized for that task."

"It's child's play, my friend. No need for improved furnaces or cumbersome apparatus. Haven't you heard mention of the new metallurgical procedure invented by the German Hans Goldschmidt, which is known as aluminothermics?[33] It dates back about two years."

"Two years ago, alas, I was on Île du Diable, and believe me, chemistry wasn't my primary interest. We didn't keep up to date."

"I beg your pardon, my friend—I forgot! Let it suffice for you to know that it's a method of sovereign elegance and incomparable convenience, which permits a child to found and weld the most refractory metals—not only gold but chromium, manganese, tungsten and so on. A few pinches of powdered aluminum, any crucible whatsoever, and a friction match to start the reaction; I can develop the temperature of an electric furnace in a drawing room, and the job's done!

"Everything has been anticipated, I assure you, and we really do possess the long sought-after secret of the philosopher's stone. Without a doubt, I could mass-produce gold, as others manufacture chocolate, bricks or soap. We'd have to build a factory for that, hire workers and, in consequence, bring everyone up to date—but by myself, with one or two reliable companions, I can take responsibility for sustaining the situation and furnishing the sinews of war, as we go along, for the financial campaign that you alone can organize and direct.

"I can. In fact, count on transmuting, every twenty-four hours, ten kilograms of silver into nine kilograms of fine gold. Nine kilograms of gold are worth about 27,000 francs. Let's deduct the price of the silver and the expenses

---

[33] Aluminothermy, in which aluminum is used as a reducing agent to separate other metals from their oxides at high temperatures, was actually pioneered by Nikolai Beketov, but Hans Goldschmidt improved control of the relevant reaction and took out a patent in 1898; it was mainly used in welding railway tracks.

of manufacture, which are about 4,000 francs. That leaves, per day, 23,000 francs. Given that it's impossible for me to work around the clock, let's say 15,000 francs, leaving a wide margin for unforeseen contingencies.

"One can undertake great things and bring them to completion with an assured income of 450,000 francs—near half a million—a month!

"By the way, if I fall ill, fall victim to some accident or die, the explanation of the method, with my calculations, the record of my experiments, dosages and all manual operations, down to the last detail, is here in this drawer..."

Rozen became thoughtful. A sudden thought had just occurred to him. There was a livid pallor in his face; his large eyes were shining with a singular phosphorescence.

Why, he thought, *since I'm now the master of the famous secret, should I share it with others? Why even encumber my life by trailing this Russian mystic in my wake—this old madman who bores and compromises me with his revolutionary dreams? We're alone...the house is surrounded by derelict land, where no policeman ever ventures...Rozen, my lad, the time has come to demonstrate that you're a man. Fortune is at hand; don't let it escape.*

A sharp awl, a terrible weapon at the end of a robust arm, was lying on the workbench.

The former convict slyly reached out a hand, and, with the rapid movement of a pickpocket's fingers, slipped the implement into his sleeve—but it was only a gesture, followed by a rapid change of mind. The bandit was too intelligent and far-sighted to risk killing the goose that laid the golden eggs in that fashion. As rapid as a lightning-flash, it occurred to him that he might have further need of Sokoloff, whose marvelous and fecund genius he had come to understand. No instrument of fortune was worth as much as him, superior to the most skillful and audacious speculations. His very mysticism and revolutionary monomania were as many trump cards—and what trump cards!—in his hand.

And did he not know better than anyone else how to manipulate people, especially the naïve and trusting, and make them do, almost unconsciously, what he wanted? Not to mention that murder, always dangerous, was repugnant to his practical mind.

He put the awl back.

Sokoloff, entirely absorbed in his work, had not seen anything. Even if he had seen, in fact, he would not have understood, would not have guessed.

XVII. An Annoying Encounter

"Well, my dear master," said Rozen, as he went into Sokoloff's workroom, "are you satisfied with tonight's experiments? Is the Great Work making progress?"

On arriving in England, the Levantine had significantly modified his appearance. He resembled neither the young Parisian socialite nor the Cayenne convict. His hair, slightly discolored and yellowed by hydrogen peroxide, was divided by a parting that extended from the middle of his forehead to the nape of his neck. His beautiful black beard, now chestnut-brown, was cut into two sideburns, which, fusing with his moustache, gave it an exceptional length and thickness. The scar on his cheek, which he took care to leave clearly visible, contributed to giving him a very different facial expression.

The commencement of baldness, of the most distinguished kind, also uncovered the crown of the head, formerly hidden by a naturally curly fleece. That result, which would have been almost sufficient in itself to give him a new physiognomy, had been systematically obtained by means of a skilled and prolonged application of radiography. Rozen had paid for that with a slight irritation of the epidermis; on the other hand, he was bald—not excessively bald, but mercilessly bald—for everyone knows that wherever X-rays have passed, hair, mysteriously afflicted in the sources of life, never grows again.

These facial transformations, however, all superficial, had not sufficed for the mistrustful subtlety of the prudent adventurer. Under the pretext of curing a dolorous double facial tic—and he could play wonderfully, when necessary, the comedy of spasmodic convulsions and rhythmic quivering of the skin—he had put himself in the hands of a renowned Swedish therapeutic masseur. For about an hour every day, for weeks on end, the skillful practitioner had kneaded his forehead and cheeks repeatedly, to such an extent that, with the best will in the world, without suspecting for an instant what his strange client had in mind, he had made him a new head. Beneath his magical fingers, modeling the flesh like soft wax, the slight puffiness that often characterizes Levantine beauty was gradually resorbed; new contours had appeared, while the features, liberated from cumbersome fatty tissue, had been refined.

"As good work goes," Macaron had declared, "it's good work."

Even Sokoloff, ever-sensitive to the marvels of art and science, had not spared his approving smiles for that masterpiece of sculpture in flesh.

The fact is that the transformation surpassed Rozen's hopes. Every day, he had followed the progress of his pretended cure in a mirror.

"I wouldn't say hello to myself in the street," he said.

On the day when his so-called tic was definitively cured and he said good-bye to the Swedish masseur—who was generously paid and heaped with compliments—he was a different man.

Even his voice had changed. It still had the same charm, the same strange and gripping timbre, but a deft electrical stimulation of the vocal cords, patiently applied over weeks, had made it deeper, with a kind of slight vibrato reminiscent of the sound of a harpsichord.

"One can do anything one wishes with living matter, as plastic as clay," said Sokoloff, willingly.

Rozen was the living proof of that paradoxical axiom. His own mother would not have recognized him.

Elegantly dressed, he looked sufficiently like a gentleman of pure Anglo-Saxon descent, solely occupied in the business of spending his income.

Sokoloff, by contrast, looked more like a worker than a gentleman, with his untidy hair, his long untrimmed beard, his smock of coarse black fabric spotted with red acid-burns, whose sleeves, rolled up to the elbows, bared formidably muscled arms, but for the slenderness of his wrists, the innate distinction of his manners and the grace of his gestures—in sum, all the subtle *je ne sais quoi* produced by long hereditary refinement that betrayed his origins to a perspicacious observer.

He was sitting in front of a workbench laden with papers covered with calculations, beside which were scattered capsules, test-tubes and phials filled with liquids of every color.

He raised his head and, recognizing Rozen, smiled with ineffable bounty. "How handsome you are, my dear Rozen, he said, looking at his interlocutor. Where are you going dressed up like that?"

"To a garden party at Sir Rowland Drake's."

"Always partying, eh?"

"Always!" said Gaston, laughing.

"It's necessary to remember the cause. Pleasure ought not to make you forget duty."

"Pleasure!" said Rozen, shrugging his shoulders. "Pleasure! Come on, my friend, do you imagine that it's for my personal pleasure that I hang around with these arrogant fops and lunatics, puppets without hearts or brains, whose friend I'm becoming. No, no…make no mistake. Although I mingle with them, seeing their life of dissipation, and constrain myself to befriend them, it's because it's necessary, in order for me to attain my goal, that they believe me to be their peer."

"Do you really think so?" asked the scientist, unsettled by that loquacity.

"Certainly. I believe it more than ever. Isn't it the best trump card in the hand of a general laying siege to a town, to have a man of his own in the heart of the town, a damned soul who knows all its secrets? Well, the general is you; the town is this rotten society that we want to destroy; the damned soul is me…"

"Perhaps you're right," Sokoloff declared, looking at Rozen admiringly.

"Believe me, then, once and for all, old chap. I'm making myself more useful in acting like this than by going, like so many agitators of our acquaintance, to bark in meetings or howl in the street. You'll see, when the moment of the great upheaval comes, and we'll be able to give it its full force..."

"All right, I believe you," said the scientist, convinced. "Go and do your job in your own fashion. By the way, do you need money?"

"I shouldn't ask you for any," Gaston relied, with feigned hesitation. "But, reluctantly, to maintain me at the level of those privileged by fortune..."

Sokoloff opened a drawer. He took out two rolls of gold coins and handed them to the Levantine. "Take them," he murmured, "and don't spare them."

"Thank you, comrade!" exclaimed the hypocrite, as his pockets swallowed the gold.

"And now let me get on with my work," the scientist concluded, extending his hand. "I've got a lot to do today."

Rozen could not help smiling with pity. He was amused by the transcendent but naïve scientist, whose blind confidence he was exploiting. Since he had come to England, he was leading a joyful life. With the money Sokoloff handed out lavishly to him, in order that he might work for the future triumph of the revolution, he was cutting a dash in English society. And whenever Sokoloff, a simple man *par excellence*, expressed surprise at that luxury, Rozen explained his personal theories, demonstrating to him that it was necessary to have the appearance and power of the great in order to get one's hands on the levers of the world.

Sokoloff, seduced and stunned by his verve, believed him.

That morning, once again, the bandit had come to obtain by fraud the large sum he needed.

Happy with his success, he was about to take his leave of the scientist when three spaced raps sounded on the workroom door.

"See who that is," said Sokoloff, frowning.

Rozen went to open the door.

"It's only me, Boss," croaked a hoarse voice—and Bastien, alias Macaron, made his entrance, wearing a self-important expression.

"You, here? What are you doing here?" Gaston demanded, in an irritated tone. "You know very well that the master doesn't want to be disturbed."

"More impious words!" Sokoloff protested. "Master, boss—there are no masters or bosses in anarchism. There are only free and equal comrades. When are you going to rid yourselves of that vile language, out of place in the mouths of men carful of their dignity?" In a lower voice, he added; "And you know very well that it wounds me."

Flustered by this assault, Macaron said nothing. *When that animal talks to me*, he thought, *I'm confused. He's always telling me what not to say, although it's not anarchism for one person to tell his fellow what to do!*

But Rozen did not have such scruples. "Don't get annoyed, my dear friend," he said, in a soothing tone. "It's a manner of speaking, of no importance. The words signify nothing in themselves. What we salute in you, in calling you 'master' or 'boss,' isn't some kind of authority—which we don't tolerate in anyone, even Sokoloff: Neither God nor Master—but the superiority of knowledge and experience; it's the excellence of the advice of the man who preceded us into the revolutionary arena and who continues to steer us there. It's the professor, the guide. And let's not forget that we're living in bourgeois society and we have to play a role, so that no one suspects us. How, then, can we dispense with speaking its language?"

Sokoloff could not help smiling. "You're right," he murmured. "You're always right, and you're wiser than me. It's necessary to howl with the wolves; the end justifies the means."

"But anyway," Rozen continued, this time addressing Bastien, "tell us what brings you here. Have you forgotten the orders?"

"I know the orders," the other replied, still slouching in the doorway, "but I've got important news to tell you."

"News?" said Sokoloff, turning round. "What news?"

"Citizeness Eléna is here."

"Eléna!" cried Rozen, going pale. "You're mad!"

"Certainly not!" Bastien sniggered. "It really is citizeness Eléna, our good and brave comrade from Cayenne."

"The young woman you mentioned to me, Gaston?" Sokoloff put in. "The one who rendered your captivity less harsh and helped you escape?"

"Of course!" said Bastien. "Our good angel, if I might put it that way."

By a violent effort of will, Rozen mastered his surprise, and reined in his anger, which had been about to burst forth. It was in an almost affectionate tone that he asked Macaron: "And where did you meet her?"

"Oh, that's quite a story. Imagine that, yesterday evening, I was going to pay a visit to two or three public houses in Soho, where I hoped to run into French refugees..."

"In order to get yourself recognized!" Rozen interjected, shrugging his shoulders.

"No danger...they're all Parisians and, as you know, I've only every worked in the provinces. No one knows me, so to speak, and they all take me for an Englishman. Even though I laugh myself silly when I hear them talking in argot, imagining that I don't understand them—me, who learned it at the teat!" Bastien burst out laughing.

"Enough reminiscences," said Rozen, severely.

"So," Bastien continued, "I'd visited three pubs and was coming back without having found anything, a trifle vexed, when I suddenly bumped into a pauperess holding a baby in her arms."

"A baby!" exclaimed Sokoloff, who was listening with interest to Macaron's slightly ironic story.

"Of course! Yes, a baby…whose author is not a million miles away from here—isn't that right, Boss?"

"What, me? I'm a father?" Rozen replied, feigning an emotion that he was far from experiencing. "Go on, Macaron, talk. Was it her who said that?"

"Oh, not right away. She didn't recognize me, the poor dear. Imagine that! She was dying of hunger, and her poor kid too, for, not having had anything to load her guns for two days…"

"That's horrible!" Sokoloff murmured, his generous heart deeply stirred.

"Yes, horrible!" Rozen repeated, putting his hand to his eyes as if to wipe away an absent tear.

"But I recognized her right away," Macaron went on, "in spite of the alteration of her features and the ravages that poverty had inflicted. Too bad. To her, I named myself right away, without fear—no danger that she'll spill the beans, eh?"

"And then?" asked Sokoloff.

"She uttered a cry of joy: 'Saved! Saved!' 'Yes, my dear citizeness!'—I said it just like that. And, as it was necessary to take care of the most urgent need, I took her into the bistro I'd just left. She ate and drank to her heart's content, weeping with joy, so much that it made me cry too…and I'm till crying…" Macaron blew his nose noisily, and patted his eyes with a handkerchief.

"You're a good lad, Bastien." said Sokoloff, shaking the anarchist's hand. "That was a good thing you did…"

"Yes, very good," said Rozen, "but what have you done with her? Where is she?"

"Where is she? Why, at home, of course. I couldn't take her anywhere else, could I?"

Gaston stifled the curse he was about to utter, and shook Bastien's hand affectionately. "You did well," he said. "She's there, then?"

"In my bedroom, sleeping like a contented soul. She was exhausted by fatigue, the poor girl, and when she'd eaten, her eyes were closing involuntarily. I gave her my bed and slept in an armchair."

"This changes everything," said Rozen. "I won't go out—I'll leave partying for another occasion. My duty is to go to Eléna—isn't that right, friend?"

"Certainly!" Sokoloff exclaimed. "And when you've seen her, and exhausted the joy that you'll both experience in this happy and fortuitous reunion, tell me, so that I can go in my turn to tell your heroic friend how well I think of her."

"Don't worry, my friend. But I'll leave you…I'm in haste to see Eléna again, to hold her in my arms. Lead the way, Macaron."

"Lead yourself, Boss," said Bastien, as he went out in the corridor. "I've told her you're here."

Rozen followed him, with rage in his heart.

On abandoning Eléna during his escape from Cayenne he had hoped never to see her again, nor to hear any mention of her. And here she was, having reappeared, finding him in London, where he had created a new identity. She had surged forth like a living pang of remorse, like an accusation of the ignominy of the way he had treated her, his ingratitude and perfidy; like a danger, a sword of Damocles suspended over his head.

Oh, he said to himself, *how unfortunate that it wasn't me she met. I'd have let her and her child die of hunger—whereas this idiot, with his sensibility, brought her to me. And Sokoloff is delighted by it! So that it's necessary for me to face misfortune with a stout heart, feigning joy and tenderness...*

Thus disposed, he went into Macaron's bedroom, where Eléna was lying.

The poor woman was asleep. As Macaron had said, suffering had made her thin and her face pale, but she was still beautiful, and Rozen could not help a start of admiration on seeing her lying, full dressed, on the bed, with her baby beside her—a delightful child.

She loves me, after all, the bandit said to himself. *Perhaps she still believes in me, since she thought she was saved when Macaron told her I was here. With a few fine words, I could do whatever I wished with her...pooh! My star's still shining and hasn't yet gone out.*

He drew nearer, and lightly touched the young woman's shoulder with his finger. She opened her eyes and looked around anxiously. Gaston's physiognomy seemed striking, although she did not recognize him at first, so skillfully had he built himself a new head. Suddenly, though, her eyes fixed themselves on Rozen's.

His velvet eyes betrayed him, and she hurled herself into his arms, crying: "Gaston! It's you! It's you!"

"The very same, my dear beloved," said Rozen, with a marvelously counterfeited affection. "The man who has been searching for you, as you have doubtless been searching for him—and who blesses the day that has finally brought us together again!"

She was unable to reply. Her anguished heart was beating as if to burst beneath the excess of happiness that had arrived too suddenly.

She hugged her beloved convulsively to her bosom, and covered him with crazy kisses. Eventually, a flood of tears surged from her eyes, soothing her. Her voice returned.

"Oh, yes, bless the day, for I'd given up hope long ago, Gaston, my love, my spouse."

"You're right: your spouse—for this dear little creature, your son and mine, will tighten the ties that bind us even further," said Rozen, in an emotional voice, the tone of which even deceived Macaron, who had remained discreetly by the door, quite overwhelmed.

And the hypocrite, picking up the child, deposited warm kisses on his cheeks.

Was it surprise, or fear of that unknown man? Was it the prescience that those naïve little beings, much closer to nature, possess? Beneath the kisses, the child began uttering terrible screams.

The mother took him back and did her best to console him.

"But what became of you?" Rozen asked, sitting down on the edge of the bed. "How did you come to leave Cayenne and Guiana?"

"After your escape there was an active search, and a few days later, your clothing was discovered with the bones of a corpse eaten by animals. The general opinion was that you had gone astray in the woods and had fallen there, dying of hunger. That had happened so many times before to unfortunate convicts trying to escape from the bagne that no one was surprised by it."

"Yes," Rozen murmured, smiling. "The idea was as simple as it was good."

"Your death-certificate was drawn up, and that was it. On the contrary, I had a secret conviction that, with your energy, courage and strength, you had succeeded in reaching hospitable territory safe and sound. So what had happened?

"I didn't know anything, but what was for others the proof of your death was not that for me. I believed that you were alive. I waited for your communication. I counted the days, still hoping to receive the signal in response to which I was to leave to join you. Alas, the days went by and that communication did not came.

"Was it necessary, then, to believe in a catastrophe? It was then that an unexpected complication arose. I realized that I was going to become a mother. Certainly, it was a great joy and an ineffable consolation to me, that child who was about to come into the world—your child, your flesh and blood, the pledge of our brief love—but it was also a cruel embarrassment for my plans. How, in that situation, was I to travel the distance that separated me from you, and vanquish the obstacles that would emerge during the journey?"

"Poor, dear heart!" sighed Rozen tenderly, cleverly giving his fine dark eyes an expression of infinite softness.

"My misfortune was even greater that I was able to suppose," Eléna went on. "In spite of all there care I took to hide it, it wasn't long before my condition was noticed. I was summoned, and after an interrogation to which I refused to reply, as you will understand, I was dismissed ignominiously from the director's house."

"The villains!" exclaimed Rozen.

"The blackguards," Macaron muttered, clenching his fists. "If I'd been there..."

"Don't insult them too much," said the exquisite creature, softly. "I owe it to them that I've found you again. What would I have done, thrown back on my own resources? I don't know. When he sent me away, the governor was generous, and gave me enough money to pay for my passage on a Dutch sailing-ship that was leaving Paramaribo for Europe, and which had stopped at Cayenne to take on a cargo of ironwood.

"Oh, that long and horrible crossing! How I suffered, malnourished, deprived of air, sleeping on the floor, shaken by the pitching to the point of believing that the child I was carrying in my womb might be born prematurely at any moment, only to die immediately.

"Finally, my suffering came to an end. The captain, who only wanted to be rid of me, deposited me on the English coast as he passed through the Channel, and wished me *bon voyage*. I was utterly penniless, and it was in a hospital, where I was taken in, that my little Gaston was born...

"Since then, I've lived by begging, but it was just in time that Macaron recognized me, for I was at the end of my tether and I really believe that we were going to die..."

"And in the meantime," Gaston continued, having finally succeeded in forging a story, "once having got out of trouble, I sent you letter after letter. I had someone look for you in Cayenne. I learned about your departure indirectly, without knowing the cause, and lost myself in conjectures..."

"Oh, I knew that you hadn't forgotten me," said Eléna, covering the liar with an amorous and grateful gaze."

"Now, we'll be happy. I have a position, money..."

"What does that matter?"

"It matters a great deal. In order to live, is it not necessary to forget past sufferings and think of our child's future?"

"You're right, as always, my beloved."

"Get some more rest," Rozen declared, "While I take care of your installation here. You need clothes and underclothes. Macaron will take care of that. Personally, I shall go to tell my friend—our friends—about your arrival. I'll introduce you to them when you're completely recovered and in a fit condition to receive visitors.

He embraced her again and went downstairs.

Good, he said to himself. *It's going better than I could have imagined. She's absolutely devoted to me. She'll be my slave, as before, and that might be useful. And how much difficulty she had recognizing me! I must really have changed a great deal. It goes without saying; Macaron was right: it's work well done.*

An hour later, Macaron came back, carrying a costume that, if not a model of elegance and taste, was at least comfortable. Eléna put it on, adapting herself to the fit as best she could, for Bastien had only been able to offer a very approximate description in the dressmaker's shop to which he had been. Then she declared that she was ready to visit Sokoloff.

The scientist welcomed her with open arms. He knew her story. Had she not been a providence for the unfortunates in the penitentiary in Guiana, the angelic savior of companions sent to the bagne for their ideas, which were also his? That was sufficient from him to love her, but there was something else too: the young woman's beauty, and the charm of her voice, almost as musical as Rozen's; and when she retold in his presence the story of the sufferings she had endured before rediscovering the man she loved and the father of her child in London, real and sincere tears ran from his eyes, fatigued by work and late nights.

From that moment on, Rozen knew that he had been right to take Eléna in. At the first stroke, the Cuban woman had acquired a sympathetic influence on the scientist, and that influence could, if he was so minded, be combined with the one he already exercised in order to be the absolute master in the house. He promised himself to use it, and even to abuse it, if necessary.

To begin with, it was necessary to quit London, where, in spite of the money that Sokoloff gave him, he could not lead the existence of which he had dreamed. In spite of the good connections he had been able to make, he felt perennially restricted and anxious by the possibility of danger. English society is suspicious, and not as gullible as that of Paris. Someone might take it into his head to research his origins and antecedents.

Then again, he did not have Paris.

He was nostalgic for the boulevards, with a kind of sadistic need to appear there, transfigured, as a master and conqueror. It was in Paris that he had lost the first round of his contest with society; it was in Paris that he ought to take his revenge! It was therefore necessary to persuade Sokoloff to leave London.

That would not be easy, for the scientist was fond of his house, his marvelously equipped workshop, and his habits.

With Eléna's aid, however, he was certain of success.

Part Two
COSMOPOLITAN PIRATES

I. In Grandeur

The very next day, when he went to visit his Chelsea laboratory, Rozen raised the question with Sokoloff, carefully refraining from mentioning his personal interest, but putting forward that of anarchist propaganda.

"It's true that one enjoys a relative freedom in London," he said, "but one is surrounded by spies. Among the political refuges with which one is in communication, it's difficult to tell the difference between the true and the false. Besides which, what can we organize here? How can we bring change to this ponderous British society, in which everyone believes that the different social classes are set in stone?

"Look at the miserable inhabitants of Whitechapel. They're dying of hunger and poverty. Do they complain? No? They brutalize themselves in drunkenness and think men, women and children are happy who, at the end of a day of begging, have succeeded in finding enough to allow them to roll in the mud, felled by whisky.

"What can be done with such elements? It would take years, perhaps centuries, to achieve their regeneration. In any case, one can only attempt that by example. When only the English aristocracy remains standing, it will collapse like the rest, but it's necessary to attack the rotten society at its most vulnerable point, and the only place in which we can attempt the struggle is Paris.

"Paris! Where, in spite of the police and their surveillance, it's easy to centralize all the anarchist forces. Paris! From which one can send emissaries into every capital in the entire world. Paris! Whose revolutionary prestige hasn't weakened in the last century. Paris! From which action can radiate everywhere, from which the word of command can be launched and in which, given the nervousness of the people, the movement will easily depart, giving the example and the signal to all the disinherited of the world. Paris! Perhaps the only city in the world from which the signal for universal revolution can depart, because it's the only one whose example would be contagious, the only one whose prestige, doubtless due to its tragic history, could become an apostolate and a radiant force.

"In order to unleash the tempest, it's necessary to live in Paris, in a situation high enough to have nothing to fear from police harassment, and to have connections everywhere, ostentatiously, without exciting suspicion, in order to be able to dispatch news, orders and indications, with a view to the liberation of humankind, on an everyday basis, concurrently with the leaders of bourgeois tyranny.

"It's necessary, in order to do battle with the capitalist and monetary power that rules the world, to be equal in strength, and superior..."

"That's all very well in theory," Sokoloff replied, "but how can we apply it?"

"It's quite simple. With the resources that science furnishes, we'll have almost as much gold as we wish. In Paris, I'll found a colossal bank. I'll move into the marketplace, and start a war that I don't believe I can lose, since gold costs me nothing.

"As for others—there are a thousand ways of ruining them. Do you remember what Napoléon attempted to do to England? If he had been able, as he wished, to drain all the gold in England into France by substituting the false banknotes that he had manufactured, that would have put paid to British power. Today, thanks to photography, heliogravure and a thousand other means that science had given us, forgery is mere child's play for men like us.

"There will, in any case, be no need to resort to extreme measures. Nothing can resist the power of gold; it gives a seeming intelligence even to imbeciles, who have no need of any other trump card to win all games and hoist themselves up to the pinnacle. How much will we have in our hands? It won't take long, I swear to you, for me to become the master of the world. When one holds the marketplace, when one holds credit, one holds everything else; one is the supreme power!"

"You're right, my son. But what if you don't succeed, in spite of your skill?"

"I'll only compromise myself, and will fall alone, without the party receiving the slightest affliction!" Rozen exclaimed, in the inspired tone of an apostle.

"Good lad!" said the old scientist, enthused. "Go on; I yield to your reasons. You have *carte blanche*—act!"

Rozen had reached his goal. He was going to leave London, which he had never felt to be his true terrain, and go to Paris, where he would forge a new identity

Then, the prospect of the magnificent situation that he was going to create for himself intoxicated him...

Only one thing cast a shadow over the picture. Sokoloff wanted to stay in England.

"I'll be no use to you over there," he said. "I'd rather remain here, in my workshop. I don't want to move my books, my papers and my phials...go on your own. When you need something from me, send Macaron."

No, that could not be—far from it. One day, Sokoloff might see through him. It was necessary to maintain him under his own domination, not to lose sight of him for a single day, to stun him incessantly with protestations of devotion.

It was Eléna who, on his orders, was charged with changing Sokoloff's mind.

From the very first moment, the scientist had acquired a quasi-paternal affection for her, and as they came into contact more frequently, that affection changed into a veritable worship. She reminded him, by virtue of her ideas, her energy and her abnegation, of the woman he had loved so much, the one who had initiated him into nihilist ideas, who had paid with her life on an ignominious gallows for her attachment to the revolutionary cause.

The child also acquired an important place in Sokoloff's golden heart. He wanted to adopt that innocent, gentle, supple little creature as his pupil, to mold him and train him in order to create in him a pure apostle of Anarchism.

In spite of the influence that Rozen had been able to acquire over him, Sokoloff would have refused to leave London. One plea from Eléna, one kiss from the child, and he was convinced.

Rozen did not want to lose any time. That same evening he took the train to Dover; the next day he was in Paris, preparing for everyone's arrival.

As he had said, he did things on a grand scale. There was a large vacant property for rent in one of the finest houses on the Place Vendôme; he rented it immediately in order to set up the Banque Saint-Magloire & Co. Saint-Magloire! That was a name he could wear without fear. The gaucho from which he had stolen that identity would never reclaim it.

Under that name, his own from now on, he bought a house on the Champs-Élysées, in which he installed his and Eléna's personal household—for he wanted to retain Eléna. More than that; he had resolved to represent her as his wife. A banker who is married and a father inspires much more confidence. Then again, would it not necessary to play host, to throw parties, in order to make an impression in Parisian society? With her superior education, her intelligence and her grace, Eléna would do honor to his drawing rooms and would seduce his guests.

As for Sokoloff, what was necessary for him was an exceedingly tranquil retreat, where no external noise would disturb his work. That retreat he found under the tall trees of Auteuil, and it was to a charming villa, isolated in the midst of lawns and trees, that the scientist transported all the material brought from London.

Six months after the arrival in France, everything was going exactly according to Rozen's plan. He had begun with a masterstroke: the launch of a sugar-manufacturing company, the Société Sucrière du Nord, which, by good luck, turned out to be an excellent speculation. The shares had paid a dividend and stayed well above the issue price. It had not required any more to affirm the reputation of the Banque Saint-Magloire from the viewpoint of commercial security.

As for the investment side, as Rozen had told Sokoloff, the certainty of never lacking funds had given him every audacity. He launched himself head-first into the most hazardous speculations, and, as if Fortune had extended her hand over him, he succeeded nine times out of ten. Besides which, he knew how to make his own luck. If an unexpected drop in share-price threatened his position, instead of liquidating it at any price, as a naïve individual would have done, he hung on to the depreciated shares, waited for a while, and, taking advantage of a temporary and artificially-engineered rise, he made a profit where another would have been ruined. Thus, people in the world of finance began to consider the Banque Saint-Magloire as a kind of barometer, whose indications it was necessary to consult before undertaking anything.

What permitted the bold speculator always to be in advance was that, thanks to the discovery of argentaurum, he was already able to procure immense resources, even though the operation was delicate. The ingots or powder of artificial gold that Sokoloff fabricated was easily sold abroad and transformed into beautiful coins of the finest ring. The profit resulting from the difference between the prices of gold and silver in the precious metals market, less the price of manufacture, was considerable. It was, however, necessary to limit that augmentation of funds in order not to alert the world of finance by throwing too many bars of gold into the market or buying too much silver—but the business genius of the Baron de Saint-Magloire compensated for that.

Eventually, he entered into a relationship with the celebrated Henry Albert, the famous "thieves' banker," who centralizes the operations of his associates throughout the world in London. As has been seen in a large number of judiciary affairs, it is a veritable syndicate and, so to speak, a veritable administrative organization

In a movement as important as that of the Banque Saint-Magloire, the flow of stolen bonds sent from England to France was mere child's play, all the more so as the preliminary precaution was taken of modifying the numbers. That too was a enormous source of profits for the operation.

On the other hand, scarcely had he installed himself in the house in the Champs-Élysées, furnished in a princely fashion, than Saint-Magloire threw a series of parties to which he invited all the important people that Paris contained, in the aristocracy, finance, big business, art, literature, and so on. People had come, timidly at first, out of pure curiosity; then they had got used to it. The food was good, the master and mistress of the house welcomed guests with the cordiality of an impeccable distinction...

Soon, Saint-Magloire's dinners were the most sought-after in Paris, and when, better able to do so, he began to be more selective in compiling his guest-lists, that quest became a fury; the best-placed individuals would have resorted to any baseness to have their name figure the following day in the newspapers' account of the reception.

Saint-Magloire had attained his objective. He already dominated Paris. Soon he would dominate the entire world—not, as Sokoloff believed, for the sake of the regeneration of the unfortunate and universal equality, but for the satisfaction of his own pride and passions.

Eléna was happy too. That luxury, that life of gaudy parties, wearied her and was a burden to her—but she was reunited with the father of her child. She passed for his wife and, disdainful of laws and social convention, considered herself as such. Her child's future was assured. What more could she want?

She was, moreover, kept at a distance from all her pseudo-spouse's shady operations.

Dulac, who had also been part of the emigration, was pursuing the realization of his most cherished dream: the creation of a lyric theater. Artfully, without haste, he had already charged the theatrical correspondent of an influential newspaper to inform Germaine, the singer, whom he still loved in spite of everything—Germaine, of whose ambition he was well aware, for whom he was ready to make any sacrifice—that she could come back to him, and that he would be able to conquer her.

Germaine, however, was at the Opéra, where, although she was not a leading player, she considered her position too good to dare to desire another. She was Mademoiselle Germaine Reyval of the Opéra; that always worked wonders on a visiting card. The banker who had stolen her from Dulac had succeeded, by means of his influence, and by setting the theatrical correspondents of the newspapers to work, in getting her into the Académie Nationale de Musique. If she left, even passing over a bridge of gold, even to see her name displayed in large letters on polychromatic posters three meters high, would she have enough success elsewhere not to regret her departure?

Dulac bided his time, maneuvering with a patience and diplomacy that was truly extraordinary in a man as violently infatuated, and, as the idea of the creation of his lyric theater won converts—which is rare for lyric theaters, especially unsubsidized popular theaters—he hoped that, sooner or later, the young woman would decide to become its star.

For his part, Bastien, alias Macaron, for understandable reasons, had become Mr. John Robertson and set himself up as a bookmaker. We ought to say, in order to be accurate, that Macaron-Robertson was somewhat out of step with the general tone of his former companions in misfortune. Careless of aristocratic connections, he spent his life in a very mixed society, at racecourses by day, and in bars by night, where he drank like a bottomless pit, perorated in an Anglo-French jargon in which the argot of the barrières mingled in picturesque fashion with the language of Shakespeare, and only went home when he could no longer stand up...

Macaron was a subject of perpetual terror for Saint-Magloire, who feared that he might compromise everything one day by some drunken indiscretion. Drunk or not, however, the former convict knew how to hold his tongue, and only said what he wanted to say.

In sum, he was inconvenient, but it was necessary to tolerate him, and Saint-Magloire consoled himself for that by using the bookmaker as an informer. By virtue of his connections with grooms, jockeys and stable-lads, he often had channels of information that were not to be disdained.

II. The Man of the Day

"Well, my son, what's new?" Sokoloff asked Rozen one morning, when the latter was sitting facing him in his workshop.

In spite of his vast fortune, Saint-Magloire did not neglect the scientist. He often had need of him, of his advice and his science, which, in spite of his immense vanity, he was forced to recognize as superior to his own.

Sokoloff had not changed. He was still the same simple and affable man, simply dressed but nobler in his chemist's smock than many people in the most elegant costume.

"Come on," he said, pushing away the sheet of paper on which he had spent the morning setting out hundreds of formulae, "When are we going to start the great war?"

"Soon, my friend, soon," Saint-Magloire replied, confidently. "And..."

"It's just that I've been waiting for a long time."

"Don't you trust me anymore?" the banker exclaimed, hotly.

"Yes, but impatience is clawing at me. This old world is so perverse, so worm-eaten..."

"Well," said Saint-Magloire, "we'll shake it from top to bottom, so that nothing will remain of it but dust. Listen: thanks to you, I have power, but it's necessary to bring that power to its apogee, in order that I have in my hand, at my discretion, not only the bourgeoisie and the financiers, sheep for shearing all the way down to the skin, but also those who lead the others: civil servants, parliamentarians, senators, ministers, ambassadors, princes and kings. It's necessary that, with the blink of an eye, I can make Europe tremble, that with a flick of the wrist, I can change everything, turn everything upside-down at my whim..."

"You see the big picture, my lad!" said the naïve scientist, dazzled by that eloquence. "Is your back strong enough to bear such a burden?"

"Burden! Get away! Have no fear. What does it matter? Am I not your pupil, your creation? If I should succumb before having completed my task, you'll be here to put another disciple in my place, who will follow in my tracks and conclude the great work."

Sokoloff shook his head. "Where would I find an organization of the same value as yours? Where would I find an intelligence that understands me as you understand me? Be prudent, my friend..."

"Don't worry! I shall only give the signal when all my batteries are so well-aimed that nothing can go wrong. We mustn't leave the slightest thing to chance—and that's why I repeat: trust me, be patient, and give me the time necessary to be sure of success."

Having once again lulled the suspicions of the man of genius he had made his dupe, Rozen returned to his business and his pleasures.

He had not lied in talking about the ever-increasing magnitude of his power and influence. Once his bank had been launched, with the wind behind it, everything he had done had succeeded. Success breeds success, as the English proverb has it. Rozen had taken advantage of his financial connections to insinuate himself into every corner of society and take root there.

The case was not knew. In every epoch, we have seen financiers dictate in this fashion to the most powerful people in the world. To name only one, Jacques Coeur, the son of a fur-merchant in Bourges, had arrived at his apogee possessing thirty lordships, covering the Mediterranean with his ships, giving orders to the Parlement de Languedoc, treating as an equal with the Republic of Genoa, and having princes, courtiers and the king himself as debtors—who, being unable to repay him, were at his mercy. His fall was terrible, to be sure, but for long years his power as limitless, and the daring always hope to be cleverer than their forebears.

Later, Fouquet had dared to compete in ostentation with the Sun King. And there was John Law, who, if he had had more "guts," as one says today, could have bought all of France as one buys a country house. And even closer to our own time, Cornelius Herz, for whom our great politicians were merely puppets whose strings he held.[34]

The Baron de Saint-Magloire wanted to be Jacques Coeur, Fouquet, Law and Cornelius Herz all rolled into one, but on condition of only having their wealth, their power and their predominant situation, He believed himself to be cunning enough and sufficiently hardened by experience, prudent enough and strong enough, not to have to fear their fate. From the outset, in fact, he had sought to procure weapons against all those from whom he might have something to fear.

Bastien, alias Macaron, had been a useful resource for that. There are few people in high society who can keep a secret for long from their chambermaid or valet, and secrets fly from the antechamber to the kitchen and the stables. By virtue of his connections in the servant class, for whose drinks he paid generously, John Robertson not only decanted racing information, but also intimate gossip. While regarding him as an "old concierge" because of his passion for gos-

---

[34] Cornelius Herz, the great pioneer of electrical technology in France and throughout Europe, was not as rich as the other three men cited, but he had an equally spectacular fall when he was caught up in the Panama scandals of 1892; he was subsequently vilified in the French press and ruthlessly persecuted by the courts. The authors of the present text could not have anticipated that in 1906 (eight years after his death) Herz would be officially exonerated of all blame, having been set up as a scapegoat, but they must have had some inkling of his probable innocence.

sip, they gladly told him that Madame la Comtesse de X*** had had a row that morning with her husband with regard to young Duc Z***, who, for his part, had virtually set up house with Mademoiselle L of the Opéra, with whom he had an eight-year-old son at school with the Pères; that Madame de C had pawned her diamonds to pay the Vicomte de M***'s gambling debts; that Monsieur P***, the député for the Rhône-Inférieur was sharing with his mistress in profits made at the Folies-Bergère, the Palais de Glace and he Casino de Paris.

A thousand items of information that Macaron brought the Boss, and of which he made use in his own fashion, redeeming Madame de C***'s jewels in order to return them, congratulating the Comte de X*** with feigned naivety on the good looks and intelligence of his son, inviting the député's mistress to dinner at Paillard's or Maxim's…showing each of them that he knew of a "skeleton in the cupboard," and thus inspiring, in turn, gratitude, dread and anxiety.

In that complicated enterprise, gambling served him equally well. Into the hand of a gentleman who has just "lost his shirt" and to whom the club refused any further credit, you slip the twenty-five louis required to get back into the game and take his revenge, and from then on, that gentleman cannot refuse you anything, especially if, when the losing streak continues, you forget to reclaim the loan. He is a slave, attached by the contracted debt and the cleverly fanned hope of further subsidies in case of need…

With a gambler, one can do anything, when one has the necessary cash.

One can say the same of women.

Always seductive, more the charmer than ever, the Baron de Saint-Magloire had, in his own interests and for his personal pleasure, numerous connections in the demi-monde and even in high society. In addition to his handsome features, which the changes to his face had metamorphosed and matured without significant attenuation, his generosity was proverbial.

It was said that the director of one prestigious Paris shop had nearly gone mad by virtue of the excess of his good fortune—so many lovely women coming to visit his establishment every afternoon. The same misadventure might have befallen Saint-Magloire if he had not had a Herculean constitution, thanks to which no excess could weaken his nerves or trouble his mind.

If Macaron had the confidences of the tavern, he was able to obtain for himself those of the pillow, and they were no less interesting.

Finally, thanks to his connections, the facilities provided by his admission into the offices of the Prefect of Police—who had become his friend—ministers and various important civil servants, he had easily plundered a few state secrets, which he has hastened to communicate, clandestinely, to the ambassador of a great foreign power, a rival with little love for France.

In exchange, he did not ask for anything. What, in any case, could have been offered to a man who juggled with millions? But he solicited the honor of continuing his "disinterested" services, which he rendered solely, it appeared, by virtue of the duty of friendship and in the interests of international peace. And as, for that reason, the ambassador was obliged to keep him up to date with the state of affairs, and make him certain confidences and confessions when he, incognito, to wait in private rooms where precious documents were sometimes left, he had been able to play a double role and report much information of inestimable value to the French government...

Gaston had continued in this fashion, having personal and occult relationships with various diplomats, betraying one to another and *vice versa*, according to whatever was in his interests for the moment, increasing in political influence as in financial influence, honored with decorations from many countries, feared and respected, dictating to the most arrogant...for, while he found means of collecting what he needed to compromise others, he was careful never to risk being compromised himself.

One day, when a young and rather impatient embassy attaché, complained of having had to wait too long in his antechamber, the Baron had replied, dryly: "Everyone takes his turn here, Monsieur."

"But it seems to me that in my position, I have the right to certain prerogatives..."

"Why is that, if you please?"

"Are you not at the service of the man who sent me?"

The Baron had fixed him with his large dark eyes, whose soft expression had disappeared, to give way to a frightful hardness. "Know, Monsieur," he pronounced, emphasizing his words as if to give them greater range, "that if I have the honor of being the friend of your ambassador, and if I wish, on occasion, to render him some small services, I do not depend on him in any fashion, any more than on anyone else..."

"However, Monsieur..."

"His Excellency, I can tell you," the Baron continued, implacably, "has considerable obligations to me. If I inform him of your indiscretion, it would cause you considerable difficulty. Let us say no more about the subject, I beg you, and tell me what brings you here. My moments are precious, and you have already wasted, by virtue of this futile incident, half the time that I had allocated to your audience..."

The attaché took it as read, and never dared complain again.

Two or three events of that sort sufficed to convince Rozen of his invulnerability. Who would dare to attack him henceforth? As he had told Sokoloff, the former convict of Cayenne, once sentenced to lifelong hard labor, had become the king of Paris, the king of the world: a king without responsibility.

III. One Morning at the Banque Saint-Magloire

Even though it was only half past nine in the morning, visitors and solicitors were already presenting themselves in the large reception room that served as a antechamber to the celebrated banker of the Place Vendôme, to whom they were introduced by two liveried lackeys.

In summer and winter alike, whether he had spent the night working or partying, the Baron de Saint-Magloire always granted his audiences at ten o'clock in the morning. It was an inflexible rule.

At ten o'clock precisely, the office door would open, and a dignified senior usher in a black coat tailored in the France style with a silver chain around his neck would appear, list in hand. The receptions began and succeeded one another rapidly, but the list was rarely completely exhausted. It was almost always too long for him to see more than half or two-thirds of the people thereon, all the more so because it did not only comprise the people sitting in the waiting-room. There were others, individuals of note, waiting in two further rooms in order not to be recognized. There were several small rooms set aside for that purpose, in which only one person could be accommodated.

At a quarter to noon, the senior usher put a cross by the name of the last person admitted, folded up his list and announced in a solemn voice that: "Monsieur le Baron is no longer receiving anyone." Thus, for fear of disappointment, people arrived early, in order to obtain a good place in the queue.

This morning, as usual, the Baron de Saint-Magloire had arrived at his office a few minutes before ten. After having arranged his papers and cast a glance over his personal correspondence—for the bank's correspondence was opened and read in the offices by secretaries—he rang. The usher appeared.

"Are there many people today, Florent?" the Baron asked.

"About fifteen, Monsieur."

"Known?"

"If Monsieur le Baron will cast an eye over the list..."

The Baron took the list from the usher's hand and scanned it. "These first, he said, making little blue crosses after a few names; the others later, at random." Then, pointing at one of the names on the list, he said: "Send in Monsieur Baker first; he has an appointment."

Mr. Baker was an employee of the famous Henry Albert, the thieves' banker. He was the man personally responsible for altering numbers and forging all possible signatures. The transformation of a zero into a six or a nine, according to circumstance, or the suppression of the tail of a six or nine to make an irreproachable zero was child's play for that talented accountant.

"Madame Blanchardières?" the banker went on, continuing his reading. "Send her to see the head of the legal department—Monsieur Pamproux too. Who is this Monsieur Vaulnier?"

"An old white-haired gentleman of respectable appearance. Monsieur le Baron saw him last week."

"Oh, I remember…he has an iron-bearing spring to be floated. Send him in right away—I'll get rid of him."

The usher bowed, took the list and went out.

Saint-Magloire took his place at his desk—one of those marvelous "business models" recently imported from America in which everything is planned for the comfort of the person making use of it, in which ever paper, note and document has its place within arm's reach and whose drawers and secret compartments are so numerous that an examining magistrate conducting a search would spend an entire day going through them. The desk was placed near a large window, in such a fashion that the banker was half in shade while his visitor, sitting opposite, received the light full in his face—which made the examination of his physiognomy easy.

Once seated, he opened a drawer and took out a snub-nosed revolver, whose chamber and mechanism he checked carefully, and which he placed within easy reach of his hand, beneath a file that hid it from view. With that done, he cast a glance at the mirror, and waited. He did not have to wait long.

The door opened and the usher announced: "Monsieur Vaulnier!"

The visitor had ever appearance of an honest man. He was about sixty, slightly portly but not too much for his height, with a placid face, carefully shaven, and snow-white hair, still quite abundant, correctly dressed without aspiring to elegance, like a rentier from the Marais or a provincial land-owner.

"Well," Monsieur Vaulnier began, "Monsieur le Baron has kindly take an interest in my mineral-water enterprise…"

"Speak without circumlocutions," Saint-Magloire interjected. "No one can hear us."

"Oh! Well, then…I've undertaken all the research with which Monsieur le Baron charged me with regard to the Banque de France's delivery vehicle."

"And what have you learned?"

"The coup was carried out as the police supposed. A man dragging a small handcart hooked himself on to the back of the truck as if to take advantage of the horse's aid. That didn't awaken any suspicion. The handcar was covered with a tarpaulin, under which a second man was lying. In the course of the journey the latter got into the truck and passed the sacks and wads to his comrade."

"That's what the Sûreté report said," observed the Baron, indifferently, toying with his paper-knife. "Don't you know anything else?"

"Yes, but I wanted to check the enquiry," the gentleman replied, slightly nettled. "Although I have every confidence in the Sûreté, to which I've had the honor of belonging, I don't trust anyone but myself."

"So?"

"When the job was done, the man got back under the tarpaulin with his booty. The handcart was detached from the vehicle, which continued on its way, and the two men—the second having got out in order to push the cart, which was now heavy—headed for the Gare du Nord."

"You think so?"

"I'm certain of it, Monsieur le Baron. I found traces of their passage myself. I could almost give you're their description..."

"No need," the Baron interjected, swiftly. "I know that you're a skillful policeman, Monsieur Vaulnier—but what I want to know is what became of the stolen money and bonds. You know that the bonds included a certain sum originating in this establishment."

"I know that, Monsieur le Baron."

"In consequence, I'm one of the victims of the theft. What interests me above all isn't having the thieves arrested—that's up to the police—but knowing whether I can recover anything."

"Oh, as to that, Monsieur le Baron, you can put on your mourning-dress. At present, everything is in a safe place in England."

"Then let's say no more about it," said Saint-Magloire with a sigh. "Thank you, Monsieur Vaulnier. This is for your trouble." He held out a hundred-franc note.

The other took it, examined it as a matter of habit, and put it in his wallet. "I should stop making enquiries, then?"

"Absolutely."

"If Monsieur le Baron needs me or anything else..."

"That's understood. I have your address. *Au revoir*, Monsieur Vaulnier."

"Your humble servant, Monsieur le Baron," the gentleman said, as he withdrew.

Saint-Magloire pressed the button of an electric bell. "Send Monsieur Baker in," he said to the usher.

A few moments later, the door opened and Baker, a tall thin Englishman, fair-haired and phlegmatic, made his entrance.

"It all went without a hitch," said Saint-Magloire. "I've kept track of the investigation under the pretext of being one of the victims of the theft. The funds have arrived safely over there. It's up to you now."

Without saying a word, Baker bowed and went out.

The Baron rang again and made a sign.

The usher announced: "Monsieur le Prince Coriolan Bocconi."

A slim young man, buttoned up in an elegant morning-suit, presented himself. Had his name been lacking, his tinted complexion, his large black eyes and his curly hair would have identified him as an Italian. He bowed profoundly. The Baron greeted him with a simple nod of the head.

"Monsieur le Baron..." he began.

"Sit down Prince," Saint-Magloire interjected, "and tell me what brings you here."

"Monsieur le Baron," the young man continued, having taken his place in the armchair situated directly opposite the desk, "I believe that I need no introduction, I am, as you know, Prince Coriolan Bocconi, of the Palermo Bocconis."

"Indeed," said Saint-Magloire. "I've had the pleasure of meeting you at the Cercle des Étrangers."

"My family is rich," the Prince went on. "I own a great deal of land in Sicily…but the farmers are having difficulty paying, the rents are late…in brief…"

"In brief, you need money," Saint-Magloire put in, again.

"Alas, yes, Monsieur le Baron."

"Madame Morvillars doesn't want to fork out any longer?"

Stung by the directness of that remark, the Prince started as if he had received a electric shock. His eyes flashed in such a manner that, without losing his apparent impassivity, Saint-Magloire put his hand under the file to grip the revolver—but it only lasted a moment. The flash died away, and Coriolan Bocconi resumed his obsequious expression.

"I don't understand, Monsieur le Baron," he said.

"Of course not," said Saint-Magloire sarcastically. "There are no mysteries between us. Everyone, including me, knows that, although your family goes back to the crusades and was once very wealthy, that wealth as dissipated a long time ago. All that remains of it are a few pieces of land in the mountains, which produce little and are burdened more mortgages than they're worth. Finally, you've exhausted your credit with all the money-lenders in Paris. You're signature is worthless."

"Monsieur le Baron!" cried the Prince, who had gone white.

"I'm not saying this to offend you. We men of finance know nothing but balance-sheets, and it's your balance-sheet that I'm establishing. You would, therefore, be utterly without resources if you did not have the aid of a woman who thinks you handsome and proves it with her liberality…"

"This is too much!" Bocconi roared, rising to his feet. "You'll make me forget that I'm in your house…"

"Sit down, my dear Prince," the Baron continued, his tone still placidly ironic. "I'm not criticizing you, I'm congratulating you. You're not the only one who's playing the role of Rubempré.[35] How many of our companions at the club, including the most brilliant, only owe their luxury to their elegance and good looks?"

"Well, yes," murmured the young man, lowering his eyes. "I've fallen out with Madame Morvillars, and that's why I need money, for I want to pay her

---

[35] The name assumed by a character in Balzac's *Comédie humaine*, who embarks reluctantly on a career as a dandy and gigolo; he plays central roles in *Illusions perdues* and *Splendeurs et misères des courtisanes*.

what I owe her...what she lent me...because it was only a loan that I accepted, of course."

"I'll believe anything you wish," said the Baron, with a hint of mockery, "but I beg your pardon; while chatting we're forgetting that time is passing. How much do you need?"

"Oh, not much. Fifteen or twenty thousand francs."

"You call that 'not much,' do you? Damn. Well, let's assume that I agree to lend them to you—what guarantee will you offer me? Not your land, I assume? I've told you what I think of that."

"But..." The embarrassed you man murmured.

"Well, personally, I have something better than that to propose to you. You're very good friends, if I'm not mistaken, with ***'s *chargé d'affaires*?"

"Yes, indeed."

"You can call on him whenever you wish?"

"Yes—but so what?"

"Well, my dear Prince, it might happen that a piece of paper left on a desk—a letter, telegram...cast an eye over it, take note of its contents..."

"I don't understand," stammered the Prince.

"You will. I deal on the stock market. A new political decision, known by me twenty-four hours before anyone else, might permit a fruitful operation."

"That's true."

"And in that operation, you'd have your share."

"Yes, but..."

"One recommendation: don't forget the waste-paper baskets. One sometimes finds treasures therein...torn up notes that can be pieced together, and which are of pulsating interest..."

"But you're proposing that I become a spy!" exclaimed the young man, astounded.

"Oh, what an ugly word! Don't pronounce it, my dear Prince. It's as if, with regard to your liaison with Madame Morvillars, someone called you a..."

"If I consent," the Prince interrupted, abruptly reaching a decision, "What will be my reward?"

"I've told you: a share in the profits you make me. Perhaps fifty or a hundred thousand francs a year. That depends on you—your luck, your flair..."

"I accept," Coriolan concluded, offering his hand to the Baron.

The latter, taking two thousand-franc bills from his pocket, put them in the beggar's hands, and, rising to his feet to indicate that the interview was over, said to the prince: "Take that on account, but try to have something soon. I'll give you a substantial immediate advance on your fifty thousand francs."

"Monsieur Dubois du Rhin," announced the usher.

Monsieur Dubois du Rhin's real name was simply Dubois, but as the député of the département of the Rhine, he had, like several of his colleagues, added the name of his constituency to his own, in order to distinguish himself from his namesakes.

He was a short, plump man, ruddy in face and hair, with a self-important air and a very common appearance, a type-specimen of the vain, pompous and impertinent upstart.

When he came in, the banker stood up to shake his hand.

"Bonjour, my dear député," he said. "To what god fortune do I owe the honor of your visit?"

"Hmm...the thing is..." said the député, who did not exactly have the gift of eloquence and whose entire role in the Chambre consisted of voting for the minister whatever the circumstances, "the thing is that I've come to ask for a small favor."

"Speak freely. I'll be happy to help."

"Thanks very much! You know that, for my election, having to compete with an adversary anchored in the region, I had heavy expenses to meet. You were kind enough to help me..."

"It was a duty for me to support a friend of the minister."

"Yes, yes...so I gave you some promissory notes..."

"Some of which have fallen due," the Baron put in. "I understand. You've come to repay them and thank me..."

"No, it's not that!" said the député, whose assurance had completely departed. "Those notes..."

"Well?"

"I'm a little hard up; I had to spend a great deal to take up residence in Parris. So...you understand?"

"You want to renew them?" said Saint-Magloire, graciously. "Just come right out and say it..."

"You consent?" exclaimed Monsieur Dubois du Rhin, whose face reddened more deeply with pleasure.

"I can refuse you nothing. You can go into my officers immediately; my employees will have their orders. But I think that, in return, you might be useful to me."

"Gladly!" said the député.

"You're still well in with the Minister of the Interior?"

"As well as it's possible to be."

"Then do me the favor of recommending a worthy fellow to him, in whom a lady of my acquaintance is interested. He wants to be appointed Commissaire of Police in your département..."

"Nothing easier," said Dubois du Rhin, swelling with pride. "It's as good as done. What is your protégé's name?"

"Albert Petitpierre."

"Petitpierre!" cried the député, starting. "You can't be serious!"

"On the contrary. I'm very serious, as you can see."

"But he's a scoundrel..."

"Pooh! That's a harsh word, for a man who had committed a few peccadilloes."

"It's accurate, Monsieur le Baron—perfectly accurate. I know this Petitpierre very well. He was a businessman, and went bankrupt in a fashion that many people considered to be fraudulent. I don't know why he wasn't sent to the Assize Court! It's impossible to make him a man of law."

"Bah! I thought that, thanks to your influence..."

"Nothing in the world could persuade me to support such a candidate."

"That's unfortunate," said the Baron, dryly. "Very unfortunate—for in that case, being interested in the poor fellow, I'll be obliged to give him what he needs to get out of trouble—and I shall consecrate to that good work all of your overdue promissory notes."

"My debts..." Stammered the astounded député, "but since I've renewed them...that's agreed..."

"It was agreed a little while ago, but you're really not very obliging. Tit for tat. I'm obliged to recover the money and I beg you to return it right away."

"But it's impossible," moaned Dubois du Rhin, whose fine coloration had vanished.

"Everything seems to be impossible for you today, my dear député," observed the Baron, sarcastically. "Well, too bad. That's my ultimatum: have Petitpierre appointed commissaire, or I'll take you to court. You're greatly exaggerating Petitpierre's record. The Prefect of Police has told me that his judiciary file is blank, and I know that the court made a decision saying that there was no case to answer. Damn it, you shake the hands of people who've gone the same way every day."

"All right, I admit defeat," said the député, piteously. "I'll go to the minister; I'll try..."

"Good! I knew that you'd be reasonable. I'll see you soon, my dear friend; bring me good news for my protégé—who, I assure you, has been persecuted in a most unjust fashion. The notes will be all ready for renewal..."

The député withdrew, his head bowed.

The Baron rang the bell. The usher appeared.

"Is Monsieur Petitpierre here?" the Baron asked.

"He's waiting in the next room."

"Send him in."

Tall, thin and jaundiced, with angular features and a hesitant step, the Baron's protégé had the most villainous face imaginable. The gold-rimmed spectacles he wore instead of masking his evasive gaze in order to make it seem franker, added to the somewhat unsavory impression of his physiognomy. He was dressed in a long frock-coat, worn by brushing and showing its threads. Under his arm he was carrying a voluminous briefcase stuffed with papers, which gave him the appearance of one of those shady businessmen that one sees so often in the vestibules of justices of the peace, on the lookout for clients.

Petitpierre bowed, folding his lanky body in two as if he wanted to touch the floor with his forehead, and darted a glance at the desk on which the banker was leaning his elbows.

"Monsieur the Baron sent for me?" he said, in a honeyed voice.

"Yes. Where are we in our endeavors?"

"Making progress; I have every reason to hope that Monsieur le Baron will be satisfied."

"Let's see!"

Petitpierre sat down, put his greasy hat on the floor, set his briefcase on his knees, opened it and took out two pieces of paper, which he handed to Saint-Magloire.

The latter placed then on his desk in order to examine them. They were two letters—or, rather, one letter, reproduced in two identical exemplars.

"Not bad, truly," said the Baron, after a few minutes. "You have talent, Petitpierre."

"Monsieur le Baron is too kind," murmured the forger, taking on an equivocal expression.

"Except that this is only a copy, word for word. Could you imitate the handwriting as well in a different document?"

"If Monsieur le Baron wishes to take a look," said Petitpierre, taking another piece of paper from his briefcase.

"Very good!" exclaimed Saint-Magloire, taking the piece of paper. "This is superb!"

The sheet he was holding was a document bearing the same heading, written on similar paper and with the same handwriting as the letters, but different in its import.

"I think," Petitpierre insinuated, lowering his eyes with feigned modesty, "That the lady would have a great deal of trouble denying that it's her handwriting...I'm not talking about experts; they're of no account to me."

"It is indeed well-indeed," said the Baron, examining it with a magnifying glass. "The bold strokes and the upstrokes are perfect."

"And it will always be thus—but Monsieur le Baron is doubtless unaware of how much work is necessary for that: the failed attempts, the long nights. It's worth..."

"Monsieur Petitpierre," Saint-Magloire interjected, abruptly, "You're forgetting that I've saved you from the bagne..."

"Monsieur le Baron," Petitpierre murmured.

"I have here," Saint-Magloire continued, pointing to his desk, "more than is required to send you there whenever I wish. I have, therefore, every reason to count on your devotion."

"Oh, Monsieur le Baron, I belong to you body and soul," protested the other, putting his hands together as if he were saying a prayer.

"That's good. I can use your remarkable talent for forgery, but I don't want you to raise your voice. Nor do I want you ever to try to find out any more than I tell you..."

"Mute as the tomb."

"I'm undertaking a diplomatic campaign; you'll help me to accomplish it. You'll furnish me with the documents I need—but never keep a single note, piece of paper or copy for yourself to use a weapon against me. That would be a waste of time; I've taken my precautions. You'll doom yourself without hurting me."

"Understood, Monsieur le Baron."

"And now, in order that you'll rest easier, and can work without being disturbed, I've arranged for you to leave Paris and have obtained a position for you, which will shelter you from any suspicion, and give you an entrée into the Sûreté Générale, where you'll try to make friends. You're going to be appointed as a special Commissaire of Police."

"Me?" exclaimed Petitpierre, bewildered.

"You—and in your own homeland. I need to have a man of my own out there who will close his eyes to certain comings and goings at the frontier...who can help out with them, if need be. Understand?"

"I'm at Monsieur le Baron's orders."

"Good. Go—I'll tell you when the time comes; in the meantime, continue to work on your...imitations."

When Petitpierre paused, standing up with his hat in his hand, Saint-Magloire looked at him in annoyance. "Well, what are you waiting for?" he demanded.

"I have a few words to say to you." Without waiting for authorization to speak, Petitpierre continued in a tearful tone: "I've been obliged to give up the work that nourishes me, and if I'm obliged to leave, I'll need to make a few preparations."

"I understand." Saint-Magloire took fifty louis from a drawer, which he placed on the edge of the desk.

Petitpierre reached out a hand, and the louis disappeared into his pocket. Then he bowed, as emphatically as before, and walked backwards to the door through which he had entered.

"What a scoundrel, indeed!" murmured the Baron, shrugging his shoulders. "A stupid scoundrel. He doesn't even have the courage to dispute his ignominy. At any rate, I have him tied up, ankles and wrists..."

The usher appeared at the door again.

"Who's next?"

"Monsieur Briançon, the old bespectacled gentleman the Baron sent away yesterday."

"Tell him to come back tomorrow...or, rather, to wait until I send for him. Next?"

"Madame de Saint-Lai," said the usher, after consulting his list.

"Send her in right away."

The usher went out, to return almost immediately, escorting the visitor.

Mademoiselle Joséphine Lai—de Saint-Lai in society and "Fifine" in private—was a pure-blooded product of the Butte de Montmartre. Of medium height, still fairly slim, as restless as a viper, she had the unhealthy pallor of children brought up in the vitiated atmosphere of workers' hovels—a pallor that certain Parisiennes would like to pass off as distinction, but which is nothing but chlorosis.

Her features were far from symmetrical, her upturned nose being a trifle rascally and her mouth too wide, but that mouth opened on two rows of pretty white teeth, while cleverly fluffed-up red hair and two wide eyes gave the whole a pert appearance that was not without charm.

Joséphine as thirty-eight years old, but her face had not been wrinkled by the adventurous life she had led. At a young age, she had been apprenticed to a dressmaker. Her vicious tendencies had been rapidly awakened by the spicy talk of the seamstresses, and one evening, when one of her brothers returned to the paternal dwelling where everyone went to bed in a reckless promiscuity, Fifine became his mistress. It was a promising debut.

Soon she left Papa's home to live with a shop-assistant, who kept her for three months; then she lived for a while with a professional cyclist, who initiated her into the secrets of the pedal and obliged her to "play the music halls" in order to help out with the household expenses. Routinely beaten, she quickly wearied of that lover and crossed the river.

In the Latin Quarter, she lived for two years with a law student and, as she had a keen intelligence, the latter succeeded in educating her to some extent. When his studies were concluded, the student left the Quarter and his mistress to go to some principal hole to make his debut in the local magistracy. Gradually, Fifine fell into black poverty and finally ended up in a brothel, where she had some success between two o'clock and seven as the "*plat du jour*." There, her luck turned in the form of a rich old gentleman who, finding her to his taste, set her up in a furnished apartment and launched her into gallant society.

For a few years, Fifine was counted among fashionable whores. She led a life of parties, took superb trips with important foreigners quilted with gold, and was prudent enough to put a few thousand francs to one side.

Thanks to that precaution, she found herself sheltered from poverty, and when the day came that she had to renounce her status among the *horizontales* of note, she went to find the madam of the brothel where she had encountered hr first serious protector. She entered into partnership that entrepreneur, who was a good businesswoman, and when the latter died, she continued to run the house, which was perhaps the best-patronized in Paris. Very amiable, with a rare skill, she was able to put herself on the best possible terms with the Administration by rendering some small but much-appreciated services to the Prefecture.

Naturally, Saint-Magloire, who did not neglect the smallest detail in order to perfect his gigantic enterprise based on blackmail, had made the acquaintance of this remarkable professional. It had not taken long, thanks to a few liberalities and taking care not to be numbered among her clientele, to have Fifine entirely at his disposal, to such an extent that the best tips were reserved for him. The Levantine came before the Prefecture of Police, to which Madame de Saint-Lai no longer gave any information except that of which her friend Saint-Magloire had no need.

Rozen paid generously, moreover, and his purse, always open, assured him of the devoted collaboration of the retired *horizontale*.

Such was the woman that the usher had just introduced into the banker's office.

Fifine was radiant. She had brought a good tip, which she has got from one of her clients, a chambermaid in the home of the Marquise de X. The latter was the wife of a highly-placed Statesman, who had the most complete influence over her husband. Malicious tongues said that she led him "by the nose," and even added "by the horns."

"How beautiful you look, my little Fifine," said the Baron, getting up in order to chuck Madame Saint-Lai under the chin in a familiar fashion. "Do you have the secret of eternal youth?"

"Too flattering Baron—you don't believe a word of it."

"You're wrong to think so, my dear." And he added, with a well-feigned grimace of disappointment. "Be nice!"

"Baron, you're a truly marvelous man. What a pity you aren't one of my clients!"

"All right, all right!" said the banker. "You haven't come here to hawk your wares. What have you brought me?"

"A real treat!" said the visitor, taking a letter out of her bosom. "Judge for yourself."

"Indeed," said the Baron, taking the letter from her hand. "It's from the Duc. But look—the seal isn't broken"

"No, but that won't pose any difficulty, will it? Just be careful. Last time, the escutcheon wasn't replaced perfectly. My client had a scare. She costs me a lot, you know, and she's fond of her job..."

"Don't worry," said Saint-Magloire, laughing.

The letter was closed by a large wax seal bearing a coat of arms. He put it, address down, on a shelf covered with a piece of white paper. Then he took a sheet of led from one of his drawers, which he carefully placed over the seal.

"It sends shivers down my back," said Fifine, "to see you do that."

"Don't be silly," said the Baron, shrugging his shoulders. He took a stout hammer from a cupboard and brought it down with a smart tap ion the lead sheet. "Here," he said. "Look."

The wax was reduced to dust, but in the plate, the imprint of the seal appeared distinctly, like a sculpted engraving.

"Marvelous!" said Fifine.

"The rest's no more than a joke," the Baron continued, putting a little bowl filled with water on top of an alcohol lamp. "Two minutes of steam, and the gum comes unstuck...

"There you go—we're the masters of the precious letter."

Indeed, he took it out of the envelope he had opened by the methods he had explained to Fifine and started scanning it.

"Very funny...he's jealous...he's heaping reproaches upon his mistress."

"Jealous of whom?"

"Of the husband."

"Oh, what a farce! One would pay money to see it!"

"Wouldn't one just? Now, as it's necessary to return the letter, let's make its portrait."

Saint-Magloire put the hammer back in the cupboard and took out a small camera. The daylight as poor but the apparatus was equipped with a powerful electric lamp manufactured by Sokoloff, which could replace sunlight advantageously. The Baron connected the wire of the lamp to the electric socket on his desk, and the light appeared, dazzling. Then he placed the letter that he wanted to photograph at an appropriate distance from the apparatus. "Don't move!" Fifine's mocking voice called out.

"It's done," said the Baron, going to replace the camera in the cupboard. "Now I'll seal the letter again." He replaced it in the envelope, gummed the edges, and closed it up. Then he took some red wax, similar to that of the seal, melted it, and used the lead sheet to seal it.

"Look," he said to Fifine.

"No doubt about it, it's perfect," the latter replied. "It would fool the Duc himself."

"Now go, quickly. I have lots of people to see."

"Hang on," said Madame de Saint-Lai. "You're forgetting something."

"Yes, that's true," the Baron replied, smiling. He reached into his pocket and took two hundred-franc bill from his wallet. "Here, that's for today. Next time, we'll see."

"Thanks, Baron," said Fifine, sketching a comical curtsy. "A pleasure."

"Go, go!"

Madame de Saint-Lai disappeared into the corridor.

The usher came in.

"Who's next?" asked the Baron. "Hurry up, it's getting late."

"There's a gentleman who insists on being seen today, before leaving, he says, for the provinces."

"What's his name?"

"Charles Lavardens."

V. An Old Comrade

Saint-Magloire could not suppress a start of surprise.

Lavardens!

That name immediately reminded him of the compatriot he had known in London, so miraculously rediscovered in Cayenne, and then in Venezuela—and then lost to sight for years.

What could he be doing in the establishment of the Baron de Saint-Magloire?

Could he have recognized me? Rozen thought. *No, it's impossible...*

He darted a glance at the mirror placed opposite his desk, and the mirror sent back his banker's face, so different from that of the convict of Cayenne. He smiled in satisfaction. *Why refuse to see him then?* Saint-Magloire said to himself. *Have I anything to fear?*

He shrugged his shoulders proudly.

No, the man who had accomplished all the magnificent feats of his life was no coward. The audacious man who, on the same evening that he had escaped from prison, had gone to show himself off with a woman at the theater before setting off for the frontier; the reckless fellow who had organized the anarchist revolt at the penitentiary in order to betray it to the governor; the madman who had coolly risked that escape from Cayenne, in which so many others had found, instead of liberty, a hideous death...that man could not be fearful of any peril whatsoever...

Saint-Magloire—or, rather, Rozen—was one of those who, on the contrary, found a keen pleasure in braving danger.

"Have Monsieur Lavardens come in," he said to the usher.

The only precaution he took was to veil his gaze by means of a pince-nez with smoked lenses.

Charles Lavardens came in, and made the profound bow of a solicitor. That reassured Saint-Magloire fully.

He doesn't suspect a thing, he thought. *So what is he doing here?*

"Monsieur," Lavardens began, "I've heard mention of you as a man favorable to bold enterprises..."

The banker nodded his head without making any reply.

"So, I've come to seek you out without hesitation. My name is Charles Lavardens. I'm a former non-commissioned officer in the marine infantry, and for several years I've been the principal agent of the rubber manufacturer Hubaut and Company—but Hubaut and Company. Having made some bad investments, had to be liquidated, and I found myself on the sidewalk..."

Why, Saint-Magloire said to himself, *he's come to ask me for a job! That's funny!*

"Then," Lavardens went on, "I thought of a business proposal that I believe to be very good. Do you know Cayenne, Monsieur?"

"What?" said Saint-Magloire, unable to suppress a start of surprise.

"If you had studied the resources of that sacrificed colony, even if only in books, you would have taken account of the immensity of its resources, which are unfortunately neglected. Charged by my company with purchasing liquid rubber, I traveled through Guiana in all directions. I've seen forests of mahogany and ironwood there, and, in addition, essences, that are very easy to buy and only cost the trouble of taking them...

"I've dreamed of a large-scale exploitation of those forests, and I've come to ask you for the modest capital that will be necessary to begin it...a capital that will be doubled in two or three years...for the more one puts in, the greater the profit will be..."

Saint-Magloire was hardly listening. He was thinking about something else.

Lavardens had lost his job. Lavardens was devoid of resources. He was an intelligent and honest man. Saint-Magloire also knew that he was endowed with a confidence sometimes extended to naivety; he was not unaware that the ex-non-commissioned officer in the marine infantry was, in spite of his audacity, a man of weak character, easy to manipulate. The business proposal he was offering was evidently feasible, as Saint-Magloire knew better than anyone, having also studied Guiana...

But the exploitation required preliminary steps, a voyage, an installation, wasted time...

And Lavardens might be useful for much more rapid and no less fruitful work. It ought to be possible to recruit him to assist an enterprise with which Sokoloff had endowed the association.

The flow of gold ingots emerging from Sokoloff's workshop offered no difficulty or peril for the excellent reason that the gold was real, authentic and honest, only different from gold from the Transvaal or Alaska by virtue of its genesis. The most skillful chemist and the most experienced assayer would have been absolutely incapable of discovering the slightest inferiority or flaw in the synthesized gold. In addition, all the nuggets offered for sale went through the mail, like letters.

There was, however, reason to fear that the abundance of the precious metal would eventually awaken suspicion in the restricted society, always quick-witted and suspicious, that was involved in the trade in non-monetary gold. Eventually, they would wonder how much gold could be emerging "into the wild" from the coffers of the Banque Saint-Magloire.

The bank was certainly rich enough; it was notoriously interested in a large enough quantity of auriferous deposits for the matter to be explained without too much difficulty, and could not even be challenged on the legitimacy of those reiterated operations. However, the small game hunters might become inquisitive, make enquiries, and try to trace the source. Who could tell whether they might not get as far as Sokoloff and penetrate part of his secret? That would put the cat among the pigeons!

Undoubtedly, of course, everyone had the right to make artificial gold, if that artificial gold had all the physical, chemical and salable qualities of natural gold. Strictly speaking, it ought to be more valuable, because of the genius and effort expended in its manufacture. Had not the question already been raised with regard to artificial rubies?[36]

But the spell would be broken. There would be indiscretions, scandals...

It was better to defend, jealously, the mystery that hid the source and course of the Pactolus from profane eyes.

To that effect, Saint-Magloire had thought for a long time, the wisest thing to do would be to have a trustworthy man who would go from market to market, letting ingots out at a maximum of four or five at a time, in such a way as not to awaken any suspicion or eve any surprise. The snag was finding that trustworthy man.

Abruptly, the banker sensed that Lavardens could play the role admirably. The difficulty was simply a matter of raising the question. Given his ignorance of scientific matters, might he not think that it was a matter of forgery? Might he not imagine that a trap was being set for him, and seek to avoid it?

The idea then occurred to Saint-Magloire to play the great game boldly, in order to try to find out what Lavardens thought of him.

"You tell me, Monsieur," he began coolly, "that you've made numerous voyages to Guiana. You must have heard mention of a detainee whose name generated a god deal of talk a few years ago..."

"What was his name?" asked Lavardens.

"Gaston Rozen."

"Rozen!" exclaimed Lavardens. "I've done more than hear mention of him, Monsieur—I knew him intimately."

"No!"

"Yes. I happened to meet him before his misfortunes, when he was in England, and I ran into him again in Cayenne. But why mention the man to me?"

"Because I too knew the poor fellow, whose misfortunes saddened me."

This was said in an emotional tone, by which Lavardens allowed himself to be caught. "That unfortunate," he continued, "I mourned wholeheartedly. Endowed with an extraordinary intelligence and qualities of the highest order, he would have gone far if he had employed his remarkable faculties better."

"I've been told that he met a frightful end," Saint-Magloire put in.

---

[36] Although the first artificial rubies were produced in 1837 it was not until 1903 that Auguste Verneuil industrialized the process and began to mass-produce stones commercially, so the text is slightly ahead of developments.

Lavardens did not reply immediately. The timbre of his interlocutor's voice, and certain mannerisms has awakened a confused memory in him. Instinctively, he raised his head and looked the banker in the face, long and hard.

"That's strange," he murmured.

In spite of his self-confidence, the Baron started. "What are you thinking, Monsieur?" he asked, slightly disconcerted. In his anxiety, which he only succeeded in hiding at the cost of a violent effort, he carelessly dropped the pince-nez that was masking his gaze. He replaced it immediately, but, rapid as his gesture was, Lavardens had had time to see that gaze, of which he retained an ineradicable memory.

"Oh!" he repeated. "That's strange. It seems to me..."

"What does it seem to you?" enquired Saint-Magloire, increasingly anxious. At that moment, the banker sincerely regretted the desire he had had to know what Lavardens thought about Rozen. He understood that he had to pay for that audacity, to discover whether he really had been recognized. "Explain yourself, Monsieur—tell me, I beg you, to what I ought to attribute your surprise."

"Forgive me, Monsieur," said Lavardens. "I just had a crazy idea. I..."

"What do you mean?" Saint-Magloire demanded.

"Once again, Monsieur, I beg your pardon. I must be the victim of a hallucination...but I thought just now, at the sound of your voice, although slightly changed, but most of all at the gaze that I was able to meet when your pince-nez fell...that I was once again in Rozen's presence."

"I don't understand," said Saint-Magloire. "You know as well as I do that Rozen is dead. His decease has been officially established. You were dreaming, my dear Monsieur Lavardens."

"I was dreaming!" Lavardens repeated. "And yet, in the short time I've been talking to you, I've found the inflection of his voice in yours; during the few seconds that I was able to see your eyes uncovered, I recognized his gaze, perhaps unique in all the world, which rendered him so seductive and terrible at the same time." Carried away by the situation, he added: "Finally, even though it might irritate you and get me thrown out, I tell you with the utmost conviction: you are Gaston Rozen!"

"You're mad!" the banker growled, with an angry gesture. "Rozen is dead."

"I can affirm the contrary. I saw him in Venezuela after his escape from the penitentiary. He told me about his escape himself. He told me his dream for the future, of winning back an enviable place in the world. He asked me for help. I helped him. Oh, I know that he has skill enough, even genius enough, to have accomplished that prodigy. Baron de Saint-Magloire, you are definitely Rozen."

The banker had recovered his self-composure. What did it matter, after all, that he had been recognized by Lavardens, whom he knew to be a good man, incapable of betraying him, and over whom he would soon have a hold, by virtue of gratitude.

"Well, yes," he said, facing up with his habitual audacity to the peril that he had so recklessly provoked. "It's me. And now that I'm at your discretion, you've won the game. What you were imploring, you can now demand..."

"No!" cried Lavardens. "No! God forbid that I should profit from a surprise to demand anything whatsoever from you. You've committed serious wrongs, it's true; you've escaped punishment and you've become, thanks to your intelligence, better employed this time, a man of the elite. Rozen really is dead, in fact. It's the Baron de Saint-Magloire that I salute. I remain the solicitor that I was when I came in."

"Thank you," said the banker, extending his hand. "You're a superior individual, Lavardens. Social prejudices have not eroded your fine generosity—and the Baron de Saint-Magloire only asks, in consequence, that he might prove his gratitude to you

"Just now, you talked to me about a business proposal that I believe to be excellent, but which requires time and effort—a great deal of time and effort. For myself, I'll propose one to you that will yield results must finer and more immediate. It's a rapid and brilliant fortune that I'm offering you."

With his facility of speech and his habitual fluency, extended to the point of eloquence, he explained the project that he had conceived.

As he had feared, however, his interlocutor's physiognomy, instead of expressing enthusiasm and joy, darkened instead, depicting the most vivid opposition.

"I greatly regret," Lavardens said, uncomfortably, when Rozen had finished his explanation, "that I am unable to accept what you propose."

"But think," said the banker, annoyed. "Our gold is real gold, in no way distinguishable from gold found in placers." He took a small ingot from a drawer and threw it on to the desk. "Here," he added, "can you see any difference?"

"I know that it's false gold, and that's enough for me," Lavardens replied, softly. "There's no getting away from that." He had jumped to the conclusion, from the very beginning, hat he had fallen into a forgers' den. It was, therefore, by criminal means that Rozen was offering to make his fortune.

Lavardens almost regretted the generous impulse that he had made previously.

All Rozen's eloquence, all his power of suggestion, had been thwarted by the irreducible stubbornness of that honest man.

Abruptly, however, with his usual decisiveness, the banker changed tack. "Still the same, then, my dear Lavardens! Still riding high on virtue! I suspected as much, but I wanted to test you. Forgive me. I've seen the rascality of men at such close range, and have suffered so much from it, that I've become terribly misanthropic, pessimistic and skeptical.

"Do you know that nine out of ten of those who pass in society for honest people, in every social class and society, would have jumped at the proposition I've just made to you? You, on the contrary, didn't flinch. What a pleasure it is, in the work of rehabilitation that I've undertaken, and what a consolation, finally to find a man of integrity, resistant to all temptation, especially when that man is the only one who has already offered me a helping hand when I was in distress...and also, alas, involved in crime."

Rozen smiled, and added: "You know, Lavardens, if it were possible to make artificial gold, as I affirmed to you just now, that gold would not be in the least false...now, now! Don't protest. It would be different from natural gold, that's all, but it would be just as dear, since it would be identical. Unfortunately, the manufacture of gold is an alchemist's chimera. That ingot comes from the Ivory Coast; it emerged from the crucible of nature."

Lavardens gradually relaxed. His trusting nature—weak-minded, even— put him at the mercy of the Levantine's guileful coaxing. He was glad to believe that he had been mistaken. No, Rozen was not a criminal, and that filled him with joy, for he would be able to re-raise the question of the proposal that had brought him to the Place Vendôme, which he had not forgotten.

Saint-Magloire had not lost sight of it either, and while a flood of soothing words escaped his mouth, he told himself that it might be the means of retaining Lavardens' discretion and prevent him from abusing the terrible secret that he had just had the imprudence to let him suspect.

Henceforth, Lavardens had a hold over him. He could doom him with a word...but Rozen had seen other possibilities. Soon, the game was won.

"I told you, my dear Lavardens," he went on, "that you aren't dealing with an ingrate. You need funds for your project in Cayenne. I shall put them at your disposal in advance. When do you want to leave?"

"As soon as possible."

"Which is?"

"A ship is leaving in ten days. If I could take it..."

"You'll take it. Come back in a week. How much will you need?"

"Sixty thousand francs should suffice."

"You'll have a hundred thousand."

"Oh!" exclaimed Lavardens, joyfully. "That's truly superb!"

"Isn't it natural?" said the banker, smiling. "I don't forget my debts." He offered his hand again.

Frightened and bewildered, Lavardens felt as unsteady on his feet as a drunken man. Without knowing exactly why, it pained him to accept money from that man, simultaneously so seductive and disquieting. A scruple came to him at the last moment. But how could he refuse, when the money would get him out of poverty, permit him to give the wife he adored security, and even luxury?

Then again, his hesitation vanished when he told himself that the money, employed in his honest enterprise, would soon be reimbursed with good interest.

"In a week—don't forget," Rozen repeated. Just as Lavardens was leaving however, he called him back. "First, my dear friend, allow the Baron de Saint-Magloire to pay Rozen's debt." And he handed him a thousand-franc note that he had taken from his wallet.

"But..." Lavardens replied.

"You're not going to refuse, I suppose. It's the thousand francs you so kindly advanced to me in Venezuela. I beg your pardon, but I dare not mention interest in regard to that amicable loan. *Au revoir*, my friend...oh! I almost forgot. When you come back, don't give your name. I don't intend to involve my associates in this affair, which is between the two of us. Be kind enough to send in your card in a envelope. I don't want any indiscretions, you understand. I intended to handle the matter personally, with you."

He went with him to the antechamber and shook his hand warmly.

Then, as soon as he returned to his desk, he pressed the button of the electric bell nervously.

"Send someone to look for Monsieur Robertson," he ordered, "and have him brought to me immediately."

VI. Mr. Robertson

Finding Robertson in Paris would not have been easy if the employee to whom Florent, the usher, gave the commission had not had a precise indication. It was, in any case, not the first time that Joseph, the Banque Saint-Magloire's young groom, had undertaken such a search.

Several times, already, he had been sent to run after Robertson, and knew by now where to find him, according to the hour. Until ten o'clock in the morning he was at his domicile—his "home," as he called it—from ten till midday at the bar in the Rue de Hanovre where the bookmakers met; from noon to two at the restaurant; after that, except for race days, at the bar, until seven in the evening. Then, if he was not too drunk, he returned to the restaurant. In the opposite case, he spent the evening sitting on a stool in the bar, leaning his elbows on the table—unless, which was not rare—he slid underneath it.

Mr. Robertson—alias Bastien, alias Macaron—had, as one can see, very regular habits.

It was, therefore, at the bar in the Rue de Hanovre that Macaron spent the greater part of his time, drinking all kinds of beverages, smoking cigarettes and holding forth. It is appropriate to add, however, that in spite of his loquacity, even when he was drunk, he never committed the slightest indiscretion regarding his past. As he said in his picturesque language "it needed a powerful corkscrew to get verses out of his nose."

Unable to speak sufficiently correct English to pass himself off as a veritable islander, he had made up a story. He had, he said, come to France at a very young age, with his parents, pure-blooded English folk, and it was not until they died that he went back there. That explained why he spoke French with a British accent, and his pretended other tongue with a French accent. In consequence, no one had any suspicions about his true identity. On the other hand, it was in the provinces that Macaron had always operated as an anarchist. The Parisian police, therefore, never thought of paying attention to him.

Bastien, alias Macaron, having become Mr. Robertson, spent his days very happily, dividing his existence, like the soldiers in Adolphe Adam's comic opera *Le Chalet*, between "wine, amour and tobacco"—with the variation that wine gave way to a series of varied liqueurs, among which absinthe occupied a preponderant rank. As for amour, it is better not to go into overmuch detail.

As it was not yet midday, Joseph was certain of finding him still in the bar in the Rue de Hanovre. Besides, it was race day at Pau, and that morning there was a big meeting in the bar. The merits of two favorites were being discussed there: Caménste, by Avor out of Miss Catherine, and Aubépine II, by Salvator out of Madame Angot. Aubépine II had a dozen wins to his credit, but all in the provinces; Camériste had run at Auteuil, coming in third, to be sure—but that constituted an advantage in the eyes of many people...

Mr. Robertson was in favor of Aubépine II.

At the most animated point in the discussion, Joseph, pushing through the crowd of punters who, in spite of the law, had come to bring their hundred sous or ten francs to the illicit bookmakers, went up to Macaron and whispered in his ear.

"Oh, my God!" said Bastien, Addressing his friends, he went on: "I beg your pardon, but this little boy has come in search of me on an urgent matter."

He went out.

"What does the Boss want?" he asked Joseph, when they were in the street. With the employees of the Banque Saint-Magloire, Macaron conserved and even emphasized his English pronunciation.[37]

"I don't know," the groom replied. "It was Monsieur Florent, the usher, who told me to come and fetch you right away. Monsieur le Baron is waiting for you."

"Oh, I understand; it's a racing tip—very good!"

"That's quite possible," said the groom. "Have you got anything good for today?"

"Yes—Camériste's a good thing."

"Kemerist," said the gamin. "Good. During my lunch-break, I'll go see my bookie."

"You gamble, then, young fellow?"

"Are you kidding?"

They arrived at the bank; it is only a short distance from the Rue de Hanovre to the Place Vendôme. Macaron ran up the stairs.

Florent was waiting at the top. "Go in, quickly," he said. "Monsieur le Baron wants to talk to you immediately."

The Baron was in his office, pacing back and forth, slightly agitated. He almost regretted summoning Bastien, but it was necessary to take action. Lavardens seemed dangerous. Perhaps Macaron, he thought, with his decisive and free of prejudices would find a means to ward off the blow...

"Well, what's up, Boss? Macaron asked, having closed the door behind him. With Saint-Magloire, Macaron judged that there was no need to retain his fake accent.

"I've just done something stupid," said the banker, angrily.

"Go on! Impossible!"

"I did, I tell you."

---

[37] In this sequence, and some later ones, the author equips Macaron's speech with an eye-dialect crudely suggestive of an English accent, which inevitably defies translation, although I have preserved the groom's misunderstanding based on Bastien's mispronunciation.

"That's not your habit, though," said Macaron, casually sitting down. "How the devil did it happen?"

"I let someone guess my identity."

"Your identity?"

"Yes, my real name, Gaston Rozen."

"Aargh! And this someone knows..."

"My entire past, thoroughly."

"Bloody hell! But is he a friend or an enemy?"

"A friend...at least, I have reason to think so."

"Then there's no harm done."

"Who knows?"

"Damn! Since he's a friend..."

"All the same, I'm furious with myself...it was me who pushed him to recognize me. You know that I like playing with fire. Danger amuses me—but here I went too far, stupidly insisting..."

"The fact is that such an imprudence on your part astonishes me," Macaron said. "At the end of the day, even if he's not indiscreet...may one know?"

"What?"

"The name if the individual and how it happened."

"I don't have any secrets from you. Do you remember Lavardens?"

Macaron scratched his head.

"Truthfully, no," he said. "Lavardens, Lavardens...unknown to the battalion."

"He's a comrade I knew during my time in London, and who met me again in Venezuela."

"Oh yes—you mentioned him to me. The former NCO in the marines, who lent you a thousand bullets. He doesn't wish you any harm, that one."

"No, and if I'd contented myself with letting him recognize me, I wouldn't be overly worried—but was imprudent enough to try to enlist him."

"As an anarchist?" Bastien asked.

"Yes," Saint-Magloire replied, biting his lip. "Yes, exactly—as an anarchist."

"And he didn't bite?"

"No, he refused, indignantly."

"You saw that?"

"Naturally, I didn't persist, and in order not to excite him, I promised to give him some money..."

"Bad business," Macaron observed, sententiously. "When the money's gone, he'll come back."

"No, he's an honest man. With him, there's no fear of blackmail."

"There are no honest men when it comes to money. Look, Boss, the best thing would be..."

The Baron understood exactly where his acolyte was going, but he feigned ignorance. "To do what?" he asked.

"Where's he lodged, your honest man?" Bastien asked, responding to the question with another.

"He's due to return to Le Havre soon."

"And you let him go?"

"Don't worry—he'll come back. He hasn't got the money I promised him yet."

"Then there's no problem, Boss. But when is the poor chap coming back?"

"Next week."

"Well, on that day, warn me and let me hide in a corner. I'll examine your honest man, and give you my opinion. I'm a *physiolomist*, I am, although I don't look it."

"Agreed. And now, goodbye. I'm going to lunch."

"You don't say, Boss!" said Macaron, brazenly. "Aren't you going to invite me?"

"Impossible, my friend. I'm expected..."

"In that case, if, by chance you still have a few gold pieces lurking in the depths of a drawer getting bored, I can give them an outing to cheer them up, and myself too..."

"You need more money?" said Saint-Magloire.

"One always has needs," Macaron observed.

Saint-Magloire threw him three louis, which he caught in mind-air with surprising skill. "One hasn't forgotten one's little talents," he said, juggling the coins. "*Au revoir*, Boss. See you next week."

"And try not to be too drunk that day."

"No danger. I'll drink nothing but pure water."

He went back to the bar at a run.

During his absence, the assembly had continued discussing the merits of Aubépine II and Camériste. They had drunk a little more and smoke a little more, but there was no more agreement between the two opposed camps.

"Is there still time to bet?" asked Macaron, as he came in.

"Yes, Mr. Robertson."

"Well, put two louis on Aubépine to win and one on Camériste to place..." And he threw the three twenty-franc coins that Saint-Magloire had given him on to the counter, superbly. It was a decisive move in favor of Aubépine II. In the eyes of all the punters, Mr. Robertson must have received a first-hand tip. Bets flooded on to Madame Angot's daughter.

To be honest, we ought to admit that Mr. Robertson had indeed received news from Pau. He knew, beyond a doubt, that Aubépine II was off color, in a state of notorious inferiority, and, in spite of her great ability, did not stand a chance against Camériste, who as in fine form—but as he was in cahoots with

192

the bookmakers, he had every interest in steering the punters in the direction of the horse that could not win.

His two louis were simply bait.

When he saw that the coup had succeeded, he tapped on the counter. "Now, lad," he commanded, "a mominette"—which means a small absinthe—"but in a large glass, with plenty of absinthe inside. I'll tell you why..."

The week went by. The time arranged with Lavardens arrived.

Saint-Magloire was perplexed. What should he do?

All things considered, he had nothing to fear from the man, who had always given evidence of sentiments of sincere generosity toward him...would it not be better to give him the promised advance and let him leave quietly for Guiana? In sum, the enterprise that he wanted to undertake might and ought to be profitable, and if it were to fail, a hundred thousand francs was not a huge loss for the Banque Saint-Magloire.

Except that Lavardens knew too much.

Apart from knowing Saint-Magloire's real name, he had a suspicion of the gold fabrication. Undoubtedly, he must have taken that story for a fairy-tale, a hoax or a joke, but if he talked about it to others he might, sooner or later, put some clever devil on the track...

Saint-Magloire had given orders to his usher to reserve a private room for a visitor who was hand him a recommendation in an envelope. In an adjacent room, separated by a doorway fitted with thick curtains, Bastien, alias Macaron, was stationed. By opening the door gently, he would be able to part the curtains slightly and see without being seen.

Ten o'clock chimed.

As usual, Saint-Magloire opened his mail, received a couple of division heads, and summoned the usher who had replaced Florent. The Baron had taken the precaution of sending the latter away. He did not want Lavardens to be recognized in his establishment.

"Has anyone come yet?" he asked.

"I beg your pardon, Monsieur, there's a gentleman who didn't want to give his name. He asked me to give this envelope to Monsieur le Baron. Following Monsieur le Baron's orders, I put him in the private room."

For form's sake, Saint-Magloire opened the envelope and glanced at the card. "Show him in," he said.

Lavardens appeared, his face radiant with hope.

"Bonjour, my dear chap," said Saint-Magloire. "Everything's in order. The steamer is still leaving tomorrow?"

"Still."

"What time?"

"In the afternoon."

"But I don't know of a direct line from Le Havre to Guiana...unless there's a sailing ship..."

"I'm not going directly to Guiana. Otherwise we'd be leaving from Saint-Nazaire. I have friends in New York who'll be very useful to me, and moreover, that's where I'll be able to purchase the tools I need at the best price."

"I understand."

"Then again," Lavardens added, "my wife is in Le Havre, and I'd rather get her aboard right away than make another long journey overland..."

"She must be very happy, your wife?" Saint Magloire interjected, wanting to know whether Lavardens had talked about him.

"Delighted, Monsieur le Baron. She blesses you, without knowing you."

"You have, however, been obliged to tell her..."

"Oh, I didn't tell her your name. I know how to keep a secret, even from my wife. I simply told her that I'd met a childhood friend in a brilliant position, and that the friend in question had generously offered me a hand..."

"Good, good," said Saint-Magloire. "I'm sure I can rely on you, my dear chap. Now, let's talk business. In a few hours, this evening, I'll give you the sum."

"This evening...it's just that I have many preparations to make."

"Well, what's preventing you?"

"The money...I have numerous purchases...having been obliged, for several months, to live very economically, we're scarcely prepared for such a long voyage, and I counted on making some necessary purchases this afternoon. With the thousand francs you gave me, I settled a few arrears."

"That's very annoying," said Saint-Magloire. "Had I foreseen that, I'd have realized the funds. I told you that I would make the investment personally, and wouldn't take the money from my own bank...you see, my dear Lavardens, I've been so absorbed by important concerns in the last few days that I find myself caught unawares..."

"Oh, my God!"

"Don't despair. Haven't I just told you that everything's in order? One telephone call and I'll be able to give you a check that you can bank in Le Havre. Come back between six and six thirty. I'll be waiting. In the meantime, make a list of the things you need."

"Oh, it's already made," said Lavardens, taking a piece of paper from his pocket.

"Good, that's even better. Go to the shops, make your choice, negotiate the prices and have the equipment sent to your hotel after six. Where are you staying?"

"I confess that," said Lavardens, "because I was only coming for the day, and being on a very tight budget, I haven't booked a hotel room. I'll have lunch shortly at some restaurant, probably a Bouillon Duval, and since I have to stay, I'll do the same for dinner. Then a simple change of clothes."

"Go to lunch, take care of your purchases. How much do you need for that? A thousand francs?"

"Much less—I'm only taking what's strictly necessary for the voyage. Once in New York, as I said, I'll get the full complement."

"In conclusion, you need pocket money?"

"Five hundred francs will suffice."

"Here you are," said the banker, rummaging in his wallet. Go, and don't cut corners with regard to what you need..."

"Oh," said Lavardens, whose eyes were gleaming with joy, "how can I thank you for your kindness?"

"Bah! You're joking. Am I not in your debt? One final word—would you do me a favor?"

"Can you doubt it?"

"Well, since you're not in a hotel, have your purchases sent directly to the railway station and come and dine with me, informally, at a tavern. Until the time of your departure, we can chat entirely at our ease about the past and the future."

"I accept gladly," said Lavardens. "Where shall I meet you?"

"I'll be at the Restaurant Paillard at six o'clock—ask for me at the cash-register. I'll give you your check while we eat."

"Six o'clock...agreed."

"Now, forgive me for sending you away, but I have ten people waiting for me. Until this evening. Here, my friend, go out this way." He led him to a small room that opened directly on to the staircase.

"Until this evening," Lavardens said, shaking the hand that the banker held out to him effusively.

As soon as the door had closed behind him, Saint-Magloire went to the small room where Bastien was waiting.

The latter had a singular smile.

"Well?" the banker asked. "What do you think?"

"I'll think what you think yourself, Boss," Macaron replied, with the same smile.

"That way of avoiding the question is perhaps very clever, but it doesn't help me much," Saint-Magloire riposted, indifferently.

"You know the man better than I do, and you ought to know whether he can be trusted."

"I think so. The fellow's honest and frank, incapable of lying..."

"Oho! A white blackbird, then!"

"Don't joke...it's rare, indeed, in this day and age, an honest man..."

"Damn it, Boss, it seems that the weather-vane has turned around, and the wind is blowing in the direction of virtue...you're going to give him your hundred thousand bullets, then?

"I have a strong desire..."

"As you wish—it's not my wallet the notes are coming out of, and for good reason. Only, will you permit me to make one small observation?"

"That's why I'm consulting you."

"Well, the fellow might be frank and honest, and all of that, but he has one fault—a wagging tongue."

"Bah! He hasn't said anything to his wife..."

"That's too much. She'll get it out of him...and if you know a woman who can keep a secret, you'd do well to have her cast in bronze."

"Why do you think he'll talk?" said the banker, shivering involuntarily.

"The sly beauty," said Macaron. "Oh, Boss, I no longer recognize you. He won't have been back in Le Havre for a quarter of a hour before she knows your name, even assuming that he hasn't told you a lie."

"Go on!"

"Follow my reasoning. You're going to give him a check, aren't you? She'll want to see it, examine it, feel it, embrace it...and she'll read your signature...and, as women are clever when they want to know something, as she knows that he knew you in London, and doubtless in Venezuela, she won't need to be a sorceress to divine that Monsieur le Baron de Saint-Magloire and the late Gaston Rozen are one and the same."

"That's right," murmured the banker, with a regretful sigh. "In that case..."

"In that case, what, Boss?" I'm listening.

"What if I gave him the money in banknotes?"

"That would be better, but it wouldn't put my mind at rest."

"So you think..."

"When I heard you informing yourself so artfully about the circumstances of his sojourn in Paris, Boss, I thought your decision was made...you know that there's no trace of his passage here. At Paillard's, where you're going to dine, a hundred people pass through that no one knows. Here, he's been seen once, a week ago. Florent wasn't here today to see him again, so there's nothing to fear with regard to a trail. You're taking him to the station. I'll be there ahead of you. I have his face engraved in my eye...and believe me, dead the beast, dead the venom."

"What about my check?" asked the banker.

"I'll bring it back, of course, and you'll tear it up. No one will ever know that it existed."

"There'll be the counterfoil..."

"You'll stop it. It's done every day. A bearer check, of course...no one's going to search your papers."

"You know, I'm beginning to think that you're right," said Saint-Magloire. "But what if you fail?"

"Never. I'd lose my skin first. And if, by some impossibility, I'm caught...you can rest easy. I'm not one of those who turns informer."

"All right, do it," said the banker, with a sigh. "But I'd rather have spared the poor devil."

"He had to get in our way!" Macaron observe, philosophically. "There's only one thing to settle. Which train is he taking?"

"That's up to him."

"No, it's up to you to hold on to him until the moment you want to send him. Let's see." Macaron took a train timetable out of a notebook. "We have a train at nine o'clock." That's too soon—out of the question. There's the eleven-ten express, and after that there's only the half-past midnight stopper. That would be too late. If I were you, I'd advise him to take the eleven-ten.

"You're in command, obviously," observed Saint-Magloire.

"Have to be, Boss, since you're going soft. Damn it, I no longer recognize the man of old. Come on, it's settled, that we're sending him on the express, isn't it?"

"I'll arrange that."

"And I'll make my own arrangements to get to the station before him. *Au revoir*, Boss—and rely on me. It's nice to be back in action again, eh?"

Saint-Magloire made no reply. There was still a scruple, deep down; he was reluctant to leave another corpse along his route—but that was a momentary matter, and when Macaron had gone, he pressed the button of the bell and said to the usher who came in to receive his orders, in an assured voice: "Send in the first person on today's list."

VII. The Tribulations of a Head of the Sûreté

With his elbows on his desk and his head in his hands, chewing on an extinct cigarette, the head of the Sûreté was extremely annoyed.

It is well-known that the offices of the Sûreté, once narrowly lodged in a dark and dingy apartment on the Quai de l'Horloge, were transferred some years ago to the other side of Paris, into a much more spacious location, much better provided with air and light, on the Quai des Orfèvres.

The head of the Sûreté is no longer the scarcely-recognized hybrid policeman of the Restoration and the July monarchy.[38] Today, he is a worthy magistrate, highly-considered and chosen from among the most deserving Commissaires de Police.

His comfortable accommodation, however, did not prevent Monsieur Cardec, the head of the Sûreté, from being in a terrible mood. A man who, in the early days of his service, had given proof of a skill to which everyone rendered homage, and who had had a veritable prodigious success in his enquiries, he had been the victim for several months of persistent bad luck. One might have thought that some evil spirit was dogging his footsteps.

To begin with, he had had to seek the authors of a series of burglaries carried out with mathematical precision in houses whose owners were absent. One could have sworn that the thieves had been guides by their victims, so rapid and precise were their operations. And even by promising double or triple rewards to the "snouts"—which is to say, the most experienced informers in the "underworld"—he had been unable to obtain the slightest result.

That would have been quite enough—but someone had robbed a Banque de France transport vehicle in broad daylight, and the Prefect of Police had thrown a fit, declaring that it was necessary, at all costs, to discover the thieves.

It was all very well for the Prefect of Police to talk. The thieves had not left their visiting card in the plundered vehicle.

For want of anything better, half a dozen villains who were quite capable of such a coup had been arrested, but they had all been able to prove their innocence.

It was known that the stolen bonds had been taken to England—but by whom?

---

[38] This refers to Vidocq's supposed tenure in that position; at the time, the whole basis of police procedure was reliance on informers. Vidocq, although he presented himself in his memoirs as a proto-detective which a fondness for planning *razzias* [raids], actually seems to have been the Prefecture's go-between with a gang of fellow ex-convicts who were collecting information from their old friends.

And to crown the Head of the Sûreté's distress, another mysterious crime had just been added to all of that. The torso of a woman had been found in the Seine, covered in stab-wounds.

In one of the principal churches of Paris, the panic-stricken sacristan had discovered two legs hidden in a confessional, which appeared to belong to the same victim—whose head, frightfully mutilated, had been thrown by the murderer or an accomplice under a bench in one of the leading cafés in Paris—and there was no clue to permit the establishment of the unfortunate woman's identity.

The brigade was exhausted; the chief passed his days and nights raking his brains—and it was all in vain. Every morning the Prefect asked whether there as anything new, and when he invariably received a negative reply his impatience was further exasperated.

The newspapers, which had once sung the praises of the "skillful policeman" to his heart's content, were now beginning to joke about his lack of success. One reporter had insinuated that the staff of the Sûreté were recruited among Offenbach's legendary carabiniers;[39] another recounted in all seriousness that the Prefecture specialized in *"petits fours;"* a third, extending to black comedy, recalled the great deeds of the celebrated Monsieur Jackal, who had only ever existed in Alexandre Dumas' *Les Mohicans de Paris.*

All this criticism and mockery was exceedingly disagreeable for poor Monsieur Cardec, who, although having nothing for which to reproach himself, nevertheless felt that his reputation had been compromised and that his position was under threat. He was thinking about all that, searching in vain for a means of getting out of difficulty and recovering his lost prestige, when someone knocked discreetly on the door.

Monsieur Cardec made a gesture of annoyance. "Come in!" he said.

The door opened hesitantly, and the orderly on office duty came in.

"What is it?" said the magistrate, in a surly tone. "I told you not to disturb me."

"There's a lady asking to talk to the chief."

"A Lady? Did she give her name?"

"Here is it," said the orderly, holding out a black-edged card.

Monsieur Carden read: *The widow Lavardens.*

"Don't know her!" he said. "What does she look like?"

"A pretty woman, brunette, in full mourning-dress."

"Some widow come to ask for my protection," Cardec murmured. "She's picked her moment! Take the lady to the deputy chief, or simply to the secretary. I don't have time to see her."

The agent bowed and left.

---

[39] In *Les Brigands* (1869)

The widow Lavardens, the chief said to himself. *Who's that? My word, everyone imagines that they have a right to disturb you.*

The door opened and the orderly reappeared.

"What is it now?" demanded Cardec, impatiently.

"The lady insists. She says that she has to talk to you in person. She says that she has something of the utmost importance to tell you."

"Go on, send her in. Perhaps she does have something interesting to tell me."

The orderly went out, and returned preceding a woman dressed in black. He stood aside to let her pass and then left.

The chief of the Sûreté cast a rapid glance over the obstinate visitor.

Beneath her long mourning-garments, Oliva Lavardens was perhaps even more beautiful than when we saw her at the beginning of this story.

The head of the Sûreté was struck by the appearance of sadness and dignity expressed by her features, and experienced a kind of instinctive sympathy for her, mingled with profound respect.

"Please sit down, Madame," he said, indicating an armchair with his hand, "and tell me what brings you here."

Madame Lavardens sat down, and, raising her large dark eyes to look at the magistrate, began: "Excuse me for having insisted on speaking to you personally and not to one of your employees, Monsieur, but as I told your agent, what I have to tell you is of the highest importance."

"Speak quickly, then, Madame."

"I've come to denounce a great criminal."

The head of the Sûreté sat up straighter. A great criminal. Might it, perhaps, be the murderer of the dismembered woman?

"A great criminal?" he repeated.

"Yes," said Oliva. "I will even say one of the most audacious bandits that has been seen for many years.

"And what is his name?" asked the magistrate, intrigued.

"Gaston Rozen."

"Pardon me, Madame," said the head of the Sûreté, looking his interlocutor in the face. "I must have misheard. You said...?"

"Gaston Rozen. Oh, I know, you're going to object that Rozen is dead, that he perished trying to escape from Guiana, that his body was found on the bank of the Maroni. I know all that, but I'm certain that Rozen is clever enough to deceive the most clear-sighted police, and that, taking advantage of the fact that everyone is convinced of his death, he is living in tranquility and committing new crimes without fear."

"I'd like to believe you, Madame, but would you care to tell me, please, on what you base your assertion?"

"On a fact that is very painful for me," Madame Lavardens continued, raising her handkerchief to her eyes. "My husband has been murdered, and Rozen is his murderer."

"Another crime!" exclaimed the head of the Sûreté. "A murder in Paris?"

"No, in the provinces, between Rouen and Le Havre, on the railway line."

"The line to the west? I read something about that, in fact—but it seems to me that was mention of an accident?"

"That's what the local legal authorities claimed—but I, Monsieur, know what I'm talking about, and I maintain that it's a case of murder."

"But if an investigation has been carried out..."

"It was carried out with a decision made in advance. Only one of the magistrates had the slightest desire to seek the truth; the other and the physician—especially the physician—prevented him from doing so.

At first, the head of the Sûreté had had a glimmer of hope. If the woman was telling the truth, if she had had some proof to support what she said, and if the celebrated bandit Rozen really had deceived the law by some old maneuver, one might unhesitatingly attribute all of the recent crimes whose authors remained undiscoverable to him.

But she was talking about a banal accident that had happened near Le Havre, which the newspapers had scarcely mentioned. What connection could that have with the legendary crook whose memory she was evoking?

"I will point out to you, Madame," he said, in a slightly chilly tone, "that you're talking about a matter that is outside my jurisdiction. Except for special missions, I can only occupy myself with what happens in Paris."

"But it's in Paris that Rozen is living. It was in Paris that he planned the murder of my poor Charles. Please, Monsieur, give me a few minutes of your time and you will, I hope, be convinced, as I am, of the truth of what I am saying."

The head of the Sûreté made a resigned gesture.

"Speak, Madame. I'm listening."

The widow then recommenced the story that she had told the magistrates from Le Havre at Beuzeville-Bréauté station. In her desire to avenge the death of her husband, the poor woman searched for the most persuasive words and the most convincing evidence in order to communicate to the head of the Sûreté the conviction she had herself of Gaston Rozen's existence and culpability.

As he had promised, Monsieur Cardec listened attentively, and seemed interested in her story. Even better—from time to time, he made a note on a piece of paper in front of him: a kind of hieroglyph, comprehensible to him alone.

When she had finished, he reflected momentarily, rapidly scribbled a few lines on a notepad and rang.

The orderly appeared.

"Take that to the deputy chief," Cardec instructed. Then, addressing Madame Lavardens, he said: "Excuse me, Madame, I have something urgent to do. We'll resume this conversation afterwards."

"My God, Monsieur, I think it's futile for me to disturb you any further. I've told you everything. It's up to you to take action now. I'll go."

"No, Madame, stay; I shall have to reply to you, and perhaps ask for further information in a little while."

"Oh, thank you, Monsieur. I'm at your orders...for I can see that I've finally been able to put a finger on the truth that others didn't want to hear. Bless you, for consenting to aid me in punishing my poor husband's murderer."

The head of the Sûreté made no reply. He was waiting until he had examined the files.

Madame Lavardens, sitting next to the desk, became pensive, her gaze lost in space.

A quarter of an hour went by. The office attendant came back, holding an envelope. The head of the Sûreté took the envelope and rapidly scanned the letter—or rather the note—that it contained.

The note said: *I've just telephoned the Sûreté Générale, as requested. The report of the Special Commissaire in Le Havre is in due form. The death of M. Charles Lavardens was due to an accident. He fell from a carriage through an open door. The medical evidence is precise, and the reports of the employees leave no doubt on the subject. As for the widow, grief has caused her to lose her mind. She's a poor madwoman who should be turned away gently. With regard to the convict Rozen, there is no more doubt. His death is officially established.*

The head of the Sûreté put the piece of paper down on his desk and turned to Oliva Lavardens, who was waiting anxiously.

"To my infinite regret, Madame, I'm unable to occupy myself with the research about which you came to talk to me."

"And why not, Monsieur?" exclaimed the young woman, rising to her feet, amazed.

"It is, as I told you, the court in Le Havre that has sole jurisdiction over the investigation. I can't trespass on their preserve; it would be an impiety."

"But since they've abandoned it! Since they don't want to believe in the existence of the murderer!"

"Calm down, Madame, I beg you," the head of the Sûreté continued, rising to his feet in his turn. "Calm down and think hard. Imagine that you could—that you must—be mistaken. Your memory is doubtless serving you poorly. Your husband mentioned Rozen to you, but could not have told you that he is alive."

"Rather think, Monsieur, that Rozen is powerful enough, thanks to his stolen wealth, to have imposed silence on the law!"

"Madame!"

"That's all right, Monsieur—I'm leaving. But I'm not abandoning the struggle. And we shall see whether, on the day when I prove that Rozen is alive, when I point him out to you, in spite of his disguise, whether you will dare to close your eyes."

"On that day, Madame, I swear to you that I will do my duty, whatever position the guilty party holds."

"That's good, Monsieur. I shall rely on your word. *Adieu*—or rather, *au revoir!*"

Oliva Lavardens withdrew without looking back.

"Poor woman!" murmured the head of the Sûreté. "So young, so pretty, and out of her mind..." And he began rereading the note that contained the reply of the Sûreté Générale.

VIII. The Good Doctor

At that moment, the office attendant knocked again and came in. He was holding a card in his hand.

"What is it now?" demanded the head of the Sûreté. "I'd like a little peace."

"It's a gentleman who's already been waiting for some time. He says that he's one of Monsieur le Chef's close friends.

"Doctor Lemoine!" murmured Cardec, casting a glance at the card. "Send him in right away."

"Come in, Monsieur," said the employee, ceding passage to the visitor who had followed him.

"My God!" exclaimed the doctor, as he came in. "My dear comrade, one can't even come to shake your hand—you're better guarded than the President of the Republic!"

Dr. Lemoine was a tall, handsome man, nearing forty but vigorous, solid, well-built and having, as they say, a magnificent bearing.

A scientist of great breadth—for the Académie had already crowned two of his numerous scientific discoveries and had charged him with delicate and dangerous missions—he took no pride therein, and was the most modest, mildest and most affable man one could wish to meet.

In possession of a considerable personal fortune, Lemoine could have lived in one of the most elegant quarters of Paris, but he preferred Montmartre, where, on the crest of the "sacred Butte," he had constructed the most comfortable and most elegant of hermitages. There, as he loved to repeat, the air was very good and there was a lovely view, two points that he deemed essential. His detached house had a beautiful garden—something rare in Paris—with true verdure and tall trees.

It was there, in the meditative tranquility of his laboratory, exempt from all indiscreet neighbors, that he was able to work at his ease on research useful to humankind.

Dr. Lemoine had a restricted clientele, among the rich. He did not like to treat the maladies of mistresses and the dolors of neurasthenics. On the other hand, he was a physician to all the poor, and in the Grandes-Carrières quarter as well as Clignancourt and Épinettes, popular gratitude had nicknamed him "the good doctor."

Such was the visitor who had just come into the office on the Quai d'Orfèvres, the friend of the head of the Sûreté.

"Excuse me," said the latter, shaking the hand that Lemoine held out to him. "I was very busy."

"I could see that…clearly. It's not surprising, old fellow, that you had me wait for such a long time. I saw your visitor leaving. A pretty woman! I might even say a very pretty woman. I understand that the time didn't seem long to you."

"In which you're mistaken, my good friend," Cardec replied, "for the poor woman's visit was far from enjoyable."

"Get away!"

"She's a widow whose husband's tragic death has disturbed her mind."

"Oh, the poor woman! At her age, and so pretty. Is there no remedy?"

"You'd have to answer that, my good doctor," said the magistrate, smiling.

"I wouldn't say no. It's a cure that would make me smile. Where does your sick woman live?"

"To be honest, I didn't think of asking for her address—but she'll certainly be back."

"You think so?"

"I'm sure of it. She has an obsession, and people like that never give it up."

"That's true. And what is her obsession?"

"She thinks that her husband was murdered and she wants me to find the murderer."

"Then you're right: she'll come back. When she does, ask for her address and let me know."

"With pleasure."

"But with all that," said the doctor, "I haven't asked for news of your health—something unpardonable for a physician. How goes it?"

"Badly."

"Badly! But you seem to be blooming—eyes somewhat fatigued, it's true…overwork, probably."

"Yes, work and tribulations."

"Go on! What's happened."

"You don't read the newspapers?"

"I don't have time. I subscribe to a few papers, but I only cast an eye over them at lunch time to keep up with current events, and then never look at them again."

"Well, my friend, if you had read certain articles, you'd see that there is no man more stupid and idiotic—more incapable, in a word—than your humble servant…"

"Bah! And that gets to you?"

"Certainly, for the articles directed against me are read in high places, and in the Prefect's entourage, they don't like men who attract criticism of the administration."

"That's more serious. But why this bitter criticism of you, whom they were covering with flowers not so long ago?"

"For two or three affairs of that I'm unable to bring to a close. One would think that the devil were mixed up in them."

"Perhaps he is. Come on, tell me your troubles."

"What's the point?"

"My friend, to be a good physician for the body, it's necessary to be a good physician for the soul."

"You want to? Well, listen..."

"I'm all ears," said the physician, settling into an armchair.

The head of the Sûreté told him, in detail, the story of the burglaries, the robbery of the Banque de France delivery truck and the strange discovery of the woman's body-parts. He told him about the failure of the investigations of these affairs, for which the Prefect was extremely displeased with him. "You understand," he said, in conclusion, that with all these embarrassments, I wasn't in the mood to listen to the fantasies of that poor madwoman."

"Who knows?" he murmured.

"What? You'd have believed her?"

"My dear friend, the Orientals—who aren't as stupid as us, you may be quite sure, for they're capable of arranging their existence in such a way as to shelter them from all distress that harasses us—claim that the word of the insane is that of God, who chooses them for his intermediaries."

"If that's the only means of getting me out of this mess..." said the head of the Sûreté, smiling.

"Eh! Let me finish, damn it! Your pretty visitor of a little while ago is mad, you tell me—fit to be tied, I'll grant you, although, according to the rapid glance I was able to cast over her in passing, nothing denotes mental alienation. A physician can't judge anything, though, by a superficial examination. Are you sure, though, that it's only the death of her husband that has unhinged her mind?"

"I only know about that what I've been told—or, rather, what was telephoned to my deputy by the functionaries of the Sûreté Générale, informed by the report of the Special Commissaire in Le Havre."

"Good—that's a first point that will serve me as a base. What would you say to me, a physician, if I assured you that the people who claim to have had their houses robbed are simple lunatics who upset everything themselves and imagined that they had been the victims of non-existent burglars? What would you say if I told you that the woman hacked into pieces was merely a vulgar suicide-victim?"

"What are you getting at?" asked the head of the Sûreté, amazed.

"Never mind the implausibility, and tell me sincerely that you'd be overwhelmed with joy, since the madness of the burglary-victims would explain your lack of success in the search for the pretended burglars."

"That's true."

"Good. Well, why shouldn't we admit that, to avoid searching for the unknown murderer of whom that woman speaks, the investigators out there found it more convenient to pass her off as a madwoman?"

"On, on that point, I stick!" exclaimed the head of the Sûreté, fervently. "There might be incapable or negligent magistrates, but none would trample his duty underfoot to the point of acting like that!"

"Don't get excited. "I didn't intend to insult the magistracy. It's only a hypothesis—nothing but a hypothesis. But I'll gladly cross it out, since it annoys you."

"Good!"

"Only, I'll replace it with another."

"Which is?"

"Madame Lavardens...that was the name you mentioned? Madame Lavardens is mad...her husband's death has disturbed her mind...but victims of madness of that sort, resulting from cerebral commotion, generally have an obsession..."

"That's the case."

"Let me finish: an obsession related to the catastrophe that has struck them."

"So what?"

"I once knew a young woman whose fiancé had been killed in a duel. She continually saw an épée applied to her breast. Another woman whose child had perished in a fire saw herself surrounded by flames, and cried: "Fire!" And so on. Madame Lavardens says that her husband has been murdered. There must be some circumstance that has engraved that monomania of murder on the sick brain of the young woman."

"What you say is perhaps accurate in psychological terms, but the police can't operate on such subtle bases."

"Why not? That a judge can only pass sentence on the basis of material evidence, I agree wholeheartedly—but a head of the Sûreté, a ferret, should not hesitate to make use, as you say, of psychology, ready to stop when he sees that it has led him too far...

"Look, I remember an anecdote I was once told, with regard to a famous criminal, by my colleague Couty de Pommeray.[40] When the examining magistrate arrived with your predecessor, the head of the Sûreté in that era, Monsieur

---

[40] This seems to be a garbled reference to the notorious murderer Edmond Couty de la Pommerais, a physician convicted of poisoning his mother-in-law and his former mistress, who was guillotined in 1864 (and with whom Lemoine cannot possibly have been acquainted). The case became famous because the murderer was one of the first people convicted on the basis of expert forensic evidence, supplied by the forensic pathologist Ambroise Tardieu, using a method subsequently replicated in the present text.

Claude,[41] to search his study, he found all the books and papers in such perfect order that he deduced that they had been arranged very recently. Do you know what was the first thing the policeman said?"

"No."

He cried: "We won't find anything, because the man really is guilty."

"That was, indeed, judiciously reasoned," observed Monsieur Cardec.

"You see that it's necessary not to rely too much on material things," the doctor went on, "since, in the case I mentioned, it was the certain absence of evidence that proved guilt."

"Good. But to get back to our affair..."

"I'm certain that Madame Lavardens must have heard mention of this Rozen as a man from whom there was everything to fear."

"But as he's dead."

"He might, as she claims, have escaped. He might have come back to life."

"Oh, that seems to me to be overstepping the mark."

"Not at all. When I say 'come back to life,' I'm talking about an imitator, a successor. Famous bandits are like kings—they have dynasties. Don't you en-counter, in the gangs that your agents arrest, night-prowlers who have taken the name of Cartouche, and others who call themselves Mandrin, or, more recently, Marchandon, Campi, or Prado?"[42]

"Indeed."

"Well, how do you know that some convict, escaped or liberated, envious of the aureole that Rozen created, hasn't adopted his name?"

"It's possible. What's the conclusion?"

"The conclusion is that it's necessary to accept gratefully all that the good Lord, or chance, as you wish, sends us to serve as materials for the edifice we're trying to build. In other words, instead of shutting your door on that you want, for your own pleasure, still to call 'the madwoman,' it's necessary to bring her in, flatter her obsession, interrogate her as gently as a child, and extract infor-mation from her that might perhaps be precious."

"But it's a provincial matter, and that's not what the newspapers are hurl-ing at me. Would they let up on me if I'd discovered the murder...if I do discov-er him."

---

[41] Antoine Claude was the head of the Sûreté from 1859 to 1875, and could not have been Cardec's immediate predecessor; he is surely mentioned here because he was the first authentic head of that organization to publish his (ghost-written) memoirs, thus providing the key precedent for Goron's endeavors.

[42] The three "recent" murderers, who were guillotined in 1885, 1884 and 1889 respectively, were not in the same league as the legendary bandits Cartouche and Mandrin, being common criminals of no great distinction; it seems highly improbable that any self-respecting criminal would have deigned to borrow any of the three names.

"It would prove, at any rate, that you're not as incapable as they say. And who knows whether, in putting your hand on this man that Madame Lavardens claims to be rich and powerful, you might not find the key to the enigma in question: the mystery of the occult protection covering the authors of the crimes that are putting you in such an awkward situation?"

"I'm afraid that I might be undertaking an exceedingly difficult task," said the head of the Sûreté, shaking his head in discouragement."

"My friend, as the gospel says: 'Seek and ye shall find.'"

"It's easy for the gospel to say that. I've done so much seeking already!"

"There's a well-known phenomenon: when an accountant has messed up a calculation, he can do it again twenty time over, always saying sat the same place: two and two make five, or six—and he never succeeds in finding his mistake, although any schoolboy could rectify the fault...

"You're a distinguished policeman, but you might have taken a false track. Would you like me to be the schoolboy who can put you back on the right one?"

"With all my heart."

"Well," said the doctor, "let's begin right away. In the story you've just told me, two principal points stand out. It's necessary to clarify them."

"Go on."

"Firstly, the telegram sent by Lavardens. Secondly, the sum of a hundred thousand francs that the traveler should have had on him, which was not recovered. Did that not strike you?"

"Lavardens had certainly told his wife that he would get a hundred thousand francs, but what proof is there that he received them? Go on."

"The telegram that Madame Lavardens received must have the name of the office from which it was sent. In any case, it will be easy to discover. That will give us a starting-point for the operation. Since, we'll know where Lavardens was when he sent it. Perhaps, by making enquiries in the vicinity, we'll find someone who saw him. Perhaps we can find out with whom he spent the evening—especially if it's a well-known individual, much in society."

"Good for the first point. What about the second?"

"The money must be important to the investigation. Madame Lavardens told us that. What also helped the version of the accident is that a wallet, purse, watch and chain were found on the body, which seemed to exclude any idea of theft. But how do we know that wasn't cunning on the part of the murderer, who left the pocket-money in order to defect suspicion? What is certain, in my opinion, is that Lavardens had the hundred thousand francs on him, since the telegram said: *Business concluded.* Thus, Lavardens had received, from someone—Rozen or someone else—a hundred thousand francs. A sum of that size doesn't emerge from a cash-box without any mention of it being made in the books, does it?"

"That seems fair to me," the head of the Sûreté replied. "But what are you getting at?"

"This: that by going to check the account books of the banks, one could find the one that issued a hundred thousand francs on the day of the crime to Monsieur Lavardens, and the trail would then be discovered."

"Unfortunately, that's impossible," said Cardec.

"Impossible? Why?"

"I can't just go inspect the books of all the banks in Paris, out of the blue."

"What prevents you?"

"Their number, to begin with. Open a Bottin—you'll see that their names alone take up thirteen pages. At an average of forty names per page, that makes more than five hundred. The search would take a month."

"Well then, one can sacrifice a month."

"You can, perhaps—not me. I, unfortunately, have work in hand that doesn't permit me such a whim. Oh, if it were by order of a judge...if the investigation were reopened...I wouldn't say no—but it's closed and filed away, and I wouldn't be forgiven for treading on the toes of the magistrates who think they've judged it soundly and irrevocably."

"You don't need to say why you're carrying out the search."

"Oh, you think so! You imagine, then, that the head of the Sûreté is an absolute potentate who has the right to do whatever he wishes?"

"Why, that's exactly what I understood his function to be."

"Well, it's necessary to cross that out of your notes. That head of the Sûreté only exists in novels. There he comes and goes and maneuvers his agents as he likes, strewing gold around and not having to account to anyone, provided that he succeeds. In practice, it's different. He must make a report on everything that he does, and his expenses are subject to carefully checking, which does not permit unnecessary prodigality."

"Too bad! When one gives a man responsibility for public security and the prosecution of crime, he ought to have *carte blanche*, and be responsible only to his conscience. But since that's the way it is, set aside the question of money— I'll take charge of that."

"You?"

"Me. I'll gladly sacrifice a few thousand-franc bills to my apprenticeship. That leaves the personnel. Can you give me two or three men?"

"Perhaps."

"You wouldn't want me to be obliged to recruit staff-members who are as much novices as I am."

"All right—I'll arrange it."

"Well, take your steps tomorrow. What time is most convenient for you?"

"Between two and four, unless anything comes up."

"Understood. Until tomorrow."

The two friends shook hands, and the doctor left, saying to himself joyfully: *Now I'm a policeman! People are right to say that everything happens, especially the implausible!*

IX. Saint-Magloire's Amours

A week after the alliance contracted between the head of the Sûreté and his friend, the "good doctor" Lemoine, there was an important performance at the Opéra.

It was not a gala performance, nor even an extraordinary one, but that Saturday saw the debut in a leading role of a singer who had thus far only played secondary parts. Germaine Reyval was singing Marguerite in *Faust*.

It was her lover the banker who had obtained that result, by means of pleas, bribes and even intrigues. Needless to say, he had worked hard on publicity, had inserted notices at considerable cost in all the newspapers and boasted everywhere—at the Bourse, in ministers' antechambers, the big clubs and fashionable cabarets—about the talent of the new star. Thus, the hall was crowded by the time that the public is ordinarily just beginning to arrive.

It was, very nearly, a first-class audience, half-artistic and half-socialite: fashionable authors, critics, diplomats, the Faubourg Saint-Honoré and the Faubourg Saint-Germain, great lords and flashy foreigners, duchesses, marquises and demi-mondaines—the entire multivarious mixture known as "All Paris."

In one of the side boxes, Dulac, who had come to hear and applaud his idol, considered that supposedly "select" audience with a mixture of joy and resentment. He loved Germaine too much not to be happy about her success, but he was chagrined by the thought that the young woman would become even more successful at the Opéra and increase the difficulty of the negotiations into which he had entered to engage her at his own theater. He was, therefore, torn between the desire for her triumph and the fear of the results that triumph might have for him.

In two fine orchestra stalls placed in the very center, from which the entire auditorium could be examined without difficulty, Monsieur Cardec and Dr. Lemoine were stationed.

"I may seem to you to be something of a Danube peasant, my dear friend," said the doctor to the head of the Sûreté, "but I haven't set foot in a theater for I don't know how many years, occupied as I was in my work, and I no longer know anyone. You'll have to serve as my cicerone."

"Gladly," the policeman replied, laughing. "What would you like to know?"

"Well, to begin with, who is that little woman over there in pink silk who is fluttering around and seems to be doing everything possible to attract attention to herself? An expensive prostitute? An actress?"

"Shh, fool! That's the Marquise de X***, wife of the ambassador of..."

"Damn! And that tall stiff gentleman over there in rear, with his waxed moustache and his rosette of the Légion d'honneur? A general, undoubtedly, or at least a senior officer?"

"Not at all, my dear friend. That's Victor J***, the celebrated composer of music, to whom we owe two highly-esteemed operas."

"And that fellow two steps away from him, similarly decorated?"

"Colonel T***."

"The hero of Tonkin—that worthy bourgeois with the placid expression!"

"Exactly."

"Well, I'm definitely no physiognomist...and I no longer dare ask anything else. One last question, though. Who is the individual with such a proud expression, at whom all gazes were directed just now, when he came into the box between the columns?"

"Oh, that, Monsieur, is a person much more important than all the rest: the King of Paris."

"The King of Paris?"

"Exactly—the famous Baron de Saint-Magloire, the rich banker of the Place Vendôme."

Saint-Magloire had, indeed, just made his veritably triumphant entrance. As the doctor had said, he had scarcely appeared in the intercolumnar box than all heads had turned toward it and every pair opera-glasses aimed at him, while a whisper had run around the hall. From the seats and other lodges—everywhere—respectful or amicable salutations had been addressed to him. His acclaim was almost worthy of a sovereign. Less constrained by etiquette, he had limited himself to responding to the general enthusiasm with a slight inclination of the head, aimed at the entire audience at once.

"Oh, that's the famous Saint-Magloire," said Lemoine, looking attentively, with the aid of his opera-glasses. "Well, to tell the truth, even I'm obliged to recommence my heresies, I declare that I don't like his face. He's a handsome man, I admit, but...there's something strange about his physiognomy—I don't know exactly what—that's antipathetic to me."

The head of the Sûreté smiled ironically, for, deep down, he was of the same opinion as the doctor; although he had nothing with which to reproach Saint-Magloire, that had not prevented him from also being slightly repelled by the banker's arrogance.

"Come on, my dear chap," he said. "The baron is the most charming man in the world. He gives diners to which the greatest names in France are honored to be invited, parties whose invitations are hotly contested. He taps ministers in the belly and addresses ambassadors as *tu*. What more do you want?"

"I'd like to know, for instance, whether he's charitable."

"Consult the subscription lists. You'll always see his name at the top."

That's not what I mean. Loudly-publicized charity is part of the program of every man on public view...but I'll wager that that man, who ostentatiously puts himself down for a thousand francs for flood victims in Hungary or earthquake victims in Caracas wouldn't give ten sous in the shadows of night to some poor devil dying of hunger."

"You've definitely taken against him."

"To begin with," the doctor continued, "how do you explain that light-colored hair and beard with those dark Oriental eyes?"

"Ask his parents."

"I like the young woman who is with him a great deal better! There's a frank and honest face, and, at the same time, a true type-specimen of pure beauty..." Lemoine stopped, simultaneously surprised and moved. *That's strange*, he thought. *I must be the victim of a hallucination. What connection can there be between the Baronne and...the other? I'm dreaming...and yet, the resemblance is truly extraordinary.*

"What's the matter?" Cardec asked. "You're cultivating a monologue now?"

"No," my friend, "it's just an idea that occurred to me. I was mourning that pretty woman, who can't be happy with such a husband."

"Bah! He gives her luxury. What more to women desire?"

The first chords of the orchestra cut off Dr. Lemoine's reply. He turned back to the stage, getting ready to listen.

If the doctor had shown himself to be a poor physiognomist in his initial appreciations, it is evident that he had been better inspired with regard to Saint-Magloire and Eléna, who was accompanying him.

Eléna was, indeed, far from being happy in spite of the luxury that surrounded her. She was suffering, afflicted in the utmost depths of her heart.

Saint-Magloire, that man of steel, devoid of conscience and of heart, had one weakness. He loved women. He loved them without restriction, without limits—and thanks to his situation as King of Paris, as Monsieur Cardec had described him, he had only to choose: women from high society, women of the demi-monde, actresses, bourgeoises...none resisted him.

As for the one who was installed beside him, whom he introduced to everyone as his legitimate wife, he limited himself in her regard to conventional politeness; she no longer meant anything to him intimately.

Eléna was suffering cruelly from that abandonment. Her lover had cast her aside, but she still loved him.

Then again, she retained an immense gratitude to him for having saved her child, who was about to die of starvation, in London. She did not suspect that that he had only carried out that pretended act of benevolence by virtue of the force of circumstances, and that all the honor of it reverted to Bastien, alias Macaron—a bandit, a thief and an occasional murderer, but who still had a hundred times as much humanity in his heart as his companion.

At any rate, Saint-Magloire's amours had no tomorrow. They were amours of the senses, not of the heart. Blasé in respect of everything, Saint-Magloire considered women merely as instruments of pleasure. Even though her heart was incessantly stabbed by suffering, therefore, Eléna was able to believe that she still possessed her ,lover's affection—and being thus persuaded, she pardoned his incessant infidelities.

That evening, proud of being on the arm of the man she loved, happy to be in his presence and at his side in that box, she had resumed the full glare of her radiant beauty, so often temporarily tarnished by suffering and tears. If Saint-Magloire was the King of Paris, Eléna could pass for the Queen of Beauty in the midst of the many pretty women who were garnishing the auditorium of the Opéra.

The curtain had risen, however. *Faust* began, and the audience, so noisy and restless a few moments earlier, was listening in a religious silence.

Marguerite's entrance was greeted by a murmur of astonishment. Beautiful as she was, Germaine was far from possessing the grace, so candid and so touching, that the lamented Miolan-Carvalho had been able to conserve in that creation until her final years.[43] She had, instead, an inebriating beauty that did not fit the character, in spite of her luxuriant wig. She was not the gentle Marguerite of the German poets. She was a Marguerite in the Parisian mold.

She had, however, worked long and hard on the role. She had mastered it so well that, as the first notes emerged from her throat, the first impression disappeared and everyone remained under the singer's charm.

Two people in the hall had been entirely subjugated instantly: Dulac, who, madly infatuated with Germaine, could find no fault in her; and Saint-Magloire, for whom the sight of the superb creature had caused the blood to rush to his brain. From the moment she came on stage, he devoured her with his eyes, seemingly insensible to anything else, and scarcely replying to Eléna, who had asked him a question.

When the first act ended, he could no longer hold back, and while the claque, with which numerous spectators joined in sincerely, recalled the debutante, Saint-Magloire, precipitately quitting his box, had himself introduced into the wings.

Audacious and sure of herself as she was, Germaine nevertheless experienced a profound emotion. So, intent on conserving the full complement of her means for the second act, she had forbidden entry to her dressing-room, postponing until the end of the performance the compliments of admirers, and not even wanting to receive the bouquets of flowers that were accumulating on a bench. Before the name of the Baron de Saint-Magloire however, the prohibition

---

[43] Marie Caroline Miolan-Carvalho played Marguerite in the 1859 première of Gounod's *Faust*, at the Théâtre Lyrique, but that version was not a great success; the piece only became part of the standard repertoire after being performed at the Opéra, in a revised version with an additional ballet, in 1869.

fell and the door opened wide, to the great resentment of the visitors who had been sent away.

"Excuse me, Mademoiselle," said the banker, bowing to the cantatrice, "but I was so impressed by your great talent that I could not resist the desire to come and present all my compliments to you..."

Germaine was exultant. A woman for whom money was god, and replaced everything else—love, honor and honesty—saw the celebrated banker, Baron de Saint-Magloire, the multimillionaire, the King of Paris, coming to her!

A brilliant mirage passed before her eyes. She saw herself dominating that man, sifting handfuls of gold, able to satisfy all her fantasies, crushing her rivals with her luxury. Not for a moment did the ambitious woman think about the debt she had contracted to her protector, the banker who had raised her to this level. She had sacrificed Dulac's love for him, she sacrificed him without hesitation for the other. Is it not sung in *Faust*, accurately, that the Golden Calf is still standing, and that its power is praised?

Between her and Saint-Magloire, those two natures gangrenous with vice, an understanding was easily and rapidly reached. Ten minutes after his entrance—which is to say, at the moment when the summoner came to warn the actress that the second act was about to commence, Saint-Magloire went back to his box, bearing the promise that Germaine would come to sing in his home at his next soirée.

During the interval, the head of the Sûreté and the doctor, remaining in their seats, had resumed the conversation.

"The famous Baron has left his wife alone," said Lemoine. "That's not polite."

"Well, my dear chap, after several years of marriage, one no longer pays attention to niceties."

"That may be so, but if I had such a wife, I'd worship her from dawn to dusk."

"And from dusk to dawn," added Cardec, laughing. "But it seems to me, my dear friend, that you're very smitten with the Baronne."

"If she were free, I'd go crazy for her."

"Good! The other day it was the murdered man's widow."

"Oh, it's not the same thing. They're both pretty...there's even a point of affinity between them, their southern origin—but Madame Lavardens only inspires a great sympathy in me, whereas Madame Saint-Magloire..."

"Oh, stop, my friend. Too much!"

"Pooh! I can admire a fine Rubens in a princely gallery without the slightest hope of possessing it. I can do the same with a beautiful woman."

"Then it's a love..."

"That's Platonic...for want of a better word," said the doctor, smiling. While speaking, he had directed his opera-glasses at Eléna, and once again, was struck by surprise. Forgetting his friend, he embarked on a monologue.

"Truly, it's prodigious; the more I look at her, the more I'm tempted to believe that it's her. It's true that resemblances among creoles are frequent...but this one is truly prodigious..."

"Well," said Cardec, "when are you going to stop staring at the Baronne? Her husband's coming back...anyway, the second act's about to begin. You'll see a third beautiful woman."

"Oh, I don't like that one at all. Her blonde beauty has something satanic about it, and her yellow eyes—for they are yellow; look!—have reflections of falsity that frighten me. I'd willingly swap her with Monsieur de Saint-Magloire for his beautiful creole."

The orchestra attacked the first bars, and the two friends interrupted their conversation again.

A few days after the performance of *Faust*, Germaine Reyval, keeping her promise, came to sang at the Baron de Saint-Magloire's home. There was, apparently, nothing extraordinary in that. The most highly-esteemed artistes in Paris came to be heard at the Baron's receptions. On several occasions, at his salons, he had even given his friends the first glimpse of lyric works not yet presented on the stage. There was nothing abnormal about Germaine's presence, in the eyes of the guests.

For one of them, however, the arrival of the cantatrice came as a great surprise. The name of that guest was Dulac. Although he was unaware of Saint-Magloire's new passion for Germaine, his heart received a violent shock at the sight of the young woman.

For her part, the cantatrice was no less astonished by the sight of her lover, whom she believed to be far away.

In fact, Dulac, even though he had never been sentenced in Paris, had been wary of revealing his name, or at least of making it evident, and it was under that of an administrator, his straw man, that he was seeking to found his theater. Germaine had not the slightest expectation of running into him.

With the skill she had been obliged to develop in controlling her face, however, instead of turning her gaze away from him, it was her who, in the midst of the complimentary crowd, addressed the most seductive of smiles to him.

Dulac, who was wondering what attitude he ought to adopt toward her, no longer hesitated. He went toward her, in order to speak to her—but Saint-Magloire had already taken possession of his guest's arm. To intervene would have been indiscreet.

Germaine had gone to the piano and, at the banker's request, launched into the "Spinning-wheel song," her triumph at the Opéra, then the "Jewel song," and finally the "Seduction duet," in which Saint-Magloire provided the counterpart with his warm and vibrant voice.

There was a thunder of cheers in the salons. No one knew whether to lavish more eulogies on the banker or the diva.

When the chorus of felicitations had eased slightly, leaving Saint-Magloire in the midst of his court of flatterers, Germaine took Dulac's arm. He, charmed and intoxicated by joy, let her take him to one side.

"Do you still want me, then?" she said, addressing him as *tu* and putting all her seductive voice into the question.

"Why do you want to know?" he replied, addressing her as *vous* and making an effort to conserve a false coldness. "You no longer loved me; it was only natural that you should leave me."

"Why talk like that? In default of love, isn't friendship possible?"

Dulac turned his head to look her in the face. There was an expression of such sincerity on her face that he felt moved to the utmost depths of his soul.

"Poor dear!" the charmer continued. "Do you think, then, that I've forgotten he happy times I spent with you? Do you think that the man for whom you think I sacrificed you had the smallest fraction of the affection I devoted to you? No, no! God is my witness that many a time, in the midst of the luxury with which he surrounded me, my heart returned to you, like my thoughts, while tears of regret pearled beneath my eyelids."

Dulac listened to these words like delightful music—even more delightful than the symphonies that he had just heard, when Germaine had interpreted the genius of Gounod and held an entire audience suspended from her lips.

"Why did you run away from me, then?" he said, trying to resist. "Why didn't you reply to my imploring letters? Why condemn me to that agony worse than death?"

"Why? Do I know, my poor friend?" the cantatrice riposted, moving her face closer to Dulac's—so close that the young man felt her perfumed breath, the breath that intoxicated him with love.

"Oh, you want to hook me again with more lies!" he exclaimed, maddened.

"No, I don't want to lie, I want to bring peace to your heart, to make you forget past suffering... In the midst of all these rich men, proud of their fortunes, their titles and their ranks, I've come to you spontaneously, not wanting you to be unhappy."

"Chance..." Dulac tried to object.

"No, not chance! My will. I knew you were here; I wanted to see you again. I wanted to heal the wound I've inflicted. And then...who knows...?"

The appeals of the guests, clamoring for the cantatrice, interrupted the conversation. They reproached Dulac amicably for taking possession of the heroine of the soirée.

"Soon," Germane said to him, with a last squeeze of the hand.

Lovers want nothing more than to be convinced. Dulac believed in Germaine's sincerity. And while he lulled himself with gilded dreams, the perfidious woman resumed the comedy of seduction with the wealthy Saint-Magloire.

It was an easy role to play, for the banker, to whom sentiments of the heart were of no consequence, contenting himself with carnal possession, could not believe for a moment that a mistress royally rewarded by him might deceive him.

So Germaine Reyval was able to continue her double game, really having Saint-Magloire for a lover, who gave her money generously, while assuring herself of Dulac's trusting silence by means of promises she hoped never to have to keep.

X. The Mute

The office of the international bank had just closed. After having given his final verbal instructions to his division heads, Saint-Magloire climbed into his coupé and gave the coachman the order to take him directly to his house.

Nervous, and visibly preoccupied, he rapidly climbed the ten steps of the monumental perron of the princely residence and went into the hallway on the ground floor like a gust of wind. A Chinese domestic, exclusively devoted to his service, swiftly relieved him of his hat and cane, and helped him remove his overcoat.

"I'm not at home to anyone, Yu," the adventurer said dryly, heading toward the mysterious study in which, every evening, when the day's work was done, he locked himself away in silence in order to plan the shattering coups on the Bourse, and the cunning political and financial schemes, that had made the escaped convict, in a few years, a fortunate rival of the Hirsches, Bleichroeders and Vanderbilts.

The Oriental bowed and went back to take his place in a little glass-walled office opening into the hallway, and linked to the Baron's study by a special system of electric signals in which the telephone was completed by one of those items of telegraphic apparatus know as a telescripter,[44] which permits the near-instantaneous transmission of a written message at a distance.

There was a particular reason for that unusual facility, which was that although Yu was perfectly capable of receiving orders by telephone, he was incapable of replying by the same means. The poor man was mute, completely dumb, because he no longer had a tongue.

Yu had followed Saint-Magloire everywhere for several years, marching silently in his shadow and serving him with a fanatical devotion. His story was a veritable romance, both tragic and macabre.

At the time when he had still been in China, Yu had been a mandarin of the highest rank: a sapphire button mandarin. He had a lucrative and envied position, analogous to that of a Prefect, in a province at the heart of the Celestial Empire. Infected with revolutionary ideas, however, he had become the secret instigator of one of the principal chiefs of the innumerable secret societies, which, since the famous Tai-Ping insurrection, had worked incessantly in the

---

[44] This term was probably improvised by the authors; at any rate, it was not in common use in 1901, although early examples of what would now be called fax machines did exist, including Shelford Bidwell's "scanning phototelegraph," invented in 1881 and Arthur Korn's recently-launched "bildtelegraph," which had much greater success in the subsequent decade.

shadows to bring down the Mongol dynasty and overturn all the religious, political, economic and social institutions of the Middle Kingdom.

Out there, where everyone is a conspirator to some degree, and where the police lack zeal even when they are not in on the plot, it is not a mortal sin. Nevertheless, Yu, who was easily roused, went a little too far. One day, armed bands, surreptitiously stimulated by him, expanded out of his jurisdiction, drawing in their wake all the vagabonds of the region, massacring the imperial functionaries, pillaging the shops, holding the rich to ransom and proclaiming, along with the communal ownership of property, a kind of egalitarian democratic republic, in the name of universal peace.

Yu counted on the movement becoming generalized, gaining ground all the way to Peking, and that all of China—or, rather, all the Chinese, for the country is nothing but a mosaic of disparate pieces more or less solidly cemented together—would catch fire like a pile of straw. And as he was both a fanatic and a practical man, he did not despair of fishing a little honor and money out of the turbulent blood in the midst of the ruins heaped up by his party.

Unfortunately for him, the mob was rapidly circumscribed, with the result that the imperial troops had no difficulty crushing it. Thousands of rebels were decapitated, without any kind of trial. Yu, in his double capacity as a mandarin and leader of the revolt, was entitled to greater ceremony. He was kept for the choice morsel: which involved his first being imprisoned, and submitted to horrible tortures, on the basis of well-founded accusations of the crimes of high treason, forfeiture and sacrilege.

Threatened with being cut into two hundred and seven thin slices if he did not confess his participation in the insurrection and denounce the other mandarins who were suspected of complicity, and fearing that he might weaken, he had the atrocious heroism of severing his tongue with his teeth and spitting the bloody fragment into the face of the magistrate.

Transported by fury and desirous of savoring his vengeance over a longer period, the latter had Yu thrown into a dungeon where he was imprisoned in an iron cage too narrow and too low for a man to do anything other than crouch inside it. The mutilated man remained in that frightful situation for months on end, until his relatives, having bribed his jailers, succeeded in getting him out.

He was kept hidden in an isolate country house for a long time. There, thanks to the extraordinary endurance and prodigious vitality characteristic of the Chinese, he was eventually healed. Once on his feet, as the air of China continued to be dangerous for him, he made the utmost haste to reach Shanghai, with the firm intention of emigrating to America.

Unfortunately, as he had been completely ruined, he could not even pay for his passage, and he was obliged, despairing of his cause, to embark as an assistant cook on a German ship bound for Montevideo.

From there, after various misadventures from which he had cleverly extracted himself, he had ended up running aground in Buenos Aires, where he had accumulated professions more honorable and more remunerative than sandwich-maker and meat-baster. It was there that hazard had thrown him into the arms of Rozen and Macaron, after their return from the Grand Chaco.

One night, when the two colleagues had got lost in the outskirts of the great city, they had gone into a kind of wooden cantina with a corrugated iron roof, lost in the middle of waste ground, to ask for directions. No other light was shining in the vicinity; they had no choice. It transpired that the cantina was a low dive of the worst kind, where people in rags of all nationalities were gambling and singing while drinking *aguardiente*.

Amused by the spectacle, which was not unpicturesque, after having received the directions they needed from the *almacenero*, had taken time out to sit down and drink a *copita* at a table where a Chinaman—you will have recognized Yu—was playing cards with a *vaquero*.

The vaquero, a thickset and broad-shouldered fellow with prominent muscles like the knotted branches of a vine-stock, answering to the name of Ramon Cajal, was winning as he liked from the Chinaman, who seemed to be having the worst possible run of bad luck.

Rozen, who took an interest in the game, did not take long to discover the secret of the vaquero's luck. Skillful in the card-sharp's art, he was giving fortune a helping hand, and poor Yu could not see anything but smoke.

Not the least curious aspect of Rozen's obscure and complex character was that he was sometimes in a mood to right wrongs. The bandit must have numbered among his distant ancestors some rival of Don Quixote, a few drops of whose blood were still flowing in his veins. That evening, confronted by the distress of the poor Chinaman, who was being basely robbed, the old blood in question only needed one turn.

"It seems to me that you're cheating, *hombre*," he suddenly exclaimed, in a strident voice, putting his hand on Cajal's arm.

"Cheating, me!" retorted the latter, pale with anger. "I'm cheating! Say that again, and I'll ram the words down your throat."

Complete silence had suddenly fallen in the *posada*. The bacchic chants had ceased; all the drinkers, keenly interested by the quarrel, had quit their seats to form a circle around the vaquero, with whose violence and vigor they were familiar.

"Oh good!" murmured Macaron. "Another fly in the ointment! Now we'll have a dust-up, when we could have had a nice quiet time." As he "had blood in his veins," to use his own expression, however, and was not at all afraid of a "dust-up," he took his place by Rozen's side, ready to play his part in the henceforth-inevitable brawl that he anticipated.

Rozen had no need of anyone's help, though. Standing up with his arms folded across his chest, with is legs braced, he fixed his magnetic stare on the vaquero, almost as phosphorescent as the eyes of a cat. "If I said you were cheating, it's because you were cheating—and I'm saying it again."

"*Carajo!*" howled Cajal, drawing a huge flick-knife out of his right boot, which he opened—*click clack!*—with a familiar twist of the thumb. "I'll have your hide!"

He raised his arm, but he did not have time to strike. With lightning rapidity, Rozen had got in ahead of the attack and had knocked the vaquero over with a head-butt in the midriff. The latter, surprised by the impact, dropped his knife, on which Rozen immediately put his foot.

"You can get up," he said, in a voice that no emotion caused to tremble. "A Frenchman never hits a man when he's down…but you won't be doing any more stabbing!" And gripping the blade of the knife between his fingers, he snapped it in two and threw it outside through the wide-open door.

Meanwhile, Cajal had regained his feet and, bruised and tottering, with foam on his lips, would have tried to take his revenge if, with a terrible blow of the fist full in his face, Rozen had not immediately laid him out at his feet. There was a sound like the cracking of a nutshell, and blood spurted forth, as the man collapsed; this time, he was out for the count.

"Bravo!" cried Macaron, sketching an entrechat. "Nicely done, mate." The regulars in the cantina, were not far from sharing Bastien's enthusiasm. Not only did they admired Rozen's strength, agility and fury—all things that always make a big impression on coarse natures—but they were not at all displeased by the lesson handed out to the vaquero, who had terrorized them all until now.

It was, therefore, in the midst of a sympathetic murmur, while Cajal continued to spit out teeth with a groan, that Rozen and Bastien left the battlefield in order to return to the city center. They had scarcely reached the lighted areas when Rozen heard furtive footsteps behind him, at the same time as a hand tugged gently at his sleeve. It was the Chinaman for whom he had just risked his life, but whom he had already forgotten. It was poor Yu, who, his face illuminated by a broad smile, handed him a piece of paper on which was written, in bad Spanish:

Mute by virtue of an accident of which I will give you all the details in writing, I cannot thank you orally for your generous action, but I beg you to believe in the eternal gratitude of your devoted servant.

It was signed: *Yu.*

Struck by the keen intelligence shining in the mute's eyes, Rozen had wanted to know his story. Then with a superior diplomacy, he had revealed his own, which he considered to be of a nature to impress and seduce him—which is to say, of course, the revolutionary legend concocted for the needs of his cause.

The cunning fellow knew what he was doing. By thus combining, in the simultaneously mystical and positive mind of the ex-mandarin, admiration, gratitude, fanaticism and enthusiasm, he inevitably made him into his creature, his slave—an incomparable slave, since he could be both a guard-dog and a confi-

222

dant. And what a precious confidant!—a man who did not even need to hold his tongue, at the psychological moment, because he no longer had one.

Rozen had truly put his hand on a rare bird. After a few weeks, Yu was irrevocably devoted to him, body and soul. He would no longer have sworn by anyone but Rozen, for whom he professed a fervent and jealous worship, if he had still had anything in his mouth that could perform that function.

When the three anarchists left South America, the Chinaman, whose life without Rozen would have been pointless, hastened to follow them. In London, where he had immediately found employment in one of the clandestine but luxurious opium-dens in the West End, whose clientele is recruited from the "gentry," scarcely a day passed without him going to find the master of his choice and offer him his services. So, when Rozen came to take up residence in Paris, he took care not to forget Yu. He brought him with him and took him into his household, promoting him to the role of butler or factotum. It is under that title that we find him in the house in the Champs-Élysées, more enslaved than ever to Saint-Magloire, whose orders he was ready to carry out at any hour of the day or night, whatever they might be, without hesitation, weakness or remorse.

In the eyes of the former chief of the Brotherhood of the White Lotus, the astonishing individual to whom he had given himself, as one gives oneself to the devil, effectively personified the pandemic revolution, which, from North to South and from the Far East to the Far West, would sooner or later end up taking its justiciary and vengeful scythe to all the decrepit old institutions whose burden is crushing the disinherited of all nations.

In his superstitious conception of history, Yu considered Rozen to be the messiah of revenge, something akin to the emperor of the Occidental Tai-Pings, destined to found, eventually, in the ruins of the Old World, the supreme reign of universal peace, justice and equality. What did it matter to him if, in order to attain that sacred goal, it was necessary to oppose force with force, crime with crime, cunning with cunning, theft with theft and even treason with treason? Does not the end justify the means?

Besides which, everything that Rozen, the hero, the prophet, the God, did, was necessarily justified...

The bell of the private telephone that linked his kiosk to the Boss's study abruptly wrenched Yu out of his dreams of general upheaval and fraternity. With one hand he stuck the receiver to his ear, while the other briskly pecked out a kind of arpeggio on the keyboard of the telescripter. It was the agreed signal to advertise at the other end of the wire that he was all ears.

"Go tell Madame," said Saint-Magloire, "that I regret not being able to dine with her this evening. I'm expected at the Ministry of War, and I shall doubtless not be back until late at night."

Yu telescripted that he had understood, and then went at his soft, lithe pace to Madame de Saint-Magloire's apartment.

223

Meanwhile, seated at his desk—a superb Empire design copied with scrupulous fidelity from the famous desk ornamenting the office of the Minister of Foreign Affairs on the Quai d'Orsay—Saint-Magloire seemed to be taking the greatest interest in reading a dossier relating to a lucrative business in military equipment, which he was leafing through feverishly.

His mind was elsewhere, however. He yawned and rubbed his eyes. Suddenly, gripped by an abrupt malaise, he slumped back in his armchair.

"Another of these accursed dizzy spells," he murmured. "For three weeks, I haven't been on the ball; my head is empty; I can no longer work. I'm becoming positively sickly. Will it be necessary for me to retire to the country, where I can live in bourgeois comfort on my petty pension, planting my cabbages? A cruel enigma, as the other would say."

The bandit sniggered, got up from his seat with an abrupt movement, and started pacing back and forth. "No, I'm neither old nor exhausted," he said to himself. "My muscles have all the energy and elasticity of old; my mind is still as clear. I know what I want, more than ever, and I still have the same thirst for wealth and power. My scorn for men and laws hasn't wilted. I have Paris at my feet; tomorrow, I'll be the arbiter of the world. Why try to hide from myself any longer the causes—or, rather, the cause—of this enervation from which I'm suffering? I'm infatuated with Germaine Reyval, that's all!

"That creature has awakened a sentiment in me to which I thought I was immune. I'm jealous, stupidly and ferociously, like some poet or grocer, jealous of a girl who's been on familiar terms, previously, with all of Paris: an actress who, just yesterday, was them mistress of Gouspin—the hideous Gouspin of the Japanese Divan.

"What does it matter? I love her, and I want her all to myself. She's said goodbye to her clown, I know, and in default of love, self-interest commands her to keep the swarm of her suitors at a distance. Three days ago, though, when she came to sing here, my joy in seeing her and hearing her as spoiled by the tender gaze with which she enveloped Dulac, the first to run to compliment her.

"That Dulac! Didn't he bore me to death once with the story of his love-affair with a singer who, after ruining him, dropped him for a poseur? I'm sure that singer was Germaine! Curse him! If he's found her again, got her back, in my house...oh, triple brute that I am, I'll have lit the candle...if it's true, woe betide Dulac!

"But my God, one would think I'd been gripped by sentiment...here I am, declaiming like a lover in a melodrama, without thinking that the clock is turning and that Germaine's waiting for me..."

At that moment, the ringing of a telephone interrupted his monologue.

"Hello?" said Saint-Magloire, suppressing a surge of impatience. "Who's that? Great—it's Eléna now. That's all I need."

"You're not dining at home?" Madame de Saint-Magloire enquired.

"No, darling—impossible. I've been invited by the Minister of War. It's a fag, but I can't get out of it. I need o hurry, too, for I'm already late. Excuse me—I don't have a minute to spare."

"Come, I beg you. Pepe is ill."

"Impossible, I repeat. I have to run. Goodnight, and a thousand kisses to Pepe."

"Our child is ill, Gaston, very ill. He wants to see you. Come, I beg you."

"Surely you're exaggerating? This morning, Pepe looked superb. It can't be serious, this sudden indisposition...but since he wants to see me, I'll come immediately."

I'm heading for a scene, the Baron thought, as he climbed the stairs. *Eléna must have caught wind of something; some charitable soul has mentioned Germaine to her. I'll wager that she's going to throw a fit, and that the child's illness is just a sham, a pretext to pin me down.*

He shrugged his shoulders, and continued: *Bah! It's not the first time it's happened. I know the routine...Eléna adores me; she'll forgive me, as always. It's only a matter of playing the game. Let's go see her.*

XI. Lover and Mother

At a deliberate pace, with a smile on his lips and a tender expression in his eyes, he went into the nursery.

Eléna had not deceived him; little José—Pepe, as his mother called him—really was ill. Gripped by a violent headache, fever and shivers that afternoon, the child had had to be put to bed.

The family doctor, the illustrious Dr. Faldin, had been urgently summoned and had diagnosed a gastric disorder that was not serious, but an hour ago, the child had fallen into a kind of torpor that had frightened Eléna.

"So it's true that Pepe's not feeling well," said the father, drawing nearer.

"You know that I never lie," sighed Eléna, whose beautiful eyes were veiled with tears. "José is ill." In a low voice, she added: "Dangerously ill."

Rozen leaned over the child, whom he kissed with an effusiveness that softened the mother's heart.

"What is Mama telling me?" Rozen went on, in his charmer's voice. "My Pepito isn't feeling well?"

"Yes Papa," sighed the child, with a sad smile.

"What is it? What is it? Here's a naughty Monsieur Pepe, who's pretending to be ill in order to be petted...."

"If you knew how I'm hurting...Father."

"Sleep, my darling; that will do your tummy-ache good. It must be tummy-ache. Tomorrow morning you'll be better, and we'll go for a nice ride in the Bois. Isn't that right, my Pepe?"

"Yes...the Bois...in the little carriage...tomorrow," said the child, in a plaintive voice.

"I'm going to leave you for a little while," the Baron added. "I've been called away on urgent business. Go to sleep; be good; I'll be back in an hour."

"Soon, Papa..."

"I told you—in an hour, perhaps before." To his wife, Saint-Magloire said: "You were wrong to be alarmed. Pepe's indisposition won't have any serious consequences." He headed for the door. "I'm leaving now, my love."

"You're in a great hurry to get away from me, then?" Eléna said.

"I'm not getting away from you," said Rozen, dryly. "I'm going to dine with the Minister of War."

"Don't leave your child, I beg you."

"Impossible! I have to talk to the minister tonight, about some equipment business."

"The minister's only a valet, at your orders, as you know full well. He won't make any deal without having asked your advice."

226

"It's true that I have an influence over him," Rozen said, smiling, "But he has his eccentricities, and..."

"Grant me a few minutes," Eléna implored.

"Two minutes—but no more."

Eléna confided José to the care of a chambermaid, and drew her lover into the next room. "I need to talk to you," she said, abruptly.

"Be quick, then. I'm in a tearing hurry—I'm expected."

"You mean that Germaine Reyval is expecting you."

"Germaine Reyval!" Rozen exclaimed, laughing. "Perhaps you imagine that I'm that young woman's...friend?"

"She's your mistress, Gaston—don't try to deny it. For months, my instinct, of a woman in love—for I love you with all the might of my heart and my flesh—has been able to divine beneath the deceptive effusion of your words and the studied exaggeration of your caresses, the indifference, and perhaps disgust, that I inspire in you. Besides which, all of Paris knows about your love-affair with Germaine, and in the presence of the scandal whipped up by the follies you've committed for that creature, it would be very naïve on my part to be unaware of your betrayal."

"My dear Eléna," Saint-Magloire interjected, taking a few steps toward the door of the room, "you're an adorable woman and a sublime mother, but permit me to tell you that you haven't a shadow of common sense. If you want to, we'll talk again tomorrow, at leisure, about the great treason of your humble servant and friend. I have repeated to you until I'm weary: a very important business matter that I cannot neglect has summoned me to the Ministry of War. Goodbye, then, and I'll see you soon."

"You won't go until you've heard me out!" Eléna cried, seizing Saint-Magloire's arm with an energetic hand.

"Speak then—what do you want?" said the latter, disappointed by this unexpected resistance, and addressing Eléna as *tu* in order to inspire more confidence in her.

She believed she had already won her cause and, her eyes shining and her face transfigured by the memory of the past times that she was evoking, she began: "Ten years ago, when I met you in Cayenne, in the home of the director of the penitentiary, touched by the story of your misfortunes, seduced by your beauty, subjugated by the grace of your manners, conquered by the charm and power of your mind, I gave myself to you, body and soul. On the strength of your promise to join me in the United States, I facilitated your escape from the bagne. After several years, when I believed you were dead, I found you again in London, rich and well-known in London's high society. You could have pretended not to recognize me and thrust me brutally into the gutter, but you were generous and good.

"Since that day, having become the King of Paris, rolling in gold, you have wanted me to share your luxury, you have presented me to the world as your legitimate wife. In default of the insensate love that I have for you, the affection that you have lavished on José, our dear child, has redoubled my admiration and my devotion. I have never attempted to penetrate the secrets of your life, or tried to discover the motive for your actions, some of which have appeared to me—why not admit it?—singular, and even suspect.

"I am your plaything, your slave, a passive instrument in your hands. You are a superior man, whose actions I do not measure, and whose orders I do not dispute—but I love you. I love you, and I'm jealous. I will not tolerate another woman stealing you from me!"

Exhausted by emotion, Eléna burst into tears. "Tell me, Gaston," she moaned, "tell me that Germaine is not your mistress. Swear to me that the world is lying…that you only love me."

The seducer went to her and, taking her hands in his, he drew her to a sofa and sat her down beside him. "Has the chagrin that José's illness has caused you obscured your reason, ordinarily so clear and direct?" he murmured. "Why insult me by believing that I am forsaking you for a venal woman? Since the day when your love and your unselfishness extracted me from the horrors of the bagne, I have vowed to you an attachment that no power in the world could every succeed in breaking or diminishing.

"With you, dear heart, you who are my entire life, I must not lie. I swear to you that your love for me is wrong to be alarmed. Certainly, all the appearances are against me. I understand that, in the eyes of society, my pretended liaison with Germaine Reyval is a proven fact…but if I allow it to be talked about, if I allow it to be believed, it's because I have to. The woman is useful to me; in my hands, she's an instrument, nothing more. Her, my mistress! Perish the thought! The day when that happened, I would have abdicated my power; she would hold me…but it's necessary that the gallery is unaware of the real objective of my relationship with Germaine. Yes, I spend money on her, that's true…"

He shrugged his shoulders. "You know full well," he added, "that in order to maintain he preponderant situation I have acquired, I must condescend to things that I find repugnant, but which are indispensable.

"People are saying that the banker Saint-Magloire has the most sought-after woman in Paris for a mistress, and that augments, in the eyes of the vainglorious—who form the majority—the prestige of Saint-Magloire. But if the Baron is associated with that woman of the theater, the heart of Rozen belongs to you forever, and beats for no one but you…"

"It's my turn," Eléna said, interrupting him, subjugated by the soft words and the soothing tone in which her lover pronounced them, "it's my turn to ask whether your reason is not going astray. What motive is powerful enough to drive you to court this woman?"

"No," said Rozen, in a grave voice vibrant with suppressed emotion, "what I have told you is dictated by reason itself. I am, as you know, the foremost promoter of enterprises in the entire world, one of the kings of cosmopolitan finance, and I am the one, I dare say, who pulls the strings of European politics from behind the stage.

"It's not an unhealthy ambition for wealth and enjoyment that has made me swear to amass a fortune without parallel—in which I have almost succeeded. Behind the Baron de Saint-Magloire, the director of the Banque Internationale, hides the anarchist Rozen—who, when the time comes, will put his immense capital, his political influence and his worldly relationships at the disposal of the social revolution.

"That moment, so ardently desired, will not be long in coming. The knowledge of certain diplomatic secrets will permit me to unleash a general conflagration in which the monarchies and political and social institutions of Europe will be consumed.

"Now, those secrets, which, in spite of my efforts and those of my usual collaborators, I have not yet been able to discover, are consigned to a single document, which is in the hands of diplomat I cannot name. It happens that the statesman in question is infatuated by Germaine, who, on my orders, has thus far resisted the solicitations of her worshiper.

"That man—who, like everyone else, believes in my liaison with the woman he covets, is gradually going mad. To possess her, he will commit the worst stupidities. That is what I'm seeking, what I'm waiting for. Thanks to the influence I've obtained over Germaine, I am master of the moment when she will finally consent to crown the diplomat's flame.

"Then, in the intoxication of the possession, he will forget all prudence and it will be child's play to rob him of the document he possesses, which will permit me to precipitate the ruination of the Old World and see the dawn of the social revolution, to which I have devoted my entire life.

"Do you understand now that I am no more mad than you are? Do you understand that Saint-Magloire's love-affair with the fashionable cantatrice is pure comedy? Come on! Jealous! Come into the arms of your Rozen, who will forgive you for having doubted him…for it's further proof of the love that you have for him…"

Vanquished by the charmer's persuasive eloquence, the naïve Eléna dissolved in tears, and covered the man she loved with kisses. "Forgive me, my love, forgive me," she stammered. "Go…I love you…and you're right to sacrifice my self-respect to the great cause that you and Sokoloff are defending…

"But I'm afraid, my love…I'm afraid…"

"Child!" he said, with a smile full of promises. "What will it take to convince you, then?" He hugged her tightly to his breast, caressing her with his hypnotic gaze, carefully avoiding interrupting the flood of words that rose to the lips of his generous and gently lover.

"Yes," Eléna continued, "I understand and I admire you. You are the sole judge of the means to be deployed to bring prompt destruction to a social order from which we have both suffered so much. Go where duty calls you, my idol. I don't want to know any more, I tell you! I no longer want to know whether Germaine Reyval exists..."

When she had finished, Rozen took her hands and held them affectionately in his.

"In your turn," he said, "forgive me for having employed wounding words in your regard. I do not love and never will love any other woman than you—but it's necessary that I accomplish, fully and without weakness, the glorious mission that I have undertaken."

Then, drawing Eléna toward him again in a passionate embrace, he deposited a long and ardent kiss on her lips.

"Before leaving," Eléna said, with a delighted smile. "Come and see José."

"Let's go and see the dear child," Rozen agreed.

"How is Pepe?" asked Eléna of the governess charged with looking after the child.

"He's been asleep for half an hour, and only has a slight fever now."

The Baron resumed the formal mode of address before the boy's nurse. "You see," he said to the Baronne, "that you were exaggerating the gravity of José's illness. I'm leaving. Get some rest, my dear. See you soon."

But she held him back again. "Oh, stay, stay!" she begged. "I don't know why, but I'm haunted by sinister presentiments. It seems to me that our child is going to die!"

"You're being unreasonable," he said, softly. "Pepe only has a slight indisposition. Do you think that if he were seriously ill, I'd have the heart to occupy myself with business matters?"

"You'll only be absent for as short a time as possible, won't you, my love? And as soon as you come in you'll come to see how he is?"

"I promise," said Saint-Magloire—who, after having brushed Eléna's hand with his lips, made haste to go away and climb into the carriage that was to take him to Germaine's abode.

"I'll watch my son," said Eléna to the governess. "You can go to bed. If I need you during the night, I'll ring."

"As Madame pleases."

Two hours went by.

Reassured as to the condition of her son, who seemed to be sleeping peacefully, Eléna lay down on a chaise longue to doze, but she wanted to make sure once again that the child was not troubled, and, drawing nearer to José's bed, was frightened by the little boy's pale face and the extreme dilation of his pupils.

At that moment, Pepe was seized by a violent coughing fit, and his lips were fringed with foam.

"Pepe!" she said, picking him up in her arms. "Pepe, my dearest! Look at me! It's your Mama..."

But the little boy's eyes were fixed, as if obscured by a veil.

Then, the mother became aware of the gravity of the illness. She stood up, with a tragic expression. "My child is dying!" she cried, mad with grief. "Help! Fetch a doctor!"

She ran to the bell, and then returned to the sick child's bed.

José had lost consciousness, and was agitated at intervals by a dolorous tic.

"The governess appeared. "Run and fetch Dr. Faldin," she ordered. "My son's dying! Quickly! Quickly! It might already be too late." And, remaining alone with José, breathless with desperation, her eyes riveted to the child's face, she murmured: "Oh, if only I knew what to do while waiting for the doctor! As long as he comes right away...I should have stopped Gaston going out. He would have known, without a doubt, what to do to save my son...but me, I'm powerless..."

At that moment, Pepe was breathing more easily; his eyes were closed; he seemed to be asleep—but a continuous plaint emerged from his discolored lips.

Meanwhile, the mother wanted to clutch at one final hope. Even though she had, by virtue of contact with Rozen and Sokoloff, lost all religious belief, she experienced in her distress the need to request help from the God whom she had been taught in her infancy to implore. It was not for nothing that she had Spanish blood in her veins.

She knelt down beside the bed and, with her hands joined and her eyes raised toward the heavens, toward infinity, she murmured a prayer into which she put her entire soul.

"My God...my God! You permit, do you not, people to be saved? Have pity on him! Have pity on me!"

XII. A Light in the Darkness

"What a miserable dinner I'll be serving him!" complained Dr. Lemoine's maidservant, looking with an expression of consternation at the wall-clock in the dining room. "Half past nine! He promised me that he'd be back at eight o'clock! His lateness is inexplicable. The lady who is in the drawing room has an appointment with him, and he never makes anyone wait...God forbid that he's had an accident! One can never be tranquil in Paris, where there are so many carriages and rogues!

Thee reflections did not prevent old Perrine from casting a glance at her oven, and after having observed with a sigh of satisfaction that the chicken fricassee, the main dish of the compromised dinner, was not in danger of immediate desiccation, she went into the drawing room.

"Is Monsieur le Docteur here?" asked the unknown woman, rising to her feet.

"Not yet, Madame," but he can't be much longer. Monsieur usually dines at eight; he's doubtless been retained at the bedside of a patient. Don't worry, Madame; given that Monsieur has given you an appointment, he won't break his word. If he's going to be too late, he'll send you word—and that, thank God, will reassure me...

"He's bound to arrive at any moment..."

While delivering this monologue, the worthy woman went to the electric radiator—a kind of curiously-wrought copper grille—that Lemoine had recently installed, in place of a screen, in front of the fireplace.

"It's one of Monsieur's inventions," she said, "and see how it warms! Properly, you know! No smoke, so ashes, no odor of charcoal, no dirt. It's jolly convenient, you know."

"Is the doctor an engineer, then?" asked the visitor.

"Engineer!" exclaimed Perrine. "Yes, of course he's an engineer. To begin with, he's everything. Monsieur does whatever he wants—and with that, he's generosity itself, a saint!"

Once launched upon a eulogy to her master, the worthy woman was not easily stopped.

"It wasn't yesterday that I met him," she continued, happy to be able to talk about the object of her worship yet again. "I was in service in his father's house, and I knew him when he was very young—see, no bigger than this...and now he's a scientist, a fine physician. He could make millions if he wanted to, but no! He only looks after the poor people, all the people who haven't a sou. And the rest of the time, he works for himself, reading big books and making machines such as have never been seen..."

A ringing bell cut off Dame Perrine's verbiage.

"It's Monsieur!" she cried, precipitating herself toward her master.

"Bonjour, my dear Perrine," said the doctor, "I'm a little late...and you're going to scold me again..."

"Well! If you think it's pleasant to die of anxiety like this every evening..."

Lemoine could not help smiling. "Come on, come on, don't argue. For this evening, hold your peace...show me mercy...I'm expecting someone..."

"She's been here for a long time...poor lady...and I told her that even a physician..."

"Good, good...leave your recriminations for later, Perrine. Serve my dinner, quickly."

"It'll be jolly, that dinner...if you make that lady wait much longer..."

"No, I'll ask her to come and talk to me while I'm at table. Hurry up—I'm dying of hunger."

The doctor went into the drawing room and advanced toward the stranger. "Madame Oliva Lavardens?" he said, bowing.

"Yes, Monsieur le Docteur. This morning, your pupil, Monsieur Martin came to tell me that you wanted to see me...with regard to a matter of interest to me."

"And which interests me too, Madame, for I've promised to help you with all my strength...no longer to leave you alone...to undertake..."

The young woman did not mistake the meaning of what the doctor was saying for an instant. "Oh, Monsieur!" she exclaimed. "have I finally found a man who will consent to lend me his support in discovering my poor Charles's murderer—for this is about the crime in Bréauté, isn't it?"

"Your presumption is correct, Madame—it is indeed the crime in Bréauté that I want to discuss with you. I desire to know the details of it, in order to give you, if possible, the means to avenge yourself."

"Oh, thank you...thank you!" Oliva could not say any more. Emotion, the joy of finding someone willing to listen to her, to encourage her in the work of vengeance she had undertaken, prevented her from articulating any but a single phrase: "Thank you."

"I will, however, ask you, before the conversation that I need to have with you, for permission to go into the dining room. You will excuse me, Madame, for you know how pressured our time is...we physicians..."

"I am at your disposal, Monsieur," Madame Lavardens replied.

They both went into the dining room.

It will be remembered that Dr. Lemoine, after encountering the widow Lavardens at the door of the office of the head of the Sûreté, and with the latter's authorization, had promised to question the unfortunate woman who had been represented as a madwoman.

Desirous of shedding light as soon as possible on the mysterious crime of which the Sûreté and the court had long ago enounced searching for the author or authors, Lemoine had asked his assistant Martin to go to see Oliva and ask her to come to his residence, at number 115, Rue des Dames, Batignolle, at eight-thirty in the evening.

Fearful of a trap, Madame de Lavardens had come to the Rue des Dames during the day and, under the pretext of making some purchases of small importance in various local shops, had obtained information regarding the doctor.

"Monsieur Lemoine is an incomparable physician, a great scientist, a perfect honest man!" she had been told, everywhere.

Reassured as to the doctor's intentions, and somewhat intrigued by the mysterious aspect of the rendezvous, she had not hesitated to respond to Martin's invitation.

After having excused himself again, Lemoine offered Oliva a chair, and sat down at table, served by old Perrine, who was slightly discontented to see that her master was only going to eat the dishes she had so carefully prepared for him in a distracted fashion.

There was a momentary pause, during which Oliva collected herself and the doctor studied her.

This woman, he said to himself, *seems to me to be of sound mind. And it would require the men of law to be superficial and hidebound—as they often are—in order for them to attribute to mental alienation the insistence with which the pretty lady demands the pursuit and punishment of her husband's murderer. There is no external sign suggestive of the derangement of her faculties.*

Oliva was the first to break the silence. "I was greatly surprised," she said, "being unacquainted with you—even with your name—by the rendezvous to which you have summoned me. I hesitated at first as to whether to accept the invitation, but having determined that you are a benevolent and charitable man, always ready to take an interest in the unfortunate, materially or mentally, I overcame my hesitation. I am ready to answer you now that I know the motive for your summons. You will help me to avenge the husband I adored. Speak, Monsieur—question me."

"Madame," Lemoine replied, "you have the guarantee of my most active collaboration, but I beg you to remain calm and not to recriminate against the magistrates who have, in good faith, abandoned an affair that they thought quite simple. They concluded that it was an accident, but you are sure that it was not. I have a vague intuition that you might be right, and I want to enlighten myself with regard to this tenebrous story.

"I shall therefore proceed with an interrogation as meticulous as possible, and you must not be astonished by questions put to you be a man without a judiciary mandate..."

"What does that matter to me?" said Oliva, fervently. "What does it matter whether someone who takes an interest in me, and consents to hold out a hand to permit me to reach my goal, is official or not?"

"However," the doctor interjected, "I can tell you that the secret enquiry that I am beginning this evening has been given the agreement of the head of the

Sûreté. He has promised me the broadest cooperation and the most devoted of his sleuths."

"I shall be eternally grateful to you for the interest that you are taking," Oliva stammered, her voice choked by emotion. "You may interrogate me. I will tell you, without reservation, everything I know about my husband's murder."

"Your name is Oliva Ossona, widow of Charles Lavardens, former non-commissioned officer in the marine infantry, and more recently a commercial representative?"

"Yes, Monsieur."

"Where were you resident at the moment when your husband was found dead a few hundred meters from Beuzeville-Bréauté station?"

"We were about to leave for America, and we had left our lodgings at 125 Rue Lepic to stay at the Hotel Frascati in Le Havre."

"According to the notes furnished to me by the Sûreté," Lemoine continued, rifling through a file, "Lavardens, traveling on the line from Paris to Le Havre, fell accidentally through the door or the compartment in which he was traveling, and was killed in consequence, not far from Beuzeville-Bréauté station. I have a copy of the statement drawn up by the medical examiner. Summoned to give his opinion as to the cause of your husband's tragic death, the professional concluded that it was a purely accidental but explicable death due, according to him, to internal lesions determined by Lavardens' fall."

"That physician is wrong!" Oliva replied. "When, after six mortal hours of waiting on the platform at Le Havre station, I learned from the Company employees that the body of a traveler had been found on the track at Beuzeville-Bréauté, I immediately went to the scene of the incident, although they tried to dissuade me. Alas, my presentiments had not deceived me. The cadaver lying in the improvised bed in the stationmaster's office was indeed my husband's.

"The official statement affirms that Charles Lavardens' body bore no apparent wound that could have caused death..."

"That's true," said Lemoine. "No trace was found of any knife wound or gunshot wound. But pray continue, Madame."

"The place where Charles's body had been found was very close to the station at Beuzeville. At that point, the train must have been moving quite slowly..."

"Indeed, it is usual, on arrival at a station, to stop briefly and put on the brakes in order to reduce sped and bring the train to a smooth halt in the station."

"Suppose that, woken up with a start by that deceptive stop, and induced by the sight of the lights on the track to believe, erroneously, that he had arrived at his destination, poor Charles had opened the compartment door and jumped down. Don't you think that a man of his agility could not have done that without accident? Getting off a train in those conditions was child's play for Lavardens. But even if, only half-awake, he had miscalculated his leap and fallen, the fall could not have been serious enough to cause death. He might have broken a leg or perhaps dislocated an arm..."

"It's the head that hit the ground first," the doctor objected.

"And it's for that reason that I persist in affirming that my husband was killed in the carriage. His cadaver was thrown on to the track by the murderer with the objective of creating the belief that the death was accidental. The wretch was well-served by the circumstances, and by the negligence with which the medical examiner inspected the body. That man only had one thing to say: 'No trace of violence; no wound.' Does one need a knife or a pistol to kill someone. I am convinced that science offers criminals mean of killing as sure as weapons..."

"We'll return to that grave question later," Lemoine observed. "There's another point on which I want to question you. If the documents I possess are accurate, you told the examining magistrate who assisted in the initial investigation that the author of the murder was one other than an individual named Rozen, a famous bandit escaped from the penitentiary in Guiana. Now, according to the reports of the colonial administration, that man died in attempting to traverse the virgin forests of the Maroni. His death certificate has been issued."

"I identified Rozen as Lavardens' murderer," said Oliva, emphasizing her words, "in spite of the administration's reports, because, in spite of his death certificate, Rozen is alive, and because he alone could have had an interest in killing Charles."

"That demands explanation," said Lemoine, keenly impressed by the widow's definite declaration."

"I'll explain. Charles had often talked to me about Rozen, whom he once knew in London. He had rediscovered him later in the penitentiary in Guiana, to which he had been sent after a series of crimes that earned him a sentence of hard labor. Charles, who was then a non-commissioned officer in the marine infantry, had not wanted to be recognized by Rozen. He was guided by a humanitarian sentiment."

"I understand," Lemoine put in. "He did not want the convict, clad in the uniform of the bagne, to blush before a former comrade."

"In any case, Madame Lavardens continued, "Charles was only in the Îles de Salut for a while. When his term of service concluded, he returned to France and was discharged. Enterprising and active, he left again almost immediately for America, this time for Venezuela, where he was to set up an establishment to buy raw rubber. There, he learned from the newspapers about Rozen's escape and death. Sometime after that, however, he was surprised to find himself in the presence of the escaped convict who was believed to be dead. Rozen, who had no money, and therefore no objective, was wandering aimlessly.

"He was, and must still be, a clever actor, so he succeeded in interesting Charles in his fate, and poor Lavardens gave him some money to help him start a new life. Charles was good and trusting. He believed in the convict's repent-

236

ance, and had a certain sympathy for the fallen man—so intelligent, he said, and so charming—whom he sincerely believed to be capable of great things. 'What a pity he turned to the bad,' was what he said—and he said it to me often."

"All these details, very interesting from the viewpoint of the case, offer proof that Rozen really did succeed in his escape. The fact is established, so far as I am concerned. Please continue, Madame."

"After many misfortunes which would take too long to relate and would not add anything to the clarity of the story I'm telling you," Oliva went on, "we ended up in a tiny apartment in the Rue Lepic, where we had been living for some months on meager commissions that Charles obtained here and there. Then, one day, I saw him come in radiant. 'I've just taken a step that will assure our future,' he told me. 'I've finally found a backer in order to go to Guiana to undertake timber exploitation.'

"Driven by a natural curiosity, I tried to discover the name of the generous banker to whom we owed that happiness, but Charles remained mute. To my pressing questions he always replied: 'I can't reveal that, even to you. Later, perhaps, you'll know, and you'll be astonished. In sum, we're going to Le Havre, where we'll embark for America.'

"Two days before the departure of the steamship, Charles traveled to Paris; I received a telegram—the last—saying: *Business concluded.* You know the rest. He was killed in the carriage that was bringing him, joyful and triumphant, to Le Havre. My husband's tragic end was due, in my conviction, to a murder committed by Rozen, or an accomplice. Everything causes me to suppose that: the mystery with which Charles had surrounded his negotiations with his backer; the few words escaped by virtue of the impatience caused by my insidious questions: 'You'll be astonished.' I'm certain that it was Rozen that Lavardens encountered again in Paris: Rozen, who had succeeded, by a series of audacious coups, in recreating a situation; Rozen, who, doubtless fearing a denunciation—as if Charles were capable of that!—wanted to avoid the possibility, to make an inconvenient witness, a man who knew his true identity, disappear permanently."

"That's plausible," said Lemoine, "but you have no proof to support..."

"It's proof for which I'm searching," Oliva said. In a discouraged tone, she added: "You doubt me too, Monsieur, but think: who could have so rapidly advanced a hundred thousand francs to Charles, without any preliminary study, if not Rozen? Another man, assuming that he had consented to that large advance, would have come forward after the murder; he would have reclaimed his money—which was, moreover, not recovered, since Charles had no trace of that vast sum on him when his body was found. On the part of any capitalist, that silence would be incomprehensible. On Rozen's part, by contrast, it is quite understandable.

"Alarmed by the appearance of Charles, his first move was to give him money, to do him a great favor in order to buy his discretion. Then, on reflection, he took fright. He told himself that only the dead can keep a secret, and that, besides, it would be good to recover the hundred thousand francs. For a man like him, one crime more or less scarcely counts, especially if it gives him security..."

"All that is, in fact, quite logical," murmured Lemoine, "but I return to this point: what material proof is there? We don't even have a serious clue: not the slightest thread leading to the trail that might be followed in order to lay hands on the guilty party. Everything is dark. Yes, you must be reasoning correctly, but we must not be content with reasoning. In such a matter, the most expert and most ingenious deductions only serve as a basis for a moral conviction. Everything remains mysterious and ungraspable, including the accomplishment of the crime...the discovery of the body bearing no trace of wounds..."

"I repeat, Monsieur, that one has no need of weapons to kill someone..."

"Yes, I know...poison...perhaps there's something for which to search...we'll see. Rozen, if he really is guilty..."

"It's him!" Oliva exclaimed. "That, I swear to you."

"Yes," Lemoine continued, without contesting the widow's affirmation. "Rozen is knowledgeable; he might have employed means that leave no trace. We'll try to investigate that. You mentioned an accomplice just now...I think we ought to set that hypothesis aside, for I can't see Rozen entrusting such a task to an accomplice. It's not possible because it's not logical. As I see this bandit, in accordance with the legend that formed his silhouette like a legendary aureole, Rozen must have operated alone, and we'll discover, I promise, the means that he employed...

"In any case, what appears to me to be indubitable, is that Rozen, if your husband saw him in Paris, evidently committed the crime to get rid of a possible denouncer. It's therefore necessary for us to find some trace of the negotiations that might have taken place between the two men. For that, it's necessary to discover the name under which the revenant is currently hiding. That's the first thing we have to look into; before anything else, we need that point of departure.

"Collect all your memories, Madame, search the depths of its most secret recesses, and try to recall whether your husband ever said anything that might guide us in that enquiry."

"Alas, Monsieur," Oliva replied, "I haven't waited until now to ask myself that question, to which I have no answer. My husband always talked about Gaston Rozen, or simply Gaston, nothing more and nothing less."

"But in the absence of a name, and address or a nickname, can't you recall some characteristic feature of Rozen's physiognomy?"

"I only know one thing, and that is that he was a very handsome fellow, or a rare beauty, tall in stature, with extraordinary eyes: 'of velvet and flame,' my poor Charles said. He said that he had never seen such a gaze. Not very precise, as a description, is it, Doctor? Oh—I forgot: Rozen, who must now be thirty-seven or thirty-eight years old, speaks all the languages of Europe fluently. He is, in addition, a scholar and an artist. He has a superb voice, and plays the piano like a virtuoso."

"All that is doubtless very vague," Lemoine went on, "but one never knows. In the event, one or other of those details, which seems at present to be insignificant, might clarify the situation in a dazzling fashion. Tomorrow, I'll begin my campaign."

Lemoine had been so strongly gripped by the situation that he had not thought of moving to another room. Oliva and he had remained in the dining room, at the table that Perrine had just cleared.

"It's getting late," the doctor declared. "I'll accompany you to the cab-rank."

"Don't take the trouble," Oliva replied. "I'm brave, believe me, and the Rue des Dames isn't cut-throat territory."

"It's nearly midnight," Lemoine replied, getting up, "and it would be negligent on my part to let you go alone."

The doctor put on his overcoat, and headed for the door, followed by Madame Lavardens.

"The affair whose delicate solution we're pursuing demands absolute prudence," said Lemoine, as he left the house with his protégée. "Don't visit the Sûreté again and tell anyone who asks that you've given up trying to discover your husband's murderer. When I need to confer with you, I'll arrange a time and place for the meeting via my pupil, Monsieur Martin."

"I'll follow your instructions to the letter," the window replied. "Until we meet again—and once again, permit me to thank you for your generous devotion."

In the street they walked in silence, and went down to the level of the exterior boulevards, where Oliva climbed into a fiacre. Then the doctor headed back to his domicile.

We may suppose, he thought, *that Charles Lavardens must have been murdered by Rozen or one of his companions. On the other hand, it's certain the wretch occupies, or has occupied, a prominent position in the world of finance, and if he had not left Paris in the wake of one of those catastrophes that generally put an end to three cosmopolitan tricksters, I should be able to locate him. Once his identity is recognized, I'll be able to set a trap in which, no matter how clever he is, he can't fail to be caught.*

Lemoine was only a few steps from home when a luxurious carriage drew up outside his door. A footman leapt nimbly from the seat and, after having checked the house number leaned hard on the doorbell.

"Who are you looking for?" asked Lemoine, intrigued by the nocturnal visit."

"Monsieur le docteur Lemoine."

"That's me."

"So much the better," the footman replied. "It's on behalf of Dr. Faldin. Come quickly, Doctor—Madame's little boy is dying..."

"Is it far?" Lemoine asked.

"The Champs-Élysées, Doctor, but with our horses we'll be there in ten minutes. Oh, come quickly. I've been to Dr. Faldin's—they told me that he was visiting a patient in the Rue des Dames. I've just come from there, because Madame only wants him, but the Doctor can't come. He gave me your address, and told me that you'd go on his behalf..."

"Who are your employers?"

"The Baron and Baronne de Saint-Magloire."

"I'll come with you," Lemoine said, simply, getting into the carriage, which drew away at top speed toward the Champs-Élysées.

"What a strange coincidence!" Lemoine murmured. "Saint-Magloire! Isn't that the name of that Levantine financier, the director of the Banque Internationale, who lives in a sumptuous house in the Champs-Élysées, where hazard is taking me? I've glimpsed that equivocal individual several times, whose hand is in every great financial and industrial enterprise, and exercises, so I'm told, a sovereign and occult influence over ministers and Parliament."

Involuntarily, the doctor made a connection between certain details that he knew about Saint-Magloire and the description of Rozen that Oliva had given him: a handsome man with seductive manners, by virtue of his voice and singular dark, brilliant and expressive eyes, an excellent musician and polyglot. Moreover, Saint-Magloire had, in Lemoine's eyes, a shady side. He must be a high-flying rogue—but from there to seeing his as the former convict that Charles Lavardens had known, to his misfortune, was a great leap...

A man escaped from the bagne, a celebrated thief, sought by all the police in the world, does not become a banker and politician overnight.

I'm dreaming, the doctor concluded. *What point is there in trying to establish a far-fetched comparison? Evidently, Rozen must have established a new identity; he's perfectly capable of occupying an enviable in the population of interlopers that lives the high life in Paris, but the millionaire Baron de Saint-Magloire must have an origin different from Rozen...however clever he is, he hasn't had time to rise so high. He might have been the king of the bagne, but he could never be the King of Paris.*

XIII. A Mother's Curse

"Save my child, Doctor!" cried Eléna, precipitating herself toward the doctor that the valet had just introduced into José's room...but she stopped dead, fixing the newcomer with a gaze in which there was an expression of extreme surprise.

For his part, the doctor felt himself invaded by a strange disturbance. Eléna's voice had made him tremble, and there, very close to him, in her simple indoor costume, Saint-Magloire's wife reminded him even more of the features of the woman he had once loved, from whom Destiny had separated him, but whom he had never forgotten.

Both of them remained indecisive, their hearts overflowing with memories, no longer daring to speak, for fear of seeing the vision of the past vanish...

Were they not both, perhaps, the victims of a hallucination?

Eléna was the first to resolve to ask a question. "Monsieur," she said, "this isn't the first time we've met. In New York, some years ago, I knew a Frenchman...also a physician...whose name was Lemoine..."

The doctor interrupted her. His heart was beating violently: a name rose to his lips: Eléna. And that name he repeated, extending his hands toward the woman he had adored: "Eléna Ruiz!"

"You...you! Lemoine!" stammered the Baronne, prey to a violent emotion, in which there was both joy and pain: the joy of seeing a friend again; the pain of finding him when she was not free, when she belonged to another...

A plaint from the child brought her back to reality.

"Heaven be praised!" she said, taking the doctor's hand. "You'll save the child as you once saved the mother."

Those words brought back all Lemoine's self-composure and mental lucidity. He remembered that he had been urgently summoned for a desperate case. The man gave way to the physician.

In two seconds, forgetting Havana and New York, even forgetting the love that fatality had just reanimated within him, he absorbed himself entirely in the exercise of his art.

"Let's see," he said, softly, drawing nearer to the bed where the child lay, wrought by pain and delirious, with strange sighs that resembled death-rattles.

In the blink of an eye, Lemoine was conscious of the gravity of the malady, but he did not let his impression show, in order not to alarm the mother.

"Bring me the lamp," said, throwing his coat on to a chair with an abrupt gesture.

Scarcely had the chambermaid assisting the Baronne brought the lamp, however, than the little invalid began uttering shrill cries.

At the same time, his eyelids convulsed, while his teeth were grinding in a sinister fashion.

Oh! thought Lemoine, whose experienced eye had not missed the slightest of those significant symptoms. *Rapidly-progressing meningitis! The poor child is doomed...he'll be dead in two hours...unless...*

"You'll save him, won't you, Doctor?" Eléna implored, in a tremulous voice.

Lemoine did not answer the question. Straightening up, he commanded, curtly: "Leeches! Ice! And quickly!"

"Quickly! Leeches! Ice!" Eléna repeated. "Do as the Doctor says!"

"Yes, yes," the latter went on. "And don't waste a second."

"Is my child going to die?" asked Madame de Saint-Magloire, disturbed by the physician's tone. "My God! My God! He's going to die?"

Lemoine was reluctant to break the mother's heart with too brutal a reply, but neither did he want to hide the dolorous truth from her.

She sensed the hesitation, and her anguish was further increased by it. Shaken by sobs, she persisted: "Doctor...my friend...I beg you, don't lie to me. I must...I want...to know!"

"My God, Eléna... Madame," Lemoine said, pulling himself together. "I won't hide the fact that it's very serious, but by acting energetically, I hope we might yet save him. Calm down, I beg you. It's necessary that you reply to a few questions that I need to ask."

"I can do that, Doctor," Eléna replied, holding back her tears by means of a heroic effort. "I'm listening."

"Can you tell me the first symptoms that the child exhibited."

"This morning, at lunch time, José was quite well, as cheerful and turbulent as usual. He ate with a good appetite. It was only at about three o'clock, this afternoon, after his lesson, that he complained of having a bad headache. I thought at first that it was one of those insignificant and temporary headaches that all children get, especially when they're growing, but I was mistaken.

"The fever began, with violent shivering, nausea, and I sent for our physician..."

"Dr. Faldin," Lemoine put in, "is one of our most experienced and perspicacious physicians. That's odd. What time did he come?"

"Six o'clock."

"And what did he say?"

"He said that it was a slight indisposition—a colic, I think. He prescribed powdered quinine hydrobromide and a tonic potion of cola."

"That's extraordinary," Dr. Lemoine said, *sotto voce.* "At six o'clock, he should not have mistaken the symptoms, and he still had time to take action. It's incomprehensible. My word, I think that fashionable great physicians sometimes don't pay attention to what they're doing. The hurry around, listening to their patients' chests and writing their prescriptions too rapidly…they have too many patients to see..." He went on: "He's been vomiting, hasn't he, Madame?"

"Yes, Doctor, with the frightful screams that you've heard—that's what frightened me. Terrified, I sent for the doctor urgently. He must not have been free."

"No—he recommended that your servant come and ask me to substitute for him."

"And here you are, Doctor—you, to whom I owe my liberty, my life, whom I thought I would never see again. God is good! He doesn't want my child to die! He's sent you to save him."

At that moment the child, who had remained silent for a few minutes, uttered a more violent scream, even shriller—a veritable howl, of a slaughtered beast. Crazed with anguish, Elena threw herself on José and began covering his poor distressed and grimacing face with mad kisses.

"Be careful, my dear friend," said Lemoine, in a grave voice, "be careful! Master your grief, I beg you. Let me be the only one to touch the child, to whom your caresses risk doing harm. Perhaps it's still not too late, but I'll need your help shortly. Control yourself, I beg you."

At that moment, out of breath from the rapidity of his run, the valet brought an ice-bucket and a jar of leeches. He began to recount in detail that he had had difficulty waking up the pharmacist, but the doctor cut off that futile verbiage with a curt word. Then, with consummate skill and an admirable dexterity, he placed four leeches behind each of the child's ears, and covered his skull with a rubber cap full of crushed ice.

Almost immediately, the hoarse gasps eased, the muscle-contractions in the face ceased, and the little invalid, ceasing to moan, fell into a deep sleep, troubled only—at long intervals—by feverish spasms.

"My role is concluded," said Lemoine then. "Everything that had to be done urgently has been done. You have time enough to summon your usual physician. This time your people will doubtless find him at home, and he'll no longer be mistaken as to the diagnosis. I have nothing more to do than withdraw, blessing the providence that has permitted me to see you again…even though it is as painful for me as it is, perhaps, for you..." He added, in an imploring tone: "Will you permit me to come and ask for news of the dear child?"

"My dear friend, I beg you, don't go! I'm afraid…I'm afraid…some complication might arise before Dr. Faldin arrives. I wouldn't know what to do. Besides, I no longer have any hope or confidence in anyone but you."

The professional overexcitement had eased, and Lemoine felt himself invaded by a strange disturbance in the presence of the woman whose cherished image had often haunted his dreams, and whom he had just rediscovered, so miraculously, in anguish and despair.

Too emotional to speak, he nodded his head to indicate that he would stay; then, still mute, his blood seething and his throat constricted, having great difficulty in slowing down the beating of his heart, he went to sit down at the child's beside, while Eléna, having murmured a word of thanks into which she put her entire soul, sat down in an armchair, hiding her face in her hands.

Stifled by the thick hangings that covered the walls and hid the windows and the door, the noises from outside did not penetrate as far as that room, in which a heavy silence weighed upon the warm air, redolent with pharmaceutical odors, scarcely troubled by the regular ticking of clock and poor little José's occasional sighs and coughs.

Plunged in the shadow of the curtains, Dr. Lemoine, who gradually pulled himself together, recovering his ordinary calmness along with his self-possession, was able to examine the Baronne de Saint-Magloire at his leisure. Slumped in her armchair, the poor woman would have seemed to be unconscious if a convulsive shudder had not agitated her body from time to time.

What a romance her life has been! Lemoine thought. *Eléna Ruiz, the ardent patriot, daughter of a martyr to independence, the heroine of Cuba, now the wife of a cosmopolitan business magnate, that Saint-Magloire one finds everywhere, whose name is on everyone's lips, the King of Paris who inspires both suspicion and respect in the police...a female revolutionary ending up in the guise of a millionaire socialite! How...as a result of what imperious and tragic circumstances...in consequence of what drama...has that come about?*

And the doctor thought that if his mother's death had not obliged him to leave New York so hurriedly, if destiny had permitted him to correspond with the young wma he had abandoned in that American city, that adorable creature would now be his wife!

That thought made him shiver; then, his eyes staring into the void, he continued dreaming.

My God! How I loved her! She even seemed to share that love! And I lost her! She belongs to another...to that accursed Saint-Magloire, whom I suspect of being the worst of bandits! She was so pretty, with eyes of such an infinite softness, a charming voice, lips begging to be kissed... Today, she's perhaps even lovelier, more troubling in her radiant maturity...

Do I still love her? Lemoine wondered. *Should I not crush this affection that is reigniting in my heart? Should I not distance myself from her forever? Better to do that, to accept destiny...*

Why disturb her life? Perhaps she loves and esteems her husband. Not to see her again would give her a proof of love greater than any other...

Lemoine recalled the suspicions he had had the other evening, at the Opéra.

Oh! he concluded. *The heart has instinctive leaps that are not deceptive.*

Eléna too was pensive, her soul in turmoil. A dolorous disturbance mingled with her maternal anguish. At that moment, she seemed to be living in a nightmare.

244

She evoked the memory of the terrible drama in Cuba, which had enabled her, after so many vicissitudes, to meet Lemoine, her savior. She saw once again, with gripping clarity, the tent of the Spanish general, whom she had begged for mercy for her father, the outrage, the firing squad, the condemnation to death, the last-minute delay—and then, the appearance of Lemoine, the escape, the flight to New York.

I loved him and he loved me, she said to herself. *I could have, I ought to have been, his wife...*

That was before the voyage to Guiana that was about to turn my life upside-down...

What must he think, finding me here in the midst of this luxury? My God, he would doubtless despise me if he knew the whole truth!

Suddenly, she felt a mad terror. She recalled all of Dr. Lemoine's perspicacity, his psychological subtlety, his liking for obscure and complex problems. Surely, he would be led to want to know the truth—and it would be a mere game for him to succeed. He had deciphered other enigmas just as tenebrous! Then she would be doomed, dishonored, in the eyes of one of the only man in the world whose esteem was precious to her...

At that moment, a feeble plaint, followed by an agonized groan, recalled the mother and the physician to the immediate reality, even crueler than their dream.

"My José! My Pepito!" moaned the Baronne, on seeing the poor child, his body abruptly stiffened ad his features congealed in a macabre rictus, writhing on bloodstained pillows.

Lemoine had leaned over the bed.

"Neither the ice nor the leeches have been effective," he murmured. "It was too late."

Eléna had not heard him, but when the doctor straightened up, his brow furrowed and his gaze bleak, she understood that it was all over.

"He's dead, isn't he?" she asked, in a breath.

The doctor nodded his head.

The poor woman had ceased weeping. In her eyes, abruptly dry, an ardent flame was ignited, illuminating a hollow face the color of ash.

She rang.

The valet came running.

"Go fetch Monsieur," she said, in a changed voice, whose hoarseness was astonishing in that angelic mouth.

"Monsieur le Baron has not yet returned," the man replied.

I suspected as much, Eléna thought. *The cheat lied to me. He certainly wasn't dining with the minister. Where can he be? With that slut, no doubt. But there or elsewhere, what does it matter? What's frightful, criminal, is that, knowing that his child was in agony and his wife in despair, he dared to run to his pleasure...the man has no heart. He deceives me as he deceives everyone else. Oh, I feel at this moment that I hate him, that gutless father! Alas, every-thing's falling apart at the same time.*

My child is dead...

My love is dead too...

Faith is dead!

"Be strong, Eléna," said the doctor, seeing the unfortunate creature totter.

"Oh, my friend!" she replied. "If you knew! If you only knew!"

And, falling to her knees at the foot of the bed, she began to press the child's inert and already cold hands to her lips.

A few seconds later, the door opened abruptly, and, his face contracted and pale, but correct and haughty, Saint-Magloire came into the room, in evening dress, with a gardenia in his buttonhole, and advanced toward Eléna, who was still on her knees.

"What's this I hear?" he said, in his seductive voice. "Has Pepito's condition got worse?"

"Your child is dead," replied the Baronne, harshly, getting to her feet as if moved by a spring. And with a tragic gesture, she showed him the corpse.

Immediately, with the presence of mind and art of composition that were not the least of his skills, the financier had adopted an appropriate expression; his lips were pinched, while a light mist moistened the velvet of his pupils.

He leaned over the bed, and with a sob in his throat, he deposited a kiss on Pepito's icy forehead.

Eléna, with her arms folded and her features hardened, followed all his movements, so spontaneous in appearance, with eyes in which there was both scorn and hatred.

A subtle observer and a past master in the art of analyzing sentiments, Dr. Lemoine had even been able to remark, in spite of the intense emotion that gripped him and perturbed his psychology somewhat, more scorn than hatred. He saw that, doubtless rightly, as a grave symptom; hatred, in fact, is often merely love gone awry and disfigured, while scorn stifles within us any vestige of tenderness. It even seemed to him that he had heard the word "blackguard" pass, like the crack of a whip, between Eléna's clenched teeth.

Suddenly, the Baron de Saint-Magloire—who, at the moment of his entrance, like a gust of wind, had not appeared to perceive his presence—took a step toward him, and, continuing to mop his eyes with his handkerchief, bowed courteously.

"Monsieur le docteur, undoubtedly?" he asked.

"Yes, Monsieur," Lemoine replied. "In the absence of your usual doctor, your people came to look for me, affirming that it was an urgent matter. They were only too right, alas. It was too late...a fast-developing meningitis. Nothing could be done. Science is impotent in the face of certain fatalities, and it is not always given to physicians to grant a mother's prayers..."

"I'm infinitely grateful to you for what you have done, Monsieur...?"

"Lemoine."

"That's a name I shall never forget," Saint-Magloire continued. "I would be honored if you would consent to consider us as friends..."

The doctor went out, having bowed respectfully to Eléna, who shook his hand with a feverish grip. The Baron escorted him to the vestibule, continuing to shower him with the most urgent manifestations of gratitude and amity.

The Baron ordered his coachman, who was waiting at the door with the hitched-up coupé, to take the doctor home. Then he went back to the mortuary chamber.

"My poor love!" he said advancing toward Eléna with his arms wide. "Poor dear!"

The Baronne recoiled with a gesture of disgust, as if at the approach of a reptile.

"Wretch!" she murmured.

Momentarily amazed, the adventurer quickly pulled himself together. He thought it was a fit of nervous fury provoked in Eléna by grief. "Come on, darling," he said. "Grief is leading you astray. This is a great misfortune, which I mourn as much as you, but it's not my fault. You couldn't push me away more cruelly if I had killed Pepito!"

"You haven't killed him, but your indifference, your lightness of heart, are atrocious—as atrocious as a murder...didn't I beg you to stay to watch over Pepito with me? You knew that he was going to die, and you left anyway, inventing the excuse of urgent business...a lie."

"But you're crazy, my poor Eléna. How could I have believed that the poor dear, who was so healthy yesterday, was in danger of death today? Could I have saved him, in any case, if I had been here? Like you, I would have had to wait for the doctor..."

"In default of affection, a father ought to have enough respect with regard to his son to remain at his bedside when he's stricken by illness. You don't understand that...which proves that you have no soul!"

"But I told you, my love," the Baron continued, still in a honeyed tone," that it was a matter of the highest importance. I didn't have time to call off the appointment. I understand perfectly that a father's place is beside his sick child, but the head of a family, especially one in my position, has imperious duties to fulfill, to which he must often sacrifice..."

"You're lying! You're lying!" roared the Baronne. "You haven't come from the Ministry! You've come from your mistress, and I wonder that you consented to come back so soon, since the night isn't yet entirely over." Then, stinging him with her scorn, she added: "So what new infamy do you have planned for this morning, to have returned so early, to have quit your shameful pleasure?"

"Shut up, woman, shut up!" growled Saint-Magloire, whose mobile features had suddenly taken on a frightful expression of anger and menace. "Shut up!"

But Eléna, beside herself, exasperated by despair, was no longer listening.

"Oh, I know you now. During those hours of cruel anguish, I felt the sinister presentiments that have obsessed me for such a long time confirmed. I've seen through you. I've understood…you're a monster, devoid of soul or entrails. You've never loved anyone, except yourself…

"You didn't even love your child. As for his mother, you've played the comedy of love to serve your own interests—oh, don't protest; that would only be one lie more!—his mother who gave herself to you, who saved you from the abyss…but who would only have to say a word today to plunge you back into it!"

A flash of fury sparkled beneath the furrowed brows of the Baron de Saint-Magloire; the rictus of a wild beast contracted his seductive physiognomy. With a rapid glance he inspected the room, to see whether anyone was listening—but since he had come in, the chambermaid had retreated in company with the valet. They had other things to do than listen to the bosses tell one another home truths. Rozen leapt to the door anyway, and opened it wide.

Having neither seen nor heard anything suspect in the antechamber, he came back to Eléna, fists clenched.

"You'd dare to betray me?" he said.

"Oh, have no fear, Gaston Rozen," she said, in a duller tone. "Have no fear that I'll unmask you. I have loved you, unhappily, I have believed in you, Besides, I belong to a race for whom informing is unthinkable. The daughter of an outcast will not betray the secret of an escaped convict. But henceforth, know that I am your irreconcilable enemy; know that I hate you! And before the corpse of this little being, who was the flesh of our flesh, I curse you—I curse the day that I met you…"

Saint-Magloire wanted to cut short that scene, which he considered to be a fragment of melodrama.

"Eléna," he begged, in a tone pierced with a certain irony. "Cease these insults…"

"Yes, I curse you, and may misfortune descend upon you…"

Absolutely certain that his companion would keep her word and would not betray him, the bandit had recovered all his self-composure.

"I forgive you, my dear," he said. "Grief has caused you to lose your head. Would you like me to ring, to send for guardians to keep watch in this mortuary chamber?"

"I shall keep watch on my own," the Baronne replied, harshly. "No, I'm not mad. I'm not acting under the influence of nervous excitement. I hate you…and every time you are in my presence in future, I shall spit my scorn in your face."

"Poor woman," murmured the banker. "I feel sorry for you, sincerely."

With an ironic smile, he went out backwards, while poor Eléna, her strength exhausted, fell on to the floor in a faint.

"Well, my little one," muttered the bandit, as he strode along the corridor, "you'll pay for that, of course. One such scene is enough; twice would be too much. We shall see..."

XIV. A Thunderbolt

All gamblers tell themselves that there are streaks of good luck and streaks of bad luck.

When luck is on your side, everything succeeds, even imprudence, even mistakes, even faults. At a given point, a fortunate card will bring you the win on which you were no longer counting. It is the old story of the gold ring of Polycrates, tyrant of Samos.[45]

When, on the contrary, bad luck gets the upper hand, the cleverest plans go awry. The most skillful calculations are defeated by chance.

Saint-Magloire had had a lucky streak. He had exhausted it, for the greater satisfaction of his pride, for the slaking of his desires. The change of fortune arrived, implacably.

Locked in his study, having forbidden his door to all visitors, he was conversing with Mr. Baker, the employee placed in his establishment by Henry Albert. Saint-Magloire was sitting at his desk. Opposite him, the Englishman was standing up, impassively, his pale face—which one might have thought carved in hard and rigid wood—not expressing the slightest sign of pleasure or annoyance,

"Père Vaulnier has just left," said the Baron.

"I know; I met him in the anteroom."

"Do you know what he came to tell me?"

"Not yet, Monsieur le Baron."

"That several of the bonds returned from England have been seized by the French police."

"Oh!" said Mr. Baker, without losing his tranquility. "How does he know that?"

"Vaulnier's a former agent of the Sûreté, who retired and now does police work on his own account."

"An amateur detective?"

"A very worthy man, who has never suspected for a moment the role I'm making him play. After the robbery of the Banque truck, I commissioned him to carry out an investigation, on the pretext of having an interest in the theft. He's

---

[45] According to Herodotus, Polycrates was advised by the Egyptian Pharaoh Amasis, who thought he was too successful, to throw something valuable away in order to strike a balance. The gold ring that he threw into the sea was, however found in the gut of a fish offered to the tyrant by a fisherman, and Amasis promptly withdrew his alliance, on the grounds that such a lucky man was bound to suffer a drastic reversal of fortune.

done well, the old fox, for he came to tell me, point by point, how the thing was done."

"But he hasn't found the two men who brought off the coup," observed the Englishman, glacially.

"No, fortunately...although they didn't know who they were working for, having been set up for it by a foreigner..."

"Who was back in London the same evening."

"Except that our correspondent has committed the imprudence of sending us a considerable quantity of the bonds the truck contained."

"As always."

"And they hadn't been sufficiently doctored!"

"I beg your pardon, said Mr. Baker, slightly offended. I took care of the work personally. The numbers were altered by me with the care that I always bring to affairs of this sort, and I think I know my trade. You know that the printing was perfect."

"Then how was the doctoring discovered?" demanded Saint-Magloire, impatiently.

"It appears that they've found new methods—chemical or photographic, how do I know? One can never have exactly the same ink, as you know. Then again, some of these rascals are good..."

"In the meantime, an investigation has been launched, people arrested..."

Mr. Baker shrugged his shoulders philosophically.

"And what if they talk, those people, if they identify others? What if, by following the thread, they reach the source—which is to say, us?"

"You've nothing to fear on that score," said the impassive Baker. "Between them and you, there's a barrier: me."

"What do you mean? That you'll be arrested in my stead? Some advantage! As if the connection between you and me weren't fatally established."

"That's not what I mean. I like my liberty at least as much as you do, but at the first sign of trouble, I take my precautions. All the bonds recognized as coming from the Banque Saint-Magloire have been reimbursed. So far as anyone knows, the Banque Saint-Magloire will have committed the imprudence of receiving them in good faith, and passed them the same way. On learning that they've been falsified—by whom? no one knows—it reimburses them, with interest. It accepts the loss. The Banque Saint-Magloire is impeccable; it's a victim, that's all."

"That's all is easy to say. Is it a big loss?"

"Two and a half million."

"That's a lot—but in sum, if that's all..." said the banker, slightly reassured.

"Pardon me," said the phlegmatic Baker. "There's still the reserve..."

"What reserve?"

"The bonds we haven't passed on, because I stopped the sale at the first alarm."

"And they're worth?"

"Between seven and eight million."

"Eight million!" groaned Saint-Magloire, unable to suppress a nervous gesture so violent that the paper knife that he had picked up a few moments before snapped in two.

"Oh, we've only paid fifty per cent for them," observed Mr. Baker, mildly. The total loss might rise to five or six million, that's all..."

"That's enormous!"

"It's the risks of commerce, Monsieur le Baron."

"Oh, your English calm makes my blood boil!" exclaimed Saint-Magloire. "Get out!"

"Very well, Monsieur le Baron." Mr. Baker pivoted on his heels and went to the door as calmly as if he had been sent to relay an order to the offices.

"Six million! The brute! The triple brute!" roared the Baron, stamping his feet, when Mr. Baker had gone. "Six million! And he told me that in a blank voice, as if it were trivial. Six million! When I've dipped into my own coffers to ward off the Bourse's recent drop in coppers, while waiting for the price to rise again. Six million lost, when I was counting on that very return to cover some heavy expenses, especially the draft a signed when buying Germaine's house!"

He passed his hand over his sweat-bathed forehead—which caused his anger to rise again.

"And it goes without saying," he went on, "that the draft has to be paid on presentation, no matter what the cost, or else it'll mean a quarrel with Germaine...and the beginning of the end...

"The slut would shout from the rooftops that the Baron had failed to keep his word, and my credit would be shaken...and once a breach is opened...it's impossible to retreat, to delay, to request an extension! The shock would be almost as rude for me." He wrung his hands. "Oh! To think that I can't get over the woman who's ruining me! Here's me, for whom a woman has never been anything more than a plaything, and love a pastime, transformed into a troubadour of romance, timid, and terrified by the idea that she might leave me...for that thought torments me even more than the most disastrous of bankruptcies...

"And she doesn't love me! It's my money she wants. I know that she's making a fool of me. No, she loves that accursed Dulac, on whom I daren't avenge myself! Oh, to kill him, to kill both of them if necessary! Dead, she'd be mine forever...I'd still have her memory..."

He got up and started pacing agitatedly around his study. "Come on, Rozen!" he said to himself. "You're hit, old man. You'll have lead in your wing if you don't bring off a major coup!"

"Then again, it's necessary to get Sokoloff moving. He's got scruples...he has to vanquish them, or I have to vanquish them for him. Why hesitate to inundate the argentaurum market? The thing is to do it cleverly."

Someone knocked discreetly on the door. It was Florent, the usher with the silver chain, who reminded his employer that time was passing and that his visitors were waiting.

It was a salutary diversion. Making a supreme effort, Saint-Magloire succeeded in restoring an appearance of calm to his face.

"Come in, Florent," he said, in a voice that was still slightly tremulous.

The usher came in.

"Tell them that I can't see anyone else this morning. I have work to do...important work. Put them off until another day."

"I beg Monsieur to excuse me," said the usher, "but there's a man here who insists, saying that he absolutely must see Monsieur le Baron this morning."

"A man? Who is he?"

"This is what he gave me." Florent presented the tray, on which there was an envelope.

The baron took the envelope and tore it open. It contained a simple card with the inscription:

Bourguignon
Senior Inspector in the Service of the Sûreté
36 Quai des Orfèvres.

A frisson ran through him from head to toe.

"This gentleman wants to talk to me personally?" he asked.

"Yes, Monsieur le Baron, to Monsieur le Baron in person."

What does this mean? Saint-Magloire asked himself.

In a trice, with the vertiginous rapidity that thoughts have in certain circumstances, Saint-Magloire posed all the hypotheses to which a visit from an agent of the police, and his insistence on speaking to him personally, might give rise.

Was his true identity suspected? Might his rival, Dulac, have denounced him in a fit of jealousy? Or was it about the matter of the intercepted bonds? Was the law, in spite of Mr. Baker's assurances, on the point of finding the trail? Perhaps, again, it was about the famous burglaries that he had organized so cleverly? Had one of the members of the gang for whom, thanks to his social relationships, he had been able to identify rich people absent from Paris, been caught and talked?

That was over in a flash; expelling all those depressing ideas, he wanted to become, and did become, the strong man of old; he was ready to confront the danger, whatever it might be, feeling sturdy enough and strong enough to avert it.

"Show him in," he said, in a confident tone.

Monsieur Bourguignon came in.

He was a man of about forty, not tall but solidly built, broad-shouldered, with a ruddy face, and seemed possessed of an uncommon vigor and energy. His costume, without being elegant, had a certain correctness and meticulous neatness that denoted a former military man. He bowed, stood up straight, his feet positioned at right-angles, and waited.

"You asked to speak to me, Monsieur?" said Saint-Magloire. "What is the reason for your visit?"

"I owe you thousand apologies for my insistence, Monsieur..."

Not a very reassuring opening, Saint-Magloire said to himself.

"...But," the senior inspector continued, "I have a communication to make to you on behalf of the head of the Sûreté that will suffer no delay."

"Speak, Monsieur," said the Baron, seized by a vague anxiety. "I'm listening."

"Do you know," asked the policeman, bringing a slip of paper out of his pocket, "a man named Robertson?"

Ah! thought Saint-Magloire. *It's about Macaron.*

"Robertson?" he said, aloud, as if searching his memory. "Robertson? The name rings a bell, but I can't put a face to it."

"And Englishman who takes bets on racehorses."

"I do gamble a little on the course, but when I do, I go to the *parimutuel* like ordinary mortals. Apart from a few sportsmen that I meet at the club or in society, I don't know anyone in that world..."

"The man claims that he knows you, and is asking for you."

"Me?"

"Yes, Monsieur le Baron."

"In what connection?"

"This Robertson, a regular in the bars frequented by stable-lads, tipsters, sellers of information..."

"A fine society!" Saint-Magloire put in, with a well-feigned gesture of disgust.

"A trifle mixed," said the agent, smiling. "Well then, this Robertson has the habit of drinking, even of getting drunk, and often, when he's drunk, he has fights..."

"So?"

"He's been taken to the police station several times already, but as he has a domicile, and his concierge, always well-paid, gives him excellent references, he's been released. Yesterday, however..."

"Yesterday?"

"Yesterday, the matter was more serious. Not only was Robertson drunk, not only did he get into a fight, but he put up desperate resistance to the agents who wanted to take him to the station."

"And he's asked for me?"

"Continually. 'You don't know who you're dealing with,' he said. 'I'm a close friend of the Baron de Saint-Magloire, who dines with the Prefect and ministers. I'll have you all sacked.'"

"Drunken boasting," said the Baron, disguising the keen annoyance that this news caused him. "There are people who, when they drink, give as a reference the first name that comes into their head. Now, I've had a great many people in my service. It's not impossible that this man..."

"That's what the commissaire thought. Nevertheless, he thought that he ought to pass the information on to the Prefect of Police, and that's why I've come..."

"And what is this man's present situation?" asked the Baron.

"His situation?"

"Yes. Has he been released?"

"No, Monsieur le Baron. This time, there's not only manifest drunkenness but resisting arrest. And he has no identity papers...so an investigation has been ordered, and it's for that reason that Monsieur Cardec has sent me to see you..."

"Listen," said Saint-Magloire. "I do indeed remember, vaguely, having had an Englishman by the name of Robertson in my service when I was in London...he looked after my horses. That Robertson had a son...a hothead...

"When I returned to Paris, I was very surprised to see the young islander come into my study one day. I had repaid his father for some services by advancing a small sum of money to establish himself as a bookmaker, and the son, who had succeeded the father, came to offer me some 'incredible tips.' Now, as I've said, I only bet at the course. I thanked the young bookie, and never saw him again. Perhaps he wasn't wrong, after all, to mention my name...if I can be useful to the poor devil and get him out of trouble, I'd like nothing better...do you think this business can be settled? It's a peccadillo, after all."

"Certainly," said the agent, happy to please such an important individual. "Certainly, of Monsieur le Baron cares to say a word to Monsieur le Chef de la Police Municipale..."

"Well, so be it. If necessary, I'll talk to the Prefect, whom I have the honor of knowing."

"Oh!" the inspector went on. "If he apologizes to the guardian of the peace, he'll be released...the investigation will be halted. He's lucky to have picked a man as generous as you, Monsieur le Baron! It only remains for me to beg your pardon again for having disturbed you. I have the honor..."

"Bah! It's nothing," said the Baron, with a paternal bonhomie. "*Au revoir, my friend, au revoir!*"

The agent bowed, and went out backwards."

"That's the limit!" exclaimed Saint-Magloire. "Now Macaron's getting drunk and jabbering. That's all I need. And I have to get involved and have him released! Once in the hands of a judge, the fool's capable of getting himself recognized...and with him recognized, the romance of our escape vanishes..."

This time, the Baron closed his doors conclusively. Then, putting on his coat and hat and picking up his cane, he left the building.

"Shall I summon Monsieur le Baron's carriage?" asked the usher.

"No need, I need to take a walk."

When he was in the street, he said to himself: *I've been neglecting old Sokoloff. He's a wise man, and might be able to give me a means of arranging things for the best. Let's go see him.*

He went along the Rue Saint-Honoré and the Rue Duphot and arrived in the Place de la Madeleine. There he went into Durand's and ordered a partridge and a bottle of Bordeaux.

While was waiting for the meal to arrive, he telephoned his house in the Champs-Élysées to say that he would not be in for lunch.

A quarter of an hour later, having had coffee he sent the bellboy to find him a cab.

Sokoloff, it will be remembered, lived in Auteuil. Saint-Magloire had found him a very tranquil villa whose residence was situated in the middle of a large garden, almost a park, with tall trees and bushy hornbeams, so that he had been able to set up his laboratory with plenty of space, sheltered from any curious gaze, and that none of the suspicious noises that his experiments in chemistry might produce could be heard by any indiscreet or suspicious ear.

Saint-Magloire had the cab take him to the Rue de la Galiote, facing the Pont Mirabeau. There he paid the coachman, and, went on foot along the Rue Mirabeau, which goes past the Institution de Sainte-Perrine to the villa situated to one side, where Sokoloff was living under the name of Smithson, passing himself off as an American businessman.

As always, the old scientist was at work. On recognizing Saint-Magloire's voice, he raised his head—but instead of addressing him in a familiar fashion, as usual, he said, harshly: "Ah! There you are, *Monsieur!* Have you come to tell me that the time for action has finally come?"

XV. A Summons

Saint-Magloire was momentarily disconcerted by that welcome, very different from the one he was expecting—but he did not take long to collect himself.

"Not yet, alas, my dear friend," he said, giving his voice the tender inflection that had always seduced Sokoloff, "but we're getting there. Another few days of patience."

"Patience!" said Sokoloff, bitterly. "It's necessary, indeed! For month after month you've been telling me about the imminent completion, and it continually retreats, like the water before the lips of Tantalus..."

"But my dear friend, I assure you..."

"What are you waiting for?" cried the old revolutionary—and did not stop at that interruption. "Yes, what are you waiting for? Back in England you objected that the country was not propitious, and you made me come to France, where, you said, imaginations and overheated brains, appetites for luxury and well-being would render proselytism easier.

"Reluctant as I was to move, I came with you to Paris..."

"And you're a thousand times better off here than in London..." Saint-Magloire tried to say.

"Once in Paris, you wanted a fortune, power; you've had them. Everything has succeeded as you desired. For my part, without abandoning my work, I've activated friends. I've organized groups of anarchists, not only throughout France but throughout Europe. I've woven a colossal spider's-web, whose center I occupy, and whose threads are in my hands,

"And when I ask you to move, when everyone, everywhere is getting impatient, you have only one reply to make to me, one response, always the same: *Wait!*"

"Well," said Saint-Magloire, "don't condemn me without hearing what I have to say. Let me tell you what's happening."

"What is happening? Speak!"

"As you've just reminded me, everything was going well at first. Thanks to your collaboration, I was the spoiled child of fortune. I had the confidence of the powerful in this country, and the governments of the principal nations of Europe. One false word cleverly confided to diplomatic indiscretions would have been sufficient for me to sow discord between all the peoples, to unleash a European war, by virtue of which the Revolution might finally burst forth."

"Why haven't you done it?" Sokoloff interrupted, slightly soothed.

"Because I only wanted to strike a certain blow, because a failed attempt would have been another crushing defeat for our party, terrible this time, perhaps irremediable."

"Bah! Like the Lernean hydra, Anarchism has a hundred heads, and those that are cut off quickly grow back. But go on."

The scientist had calmed down. Subjugated by Rozen's warm voice and eloquence, he had reverted to addressing him in the familiar manner. Gaston understood that he had won his cause yet again.

"I saw the propitious moment approaching," he went on. "I was about to come and tell you the good news when my luck suddenly turned and disaster fell upon me."

"Disaster? What disaster?"

"You know, Sokoloff, that I was counting heavily on the argentaurum for the success of our common endeavor, but—and I truly don't know what pusillanimity has held you back—you have still only produced insignificant quantities...[46]

The Russian frowned.

Saint-Magloire sensed that the reproach was maladroit at that moment, and swiftly added: "I only say that, Master, to explain to you why I've been obliged to launch myself into business...but I've suffered heavy losses on the Bourse and elsewhere. This very morning, I learned that an operation on which I was greatly reliant had gone irredeemably awry, and I have considerable obligations to meet..."

"Well?"

"Well. I'm busy fending off these blows of fate."

"Get away!" cried the old apostle, rising from his chair. "Why? Circumstances have never been more favorable."

"I don't understand," stammered Saint-Magloire, utterly nonplussed.

"Go bankrupt!"

"Bankrupt! But I'm not yet reduced to that, thank God."

"What does it matter? File for bankruptcy—the bigger the deficit, the better."

"You must be joking! When you put..."

"Of course! It's quite simple, though! What thunderclap could terrify the financial world more than the failure of the Banque Saint-Magloire!" cried Sokoloff, enthusiastically. "It would be a crash as catastrophic, as shattering, as that of Metals or the Union Générale. There are thousands of families in France who have all they possess invested with you or your businesses, hundreds of bankers and businessmen whose bankruptcies would follow hot on the heels of yours...

---

[46] This omission on Sokoloff's part is never explained; the true reason is, of course, that the authors have realized belatedly that it is a tactical mistake to provide a fictitious master criminal with a perfectly legal means of amassing millions, thus relieving him of any real motive to commit crimes and thus maintain his status as an arch-villain.

"That will form an army of malcontents and desperate individuals, who will come to swell our ranks…you can see that no hesitation is possible."

Saint-Magloire, needless to say, was far from sharing Sokoloff's enthusiasm. His devotion to the anarchist cause, and to the Revolution, had never been anything but an artfully-played comedy intended to serve his personal interests. In Guiana, he had only fomented a rebellion in order to betray it for his own profit.

As for Sokoloff, he had pretended to associate himself with his ideas because he had sensed that he as a powerful support for his success…and now that he had wealth, luxury and pleasure, it would be necessary for him to smash it all, to renounce his fortune, power and Germaine, with whom he as madly in love!

Ah! Rather smash Sokoloff himself, rather betray his benefactor!

What did that further crime matter to him, after so many others?

Except that it was necessary to find the means, and, in order to find that means, to gain a few more days, a few more weeks of respite.

"Perhaps you're right, Sokoloff," he said, affecting, with his sovereign science of deception, a tone of conviction. "It would certainly be a major blow to society: the collapse of a bank reputed to be the richest and most solid of them all…"

"Well, then—why hesitate?"

"Because it's necessary that the coup has its full effect, that it really is a terrible hammer-blow, working to our advantage while crushing others…but that's not the case at present.

"Why is that?"

"As I've just told you, I've suffered considerable monetary losses, and if I file for bankruptcy now, I'll end up with a serious, real and deplorable failure, which will quite possibly ruin others, but will leave us without a sou."

"Without a sou!" cried Sokoloff, seized once again by suspicion. "But where has all the money that I've given to you gone?"

"I've been obliged to make enormous expenditures in order to sustain my status, and I repeat once again that the production of argentaurum, and the flow of that metal on to the market have not been in conformity with the promises that you made me…"

"It was understood," said Sokoloff rudely, "that the manufacture would be slow. I haven't hidden the difficulties of its manufacture from you, and the dangers of throwing too great a quantity of argentaurum on to the financial market. I have, however, given you sufficient to constitute a considerable capital—and what have you done with it? You've squandered it for your personal satisfaction. Is that how one serves a noble cause?"

"Sokoloff, my friend!" Rozen interrupted, with an admirably feigned emotion.

"I have been a prince, Monsieur," pronounced the scientist, sharply, "and a real prince, in a land where money is not obtained for nothing. Life at the Russian court is certainly as expensive, you may be sure, as life in Paris. Well, while throwing money out of the window, like my friends, I did not exceed my income, which was far from being as large as yours..."

"Time has moved on since your youth; you can't know..."

"Yes, I know...I *know*," said Sokoloff, emphasizing the word. "I know now that what people have told me about you, and what I have heard from malevolent tale-tellers, was the truth. Instead of occupying yourself with the work of regeneration, to which I have devoted my life, you have no other concern than the maximum possible enjoyment. Your insane dissipation is alimenting all the gossip in Paris, and your love-affair with a renowned singer—a slut without a heart or a brain—is no mystery for anyone."

"I have no pretention to pose as a puritan," said Saint-Magloire.

"Nor have I to play the moralist. It is not, in fact, from the standpoint of austerity that I scrutinize your private life, although I have a profound and respectful affection for our sister Eléna, whom you have abandoned and who must be suffering cruelly..."

"Ah! Eléna has confided her woes to you," Saint-Magloire sniggered. "I should have suspected it!"

"No! Eléna is too noble and generous a soul for a single word against you to emerge from her mouth. I repeat to you that it's from every direction that the details of your existence reach me. I would not have spoken to you had I not acquired the conviction that you have forgotten your promises and your engagements, in order to think only of your pleasures..."

"You're mistaken. I swear to you that you're mistaken on my account."

"Prove it to me by action. It's high time!"

"Give me a few days..."

"All right! But put yourself seriously to work, then!"

"Give me a fortnight."

"Come to see me in two weeks, then—and I'll know whether I ought to keep you or withdraw my confidence in you..."

And, sitting down again at his workbench, the old scientist made a gesture with his hand to signify that the visit was not to be prolonged.

The banker, however, thought that he ought to make one last effort.

"Friend," he said, "one more plea..."

"I'm listening," said Sokoloff, curtly.

"I need a few ingots..."

"I've told you that you shan't have any more!" exclaimed the scientist. "And to keep my word, I've smashed my apparatus. I've annihilated those marvelous machines, the fruit of so many years of labor...

"It's finished...finished!

"You asked me to give you the initial foundations of a fortune. I've done that. Today, you're acting as you intended. I'm no longer getting involved in your shady scheme...

260

"If, in two weeks, you haven't realized my desire—if you don't bring me the means of giving birth to the social revolution, I shall act on my own.

"That's my final word!"

"Master! Anger is giving you bad advice. You've misunderstood the services rendered..."

"Not at all, Monsieur. I've seen in you an admirably-endowed man. I've considered you as a mainstay of anarchism. I've treated you like a son. You've preferred the odious life of sybarites. That's your affair, not mine...but you've lost my confidence. I've give you two weeks to get it back.

"Go...act...and we shall see..."

Sokoloff shook the hand that Saint-Magloire held out to him with his fingertips, and the Baron left the scientist's home somewhat disconcerted.

The streak continues, he said to himself, in a melancholy fashion, as he drew away from the villa. *I come to ask him to get me out of trouble and I get a sermon and an ultimatum. Bankruptcy! He's got some hope! I'd rather have all the anarchists in the world shot, starting with him!*

In sum, I have a fortnight in hand. That's a little more than twice as long as God took, it's said, to create the world. The devil may take me if I can't find a way to get afloat again...

He hailed a cab, and this time, without hesitation had it take him directly to the Place Vendôme. He found Bastien, alias Macaron, there, waiting for him.

As he had promised, Inspector Bourguignon had gone to report the Baron de Saint-Magloire's merciful words to the commissaire, and the magistrate, delighted to please a person he knew to be on the best possible terms with the Prefect of Police, had hastened to set the false Robertson free, merely enjoining him, after having addressed his excuses to the agents, to go and thank the generous man whose name he had almost compromised.

Macaron, having sobered up, had obeyed, and waited for the banker's return, ashamed and crestfallen, suspecting the kind of reception he would receive.

Without saying a word, Saint-Magloire gave him a sign to follow him and headed for the private entrance that permitted him to go up to his study or come down therefrom without meeting any of the bank's clients or visitors.

Bastien went up behind him, sheepishly.

Saint-Magloire opened the door of his study, shoved Macaron gently into the room, and closed the door.

Damn! Macaron said to himself, that unexpected calm frightening him more than an outburst of wrath. *What will I have to take for my cold?*

"Bastien," said Saint-Magloire, planting himself in front of his interlocutor, "you're doubtless unhappy in the skin of the identity you've adopted. This Robertson mask is burning you; you want to get rid of it."

"Beg pardon, Boss, but I don't quite get your meaning..."

"It's clear, though. What I mean is that although I got you out of the bagne, you're doing everything possible to get back there..."

"Certainly not!" Bastien exclaimed.

"If it were only you, animal, I wouldn't be overly worried, but your arrest might seriously compromise me, compromise Sokoloff, compromise the cause...I don't want that."

"You're right, mate..."

"No joking. The situation is serious—much more so than you seem to think."

"What!" moaned Macaron, piteously. "For a little drop of booze that I've paid for!"

"When one can't drink, one sucks one's thumb. You no longer recall, imbecile, that while you were drunk, you fought with the police and talked...and talked in French, although you pass yourself off as an Englishman."

"Damn! That's bad."

"If it were only that! But you talked about me, our past relationship."

"Impossible! I must have been very drunk, then."

"Do you imagine that it didn't seem strange to the agents, and especially the commissaire, that a prince of finance should be the comrade, the intimate friend, of a drunken and violent bookmaker?"

"The fact is," said Macaron, scratching the back of his neck, "that it might give them the idea of looking into the matter...and when nosey individuals begin to search you for head-lice, one never knows where they'll stop."

"You can see, then, triple brute as you are," Saint-Magloire finally burst out, "that you've stirred up the waters, and that you need to disappear!"

"Disappear...me?"

"Would you prefer to have the police on the case? I've got you out of their claws once, but who knows whether the second time, or the third..."

"Oh!" said Macaron, with a sincerity that was not feigned. "I swear that I won't drink anymore."

"A drunkard's oath..."

"No, a serious oath. Haven't I kept my word? Didn't the business on the Le Havre train go with a bang?"

"Not so loud, wretch!"

"You'll see..."

"And if I believe you—even if you keep the oath you just made—do you think that's the end of it?"

"Go on! What else is there?"

"Are you a true anarchist?" demanded Saint-Magloire, answering one question with another.

"For sure, Boss."

"Are you prepared to make the greatest sacrifices for the cause?"

"Well...obviously."

"Then you'll abandon your quiet life, your habits and your pleasures without regret, to resume the battle against society?"

"Listen, Boss," said Macaron. "Necessary to be frank, no? Well, anarchism like that's all right when one's young..."

"Aha!"

"But when you get to my age, when you've tasted misery, when you've had the dirty deals that we've had, and then, when you've found almost everything you need to be tranquil, then..."

"Then? Go on—finish."

"Well, it's hard, yes, it's hard..." Misunderstanding Saint-Magloire's intentions, Macaron started again. "Oh, I'm not ducking out. If it's absolutely necessary to get stuck in again, I'll do it—but it'll be hard, very hard. I'd prefer something else."

"I'm not displeased to hear you say that," said the Baron, in a gentler tone, "because I, too, am finding the sacrifice of everything exorbitant, renouncing everything for a...dream—and a dream that might end badly, for, after all, remember what happened out there..."

"It's true that we had a narrow escape, Boss," Macaron agreed.

"I believe that, out there, I showed sufficient devotion..."

"For sure!"

"And that today, by means of our operations, we're fighting a war against society more dangerous than any that can be fought by means of dynamite..."

"That's my opinion...and I share it!" Macaron exclaimed.

"Well, then! Sokoloff, however, is getting impatient; he thinks that we've gone to sleep in the enjoyment of life, and he wants to give us the signal for the general conflagration."

"Shit! It's easy for him to talk..."

"He doesn't want to know anything any longer, and yet he wants everything to move on regardless."

Bastien, alias Macaron, made no reply, but he face expressed a profound consternation.

"There might be a means..." said Saint-Magloire, after a moment's silence.

"What?"

"A means, if not of getting us out of trouble, at least of delaying the collapse we fear."

"Keep talking, Boss. What do we need to do."

"You need to go see Sokoloff."

"Al right—I'll go. What then?"

"You'll tell him that I've decided to bring matters to a head."

"Eh? What? It's not a joke?"

"No, but you'll add that you've been in communication with all the comrades in Paris and France, and that you believe—that you know—that they're not ready."

"That's fine by me. But will he believe me?"

"He's only in communication with correspondents in the big international centers. He doesn't know the comrades. Persuade him, and he'll be the one asking us to wait. It will be another few weeks gained. After that...well, we'll see..."

"I'll get on with it!" exclaimed Macaron, joyfully. "And you can count on my eloquence, Boss. I'll be irresistible."

"On that condition, I'll forgive your imprudence. But be careful!"

"Have no fear. I'm on it. *Au revoir*, Boss!"

"*Au revoir.*"

Saint-Magloire opened the door. Bastien went out via the private exit.

Under the porch he met Joseph, the young groom. "Oh, there you are, Mr. Robertson!" exclaimed the boy. "You've just been to see the Boss?"

"Shut up, brat. I've been to thank the Baron for a great service he's done me. I'll thank you to hold your tongue."

"Fine," said the groom. "Got any tips?"

"No tips. I'm no longer a bookmaker; I'm not having any more to do with the races."

"Oh!" said Joseph, disconcerted. "What are you doing, then?"

"Nothing!" said Macaron, as he went away.

In the meantime, Saint-Magloire was asking himself: *Will he succeed? In any case, through him, Sokoloff will believe that I've decided to hasten matters along, and that will restore his confidence...if I can just gain a little time, I'll be safe! I can still bounce back, and I've triumphed in situations more difficult than this!*

That was true—but Saint-Magloire was forgetting that, in the era in which he had successfully undertaken the struggles to which he had made allusion, he had been younger, more vigorous, and not so softened by the abuse of physical satisfactions of every sort. And above all—above all!—he had not been in love.

For that was where his greatest strength had always lain: in having no heart; in sacrificing, if necessary, men or women, friends or mistress, all those who loved him, all those who were devoted to him, without hesitation or regret...

In Cayenne, to acquire the favor of the administration, he had had the anarchist comrades, who trusted him, massacred; in London, but for Sokoloff and Macaron, he would have left Eléna and her child to die of hunger. And that very child he had just seen perish of a frightful malady, without a tear, just as he had, after a momentary hesitation, ordered the murder of his friend and benefactor Lavardens, remorselessly.

He had abandoned everything, to think of nothing but Germaine—and yet, at that moment, there were many dangers to ward off.

Sokoloff was quieted for a while, that was certain—but there was Macaron, who, in spite of his oath, might let himself go, might even be provoked to drink by some enemy, and might talk in an even more dangerous fashion.

There was Dulac, attained by the madness of jealous lovers—the madness that, at times, tortured Saint-Magloire himself, with whose perfidious advice he was familiar. There was a risk that Dulac might spoil everything, in a fit of amorous delirium.

Eléna herself, the virtuous and meek Eléna, was weary, as Rozen could see only too well, of being abandoned and betrayed. The devotion of that woman of heart still held sway over her…but what if the end of grief brought scorn sand hatred? Eléna might then become the most redoubtable of enemies…

Since the tragic night of José's death, it was necessary to keep an eye open in that direction, and keep a close watch.

Come on, Saint-Magloire said to himself, after a moment's reflection with his head in his hands. *Nothing's broken yet, but there's no time to lose. To work, immediately!*

He rang. The usher appeared. "Is there anyone still in the offices?" he asked.

"All the gentlemen are there. It's only four forty-five, and they don't leave until five."

"Good. Tell them that no one is to go without my permission, and send in Monsieur Baker."

The usher bowed and went to carry out the great chief's orders.

XVI. Moving Fast

Five minutes later, Mr. Baker came into the Baron's study.

Singular as it might seem to receive a summons just as the offices were about to close, when his employer was supposedly no longer at the bank, he maintained the tranquil expression of a man incapable of astonishment.

"Mr. Baker," said Saint-Magloire, "have you taken care of the matter you mentioned to me this morning?"

"I've been busy with it this afternoon, Monsieur le Baron."

"The suspect bonds have been withdrawn?"

"Some of them. The others will be back tomorrow, except for those that have been sent to the court to support complaints."

"They need to be withdrawn too. I'm seeing the public prosecutor tomorrow; the complainants being disinterested, the case needs to be closed."

"Obviously."

"That said, what is the total sum of the retracted bonds?"

"Including those we haven't yet liquidated?"

"The entire total."

"Exactly seven million, five hundred and forty-eight francs."

"Good. From the viewpoint of sale, those bonds are dangerous...but they can still serve as collateral."

"Hmm!" said Mr. Baker, dubiously.

"Come on," said the Baron. "The moment that the Banque Saint-Magloire didn't hesitate to reimburse the suspect bonds that it received unwittingly, and passed on in the same way, its reputation could no longer be in doubt—so no one will examine them too closely..."

"It's possible. All the more so as it's difficult to perceive..."

"It's settled, then," the Baron interjected. "Would you ask the cashier and the chief accountant to come in?"

"Immediately, Monsieur le Baron."

Baker went out, and returned almost immediately with the two division heads.

"How much do we have in the safe?" the Baron asked the cashier.

"Liquid, Monsieur le Baron?"

"Yes."

"Five hundred thousand francs."

"That's not much."

"I would point out to Monsieur le Baron that we've just had to reimburse..."

"About two and a half millions for the bonds in litigation—I know. But it doesn't matter. Let's rely on what we have. Tomorrow morning, a bill signed by me to Renard, an architect, will be presented to you. Pay it."

"It's just," said the cashier, "that we need to liquidate the Van Westyne of Amsterdam account..."

"So?"

"And the Millarès of Lisbon account, which we ought to have settled some days ago."

"What does that matter?"

"I'm afraid of finding myself a little short, given that I'm not expecting anything to come in."

"Don't worry about that—that's my business."

The cashier bowed without further protest, like a man habituated to obedience. Besides which, Saint-Magloire's employees had unlimited confidence in "the Boss."

"Let's see how things stand on the Bourse now," the Baron continued, signaling to the book-keeper in charge of that important business to come forward. "Where are Styrian mines?"

"At 309.25, Monsieur le Baron."

"And where were they yesterday?"

"At 320."

"The fall's accelerating?"

"Unfortunately, yes, Monsieur le Baron. We have a large holding, and the difference amounts to an appreciable loss."

"Easy to remedy," the banker murmured. "Tomorrow, you'll go to see two or three brokers and tell them to buy as many of the shares as possible."

"Buy?" exclaimed the stupefied employee. "But I just told you..."

"That coppers are going down. You haven't told me anything new. My intention is to provoke a steep rise."

"I don't understand."

"I don't require you to understand," Saint-Magloire said. "Carry out the order exactly."

"I understand" exclaimed the cashier, glad to mark his superiority in front of the Boss. "On seeing demand abundant, the holders, reassured, will no longer want to sell, and the price will rise sharply..."

"You're an intelligent man, Monsieur," said Saint-Magloire, smiling. "I won't forget your powers of observation."

The book-keeper, extremely vexed by the compliment paid to his colleague, which was an indirect criticism of his own skill, hazarded: "But the brokers will ask me for collateral!"

"Do you think I haven't anticipated that? You'll confer with Monsieur Baker, who has my instructions...that's all, Messieurs—you can go."

The three employees bowed respectfully and withdrew, privately admiring their employer's composure and clear-sightedness.

Another danger averted, Saint-Magloire said to himself, when he was alone. *I haven't wasted my afternoon. Now I can go, with a light heart, to pay my homage to Germaine...*

The Baron was not mistaken in is anticipations.

Glad to be entrusted with operations by the celebrated and powerful bank in the Place Vendôme, the stockbrokers had no objection to accepting the bonds as a guarantee. On the day after the bank had generously made the sacrifice of two and a half millions to compensate the purchasers of suspect bonds, no shred of suspicion could be raised against it. Collateral? Guarantees? Did one even need them, when dealing with the Baron Saint-Magloire? Was one not certain, in his establishment, of being paid open-handedly?

The next day, therefore, the coup on the Bourse exceeded his expectations. On seeing demand for coppers increase again, the shareholders thought that there must have been some confidential dispatch known only to the favored few, and marked up the prices. As Saint-Magloire already had such a large shareholding, there was soon a scarcity. At the next day's close, Styrian coppers had risen to 321; the following day, they jumped to 355. Everyone wanted them.

It was only then, in small parcels, without attracting attention, that he began to sell at a profit the stock whose possession might have ruined him.

As for Westyne of Amsterdam and Millarès of Lisbon, they raised no objection to a delay in the settlement of their accounts. Could one recriminate against the Banque Saint-Magloire? Everyone had faith in the star of the banker who made fantastic gleams of self-interest shine in his clients' eyes.

The Baron sensed that it was necessary to forge ahead, and from that day on, it was not with the reasoned audacity of the early days but with temerity, at break-neck speed, that he launched himself into the most hazardous speculations. No venture frightened him. All were good. Beaters in his employ traveled around the provinces and abroad, searching for mines to exploit, factories to be taken over by holding companies, casinos to found and railways to construct in the most bizarre territories.

Taking up Lavardens' idea, he set up a company to fell virgin forests methodically—except that, as Guiana as too well-known and the preparatory work too laborious, it was on the shores of the Black Sea that he discovered hundreds of leagues of unexplored forests, belonging to a Russian prince who was unaware of their value, and from whom, at little more than the price of the manual labor, obtain enough pine-wood to supply the whole of Europe for twenty years.

The reports of the engineers sent forth to investigate were so precise that Black Sea shares were selling at a premium.

Needless to say, not a single tree was ever felled.

That affair, launched as that of the Moroccan auriferous sands had been, was abandoned by Saint-Magloire to the hands of titled mugs who served as bait to attract the public. He swiftly formed a company, prudently withdrew his name from the business…and went on to something else. He would able to say, if the enterprise crashed, that it was due to the incompetence of the administrators. He was only an initiator; he was too busy to see all the enterprises to which his genius gave birth through to end…

And that ingenious policy permitted him to profit from a hundred prodigious share-issues…

He went on and on, imperturbably, aided by monstrous advertising, draining wealth from the rich and the savings of small capitalists. When a business collapsed, he did not give the financial world time to listen to the complaints of the shareholders; he immediately set up another—and the dazzled capitalists came running every time, like moths to a flame…

In any case, if the collapse of each company was disastrous for the naïve individuals who had invested in it, its liquidation took place quietly, without a scandal, without the concert of recriminations and imprecations that destroyed the credit of an ordinary financier forever. Saint-Magloire, the owner of several financial newspapers, and a major shareholder in several others, had sown up all the organs of publicity with princely largesse. He was assured of the collaboration of the press, and the anger of the dupes was never directed at him.

At one time, however, it nearly collapsed.

Among the numerous companies spawned by his bank, two in particular had obtained a colossal success, thanks to their prospectuses and advertising.

The former was set up to exploit a geodynamic motor based on the utilization of terrestrial magnetism. At first sight, it seemed fanciful, but in view of the immense progress made by science in a few years, the magnetic motor seemed more impossible, in sum, than the telephone, the transmission of power at a distance and, especially, wireless telegraphy.

On the other hand, what an economy! No more combustibles and manual labor to pay for, no more unemployment, no fear of strikes in the factories! Power would be obtainable for free—the dream of all engineers—becoming, with no further ceremony, a natural element: which, after all, had already accomplished so many other miracles. People rushed to buy the shares.

There was no less enthusiasm for the second company. The business was by no means banal; it seemed miraculous. It was a matter of extracting the gold contained in sea-water: an inexhaustible source of wealth, more productive than all the terrestrial mines put together. The prospectus skillfully sowed the illusion among the public.

"There must be gold there," it said, "just as there is arsenic present, as Raspail once demonstrated, in the course of a famous trial,[47] in the armchair of

---

[47] The chemist François Raspail made this famous observation in connection with the sensational trial of Marie Lafarge, charged in 1840 with having poisoned her husband; Raspail was summoned by the defense to challenge the fo-

the president of the Court of Assizes. It is everywhere, in a greater or lesser dose. There is no need, in order to discover it, to emigrate to Guiana, the Transvaal, the Klondike or the Ivory Coast; the universality of things is nothing but an immense placer, whose non-exploitation is solely due to the fact that the exploitation often fails to cover the cost of extraction, so that the game isn't worth the candle.

"But sea-water contains gold in considerable quantities; it must not be forgotten, in fact, that the Earth, which only solidified after having passed through the gaseous and liquid states is, like Venus—but not metaphorically—the issue of the briny wave, from which it proceeds legitimately, and which was its matrix and its cradle. It is therefore natural and necessary that the Ocean conserves, in the bosom of its mysterious intimacy, specimens and traces of all the elements, without exception, up to and including gold, that share in the composition of the globe's fabric. It is a kind of genealogical museum in which everything that exists has its anticipated representation, as in the legendary ancestral gallery..."

So said the pamphlet, the writing of which had been entrusted to the prince of popularizers, the man who was known as "the most scholarly of litterateurs and the most literary of scholars." He had put into it, along with the magic of his good faith, all the resources of his prestigious eloquence.

It was by means of electrolysis—which is to say, the decomposition by an electric current of the auriferous liquid—that the feat was to be achieved. Across a channel sixty meters wide, between two rocky points, like those that abound along the granitic coasts of Brittany, sixty plates of galvanized iron, two meters by three, would be disposed, at an angle of twenty-five to thirty degrees from the direction of flow, so as to constitute the negative electrode and carry out the electrolysis. It would only require half of one horse-power to provoke the precipitation of an increasingly thick layer of the various metals—up to and including gold—dissolved in the sea-water. There would be no more to do thereafter than collect and separate it by ordinary methods.

In brief, gold would be not much more difficult to extract from sea-water than salt. The cost of the installation, in any case, would be almost insignificant. The motive force would be borrowed, with no further ceremony. From the tides themselves, and as sea-water costs nothing, the profits would not take long to mount into dozens of millions. Great piles of gold would soon be seen, shining in the sunlight, all along our coasts, as salt-stacks can be seen today.

Needless to say, foreigners would not be allowed to enjoy a similar windfall.

"What a beautiful gift, in truth, to make to our beloved fatherland!"

And strike up the band!

---

rensic evidence offered by the toxicologist Mathieu Orfila, but by the time he reached the court the impatient jury had already delivered a guilty verdict, which seems to have been correct.

The capital of the limited company, created with the suggestive name of the Compagnie Française des Trésors d'Amphitrite, was covered five or six times over.

It must be said that to begin with, all went well. The results yielded by the geodynamic motor—which was carefully hidden from the eyes of the profane—were such that, to judge by certain witness-statements and the reports of certain engineers that were surreptitiously passed from hand to hand, that speculation took possession of the shares, which would soon have surpassed parity before a single machine had even been exhibited, let alone put on sale.

As for the Compagnie des Trésors d'Amphitrite, it paid a dividend as soon as the first trial!

But when Saint-Magloire had got rid of all his shares, the fall commenced. The motor no longer worked. It had only ever worked with the aid of trickery—a mysterious channeling of compressed air!

A million cubic meters of sea-water yielded about a gram of gold, worth three francs—and that gram of gold was obtained at the cost of labor worth at least six francs.

There was a terrible crash.

This time the dupes were enraged.

It proved that the initial dividends of the Compagnie des Trésors d'Amphitrite had been fictitious dividends, and that the banker of the Place Vendôme had deceived his shareholders odiously. Complaints were lodged; an investigation was launched.

A skilful campaign in the newspapers put a new face on things, and, in spite of the utterly crushing investigation mounted by Monsieur Cardec, supported by his friend Lemoine, Saint-Magloire emerged from the Palais de Justice exonerated and triumphant!

The Baron, who had connections in all milieux, had been clever enough to interest the most influential people in his financial enterprise. Incentives, cleverly distributed, had worked wonders. He had been able to manipulate the magistracy with an admirable dexterity. Knowing that, no matter what certain people claim, it is not corrupt, he had carefully refrained from any appearance of trying to buy it, but he had interested a few needy functionaries in the affair, and for those who could not resist the attractions of beauty he had "deployed the skirt."

For that delicate task, he had had recourse to the rare qualities of Madame de Saint-Lai and the brothel-keeper had achieved prodigies. Her entire feminine general staff had been devoted to it. An entire battalion—a veritable army—of pretty women had sung the genius of Saint-Magloire to their lovers with gracious abandon. A leading role in that gigantic comedy had been attributed to Germaine Reyval. She was intimately linked with the mistresses of senior functionaries in the Prefecture.

In brief, Saint-Magloire had cast an immense net over the whole of Paris. And when the bankruptcy came, all the Baron's friends—who, forewarned, had already sold their shares and had not been "caught on the hop"—commiserated with him, defended him and boasted of his perfect honesty. Who, then, could possibly accuse of theft or fraud the man who had attempted to realize for France the most sublime enterprise of the century?

Those whom money and women did not tempt in the least had been captured by the satisfaction of some vanity or vainglory. During the issue of shares in the Compagnie des Trésor d'Amphitrite, a veritable rain of decorations had descended upon Paris. The *Officiel* registered a continuous jet of rosettes and red or violet ribbons.

The press had been rendered incapable of action. Unanticipated partnerships had saved newspapers that only had a few days to live from ruin. The powerful dailies had seen their advertising revenues rise to hitherto unknown levels, and it was impossible for independent journalists to "smear" Saint-Magloire.

Nothing had escaped the perspicacity of the Baron; he had created, without seeming to be involved, such fervent defenders that the official investigation opened into his affairs ended, in a matter of days, in finding that there was no case to answer.

It was recognized that he had been imprudent, but his good faith and honorability was blindingly obvious...

There was, however, no doubt that he had lead in his wing...

In the course of the investigation mounted by the head of the Sûreté, and in which he had been involved in an amateur capacity, by way of dilettantism, Dr. Lemoine had had the intuition that the Baron de Saint-Magloire and the escaped convict Gaston Rozen were one and the same.

Already, on that tragic night when he had rediscovered Eléna at the beside of her dying son, a sort of presentiment had troubled him at the sight of the extraordinary type-specimen of the flashy foreigner who had become the husband of the woman he had loved; a suspicion had crossed his mind with the dazzling instantaneity of a lightning flash.

He had said to himself that the man before him, whose strange gaze was so impressive, might be the fantastic Rozen, the convict risen to grandeur, the murderer sought by Oliva Lavardens—but Dr. Lemoine was not a man to allow himself to be hypnotized by a first impression. Precisely because he was afraid of being influenced by his own sentiments, by what he called the "personal equation," he reacted against that troublesome impression.

Besides which, neither the physiognomy nor the general appearance of Saint-Magloire corresponded exactly with the portrait of Gaston Rozen that he had built up from the information—furnished second-hand, to be sure—emanating from individuals who only knew him by hearsay themselves. He seemed to recognize in him the same consummate skill, the same audacity, the same mastery, the same brio, but was that not a romance, a dream? If it were necessary to condemn men on indications as fleeting and deceptive as that, no one would be sure of tomorrow.

In spite of his defenders, however, and in spite of the general silence of the press, the complaints of Saint-Magloire's victims had risen to such a pitch that the law and the police had been obliged to intervene, albeit without obtaining a conviction, while Dr. Lemoine, at the invitation of his friend Monsieur Cardec, launched on his trail, had begun to believe that his presentiments had not been mistaken.

Certain details, presumptions rather than facts, continually seemed to confirm that which his instinct had suggested in the course of the sad night whose memory had not ceased to obsess him. He imagined, moreover, that, one way or another, he would eventually penetrate the secret of Saint-Magloire's past. Nothing, in fact, prevented an investigation, and the great financier had no more protection than anyone else against an investigation by the police.

We have just seen how that calculation was undone by circumstances, and how Saint-Magloire, saved by his connections and a host of unwitting accomplices, had slipped through the mesh of the net—but the worm was in the fruit.

Suspicion had conclusively entered Lemoine's mind, and he was henceforth determined to do anything to ascertain its exactitude.

Although he was solidly hardened, the Baron de Saint-Magloire would have been afraid if he had even been able to imagine that such a redoubtable spy was now dogging his footsteps and marching in his shadow. In all the joy of having some out of the affair so fortunately, however—with a few million in his pocket—the Baron had no such suspicion.

Lemoine was still perplexed, however.

If only Eléna had been willing to talk! But the doctor had too much tact, and, above all, too much respect for Eléna to question her on the subject. How could such a conversation be undertaken? How could they talk about the past?

And yet the young woman, who lived almost in seclusion, received him. He often returned to the house, from which Saint-Magloire was absent with increasing frequency.

So far as Eléna was concerned, Lemoine conserved the role of a friend, a comrade. Her upright character refused to push the young woman to resume the duet of love so unfortunately interrupted all those years ago. The doctor believed that she was married and he would have considered the slightest attempt to tempt her away from her duty to be dishonest

In the meantime, one point appeared clearer with every day that passed, which was that Saint-Magloire was an adventurer of the most dangerous kind, a veritable scourge for Paris and France. But how could he be attacked? One might have thought that the entire society around him was blind. To try to share his suspicions with others would no more harm than good. It was better to wait and search patiently for some weak spot in the apparently-mighty colossus. The doctor was, therefore, determined to track Saint-Magloire's life with the same attentive curiosity that he would have devoted to tracking a disease, watching for an opportune moment to intervene.

He did not think he ought to share his ideas with Madame Lavardens, whom he saw every day and whose thirst for vengeance had not been appeased by time—far from it.

She too felt certain that she would finally succeed in unmasking Rozen. Where? When? She had no idea. She was under no illusion as to the difficulty of the task, but a secret inner voice told her: "You will succeed!" And Lemoine, who had been able to assess her character, all nervousness and enthusiasm, had judged it prudent to hide his suspicions...

If Oliva had learned that he suspected Saint-Magloire of being Rozen, no reasoning or influence could have prevented the impetuous young woman to have gone proclaiming it to the law; then all would have been lost, because no one would have listened. They would have fallen back on the accusation of her madness. And Saint-Magloire, alerted and put on his guard, would have taken measures... fleeing if he sensed that he was imperiled, going on the offensive if he thought himself strong enough.

That was, in any case, the opinion of Monsieur Cardec, the head of the Sûreté, the only person to whom Lemoine had communicated his ideas. They were, therefore, alone in deciding what strategy to follow.

With regard to Madame Lavardens, Lemoine kept he hopes up, gaining time, as Saint-Magloire was gaining time with Sokoloff. "Wait," he repeated, at each new visit. "Success is certain, if we don't rush. Wait!"

Unfortunately, he could see quite clearly that, although Madame Lavardens was as strong mentally as she had been at the beginning, she was physically exhausted. She lived modestly, and restricted herself severely in order not to run up debts. Lemoine had understood that the young woman was too proud to accept any help, but gradually, though his connections, he had procured her—without her suspecting his intervention—pupils for piano lessons among rich people who paid well. Then, one day, after having seen Eléna Ruiz again, the idea occurred to the doctor of placing Oliva with Saint-Magloire's companion. There, it was possible that the widow Lavardens might be useful to the goal that he was pursuing on her behalf.

Since the death of her son, Eléna had suffered, mentally rather than physically. Her increasingly marked abandonment by Saint-Magloire, absorbed by his business affairs and his passion for Germaine, only aggravated the situation. Eléna needed continual care, a devote affection. Who better to provide it than Madame Lavardens? The two young women were similar in character, and their situations had a marked resemblance. Both were lively and energetic, but good, sensible and capable of great devotion—and both had an immense dolor in their hearts. Oliva was mourning her murdered husband, Eléna dying for her vanished love.

And at the back of his mind, Lemoine persisted in believing that they both had the same torturer: Rozen. He therefore resolved to bring them together.

For Eléna, that would be easy. From the hand of the "good doctor," the man who had cared for her son with as much devotion as he would have done for his own child, Eléna would accept a friend blindly. It remained to convince Oliva.

"More than ever," he said to her, one day, when he young woman had come, as usual, to ask whether his research had produced any result, "More than ever, I think I'm nearing the goal."

"You've been saying that for a long time," murmured Madame Lavardens sadly.

"That's because I've been on the same track for a long time—and the more I advance, the stronger my conviction becomes."

"Whom do you suspect? Why won't you tell me?"

"Because you'd go too quickly and break the conductive wire. Suffice it to say that the man in whom I believe I've recognized Rozen is rich, powerful, bold and clever. He must therefore be combated with patience and guile, so wait a little longer."

"I've waited so long already!"

"Today, I have a proposal to make to you that you ought to accept, in the interests of the task we've undertaken."

"Speak, Doctor," said the widow, anxiously. "Speak."

"I have a rich friend, who is suffering, as you are. She needs to have someone close to her who can give her the necessary care, more moral than physical. It's merely the work of a lady's companion..."

"Explain."

Without mentioning any names, Lemoine acquainted her with Madame de Saint-Magloire's situation—abandoned by her husband, grief-stricken by the death of her son. He told her how good Eléna was, and how unhappy she was.

"In her employ," the doctor added, "you'd no longer have to worry about ensuring your livelihood; you could then devote yourself entirely to your vengeance. I am convinced, moreover, that Rozen must be a member of the cosmopolitan circle that frequent the house of the woman of whom I speak, and that you'll be admirably placed to observe."

"I accept," said Oliva, whose eyes were glinting, "and I swear to you that I'll keep my eyes open."

The doctor had almost attained his objective. His dear Eléna would have a devoted companion...and the actions and gestures of Saint-Magloire would be closely observed.

He was determined to hasten the realization of his plan.

It would be a major step forward, he said to himself, with satisfaction. *Once my protégée is installed in the house in the Champs-Élysées, I'll be able, by interrogating her cleverly, to find out many things about Saint-Magloire, and what Eléna thinks...perhaps, thanks to that unconscious witness, I'll reach my goal.*

XVII. Amour, When You Grip Us. ...

As soon as the bank in the Place Vendôme had taken off, the Baron de Saint-Magloire had had nothing more urgent to do than open for Dulac the million-franc credit he needed to realize his artistic dream, the creation of a popular lyric theater.

If, as was probable, the first million was insufficient, further capital would eventually be placed at his disposal. In reality, Dulac's credit was, so to speak, unlimited.

Saint-Magloire was not sparing with what Macaron called "the *galette*" when it was a matter of obliging a brother—but sentiment counted for nothing in that generosity, which was all the more princely because it was effected with the community's funds.

Saint-Magloire did not throw money out of the window needlessly. He knew full well that the best, simplest, surest and most conclusive way of liberating himself from Dulac's scrutiny was to give him the means of pursuing his hobby-horse.

His ideal was, in fact, to have his own lyric stage. He wanted to create an absolutely independent theater, with enough cash in its coffers, having enough prestige and influence, to oppose the outdated prejudices of the public: a theater in which the works of young and audacious composers would be performed, who, shaking off the yoke of tradition, deeming Boïeldieu, Gounod, Meyerbeer and Rossini, not to mention the demigod Wagner, to be so many old fools and tom-tom beaters: in a word, the works of the anarchists of art. Dulac was ambitious to be the happy Antoine of that new Théâtre Libre.[48]

That was, at least, what he said, with a great luxury of specious arguments, and perhaps what he thought. Fundamentally, however, he was only obedient to one motive; half-unconsciously, he was pursuing an obsession: getting Germaine Reyval back. His goal was to be able to offer her a marvelous engagement; he intended to give her heaps of gold with a great deal of glory around it, in order to bring her back to him and make himself beloved, even if it swallowed up a fortune.

---

[48] The actor-manager André Antoine had founded an eponymous theater dedicated to the ideals of "Théâtre Libre" in 1887. It was a pioneering and radical "workshop theater," in which the director promoted a kind of psychological realism. It closed in 1894, but Antoine was still trying to put his ideas into practice in other Parisian theatres in 1901; he subsequently diverted his attention and talents to the cinema, where the application of his naturalistic theories became significant influence.

Saint-Magloire had divined all of that. He had anticipated that Dulac, once his finger was stuck in the gears, would be entirely devoted to his chimera, and would cease to an inconvenient accomplice, too idealistic, too timid and too burdened with scruples—and he had given him a golden bridge.

In fact, Dulac was more of an artist and dilettante than a man of action. His anarchism was only skin deep and the ultra-revolutionary doctrines that he willingly embraced, with noisy affectation, in private, were more a product of a kind of snobbery. It was even probable that, if the case arose, he would recoil before certain tasks.

Intelligent, educated and overflowing with verve, Dulac was more brilliant than profound, more enthusiastic than tenacious. He was a man for eccentric and paradoxical tasks, provided that they were light and rapid. He was capable of coups of the head and heart, and perhaps, under the influence of passion, he might even have risked physical action—but obscure intrigues, and laborious and complicated schemes, were unsuited to his frivolity, his lack of forethought and his mental idleness, not to mention his reserves of irreducible loyalty.

Attached for a few months at the secretariat of the bank, he had astonished Saint-Magloire—who was not easy to astonish—by the extent and variety of his knowledge, and especially by his facility of assimilation. In less than a fortnight, the poet, who had not previously had the slightest idea how a bank worked and had even claimed an incomprehension and scorn for numbers, had penetrated the secrets of financial mechanics, down to the slightest details.

Then, gripped one day by a nostalgia for journalism, he had dropped everything in order to become the music editor of the large daily newspaper. His articles, imprinted with a certain sarcasm, but always accurate and sure of their facts, were widely read. His eloquent criticism was appreciated.

Mingling with the artistic and worldly society, in spite of his indifference to gossip, he had inevitably learned about the exceedingly Parisian liaison between the great cantatrice Germaine Reyval and the Baron de Saint-Magloire. People had initially talked about it in whispers; then gradually, it had become a matter of public notoriety, and Dulac had had nothing more to do than gather the certainty.

At first, he had seen red, and thought of immediately taking vengeance on what he considered to be an infamous treason. All the "comrades," and Saint-Magloire better than anyone, knew where his sentiments were directed, and the state of his soul. Vengeance would have been easy, although the Baron was careful to keep him in the dark with regard to his clandestine exploits. He knew enough to destroy him with a word. Thanks to Macaron's indiscretions he had found out about the installation for the manufacture of artificial gold. He was not unaware that it was functioning regularly in the mysterious house in Auteuil, which Sokoloff's genius had surrounded with a network of warning devices and automatic traps, in which intruders unenlightened as to what precautions to take would inevitably would inevitably be caught.

In any case, even if he had been incompletely informed regarding the present, he knew enough about the past for a single word addressed to any man law to precipitate the catastrophe. That word, however, which would have compromised everything while bringing down his rival, he was too hesitant to pronounce.

To begin with, he did not believe that the Baron's liaison with Germaine was serious. He saw it as nothing but a flirtation, in which vanity played the leading role on either side—and that thought, which squared so well with his irresolution, permitted him to hope that Germaine's heart had not been conquered and might belong entirely to him.

Then again, to avenge himself it would have been necessary for him to take action, to make a decision, to do something energetic. As usual, he procrastinated, limiting himself to treating Saint-Magloire frostily when he encountered him, to make him aware of his discontentment.

The financier was too subtle not to perceive Dulac's jealousy.

That was the moment—truly psychological—that he chose to strike the great blow he had already been meditating for a long time. One morning, without any warning, he summoned Dulac, and, playing the game of amicable devotion, at which he was a past master, he told him of his intention to back the Théâtre Lyrique Populaire, and to confide its sole direction to him.

It was more than an intention; the financier had prepared everything in advance and set up the partnership; the deal was done. The Théâtre Sarah-Bernhardt had been rented, having become available by reason of the tragedienne's recent flight to Australia.[49] The lease was signed, a year's rent paid in advance, and all the formalities completed. The new impresario had no more to do, if his heart told him to, than take possession of it that same day, with all the force that credit gives and all the confidence inspired by the certainty of having assured backers.

With the persuasive voice that charmed his interlocutors, Saint-Magloire made Dulac understand that his "coquetries" with regard to Germaine had no other objective than to persuade the capricious actress to become the star of the new theater.

Naturally, Dulac was moved to tears. Forgetting all rancor and jealousy, he fell into Saint-Magloire's arms.

Ever the rogue, the latter also pretended to be deeply moved. He was, at any rate, delighted with his idea. It was one more obstacle—and not the least—out of his way. That was worth the sacrifice of a million.

---

[49] This evidently refers to a fictitious event in the near future that the novel's internal chronology has now apparently reached. Sarah Bernhardt had visited Australia in 1891, while on a flamboyantly-publicized World Tour, but she did not return after taking over and renaming after herself what is now the Théâtre de la Ville in 1899.

The very next day, scarcely installed in his directorial office in the Avenue Vitoria, Dulac telegraphed Germaine to tell her about the happy event and propose an immediate engagement on conditions that she could name herself.

Since joining the Opéra, Germaine had only made rare appearances on our great lyric stage, where she had only had a relative success: a few repertory roles, a few creations in which she had been ferociously criticized, and that was all. In spite of her prestigious beauty and her real talent—for, although she was slightly lacking in lung-power, she was a stylish singer and excellent musician—and in spite of the unanimity of the praise in the press, vaguely suspected of complacency by the skeptical and blasé public at large, she had not attained the artistic glory of which she had dreamed.

She had not been forgiven, in melomaniac society, for her caustic impertinence with regard to her comrades, some of whom had powerful protectors in the aristocracy of subscribers, and who strove to attenuate the veritable success of her debuts.

It had, therefore, been easy for Saint-Magloire, by exaggerating all the little annoyances that plagued the artiste, to persuade her that she ought to quit the Opéra to become the first-magnitude star of a theater of new art, where her superb talent would find an open arena, in which she would create unforgettable roles. And she hastened to respond to Dulac's appeal. Without losing a minute, after having made herself supremely beautiful, she ran to the Théâtre Lyrique.

"It's truly kind of you," she said, extending her hand to her former lover, "truly kind of you to have thought of your little Germaine. You don't hate me anymore, then?"

"I never hated you. I've always loved you. I adore you—you know that. You've made me suffer cruelly, but I forgive you. I'll forget everything, since you've consented to be my star...and I hope that you still love me...a little tiny bit."

"You're a man of spirit, and I know your good heart," the actress replied. "I'm ready to create any role that you desire, whatever it might be. As for the rest, it's more delicate. I promise to love you a little, even a lot, but as a friend, as a comrade..."

Although he ought to have expected that response, Dulac went pale; his face contracted and his lips trembling. "Is it over, then, our dear romance?" he asked, in a changed voice.

"My dear, one can rarely resuscitate the dead. But tell me, it wasn't only, with the goal of playing court to me that you invited me to come with such urgency was it? Suppose we talk business?

"So, here you are, a theater director, master in your own home, free to make art for art's sake, and naturally, you want me to fight the good fight under your flag, in your company! That fits me like a glove, you know?"

A glimmer of hope lit up in Dulac's face. "Yes," he said, "it's true that I have a theater of my own. I no longer have to depend on anyone—I have money, a lot of money. I can finally put flesh on my life's dream. The Théâtre Lyrique Populaire will soon be the foremost lyric theater in Europe. People will make pilgrimages to it, as they do to Bayreuth—bear that in mind! You can imagine that I'm not going to begin stupidly with some banal revival. What point is there in getting bogged down in the old ruts of beaten tracks? The sole reason for being is to do something new, and more new things, and always new things! So I shall inaugurate the season with a magical opera in which everything will be utterly original and utterly delightful, as you'll see. The libretto is adapted from Shakespeare's *The Tempest*, by the fine poet Symphorien Lacaze. The music is by Joseph Bucquoy, the young composer who..."

"I know him," Germaine put in. "He has talent, but what a eccentric! A trifle bizarre, your Bucquoy, in the final count. You know that he's never been able to get a single sheet of his music performed..."

"I know—and it's for that very reason that I'm taking him on. And you can be tranquil. Launched as I shall launch it, his opera will be the talk of Paris. Only I need you to play Titania."[50]

"That's flattering for me, my dear director, and I'm proud to have the future of the new art by the throat. Hurrah for the new art!" Perhaps unconsciously, and perhaps with a certain malice, she added: "But I'm wondering to what Maecenas we owe this windfall?"

"To someone you know well," riposted Dulac, with a forced smile that resembled a grimace. "To a Baron quilted with gold, whom you've made your God!"

Germaine burst out laughing. "Dear Gaston! Are you jealous of him? My poor friend, how silly you are. I'm not in love with the Baron de Saint-Magloire. He's too handsome! But I'd be lying—and you wouldn't hold me in esteem any more—if I said that I'm not infinitely graceful for the services with which he's overwhelming me. In truth, that's all...nothing more...nothing else."

With a delicate gesture, a trifle roguish, she clicked her pink thumbnail on the nacre of her teeth. Then she went on: "He pays court to me, of course, as he does to all the women; we've flirted a little; when I sing at his soirées, he pays me royally..."

"I'll pay you more than royally," Dulac interjected, in a singular voice, in which there was both a caress and a threat. "I'll pay you as no singer has ever been paid by any theater in the world. The Théâtre Lyrique can provide all luxuries, and its director can refuse Germaine Reyval nothing."

"You need your head examined!" the actress riposted. "Would you like me to call a doctor?"

"Woman of marble!" moaned Dulac, seized by a fit of discouragement.

---

[50] It is presumably in accordance with Dulac's principles of anarchist art that Titania has been relocated to *The Tempest* from Shakespeare's other fairy play.

"Come on, come on, my darling," Germaine murmured, moving her chair closer and taking Dulac's hands in hers. Don't make me out to be worse than I am. You love me, I don't doubt it. I can sense it; I can see it. You hope to triumph over my explicable resistance, alas, and by force of love, reconquer a heart that was once yours. Have I the right to destroy that tender hope? Would I be sincere in so doing? Only, let's be patient. Let me think; let me pull myself together. If you knew what a fever, what a whirlwind, I've been living in recently!

"But now I've become your resident. We'll see one another every day; you'll have a thousand opportunities to pay court to me. I promise that I'll let matters take their course. The esteem and affection I have for you will facilitate the sacrifice. Eventually, a day might come when…perhaps…who knows?"

That carefully measured declaration, full of promising reticence, brought a flood of blood to Dulac's face. The anarchist director's eyes glittered.

He got up abruptly, as if moved by a spring, with the visible intention of taking Germaine in his arms—but at a sharp glance from the beauty, he sat down again, his hands feverish.

"You're right," he said. "I need to reconquer you. In the meantime, let's talk business. Here's the score for *The Tempest*. Please read it at the piano with your accompanist, and learn it as quickly as possible. When you know it, you can rehearse your role with the orchestra. Bucquoy will come…to establish the continuity, to settle the nuances of interpretation with you…you'll see that he's a genuine artist. Afterwards, we'll think about your costumes, which I imagine as magical, dazzling, unprecedented…for nothing is beautiful enough for you!"

"My darling, you're so kind that I no longer know whether you make me feel pity or fear! I'll run away, for I fear that I might allow myself to weaken— and I mustn't weaken any longer! Soon!"

She held out her hands to Dulac, who, intoxicated, covered her fingers with mad kisses—and she ran to the door amid a joyful rustle of petticoats. There, looking back in a melodramatic pose, she exclaimed; "She resists me! I shall murder her!" Then, changing her tone, with a slight faubourgian accent, she cried: "*Au revoir*, Antony!" shutting the door in the director's face.

The she launched herself into the corridor, with a volley of crystalline laughter.

Slightly disconcerted, Dulac returned to sit down at his desk, delightedly sniffing the subtle perfume of tuberose and violet that filled the room.

"It's not over yet," he said to himself. "All is not lost…she's more emotional than she wants to appear. She laughs to cover up her disturbance…and I love her so much that she'll end up loving me too!"

XVIII. A Further Crime

Staged with extraordinarily luxurious scenery and interpreted by a first-class company, *The Tempest* was a triumph, celebrated in every tone by the press of the entire world.

At a stroke, Joseph Bucquoy had been established as a grandmaster, and the Théâtre Lyrique Populaire, having become the theater in fashion, had to turn people away. It was full to overflowing.

Every evening, a triple salvo of applause greeted the entrance of Germaine, adorable in grace and fantasy, in the role of Titania, which seemed to have been positively written for her, as anticipated by Dulac, whose love had only refined his artistic sensibility and sureness of judgment.

When the performance ended there were three, and then four curtain calls, veritable ovations, in the midst of an enthusiastic stamping of feet. The radiant beauty of the woman had at least as much to do with that as admiration for the artiste's talent.

Saint-Magloire's passion had only been further excited, to a paroxysm surprising in a man of his kind. He could no longer live without Germaine. Almost every evening he sent his carriage to wait at the theater door in order to taker to super with him at some fashionable cabaret, and he counted the hours until he would sleep with her again.

This crazed love became the talk of Paris and Dulac, in spite of the tenacity of his illusions, soon reached the point of no longer being able to hide the extent of his unhappiness from his oblivious lover. Maddened by the desire that was boiling his blood, however, he continued to forgive, and would have accepted everything, including sharing her, provided that Germaine consented in the end to give herself to him. Something told him that, one day, that indulgence—for which he sometimes reproached himself as cowardice—would have its reward, and that Germaine would eventually provide him with an exquisite revenge.

He was, moreover, not entirely wrong.

Softened by success, Germaine was attracted once again, by insensible degrees, to the man to whom she owed so much intoxication and whose contagious tenderness, so touching in its resigned humility, eventually had an effect on her. Sooner or later, she would have finished up tumbling into Dulac's arms, partly out of pity, partly out of gratitude, and partly out of sensuality, if the dread of allowing herself to be caught in a trap of a return of passion, whose consequences she feared, had not made her continually defer the rendezvous implored by the poor "limpet"—a rendezvous put off a hundred times, cancelled by means of the feeblest excuses.

Then again, Saint-Magloire was not a man to be deceived with impunity.

At length, however, Dulac lost patience. From the depths of his heart he sensed one of those violent, impulsive and ferocious hatred rising, which emerge therefrom in despair, which turn the tender and the feeble into "rabid sheep." And that hatred was directed not so much against Germaine as against Saint-Magloire, the thief of love!

He reverted then to nihilist traditions and reminiscences of propaganda by action. Why should he not manufacture one of those infernal machines, for which Sokoloff had once revealed the terrible recipes to him? Why should he not blow up the house in the Champs-Élysées, with all its contents, or the offices in the Place Vendôme, or even the little house in Auteuil, one night when he knew that the lovers were spending the night there, as they often did?

He had even made a few preparatory trials to that effect, but he did not have the heart. Besides which, it only required one word from Germaine, one glance, one handshake, the calm the storm that was rumbling beneath his skull, and give him hope. Then, his projects of vengeance came to seem chimerical, ridiculous and absurd, and his anger instantly gave way to a puerile confidence.

Deep down, he thought, *Germaine can't love Saint-Magloire...any more than the so-called Baron is capable of a genuine sentiment. Between them, it's a question of vainglory...it is, as they say, playing to the gallery. Why, then, get alarmed? Germaine will return to me, entirely... She'll break definitively with that Saint-Magloire, whom she accommodates, perhaps, because of me...because she fears that he'll withdraw the credit at my disposal...*

And with the versatility that was the bedrock of his character, Dulac re-solved to have it out with the financier. *It's time*, he concluded, *to put an end to this comedy...*

In the meantime, however, because he took pleasure in irritating the jeal-ousy of the director of the Théâtre Lyrique, the Baron treated him increasingly as a stranger. He affected no longer to encounter him except at the theater, or exchanged a few brief words of banal camaraderie with him—but Dulac did not seem to notice it, and continually put off the moment of the reckoning that he had promised himself.

One evening, however, more nervous than usual, he grasped the Baron's hand when the latter nonchalantly offered him his fingertips. "I need to talk to you seriously," he murmured in the adventurer's ear.

"I'm listening," the other replied, with a gesture of annoyance. "What is it about?"

"Germaine."

Saint Magloire understood that he was about to have a thorny conversation. Following his custom, he resolutely took the offensive. "My dear fellow," he sniggered, fixing Dulac with his magnetic gaze, "You'll permit me not to follow you on to that terrain. My relationship with Germaine is no concern of yours. I've given you a theater and you're free to direct it as you wish; I've permitted you to create operas, to renew the art, and to win as much as you like at that game, for which I've furnished you with all the trump cards. Stuff yourself with glory and money, but for God's sake don't stick your nose into my business, for it'll get you into trouble!"

"That's my intention, however," Dulac growled, exasperated by the Baron's patronizing attitude. "You need to hear me out."

"*Bonsoir*, my dear director," the banker retorted—and, pirouetting on his heels, he went deliberately to knock on the door of Germaine's dressing-room.

The lovely woman, completely swathed in lace, emerged at that very moment. Going past Dulac, whom she brushed past without appearing to notice, she took the Baron's arm.

The poor lover, absolutely beside himself, but not wanting to risk losing Germain irredeemably by causing a scene, saw the two of them climb into a coupé hitched to two magnificent thoroughbreds. He heard the financier call out to his coachman: "To Maxim's"—and it seemed to Dulac that a double burst of laughter escaped from the carriage when the horses departed at a rapid trot.

Ah! They were mocking him.

This time, he had reached the end of his tether. Mad with rage, obedient to an irresistible impulse, Dulac leapt into a fiacre and had himself taken to the Rue Royale at a gallop.

His initial idea was to get into the private room where his rival was enclosed with Germaine by any means possible, including force, and kill them both, without ceremony, like dogs, and to blow his own brains out immediately afterwards. He had even checked that the revolver he carried in his pocket was suitably loaded, and had taken off the safety-catch.

If Maxim's restaurant had been closer to the Théâtre Lyrique, the Baron and Germaine's little party would certainly have ended bloodily—but there is sufficient distance between the Avenue Victoria and the Rue Royale for a heroic resolution to be unable to persist without modification in a man as hesitant as Dulac. He had scarcely reached the Palais-Royal than, aided by the coolness of the night, instead of searching for a means not to miss the Baron and Germaine, he was already considering the material impossibility of carrying out his double murder.

He found a host of good reasons to calm himself down.

The waiters at Maxim's, who know me and have always seen me in control, can't fail to notice the sate I'm in. I'm trembling, my teeth are chattering; I must be pale. Seeing my haggard eyes—frightening—they'll suspect something, follow me, and stop me at the crucial moment... The drama will turn to ridicule... I'll be mocked... Vengeance will escape me, and I'll only have achieved one thing...to make all of Paris laugh derisively. That's not the place to strike!

A violent temptation gripped him to get a piece of paper instead, and to scribble a few laconic words on it, certainly more terrible for Saint-Magloire than all the bullets in a revolver.

Why not denounce the bandit who had stolen Germaine from him? Why not reveal to everyone the origin of this Saint-Magloire, alias Gaston Rozen, escaped convict, filibuster and forger? Was it not sufficient to go into a café and calmly address that denunciation to the Prefect of Police or the public prosecutor?

If Dulac had often rejected that form of vengeance, which his natural rectitude had always made him consider as unrealizable, he had, however, envisaged it, and during the sleepless nights of his sharp jealousy he had weighed up the pros and cons.

His imagination worked like that of an author planning a novel, and his nervous overexcitement eventually found a fortunate derivative in that scheming. Germaine's lover had often told himself that Saint-Magloire was too powerful, and occupied too high a position, that he had too much prestige for a banal anonymous letter to be able to awaken suspicion. The letter would be thrown in the waste-paper basket without being read all the way through, or at least without the slightest importance being attached to it. Perhaps it would even be shown to Saint-Magloire, who, with a disdainful gesture, would have handed back the "filthy paper," the work of some envious wretch or madman...and that would be all...

It would have been a complete waste of time for Dulac to have resorted to that cowardly weapon. He would have fallen into infamy for nothing...

Not to mention that, if the impossible happened, and the denunciation were to be taken seriously, Saint-Magloire would not be the only one compromised. The police would not fail, in following the indicated trail, to encounter Sokoloff, Bastien and himself. That would be a means to lose Germaine, this time without appeal.

Meanwhile, the fiacre had stopped at the door of the famous cabaret, from which a dull rumor of celebration emerged.

Dulac leapt nimbly down to the sidewalk, threw a hundred sous to the coachman, who dissolved in noisy thanks, and, brusquely brushing aside the young groom who presented himself in front of him, cap in hand, he began pacing back and forth, looking in t the lighted windows of private rooms, in which imprecise silhouettes were moving like Chinese shadows.

Soon, at the last widow in the direction of the Place de la Concorde, the partly open curtains of which let out the bright gleam of a chandelier, the director of the Théâtre Lyrique perceived a woman he recognized immediately.

Then a man appeared and took the woman in his arms.

"Germaine! Oh, Germaine!" murmured Dulac, clenching his fists.

Slightly astonished, the coachmen whose carriages were parked in front of the restaurant gazed at the gentleman in evening dress, hypnotized in front of a widow like a starving man before victuals...

"Well, old chap," said one, "whoever dropped that fellow off for a drink hasn't stolen his wallet. Should have—he's had enough already...."

"You don't get it," replied another. "You can see that he's not drunk. I bet he's some sucker looking for his old lady, who's doing the dirty on him with some gigolo…maybe there'll be a dust-up, and we can all have a laugh."

But Dulac did not hear anything. Less resistant than usual, he did not even notice the jokers who were looking down their noses at him, making fun at him and drawing away, splitting their sides.

He no longer new anything; he was no longer thinking about anything…

No sentiment or sensation subsisted in his distress, save for a frightful anguish that was brutally squeezing his throat, stomach and entrails. It seemed to him that his heart, immeasurably swollen, was filling his entire breast, ready to burst.

In order not to fall over, he leaned instinctively on the gas-lamp opposite the window in which he had seen Germaine in the Baron's arms. Then, by virtue of gazing at the same spot, a kind of torpor overtook him; his eyelids fluttered, exhausted. He seemed to be asleep, agitated by a nightmare.

Passers-by were becoming increasingly rare; only a few coachmen—cab-drivers or servants—sleeping on their seats were waiting for the emergence of diners. Dulac stayed there, leaning against the bronze lamp-post, his head empty, unsteady on his stiffened legs, twitching.

Suddenly, the window darkened like a closing eye, and there was a bustle in the red-carpeted stairway of the private rooms. People were about to come out…they came out…

At that moment, a coupé hitched to a single horse, which would not have attracted any attention if it had not been driven by a Chinaman in national costume, turned the corner of the Place de la Concorde and came to draw up alongside the sidewalk. It was Saint-Magloire's coupé, brought at the appointed time, to within two minutes, by the faithful Yu.

Immediately, the financier appeared, with his arm around Germaine's waist. Without a word, he pushed the actress into the carriage, and briskly climbed in after her. The coupé departed immediately in the direction of the Seine. The Chinaman was driving fast.

The sight of the woman he loved on the arm of his fortunate rival had roused Dulac abruptly from his torpor. Bounding, with an agility surprising in a man of his corpulence, out of the dark corner into which he had plastered himself when the noisy crowd of belated celebrants emerged, he ran after the coupé, which was evidently heading toward Auteuil.

He did not feel tired or short of breath. Carried away by a superhuman force, he flew with the speed and lightness of a roebuck, his feet scarcely touching the asphalt.

The coupé had not yet passed the obelisk when he caught up with it and, with a vigorous thrust, hooked himself on to the rear springs. The Chinaman and the couple inside did not seem to have noticed anything.

The horse, vigorously urged on, had not felt the increase in load.

Once again, Dulac had obeyed one of those nervous impulses to which he was accustomed, and which might, in the right circumstances, have made him a murderer. As always, however, once the physical effort was expended, the faculty of examination returned, and he began to reflect about the eventualities of the adventure on which he had dazedly embarked.

Yes, the house in Auteuil. It was there, obviously, given the route it was taking, that the carriage was heading. Had Saint-Magloire succeeded, then, in having his liaison accepted by Sokoloff? The charmer was quite capable of having made the naïve savant believe that Germaine was indispensable to their plans....and for the good of the common cause, the Russian had probably closed his eyes and let the Baron do as he wished.

Given that, the situation was quite simple. Dulac would get into the house, hidden behind the body of the coupé he would swiftly jump down to the ground and hide in the bushes in the garden—and when the villains were in bed, he would, if necessary, force the door of their bedroom, breaking it down with his shoulder for want of any other means.

Then, they would see!

Overexcited by his desire for vengeance, he felt sufficient vigor and audacity to lift up a world!

A second later, however, a jolt of the carriage's rubber-tired wheels on the irregular carriageway interrupted that violent project. Objections flowed rapidly into Dulac's mind.

He recalled with an extraordinary clarity the nature of the mysterious house, in which he had never set foot, but which Bastien had described to him twenty times over in his picturesque language: a genuine fortress constructed like some annex of the Châtelet. Saint-Magloire and Sokoloff were not men to let themselves be caught unawares. They had anticipated everything, taken all precautions, and intruders would not find it easy to get into the house in Auteuil.

Invisible from the street, the villa was situated in the middle of vast grounds planted with hundred-year-old trees, limited on two sides by the think walls of a convent of cloistered nuns. The property, itself enclosed by a rather thick wall crowned by broken bottles, formed the corner of two almost-deserted streets, whose length was entirely occupied by waste ground, fallow gardens and vegetable-plots.

A small postern opened on to the Avenue Raffet, but only Sokoloff and Saint-Magloire went in that way, for the lock was controlled by a secret mechanism known only to them. The rare visitors occasionally admitted to the sanctuary—Bastien, Germaine, Yu and a few reliable domestics—went through the coaching-entrance in the Rue Jasmin.

When anyone rang at that door an electric bell immediately rang inside the house, while a copper plate appeared in a groove above the bell-push bearing the word: *Enter*. The small door fitted into one of the bronze battens of the coaching entrance would immediately open of its own accord, and then close again automatically as soon as the visitor, henceforth imprisoned, had crossed the threshold, while the copper plate disappeared.

The various chimes provoked by the opening and closing of the door continued to ring for a few minutes, time enough for the visitor to be recognized by means of optical apparatus reflecting his image in a kind of concierge's lodge, where a reliable man—generally the Chinaman Yu—was permanently stationed day and night. Suppliers and casual callers never got any further. They were received in a visitors' room attached to the lodge. Only intimate acquaintances—and only if they had an appointment and had shown themselves to be empty-handed—were allowed to proceed any further; but they could not do that without a guide, the entire domain being sown with redoubtable traps.

It was, moreover, impossible to get in any other way. Climbing over the walls was particularly dangerous; in the midst of the fragments of broken glass with which their crests were bristling, numerous metallic artichokes were disposed, linked together by a network of wires through which powerful electric currents circulated—furnished not by dynamos, whose hum might have attracted attention, but by prodigious batteries of thermoelectric piles of Sokoloff's own invention, located in the cellars. Woe betide any imprudent person who touched that armature! He would suffer the fate that once befell two poor soldiers on the occasion of a charity fête held in the Jardins des Tuileries, who, having tried to climb over the gates, became entangled in the wires of the lighting, and were simply electrocuted.

Any attempt at breaking or picking the locks of the doors or windows would likewise have been immediately signaled by urgent alarm-bells. Any indiscreet individual or burglar would he exposed to being struck down, stunned or caught in a trap like a fox.

Sokoloff had even anticipated the case in which someone familiar with the house, initiated in the secrets of that defensive apparatus or having discovered it by chance, had taken it into his head to carry out a search in the absence of the masters of the house. He had set up a camera at the entrance to the vestibule, immediately behind the door, triggered automatically by a spring placed under a tile in the parquet. No sooner was a foot placed over the threshold than the system came into play, unless the precaution was taken of pressing a stop button carefully hidden in the midst of the ornamentation of the woodwork. A magnesium flashbulb went off, under the action of an electric spark, and the intruder was instantly "snapped" in passing, thus signing the confession of his indiscretion, not with his hand but his image.

Dulac knew all that, thanks to the loquacious Bastien's inability to hold his tongue, especially with a comrade. But what he did not know was the way to get through that series of accumulated obstacles with impunity. On that matter, Bastien—who, as he willingly admitted, did not understand any of that "damnable trickery"—had provided no information. Sokoloff had doubtless offered, a few weeks earlier, to show him the detailed mechanism of an installation of which he was proud, but that had not been done, Macaron having declared that he would see nothing but smoke.

In that regard, therefore, Dulac was no better off than anyone else, with the aggravating circumstance that he was aware of the danger

Again, the sentiment of his impotence invaded his soul, paralyzing his anger.

If the thought of Germaine, whom he knew to be there behind the thin quilted partition, swooning under his rival's kisses, had not returned from time to time to make his blood boil and stretch all his nerves like so many steel threads, he would have let himself slide on to the roadway and, allowing he carriage to which he had been clinging to continue its journey, he would have gone away, racked by despair, without following up his ideas of punishment.

Meanwhile, Saint-Magloire's horse, which Yu was maneuvering through the deserted streets, continued to travel at speed. It soon reached Auteuil, and when Dulac, finally emerging from his stormy dream, cast a glance around, trying to get his bearings, the carriage swept into the Rue Jasmin at top speed.

Instead of stopping in front of the bronze gate, the coachman, to his great amazement, turned the corner and came to a halt at the postern in the Avenue Raffel.

There, abruptly opening the carriage door, Saint-Magloire got down first; then, taking Germaine by the arm, almost carrying her, enveloped by a tender gesture, he put his finger in a crack in the wall. Immediately, the little door rotated silently on its hinges; the couple slipped into the gap, and, in the blink of an eye, still in silence and as if pulled by an invisible hand, the heavy batten settled back into its frame.

Dulac had not yet recovered from his surprise when the carriage, pivoting on itself with a deft maneuver, returned to the coaching entrance in the Rue Jasmin, which opened abruptly in its turn to allow it through and immediately closed behind it.

I'm inside, thought Dulac. Galvanized by the imminence and gravity of the peril, he let himself fall to the ground, where he flattened himself in the shadows while the roll of the tires on the sand of the driveway muffle the sound of his fall.

Too much knowledge is harmful, Germaine's lover continued, talking to himself, while he crawled toward a thick clump of rhododendrons, where he lurked like a wild beast in ambush. *If that damned Rozen—may the plague choke him!—had simply had his house guarded by a trust Great Dane instead of putting his faith in the fairy Electricity, I'd already have been spotted. It's true that it will still end up that way, for I can't hope to get out of the garden discreetly now, without peril. I'm inside, but I'm also in the net—except that I'll have my revenge before anything bad happens to me.*

Dulac was brave, in spite of his indecision. He was also jealous—jealous to the point of paroxysm, to the point of criminal folly. He was under the sway of the terrible passion that changes the gentlest and most inoffensive of men into a ferocious beast. The hazard of circumstances had driven him to the necessity of attempting the formidable adventure before which he had recoiled so many times. This time, retreat was no longer possible. Sooner or later, it would be necessary to act...

It was now only a question of hours, or perhaps minutes.

In consequence, he recovered his self-possession, simultaneously exciting his innate bravery and his jealousy. Caressing the butt of his revolver in his pocket, he was no longer thinking of anything but selling his life dearly after punishing the traitor.

The night was pitch dark. Thick clouds the color of ink were racing across a sky devoid of stars or moon. The silence of the grounds was only troubled by the rustle of branches shaken by the gusts of a warm as stiff westerly breeze.

A true setting for a tragedy, Dulac thought, in whom the mental agony and certainty of the imminent catastrophe had not been able to stifle the man of the theater.

At that moment, one of the ground floor windows in the house, from which the clump of bushes in which he was crouching was only separated by a lawn circumscribed by a narrow and carefully-raked path, was suddenly illuminated by a discreet glow. It was doubtless the bedroom into which Saint-Magloire had gone with Germaine Reyval.

The horrible torture of the Rue Royale began again, more cruel still for the unfortunate Dulac, whose ardent imagination showed him, with cinematographic precision, what was happening behind the curtain. He divined the gestures, the play of features, the poses...

Soon, he could no longer stand it.

Emerging from his hiding-place, he jumped over the circular path, whose gravel, crunching beneath his soles, would have betrayed his approach, and swiftly crossed the lawn diagonally, heading for the odious window, ready for the supreme assault.

Suddenly, however, his feet caught in a thin metal wire extended at ground level, which he had not noticed. He stumbled, fell to his knees, got up and re-sumed his course—too late!

The furious clamor of a special bell rang out in the lighted room, while an electric searchlight abruptly lit up and swiveled on a pivot to dart a dazzling beam of light at the exact spot where the alarm-wire had been tripped.

Immediately, the door opens violently and two shadows appeared on the steps.

The banker, in a night-shirt and underpants, raced out, accompanied by Yu, the only domestic of whom Rozen made use in his absences or his Machiavelli-an machinations.

Having made a sign to Yu to stay back, the Baron advanced deliberately toward Dulac, nailed to the spot by shock and the dazzling glare.

"I regret having kept you waiting for so long," he said, in a hissing voice, "But gallantry has its obligations. First, I had to do the honors to me companion, a lady you know…and if the delicate individual in question had not had a terrible headache, which obliged me to give her a mild narcotic in order that she might sleep peacefully, I would certainly have let you spend the night under the stars…"

"You knew that I was here?" stammered Germaine's lover, petrified by that cynicism."

"I know everything, old chap," Rozen riposted. "Nothing escapes me. Do you think I'm naïve enough not to notice that we were being spied on and followed? I saw you lying in wait outside Maxim's—but I don't like scandal and I gave orders to Yu to let you alone and let you get all the way here, where nothing could prevent me catching you in a trap. It was the wisest and safest thing to do.

"I could make you pay cruelly for your error. You'll admit that this manner of getting into someone's home by night, without warning, is a trifle boorish, even for an anarchist—but I have a longstanding affection for you, and a profound esteem. I pity you, and I don't wish you any harm, so I'll forgive you this time, but let me talk to you as a friend. What's got into you? Have you gone mad?"

"Germaine! I want Germaine!" Dulac implored, hypnotized once again by his rival's strange gaze. "Give me back Germaine—she's mine!"

"That, old man, will never happen, Germain is free, assuredly, in her heart and he flesh. That's the alpha and the omega of the anarchist doctrine, as you can't deny. She had the right to give herself to whomever she pleases. It pleased her to choose me, who loves her."

"That's a lie! You don't love her…"

"Yes, I love her! We love one another!" Saint-Magloire riposted, emphasizing the words. "She belongs to me, and you can put on your mourning-dress, my poor Dulac. Now go away. I'm a benevolent prince, and I don't want to cause the slightest inconvenience to a friend…"

Anger gripped Dulac again as Rozen stirred up his jealousy with his brutal irony.

"I could have got rid of you," he proclaimed, "by revealing the truth! The Baron de Saint-Magloire an escaped convict! Ha ha! The crook Rozen, murderer, thief, anarchist and spy…a fine scandal all that would have made! But I'm no informer…"

"I know that you're a good soul," the Baron cut in, in a voice whose softness redoubled its iciness, "and I'm grateful to you for your loyalty—but you're saying stupid things, and doing them, which is worse. You're a good lad, intelligent, an artist, on the way to becoming rich; life is smiling on you. How can you get your head twisted and irritate the comrades for a whore? Because fundamentally, as you know better than anyone, Germaine is a whore. A pretty girl, but a whore…a whore…a whore. She doesn't love you. You've had your moment. It's over. She'll never love you again…"

"I want her," growled Dulac, "and I'll have her!"

"Enough of that. It's late—or, rather, early…I have a wife at home, waiting for me. She's asleep, but it would nevertheless be inconsiderate of me to leave her alone too long, and not to be with her when she wakes up, so this isn't the time to argue with a fool who can't resign himself to being forgotten. You're acting as if you had the rights of a cuckold! As if this were the first time that it had happened to you with the individual in question!"

"Swine!" howled Dulac, decidedly exasperated, brandishing his revolver.

Saint-Magloire did not flinch. "Come on, old man," he said. "Do you imagine, perchance, that you're at the Ambigu? Would you have the heart to send *ad patres* your friend, your associate, your accomplice, poor Gaston, to whom you owe your fortune and your position? All that because he's the lover, after you, of a woman who's reputed to have received all Paris with open curtains…

"Things like that don't happen between comrades."

"I'll kill you, you bandit!" howled Dulac, increasingly excited.

"That would be a bad mistake in truth. When you'd killed me, you wouldn't be able to get out of here, as you can have no doubt. One gesture to the Chinaman, who is here and knows all the house's tricks, and you're a dead man, disappeared from circulation, without a trace, without anyone even being able to suspect where your cadaver has gone…unless you're handed over to the police.

"Either way, Germaine is lost to you forever, free again to run after the wrestlers that were her routine fare before she took me for…a protector…"

"This time, I won't miss you!" roared Dulac, drunk with fury.

He raised his arm—but Saint-Magloire was expecting the movement.

"Imbecile," he murmured. "You asked for it!"

With a vigorously-directed blow of his fist, he had already knocked the weapon out of his attacker's head. He pounced on him like a tiger, immediately knocking him down by jamming his knee into the pit of his stomach.

His throat squeezed by a steely fist, Dulac fell back, choking, without even uttering a cry.

In response to a soft whistle from Saint-Magloire, Yu came running, carrying a handkerchief with which he covered the face of the stricken Dulac. A vague odor of rennet apples filled the air.

Assisted by the Chinaman, Rozen maintained the chloroform-steeped cloth over Dulac's face. In spite of the latter's energetic resistance, manifested by contortions and spasms that Saint-Magloire's prodigious vigor had no difficulty in mastering, he ended up falling unconscious.

When he saw his enemy reduced to a state of insensibility, inert and passive, the Baron made a sign to Yu. The mute loaded Dulac's body on to his shoulders and followed his master inside the villa.

"That's that," muttered Saint-Magloire. "He wanted it this way, after all. A good dose of aconitine, an excellent drug that leaves no trace, and the inconvenient fellow will be dispatched to a world where he'll no longer have any thought of causing me any trouble..."

A short while thereafter, the Baron, enveloped in an overcoat, with a felt hat pulled down over his eyes, left the house followed by his faithful domestic clad in a chauffeur's uniform. Yu was carrying Dulac. Having put down his burden, the Chinaman brought an automobile up to the coaching entrance and, assisted by Saint-Magloire, deposited the inert body of the theater director in the back. Then the two men got into the front seat. Saint-Magloire took hold of the steering-wheel and gear-stick, and the vehicle drew away into the night at top speed while the door closed behind them, as it had opened, automatically.

Two minutes later, peace and silence reigned once again over the sleeping villa, where nothing revealed that any drama had occurred.

XIX. The Autopsy

Rising with the sun, as was his habit, Dr. Lemoine put the final touches to a long and substantial article on "The Hybridization of Plants and the Possibility of Creating New Vegetable Species by means of Grafting," destined for the Académie des Sciences. He had been working on it non-stop for forty-eight hours without going out, even to take the air on his balcony, which overlooked vast gardens full of birds and flowers, and without opening a newspaper.

The work had evidently come out well, for a smile of satisfaction and naïve pride strayed over the author's lips as he reread and tidied up the sheets.

Suddenly, the door opened. It was Perrine, the old Breton maidservant, who, with her customary familiarity, entered without knocking.

"Here's your breakfast, Monsieur," she said, putting a large tray on his desk, on which an appetizing cup of chocolate was fuming, flanked by a stack of buttered toast and a pile of letters and newspapers. Then, taking note of her master's drawn features and swollen eyelids, she grumbled: "Dear God, you've been up all night again, haven't you?"

"You're mistaken, Perrine" the doctor replied, smiling at the outburst. "I went to bed at three o'clock."

"Yes, yes, three o'clock—and up again at five, no doubt? I know you! I didn't give birth to you, but it's as good as."

"Given that I went to bed, you have no complaint to make. Two or three hours sleep—I don't need any more. I've never been so healthy. See how well I am this morning."

"Well, yes, you do have a fine look about you—I'll say! Fresh as a rotten apple! A fine thing, for a Christian, to have your eyes seasoned as if you'd been partying all night."

Lemoine was delighted. It was a veritable joy for him—a sport—to unleash futile objurgations and remonstrations from the worthy woman who adored him. This morning, however, she was too exasperated to sustain the argument for long. She left abruptly, her head tilted, slamming the door, while crying out, choking with affection and anger: "He'll kill himself! And it serves him right!"

Cheered up by that intimate scene, which was repeated four or five times a week, and which amused him more every time, the doctor drank his chocolate and devoured his toast while opening his mail, which apparently contained nothing of interest because all the letters went straight into the waste-paper basket, in pieces.

Then he lit a cigarette and, sprawling in a vast armchair, broke the rubber band on the first newspaper that came to hand.

He had only scanned a few columns, distractedly, when he suddenly uttered a muffled exclamation and, shivering with violent emotion, began rereading one particular article two or three times over, spelling out the words aloud as if he could not believed his eyes.

A PARISIAN DRAMA

Yesterday morning, at dawn, while passing in front of the magnificent residence of the celebrated prima donna Madame Germaine Reyval, in Neuilly, two policemen perceived the body of a young man in evening dress, hanging by the neck from the gate.

They quickly cut the rope, but the corpse was already cold, and in spite of all the care lavished on him at the police station, to which he was urgently transported, the hanged man could not be resuscitated.

He was searched, and on reading the papers found in his pockets, formal proof was obtained that the unfortunate was none other than one of the most well-known personalities of Parisian society; it was, in fact, Monsieur Dulac, the esteemed director of the new Théâtre Lyrique.

The medical examiner for Neuilly, summoned in all haste, established that the death, determined by strangulation, had taken place several hours previously. The body has nevertheless been sent to the Morgue.

When the news became public there was great emotion in Paris and in social circles where Dulac was greatly appreciated, as much for his character and intelligence as for his amiability and professional capabilities.

A rich bachelor with an iron constitution, with relationships in all strata of society as agreeable as they were extensive, the proprietor of a great theater, the artistic and commercial success of which were increasing by the day, it seemed that Dulac ought to have been one of the happiest men in the world. Everything, in fact, was smiling upon him, and neither fortune nor glory had betrayed his hopes. It is, however, necessary not to judge by appearances, and the most brilliant façade of happiness sometimes conceals intimate dolors atrocious enough to inspire desperate resolutions.

It is assumed that if Dulac committed suicide in the fullness of strength and triumph, it is because he had troubles of the heart. The fact of having chosen to hang himself a few kilometers from his domicile, from the gate of a lovely woman for whom he nourished, so it is said, an unfortunate passion, evidently lends weight to that hypothesis.

Amour, when you grip us...

"Poor Dulac!" murmured the doctor, dropping the newspaper. "He seemed to me to be a brave and gentle fellow, worth better than this stupid end. To kill oneself for a slut—is there anything more absurd? For she is a slut, this Reyval, a slut without a heart; one does not need a long acquaintance with her to be certain of it. And so easy to replace, for a man like Dulac! She's pretty, without a doubt, even very pretty, the bitch—but there are many as good, and even better.

Anyway, he could have had her when he wanted her, by paying the price, for she's known for 'going' with whoever pays…it's presumably for no other reason that she's with Saint-Magloire…"

When the name of Saint-Magloire hissed from his lips in the course of this monologue, Lemoine started. His eyelid fluttered and his face contracted, as if in a violent effort of reflection. Leaping to his feet, he started pacing back and forth in the study, while expressing the thoughts at the back of his mind in a low voice, as was his habit at times of bitter anxiety.

"Saint-Magloire! What an idea! What a suspicion! Why didn't I think of it right away? Doubtless everything encourages the belief that the poor fellow committed suicide. When one is hopelessly in love, without any recourse, one is ripe for the worst resolutions, alas—but on the other hand, Dulac had known the accursed Saint-Magloire for a long time. He addressed him as *tu*, I'm told. He must, therefore, have been acquainted with his tenebrous past, of which no one has been able to pierce the mystery. He might, therefore, have been a dangerous witness—an inconvenience. He was in love with Germaine Reyval into the bargain, for whom the Baron does not hide his wild and jealous passion: a double crime, in the eyes of a man who, if he is, as I have long suspected, the Rozen for whom we are searching, cannot have the shadow of a scruple.

"What if Dulac didn't give himself voluntarily to death? What if someone faked his suicide? And what if the murderer were Saint-Magloire—*cui prodest!*[51] Ah—this time I'd be on the right track. I need to know. Let's go to the Sûreté!"

Having dressed in great haste, the doctor got ready to go out.

"Perrine," he said to the old housekeeper, as he was opening the door, "I won't be in today. I might be late back. If anyone comes to ask for me, tell them that I'm in the country or in consultation—and don't let anyone into my study under any pretext."

"Understood," Perrine replied. "Monsieur can be tranquil. But what am I saying? Well, it's not reasonable for Monsieur to go running around all the sainted day long and eating out in some dirty cheap restaurant instead of staying here and resting. Monsieur must be in great need of rest, because he looks terrible today."

"Come on, Perrine," Lemoine replied. "Calm down. I won't tire myself out too much. Besides, there's something I need to do that won't suffer any delay, and which interests me enormously. It would do me more harm to stay here twiddling my thumbs, I can assure you. *Au revoir*, and don't worry about a thing."

With that, Lemoine went rapidly downstairs; then, hailing a cab, he had himself taken directly to the Prefecture of Police.

---

[51] A shortened version of *"cui prodest scelus is fecit"* [whomsoever the crime benefits is guilty of it], from Seneca's *Medea*.

There, as he was known to the office staff, he did not have to wait before going into the corridors and straight to the head of the Sûreté.

"I'll bet," said the latter, on seeing him come in and holding out his hand, "that since you're here so early, it's yesterday's event in Paris that has brought you?"

"You're right," said the doctor.

"And you're going to offer to demonstrate to me, by adding A to B, unless it's subtracting Z from X, that Dulac's death, attributed by the police reports, the press and public rumor to a vulgar suicide, was the result of a crime committed by masked men in the pay of that monster Saint-Magloire, alias Rozen, escaped convict and banker in his spare time?"

"Don't joke. The proof that my suspicions, which you were the first to mention to me, before I had even opened my mouth, are not so very ridiculous, is that you've already shared them. You even began with them."

"Oh, let's not exaggerate; shared, in this case, is a large word, which exceeds the truth. You've bent my ears so often with that romance—not so badly designed, I admit—which you've forged piecemeal for your own edification, that as soon as I heard about Dulac's death, the haunting was manifest, but only for a moment, the blink of an eye. Now I'm the first to laugh at it, as you can see, and make fun of you."

"You're wrong, for, without knowing anything, without affirming anything, I sense that we might finally be about to find the Ariadne's threat that will guide our search, fruitless for so long, and bring it to a conclusion. It's enough for me that, if only for a second, you thought as I do, for me to cling to my idea. The same hypothesis can't surge forth simultaneously, without a preliminary understanding, in the minds of two men like us—better trained than others, it must be said, in psychological observation—without there being a rational reason for the coincidence—a phenomenon of intuitive logic.

The head of the Sûreté smiled skeptically.

"Don't mock me," Lemoine continued, "without hearing me out. Let's see: Was Dulac, or was he not, on intimate terms with Saint-Magloire, who treated him with a familiarity surprising in a man of his character, who has no known friends?"

"Yes. I even know that Saint-Magloire backed the Théâtre Lyrique expressly to create a position for a man he called a comrade of hard times."

"So, Dulac must have known the ins and outs of his backer; he must have known about the skeletons in his closet, and if Saint-Magloire is the bandit we suppose, Dulac's indiscretions risked becoming singularly inconvenient, sooner or later? Is that true?"

"I don't deny it, if Saint-Magloire does indeed have something to hide. On that subject, though, I can only rely on my sense of smell, and yours. In legal terms, that's insufficient."

298

"It doesn't alter the fact that your sense of smell is worth as much, albeit not in legal terms, as any material evidence."

Secretly flattered, without wanting to let it show, the magistrate nodded his head approvingly.

"That's one motive, then," Lemoine continued. "Saint-Magloire, who can't have the slightest regard for a human life, could have wanted to get rid of a burdensome witness. But that's not all. Saint-Magloire is the acknowledged lover of Germaine Reyval, for whom he thrown money out of the widow, and with who he's madly infatuated. Now, Dulac too paid court to Germaine; he even courted her insistently: a second motive, more serious than the first, for a rejected lover is capable of doing anything to thwart a rival. Dulac had become a real danger to Rozen.

"Believe me, I'm on the right track. You'll see that if we follow it to the end, we'll hit the jackpot."

The head of the Sûreté seemed perplexed. He made no reply. He had even let his cigar go out—which was, for him, the indication of an absorbing preoccupation.

"Yes, yes," he murmured, finally, in a dull voice. "It's all very plausible. Dulac might already have been dead when he was hung from the gate of the woman he loved, in order to deflect suspicion. The scheme was very clever! I confess that your argument makes me think. But how do we find proof? You know that the cadaver exhibited no wound, no trace of violence."

"What does that prove? He could have been asphyxiated, stifled under a mattress, or poisoned. We need to do an autopsy."

"That's easy," said the head of the Sûreté. "All I need to do is open an investigation into Dulac's death. The public prosecutor is a man who sees crimes everywhere—he'd like nothing better. I can even give him the final say, because I know he's not far from sharing your views on the subject of Saint-Magloire. The persistence of the widow Lavardens has already put a flea in his ear. In consequence of our conversations, his suspicions have taken form—now they have a face, and a name. He'll be enthusiastic—and if an investigation is ordered, an autopsy is a legal requirement."

"That's perfect. But the autopsy needs to be carried out with a predetermined program; otherwise it won't lead to anything. Oh, if I were only an official medical examiner! But I'm not—although my pupil, Olivier Martin, has just been accredited as an expert...could you confide the operation to him?"

"Nothing simpler. I'll run over to the Palais right away...wait for me here. There are newspapers and cigarettes. I'll be back in twenty minutes."

And, picking up his hat, Monsieur Cardec launched himself into the corridor.

Twenty minutes went by, then thirty, then fifty—but Lemoine did not find the wait too long, plunged as he was into his thoughts; or, rather into the sole and unique thought that had taken possession of his mind since that morning.

The more he reflected, moreover, the more that unique thought took on strength and clarity in the eyes of his overexcited imagination, and the firmer his conviction became regarding the possibility of casting light scientifically on the obscure problem.

Finally, after an absence of an hour and a half, the head of the Sûreté came back in, with a smile on his lips but a frown on his forehead.

"That's that," he said. "You've got your way."

"So the public prosecutor has agreed…"

"To open an investigation and order an autopsy, which will be confided to Olivier Martin. That's not all, though—not that the public prosecutor is resistant to your way of seeing. So far, go good—except that the man is uneasy, just as I am, about the consequences of this exceedingly delicate affair. I don't think you have any illusions about that.

"If the autopsy is abortive—and there's at least a sixty per cent chance that it will be—who's going to get pilloried by the press and given a hard time by the government? Who's going to have the whole world on his back? The court, and then the Sûreté. Not to mention that Saint-Magloire—or Rozen—is going to want us dead, for he'll feel the blow, if he really does have anything for which to reproach himself. And let's not forget that he's the most powerful man in Paris, not to say the most powerful in France."

XX. The Bankruptcy of Science

As soon as Dulac had been knocked out by the inhalations of the ethyl bromide impregnating the handkerchief that Saint-Magloire had abruptly stuck under his nose, it had been easy to transport him into a ground-floor room.

For that task, the murderer had recourse, as he often did, to the aid of the Chinaman Yu, whose discretion was assured, and who had also, in the course of his Boxer existence, had seen many other murders.

Then, with the aid of the laryngeal speculum recently invented by Dr. Labordette[52] to force open the contracted mouths of victims of drowning and asphyxia, the Baron introduced the contents of a small bottle into the victim's throat, having taken it from the drawer of a sideboard.

Always keep poison in your pocket, he said to himself, with a ferocious smile; *one never knows what might happen. Vegetal poison especially, a good alkaloid like this, which leaves no distinct traces and defies the subtlety of the most skillful autopsy.*

Of course, it's necessary that he drinks it down, this fellow, and drinks every drop. Otherwise, everything would remain at the back of the mouth, for the ethyl bromide will have temporarily paralyzed the muscles of the pharynx, and nothing could be done. But we'll give nature a helping hand.

Indeed, wrapping his hand in a handkerchief, he started exercising on the tongue of the unfortunate Dulac, reduced to state of passive inertia, a number of the rhythmic tractions that serve to provoke artificial respiration.[53] The chest inflated under the action of the gusts of air thus introduced by a kind of forced entry. That sufficed to open up the esophagus for a few seconds and to give the throat muscles sufficient elasticity to determine the swallowing of the poison mechanically.

Henceforth, it was finished. If Dulac was not yet dead, he was scarcely any better, since he could no longer be recalled to life.

"All right," murmured Saint-Magloire, getting up and wiping his forehead—which, in spite of his strength and his habituation to worse sins, was streaming with sweat. "It's now a matter of getting rid of the object. Fortunately, we know what to do, and won't make any mistakes."

Five minutes later, as we have said, the door to the grounds opened without a sound and closed the same way, having let out an electric automobile driven

---

[52] Not that recently—1866, in fact.

[53] It was widely believed at the time that pulling the tongue back and forth could restore the respiration of people whose breathing had stopped, after immersion in water, choking or some other cause. The method was about as effective as sticking leeches behind the ears of someone suffering from meningitis.

by Saint Magloire in person, with the dexterity of a professional chauffeur, and which, rolling on discreet pneumatic tires, with no other noise than the dull bee-like buzz of its motor, headed for Paris at top speed along the streets of Auteuil, totally deserted at that hour, and then along the fortifications.

Yu had taken the seat beside the Baron in the mechanical vehicle.

It was nearly half past three in the morning; it was, in consequence, pitch dark when the automobile went into Neuilly via the Porte des Ternes, without being noticed by the customs officials, who paid scant attention to the elegant vehicle driven by a gentleman with a very chic silhouette and pose, with his hat pulled down over his face, who was doubtless coming back from partying. As they were about to emerge into the Rue Peyronnet, however, Saint-Magloire had a scare. Fifty meters ahead of him, almost at the gate of Germaine Reyval's house, two policemen were standing, telling one another stories that must have been funny, for their burst of laughter could be heard from some way off, re-sounding in cascading volleys.

The Baron, however, was not a man to lose his self-composure. Without hesitation, he changed direction by means of an audacious and skillful swerve; then slowing down, he took the Rue du Château, in order to double back, via the Boulevard Eugénie, as far as the Rue Peyronnet, which he found empty this time, the two policeman having gone to amuse themselves further on.

He stopped directly outside Germaine Reyval's gate; then, after having in-spected the locale with rapid glance and acquired the conviction that no peril would appear on the horizon, he opened the trunk of the vehicle and, aided by the Chinaman, took out Dulac's body, still warm, with a strong rope knotted around the neck in advance, in the form of a noose,

With all possible haste, he attached the end of the rope securely to the top crossbar of the gate. Then, assisted by Yu, he arranged the corpse, suspending it in such a fashion that, the back being turned toward the street, the feet were floating fifty centimeters above the ground. Then the Baron pulled the body down hard, in order to tighten the knot as a fall from a certain height would have done.

Having rubbed his feet against the bottom bar of the grille, in order to per-mit the supposition that it was from there that the ostensible suicide had launched himself into eternity, he made a sign to the mute, who had helped him without any sign of astonishment, and they both climbed back into the car, which drew away at top speed.

That a fine suicide, Saint-Magloire repeated to himself, privately, as he burned up the road, *and the physiologist who can prove that that animal didn't kill himself voluntarily hasn't just got his diploma.*

The fact is that, down to the smallest details, the entire tragic staging had been organized with a diabolical skill.

So, when they found themselves in the presence of the cadaver, with the official mission of extracting he whole truth from the sad remains, Doctors

Lemoine and Martin felt prey, in spite of their professional experience and knowledge, and even in spite of the ardent conviction that the master had been able to plant in the student's mind, to the most cruel embarrassment.

Coldly and systematically, they began by drawing up a methodical program, in scrupulous conformity with the most rigorous prescriptions and the narrowest rules of the art, of the operations to be carried out.

It was a matter, first of all, of establishing that death had not been determined by the hanging but that, provoked by another cause, it had preceded it. Then it was necessary to investigate the exact cause of death—and as, in the absence of any external trace of violence—a bullet-hole, razor-cut or stab-wound inflicted by a dagger, a stiletto, a needle, etc.—that cause seemed most likely to be due to poison, it was necessary to determine the nature of the poison. So many singularly delicate problems to resolve in the face of a crime committed by a man equally familiar with the most subtle procedures of science, whose rascally genius would not have left anything to chance!

A priori, all presumptions were evidently in favor of the reality and efficacy of the hanging, and it was not surprising that the official medical examiner in Neuilly, put in the presence of a hanged man, should have reached that conclusion without a moment's hesitation. That kind of suicide is, in fact, on the part of those vanquished by life, the object of a bizarre predilection that increases year by year, especially in Europe, and in France in particular, where that kind of death produces an average annual mortality of between 2,500 and 3,000 victims.

It requires very exceptional circumstances for an expert, in confrontation with a cadaver attached by the neck to a solid hempen collar, to wonder whether it might, perhaps, be a false impression.

Now, in the case in question, the circumstances were more confirmatory of than contradictory to that logical conviction—not only the psychological and moral circumstances, but also, not to say particularly, the material circumstances.

Dulac was known for an exaggerated sentimentality; he was a romantic; he was known to have been madly in love, unrequitedly; he had been hanged from the very gate of the cruel woman. What could be simpler, and what was the point of looking for noon at four o'clock?

On the other hand, the attitude of the cadaver, the form and disposition of the rope, the traces of mud visibly left by the soles of boots on the inferior crossbar of the gate, and a host of other small details, seemed to converge in support of the initial hypothesis, so natural and so plausible.

The autopsy was not to throw a very bright light into that darkness.

The examination of the region of the neck, and in particular the groove left by the noose, whose constriction—unless it was due to traction applied *a posteriori* to the legs of the cadaver—had provoked the shearing of the carotid arteries and the fracture of the larynx, was in favor of the presumption of hanging.

Undoubtedly, the two experts took note of certain interior lesions, such as sanguinary infiltrations, edema and cyanosis of the viscera, which might support belief in a poisoning. Certain alterations of the pulmonary parenchyma and the pericardium, in particular, the inflammatory appearance of the mucus membranes of the stomach and the esophagus, and other signs of a sufficient clarity, appeared to them as so many denunciatory probabilities—but it could be alleged in reply that all those signs might equally well be encountered in authentic hanging victims.

In spite of their grim discretion, in fact, the rumor of the autopsy had spread so wide outside that in the world of reporters, what was happening in the secret laboratory was tracked, as it were, minute by minute. Immediately, the major newspapers got hold of it, and thanks to ungraspable and sly suggestions, whose genesis it was no longer easy to discover, there was an orgy of physiologico-fantastic polemics everywhere, in which, in the midst of a flood of stupidities and unimaginable howlers, a few singularly powerful and documented observations floated.

The great popularizers of science, who knew their business, were irritated by the game and, not being reluctant, on the whole, to take potshots at medical examiners, whom they knew to be rather unpopular, came out squarely in favor of the hypothesis of a pure and simple suicide. They supported that view, which was, in the final analysis, highly plausible, with a host of well-chosen arguments that were, in consequence, difficult to rebut.

For their part, certain masters were all the more willing to give interviews because there were some in the medical world, where jealousies and hatreds are so ferocious, who resented Olivier Martin's rapid rise and Lemoine's independence. In all these interviews, with a touching unanimity, were directed against the experts, who were deluged by an avalanche of magisterial attestations more or less opportunely borrowed from the works of Chaussier, Tardieu, von Hoffmann, Maschka, Henri Pellotier, Cortague, Tourdes, Amussat, Lacassagne, etc.[54] The entire literature of the gibbet was included.

The Baron de Saint-Magloire, who, with his superior instinct, was not deceived for a single instant by the unacknowledged goal that Olivier Martin was pursuing, which had immediately aroused his suspicions, had, as was evident, neglected no opportunity to save face. He understood so admirably, moreover, how to manipulate the press, that the worthy individuals who served his cause with as much ardent zeal as disinterest, had no suspicion, however remote, of the

---

[54] François Chaussier published the first handbook of poisons for use in forensic medicine in 1824. Ambroise Tardieu and André Lacassagne also distinguished themselves in the field, but some of the other named on the list are much more obscure; the relevance of the chemist August Wilhelm von Hoffmann and the anatomist Jean-Zuléma Amussat is not obvious and the rest are difficult to track down; some of them might be misrendered.

role that they were playing. Reporters, columnists and scientists all went ahead unconsciously, believing with the best will in the world that they were acting on behalf of their own opinion, thus contributing to thickening the atmosphere of deception whose mirage had turned their heads.

Knowing full well that there are some currents that are irresistible, and some legends that it is a waste of time to attack as false, Lemoine and Martin bent their heads beneath the storm, and continued to pursue their ingrate task with even greater determination and passion. Convinced, in spite of the abundance and apparent force of the accumulated objections, that Dulac's hanging had been carried out *post* and not *ante mortem*, they set out in quest of the probable poison.

In that respect, the problem was even more arduous and complex. The two scientists had initially tested for the various reactions of all the usual mineral poisons, from arsenic and phosphorus to potassium cyanide, but they had, of course, found nothing.

They sensed that the murderer was too clever to have committed the imprudence of employing any of those toxic substances, nowadays so easy to discover by any chemist in possession of the rudiments of his trade. It was evidently toward organic poisons—alkaloids—that it was necessary to direct the search. But that was as clear as mud. It was as necessary to begin by extracting from the body some matter that was authentically toxic; then, after having isolated the toxin, having characterized it and determined its nature, a series of questions would arise that it would be indispensable to resolve in favor of the accusation.

Could that poisonous substance have come from any other source that a criminal and premeditated administration? Might it not exist normally in the environment? Might it not have been accidentally introduced accidentally with some aliment or medicament? Might it not have been generated post mortem by virtue of some natural and spontaneous phenomenon in the process of the cadaver's decomposition?

It was already a singularly difficult task to isolate the supposed poison, even without determining its nature. Toxic or not, in fact, organic substances, whether they are of vegetal origin, like various alcoholoids, morphine, aconitine, atropine, etc., or of animal origin, never include essential elements other than nitrogen, oxygen, hydrogen and carbon, which similarly constitute, almost exclusively, the fabric of our tissues and our humors. These elements differently grouped, in different proportions, in different forms and in different "styles," in such a fashion as to constitute an infinite variety of distinct substances, just as, with the same letters, one can form an infinite variety of words.

That's all! Work your way through that imbroglio! It is rather as if one were attempting to reconstitute the text of a newspaper article from the chaos of print characters returned to stock after their distribution in the compositor's "rack." Not to mention that, in chemical phenomena as complicated and so little understood as putrefaction, which begins as soon as life shuts down in the posthumous disintegration of being, in that return to inorganic confusion of molecules previously animated, the atoms of carbon, oxygen, hydrogen and nitrogen can recombine in the definite proportions and arrangements characteristic of poisonous substances.

Has it not been demonstrated that poisons *sui generis*, analogous to the worst vegetable poisons, which have been baptizes ptomaines, routinely form in cadavers, where they are engendered, as it were, automatically, by the fermentation of albuminoid substances? And it is not only in the putrefaction consequent on death that such substances are produced! Has not Monsieur Armand Gautier, the knowledgeable professor of Faculté de Médecine demonstrated by means of abstractions made in cases of morbid self-intoxication, that they also form in the healthiest living organisms, by virtue of the normal play of assimilation and excretion? These physiological alkaloids, routinely generated by the processes of life itself—"that corruption," as Eilhard Mitscherlich has said—are currently designated by the name of leucomaines.

Worse still, in the bosom of a cadaver, these natural poisons are not naturally separate to the point of conserving a distinct individuality. Alkaloids, in fact, when present, even associate and amalgamate with the tissues with which they form, or can form, new unstable combinations without any chemical trick being able to provide an infallible key to the enigma, the majority of reagents acting on the animal substance acting similarly on the alkaloid. A poison almost never presents itself integrally to analysis and is always polluted by impurities than can mask its character.

In sum, the juxtaposition of the vegetal poison for which one is searching and normal leucomaines, results in a source of error that is as difficult to avoid as it is to rectify.

Lemoine and Martin knew all that.

They knew it only too well.

If they had forgotten it, moreover, the press, moved by a fine zeal, would have taken responsibility for refreshing their memory.

The campaign continued, in fact, with more ardor than ever, in all the periodicals, political and medical, scientific and worldly, not even excepting the literary periodicals, which were all gripped by a desire to publish veritable courses in comparative toxicology.

The two seekers of justice were not discouraged, however. Braving the sophistry, the mockery and the insults, they ignored it all and pursued their patient search through the dead man's entrails imperturbably, stubbornly sticking to their route, thorny as it was.

The hour finally came when they believed that they had triumphed. Having made use, to dissolve that substances on which they were working, of a volatile liquid—in this case, chloroform—capable of taking up the presumed poison without simultaneously dissolving the adjoining organic materials, they suc-

306

ceeded in isolating an infinitesimal quantity of a substance that seemed to them to be a authentic alkaloid, most probably aconitine.

The fact is that the substance in question, treated successively by potassium ferrocyanate and silver bromide, in conformity with the method of Brouardel and Boutny,[55] behaved like an alkaloid distinct from ptomaines and leucomaines, giving the colorant reactions characteristic of aconitine. Was that not the proof they sought?

Alas, it was immediately necessary to retreat. Someone objected that the reactions identified were not very clear—which was true, the experts having been obliged to operate on very tiny quantities polluted with impurities, the reactions of which were inevitably superimposed on that of the so-called aconitine, denaturing it.

The argument was so precise, so scientific, that even the two experts, with their extreme professional loyalty, sensed doubt biting into their hearts. Then they had recourse, despairing of the cause and with the certainty of striking a major blow, to what is conventionally called, in the argot of toxicologists, "the physiological reaction." They took some mice and inoculated each of them intravenously with a determined dose of the alkaloid extracted from fragments of intestine and stomach macerated in glycerine, in order to test its action, as the saying has it, *in anima vili*.

They would soon see whether or not there was poison of criminal origin, the perturbatory magnetism radiated by Saint-Magloire being unable to extend to the "inferior brothers"—those violent reagents of an indisputable sincerity and a sensitivity infinitely superior to that of the subtlest chemical procedures. A few hundredths of a milligram of aconitine or strychnine are sufficient, in fact, to bring about the death, with all the characteristic symptoms, of an animal of that size,

The result was as clear as it was precise; al the inoculated mice perished in a short time, by virtue of heart attacks and paralysis of the motor nerves, which are the distinctive features of the action of aconitine.

This time, the cause seemed to be won. The presence of a poison, of a determined poison, was attested with an evident certainty that the precipitates and colorations of chemists could not furnish to the same degree.

Saint-Magloire felt the blow, and immediately sharpened the tone of the newspapers that were unwittingly inspired by his suggestions. A formal opinion appeared, signed by a scientist whose word was authoritative, evoking the recent experiments of a German bacteriologist who had just succeeded in isolating a new microbe dwelling, like the "colibacillus" in the human intestinal tract, whose cultures gave exactly the same reactions as aconitine. Such cultures, in-

---

[55] Paul Brouardel was an eminent pathologist who made a considerable contribution to forensic medicine, but I can find no trace of "Boutny."

oculated in frogs, guinea-pigs and mice, had similarly determined the deaths of the subjects, with the characteristic symptoms of aconitine poisoning.

Given that, it goes without saying, the observations of the experts no longer proved anything. And everywhere there reappeared, with an unusual luxury of detail, the old story of a suburban florist who, accused of having poisoned his wife by means of colchicine, owed his acquittal to the fact that Vulpian and Schutzemberger[56] had been able to extract an anonymous substance from a random cadaver presenting identical reactions to those of colchicine, and also to those of the debris of the supposed victim.

Another journalist discovered, into the bargain, that Dulac, very prone to bouts of rheumatism and dolorous neuralgias, sometimes had the habit of taking aconite, sometimes in the form of a potion and sometimes in the form of dosimetric granules. A pharmacist was discovered who had sold him a small provision a few days before his death. There was nothing astonishing, given that, in the fact that aconitine had been found, genuine or otherwise, in the entrails of the cadaver. Not only could that aconitine have been spontaneously elaborated by microbes in the digestive tract, but it could have been introduced by the victim himself with a therapeutic objective. On the very evening of his death, at the theater, he had complained of suffering from an atrocious headache; witnesses remembered that and recounted it.

In brief, the presence of aconitine became entirely natural. At any rate, it no longer offered anything disquieting or accusatory, and to refuse to conclude, like the experts, in favor of a suicide of which everything in the material circumstances of the death and the psychology of the deceased attested the likelihood, if not the certainty, it would have required a sin of simultaneous ignorance, neglect, obstinacy and pride. There was a general outcry, a unanimous concert of jeers, in which the songwriters of Montmartre formed a chorus with the members of the Institut, and professional caricaturists with laboratory virtuosos. It goes without saying that the most aggressive and severe were once again the profane, who had not understood any of it.

Overwhelmed with bitterness, Olivier Martin ended up abandoning the game, in spite of the supplications of his master Lemoine, whose serene valor had not weakened for an instant in the midst of that frightful tempest, by resigning his functions as a medical expert.

The last word decidedly belonged to Saint-Magloire, who was exultant—silently, of course, for his name had never once been mentioned in connection with the inquest, not even by way of discreet allusion. What crowned his tri-

---

[56] Google does produce hits for someone named "Schutzemberger" in association with the physician Alfred Vulpian, who published a book on the physiological action of poisons, but it is probable that they are misprints and should refer to the biochemist Paul Schützenberger, who did a good deal of work on alkaloids, or perhaps to his uncle Charles, a specialist in chemical medicine.

umph in completing the crushing of his adversaries was that, in the course of a search carried out of Dulac's domicile, the commissaire of police found a rough draft of a letter, lost in the midst of the deceased's papers, from which it emerged, as clear as daylights, that several weeks before his death, the unfortunate director of the Théâtre Lyrique, driven to despair by the resistance and coldness of Germaine Reyval, had already thought seriously about suicide. He could not have written the traditional phrase: "Let no one be blamed for my death!" without the document being any more significant or peremptory.

Naturally, that letter was communicated to the newspapers, which had nothing more pressing to do than to reproduce it, supplementing it with commentaries as far as the eye could see. Furthermore, a note in Dulac's handwriting, written in a despairing tone, had been found in the actress's dressing-room.

Was anything more required to prove that it was suicide?

The next day, the case was closed, as they say at the Palais, and Lemoine was summoned urgently to the Prefecture of Police by his friend the head of the Sûreté.

"Well, old chap," the latter said, on seeing him come in. "You've got us into a pretty pickle. I told you that you wouldn't succeed."

"I was right, though, and Saint-Magloire is a poisoner. I'd bet my head on that. You know full well yourself that it's the truth."

"You're right, my friend—I think as you do. Saint-Magloire must be behind it. But I'm not certain, and in any case, I don't have the proof. I'm not a scientist or a physician; I'm a policeman, it's true, and even though I'm the head of the Sûreté, I can have my personal opinions, but I'm also an officer of the law, an auxiliary of the court, and as such, I'm not independent—far from it. If I have an opinion of my own in a criminal affair, I have to keep it to myself if that opinion is not that of my superiors.

"In any case, even with the confidence they have in me, I can't carry out an investigation without their specific instruction. I can only carry out the orders I'm given. Oh, if I had proof...you can be sure that I wouldn't take long to show it to my superiors...and I'm convinced that they'd do the right thing—but I'm reduced to vague presumptions. I don't understand any of your laboratory jiggery-pokery. What's this story of microbes that manufacture unknown poisons in the depths of your guts?"

"A lie—an infamous invention. I think I know the parasitic flora of the digestive tract as well as anyone. I even made it a sort of specialty at one time...well, I never glimpsed, or even suspected, anything similar or anything approaching it. In truth, this aconitine microbe appeared at too convenient a moment for the needs for the case for me not to be suspicious. If I had time, and weren't retained in Paris by other duties, I'd set out for Germany, on the heels of this famous doctor of whom no one's heard before. I'd like to discuss it with him, if he even exists in the flesh, and see whether he's honest or not—whether, for example, he hasn't been duped by one of those illusions that are so frequent in microbiology. But it's impossible, alas. I'd like to send Olivier Martin in my stead, since he no longer has anything to do."

"Poor fellow! His first autopsy will cost him dear. Another of Rozen's victims to add to the list."

"A very incomplete list, no doubt, for we don't know everything and probably don't even suspect half of what he's done. But what do you think of that press campaign?"

"I think," Cardec replied, "that it was conceived, inspired and directed with an infernal artistry by Saint-Magloire—but what I can affirm is that he didn't pay for anything. All the newspapers went of their own accord, as if gripped by a kind of contagious hysteria."

"He's not so stupid as to pay, of course. That would have been the best way of showing the tips of his ears—but he has so many mysterious means of acting in the shadows, of spreading orders that everyone obeys without anyone guessing or even enquiring about their origin."

"Oh, he's strong, even very strong. At any rate, this time, he's won the game, since, without showing himself or compromising himself, he's been able to bankrupt science."

"The bankruptcy of science!" exclaimed Lemoine, hotly. "That's what we're seeing. First of all, I'll go to see the public prosecutor to explain..."

"Please don't do that. It's pointless to go the Palais. You'll bump your nose, because you won't even be let in. Remember that the prosecutor left all the responsibility to you. You failed—so much the worse for you."

"So much the worse for justice, rather—so much the worse for the truth."

"All right! That's your opinion; perhaps it's also mine—but what good is an opinion, even if it's absolutely accurate, if you can't instill it in others? Now, in your case, the Law has disowned you. It won't go back..."

"What if, in addition to scientific presumptions, I bring to light a new fact?"

"A new fact? What do you mean?"

"I mean that the Comte de Por-Riou—you know, the great sportsman—has told me that he saw Dulac, on the eve of the day when he was found hanged, prowling like a madman around the door of Maxim's restaurant, where Saint-Magloire was in the process of dining with Germaine Reyval in a private room."

"What does that prove? Isn't it, in fact, one more probability in favor of suicide? Dulac saw his beloved emerge on the arm of a rival, visibly authorized to take her back to his bed; he lost his head and went to hang himself from her gate. Let's not rely too much on this new item of gossip—it would be our definitive condemnation."

"It is, however, necessary to know how that bandit spent the night of the crime," muttered the doctor.

"Yes, but for that, the investigation would have to have remained open—and it's been closed, in the wake of the failure of the medical inquest that it legitimated. There's nothing to do but wait for another opportunity. Keep your eyes open and alert. I'll do that too. It'll be diabolical if the rogue isn't pinched one day or another....who knows when?"

Understanding that he had no reply to make and that it was necessary to yield to the blows of fate, Lemoine went away, his head bowed.

Thus far, he was vanquished—but he was already meditating his revenge.

XXI. At the Ministry

As soon as she had received the telegram signed by Lemoine, asking her to come to see him urgently, Oliva raced to the doctor's residence without wasting a moment. She had venerated him as the equal of a god since the day when he had consented, alone against the word, to help her in her quest for vengeance.

Madame Lavardens' heart was beating precipitately when she went into the study where Lemoine was waiting for her.

"You have news to give me?" she exclaimed, advancing toward the doctor, her eyes shining with joy and her hands extended.

"Calm down," said the scientist, gently. "Sit down first and collect yourself. What I have to tell you is very serious."

"Please, doctor...my friend...don't leave me in suspense. Oh, have no fear...I'm strong...tell me, without beating around the bush, what you know..."

"Alas, my dear Madame Lavardens, I don't yet know anything precise...but perhaps I can give you a means of unmasking your husband's murderer..."

"Speak! Speak!" said Oliva, breathlessly. "What must I do? I'm ready for anything...even risking my life..."

"I know how courageous you are. I'm not unaware of the fact that you won't recoil before any danger to avenge your dear departed...but for the moment, it's not a matter of exposing yourself to danger. What I want you to do isn't perilous; it only requires great determination on your part and sustained observation."

"I've told you, Doctor, to reach the goal...no matter what it costs..."

"Well, this is it," said Lemoine, having reflected momentarily. "If the information I've received is not deceptive—and it ought to be accurate—the criminal frequents the house of the Baron de Saint-Magloire..."

"Ah!" cried the widow Lavardens. "If I can get into the house and unmask the villain swiftly..."

"A little patience, my dear Madame. It's necessary to put a brake on your impetuosity. For the moment, it's counterproductive. It's as a friend that you need to enter the Baron's home. Do you remember me mentioning the Baronne, whose physician I've become in the aftermath of the death of her young son...?"

"Yes, I remember. You asked me whether, if need be, I'd agree to be Madame de Saint-Magloire's lady companion. I replied, and still do, that if it can help us find the wretch for whom we're searching, I'd gladly accept."

"Good," said the Doctor. "I'm convinced that the Baronne, who is an excellent woman, a sorely tested mother and an unhappy spouse, needs the company of someone devoted. 'Friend,' she has said to me, 'I'll do whatever you wish...' It has therefore been decided that, from today, if you wish, you will

312

take up your employment—forgive me for using the word—with Madame de Saint-Magloire."

"Immediately," Oliva replied, impetuously. "And I assure you that I'll mount a good guard..."

"Nevertheless," Lemoine continued, gently taking the widow's hand, "I'll only introduce you on one condition."

"I put myself entirely at your orders, Doctor. Your devotion, served by an experience that I can appreciate, demands that I obey you blindly. State your conditions; I agree to them in advance."

"*Conditions* is perhaps excessive. But in sum, the advice I have to give you is very serious, and it's important that you take great account of it.

"So, you're going to become the constant companion of the Baronne de Saint-Magloire, and that will permit you to observe everything that happens in the house in the Champs-Élysées. All of the cosmopolitan society of Paris frequents that house, and I have good reasons to believe that those people, of whom no one would dream of asking who they are, exactly, and where they come from, must include Rozen, the convict who everyone except you and me believes to be dead, the victim of his attempted escape from Guiana..."

Knowing Oliva's nervous temperament, Lemoine concealed his true thinking from her; he did not want to make her party to the near-certainty that haunted him; he judged it prudent not to tell her that, in his opinion, Saint-Magloire and Rozen were the same person. The Doctor feared, in fact, that the widow, hearing only her hatred, might precipitate matters and, by an ill-conceived attack, put the clever criminal on his guard. Forewarned of danger, the Baron was the kind of man to employ any means to protect himself, and Lemoine knew that he was capable of any crime. He had murdered Dulac, who was an inconvenience to him; he would quickly see to it that the widow of his other victim fell prey to some cleverly-contrived "accident."

What the doctor wanted was to have a reliable person in the right place—which is to say, in the Baron's entourage—able to spy on everything that happened in the house and keep him, Lemoine, up to date with what the enigmatic banker was doing. It was therefore necessary that the spy be unknown to Saint-Magloire, and it was with that objective in view that the doctor insisted to Oliva that she should be extremely prudent.

"If I'm well-informed," he went on, addressing the widow, "Rozen, whose borrowed name and new position I don't know, unfortunately, is one of the regular visitors to the house. You'll understand that he'll soon scent danger if he suspects your true identity. I've told Madame de Saint-Magloire that you were the wife of one of my childhood friends, René Vauclair, who died in the colonies, and it's under that name that everyone must know you henceforth. Without that precaution, the bandit we want to deliver to justice when the time comes would immediately disappear from Paris and wouldn't come back until he'd established a new identity—and we'd have to start all over again. We must also suppose that he'd succeed in persuading Saint-Magloire, under some pretext or other—we're dealing with a clever individual—to get rid of you, and we'd lose the benefit of your presence in the house. All these considerations might seem puerile to you..."

"No," said Oliva, "no...I understand them very well...and I promise to play the role you're giving me very well. Be certain that no one will know who I am. Even in the presence of my poor Charles's murder, I shall be able to silence my hatred. I shall have the strength not to let him suspect that vengeance is nearby...and I'll warn you before attempting anything whatsoever."

"Thank you," said Lemoine. "I'm glad you understand. Be good enough, then, to get ready to go to the Baronne's house."

"I'll only need an hour, at the most," Oliva replied.

"That's fine—go. I'll wait for you here, and I'll introduce you..."

That same evening. Oliva Lavardens was installed with Eléna, who gave her doctor's friend the most cordial welcome...

In sum, Lemoine said to himself, *that's another serious trump card in my hand. It's you against me, Monsieur le Baron! I thought I had you when you killed poor Dulac, for you did kill him, in spite of everything and everyone, but you parried the first thrust...we'll see whether you can parry the others I shall make...*

Monsieur Cardec, informed by his comrade of Oliva's entry into the house in the Champs-Élysées, approved of Lemoine's ideas in every respect.

In addition, a host of small incidents troubled the peace of Rozen/Saint-Magloire.

Since the resounding collapse of the Compagnie Française des Trésors d'Amphitrite, the banker had felt ill at ease. The worm had got into the fruit and was eating it. The Baron's business affairs were going badly.

Sokoloff was giving him the cold shoulder since Dulac's death. The disappearance of that loyal comrade had afflicted the Russian scientist sorely, and even though Saint-Magloire had emerged unscathed from the accusations made against him, a doubt still remained in Sokoloff's mind.

Rozen, who no longer had the easy profits that he had temporarily gleaned from argentaurum to aliment his enormous expenses, launched himself into the worst adventures. His instinct as a crook and his consummate skill as an expert thief still served him well. He found in Baker, who had become his damned soul, a powerful auxiliary in bringing Paris under his heel. Almost daily, the gang admirably organized and commanded incognito by Rozen, which furnished the funds of the association while remaining a myth for the associates of that new kind of Internationale, carried out some new exploit.

One night, bold burglars had succeeded in getting into the vaults of a vast credit establishment and had made off with a large fraction of the bonds entrusted to the care of the financial institution. The next morning, several safes con-

taining bonds and jewels were found to have been blown open by melinite—
bonds and jewels that rapidly traveled abroad, where, before any countermeasures could be taken, the bonds had been negotiated. As for the jewels, the thieves' bank in London had taken charge of "realizing" them in hard cash...

Naturally, that operation had brought Saint-Magloire a tidy profit.

The game was obviously dangerous. The Baron sensed that he was at the mercy of Baker, to whom he was obliged to give a considerable fraction of his profits. On the other hand, that war against society pleased the ex-883 enormously. Reading the newspapers that translated the public disquiet filled him with joy; he exulted as he perused articles in which the police were attacked with increasing virulence. And when Saint-Magloire heard the imprecations that rose up, in salons and the wings of theater, against the bandits who were terrorizing the capital, he experienced a bitter pleasure. Proudly, he told himself that he really was a king, since he commanded an army that was making the bourgeoisie tremble.

The burglars' Internationale of which he was the soul was not content, moreover, to loot Paris. The other capitals of Europe were considerably bloodied too, and the police of every country had been thrown into a panic that Rozen found very amusing.

From time to time, a cat's-paw caught in the act was arrested, but the wretch did not know whose orders he was obeying, and allowed himself to be sentenced without being able to denounce his accomplices, against whom the sword of justice remained impotent. The organization took the precaution of providing for the needs of those of its members who were unfortunate enough to be caught. They knew that their escape from penitentiaries would be facilitated, and that one emerging from prison they would find a nice nest-egg. None of them had, in any case, any desire to turn traitor. Death mysteriously struck down anyone whose tongue wagged, and the denunciation of the most trivial accomplice was punished inexorably.

That fruitful organization permitted Saint-Magloire to continue living like a lord. He was able to pay handsome dividends to the clients of his bank in the Place Vendôme, and keep those businesses that seemed the most problematic afloat.

In a word, he triumphed all along the line. Other facts had contributed to reestablish his prestige, which had tottered momentarily.

During the meticulous enquiries to which the bizarre death of Dulac had given rise, a certain sector of the press had manifested some incredulity regarding the authenticity of the title of Baron with the "speculator" of the Place Vendôme had "rigged himself out." Those were the terms employed by an intransigent journalist in a scurrilous rag.

Saint-Magloire had quickly reduced that suspicious malcontent to silence. Without having the appearance of being involved, he had had some poor devil who earned a meager living pruning genealogical trees prove beyond a doubt that his nobility was not at all fantastic, and that the baronial title he bore went back to Louis XII. In order further to confound the people who were trying to undermine the pedestal on which he stood, Rozen commissioned a book that the genealogist had dreamed of writing, a *Livre d'Or de la Noblesse Française*, and in recompense for his generous support, the author of the book devoted several chapters to the glory of the ancestors of the financier of the Place Vendôme,

All the scoffers switched to Saint-Magloire's side. Thanks to the papers of the poor gaucho whom he had murdered in a cowardly fashion in South America, it was easy for Rozen to satisfy the most difficult and to treat as infamous calumnies all the more or less malevolent insinuations regarding his origins.

Even Baker, the redoubtable adventurer's right-hand man, did not doubt that his boss's nobility was perfectly legitimate. Nor had Bastien any idea where his prison-companion's parchments had come from. It will be remembered that Gaston had not told the Parisian about the theft of the Saint-Magloire papers at the diamond mine; Rozen had let him believe that his title really was that of his own ancestors. He had told him that he had been sentenced under an assumed name, and that, once afloat again, he had the right to resume the social rank that the noble title whose heir he was permitted him to hold.

Only one man, Charles Lavardens, might have been able to see through that web, but Rozen congratulated himself on having safely reduced him to silence.

In spite of all these successes, however, Saint-Magloire, who had never trembled thus far, felt a certain anxiety. On seeing Oliva with Eléna, with whom he had fallen out completely since Pepe's death, he had been gripped by a sort of vague presentiment.

One day, Madame Lavardens had found herself alone with him, face to face, and the Baron had felt an embarrassment under the woman's gaze, which fixed upon him in a strange fashion.

Not wanting to interrogate Eléna, to whom he affected to allow an absolute liberty, he had skillfully questioned the servants, and had learned that Madame la Baronne's new lady companion was the widow of a Monsieur Vauclair, prematurely deceased in the colonies.

Why, then, feel anxious?

Why attach any importance to that gaze, which he had felt weighing upon him, and had burned him like a hot iron?

It was quite natural that Eléna, weary of being left alone, should have created company, as well with Madame Vauclair as anyone else…but his instinct instructed Saint-Magloire to be wary of the newcomer.

A fortuitous circumstance had, in any case, encouraged his suspicion.

During a visit by Lemoine—who, in his capacity as a doctor, had access to the Baronne at all times in spite of the initial opposition that Rozen had put up— the latter had observed that the physician seemed very attentive to the lady companion, and had overheard a little of their conversation.

"I don't know how to express my gratitude," Madame Vauclair had said.

Saint-Magloire instructed Macaron, alias Robertson, to follow Madame Vauclair—and he had learned that she had been to the doctor's house, where she had remained for some time.

"Good," he said, with a smile tinged with menace. "That's a woman I'll keep my eye on. It's Lemoine who placed her here, but to what end? Oh, that Lemoine...I run into him everywhere. What does he want with me? Why this determination to get mixed up in my affairs? Let him beware! If he wants war, he'll get it...like the others!"

For several days, the Baron spied on Madame Vauclair, but he did not see anything suspicious, and told himself that he had been wrong to get a bee in his bonnet. Besides which, another incident, seemingly more serious, attracted his attention. Madame de Saint-Lai, with whom he had maintained an excellent and useful relationship, had confided to him that there had been much talk about him at the Ministry of the Interior and the Prefecture of Police.

That very evening, Fifine had received a visit from Police Inspector Darbin, specially commissioned to keep watch on brothels and to collect details of their clientele.

"My dear Baron," the brothel-keeper said to Rozen, "they've resumed on the quiet what no one any longer dares say aloud; they won't soon get over the death of that poor Dulac."

"Oh, they're beginning to annoy me!" exclaimed Saint-Magloire, who no longer stood on ceremony with Fifine. "They're getting on my nerves. Dulac killed himself, because he was in love with Germaine, Is that my fault? Is it the fault of that poor girl...who couldn't prevent it? My God, one might think that he's the first imbecile who ever killed himself for a woman! I've been good enough to answer all their ridiculous questions about my relationship with the silly fool. Everything is crystal clear...and yet...

"Didn't they find a crumpled note in Germaine's dressing-room, which she'd thrown disdainfully into a corner...a note in which the idiot painted his flame in a schoolboy tirade, and threatened to hang himself from the beauty's gate if she refused to give him her heart?

"If they want anything more, let them ask the dead man! After all, I don't have anything to hide. I've generously given them all the information I could..."

The note to which Saint-Magloire made allusion had been manufactured by Petitpierre, the skillful forger to whom Saint-Magloire had had appointed as a special commissaire at the frontier. It was a masterpiece that the Baron's accomplice had forged, and which Rozen had dropped surreptitiously in the actress's dressing-room. The latter had received so many notes from Dulac that she had recognized that one in good faith, and the discovery of the piece of paper had administered the *coup-de-grâce* to the doubts raised nu the autopsy conducted by Martin, Lemoine's pupil.

"Then again," added Madame de Saint-Lai, "it appears that the Minister and the big chiefs are conferring on the means to pinch the gang of thieves that advertises itself with a new coup every day."

"I can understand why they're preoccupied with that," the Baron declared, "for their police are manifestly incompetent...not to say anything worse!" And he added, with a serious expression that initially disconcerted the delicate informer: "I hope that they're not attributing those great feats of burglary to me..." But the end of the sentence dissolved into a burst of laughter.

"Oh, Baron," Fifine simpered. "You are a one!"

"Madame, the way that wretched police force is groping, they'll end up accusing all Paris. That way, they might perhaps lay their hands on the terrible brigand who permits himself to tax the wealth of all to make the fortune of a few—unless that extraordinary malefactor has the gift of ubiquity and they find a piece of him in every capital in the world..."

Launched in that tone, the conversation between the financier and Madame de Saint-Lai became epic, and when Rozen parted company with the whore-mistress, that amiable and exceedingly hospitable individual was splitting her sides. She had never laughed so much before, she said, and Monsieur le Baron de Saint-Magloire was, in her opinion, the funniest and wittiest of men.

As soon as she had gone, however, the Baron started pacing back and forth furiously. The conversation that Fifine had mentioned to him annoyed him more than he cared to let show. A wrinkle creased his forehead, and his gaze was hard and frightening.

It's necessary to ease off for a while, he said to himself, *or throw them a small fish who can pay the price for everyone...or, which would be even better, set off a petard so formidable that all of France would be stunned...bewildered...throwing the country into such disarray that it won't think about anything else...*

We'll give that some thought. In the meantime, let's go see the delightful Germaine...

Internally, the Baron, like a sovereign, gladly employed the royal "we." A pride—or, rather, an incommensurable vanity—took possession of him when he looked back on the distance he had come since his escape. And when sometimes, the cadavers of those he had sacrificed to carve out his passage appeared by the wayside, Rozen shrugged his shoulders and said to himself: *A trifle! A few lives lost? Does that count for anything, for a conqueror?*

Although the banker of the Place Vendôme had learned from Madame de Saint-Lai, always in possession of excellent sources, that the Minister of the Interior was interested in him, the good lady had not been able to tell him exactly what had been said in the study in the Place Beauvau.

Otherwise, Saint-Magloire would have trembled.

Irritated by the daily attacks to which the police had been subjected for some time, the supreme leader of that administration had summoned the Prefect of Police to his study, asking him to bring the head of the Sûreté with him.

The holder of the portfolio of the Ministry of the Interior was still a young man. He had quickly built a reputation as a fist-class advocate at the Paris bar, and without neglecting resounding cases that would get him noticed—which had, in fact, contributed to hoist him on to the pedestal on which he dreamed of sitting—he had launched himself into the political arena, in which he had not taken long to become one of its famous gladiators.

A few years had sufficed for him to become one of the foremost and most influential of Parliamentarians, and after a couple of intermediary stages as head of minor ministries he had become President of the Council of Ministers by force of circumstance, when no one else dared take in hand the direction of the country's troubled affairs, in which one scandal was succeeding another and bankruptcies were piled upon bankruptcies...and in which resounding suicides threw consternation even into the ordinarily tranquil depths of small rural communes.

A skillful orator, devoid of the political scruples that hindered sectarians and prevented them from being statesmen, the new President of the Council, granting intelligent concessions to all the parties that formed an assembly in the Chambre without any precise orientation, had succeeded in creating a majority that he knew to be artificial, made of pieces that it was impossible to weld together solidly. It was a collage, to be sure, but a collage that permitted the minister to act with vigor.

Success had crowned the skill of the chief of the cabinet. If calm had not returned entirely to the country, peace was at last apparent, the combatants having retracted their claws. Confidence had returned, and business had picked up slightly.

One can imagine the annoyance that the Minister of the Interior had experienced on observing the impotence of the French police against the gang who, under the orders of a mysterious leader, ungraspable in consequence, were committing thefts of an incredible audacity on a daily basis.

The minister, however, knew the two men who were at the head of the Parisian police, one of whom—the head of the Sûreté—had primary responsibility for the criminal police. He had been able to appreciate their merit in numerous very delicate affairs—so he did not give a moment's thought to replacing them. It was better to join forces with them, make them feel that they had the full confidence of their superior.

The Prefect of Police was a very active functionary, fully committed to new ideas. Very Parisian, he had been able to capture the confidence of the impulsive population of the great city marvelously. He greatly appreciated the services that Monsieur Cardec rendered to the Prefecture as head of the Sûreté. He had seen him at work and supported him vigorously in certain criminal affairs in which the policeman had been obliged to struggle against the prejudices of certain courts in order to bring out the truth.

As soon as the Prefect and Monsieur Cardec had arrived, the President of the Council invited them to sit down and ordered the usher with the silver chain who had introduced them not to disturb him under any pretext, even by telephone, until further instruction.

"I called you here, my dear prefect," he said, "in order that we can decide in concert the measures to be taken with a view to capturing the bandits that are waging a redoubtable war against society—or, rather, against the capital—which is the more redoubtable because the victims are turning everyone against us, and rendering us, so to speak, responsible for their losses…and their panic.

"I asked you to bring Monsieur Cardec, whose experience in criminal matters is precious to us…"

The head of the Sûreté bowed to the Minister.

"Finally," the host of the Place Beauvau continued, "people are no longer saying in public that the bandits are audacious, but that the police are incompetent." He was quick to add: "I hasten to say that that is not my opinion. Apart from a few errors of detail that are more those of the system than its personnel, we in France certainly have one of the best criminal police forces in the world…but that police force has been found wanting against a bandit who flees like a shadow at the very moment when one thinks that he is about to be seized.

"We can speak frankly here, can we not? Well, I won't hide it from you that for I've thought for some time that we're dealing with a fantastic individual. I thought that we had finally found a chink in his armor when the autopsy of poor Dulac's corpse took place, so meticulously carried out by Dr. Martin, a young doctor of high merit, the pupil of one of our most esteemed scientists, Dr. Lemoine. I thought that we were holding the thread…

"Dulac had been seen at Maxim's; he had been seen to climb up on to a carriage that was conveying the Baron and Germaine. One can imagine the scene: a quarrel, a low blow, what do I know?"

The Minister, obedient to his slightly romantic temperament, launched into a story that he related with considerable charm, but whose conclusion was that, alas, it was necessary to yield to the confession of suicide found shortly afterwards in Mademoiselle Reyval's dressing-room.

"That's peremptory…and yet…what a pity!"

"Yes, Monsieur le Ministre, it's a pity," added the head of the Sûreté, "But I'm convinced that we'll succeed in unmasking the bandit."

"For a second time, I thought I glimpsed an opportunity to grasp the coat-tail of the redoubtable occult leader. I cried 'Eureka!' so to speak, when I saw that the night-watchman who disappeared after the theft from the vaults of the Societé *** had been placed there on Saint-Magloire's recommendation, as it would certainly have been necessary, in order to get into the bank, to have the complicity of that night-watchman, given that he alone had, in his lodge, the keys to the heavy doors of the vaults. I assumed that Saint-Magloire had placed the necessary accomplice there…but the wretch's cadaver was found in the Seine shortly thereafter, strangled!"

"Like Dulac!" murmured the Prefect.

"It's possible," said Monsieur Cardec, "but, since you've done me the honor of consulting me, I'll permit myself to make the observation, Monsieur le Ministre—and I base my opinion on fifteen years experience in criminal matters, that the murder of the watchman would be plausible even in the case of complicity on his part. If Rozen is alive, he's perfectly capable of murdering an inconvenient accomplice without hesitation."

"That's true," said the President of the Council, "but it's difficult to direct the slightest suspicion against the Baron. And as things stand, we don't even have the resource and longer of challenging his origin. He's exhibited his family documents triumphantly and we'd need a new '93 to make that noble head fall."

The Prefect and Monsieur Cardec smiled at the Minister's joke.

"In conclusion, then: on one side, an X, murderer, thief, crook, etc. On the other, worthy men exploited, trimmed, begging for mercy. Between the two, the police, whom we represent. It's absolutely necessary that we unmask X. But how? How? It's necessary to find a trap into which this terrifying X will fall."

"A trap!" exclaimed the Prefect. "He's very subtle, the fox we want to catch. Do you know that this very morning, in the heart of the Avenue Kléber, Prince Taris' concierges were found in their lodge, bound and gagged, and utterly terrified. The house had been robbed during the night. The previous evening, a police commissaire and his secretary had presented themselves to the concierges, under the pretext of making a search—and they'd stolen everything, after having put the unfortunate guardians in the state in which they were found.

"The bandits even took audacity so far as to recruit the aid, in the beginning, of two honest policemen who are now utterly distraught at having lent a hand to that incredible burglary. That, at least, is what we've discovered so far…for the poor fellows are half mad with fear."

"Is the theft considerable?" asked the Minister.

"It's been estimated at a million…at least."

"And not the slightest clue?"

"Not the smallest," said Monsieur Cardec, resentfully. "If they hadn't been in place for such a long time, one might believe that the concierges were in on it—such an operation, carried out without making a sound…no one in the vicinity heard anything at all…"

"They're phantom removal men," the Minister continued. "Decidedly, we're living in the middle of a novel! Why, then, should we have recourse ourselves to the resources of our imagination to set a fine trap for our enemy. What do you say, Messieurs?"

"We could try," the head of the Sûreté replied, "under some pretext or other, to make Saint-Magloire fall into our claws—for, in spite of all the reservations Monsieur le Ministre has just expressed, I keep coming back, involuntarily, to that mysterious banker, who gives me pause for thought every time I see him. I find his type and his appearance, which have nothing of the old French race about them, very singular. The Saint-Magloires are the true issue of the Ile-de-France, and if anyone can prove to me that their heir is an Oriental Jew…in truth, I'd be very surprised."

"If I've asked the two of you to come," the President of the Council interjected, "it's because I have confidence in your instincts. I've studied as best I can the hypothesis of a bold criminal hidden beneath the enigmatic Baron de Saint-Magloire; I thought, after everything we'd collected to falsify that hypothesis, that we were obliged to abandon the idea; but I don't want either you to leave here with even the shadow of a suspicion that I've tried to put you on another track. I'll try even harder to dig into the life of the man with you…

"In sum, we need to employ all possible means to struggle against these malefactors, and if necessary, I'll even go so far as to surround the Baron with a political plot. If necessary, the director of the Sûreté Générale can inform us in that regard; I'll send for him when I've finished with you, Messieurs."

"The main thing is to have a pretext to lock him up," Cardec went on. "Once he's under lock and key, I'm certain that the truth will burst forth from all directions…"

As the Minister and the Prefect were looking at him with visibly dubious expressions, the head of the Sûreté continued, emphasizing his words: "Messieurs, you don't appear to have any great confidence in the ideas I put forward. Monsieur le Ministre has done me the honor of summoning me, with Monsieur le Préfet, and we're not here to nod assent but to reach an agreement regarding a solution…whatever the means employed…"

"Very well, Monsieur Cardec," said the Minister, swayed by the forthright attitude of the head of the Sûreté. "You can speak freely."

"Monsieur le Ministre. I've followed very closely the enquiry skillfully conducted by my friend Dr. Lemoine. You're not unaware that he has the conviction that Rozen is not dead, as is officially believed?"

"You've informed me about the doctor's efforts, and I know that Monsieur Lemoine is convinced that the Baron and Rozen are the same…but how can we prove that? Where do we find the point of departure for an investigation? Even admitting the real existence of this Rozen, who lived in Cayenne under the registration number 883…we'd first have to discover the initial steps he took? Isn't that right?"

"Indeed, Monsieur le Ministre."

"Finding that point of departure seems to me to be fraught with difficulties…"

"Evidently," Monsieur Cardec replied. "I've done everything possible to discover, discreetly of course, whether or not Saint-Magloire is Rozen. I've arranged, under a disguised pretext, to have him watched and followed by two intelligent inspectors who knew Rozen at the time of his arrest, but neither of them recognized the convict in the banker they were watching—and I'll permit myself to add, Monsieur le Ministre, that the president of the assizes who directed Rozen's trial has been in the Baron's presence several times. Obviously, if he had recognized his former client, he wouldn't have been one of his stoutest defenders during the crash of the Compagnie des Trésors d'Amphitrite...and as, in spite of everything, I persist in my idea, I've been forced to admit the most implausible things, in thinking that Rozen has completely transformed himself, that he has modified all the contours of his physiognomy..."

"He'd be a character out of Gaboriau," the Minister interjected, smiling. Then, he continued: "In that respect, then, there's nothing to be done. We're reduced to provocation."

"With a man of Saint-Magloire's stripe, the method is delicate," objected the Prefect. "You've seen, Monsieur le Ministre, with what skill he's extracted himself from sticky situations."

"You're alluding to the Compagnie Française des Trésors de l'Amphitrite?"

"And the Moroccan gold mines," the Prefect added, "and many other wonderful affairs, veritable sucker-traps...the man has always enriched himself, and those he's plundered, far from complaining, come back every time he launches a new venture..."

"The eternal power of the mirage," declared the minister. "Of, if we only had someone on the inside...a clever auxiliary who could make the colossus slip on a bit of orange peel cunningly placed in his path..."

Monsieur Cardec shook his head.

"You don't think that can be done?"

"Within a week, Saint-Magloire would have discovered and got rid of our man...or made him go over to the enemy to a bridge of gold..."

"That's true," said the President of the Council. "The resources of the police are so modest..."

"Alas!" sighed Monsieur Cardec.

"It's necessary, however, that the thefts, the burglaries, the frauds and the murders come to an end...that we're no longer the laughing-stock of the press and the public..."

"Monsieur le Président du Conseil," said Monsieur Cardec, forcefully, "in spite of the worse-than-modest resources that are put at the disposal of the Sûreté, which permits it to dispose meager gratifications to informers of thirty to a hundred francs, and although, in budgetary terms, we're not battling on equal terms with high-flying malefactors, I have not hesitated to research the past of this Monsieur de Saint-Magloire, and if I had found a serious reason, an indubitable grievance, he would have been arrested...but what can I do on the basis of vague suspicions? If the Baron, once arrested, exonerated himself cleverly, the scandal would be enormous...

"It's impossible, in spite of everything, to attack such a powerful individual without evident proof."

"What does his power matter to me!" exclaimed the Minister, hotly. "The task we're pursuing excuses everything, even a mistake. I congratulate you, Monsieur Cardec, on your energy, and I'm ready to protect you with my authority. Given the situation we're in, it's important to do something, at all costs—even at the risk of an error. Damn it, if Monsieur de Saint-Magloire is an honest man, he'll be the first to excuse that error! Search, Messieurs, search!

"For my part, I won't remain idle. Should we promise a reward to anyone who can give us important information regarding the gang that is terrorizing Paris?"

"Hmm," said the police chief. "The leader of the gang gives too many advantages to his affiliates...he had too strong a hold over them, even when they're aught, for us to have any hope of success. Look at Dr, Lemoine: he's spent a great deal of money trying to find a trace of Rozen, suspecting him of being the murderer of the unfortunate Lavardens. Ask the head of the Sûreté how many frauds and rogues—and convicts desirous of paying for a voyage at the crown's expense—have passed through his hands."

"We've lost count," agreed the head of the Sûreté.

"There's nothing to be one, then, but bend our backs and bear the sarcasms patiently?" said the Minister. "But you know that I fear being called to account on this subject any day now. I'll be reproached for not giving the citizens of France enough protection. My ministry might be brought down...and the task I've undertaken isn't finished."

"Would Monsieur le Ministre permit me to tell him something?"

"Gladly, Monsieur Cardec," replied the chief of the cabinet, a little more calmly.

"Dr. Lemoine has succeeded in placing a woman in the Saint-Magloire household who might, perhaps, be the key to the Baron's fall. Her name is Oliva Lavardens..."

"I've been told that the woman in question is feeble-minded."

"That's a grave error, Monsieur le Ministre. On the contrary, the poor woman is perfectly lucid. She is obeying a presentiment that she has succeeded in making Monsieur Lemoine share."

"And you too, perhaps?"

"Yes, Monsieur le Ministre—and I have the firm conviction that Lemoine, an indefatigable searcher unhindered by administrative work, free to employ a host of means that would not be possible for us, will succeed in unmasking the Baron."

"My dear Monsieur Cardec, I share the confidence that you have in your friend and collaborator, Dr. Lemoine; I'm ready to encourage all his efforts, and yours—and, I repeat, I take full responsibility. Whatever happens, I'll defend you. Tell Monsieur Lemoine that we give him *carte blanche*. You may do all you can to help him. I'll cover the necessary expenses…I'll find the means to organize that.

"However, while allowing Dr. Lemoine to act, I urge you to search on your own account, Messieurs. The important thing is to reach a conclusion as quickly as possible." Laughing, the Minister added: "Here, as at the Ambigu, it's necessary that vice be punished, and that the police triumph!"

Then, gravely and fervently, he concluded: "Quite seriously, this business is the foremost of my preoccupations. Don't hesitate: all means are good against such an enemy. Invent a plot; set traps. For the moment, I only have this affair at heart. I'll find the funds. If necessary, I'll dispose of unnecessary patrols…I'll eat into the budget of the political police. People can protest…I don't care.

"What I want to know today isn't the political comings and goings of bedroom conspirators—I want to find the man who's mocking us and driving Paris crazy. The good of the nation justifies any measures that you judge it necessary to take. Have no fear: the minister will never let you down…act! Act! Put all your intelligence and activity into this affair…"

And the President of the Council, having shaken hands with the Prefect and Cardec, asked them to give him, right away, all the details of the audacious theft committed at the house of Prince Tarsis…

Then he rang for the usher, and wrote a few words on a leaf torn from a note-pad.

"Bring me the newspapers as soon as possible."

And the grand master of the French police, sinking into his armchair, put his head in his hands.

"Decidedly," he muttered, "it's easier to win a battle than to find the end of a thread in this murky intrigue. Finally, when I've read everything about the past of this Rozen before his conviction, perhaps I'll find a trap to set for this damned Saint-Magloire, who, I'm beginning to believe, like Lemoine and Cardec, must have an intimate relationship with the ex-883, dead in the marshes of the Maroni!"

Part Three
SCIENTIFIC DETECTIVES AND BANDITS

I. Medical Love

In spite of the resounding defeat of his pupil in the Neuilly affair—a lamentable failure whose repercussions had fortunately preserved his incognito, Dr. Lemoine continued to pursue the mission of justice and vengeance he had undertaken, in the shadows, with the tenacity of a Redskin.

More convinced than ever of the culpability of the Baron de Saint-Magloire, and still clinging to the hope of extracting him sooner or later from his mask, he persisted in following all the trails that he thought he had found.

He had no official mandate for that complex and thankless task, of course, and a number of doors behind which he might have been able to find a revelatory clue—the end of Ariadne's thread—remained closed to him. However, the faithful friendship of the head of the Sûreté facilitated his secret task, thanks to authorizations beyond the scope of the regulations and secret confidences, passing on rumors and "tips" obtained in clandestine ways.

The two friends often talked to one another about that obscure problem, which haunted their sleepless nights obsessively, although he did not admit it. It was thus that Lemoine heard about the conference on the subject that had taken placed in the Place Beauvau.

"I'll wager," he said to Cardec, "that the Minister had thrown a lot of legal holy water over you. Of course! You're impeccable functionaries; he owes you fine tirades on zeal and devotion. And it all terminated with a jolly: 'Above all, no stories: do what you want and I'll answer for everything, on condition that nothing happens!'"

"You've lost your bet in advance, my dear Doctor. We've found a chief quite ready to act. We have *carte blanche*—and even better, the assurance that our expenses will be covered. I can affirm to you not only that my boss and all his colleagues are convinced that Saint-Magloire is a rogue, but that their keenest desire is to unmask him, in order to see the back of that enigmatic and shady individual, who seems to them to be an indeterminate but redoubtable danger. The minister has explicitly given us to understand that we can have a free hand in ridding Paris of him—but I think we'll need to handle it delicately"

"Of course," said the Doctor. "They're putting an appearance of wanting to reach him, but underneath, they're protecting him."

"Not at all! They fear him—which isn't the same thing. The man knows certain state secrets: all the skeletons in the closet, all the small infamies that are the currency of politics—all politics. To defend himself, he's capable of anything, unless a sledgehammer blow crushes him mercilessly. According to what I deduce, and what I sense, his arrest might provoke a catastrophe, or even a series of catastrophes."

Cardec paused, then continued: "We're no longer in Venice, unfortunately, in the era when it was so easy to eliminate inconvenient individuals, who were never heard from again…today we have a mass of scruples, even when dealing with the worst villains. One has to fill in the forms…

"Oh well, we'll fill in all the desirable forms, and it won't prevent us from succeeding. You'll see! Continue your research on the subject of our man, and keep me up to date with anything new you discover about his life. I'll do the rest."

"I'll deliver the monster to you, dead or alive, or my name's not Lemoine!" the Doctor declared.

With that, taking his leaving of his friend, the Doctor went straight to Saint-Magloire's house.

Since the death of little José, it will be remembered he had often visited, always being received, as before, by the Baronne, although the master of the house was ostentatious in according him a good welcome. He took advantage of it to keep himself up to date with Eléna's health.

Always in control of himself, the Doctor put on a show of believing in the Baron's affability, but was not fooled by it. Sometimes, he observed a fugitive expression of mistrust on the banker's face. He sensed strongly that, well-served by an instinct sharpened by being always on his guard, the Baron scented an enemy in him.

The doctor, however, as much at his ease in those equivocal drawing-rooms, in that environment of high-flying foreigners, as in his laboratory or the office of the head of the Sûreté, remained impenetrable—so much so that Saint-Magloire's suspicions had gradually relaxed.

One day, however, when the polemics unleashed over Dulac's cadaver were at their height, he had taken Lemoine to one side and, leading the subject around to that burning topic of the day, had asked him point-black, with a direct thrust: "What's your opinion, Doctor, about poor Dulac's death? He was my friend, you know; his sad end has caused me a great deal of grief."

"My God, Monsieur le Baron," Lemoine had replied, mildly, having expected the attack, "You're embarrassing me somewhat. I have, of course, enormous esteem for the knowledge and skill of Olivier Martin, and I'm also sure of his good faith, but, not being a specialist in matters of toxicology, I don't think I have the right to take a side in such a delicate and controversial matter." With an admirably feigned indifference, he had added: "To be frank, I'm rather inclined to believe that Dulac, maddened by Germaine Reyval's cruelties, simply committed suicide. From the scientific point of view, at least if one can judge by the incomplete rumors that I've picked up here and there, that thesis is as sustainable as the expert's. It has the psychological probability in its favor too. It's the popular belief; it has every chance of being true."

These simple explanations, which burned the lips of the honest doctor reluctant to lie, had sufficed to convince the Baron. Deceived by his guest's false bonhomie, he had not asked him anymore.

I was mad, he said to himself, *to suspect this Lemoine. He's a naïve individual, hypnotized by science. He doesn't know anything, and doesn't suspect anything Anyway, how could a man of principle like him, pure and incorruptible, frequent a suspect house? Unless, that is, he comes for my wife...ho ho.* Quien sabe? *as Eléna says—these scientists are sometimes inflammable.*

Rozen did not know how right he was.

It required powerful motives to bring Lemoine to play the comedy to the extent of being almost familiar with the man he had sworn to bring down. In spite of his innate horror of duplicity, he had been forced to recognize that no other observation-post was worth as much as that one, since he was, in his capacity as the family doctor and friend of the household, in the very heart of things.

The end justifies the means.

However, without his being very clearly aware of it, he was also obedient to another sentiment: the desire to see Eléna again, love for whom had taken entire possession of him again. Unfortunately, the Baronne remained invisible. Plunged, since the death of her child, into an incurable despair, she shut herself away in her apartment, wearing out her eyes with weeping, and refusing to receive a living soul except Oliva Lavardens, her lady companion. Even the Doctor, of whom she could not think without a certain complex emotion, compounded out of gratitude, affection and anxiety, had not found mercy before that inflexible order.

Indeed, in addition to the fact that she could not evoke his image without seeing once again the death-bed of her adored Josecito, next to which she had so unexpectedly found, as if by a miracle, the lost but never-forgotten soul, she had been afraid of having to respond to embarrassing questions, and also of feeling the ardent sympathies of yore revive in the depths of her wounded heart: a fear of new complications, new anguish and new suffering. Lemoine, the good Lemoine, might, however, have been the confidant of whom she had dreamed, a physician of the soul even more than a physician of the body, a reliable consoler, faithful and devoted, capable of soothing the worst dolors and bandaging the worst wounds without saying a word...

More than once, Eléna had been tempted, when she knew that he was in the house, to go in search of him. Obedient to inexplicable scruples, she had always stopped herself at the last moment.

It was Saint-Magloire who was responsible cutting short those hesitations. One day, when the Baronne, in the grip of a violent bout of fever, seemed even more depressed and agonized than usual, he took it upon himself to summon the doctor, and insisted on taking him to see his wife—who made no protest.

Rozen, a subtle observer, did not even notice Eléna's sudden pallor when Lemoine came in. The latter, for his part, had great difficulty mastering his emotion.

That day, absorbed by the launch of a major affair, equivocal in its morality but likely to bring in a swift and enormous profit, which was on the point of completion, the banker was scarcely thinking about anything else. So he hastened, after a few banal remarks, to leave the patient and the doctor together in private, in order to run to the Bourse.

Eléna extended her thin hand to the doctor, who kissed it with devoted respect.

"My friend," she said, "I believe that I won't be long delayed in going to join my child." When Lemoine made a fearful gesture, surprised by that opening, she went on: "Don't protest. I sense it, and there are presentiments that are rarely mistaken. Neither your science nor your amity will be able to do anything; I've been touched by death. Thank God—for why should I remain any longer in this word, where no bond retains me any longer, and where it is burdensome to abide?

"Before dying, though, I'm happy, insofar as it is possible for me to employ that word which has the savor of blasphemy on my lips, happy to see you again, to hear your dear voice, to squeeze your loyal hands.

"Besides which, I owe you an apology. I must have appeared to you to be very ungrateful and indifferent. Forgive me—I've suffered so much, and still am! But you have not supposed, have you, that I could have forgotten, to the point of treating as a stranger, the man who once risked his life to save mine?"

Stirred to the marrow, incapable of uttering a sound, Lemoine limited himself to shaking his head as a sign of negation, while he squeezed the frail fingers that Eléna had abandoned to him ardently.

Gradually, however, he collected himself. "Poor woman! Poor friend!" he murmured, haltingly. "I have nothing to forgive you...I understood. How I mourn for you! You remember Havana, then? My God, how long ago it was! Poor Harris, you know—my friend—died in the Transvaal. I returned to Paris. Do you remember? My mother's illness...the telegram...I had to leave you over there're in New York. She died, my poor mother...I didn't even arrive in time to close her eyes. I always thought about you...why, oh why didn't you reply to my letters, Eléna Ruiz? Tell me, I beg you, why that abrupt silence...that black hole in my life? What had I done to you? Tell me..."

The Baronne abruptly raised her pale head, slumped until then on the back of the chaise-longue on which she was lying, and her eyes gleamed with a strange flame.

"You wrote to me?" she exclaimed. "You wrote to me? I never received a single letter from you... Six weeks after your departure, I too left New York, without leaving any trace. *Lo que ha de ser no puede faltar.*"[57]

"Where did you go, then? What happened to you?"

"What good would it do you to know? One cannot change what is done. Chased from New York by poverty, prey to a thousand threats, a thousand temptations, abandoned the best—like that Harris you mentioned just now, doubtless an honest man, but who didn't understand my scruples—and my father's companions in arms, I was obliged to seek refuge far away, in a remote land. It was there that I met the man to whom I linked my destiny, the man who has just left..."

"I don't like that man," Lemoine interrupted, unable to restrain himself.

"Do you think I haven't perceived that? For myself, I adored him—why should I hide it, from you, who have such a noble heart and a broad mind? Yes, I adored Saint-Magloire. I have the weakness to love him still, in spite of his betrayals, in spite of the hardness of his heart, in spite of..." The Baronne interrupted herself, and her voice choked on a sob. "Praise God, I won't for much longer! The supreme deliverance is at hand." In a softer, almost tender, tone, on seeing the doctor's features contract, she added: "Am I making you suffer, my friend?"

"Yes, you're making me suffer, and cruelly," the other replied. "For, make no mistake, I still love you. In spite of the long separation, in spite of the absence of news, the apparent forgetfulness, the turbulence of life, I've never stopped loving you. No other woman has ever occupied the empty place that your memory had left in my heart. Fatality separated us, fatality has brought us together again...and I find you belonging to another. And what another! I see you prey to despair, wishing for death. Isn't that atrocious?"

"Me too—I would have loved you, if God had wished it," she continued, in a lower voice, as if talking to herself. "I have loved you, even...but God has not wished... One cannot repair the irreparable! Believe me, death alone settles everything, because death alone can bring peace and oblivion."

"Listen to me," Lemoine said then, vehemently, enveloping Eléna with a long passionate gaze that brought blood to the poor woman's discolored cheeks. "Listen to me! I don't want you to die! I forbid you to die! You have loved me, perhaps you will love me again..."

"Alas, it's impossible!"

"Don't talk about impossibility! You love me, at least, as one loves a friend, a brother. Let me hope that amity will one day give way...I don't know, I can't tell why or how...to love...to a love equal to the one I have burning in me.

---

[57] The author inserts a footnote: "A Spanish proverb that can be roughly translated as: 'One cannot escape one's destiny.' Literally: 'That which must be cannot fail to be.'"

"But you have to live!"

Lemoine spoke in those terms for a long time, with an eloquence that the paroxysm of a noble passion made suggestive and gripping, while a strange disturbance, bitter and delightful at the same time, took possession of Eléna's soul, and she was surprised to find the taste for life that she thought she had lost forever coming to life again in the depths of her being, in a tumult of contradictory emotions.

Magnetized, in some way, by the spell of the dominating will of the man for whom she had always—even in the grip of the most powerful storms of her amorous life—retained a secret worship, she was surprised to find herself hoping again, even against hope, and confusedly anticipating the reparative dawn of better days. By the time the Doctor, proud and happy with his work of resurrection, finally bid farewell to her, he had won his cause. Still sad, melancholy and bruised, the invalid was no longer talking about dying. A mysterious voice was murmuring in her ear that something unknown, which might be peace and serenity, if not happiness, might yet return, and that life might perhaps then be worth the pain of being lived.

From that day on, Dr. Lemoine became an assiduous guest in the Saint-Magloire house.

Love did not, however, make him forget his duty as an agent of justice. On the contrary!

II. The Treasons of the Telectroscope

Although increasingly infatuated with Germaine Reyval, to the point of almost completely deserting the conjugal domicile, where he only made brief appearances at lunch time—often without seeing Eléna, who generally ate in her room—Saint-Magloire had not failed to notice Lemoine's assiduity. He even began to take umbrage in that regard.

A casual fling on the Baronne's part with some "professional flirt," of the kind that pullulate in all salons, would not have worried him, for he had detached himself almost completely from the poor woman who had never held him by the heart—for good reason—and who, impotent to withstand competition from a rival as expert in perversities as the cantatrice, had ceased for some time to hold him by the senses.

Eléna was primarily useful to him, with her refined education, her noble appearance and perfect tact, in maintaining is social image. Since the death of her baby, however, and that violent scene that had followed it, the Baronne no longer showed herself. She was of no further utility to the financier, who was entirely disposed look benevolently upon, and even to favor, an amorous intrigue, in the hope of seeing his wife discard, under that spur, the tearful attitude of a *Mater dolorosa* to resume her role as mistress of the house and charmer.

But Lemoine worried him...

He was, of course, completely unaware of the former relationship between the Doctor and Eléna. The latter had certainly told him about her adventures in Havana and New York, but, as she had believed for such a long time herself, he thought that her savior had disappeared forever. She had, moreover, never told him that the Frenchman who had been so devoted to her was a physician.

Lemoine is a very common name, the Baron said to himself. *He can't have any connection with the other. Otherwise he wouldn't have failed to take advantage of the situation.*

Instinctively, however, he sensed that the grave scientist, enthusiastic and reflective, generous and positive, willful and impenetrable, was dangerous. With a man like him and a nature like Eléna's, the flirtation risked being transformed too rapidly into passion. Although he wanted Eléna's leisure to be occupied, and her jealousy diverted, he did not want to lose his empire over her.

She knew too much!

A woman in love has no secrets from the man she loves, he told himself. *A single imprudent word from Eléna, in an expansive moment, wouldn't fall upon deaf ears. That animal of a physician, with his inquisitorial mind, would soon move from one deduction to another, and discover the hidden truth. That would be a disaster!*

Not daring, however, for reasons of prudence, to break overtly with Lemoine—which, in any case, would not have been "Parisian"—Saint-Magloire contented himself with having him closely watched. He learned nothing by that, however, that was not already public knowledge.

Lemoine often met up with the head of the Sûreté, but everyone knew that they had been friends since childhood, and that was not a detail that could frighten the Baron, since, having links himself to the upper echelons of the State, he had his own ready access to the Prefecture of Police and the Ministry of the Interior, where he never had to wait in a antechamber.

Besides which, Lemoine never spoke ill of the banker in public. Very discreet, he was careful not to let slip the slightest remark capable of equivocal interpretation, and when he had occasion to talk about Saint-Magloire it was always in the tone of facile sympathy that all Paris gladly lavishes on people who have "arrived." As for his relations with the Baronne, they were always impeccably correct, with a hint of tender gallantry never exceeding the measure of the discreet courtship due to a pretty suffering client from a family doctor and friend of the household.

Saint-Magloire, however, was not reassured. With the instinct of a hunted beast, he sniffed, confusedly, a hidden peril. So he resolved to mount a surveillance himself, and to employ any and all means.

If the Baronne, already ill, were to die *gradually*, who could have the slightest suspicion?

The idea of killing Eléna rapidly took shape in the bandit's mind, but he wanted, first, to see exactly how far her relationship with Lemoine might go. Before a new crime the former 883 still hesitated, as he had hesitated over Lavardens.

Just then, the inexhaustible genius of Sokoloff put a new apparatus at Rozen's disposal, of diabolical ingenuity, which would facilitate his espionage singularly.

Since the invention of the telephone, a number of inventors had dreamed of completing that apparatus—which, after we marveled at it to begin with, appears to us today as the simplest and most banal thing in the world—by means of a mechanism permitting the sight of the features of the person with whom one is corresponding orally at a distance of hundreds of kilometers. For many years, Sokoloff had sought to transmit visual images, with electricity as a vehicle, as one transits sounds, and after patient and laborious experiments, he had succeeded in reducing an image instantaneously to innumerable luminous points, transporting those individual elements along a wire similar to a telephone wire, and reconstituting them at the point of reception into features that were perhaps a trifle vague and fluid, but nevertheless recognizable, in the same interval of time necessary for their decomposition.

How had the scientific magician succeeded in transforming light into electricity, to the point of rendering the phenomena of vision virtually independent of distance and obstacles? It is probably useful and apposite to explain.

Just at the moment when, weary of fruitless research and failed trials, Sokoloff was about to abandon the construction of the telectroscope,[58] he thought of utilizing the singular properties of selenium, a metalloid of the sulfur family, discovered in 1817 by the Swedish chemist Berzelius.

May and Willoughby Smith demonstrated, twenty years ago,[59] that selenium, comparable in this respect to Branly's radio-conductor, which is the essential key to wireless telegraphy, is either conductive or non-conductive, depending on whether or not it is stimulated by light. In other words, its electrical resistance varies with the quantity and quality of the lighting to which it is subjected.

With a luminous beam that is controllable—which is to say that it can be switched on and off at will—one can therefore cause an electric current to pass through selenium, or interrupt it. It is thus able to transmit signals of some kind at a distance—such as, for instance, those of Morse code—by means of the intermittence of the current.

It was that bizarre property, absolutely unique to selenium, that Sokoloff, with his prodigious mastery, had thought of exploiting for the transmission of visual images at a distance.

What we call an image—which is to say, the perception by means of the intermediary of the eye and the fixation on the retina of the forms, dimensions and movements of external objects—is, in the final analysis, merely a luminous phenomenon, proceeding directly from variations in light. Instead of a living eye, therefore, those luminous variations that constitute, in reality, the whole of the image, can be impressed upon a series of parcels of selenium juxtaposed like the rods of the retina—which is composed, as everyone knows, of countless tiny cylinders known as "Jacob's rods,"[60] stuck together so as to form as many mi-

---

[58] The term "telectroscope" was frequently used in the 19th century to refer to a hypothetical telephone that would transmit pictures as well as sound. Gautier's long-time friend and some-time associate Louis Figuier used the term in 1876 to advertise a device which he believed, wrongly, already to exist. Jan Szczepanik contrived to obtain a British patent for such a device in 1897, although it was never exhibited, which prompted Mark Twain to refer to it is his story "From the *Times* of 1904."

[59] Willoughby Smith published the article containing this observation in the 20 February 1873 issue of *Nature*. Joseph May was the chief technician of the company Smith worked for, which specialized in laying electric cable, and collaborated with him on the extrapolation of the (initially accidental) discovery.

[60] The layer of the inner eye containing the rods and cones is known as "Jacob's membrane," thus licensing this slightly unusual nomenclature.

nuscule facets. They determine in each of those parcels a variation proportional to the electrical conductivity—which is to say, a difference in the intensity of the current. These electrical variations can, however, be reproduced at a distance—in other words, telegraphed.

It would therefore be possible to transmit the sensations experienced by the selenium under the tone of light over a distance, and to reproduce, in a symmetrical apparatus at the other end of the wire, the luminous variations that provoked them. One would thus have an image of the image, which, collected by a lens and projected on a screen, would permit the sight at the point of reception of what is happening at the point of transmission.

The transmitted image is not perfect, of course. Comprised of dots corresponding to each of the parcels of selenium, it forms a slightly blurred pointillist silhouette, comparable to the designs of a tapestry. On the other hand, as the luminous waves are not transmitted directly, but after transformation into electrical waves, colors are not reproduced, and one has a flat, monochromatic image, like a poor daguerrotype. Finally, such an installation costs too much to be truly practical.

These imperfections and inconveniences could not discourage a man like Saint-Magloire, however, who, in addition to not being concerned with the expense, could content himself with an approximation in this case.

He had therefore had skillful workmen—who did not understand what it was—install a checkerboard panel in Eléna's boudoir, each square of which was linked to a cell composed of parcels of selenium, disposed in such a way as to rise or fall like as many struts in a Venetian blind, according to the intensity of the electric current commanding their hinges. That electric current depending, as has just been explained, on luminous intensity, the fragments of images, reflected through a system of mirrors, were trapped, and their constituent luminous vibrations transformed into electrical radiation transmissible over a distance by the intermediary of a cable formed of as many filaments of selenium as there were "struts" in the panel.

That cable ended, by ways of a subterranean channel that the Baron had obtained permission from the Administration to set up in the drains, under the pretext of carrying out experiments with a telephonic loudspeaker, in an identical apparatus placed in a darkroom in a work-room in the Place Vendôme. There, the electrical radiation acting on a keyboard of selenium cells, which opened to a greater or lesser extent by virtue of the varying intensity of the initial luminous images, the image was reproduced in fragmentary form, more or less exactly, and projected on to a screen, on which one could see what was happening at the other end of the line, as in a broken mirror.

The field of the indiscreet apparatus was inevitably rather narrow, but Saint-Magloire had placed in such a way as at least to embrace the preferred corner that Eléna spent between five and seven hours every day, especially when she was wrapped up to keep the cold at bay.

On the other hand, Eléna, like a tropical flower, adored light. Darkness, and even shade, caused her a kind of physical anguish. In her rooms, therefore, the curtains were always wide open, so as to let the slightest ray of sunlight in, and whenever the daylight began to fade, either because dusk was falling or the sky was covered in cloud, she gave the order to light the room *a giorno*.

In consequence, the Baron had no fear that the lighting would ever be insufficient for the functioning of his telectroscope.

Sokoloff, who was very far from suspecting the usage to which his invention was destined, had seen nothing in the installation but a experiment, all the more suggestive because it closely approached the normal conditions of current everyday practice, so, he had finished it off himself, and it worked marvelously.

His insatiable scientific ambition was still not satisfied, though. He dreamed of getting rid of the wire and transmitting images at a distance without any material contact, on the impalpable wing of those mysterious Hertzian waves which serve to bear the burden of the miracles of radioconduction.

While the Russian worked to solve that double problem, the solution of which, glimpsed from time to time, but which always ended up escaping him at the very moment when he thought he was finally about to grasp and secure it, Saint-Magloire found that, as it was, with is confused Chinese shadows, its blurring, its partitioned images and its pointillism, the telectroscope was already a wonderful instrument.

The fact is that, from time to time, when the fancy took him, he was able to watch from his study, with sufficient certainty, the actions and gestures of the Baronne, who—poor thing!—had no suspicion of the inquisitorial surveillance that was being mounted on her, at a distance of several hundred meters, through the opacity of walls.

The Baron only regretted one thing, which was that Sokoloff had not yet succeeded in combining the telectroscope with the telephone amplifier, of which he had undertaken, albeit with less ardor, a parallel study, and which would have permitted him also to hear the words spoken, even in a whisper, by the woman whose movements and attitudes he was following with his eyes.

But one cannot have everything.

It was thus that Saint-Magloire was able to convince himself *de visu* that, although Lemoine was visibly paying court to Eléna, it was always in a respectful fashion, which could not in any way alarm the susceptibilities of a husband, even a husband prepared, at the least, to play the part of an Othello infatuated by preventive and umbrageous jealousy to the point of intransigence.

He would have paid dearly, however, to hear their conversation.

One day, when he was certain that Lemoine, whose path he had crossed, would be with Eléna, Saint-Magloire, more violently piqued than usual, had taken up his position in his observatory. This time, he had a flash of enlightenment.

Sitting facing the Baronne, Lemoine was speaking with an abundance of gestures unusual in that habitually cool and compassed individual. At the same time, the contraction of his features, which the fragmentation of the telectroscopic image did not prevent the distinction, testified to the most violent emotion.

Eléna, for her part, seemed utterly overwhelmed. Her furrowed brow, the convulsive fluttering of her eyelids and the trembling of her limbs revealed an abnormal state of mind.

Suddenly, Lemoine fell to his knees and, seizing the hand that the Baronne abandoned to him, bore it passionately to his lips—but Eléna pulled away immediately, and while she pushed Lemoine away with one hand, she rummaged in her corsage with the other, from which she extracted a piece of paper, which she handed to the doctor.

The later got up precipitately, clasping his forehead with a gesture in which there was suffering, surprise and horror, while Eléna, falling back in her armchair, burst into sobs.

Saint-Magloire had seen enough.

In any case, just at that moment, by virtue of one of the incomprehensible perturbations to which the telectroscope, so delicate and so capricious, was routinely subject, the vision ceased to be clear.

"That spoils things," murmured the Baron. "Obviously, Eléna has a crush on the rascal. Oh, I sense that she'll remain faithful to me, in spite of all temptations…a woman of whom Gaston Rozen has been the lover, especially a woman like that, whom I've possessed body and soul, senses, intelligence and heart, doesn't give herself to another…she'd lose too much in the comparison...

"Besides which, my suggestion dominates her, even in my absence; that empire's inescapable…so my honor is safe. My honor…!"

Saint-Magloire burst out laughing—nervous and perverse laughter—at those words, which did indeed sound in a singular fashion upon his lips.

"Honor! Come on, Rozen, no jokes! Besides, if it existed, I wouldn't reside there. But it's not my honor that's at stake—it's my safety.

"She's off the rails, Eléna, that's certain. What the Devil can the secret paper contain that she's just shown to Lemoine, the sight of which seemed to have such a bizarre effect on him?

"*Maldiga medios!* I need to clear this up."

And, having summoned his carriage, without even taking the time to take his leave of the numerous visitors awaiting his pleasure, he gave orders to the coachman to take him to the house at top speed.

The telectroscope had not deceived the adventurer. A new peril, the gravest of all those that he had impetuously defies until now, had just burst inopportunely over his head.

In the course of the conversation between Lemoine and the Baronne, one of those small, seemingly insignificant events had occurred that sometimes change the course of the destiny of a man, a family or a people.

After the conventional compliments, and in spite of the clichéd banality of formulas, there had been a surge of contained passion, and from the standard questions about the health of his beautiful client and friend, the doctor had skillfully steered the conversation to the subject so close to his heart and which he had not yet been able to bring sufficiently to light, in spite of the subtlety of his diplomacy. What had become of Eléna after her departure from New York? Why had she left his letters unanswered? Where had she made the acquaintance of the man who was to become her husband?

Ten times already he had asked Madame de Saint-Magloire those questions, more or less formally. Ten times the Baronne had avoided them, either because a domestic had come in, just in time to cut the thread of her confidences, or because, fearing that she might say too much, or yielding to a kind of modesty, she had broken the chain herself.

This time, Lemoine had sworn to press her more closely, and no matter how unfavorable the circumstances were, gently to extract the key to the enigma. That day, more nervous or more galled than usual, Eléna was visibly disposed to let something out; Lemoine's perspicacity did not miss that. So, from the very beginning, he pushed forward vigorously with his assault without further oratorical precautions.

The Baronne became emotional. "Your precipitate departure for France," she said, "caused me a considerable grief. I felt, in fact—we women can sense these things—that you were...not indifferent to me...

"Undoubtedly, since your mother was ill, the separation was necessary...but I expected to hear your news...

"Nothing...nothing: not a word! Oh, that was a cruel disillusionment for me."

"But I'd written you a dozen letters in which I tried to depict for you, in terms as respectful as they were tender, sentiments...that are still the same. Alas, all those letters came back to me with the dry inscription, which chilled my heart: *Left without leaving a forwarding address.* Thinking it was indifference, perhaps forgetfulness...I renounced writing to you, retreating dolorously into myself, and strove, while dulling my senses with work, to efface your dear memory from my consciousness." In a dull and seemingly-wounded voice, he added: "I never succeeded in that, though."

"I didn't leave an address, in fact. What was the point? The only man whose...sympathy had been precious no me seemed not to be thinking about me any longer. Nothing any longer attached me to life. It was impossible for me, anyway, to remain any longer in the United States, where I would certainly have died of starvation, unless I ceded to the abominable solicitations with which I was assailed from all directions...

"My father's friends, embittered by defeat, absorbed by the thousand jealousies and intrigues that are so often the running sore of vanquished parties, turned their backs on me. Only your friend Harris, the English reporter who helped you prepare me escape, remained faithful—but his zeal was maladroit, his amity compromising. Can you imagine that he wanted to oblige me to hire myself out to Barnum and Bailey, who would have exhibited me as 'the greatest curiosity in the world' in all the large and small towns of the five continents? To hear him, I would have earned a lot of money.

"The fact is that Bailey, to whom he had introduced me, made me seductive offers…but it was repugnant to me, you understand, to exploit my misfortunes thus. I refused. Harris, who could not share what he called my 'prejudices' did not understand that, without resources as I was, I could light-heartedly refuse a fortune…he thought I was mad, and gradually, I sensed his devotion cooling, and he left me.

"Having lost that last support—a worthy fellow, all things considered—I was definitely alone in the world, having no other prospect than poverty or shame. It was then that, thanks to a fortunate chance, I met an old school-friend, who offered me employment as a governess in…Central America…" She corrected herself swiftly: "South America, I mean. I accepted enthusiastically, and left without leaving an address…

"Spare me the continuation of the story of my sad life…of no interest to you…now that you know how and why a fatality superior to our will separated us…forever!"

Eléna's voice died away in a sigh.

Lemoine was moved to tears. His instinct as an inquisitor and seeker of justice had not abandoned him, however.

"Was it in a French family that you found a situation?" he asked, after a momentary hesitation.

Eléna nodded her head affirmatively.

"Then it was in a French colony in Central America that you went to take refuge—Guiana, perhaps?"

At that name, which evoked such terrible reminiscences, the Baronne could not help shuddering. She darted a frightened glance at the doctor, whose composed features no longer expressed anything but tender pity—but she did not reply.

Lemoine, who had not failed to notice Eléna's shudder, did not think he ought to insist, though. He resumed: "It's doubtless during your sojourn out there…with the French family…that you met the Baron?"

"No," Eléna replied, with a fearful expression, "it was while traveling…on the steamer…" She remained absorbed momentarily, and then continued, in a blank voice, her eyes staring, as if she were speaking to someone off-stage; "I thought I had found happiness…I loved him so much, and I believed s firmly that he felt the same about me! Now, it's Hell! I'm suffering like a damned soul!"

Lemoine could not bear it any longer. He fell to his knees, seized Eléna's dangling hand, and covered it with kisses.

"Poor, poor love!" he moaned.

She snatched away her hand, and, opening her peignoir with a feverish gesture, she took a small cardboard square from a thicket of lace. It was an admirable photograph representing a young man with a silky moustache, large soft eyes, a broad and pure forehead, as handsome as a god.

She contemplated it momentarily with eyes in which there was more despair than hatred, more regret than jealousy, and held it out to Lemoine, murmuring in a tremulous voice: "If you knew how seductive he was, ten years ago, in the full flower of youth and love! How could I help adoring him?"

At the sight of the portrait Lemoine leapt to his feet as if jerked by a spring. It required all his self-control, which the surge of passion had not annihilated, all his intellectual mastery and all his will-power not to utter a cry: a cry of a triumph, and simultaneously a cry of dolor and fear.

He was dumbstruck.

He had good reason.

The features of the Baron de Saint-Magloire before his transformation, which, in a fit of heat-rending coquetry, Eléna had just allowed him to glimpse, presented a strange analogy with those of the portrait of Rozen now familiar to his memory and fixed in indelible lines at the back of his mind, so intensely had he studied it with a magnifying glass in the collection of the anthropometric service.

An error was possible, however, even for an eye as perspicacious and well-trained as the doctor's.

It was difficult to deceive his memory, whose faulty of visual evocation as prodigious, and which traced, even after years, down to the slightest detail, the real image of things he had seen.

Undoubtedly, Saint-Magloire had changed his face; in his somewhat resolidified features, to which age and anxieties had set their patina and their wrinkles, the other face was no longer rediscoverable...

Furthermore, the photograph that Eléna possessed, taken before Rozen's arrest, had been "retouched," and that circumstance did not permit anything but suspicion. The imperious and seductive velvet eyes, however, were definitely the same.

Oh, if only it had been possible to enlarge the design of the ear and compare the indications to the anthropometric image of Rozen! That would have been perfect. The design of the ear, immutably in its form from infancy to the tomb, in spite of all physiological vicissitudes, resistant to the influences of education and environment, also remains, throughout life, like the intangible legacy of heredity, an inalienable characteristic of the individual.

Lemoine knew that. After Alphonse Bertillon, Lannois and Julia, Saglas and Ferri,[61] he had studied profoundly, precisely from the viewpoint of criminal anthropology, the morphology of the organ to which the profane ordinarily pay so little attention, doubtless because of the immobility that prevents it from participating in the play of the physiognomy. He had, in particular, studied Gaston Rozen's ear, of which the most tenuous features of the helix, the anhelix, the tragus, the antitragus, the lobe and Darwin's tubercle were as familiar to him as if he had them "in his eye," as the saying has it, and which he was capable of drawing freehand from memory with an impeccable precision.

The photograph that Eléna showed Lemoine, however, was not much use. The ear was seen at an angle and more than one lock of hair covered the upper part of it. Nevertheless, Lemoine felt that he was within reach of the goal that he had been pursuing for such a long time. Eléna's very reticence condemned the Baron. One more clue, one piece of evidence, and justice could be done.

But there was a shadow on that picture. In order for justice to be done, it would be necessary to trample on the heart of the woman with whom he was more impetuously in love than ever.

It might, perhaps, kill her.

Then, rapidly, another thought reassured the doctor: *But no! It will be Eléna's salvation...her salvation and deliverance...*

A painful surgical operation, no doubt, since it will be necessary to bring a red-hot iron to the quick of a bloody wound, but which will save the patient by restoring her honor, peace and liberty!

Liberty!

When she was fee again, perhaps then she would consent to be his.

Lemoine did not hesitate any longer. His decision was made. This time, he thought that he had Rozen; he would not let him escape again.

Prostrate on the cushions, her head in her hands, Eléna was weeping softly, deeply moved by the release of that confidence, of whose tragic gravity she had no suspicion. She had no consciousness of the storm that had begun to rumble within Lemoine's skull.

The arrival of a chambermaid bringing a visiting card succeeded in rendering the latter all his presence of mind—not that he feared that the maid, finding her mistress in tears, would have any suspicion. The staff of the house, habituated as they were to seeing Madame weeping all day long since the death of her

---

[61] The original text renders the final name Féré, but the context strongly suggests at the reference is to the Italian criminologist Enrico Ferri, a former pupil of Cesare Lombroso. P. E. Lannois did indeed make an extensive study of ear shape in the context of anthropological criminology, and a book entitled *De l'oreille au point de vue anthropologique et médico-legal* signed J. Julia was published in Lyon in 1889. I can find no trace of Saglas; the name might be misrendered.

child, no longer paid any attention to it, in spite of the devoted affection that everyone had for her...

But he needed to be alone again, so that he could think, and draw up a program and a plan. An opportunity had arisen to take his leave; he hastened to grasp it.

Eléna tried in vain to retain him, giving orders that the intruder should be told that she was too ill to see anyone...after a few kind words, Lemoine left.

He was just in time.

He had not reached the roundabout of the Champs-Elysées when Saint-Magloire burst into Eléna's little drawing-room like a bomb.

"Who have you received during my absence?" he demanded, in a harsh voice, without any preamble.

"That fashion of interrogating me," Eléna replied, proudly, insulted by the brutality of it, "frees me from any obligation to reply. But since you appear to want—which is, again, not customary—to know how I spend my time, I see no reason not to tell you that I received a visit from your excellent friend Dr. Lemoine. Now that I've informed you, *bonsoir!*"

And, rising to her feet with the dignity of an outraged queen, Eléna went into her bedroom, closing the door behind her."

"Aha!" muttered the Baron, surprised and irritated by that unexpected rebellion. "The lady's annoyed, it seems. It's serious, then, this little love affair...when one's annoyed, it's because one is in the wrong. It's time to set things in order...otherwise I don't know where we'll be heading...

"That piece of paper she showed to Lemoine—what could it be? Perhaps I'd find out if I told her that I'd seen it, with my own eyes...but I can't tell her that; I can't reveal my trick to her; she and he would hide thereafter...that would be easy, since they'd only have to move to another room.

"No! I've had enough! Well put an end to it...with Eléna first, since at least I her under my hand. When she's no longer here, I've no longer any need to fear the other...who won't weigh so heavily then."

Confronted by the danger that Eléna presented to him, the idea of killing her had returned to Rozen's mind—and this time, he no longer had the slightest hesitation.

She'll have asked for it—so much the worse for her!

Eléna's death-sentence had just been pronounced.

III. An Incomprehensible Illness

That scene had not had any consequence.

Ordinarily, after the slightest quarrel or observation, the Baron sulked, systematically. He sometimes disappeared from the house, without any explanation, for an entire week, as if he were seeking an opportunity to demonstrate, *urbi et orbi*, his independence from any conjugal ties—and when he took it into his head to return, as casually as a husband who had gone out for the morning on business, it was necessary that Eléna refrain from giving any evidence of discontent or sadness by a moue, a gesture, an attitude or a word. Otherwise, Monsieur seized the pretext to absent himself again with cruel words of bitterness or sarcasm, which left the Baronne bewildered and bereft.

This time, to the great surprise of the poor woman, who had expected the usual flight, he was completely different. Instead of playing truant in another bed, he went to visit the Baronne the very next morning, and began by offering his most tender apologies, in the most honeyed tone.

"Forgive me, my love," he said, "for my fit of temper yesterday. I was unjust and ridiculous. You won't hold it against me, will you? I beg you not to! Oh, I know, for some time I've been unbearable, odious—but you mustn't hold it against me. Life isn't always easy, especially for a businessman like me, overburdened with bother and responsibility.

"Things don't always go as I desire; men are so stupid...or so dishonest! Then, on days when I've had worse annoyances than usual, when I come back here, with weary limbs and a head that seems about to explode, with a fever, all my blood boiling, I have the right to be a little highly strung. Of, course, I was utterly wrong to let it show, especially to you, my beloved, whom I've never ceased to love...in spite of my faults...in spite of my infidelities..."

All that was undefined by one of those bewitching gazes that Eléna had never been able to resist.

She succeeded in forgetting the tragic circumstances of Pepe's death. Those cruel memories faded away before the protestations of love by the man to whom she had given herself. Subjugated by Gaston's eloquence, she gradually felt her heart melting, trying in vain to harden it.

After some hesitation, she ended up throwing herself into her husband's arms and weeping softly on his shoulder.

"My cherub," the bandit continued, shading the modulations of his golden voice with an infernal artistry, while he caressed his wife's hair and rocked her like a child, "my cherub, how I've hurt you! But it's over, isn't it? You don't hold it against me anymore?

Eléna shook her head, for emotion stopped her speech in her throat."

She did not want to lie, and a doubt subsisted within her; half-smiling through her tears, her lips very close to Rozen's ear, she murmured, in a tone in which neither rancor nor sharpness were any longer detectable: "It's not always business that takes you away from me. Be frank. While I weep, you amuse yourself. The other day, for example, that dinner—that orgy, rather—about which the entire press is talking, I don't know where…the Café de Paris, I think…with a troop of harlots, every one of whom found a splendid jewel under her napkin…you can't pretend that that was politics, or finance, much less the revolution…

"If you loved me, who wouldn't leave me when I'm suffering…when I need attachment to bind me to life. Instead of staying with me, you play around with whores…" In a whisper, almost a breath, she added: "How can I forgive such a betrayal?"

Rozen, a skillful actor, had a broad smile, his eyes expressing an ineffable tenderness. He took Eléna's head between his hands, and, his lips very close to the young woman's, whose eyelids were fluttering, said: "Come on, silly—you, the daughter of a conspirator, can take these stories seriously! If I were really indulging in dissipation, do you think I'd amuse myself by having it reported by the newspapers? For I'm the one who passed those rumors to the press; I'm the one who wrote them and paid for them.

"Don't you understand that it's all sham, my darling, vulgar publicity…play-acting. Given the role that I'm playing, the goal I'm pursuing…which you know…it's indispensable that I throw dust in people's eyes…

"I've often told you that it's good that everyone says that the Baron de Saint-Magloire is a spendthrift, a nabob, a peerless Sybarite, to whom the prettiest women in Paris, and the most expensive, can refuse nothing…in France, people love that; all the men who have risen to the top in this simultaneously sentimental and piratical country and have won over the masses have had a reputation as wastrels and rakes: Henri IV, Napoléon, General Boulanger…now it's my turn. Not to mention that the means aren't unpleasant…there's nothing like that sport to neutralize my exasperated nerves…I need a racket to relax me and numb me…it's a pick-me-up as well as an advertisement!

"What harm can that do you, I ask you, since it all by-passes the heart and flows over the skin, for the benefit of the gallery?"

Eléna had stopped weeping.

Seduced, in spite of herself, by the verve of the wretch, who seemed sincere, she was no longer protesting except for form's sake…

Rozen thought the occasion propitious for pushing his argument further, on to more scabrous terrain.

"It's like my supposed loved affair with La Reyval…"

At that name, Eléna shuddered from head to toe. Gaston had just touched a sensitive nerve. Softening his voice even further, which took on a strangely harmonious timbre, he persisted. "Listen to me, darling, hear me out! Yes, Germaine Reyval herself, to whom I seem assiduous, but whom I love no more than I hold her in esteem; she's a showpiece, like the rare orchid with which I adorn my buttonhole, following the example of Chamberlain, in order that everyone should know that there's no luxury for which I can't pay.

"You wouldn't want the King of Paris not to have in his collection the most costly harlot of the Opéra? The fact of passing in the eyes of idlers for having harnessed her to my chariot is more an extra two hundred million to my credit! What do you expect, darling? When one sets forth on the conquest of the world, one can't always choose one's route—but the end justifies the means."

Eléna became increasing tense. A waxy pallor spread over her lovely face. Once again, a tear pearled in her eyelashes. It seemed that she was about to faint—but a long kiss from Rozen galvanized her.

She had lost the habit of loving caresses. All the anger and resentment of an outraged woman flowed away in tender indulgence.

The Baron, moreover, had no intention of letting the advantage he had regained slip away.

"Besides," he added, "I won't leave you anymore. My reputation for lewd behavior is assured for a while. I'm all yours…I've come back to the hearth, and it will be paradise for me...

"Look—would you like us to dine together this evening, just the two of us, in a private room, in a place I know?"

In the intoxication of that unexpected return of passion, the Baronne, losing her free will, forgot all her grievances and accepted.

It was an exquisite evening—an evening of happiness that was to have several editions, for the next day, and the day after, all that week, Gaston continued to return home regularly, with all the expensiveness, refined anticipations and seductive radiance of a model husband. The honeymoon recommenced, with the charm of its intoxications, for which Eléna thought she had lost the taste forever. In the egotism of her reconquered felicity, she almost neglected Dr. Lemoine, who could no longer see her except in passing, at hazard.

It did not take long for her to be obliged to remember him.

About a week after the reconciliation, Eléna, who had been feeling strange pangs of distress since the previous evening, found herself, after a sleepless night, seriously indisposed.

An irresistible prostration overwhelmed her, with abrupt alternations of hot flushes, extending as far as profuse sweats, and intense chills. Her stiffened limbs seemed to have been transformed into leaden masses, difficult to maneuver.

However, save for a vague headache and a rather painful sensation of her entire body being trapped in an excessively tight swaddling-band, she did not experience any clearly-defined pain.

She could not get up, and when Saint-Magloire came in to dine with her, according to his new habit, he found her in bed, violently upset.

Immediately, with the suppleness of a consummate actor, he displayed a keen concern, and, in order not to abandon his "poor little wife," he had dinner served on an occasional table beside her bed—but he was obliged to do honor to the improvised lunch by himself. The Baronne was quite incapable of facing it.

She had a violent fever punctuated by frequent nauseas, without vomiting, as if she were coming down with sea-sickness. Finally, she became drowsy, but her sleep was heavy and agitated, with starts, sighs and coughing fits.

The Baron rang.

"Run and fetch Dr. Lemoine," he said to the valet, in an artfully halting voice who answered the summons, "and bring him here immediately. Take my automobile, in order not to lose a minute."

The domestic hastened to carry out the order, with all the more haste because the entire staff adored Eléna for her gentleness and generosity. When he left, though, the entire servants' parlor knew that Madame was ill, perhaps dangerously, and that Monsieur was in despair.

"For sure," the butler declared sententiously, who claimed to have as much knowledge of men and experience of life as anyone, "if Monsieur has the misfortune of losing Madame, he won't survive it."

"He won't have any lack of consolations, though," riposted the coachman. "The skirts the boss has at his heels, with gamy meat inside, don't bear thinking about. I know plenty about that, you know, since it's me who takes him to his vices! And even I don't know everything, for he also goes by automobile and on foot, when he doesn't take a cab. Like red hot pincers!"

"Shut up, lecher," said the doyenne of the chambermaids, an old woman with spectacles, shriveled, ugly and dignified. "All that's trivia, but for true love, you only have to look at Monsieur and Madame to see how they adore one another. A lovely couple! They're made for one another!"

On that point, everyone was in agreement.

Saint-Magloire was not mistaken in supposing that public opinion, even among the people who, seeing him at close range, should have known him best, still though, in spite of his resounding escapades, in the ardor and sincerity of his passion for Eléna.

While the domestics were perorating, the automobile burned up the road.

Twenty-five minutes later, Dr. Lemoine, surprised at table by the valet, arrived at top speed, distressed by the bad news.

It was Saint-Magloire who greeted him and explained the case, with the suggestive precision that he put into everything, and a considerable reinforcement of technical expressions that the most knowledgeable of specialists would not have been able to use.

"You know, Doctor," he concluded, "that I once studied medicine as an amateur. Often, in the course of my travels, I had occasion to put that aspect my knowledge into practice, and I've seen a large number of illnesses of every sort, but I don't understand the Baronne's indisposition."

"We'll find out what it is," Lemoine replied, to emotional to be suspicious.

They went into Eléna's room together.

At the sound of their footsteps, she opened her eyes, and when she perceived the doctor, to whom she extended her moist and tremulous hand, a pale smile illuminated her features.

"I'm very ill, my dear friend," she murmured, raising herself up—not without effort—on to her elbow. "You've arrived just in time!"

"We'll take care of this," Lemoine replied. "Don't worry."

While interrogating the patient and the Baron, he began a meticulous examination—but neither auscultation nor palpation, nor the explanations given, could offer a key to the enigma. He could not find anything abnormal, with the exception of an extraordinary sluggishness of organic function and a general depression incomprehensible in the wake of such a short indisposition. There was only a little arrhythmia in the heartbeat, but the skin was smooth and shiny, as if stretched, with a generalized coloration akin to chilblains, with a light hyperesthesia, especially in the face and shoulders, the breast and neck, hoarse breathing and extreme weakness.

For several days Eléna had not eaten any seafood or game, so there was no reason to suspect any alimentary intoxication.

The doctor asked to see the shoes and stockings that she normally wore. Perhaps that would enable him to find an indication of one of the tinctural poisons of which there had been much talk in recent years.

After examination, however, he was obliged to discard that hypothesis, evidently false. Besides which, he had not noticed the characteristic cyanosis of the face and extremities.

"We're only dealing with motor disturbances," Saint-Magloire insinuated, "for there's no lesion anywhere, is there?"

Lemoine nodded his head affirmatively. "For the moment," he said, I can only see one plausible hypothesis—that of an extremely violent influenza, without a determined localization. You know how periodic, polymorphous and diverse that bizarre infection is."

"In Cuba, Eléna put in, plaintively, "we call it *trancazo*."

"Yes, the 'cudgel-blow.' It certainly is. The word expresses the violence and suddenness of the illness exactly."

In Lemoine's mouth, that was merely a way of talking. Fundamentally, he was not satisfied with his diagnosis—but he stuck to it, for want of being able to find a better one, in spite of his profound knowledge, brilliant perspicacity and consummate experience. He felt, confusedly, that he was in the presence of an unusual case, evidently resembling a malign variety of influenza, but not the same…and probably worse.

Positive measures could be taken against it even so, influenza alone being in play; other assaults might be mounted later, when the latent morbid entity finally decided to reveal its true identity. In the meantime, there was nothing

348

compromising to fear, and al probabilities of therapeutic exaggeration could be set aside, since the traditional treatment of influenza, exclusively tonic and detergent, is not in the least specific.

After having administered massive dose of a judicious mixture of quinine sulfate, antipyrine and bicarbonate of soda, therefore, Lemoine limited himself to prescribing a strong purgation with a cordial potion, a little benzonaphthol to disinfect the digestive tract, and bed rest. The last item was, in any case, superfluous, the patient being incapable of standing up.

When he left, still perplexed and anxious, at least he had the conviction that that treatment of the symptoms would lead to an immediate sensible improvement, which would permit him to see more clearly the following day.

He was utterly mistaken.

The next day, Madame de Saint-Magloire's condition had worsened.

On the day after, and in the days that followed, instead of the amelioration anticipated in vain, the aggravation became more accentuated by the hour. After a week, the situation had become truly alarming. The same abnormal symptoms persisted, still with increasing intensity, but they were further complicated by a host of bizarre perturbations of a more worrying nature.

Hair was coming out in handfuls, without even the contact of a comb, as if scythed at the root. The progress of the baldness was so rapid that patches of various sizes, entirely denuded, were becoming visible on the cranium, as if shaven.

After the hair it was the turn of the eyebrows, and then the lashes. It seemed that the pilose system was being attached at its source and in its vitality by the sly invasion of some devastating trichophyton.[62] However, the bacteriological analyses carried out by Dr. Lemoine did not reveal the presence of any specific microbe. The cultures remained sterile and inoculations carried out on rabbits, dogs and guinea-pigs did not produce any effect that could serve as an indication.

The infection was not, therefore, of parasitic origin. It seemed, in the contrary, to emerge from one of these spontaneous deteriorations of living tissues—and cutaneous tissues in particular—of a chemico-physiological nature, which physicians call "trophoneuroses." Lemoine was too intelligent and too conscientious, however, to content himself with big words, which most often serve to mask ignorance. The truth is that the further he went, the less he understood.

He began to wonder whether the cruel chagrin that was tormenting him on seeing the woman he adored in such a dire condition had not blunted his powers of observation, ordinarily so subtle, and obscured his intelligence.

Meanwhile, Eléna got steadily worse.

---

[62] *Trichophyton* is a parasitic fungus that causes such human skin diseases as athlete's foot and ringworm.

After the hair, eyebrows and eyelashes, it was the turn of the fingernails and toenails, especially the former, to deteriorate. Flattened and thinned, friable and striated with longitudinal wrinkles, they no longer bore any resemblance to rose petals. It seemed that they were about to fall out, like the hair, at the slightest traction.

The skin itself was profoundly damaged. Firstly, there was a kind of generalized erythema, with a more marked intensity on the face and upper body. Dry, hard and parchment-like, clinging more and more to the bones, which it seemed to be hugging with an increasing pressure, it rose up in places in squamae or hollowed out in cracks, at the bottom of which invasive ulcers were gradually forming.

Appetite and sleep had disappeared, and the sense of touch was completely abolished.

The patient did not seem to be suffering excessively, overwhelmed by a weakness that no longer permitted her to complain, except for repetitions of nausea and frightful palpitations that threatened to break her poor shriveled body. Then, there was that perpetual horrible sensation of being enclosed in a gradually tightening sack...

Saint-Magloire affected the loudest despair. Twenty times a day he came to obtain news of Eléna, whom his presence seemed to galvanize for a few minutes. She always welcomed him with a tender and melancholy smile.

Even at night he got up several times in order to come and kiss her poor thread-like fingers piously and silently, with tears in his eyes.

All Paris, moreover, knew that Madame Saint-Magloire was afflicted with a strange illness, in danger of death, and that her husband was watching over her and caring for her with a heroic devotion.

As for Lemoine, his anxiety and distress were so violent that he had put off until later the accomplishment of his justice-seeking mission. He no longer gave it a thought, so to speak, and had not even told the head of the Sûreté about the extraordinary resemblance he had observed between the portrait of the young Saint-Magloire and Gaston Rozen's identification photograph.

Saving Eléna was his first and only thought. There would be time later to set the police on the heels of the escaped convict.

Gripped by fear and self-doubt, he finally decided to suggest to the Baron—whose excessive manifestations he had scarcely noticed, in his distress—a consultation with two other famous physicians, two princes of the science, whom he named.

"I was about to request that very step," Saint-Magloire replied. "I'll go in person immediately to ask them. A million, two million, ten million to save my poor Eléna. If necessary, I'm ready to give my entire fortune." As an aside, he added: "I'd soon have made another..."

The consultation took place the same evening, but it did not provide Lemoine with much clarification. The latter had asked for and obtained authorization to bring with him the most brilliant and most reliable of his pupils, already celebrated in spite of his extreme youth, for his impeccable diagnoses: the official medical examiner Olivier Martin.

At the name of Olivier Martin, whose role in the Dulac autopsy he had not forgotten, the Baron had made a slight grimace, but it was only a flash, which Lemoine did not even have time to notice, and he had accepted with his habitual good grace.

The two experts, naturally, were not in agreement. The first concluded that it was an exceptionally grave and tenacious case of dengue fever, a kind of malign influenza, or, rather, the particular pestilence of the Orient. It resulted, precisely, from Saint-Magloire's declaration that two or three weeks previously, the Baronne had been shown an entire consignment of superb carpets from Persia and Turkestan, brought to Paris by an Armenian salesman.

"Do you see the connection?" exclaimed Dr. Avigdor, a tall, thin authoritarian individual dressed up to the nines, with the mannerisms and gestures of a bad-tempered cavalry-officer. "Do you see the connection? It's by means of the vehicle of Oriental carpets that influenza came to Europe in the wake of the Exposition Universelle of 1889.

"Now, what is influenza if not a particular form of dengue fever, attenuated by environmental influence. But here, we're facing an acute and exceptionally serious case, because the attenuating effect of the environment has not had time to take place. The microbe has acted immediately, in all the plenitude of its virulence. As you can see, all the classic symptoms of the fever are there—to an unusual degree, it's true—beginning with the extreme depression, almost comatose at times, the feverish state, the lack of appetite, the insomnia, the emaciation."

"However," said Olivier Martin, timidly, "the deterioration of the cutaneous tissue, the baldness..."

"Even that," Professor Avigdor retorted, "even that, my young colleague. In a number of cases of pernicious dengue fever, one observes papuliform eruptions, with ulcerous desquamation of the skin and, in consequence, hair loss."

And he cited references, among others Dr. Bum of Smyrna,[63] the uncontested master in matters of maladies particular to the Orient, especially dengue fever.

The other professor, however, a cheerful fat man with a flowing beard, always in a suit and white cravat, with a velvet collar frosted with dandruff, Dr. Dominique, did not share that opinion. "Dengue fever," he said, "has never put anyone in this state. People can die of it, of course, and often do, when the case is serious, but then the dying is not as slow, nor the *ante mortem* ravages as profound.

---

[63] There was an outbreak of dengue fever in Smyrna in 1889, but the name of "Dr. Bum" does not feature in the published medical reports of the occurrence.

"Besides, hardly anyone ever dies of dengue fever itself, but of latent defects awakened by its shock—of renal or pulmonary congestion, of an embolism, a heart attack, etc., for example—the consecutive weakening of the intoxication *sui generis* having deprived the patient of the necessary endurance. The patient then falls in the direction of inclination.

"This is something else. It seems to me that no hesitation is possible. Madame de Saint-Magloire has *generalized scleroderma*. The deterioration of the tegument, nails and nervous system, the algidity, the vasomotor disturbances, the hyperesthesia, the sensation of progressive constriction, the psychological poverty and the resistance to all attempted treatments—it's all there, I tell you."

Dr. Dominique's hypothesis was, incontrovertibly, the more plausible, although it was far from being entirely satisfactory. It was unusual, for instance, for scleroderma, an insidious and terrible malady, to attack a robust young woman like Eléna, who was not apparently within the jurisdiction of rheumatic diasthesis, tuberculosis, syphilis or arteriosclerosis.

However, Lemoine and Olivier Martin rallied, at least provisionally, to Dr. Dominique's opinion. Even Avigdor, not without muttering between his teeth and expressing reservations, ended up bowing to the majority.

By common accord therefore, the appropriate treatment was begun: arsenate of soda, inoculation of artificial serum, unctions with an icthyol-based liniment to render flexibility to the skin and cause the ulcers to scar over, and electrolysis of the spine.

"We'll see what that produces," concluded Dominique, who, in his capacity of doyen, had taken up the pen. "I'm afraid, though, that this gradual weakening will continue for a few more days, or that some visceral complication will appear—always a danger with such asthenia—which will be fatal and irremediable. It's a pity! Such a beautiful creature!"

Lemoine lowered his head and blew his nose noisily. He felt tears pricking his eyes, and did not want, at any price, to let a dolor show that would have given away the secret of his heart to the malevolent and the malicious. He sensed, however, that his old colleague, with his great pathological experience, was only too correct.

"Ours is a poor science! Wretched scientists we are!" he exclaimed, when he finally went down the Avenue des Champs-Élysées half an hour later, alone with his pupil. "Come on! Do you believe, personally, my dear friend in this diagnosis of scleroderma that we've both countersigned?"

"Frankly, no, I don't believe it," Olivier replied, "but of all the hypotheses put forward, it's still the least unreasonable. It's necessary to accept it as a last resort, but I'm like you; I have my reservations."

"Alas!"

The two physicians continued to walk in silence, as if absorbed by their sad reflections. They had just reached the Place de la Concorde when Olivier Martin stopped abruptly, prey to a sudden emotion, and grasped Lemoine's arm.

"Tell me, my dear master," he said. "Don't you think that this incomprehensible case resembles, unmistakably, the effects—generalized, of course, and multiplied a hundredfold—produced on an organism by prolonged exposure X-rays of exceptional power?"

One might have thought that lightning had struck the ground at Lemoine's feet.

He shuddered, his eyes wide open, with a convulsive tremor, as if some monstrous spectacle had been offered unexpectedly to his eyes.

"Thank you! Oh, thank you!" he stammered, desperately.

And, without being able to say any more, without shaking Olivier Martin's hand, he stated running, his hat slipping sideways, waving his arms like a madman. The Porte-Maillot/Hôtel-de-Ville omnibus was passing by, almost empty; he leapt on to the platform with an acrobatic bound and, leaving his friend dumbstruck in the middle of the road, he disappeared in the direction of the Rue de Rivoli.

The veil had just been torn away.

He could see. He knew. He had understood.

IV. The Sign

Alone in his study after taking care of all current business, Monsieur Cardec was plunged in the examination of the Rozen file.

After the conference in which he had taken part in the office of the Minister of the Interior, the head of the Sûreté, to whom the moral support of the supreme master of the police had given a redoubtable energy, had devoted himself to a profound investigation.

The President of the Council had kept his word, and special resources had been granted to Monsieur Cardec in order to send the finest of his chief inspectors to Guiana, seconded by an active and resourceful agent who knew the colony well, having been stationed there several times as a soldier in the marine infantry and then as an aide to an explorer, before returning to Paris.

Before their departure, the head of the Sûreté had pointed out to the two sleuths the principal directions in which they were to conduct their research. Firstly, he had admitted as certain the hypothesis of an error regarding Rozen's death.

Indeed, in spite of the most meticulous search, nothing had been found along with the shreds of the convict uniform bearing the number 883—Rozen's number—but the debris of a single human body. Could not those remains, plausibly, be those of the boatman exile whose escape had coincided with that of the famous crook? Nothing permitted the affirmation that they were Rozen's.

In sum, the colonial authorities had issued the death certificate on the evidence of shreds of clothing found in proximity with bones. Was that sufficient?

Those bones had been exhumed. At the express request of Monsieur Cardec, the reconstitution of the skeleton had been undertaken in Cayenne.

At that precise moment, there as a young physician on a mission to the colony who had been a pupil of Lacassagne, and who was familiar with the celebrated exercise conducted by the illustrious professor in Lyon. Scientifically, Lacassagne had determined, from remains found at Millery, the exact height of the man to whom they had belonged, and that determination had permitted the identification of the cadaver of the unfortunate Gouffé, murdered by Eyraud and Gabrielle Bompard.[64]

---

[64] The murder of the court usher Toussaint Gouffé in 1889 was one of Goron's most famous cases while he was head of the Sûreté. After Alexandre Lacassagne had confirmed that the body dumped near Lyon was indeed Gouffré's, Goron eventually identified the adventurer Michel Eyraud and his girl-friend Gabrielle Bompard as the likely murderers. The trial in 1890 caused a sensation, partly because Bompard's defense claimed that she had been an unwitting accomplice acting under hypnosis.

The young physician had also interested himself in the curious anthropometric theories of Bertillon, and had cultivated a meticulous expertise in determining, to within a few millimeters, the height of the escaped convict. Now, the latter was five centimeters shorter than Rozen!

When Cardec received the telegram from his chief inspector informing him of this result, he ran to the Prefect and the President of the Council, and immediately alerted them. They agreed to keep the important information secret.

Thus, one point had been determined: if he was dead, Rozen had not perished in the place where the fragments of the convict uniform had been discovered.

What had happened there?

Moving from one deduction to another, the head of the Sûreté had arrived at the conclusion that the bandit had killed his fellow escaper in order to take possession of his clothing. Rozen had contrived a macabre stage-setting designed to deceive the authorities and pass himself off as dead.

That hypothesis was entirely natural, but it was insufficient to have established the error of the penitentiary authorities. It had been established that the recovered bones were those of the boatman—but that did not prove that the Levantine was still alive. It was not impossible, in fact, that he had succumbed after having killed his companion.

An intensive search had been carried out, and nothing had been found, but that search in the forest inevitably lacked precision. They could have passed close to Rozen's body twenty times over without discovering it. Thus, Cardec had instructed his agents to continue their investigation as soon as they knew the result of the medico-legal analysis of the bones fund on the bank of the Maroni.

A statement by Madame Lavardens revealing that her husband had had a commercial establishment in Valencia had permitted the head of the Sûreté to give his agents more precise instructions. In Lavardens' papers, the widow had been fortunate enough to find the names of the employees of the deceased's branch office in Valencia. It was, therefore, in that town that the enquiry ought to be pursued meticulously.

Success had crowned the efforts of the chief inspector and his associate. They had been able, after patient and laborious enquiries, to lay their hands on one of the accountants of the rubber business funded by Lavardens. That employee, questioned and shown a photograph of Rozen supplied to the agents of the Sûreté, had recognized the Levantine, whom he had seen on two occasions at his employer's place of business. He even remembered that Charles Lavardens had, between the two visits from the escaped convict, asked for a thousand francs from the safe, and had, to the cashier's great astonishment, justified the withdrawal by citing "advertising expenses."

In the course of their peregrinations, the inspectors had even been fortunate enough to find a tavern-keeper in Valencia who recalled having seen Rozen in the company of another man, short and thickset, whose description was unfortunately not very precise—but the tavern-owner had formally identified Rozen when the policemen had shown him the anthropometric photographic print.

Thus, there was no more doubt. 883 really had succeeded in escaping, and it was reasonably certain that he was still alive—but the results of the enquiry stopped there. It had been completely impossible to discover what had become of Rozen and his mysterious acolyte. Cardec's sleuths had explored all the drinking dens in Valencia, but no one had been able to give them the slightest clue permitting them to follow the trail of the two men, and the thread they had been following was broken just as they thought they were within sight of their goal and might be able to follow the adventurous route taken by the escaped convict.

They were compelled to return to Paris, a trifle crestfallen—but their chief had consoled them and had observed that they could not have done any more. In any case, Cardec was delighted with the enquiry, incomplete as it was. It demonstrated indubitably that Rozen had succeeded in his escape, and that was an important point.

Moreover, in addition to the facts that we have just listed, the inspectors had brought their chief other details that might be of considerable assistance in his difficult task.

The director who had employed Rozen as a secretary, and had known about his relationship with Eléna Ruiz, was dead, but there was a liberated convict in the service of the penitentiary administration—a man sentenced to ten years hard labor who, retained by the law in Guianese territory, had been taken on as an accountant in the administrative offices.

The latter was a former notary, whom gambling and women had drawn, first into indelicacy and then into theft. Quickly ruined by a life of debauchery, he had used his clients' funds to satisfy his passion for cards and the demands of his mistresses, to such an extent that he had run off one day, leaving a deficit of several hundred thousand francs. Soon devoid of resources, obliged to sleep under the bridges of Paris, where he had taken refuge in order to avoid the clutches of the police, he had been caught up in a sweep of vagabonds and the law had sent him to Cayenne to reflect on the dangers of the queen of spades and "queens of hearts."

Fundamentally, however, the thieving lawyer was not a bad man. He had only one fault—that of understanding too late that the wealth of clients is not intended to cultivate baccarat or poker and entertain loose women. His good conduct and repentance had earned him the benevolence of the authorities in Cayenne, and as he was intelligent and capable, he had rendered appreciable services as an accountant in the administrative service.

Now, that unfortunate gambler and *bon viveur*, cured of his amorous ardors, corrected by ten years of expiation under the blazing sun of Guiana, had known Rozen when the latter was fulfilling the duties of secretary to the director, but he had known nothing of the Levantine's idyll with the governess. The sacking of Eléna, when she was found to be pregnant, had taken place without any fuss; the true reason as unknown.

However, the ex-notary knew enough to be a useful auxiliary, and Cardec had immediately taken the steps necessary for the liberated convict to be authorized to return to Paris. Aided by the Minister of the Interior, he had succeeded in obtaining a pardon for him from the President of the Republic.

All that had been rapidly done, and the ex-notary, glad to see France again, where he had never expected to set foot again, had hastened to place himself at the disposal of the head of the Sûreté. Cardec, in making use of this auxiliary, had hoped to settle once and for all the question that preoccupied him. Was Saint-Magloire Rozen?

Subsidies permitted the ex-notary to dress correctly, and the head of the Sûreté entrusted him with the mission of keeping watch on Saint-Magloire's house. To avoid his informant being influenced by any prejudice, Cardec had not made him party to his suspicions in relation to the Baron.

If Rozen's companion from the bagne recognized him, the proof was in place, and the grappling iron could be put on the banker without further ado...

After several days of sentry-duty outside the house in the Champs-Élysées and the bank in the Place Vendôme, however, the freed man had been unable to discover anything useful.

He had been told: "You will certainly see the man you knew in Cayenne, the 883 we want to recapture," but every morning, the ex-notary came to see Cardec, to whom he invariably declared: "I haven't seen anyone, at close range or from a distance, resembling Rozen."

That experiment, which he was beginning to believe to be futile, disconcerted the head of the Sûreté slightly. However, he did not want to let go of the idea that the Baron de Saint-Magloire was anyone else but the famous crook escaped from the bagne. If that were true, it must be the case that Rozen had transformed himself radically.

Dr. Lemoine had told Cardec that science permitted the accomplishment of miracles of that kind—and the surveillance of the house and the bank continued, patiently.

One day, with the aim of hurrying things along, the head of the Sûreté drew the ex-notary's attention specifically to the Baron. "Oh, Monsieur," the latter had replied, "that's definitely not him. He has a long scar on his face that his beard doesn't quite conceal, and Rozen had no wound on his face."

That's not proof, Cardec thought. *He might well have been wounded subsequently...*

In brief, they were marching on the spot. There was no more to do than don his mourning for that means, on which he had founded such high hopes. It was necessary to find something else.

Nevertheless, to soothe his conscience, Cardec refrained from relieving the bagnard of his observation-post. Perhaps, by virtue of seeing the Baron frequently, the ex-notary would end up discovering a characteristic feature of physiognomy or a gesture that would cause him to recognize the ex-883.

That hope was not realized, but Cardec did not have cause to regret his perseverance.

One evening, while he was at dinner, someone came to tell him than a man was asking to see him urgently at the Sûreté. Without taking the time to finish his meal, the police magistrate ran to his office. In the antechamber, he recognized his sentinel and ushered him in rapidly.

"You have news?"

"Yes, Monsieur."

"You've recognized Rozen?"

"No, Monsieur."

"What, then?"

"I hastened to come and tell you because…it's odd, what've seen…"

"Talk, quickly," said Cardec, impatiently.

"I saw a man coming out of the house who looked like an English bookmaker. It's the first time I've seen him since you placed me at my post. I followed him. He went into a bar, where I heard someone call him Robertson…"

"Robertson?"

"Yes, Monsieur, that's definitely the name they called him by…but it's surely not his own. He's no more called Robertson than he's English…"

While the freed man was speaking, Cardec, who was endowed with an excellent memory, tried to remember when he had head that name before—and suddenly, he remembered the individual previously arrested for brawling and assaulting a policeman, who had been released because of the intervention of the Baron de Saint-Magloire.

"In the bar," the ex-notary continued, "I was able to examine him at leisure…and I no longer have any doubt. I've seen that man in the penitentiary."

"Ah!" said Cardec, keenly interested.

"I could have talked to him, allowed him to recognize me, but I thought it prudent not to do that…"

"You were right."

"Besides, he's very easy to identify. He's just the same as when I saw him…when he was in Cayenne, employed as a mechanic on the administration's launch. His name is Bastien, known as Macaron…"

"The anarchist?"

"Yes. It's definitely him. He was in the bagne for being heavily involved in propaganda by action…in Lyon, I think. At any rate, he wasn't in Paris. I don't have the slightest doubt, Monsieur. He escaped from the penitentiary shortly after Rozen…"

At that moment, Cardec made a rapid connection between the description of Bastien and that given by the tavern-keeper in Valencia of the man he had seen in Rozen's company.

The indication given by the notary was priceless. It justified Cardec's persistence with the organized surveillance a thousand times over. Light had dawned in the mind of the head of the Sûreté. He felt that he was within reach of his goal.

What interest could the Baron de Saint-Magloire have in keeping company with this anarchist escaped from Cayenne? Why, then, had he used his influence when the pseudo-Englishman had stupidly got himself arrested for drunken brawling?

In the blink of an eye, Cardec put all those facts together. It demonstrated to him that Saint-Magloire was the man he was searching for.

Delighted, he gave a handsome reward to the improvised auxiliary who had brought him such an important item of information.

Finally! They could not be far from unmasking Saint-Magloire...but it was necessary to act prudently, in order not to alert the Baron. They had to strike a sure blow, and build up in advance a sheaf of circumstances such that the bold adventurer would be confounded, and trapped.

Immediately certain of this important discovery, the head of the Sûreté went to see the chief of the anthropometric service. He had only one photograph of Rozen in his file. A copy was immediately made of the complete file of the famous crook. The head of the Sûreté studied it at leisure, but there was nothing in the record that corresponded evidently to the description of the Baron de Saint-Magloire. If he was really on the right track, the bandit had built his new identity cleverly...

Oh, if it had only been possible to subject the banker to the scrupulous measurements of Dr. Bertillon, things might take a giant step forward. There are certain indices and certain dimensions of the face and body that nothing can modify...but the Baron surely had no desire to visit the anthropometric service. No matter how adroitly the suggestion was made, he would avoid it.

On reading Rozen's file, however, Cardec noticed that it mentioned a particular sign. On his right arm, the master crook had a tattoo of a helmeted Minerva. The face of the goddess was in blue ink, the helmet in red. It was in the disciplinary companies that the adventurer had abandoned a corner of his skin to the fantasy of a specialist.

By what means can I determine whether the Baron de Saint-Magloire bears that mark? Cardec wondered.

It was impossible to think of asking the Baronne. The poor woman was, in any case, too ill for any attempt to be made to speak to her. Oliva Lavardens would obviously have been very useful in that respect, but the Baronne had been in a disquieting comatose state for some time.

On reflection, an idea occurred to Cardec.

Madame de Saint-Lai knows the Baron well, he said to himself. *She's doubtless up to date with the performances of a client for whom she has certainly procured charming temporary companions...*

Rapidly, the head of the Sûreté scribbled a few words on a sheet of headed notepaper, put it into an envelope, and rang.

The office attendant appeared. "This letter to its address, immediately," Cardec said.

"Very good, Monsieur le Chef..."

Then the orderly gave Cardec a card he was holding.

"Send him in."

A moment later, Dr, Lemoine shook his friend's hand. "I have news," he said.

"Me too," Cardec replied.

"Oh?"

"I think we have our man."

"You're as sure as that?"

Rapidly, the head of the Sûreté brought the doctor up to date with the events just related.

"Listen, my dear chap," Lemoine said, when Cardec had finished. "Of everything you've just told me, I've only retained one thing..."

"What?"

"The discovery of Macaron. That's providential. I've come here precisely to talk about him."

"No!"

"Naturally, you're further ahead than I am...I didn't know his name..."

"Or his birthplace," joked Cardec, put in a good mood by the success he had just obtained."

"Joker!" said Lemoine, laughing. "Do you know what's happened? It's extravagant. I'll give you a thousand guesses..."

"Go on."

"Mr. Robertson is in love with Oliva."

"Damn!"

"And I think that the man, who obviously knows the banker, might, if Madame Lavardens takes advantage of the situation, give us some precious information..."

"The means is heroic..."

"Oliva's a resourceful woman. She'll certainly succeed in getting the false Englishman to talk...but I didn't want to do anything before talking to you."

"That's polite."

"Well, we're collaborators; you're the great Manitou."

"Well, the great Manitou orders you to wait. There's no point in imposing a flirtation with this Macaron on poor Madame Lavardens if I can acquire the certainty that the Baron had a blue Minerva with a red helmet on his right arm..."

"Come on, old chap—you're getting carried away by that?"

"Why not? If he has the sign, I'll have no more hesitation. I'll arrest him. He'll be subjected to the terrible measures of Bertillon…and that will do the trick, for I'm convinced that a scrupulous measurement will support us. The more I think about it, the more convinced I am. It's necessary to subject the Baron to anthropometry, willingly or otherwise…"

"But the sign?" Lemoine said. "Do you think, then, that he'll have gone to the trouble of modifying his face, his voice and his gestures, only to leave that manufactured mark on his skin?"

"One doesn't always think of everything."

"I don't deny it. You've demonstrated to me several times that the most intelligent criminals. Are often doomed by a stupid mistake—a detail that a child would have thought of—but honestly, removing tattoos is so simple nowadays, by Dr. Variot's procedure by electrolysis[65]…a few subcutaneous injections, a little pain, and the sign that was long considered to be indelible gives way to a light alteration of the skin, an almost imperceptible white patch. It would require a microscope to discover the vanished design.

"You must know that many women in the highest society have momentarily given in to the mania of tattooing. It was a kind of hysteria at one time—then the vogue passed. 'It's no longer fashionable, my dear.' Then, research was done. Scientists found the means render the epidermis of these imprudent beauties, if not intact, at least almost presentable, with the aid of cold cream."

"You might be right," the head of the Sûreté put in. Nevertheless, you know my principles. Neglect nothing. So, await the results of my research—and if our man has got rid of the sign…"

"You'll tell me, and Oliva will be authorized to make a heart beast faster."

"Agreed."

"See you soon, then, old man—and good luck."

"As you can see, the business is making progress. See you soon."

Scarcely a quarter of an hour after Dr. Lemoine had left Monsieur Cardec, Madame de Saint-Lai, alias Fifine, red-faced and emotional, made her entrance into the office of the chief of the criminal police.

"As you can see, Monsieur le Chef," the procuress simpered, "I've run all the way."

"That's good of you, my dear Madame," said Cardec, ironically. "Sit down. I have some unpleasant things to tell you."

"Oh?"

"Yes, for some time, you haven't been keeping a close watch on your clientele."

"Me! I can assure you that my house…"

---

[65] The method of tattoo removal first publicized in 1888 by Gaston Variot involved the use of tannic acid; it is still in use today.

"I'm very well informed," the head of the Sûreté, smiling, "And if you continue, I shall be sadly obliged to ask Monsieur le Préfet to close it..."

"That would ruin me! Merciful heavens! But...I have nothing for which to reproach myself..."

"Are you quite sure?"

Fundamentally, Cardec was attempting intimidation. He was quite certain that the brothel-keeper, like all her peers, must have more than one peccadillo on her conscience. Even though the surveillance of brothels was not strictly within his remit, he was not unaware that Fifine, confident of the influence of some of the people she entertained, pushed her trade to the extreme limits. He strongly suspected her of procuring young girls for respectable gentlemen, who were not at all respectful of them.

The subtle informer was too clever for the law to be able to stick its nose into her underhanded practices; she took a thousand precautions when she exceeded the limits tolerated by the police—but the head of the Sûreté was lying in order to get at the truth.

"Are you quite sure?" he repeated, looking severely sat the procuress, who gazed at him pen-mouthed and trembling—and when she did not reply, either because she was too emotional or because she judged it prudent to remain silent, Cardec added: "I must tell you that our indulgence is coming to an end. You no longer have any tips except for the excellent Baron..."

"Monsieur de Saint-Magloire?"

"The very same. You're truly intelligent, and it's a pleasure to talk to you..."

"Well...he..."

"He pays generously, doesn't he? Money doesn't always buy happiness, though. There are certain immunities that are worth more than banknotes to you."

"Have I ever refused you anything? Go on—put me to the proof. You need information. Go on...I'm ready." Fifine had said that with a sincere urgency. She yielded to the temptation to avert the danger that Cardec had cleverly allowed her to suppose.

"What I have to ask you is very delicate in its nature," the magistrate continued.

"Oh, between us, why worry—there are no chaste ears here. One can..."

The head of the Sûreté stopped Fifine's speech with a hand gesture. "The Baron's one of your biggest clients..."

"Money-wise, yes...for sex, no. The lovely Reyval is sufficient for him."

"Then he's never...?"

"Never."

"That's a shame, for what I have to ask you, you can't get from Mademoiselle Reyval."

"Why not?" said Fifine, audaciously. "There are no secrets when one knows how to get them…and I know little Germaine."

"No, I can't ask you to do that."

"Is what you want to know so very terrible?"

"Well, no…it relates to an intimate detail of the Baron's person."

"Oh, if that's all it is, I know the details. Go on, then, speak! He receives me sometimes in is dressing-room, when he's in a hurry. With me, you know, that doesn't count. As he says, I no longer have a sex…I've seen the banker's anatomy. A handsome man, too…

"I'm listening."

"Well, my dear Madame, it's a trivial matter, and I don't know why I took so many detours in getting to it…but I need you to be discreet, and that's why I'm taking so many precautions."

"Mute as a carp."

"In any case, an indiscretion would cost you dear…you remember what I said to you just now…

"Yes, yes," said Fifine, anxiously. "I promise you that I'll be as silent as the tomb."

"I'll tell you, then, that one of my friends is writing an article on tattooing in high society. He's documenting it as best he can. Someone has told him that the Baron has an admirable tattoo."

"The Baron! Not him!" the procuress exclaimed, clicking her thumbnail on her teeth.

"You're sure of that?"

"Of course I am!"

"Nothing on his arm?"

"Nothing, I swear to you."

"Thank you. I'm grateful to you."

"Is that all?"

"Yes."

"You're not very demanding…"

"Yes I am…for I don't want anyone to know what we've said here."

"That silly thing…come on, I'm not a child…*au revoir*, Monsieur le Chef. And no more naughtiness like just now, eh? Life's hard today…"

"Just be careful—and above all, don't neglect the Prefecture. I'm giving you good advice."

"I hear you. Adieu…"

Fifine scurried away, the rustle of her silk shirts soon fading away in the long corridor of the Sûreté.

As soon as she had gone, Cardec picked up a postcard and rapidly traced a few words addressed to Lemoine: *You were right, my friend. The subject has practiced Variotomy. You can organize what you mentioned. Tibi. Cardec.*

The head of the Sûreté went in person to throw the card in the box at the Tribunal de Commerce, and went for a long walk along the quais.

While walking, he thought: *What Lemoine proposes might be useful, but I still think that we'll be victorious when Bertillon has spoken.*

V. Robertson's Flirtation

Discreet as the steps taken by Monsieur Cardec and Dr. Lemoine had been, they had nevertheless been discovered, at least in part, by the Baron de Saint-Magloire.

The banker did not know that those two terrible adversaries were so close to the goal they were pursuing; it had never occurred to him that he might be arrested at any moment, but he knew that in Cayenne, the bones of the boatman that 883 had killed had been identified, and that discovery made him anxious.

Momentarily, Saint-Magloire had considered the possibility of leaving Paris, buying a yacht and setting off on a long voyage, but he had abandoned the project. First of all, Germaine Reyval refused to go with him, and he did not want to leave without the woman with whom he was increasingly smitten.

That skeptic in love, that fighter for life, who had posited in principle that the slightest attachment might be fatal to him, that rake who, until now, had considered women as playthings, reproached himself all the more bitterly for his infatuation with the actress. He had often tried to suppress that passion, but his fine resolutions had always vanished as soon as he saw Germaine.

He had repeatedly called himself an imbecile and a lunatic, and told himself that the girl would one day lead him to do something irreparably stupid, but he was no less the slave of his mistress. Dulac's murder had only exasperated his passion. The cantatrice did as she pleased with the adventurer, the bold criminal for whom the lives of others counted for so little. He was like a little dog at her feet. She humiliated him be deceiving him with a second-rate actor, and Rozen accepted it, pretending not to know about it in order not to lose his idol.

He spent money madly to satisfy Germaine's slightest whims. When he had suggested buying a yacht in order to undertake a superb excursion, the singer had not only vetoed the proposal but had succeeded in having her lover buy her a magnificent item of jewelry with the money he had earmarked for the voyage that was, in his eyes, salvation.

With the turn of mind particular to people who always want to see things favorably and intoxicate themselves with hope in order not to mourn reality, however, the Baron had come to be grateful for Germaine's refusal.

It would have been stupid of me to leave, he told himself. *What have I to fear, after all? They know that Rozen isn't dead, that's understood—but am I not the authentic heir of the Barons de Saint-Magloire? Have I not established my new identity in an indubitable fashion? Why tremble? I'm still solidly on my feet, and the devil may take me if ever those gentlemen, including Cardec and Lemoine, reach their goal...*

And gradually, he was reassured...

With regard to Eléna, he had nothing to fear, and his confidence was so great in that regard that he no longer kept watch on the actions of Madame Lavardens, placed with the Baronne, as we have said, under the name of Vauclair.

Gaston Rozen was wrong, however, not to keep watch on the widow, for at the very moment when he was most tranquil on that subject, Oliva was working on her vengeance.

In conformity with Dr. Lemoine's indications, Madame de Saint-Magloire's lady companion had encouraged Mr. Robertson to pay court to her. The fake Englishman was walking on air.

An idyll! With a chic woman! That changed Bastien, who, until then, had only ever dared to chase after women with price-lists, from whom a louis or two bought much more pleasure than the most ardent declarations.

The intrepid drinker was no longer seen in the bar; he almost never went to the racecourses—to such an extent that Robertson's acquaintances unanimously declared that he had gone "loopy."

Oliva experienced an instinctive repugnance whenever the man came near her, but she suppressed her disgust and played the coquette for him; little by little, she gave him hope.

Although the role seemed painful to her honest nature, and even though her loyalty suffered in laying a trap, even for a miserable bandit, she had consented to play the comedy in order to gain Bastien's confidence. She knew that the man had been in the bagne—Lemoine had told her so—and she thought that could get him to talk, and to find out from him who this Rozen was who assiduously frequented the Saint-Magloire house.

Oliva had often suspected that the Baron might be the man she sought. She had never imparted that suspicion to Lemoine, but it had gradually gained substance in her mind.

Oh, if Macaron let slip the truth in a moment of thoughtlessness! What a triumph! And Charles Lavardens' window sacrificed everything to succeed in that.

She remembered the failure she had experienced with the magistrates involved in what they persisted in called the Beuzeville-Bréauté "accident." She had been deemed a monomaniac, dismissed as a madwoman—and she told herself that her joy would be doubled if she could finally unmask Rozen and deliver him to justice. Firstly, Charles Lavardens would be avenged, and that was Oliva's sole preoccupation; secondly, those gentlemen of the Le Havre court would receive a rude lesson for the dismissive fashion in which they had treated her formal accusation.

And the young woman had thrown herself into police work with an ardor; given herself over entirely to that rude task, guided and encouraged by Lemoine. She had become ambitious in her idea of vengeance, and, in order to achieve the result she was ready to try anything, to dare anything. It was for those reasons that she had agreed to flirt with Robertson.

Macaron thought that he was loved—and with the best will in the world, he became languorous, attentive, almost gentlemanly.

Of, if Madame Lavardens had known that the amorous swain whose dream she was caressing was none other than her husband's killer! Bastien would not have been long delayed in expiating his crime. Bow how could she suspect that Rozen had had an accomplice, and that the wretch in question was there, beside her, talking sentimental nonsense?

Sentimental! Macaron had become exceedingly sentimental. When he saw Oliva, he blushed like a girl, took the widow's slender hand delicately in his gross trembling paw, and bore it religiously to his lips.

Once, he had assiduously frequented theaters where melodramas were performed. He had been one of the enthusiastic street-urchins in the gallery, and remembered what he had often seen juvenile leads of in comedies and dramas. He strove to imitate them, certain, deep down, that such attentions capture a woman's heart. He was irresistibly funny when he murmured, in the bad English accent that he felt obliged to maintain: "Oh, my darling, your beauty brings joy to my little heart..."

It was difficult, however, for the former urchin of the faubourgs always to remain calm and correct, and a mad desire often took hold of him to take things further, to seize the object of his desire in his arms and crush her lips with a wholehearted kiss—one of those "real Parisian pecks," as he thought of them.

Once, he had attempted that demonstration, but Oliva had stopped him coldly with a severe glare.

"Shocking! Mr. Robertson. I'm an honest woman..."

"Yes, yes, milady...but amour is making my blood boil...and I beg your pardon for the sudden impulse..."

Which, in Macaron's mind translated as: *Zut! The tart's a bit of a prude!*

Instead of driving him away, however, the resistance he encountered rendered him even more amorous. He recalled that at the Théâtre des Celestins in Lyon, he had seen lovers maintain a polite restraint in that way until the day when, passion overflowing, they threw themselves into one other's arms stammering, desperately: "I love you! I love you!" And Bastien aspired with all his heart to that delicious abandonment, which was not coming soon enough for his taste.

Cleverly, Oliva exasperated her suitor. She wanted to bring him to the point at which confidences are made, in order to interrogate him about his past and find out how he had met the Baron de Saint-Magloire. She hoped that, entirely hers, he would give her the key to the mystery, and lay in wait for an opportunity to make him give himself away, to oblige him to discard the disguise he persisted in maintaining—and in order to arrive at that denouement, she favored the gallant with meaningful glances, sighs that set his heart pounding, and handshakes that set his head on fire.

Days passed in such skirmishes.

Macaron, madly smitten, could no longer control himself. In Oliva's presence, he was no longer his own master. His face lit up; his eyes shone; the phlegmatic Robertson melted by degrees to give way to the hot-headed Parisian, enterprising and bold, who mounts an assault on a heart with the same fury with which he assaults a barricade.

The widow Lavardens kept track of that transformation attentively. Finally, when she judged that the time was right, she resolved to employ more forceful means. Under the pretext of a violent headache, she had confined herself to her room, and Mr. Robertson had received authorization to come and obtain news of his "beloved."

She received him in a suggestive state of partial dress, nonchalantly lying in an armchair.

It was not without a struggle against her intimate sentiments that Oliva had consented to push matters that far. More than once, she had experienced an almost-insurmountable disgust in letting herself be courted so closely by a man the sight of whom horrified her. She had often thought that the task was beyond her strength. Her modesty was offended by delivering herself thus to the desires of the former convict—but in moments of weakness, it seemed that she heard Charles's voice saying to her: "Avenge me, my love. All means are good to punish the cowardly bandit who has separated us. There is no disgrace in pursuing a noble task..."

Finally, she had vanquished her disgust, repressed her scruples, abdicated her modesty and armed herself with courage for the definitive combat. Seemingly languorous and amorous, she waited for Bastien, fully decided to make him lose his head.

When he came in, she held out her arm to him and said, in a plaintive voice: "It's you, my friend. Thank you for coming. It does me good to see you."

Bastien, who was not prepared for this reception, lost his self-composure completely. His heart was beating precipitately; blood rushed to his face.

Oliva was adorable. The matt pallor of her face brought out the gleam of her eyes; her superb throat was provocatively detectable in the gap in her dressing-gown, and her round arms with a nacreous sheen appeared, bare, beneath the lace of sleeves cut short at the elbows.

It did not need as much to throw Macaron into confusion.

Adieu the rigid envelope of the British bookmaker. Adieu English accent...

He precipitated himself toward the young woman, fell to his knees beside her, lifted up the lace on the arm that he had taken in his hands, and in the pure tone of Belleville he murmured: "Oh, how kind you are. Truly...I'm dreaming...I'm dreaming..."

While speaking, he placed rapid kisses on the satin skin of the woman's lovely arm...

Oliva let him do it.

She was suffering cruelly; the man's kisses were burning her like a red-hot iron...but the pain was reduced by the thought that she would avenge Charles.

Emboldened by that first success, Bastien thought the moment opportune to attempt a decisive assault...but before he had time to get up, Oliva was on her feet.

If, carried away by the situation, intoxicated by the woman's perfume, enfevered by the sight of the superb creature that he thought of as already his, Macaron no longer had his free will, Oliva was, by contrast, entirely mistress of herself, and firmly determined to stop if he exceeded certain limits.

"No," she said, gently. "Later, Mr. Robertson...when I'm your wife..."

"Later! Later!" Macaron repeated. "Why not right away? I love you...I adore you, you see...of, I'll never wait so long to prove to you that I love you..."

"Shh!" Madame Lavardens interjected, coldly, shoving Bastien away vigorously. He took a few steps backward, tottering and grumbling: "Damn! What a grip!" Coldly, he went on: "Why shh! Never in my life...come on...it's not reasonable... I love you, I tell you...I'm crazy...and..."

"I'll ring and have you thrown out if you go on—and it will be over...over!"

These words had the effect of a cold shower on Bastien's skull.

Crestfallen, his arms limps, his eyes moist, he stammered: "No...I beg you...beautiful child...I'll be good...as gold..."

"Good. Look, sit down here, facing me, and let's talk, Mr. Robertson..."

"That's right," Macaron replied, *"jaspinons..."*

"What?" Oliva asked, maliciously.

"Don't get upset," muttered the anarchist. "It's argot...it slipped out..."

"Villainous expressions! How do you know argot, Mr. Robertson, and why are you speaking French without an accent now...or, rather, with the accent of natives of Paris?"

"I'll tell you...it's because...I'm English without being English...that is to say, my parents were English, but I was born here. While very young I left for England...but I sometimes have the accent of one country, sometimes the other..."

"Yes, I understand," said Madame Lavardens. "It's very odd..."

"Isn't it," Macaron riposted. And he added, privately: *What a gaffe, Emperor! Luckily, the tart's not too bright.*

"Yes, that sometimes happens. I once knew a foreigner who often reverted to the accent of his native land..."

"Of course, of course..." Bastien stammered. "And it doesn't displease you?" he asked, putting a brave face on it.

"On the contrary. I'm delighted that we're compatriots..."

"Oh! Then I'm glad now, for I was afraid..."

"Of what?"

"Well, I thought that...that you'd permitted an Englishman..."

"I'd have granted it much more gladly to a Frenchman."

"That's nice..."

"And now let's talk, Mr. Robertson, for I have some serious things to say to you. You love me, don't you?"

"Can you ask?"

"For my part, I confess that I'm not indifferent to you."

"Only that?"

"Don't force me to make a confession at the expense of my modesty. We women..."

"Yes, yes...understood...don't go on...one understands hints..."

"So we need to think about marriage...

"About...conjugal...yes, of course. Oh, I'd never get bored with a little wife like you..."

"Good—but marriage is a serious matter."

"Sure...it's a chain...what..."

"A household without fortune...is a bagne."

Bastien started and suddenly went pale.

"What's the matter?" Oliva asked.

"With   me...nothing...nothing...well...on   hearing   you   talk about...marriage...I   was   thrown   off   balance...everything...it's the excitement..."

Oliva had scored a direct hit. As we have said, she had learned from Lemoine that Robertson, alias Macaron, had served a term in Cayenne, and it was with that intention that she had inserted the word "bagne" into the conversation—but Bastien could not grasp the true import of the word.

He had pulled himself together, and went on, good-humoredly. "Marriage, a bagne? That depends. When one's truly in love...like us..."

"Yes, Mr. Robertson, you're right...but love doesn't last forever...and for a household to be solid, it absolutely must have money..."

"Yes, yes...I understand..."

"Now, for my part, I have no fortune..."

"Alas..."

"And I like luxury..."

"Me too..."

"Now, luxury...with the position you have..."

"That's true. I earn my living, though..."

"That doesn't alter the face that your situation is precarious."

"Prec...yes, certainly."

"I will only marry a man capable of providing me with clothes, jewels…my ambition doesn't go as far a demanding a house, horses and carriages…"

"Thank God!" sighed Bastien.

"But I would like at least…to keep the pot boiling, as they say, a budget of twelve thousand francs…"

"Damn!"

"That's only a thousand francs a month. If you can't give me that, it's better to renounce our…liaison…right away. What point is there in further suffering?"

"And what if I told you that I can give you them—the thousand bullets?"

"Alas, I believe that you're laboring under an illusion."

"Illusion? Oh, no! Not at all. I'll have them, I tell you. Twelve thousand a year…that makes…let's see…"

"It amounts to a capital of four hundred thousand francs, at three per cent."

"Your arithmetic is good."

"Too good, unfortunately, since I'm demonstrating the impossibility of the happiness that we had promised ourselves."

"Hang on…I can get them…"

"You?"

"Exactly. With a hundred thousand francs well invested on the Bourse…yes, of course…the Boss is ready for a coup…"

"Who's the Boss?"

Macaron hesitated just long enough to stop the name that rose to his lips.

Oliva had leaned toward him, seemingly impassive, but prey to a vivid anxiety. Was she finally about to know? Was she about to receive the certainty that her suspicions were well-founded? Would the bandit's name that she wanted to hear emerge from Robertson's mouth?

But he did not let the name slip. "M'sieu le Baron de Saint-Magloire, of course," he said. "He doesn't refuse me anything.

"Ha ha!" said Madame Lavardens.

"Ha ha!" repeated the pseudo-Robertson, piqued by the doubt she seemed to be expressing. "Since I tell you so, it's certain. Bastien never lies."

"Your name is Bastien?"

"Yes, that's my forename. Bastien Robertson."

"It's a nice name. Bastien…Bastien…"

At that moment, Bastien thought of playing a finer game; he wanted to sugar the pill for the widow, inspire confidence in her, give her the assurance that the marriage could be made. He hoped to dazzle her with the idea of having the luxury she desired…and he promised himself to elope in the English fashion before appearing before the mayor; supplying his birth certificate would certainly be a obstacle to the marriage ceremony.

"You'll see," he said. "I tell you that Monsieur de Saint-Magloire will advance me the hundred thousand bullets."

"I repeat," said Oliva, "that you're losing your head now. Think—a hundred thousand francs is a lot of money."

"The Baron will fork out. I've rendered him services, damn it."

"Yes, I know—in England."

"In England and elsewhere."

"Have you known him for a long time then?"

"Some...and he wasn't always rich. We were mates...when he was poor...out there in America..."

A violent ringing sound cut short the dialogue at the precise moment when Macaron was getting tangled up, when Oliva thought that she had finally grasped the thread that would lead her to the truth...

She already had the clear conviction that the Baron de Saint-Magloire had been Bastien's companion in Guiana—but was he the man that she wanted to deliver to justice? She promised herself that she would take further profit from the advantage that she had just gained over her suitor and resume the conversation later.

"The Baronne is calling me," she said. "We'll talk about this again another time...Mr. Robertson."

Bastien got up, utterly dazed, intoxicated by the perfume of the room and the coquettish attitude of Oliva, whose gaze generated small frissons under his skin. He kissed the charming arm that she held out to him amorously.

"Soon," he said, as he left the room, followed by Madame Lavardens. "And I'll get the hundred thousand francs, you can count on that...the Baron will fork out...and with that capital, I'll soon have made what we need..."

Oliva went into the Baronne's apartment.

As Bastien was leaving the house, however, he met Rozen, who was coming in.

"Where have you come from?" asked Gaston, looking his acolyte up and down.

"I...I...came to talk to you, Boss..."

"And for that you went upstairs?"

"Yes...no..."

Nervously, Saint-Magloire took Robertson by the wrist. "Bastien," he said, in a muffled voice, "you've been coming here too often of late. I know...I've noticed...you assiduity toward Madame Vauclair..."

"So what? I have every right...you're in love yourself..."

Rozen dragged Macaron into his study, and carefully closed the door. "Listen," he said, severely. "I understand that you're seeking to amuse yourself...but there are toys that I forbid you to touch..."

"Impossible," Bastien said, with a hint of mockery. "Me…who was counting on tapping you for a large sum…"

"What?"

"Yes—a matter of making myself a dowry."

"A dowry? You're getting married? To Madame Vauclair?"

"So what? Isn't that allowed?"

Gaston had a desire to seize his accomplice by the throat and strangle him. With his keen intelligence, he understood the danger there was in allowing Macaron to continue his maneuvers in respect of the widow. He could not sack Madame Vauclair, of whom the Baronne was very fond. Give Eléna's condition, that dismissal would have caused a scandal—but at present, he had to avoid anything that might be compromising, and Macaron's flirtation was extremely perilous. Madame Vauclair, placed by Lemoine, might be able to get the imbecile to talk, one day when he was drunk…

All those thoughts occurred to Rozen in the blink of an eye.

"All right," he said to Bastien, "But it's a bad time. Eléna is ill…she needs Madame Vauclair's devoted care. You have to wait. I can see where you want to go…this marriage…"

"A sham, of course!"

"That's your business…but take it as read that if you set foot here within a month, you'll regret it…"

"Threats?" growled the anarchist.

"No—advice. You know very well that they're taking a keen interest in Rozen at the Prefecture. They're looking into escapes that coincided with mine…"

"Damn!" murmured Macaron.

"Personally, I'm unrecognizable—but you're easy to catch. Do you want to end up back out there?"

"Oh, no! What should I do, then?"

"Well, old chap," said Rozen, softening his voice, "you'd do well to go to London for a month or two…where it's foggy. Afterwards, you can resume your little love affair, if there's an opportunity…"

Although these words were spoken in a placid tone, they were nevertheless imperious.

"That's true," declared Bastien, to whom this altercation with Gaston had returned all his self-composure, and who remembered now the imprudent words he had allowed to escape in Oliva's presence. "Your advice is good…but look…life in London is expensive, and I'm broke…"

The baron opened a cash-drawer, took a few thousand-franc bills out of it, and handed them to Macaron. "With that," he said, "you won't die of starvation."

"For sure," said the pseudo-Robertson, joyfully. "This evening, I'll decamp. See you soon, old friend…I'll write to you…"

"Yes—but banal letters, of course?"

"Don't be afraid—I'll be careful…and then, if, by chance, things get hot…sleep easy; I'm no informer."

"At this moment," murmured the Baron, anxiously, "I'd prefer to see you over there. You've nearly smashed everything once before…"

"Yes—the brawl with the cop…but I'll kept my eyes open from now on, my old mate. Give me the nod when I can come back…"

"Yes…*au revoir…*"

That same evening, Robertson left for London.

Macaron was a little put out at having to leave the lovely Madame Vauclair just as he thought he had finally touched her heart, at the precise moment when he imagined that she would no longer refuse him anything…but Rozen's order was formal; there was no messing about with the terrible Boss, and Bastien also took account of the fact that it was in his own interests to play ball.

Bah! he said to himself, by way of consolation, *two months will soon pass. I have the cash to numb myself, and when I get back, we'll resume the assault on the lovely widow!*

He intended to write to Oliva from London, to tell her that urgent business had obliged him to make the trip, and that he had only gone in order to make the large sum necessary for their marriage.

Oliva, in giving Dr. Lemoine an account of the interrupted conversation she had had with Bastien, told him how disappointed she was.

"Never mind, my dear friend," the doctor replied. "What you've obtained is very useful to us…and I thank you for having consented to play the role…"

"To avenge Charles," the widow declared, "I told you that I would do the impossible…I even sense that I have the strength to strangle this Rozen myself if I ever have the god fortune to hold him in my hands."

Madame Lavardens kept to herself the conviction she had acquired in making Macaron talk. She did not know that Messieurs Lemoine and Cardec already had strong suspicions as to Saint-Magloire's true identity.

"Patience, patience," said the doctor. "The hour of punishment is getting nearer. We'll soon get our hands on the bandit."

"May God hear you, Doctor!"

VI. Radium

All Paris knew that Madame de Saint-Magloire was ill, in danger of death, slowly being killed by an unknown, incomprehensible illness that the princes of science did not understand.

Furious at not having been able to make his diagnosis prevail, Dr. Avigdor, who was very much a socialite and got around a great deal, did not hesitate to repeat everywhere that Dr. Dominique did not know what he was talking about, any more than Dr. Lemoine, and that scleroderma had nothing to do with the case.

By the very admission of one of the consultant physicians, therefore, they were in the presence of a mysterious, almost supernatural case, defying all the resources of science and art. Avigdor no longer dared risk the hypothesis of dengue fever.

In the salons, the clubs, the editorial offices, the Bourse and Parliament, no one was any longer talking about anything but the Baronne's illness. The medical journals discussed it endlessly, evoking the most absurd suppositions—a matter of permitting their editors to put on a display of erudition. The daily newspapers limited themselves to publishing a daily health report, ever more pessimistic, for the symptoms never stopped getting worse. It was the event of the day: an event that was simultaneously political, medical and social.

At the same time, though, in the most various milieux, people never tired of eulogizing on the subject of the Baron de Saint-Magloire, whose amorous devotion was already forging a sentimental legend, and whose dolor, it was said, was painful to see.

"What a husband, my dear Madame, and what a tender heart!"

"It makes one feel better about those rascals, men!"

A few evil tongues, however, belonging to incorrigible skeptics or enemies of Saint-Magloire, whispered the ominous word "poison" in dark corners, sugared with sarcasms.

That suspicion had crossed Lemoine's mind at the very start, as soon as his first hesitation. Was not Gaston Rozen capable of anything? So the scientists had begun exercising an attentive surveillance with regard to the Baron's comings and goings, spying on his slightest gesture, when he came continually to obtain news of Eléna, to approach her bed, and when he sat down beside it.

When Lemoine was not watching himself, it was Dr. Olivier Martin who took that responsibility, or the worthy Madame Lavardens, who sat up with the dying woman almost every night.

Oliva had incredible energy and stamina; those long periods of sleeplessness and continuous fatigue did not seem to have any effect on her delicate body, which had the vigor and suppleness of pure metal. Her complexion was always as fresh, her lips as pink and her smile as heady.

If Lemoine's heart had not been gripped by a horrible anxiety, he would not have failed to remark that fine valor, and as he was normally inclined to be witty, he would probably have observed that widowhood and vengeance rather suited Oliva Lavardens.

The truth is that the pretty widow had not been insensitive to the discreet and timid court paid to her between treatments by Dr. Martin, who, without even being consciously aware of it, had been struck by lightning on seeing her for the first time. A serious but profound passion gradually grew, in spite of the sadness of the situation, between the two individuals, both young and equally seductive.

She had adored her husband, whose death she had to avenge, and had devoted herself body and soul to that work of justice, but one cannot, when one is twenty-one years old, when one is charming and one knows it, wear mourning for one's love eternally.

Perhaps, underlying Oliva Lavardens' devotion, deep down, there was a certain unconfessed desire to find herself in Dr. Martin's company, to live in his atmosphere, to breathe in his breath, to brush his hand, and to showed herself to him in the sympathetic role of a Sister of Charity.

That burgeoning romance did not prevent Martin and Oliva from observing the Baron attentively. For his part, Lemoine mounted a good guard, but he had never glimpsed anything suspect, any more than his friends. Saint-Magloire's attitude was always absolutely correct. It was that of a husband plunged in grief to the point of losing his head, no longer knowing what to do or whom to ask in order to save his adored wife. Never, moreover, did he touch Eléna, except to take hold gently of her emaciated hands and cover them with kisses; he never touched her medicaments, let alone attempted to administer them himself.

If he's tried to poison his wife, Lemoine said to himself, secretly, *it can only have been done once, at the start, at a single stroke...but what is the poison whose slow and cumulative effects could act in this fashion in a single dose, once given? And yet, that must be the case, for we don't lose sight of him, and I'm sure that he hasn't been able to do it again. He wouldn't have been able to, even if he wanted to; he's too closely watched now. We are, therefore, on a false trail!*

We know that eventually, increasingly bewildered, and no longer having confidence in his own knowledge, Lemoine had ended up becoming discouraged. It was then, on emerging from the consultation that he had organized himself, which had told him nothing, or even enabled him to glimpse anything, that Martin had, by chance, perhaps without even attaching any importance to the conjectural insinuation, mentioned the resemblance between Madame de Saint-Magloire's case and the amplified, intensified and generalized effects of X-rays.

It was as if the scales had suddenly fallen from his eyes!

He had sensed that this time, once and for all, he must have grasped the key to the insoluble enigma—and without losing a moment, he had run to the Quai des Orfèvres.

"We need," he said to the head of the Sûreté, after having made him party, impatiently and angrily, to his discovery, "to make a search of the bandit's private apartments. We'll find the coil, the Crookes tube, the entire infernal apparatus of murder that is set up there, I'm now sure, behind the wall. Then we'll have him, since we'll have the proof, visible and palpable, the crucial evidence...we'll catch him red-handed."

Cardec, however, remained unmoved by these impetuous objurgations. He had taken on the irritated expression that one adopts before a spoiled child who wants to be given the moon.

"My poor friend," he said, finally, when Lemoine, completely out of breath, saliva and arguments, let himself fall into an armchair, shivering, "passion's caring you away. How do you expect us to mount a search of the Hôtel Saint-Magloire? Under what pretext? On what evidence? We'd need a warrant, don't forget—a legal warrant. Who will sign that warrant? Who will take the responsibility? How will it be drawn up, anyway—according to what formula, with what reason?"

"But it there's a suspicion of murder...!" cried Lemoine, furiously.

"Now, now...let's not get carried away. Is there an explicit denunciation, a piece of evidence, or plausible information? No, there isn't. So let's not discuss it any further."

At a gesture of protest from Lemoine, Cardec continued: "I know that you could lodge a complaint yourself, take upon yourself the burden and the risk of the denunciation—but do you believe, frankly, that it would have any result, except to compromise you and ruin you forever? In spite of the Minister's keen desire to make progress, no matter what the cost, he wouldn't dare approve such a search. So, neither at the Ministry nor the Palais, would anyone want to go forward. No one would listen to you. Since the unfortunate business of the Dulac autopsy, you're already under a cloud up there. Once is bad enough, twice would be too much. People would say that you bring bad luck and that a wind of error and misadventure is blowing around you. You'd be out on your ear."

In spite of his excitement, Lemoine sensed the strength of the magistrate's argument. Too often, already, in the last few months, he had vaguely taken account of the fat that the agents of the law would not forgive him for leading them into an impasse. Perhaps they thought, as he did, that the Baron de Saint-Magloire was an arrant rogue, an adventurer of the most dangerous kind, of whom it would be useful to be rid, but they did not want, at all costs, to hear "stories" in that regard—and Lemoine passed for a man who had "stories" and whose "stories" turned out badly, resulting in the confusion of those who had the imprudence or poor judgment to get involved.

The orders were, therefore, to keep him to one side.

"I'll force their hand!" he cried. "Yes, I'll force their hand! The government's afraid of the press—well, I'll tell the newspapers everything. They'll have to move, when there's a public scandal."

"Are you completely insane?" replied the head of the Sûreté. "You're talking about newspapers! Where is the newspaper that will publish three lines against Saint-Magloire? Isn't the entire press, which he inundates with his sumptuous publicity and associates with is business affairs, entirely devoted to him? There's no paper, of any party, that doesn't count, in order to make ends meet, on his press releases, his advertising, his share-options, not to mention the friendships he's built with the bosses of the principal editors. There isn't, in consequence, a single paper, a single journalist, sufficiently independent to take him on. No one dares be disagreeable to that charming man, who's powerful enough to sink anyone imprudent enough to attack him. You're not thinking about the consequences—they're enough to shut the mouths of the boldest.

"You'll only find, to accept your accusation, even documented, shady blackmailers and dodgy financiers who hope to be paid for their silence—who won't get any further anyway, for the man has a large hand and a subtle eye. You'll only have succeeded in discrediting yourself and wasting your gunpowder on sparrows, with no gain at all. No one will believe your romance. They'll attribute ignominious motives to you—you'll be the villain. At the very least you'll pass for a lunatic, a monomaniac with a persecution complex."

"The press! The newspapers! You're behind the times."

The head of the Sûreté had risen to his feet. He advanced toward Lemoine, who was literally overwhelmed by this avalanche of sound arguments. The doctor was too Parisian, too much "in the know" not to grasp their excellence and range.

"Besides," Cardec continued, in a tone pierced with commiseration for his friend's profound distress, "there's something else. Let's talk swiftly, and to the point.

"Let's suppose that, with or without the collaboration of the press—a possibility whose inanity I've just demonstrated—you had succeeded in communicating your conviction to the Prefect of Police or the public prosecutor, and even to the Minister of the Interior and President of the Council. Am I not generous? Going even further, I'll assume that a legal search-warrant has been obtained, and that the Hôtel Saint-Magloire is searched from the cellars to the attics, and that we discover, in the room next door to the poor Baronne, a radiographic installation...how would we be any further forward? Is it not perfectly explicable that one should have such apparatus in one's home? It's not, if I'm not mistaken, prohibited by any law or police regulation. You have yourself—don't deny it, for I've seen it-everything necessary for radiography..."

Lemoine tried to speak, but the magistrate imposed silence on him. "Wait a second," he said. "I haven't finished. Let me ask you one question. Sincerely, between you and me, do you believe that X-rays could produce the frightful effects that you've described to me?"

"Yes," Lemoine replied. "I believe it. I'm even sure of it—provided that one has a sufficiently powerful apparatus."

"Are there precedents?"

"At that degree of intensity, certainly not—but there's a host of individual cases, less serious and localized, which permit me, reasoning by analogy, to conclude with near-certainty..."

"Yes, I understand: more induction, more theory...all scientists want to get a grip on the question of whether or not X-rays might have a terrible effect. Well, my poor friend, we haven't finished! It would be Dulac's poisoning all over again: still murky—with the aggravating circumstance that in Dulac's case, Olivier Martin had some scientific presumptions, some experimental probabilities, to throw into the balance, while this time, we're floundering in the realm of pure hypothesis.

"There isn't the slightest illusion for you to entertain. Even if—which I think improbable, if not impossible—the law were to follow you that far, you can be sure that, just as you thought, your anticipations having been confirmed by facts, you were in sight of the goal, the big prize would slip through our fingers.

"Do you want me to tell you what I think? Well, the law wouldn't have been entirely in the wrong. Don't protest! Hear me out. I'm very fond of you, Lemoine, as you know; I consider you not only as the most honest man on earth and the best of friends, but as an outstanding scientist, and I bow down before your genius. But in this case, I'm afraid that preconceived ideas might have given you hallucinations.

"Whatever you say, I can't admit that X-rays—which sometimes burn the hands of operators, I know, when they remain exposed for too long at close range to their radiation—are capable, even multiplied by a hundred or a thousand times, of killing anyone in such conditions. Do X-rays work through walls, then?"

"Certainly," Lemoine retorted, thinking he had finally found the chink in his interlocutor's armor. "Certainly! Those rays pass through all bodies with a greater or lesser facility, as if they were glass. The thickness of the screen might be an obstacle, but it's not an insurmountable obstacle. There are even some substances that put up no resistance at all..."

"All right," said the head of the Sûreté, "I understand...strictly speaking, you might be right...but in this case, it's not sufficient to be right; it's necessary to convinced others that you're right. Far from being an article of scientific faith, one of those crushing verities that impose themselves on everyone authoritatively, your theory presents itself as a paradox for which it's necessary to begin by furnishing the experimental and demonstrative proof, and which will run into universal incredulity.

"We'll fall back into polemics, contradictory evidence, all the sterilities of the controversies of legal medicine. We'll never get out..."

"There's a god for murderers!" cried Lemoine, in a despairing tone. He understood all too clearly that the head of the Sûreté was right, and that the game was lost again. Although the hypothesis that had abruptly crystallized in his mind had certainly appeared to him, the more he thought about it, more plausible and more probable, he realized that it could not be of any use to him. It was not the means by which Rozen would be caught.

"There is, nevertheless and immanent justice," the magistrate went on. "Fortunately for the police, because, without the collaboration of that immanent justice which we cal chance, we'd fail to apprehend eight criminals of out ten— but that immanent justice only acts in its own way, and in its own time. Our skill consists of always being on the alert, in ambush, ready to pounce on any opportunity that it wishes to offer us. We're not there yet; let's be patient! It will come, one day or another."

Lemoine went away, with death in his soul. He went straight back to the Hôtel Saint-Magloire, where he found Dr. Martin and Madame Lavardens sitting, not saying anything but not without exchanging languorous glances, at the bedside of the dying woman, who was asleep, as if overwhelmed by a almost comatose torpor.

Struck by the emotion that his allusion to X-rays had provoked in his master, Olivier Martin had also reflected further. Gradually, light had dawned in his mind. He was not mistaken; he could not be mistaken. The suggestion, which he had initially made lightly, without attaching much importance to it, and which he had formulated on the spur of the moment, to settle his conscience, had ended up taking on substance.

It was certainly plausible. It must even be true, for it was the only possible rational explanation for so many mysterious phenomena.

I'll make sure of it, he said to himself—and before resuming his sentry duty beside the unfortunate Eléna, he had gone to his laboratory, where he furnished himself with a screen coated with barium platinocyanide, of which he made use in his operations in radioscopy. Once back at the house, taking advantage of the Baronne's torpor, he closed the blinds and lowered the curtains in such a way as to produce almost complete darkness. Then, unfolding the piece of paper in which he had wrapped his screen, he placed it at the head of the bed, directly above the sick woman's face but slightly to the rear, a few centimeters from the partition wall.

Immediately, the plate lit up with a green-tinted phosphorescence.

Olivier Martin then placed his left hand between the screen and the wall. As he expected, the skeletal image of that hand, in which the bones appeared with the slightest details of their ridges and articulations, with a penumbral halo, was clearly projected on the fluorescent surface.

The young man could scarcely repress a cry of triumph. Scientific proof had confirmed the accuracy of his hypothesis, seemingly so hazardous. The barium platinocyanide on the radioscopic late, becoming luminous without any apparent cause, as soon as it was placed close to the all, must necessarily be in contact with X-rays, which were invisibly traversing that wall, behind which something abnormal was occurring.

Given that, there was no need to look for midday at four o'clock, no need to evoke, for the needs of the case, the specter of some kind of scleroderma or unknown influenza. The inexplicable illness could be explained quite naturally.

When Lemoine came in, the windows were still hermetically closed, with their blinds down and their curtains drawn—but in order not to lose the reflection of Oliva's lovely eyes, Dr. Martin had lit one of the electric lamps. At the sight of his master he switched it off abruptly and, picking up his screen again, he brandished it in the darkness, while he squeezed Lemoine's hand as if to crush it.

The same mysterious glow shone again, producing a light so bright in its sly phantasmagoria that their facial expressions were as clearly distinguishable as in daylight.

"Well," murmured Olivier Martin, "what do you think of that, Master?"

"Yes," Lemoine replied, in a blank voice. "Yes, it's the proof, the material justification of our suspicions. But what good is it? No one would believe us! The hour of justice hasn't sounded yet."

"The conclusion isn't useless, though. Now that at least we know what we're dealing with, now we know the source of the illness, perhaps we'll be able, if not to repair the damage, at least to interrupt its ravages. Just as long as it's not too late!"

And, leaning close to his pupil's ear, he outlined his plan briefly.

Olivier Martin nodded his head approvingly, while he looked at Lemoine with a attention in which there was a much admiration as respect.

Lemoine asked Madame Lavardens, who was following the scene with increasing interest, to switch on the light. Had they not obtained from the darkness all that they needed to know? Then he gave the order to pull the bed away from the homicidal wall and place it as far away as possible, at the far end of the room, beside one of the windows overlooking the garden.

Martin went out, bearing precise instructions. Half an hour later he returned, followed by a domestic carrying an immense three-leaf windbreaker, which seemed to be very heavy, draped in black silk, with white woodwork and glazed panels at the top.

This item of furniture, as ugly as it was cumbersome, was set up in front of the patient's bed, which it dominated by more than a meter.

"What's happening?" Eléna suddenly asked, awakened by all the fuss and raising herself up on one arm, painfully. "Why has my bed been moved?"

"Don't talk, my dear friend, I beg you—and lie down again. You'll be much better here. It's brighter, and you'll no longer be troubled by the draught from the door, as you were over there."

"Oh!" said Eléna, falling back on her pillow, as if exhausted by the effort. However, looking at the windbreaker, which she had never seen before, she murmured: "And why that horror?"

"Let me do as I please," Lemoine replied. "That 'horror' has its utility…its very great utility."

In the grip of torpor again, Eléna was no longer listening.

"Yes," Lemoine continued, *mezza voce*, as if talking to himself, "that horror has its utility. Painted in lead-based colors, glazed at the top, draped with silk down below, I'll be damned if that horror doesn't stop the accursed X-rays. And when one eliminates the cause, one must suppress the effect."

Drawn by a feverish curiosity, however, he went to stick his ear against the wall against which the Baronne's bed had previously been set. He listened for some time; then, summoning Olivier Martin, he asked him to listen in his turn.

A vivid surprise was painted on the features of the two scientists.

"That's strange," Olivier Martin finally said. "To produce such terrible effects, an enormous power is necessary, a colossal machinery…we ought to be able to hear through the wall, if not the crackle of sparks, at least the hum of the coil. But we can't hear anything—nothing at all. Perhaps he apparatus has just stopped—perhaps it's only active during the day?"

Lemoine's only response was to show him the radioscopic screen, which he had just retrieved from an armchair and as holding in mid-air, parallel to the wall.

The apartment being inundated with light, since Madame Lavardens had reopened the shutters and drawn back the curtains, the illumination was less obvious than during the initial experiment. Nevertheless, the fluorescence of the barium platinocyanide was undeniable.

Furthermore, when Lemoine placed the flap of his jacket over the plate in the form of a veil, the phenomenon reappeared with all its denunciatory intensity. The X-rays were not extinct; the homicidal waves were still passing invisibly through the opacity of the wall.

Lemoine questioned Madame Lavardens, who knew the house. What was behind the wall? But Madame Lavardens did not know, except that there ought to be a kind of library-cum-smoking-room, in which the Baron had the habit of shutting himself away with one or other of his most intimate friends to discuss confidential business matters. When he was here, alone or in company, he forbade any disturbance.

Cleverly interrogated, an old sewing-maid, who had been living in the house since the financier had taken up residence there, was a little more explicit. In the library-smoking-room, she explained, there was a kind of black cabinet, closed by a large door equipped with mirror-glass. The cabinet occupied the entire width of the wall separating the two rooms. It was always locked, and Monsieur kept the key in his pocket. It was assumed that Monsieur made use of it for experiments in photography.

Olivier Martin and Lemoine looked at one another. It was obviously one more presumption, but nothing precise—not proof.

For now, that was of little importance, for more decisive proof would not have been much use. The conviction of the two physicians was now firm, of course. It was there, in that secret cabinet, that the fabulous engine of death was set up, which had done its work all too well.

At that moment, Saint-Magloire appeared in the doorway. More cleverly composed than everyone else, he was wearing the mask of anxiety and contained dolor that he had been displaying everywhere for days—but he had o sooner noticed the displacement of Eléna's bed than the mask gave way to a rictus of fury.

His eyes sparkled, his teeth clenched, and his entire face convulsed; one might have thought it the face of a wild beast, from which some other ferocious beast of the same size wanted to snatch away its prey. It was only a frisson, as rapid as lightning—but Lemoine had seen it.

Standing in the middle of the room, with his hands behind his back, he stared at the Baron, ready for any attack. For a second, the gazes of the two men met, and clashed like sword-blades.

Olivier Martin was to say later that he thought he had seen, at the point of intersection, a spray of sparks, so taut were the two hostile wills, materialized after a fashion.

Lemoine had not the slightest doubt: the man he had before him was a murderer caught in the act. More than ever, it was a war to the death between the two men.

The Baron de Saint-Magloire had also understood. With the marvelous composure and astonishing self-control that made him, in dramatic circumstances, almost a supernatural being, he soon got a grip on himself. That diabolical man was capable, when the need arose, of controlling his own heartbeat, and slowing down the circulation of the blood in arteries stiffened by an effort of will. He could not only command his emotions, the quivering of his flesh, but also the automatism of vegetal life itself.

He had no difficulty composing his features in the face of the peril whose imminence he had sensed at first glance. It was in a natural voice, without the slightest quaver capable of denouncing the interior storm, but in which a slight hint of surprise was nevertheless distinguishable, that he demanded to know what the unexpected rearrangement signified.

"Why has the position of the bed been changed, Doctor? Were you afraid that our poor dear might catch cold over there?"

"Indeed, Monsieur le Baron," Lemoine replied, now sure of himself, and having succeeded, not without a superhuman effort, in mastering himself. "I did indeed fear air-currents. You know how sensitive Madame is to the slightest change in temperature. She has hyperesthesia to an extraordinary degree. I took it upon myself to have her transported here, where she is not exposed to the same inconvenience, and by an excess of precaution, I had this screen placed around her bed.

"Then again, there's something else. In maladies such as this one, which afflict the entire nervous system, I've noticed that the direction of *decubitus*[66] has a certain importance. Patients seem to suffer less, or at least seem calmer, when their bed is orientated in the direction of the terrestrial axis, the foot turned toward the North, parallel to the magnetic attraction. I acted in consequence."

Saint-Magloire had a politely ironic smile, which uncovered white teeth as sharp as a wolf's. "Yes, yes," he said. "I've heard mention of that theory, of which medical youth is found. Do you believe in such tricks, Doctor?"

"My God! I adhere to it without yet believing in it, having not yet collected enough personal observations to appreciate their clinical value...but there's certainly some truth in it. I've studied the subject sufficiently to be able to affirm that the day is coming when we shall have a secure grip on many of the occult forces that are invisibly active around us, and which govern our lives and our health without our suspecting it, by action at a distance, even operating through walls..."

At this point, Saint-Magloire, thinking it a direct assault, could not suppress a shudder. He leaned over Eléna, who as still unconscious, and planted a long kiss on her forehead.

When he straightened up again, he had resumed his heart-broken expression; no one could have suspected the frightful thoughts that were agitating behind that broad forehead—that of an intellectual, and artist and a leader of men—on which only dolor seemed to have cast its shadow.

"Do the best you can," he murmured, bowing sadly to Lemoine and Martin, "as long as you save her for me."

He had scarcely closed the door when all that controlled serenity, so well-feigned, suddenly vanished. The face of the wild beast reappeared. It would not have taken much for the formidable flood of rage that he had so much difficulty containing for the last ten minutes to explode abruptly.

Is that quack a sorcerer, then? he thought. *Unless he's Satan in person, how has he penetrated that secret, of which Sokoloff himself, in spite of his genius, would not have thought? But I don't have any time to waste solving the puzzle. There isn't a moment to lose. Let's begin by getting rid of the* corpus delicti—*that might be compromising, with such a bloodhound on my trail. We'll see about settling our accounts thereafter—but your goose is cooked, my little Doctor Beelzebub! Oh, you permit yourself to interfere in my game and counter my trumps! You'll what I have up my sleeve! You've just signed your death-*

---

[66] A medical term for "lying down."

arrant. You first! Later, I'll get back to the good wife. Besides, she's sinking fast now...

While muttering these silent threats, Saint-Magloire had shut himself up in the library-smoking-room adjacent to Eléna's bedroom.

The place was, indeed disposed as Madame Lavardens and the sewing-maid had described.

The Baron took a key out of his pocket; he opened the mirror-clad door of the mysterious cupboard, into which he went, emerging a few minutes later with an enormous glass jar under each arm, coated externally over half its surface by a thick layer of black varnish, and filed to the brim with fragments of a strange substance, metallic in appearance, brilliantly white tinted with pink, resembling bismuth.

He carefully placed the jars in the bottom of a suitcase; then, having closed all the doors behind him, he took the package downstairs himself, climbed into the electric automobile waiting outside the door and set off at full stream—or, rather, full fluid—toward a unknown destination.

All trace of the crime he had committed—or at least attempted—had thus disappeared.

Lemoine and Martin had, in fact, guessed correctly, or very nearly. It was not by means of X-rays that Saint-Magloire had thought of getting rid of his wife. That would have required apparatus that was too cumbersome, and above all, too noisy. His infernal genius had suggested an analogous method, more redoubtable still, while being more discreet.

He had replaced the X-rays with radium,[67] the fabulous metal whose spontaneous radiation—doubtless due to the continuous emission of imponderable particles capable of traversing the thickest and most opaque screens by means of a kind of atomic bombardment—is endowed with the same properties, but to a superior degree, producing the same effects with no sound or elaborate apparatus.

The idea had come to him on remembering the accident that had befallen a scientist—was it not Monsieur Becquerel himself?—who had brought a small specimen of radium in his trouser pocket to the Académie des Science on day, in

---

[67] Radium chloride had been discovered by Marie and Pierre Curie in 1898, causing a sensation akin to that caused by the discovery of X-rays three years earlier, but it was not isolated in its metallic state until 1910 and remained fabulously expensive thereafter, rendering Saint-Magloire's liberal purchase extremely unlikely. Marie Curie had been a student of Henri Becquerel, who had rediscovered the radioactivity of uranium (first observed in 1857) in 1896. Although the burning effect of X-rays was rapidly observed, the actual effects of radiation sickness were not fully understood until long after the publication of the present novel, which was probably the first—but by no means the last—example of a crime novel in which radiation is used as a murder weapon.

order to carry out certain experiments before the learned assembly, and had been surprised to feel a burning sensation in his thigh...

He also knew that people who handled the bizarre substance were not long delayed in seeing the tips of their fingers covered with stubborn ulcers that persisted for months on end.

He had therefore bought all the radium that he could find for sale in Germany. It had cost him very dear—exceedingly dear, in fact, for the preparation of radium is very arduous, and, in consequence, very expensive; in fact, it requires tones of mineral to be processed in order to extract a kilogram of radioactive matter—but Saint-Magloire did not care about the expense.

When his provision of homicidal ammunition was complete, he made every effort, in his laboratory at Auteuil, by means of devices of his own invention, which he had not communicated to anyone—not even Sokoloff, although he appreciated his transcendent science at its full value—to augment the power of the radium. He had succeeded beyond his own hopes. His exasperated radium had become a terrible instrument.

It was then that he disposed his batteries in the darkroom adjoining Eléna's bedroom, directly behind the head of her bed.

We know the rest.

Never had such a frightful crime been planned with such refinements of science, art and mystery. It had required all the sagacity of Lemoine and Olivier Martin, aided by a combination of fortunate circumstances, to see through the demonic plan, which was reminiscent in certain almost-magical ways of the spells of the alchemists and the sorcerers of the Middle Ages.

The next day, after having spent the night at Eléna's bedside—at which, contrary to his habit, the Baron had not shown himself again—Lemoine decided to attempt the experiment with barium platinocyanide again. This time, the screen did not light up.

The doctor, who had not thought of radium, assumed that the Baron had prudently switched of his Crookes tube. Although he was mistaken, it was scarcely necessary that he had drawn the correct inference.

Shortly thereafter, the Baronne's condition began to improve significantly.

VII. The Bird-Ship

Eléna had been saved.

Once again, the ingenuity of science, put in the service of good, had succeeded in undoing the infernal machinations of that same science placed in the service of evil.

The emanations of radium having ceased to be projected through the wall, with the appearance of continuous bombardment of fulgurant and toxic atoms, the pathological effects began to disappear. The cause of the disease having been suppressed, there was nothing more to do than let nature take its course, and the robust constitution of the Baronne de Saint-Magloire would do the rest.

The convalescence would doubtless be long—very long, terribly long. She would need weeks or months, and would require infinite precautions, for her organism, afflicted in its very sources and essential mechanisms, had suffered a frightful disruption, but the cure was sure; Eléna would certainly recover her former vigor, suppleness, youth and beauty.

The amorous joy of Dr. Lemoine would have been perfect and boundless, therefore, if he had not seen, by the same token, his vengeance escaping him. From that viewpoint, though, the game he had won so well seemed simultaneously to have been lost, until there were further developments.

Accusatory presumptions against the Baron were accumulating on a daily basis, suspicions taking on increasing precision, but material proof, the only thing capable of striking one of those sledgehammer blow from which the strongest never get up, continued to be lacking.

It was in vain that the two Sûretés—the Parisian Sûreté and the Sûreté Générale—had sent forth their most far-sighted and subtle sleuths on campaign. It was in vain that the Place Beauvau and the Tour-Pointue had unleashed the entire swarm of informers, amateur and professional auxiliaries, even grand dames and demi-mondaines, into the marsh with secret depths. The hounds always came back empty-handed, with not one vague clue, not one line baited with a quasi-certainty.

Saint-Magloire, who had his intelligence-sources, conscious or unconscious, in place, was always tipped off in good time about the investigations commenced. Immediately, he made his countermoves, with a diplomatic skill and a tactical fecundity tending literally to genius. He soon piled up tenebrous complications, imbroglios of semi-contradictory revelations, in such a fashion as to draw the investigators on to false trails ending in blind alleys.

It was at this point that the Ministry of the Interior, the Prefect of Police, the director of the Sûreté Générale and the head of the Sûreté began to suspect the fidelity of their agents and wonder whether that strange impotence had not been bought.

That was an error. The professional loyalty of police inspectors, poorly paid as the services of those useful and devoted servants of society might be, is above all temptation, and the adventurer's money had nothing to do with the abortiveness of their efforts—at least directly, for it goes without saying that the money in question served indirectly to sow in all directions the ambushes and illusions by which they were trapped with an extraordinary candor. It was only among the unofficial informers that the Baron found corruptible auxiliaries, whose indiscretions he funded. Even the majority of them were partly unaware of the importance of their treasons.

At any rate, as the convictions of the authorities became firmer, the mystery thickened even more around the filibuster of the Place Vendôme, whose political and financial power seemed, by a singular antithesis, to have reached its apogee.

Lemoine felt traces of discouragement infiltrating the metal, rudely-tempered as it was, of his justice-seeking soul. He expressed that one day, while at lunch, to his usual confidant, Dr. Olivier Martin.

"For two pins," he told him, "I'd abandon the struggle. The task is definitely beyond our strength. Only immanent justice, whose time infallibly comes, is capable of putting an end to it."

"Stick to it, my dear Master," Martin replied. "Stick to it. Last night, I had an idea."

"I'm listening," replied Lemoine. "Speak! But I have no great hope. Haven't we already studied, and even tried, the entire spectrum of practicable ideas?"

"One never knows! In any case, my idea is entirely new. Not only has it never been tried, but thus far, neither you, nor I, nor anyone else has thought of it. Follow my reasoning.

"Since police inspectors and your own agents are following Saint-Magloire day and night, we know almost everything he does, hour by hour, except when he's locked up in that infernal villa in Auteuil, isolated in the midst of waste ground and market gardens, where he spends a few hours from time to time. He even sleeps there sometimes. I'm convinced that it's there, and there alone, that we have a chance of finding the key to that ambulant enigma."

"I think so too," murmured Lemoine.

"It's there, behind those opaque walls and tall, narrowly-closed gates, that the jackpot lies. I've had that presentiment for some time. Saint-Magloire ostentatiously affects to take women with him when he goes to Auteuil. Germaine Reyval, in particular, is a regular…it's a matter of making the indiscreet believe that it's a love-nest, a small house specially fitted out to shelter the gentleman's secret escapades and debauchery—who gladly poses as a rake, affecting the morals of the ancient régime. I'll bet my head that it's a sham, though, a cover. Strange noises can be heard emerging from that accursed house, and strange lights are sometimes seen there. Something other than orgies is going on there."

"Certainly," Lemoine replied. "The house is, moreover, inhabited by a mysterious individuals, an American scientist named Smithson, I think, who's doubtless the Baron's damned soul. Alas, all that is talking without saying anything. To know, it would be necessary to see—but no one can get in. Even the cleverest have come up against insurmountable walls and orders.

"In order to get through the door, it's necessary to have a search-warrant...and to obtain a search-warrant, to extract that 'Open Sesame!' from the indecision or pusillanimity of the Law, it would be necessary to have got through the door in advance. Always that damned vicious circle."

"I'm glad to see that you share my way of seeing," Martin continued. "Given that, things will develop of their own accord, for you're bound to approve my plan. Since the supreme desideratum is to discover the secret of the house in Auteuil, we have to find a way of getting in there, by fair means or foul, at all costs.

"Well, when one can't get through the door, one goes through the window. When one can't go underneath, one goes overhead. I don't know whether I'm making myself sufficiently clear."

"To tell the truth, no," replied Lemoine, nonplussed.

"It's quite simple, though. Suppose that we could make use of a dirigible balloon, and fly over the lair, with a good telescope..."

"The idea isn't bad, in truth. We might at least be lucky enough to discover some precious clue. Unfortunately, neither you or I have a genuinely dirigible airship at our disposal...

"I only began to look at the problem myself, which seemed to me not to be insoluble as it seems...it was even going quite well, but I didn't have the time, and I'm no further forward than before. Other researchers are, I believe, at the same point..."

"That's where you're mistaken, my dear Master," Martin riposted, in a peremptory tone. "The dirigible airship exists...it will be at your disposal whenever you wish. I'm talking about the aircraft invented by my friend Leloup, the famous engineer—whom you know, I believe, at least by reputation."

Lemoine shivered. "Is it true that Leloup has completed the project whose description I once put in his hands—which was a marvel, at least in theory? I thought that, discouraged by the innumerable difficulties of detail that such a problem necessarily involves, he'd abandoned the game."

"Not at all. His aircraft has been well and truly constructed. It works delightfully well. It gives the results you anticipated, which are positively marvelous. If you're unaware of the sensational event, it's because you've been absorbed with other concerns—and also because the trials have been carried out in strict secrecy. Only a few privileged individuals, having promised to keep silent, were admitted to watch them. I was one of them, and I can tell you that, save for a little residual weakness and irregularity in the engine, the problem is solved.

"Leloup admires and likes you without knowing you personally. He can't, in any case, refuse me anything. Would you like us to involve him in our game?

"Would I like it!" exclaimed Lemoine. "I'd like nothing better. I don't really believe, to tell the truth, in the final success; in these matters there's always something that cracks or breaks down at the last minute; but let it not be said that I disdain the slightest trump card! Where it this miraculous machine?"

"At Saint-Maur, is a vast park hired specially by Leloup, far from curious gazes.

"Let's go," said Lemoine, simply.

The two friends left.

The engineer Leloup's flying machine was indeed a marvel, and his childhood friend Olivier Martin had not exaggerated greatly. On the mention of the Lemoine's name, moreover, of whom he had long been one of the most fervent admirers, the inventor did not hesitate to give his visitors a tour of his installation, where three models of different sizes but of a uniform type were only waiting for the moment to take flight.

Imagine a sort of enormous mechanical bat, whose outstretched wings, with their membranes of folded silk, extended by means of piano-wire representing so many fibers, on an articulated hollow framework of wood and steel, forming a skeleton. In front, by way of a head, each of these Beasts of the Apocalypse bears two propellers, each of which cleave the air with a gigantic plume, with quill-feathers in varnished bamboo.

It was these propellers, spinning through the air at high speed, that must drag the rest of the system behind them, by aspiration, as it were, the ensemble of which—subtracting the crew, fuel and cargo—constitutes a weight varying, according to the wingspan of the model, between 100 and 250 kilograms.

The direction obtained, thanks to the play of that gentle propeller, combined with the action of a rudder operated by means of pedals by the pilot, sitting astride the back of the machine, like a motor-cyclist on his saddle.

As for the motive force, it is furnished by a pair of steam-engines of a new model, heated by wood-spirit that vaporizes almost instantly, in consequence of a sure and simple superior mechanism, whose total weight scarcely attains three kilograms per horse-power produced. Each machine directly controls its own propeller, turning in the opposite direction to the other, of which it is completely independent although the generator is unique.

The whole apparatus rests on little wheels mounted on loose axles, in order that they can accommodate all the obliquities of the ground on take-off and landing. Before taking off, in fact, it is necessary that the aircraft picks up speed by rolling for some distance on a firm track, until that speed is sufficient to maintain it, by "gliding" in the air.

Lemoine did not hide his admiration, but with his habitual mental precision and his critical capacity, he posed a number of delicate questions, to which

Monsieur Leloup, very flattered, put a kind of coquetry into answering with all desirable frankness and clarity.

"The aviation machines on which I've been working for a long time," the inventor explained, which I call 'avions,'[68] do not belong to the family of airplanes—which is to say, flying machines in the form of inclined planes maintaining themselves in the air with the aid of a motor external to the apparatus or being built into it; their general design reproduces instead, as you can see, the wing of a bat.

"Many years ago, I observed that the wings of all flying creatures, from the bat to the vulture, and from the wasp to the sparrow, form, from forwards to rearwards, in the direction of travel, a particular spiral characterized by the invariable angle of the radius with the tangents projected at different points of the curve. That spiral presents a more or less accentuated curve, according to the load on the wings, but it is invariably found everywhere. I have therefore applied that principle, from which nature never departs, and which seems to be the essential and fundamental condition of aviation, to my own apparatus.

"The forms that I have given to the frameworks of the wings closely resemble those of bats. Their seemingly-bizarre concavities are the consequence of the efforts of multiple direction that they must support. These frameworks are hollow and established according to a special method that permits me to obtain a very considerable rigidity while assuring their extreme lightness. They're maintained in position by steel wire stays.

"The wings or membranes that serve as points of support I the air are made of silk fabric; some of them are elastic, others striped with small fibers embedded in the fabric, following lines of force. The wings are articulated in all their sections and fold up completely. While in flight, the wings do not beat; they remain extended in a gliding position.

"I can say that my mechanical bat functions perfectly. I'll give you the proof." And, fitting actions to words, he sat astride the saddle and started up the

---

[68] *Avion* has, of course, become a commonplace French word, equivalent to the American "airplane," but when this passage was written it was still an esoteric term, amenable to specific adaptation, as here, in a fashion that distinguishes it from *aéroplane*. I have left it untranslated rather than substituting the term "ornithopter," although that might be a more appropriate term for what the narrative voice is describing. The text's terminology in this respect is rather haphazard; the narrative voice and various characters also refer to the device in question as an "aerostat" and a "balloon," although it is obviously neither in a literal sense. When the novel was published in 1901, no one had yet made a pioneering flight in a heavier-than-air machine, although experiments were indeed being carried out is some profusion. This passage is, therefore, ahead of its time, although it was soon to be surpassed by actual events.

motor. Immediately, the monster, quivering throughout its network of metallic fibers, began circling around the track with increasing speed.

Gradually, the sustaining wheels lifted off the ground, above which the aircraft rose up by a few meters, with a strange rustle of silks in friction. The pilot was evidently the master of his machine, for he made it describe a host of clever spirals and arabesques, without ceasing to glide at head height. Then he reduced his speed, until the inferior castors make contact once again with the "race-track," where the aircraft, after a few circuits, finally came to a halt with a kind of shudder.

"Bravo!" cried Lemoine, sincerely enthused, while Olivier Martin clapped his hands frantically.

"You'll forgive me for not going up very high," said Leloup, getting down, "but I don't want to attract curiosity-seekers, so I always remain within the shelter of my trees."

"No matter," said Lemoine. "From the moment that you rise up by the simple effect of beating your wings above the ground, even if it's only to a height of three centimeters, the problem is solved. You can fly—you're a bird!"

But the triumphant Leloup had already picked up the thread of his interrupted lecture. "Have you noticed my engine?" he asked. "As you can see, it's four-cylinder, fifty horse-power double expansion steam engine. The generator is tubular. The vaporization is instantaneous, all the exits being closed to the steam, and the pressure climbs on the manometer at one atmosphere per second. The wood-spirit that serves as fuel is burned in the liquid state or the vaporous state, projected over the fire. A special condenser on top of the carcass, fully exposed during operation to the airflow, constantly brings the water condensed on the side-walls back to the generator.

"The machine activates two propellers turning in opposite directions placed at the front of the apparatus, driving the air backwards, partly under the wings in order to lift them, and partly over the condenser to accelerate its cooling. The wings, non-beating, remain extended during operation, and the aircraft, before taking off, has to roll on its three freely-articulated wheels and gain considerable speed on the ground under the influence of the propellers.

"Those serve, not only for traction, but also for the steering of the apparatus. With that end, a lever connected to the rudder at the rear, controlled by the aeronaut's feet, resting on appropriate supports, also controls a steam-regulator belonging to the right-had machine and another belonging to the left-hand machine. When one is opened, the other is closed to the same degree. As it's the same generator that furnishes the pressure, the sum of the energy remains constant, and the evolution of the apparatus is obtained by the division of the energy combined it the concordant action of the rudder."

Lemoine was only listening to the inventor's explanations with a distracted ear, however. He had an idea.

"Would you care," he finally asked, "to let me try in my turn?"

Leloup made a gesture of anxiety.

"You have nothing to fear," Martin put in, having noticed the hesitation. "Dr. Lemoine in the mot skillful mechanic I know. "With him, the machine won't suffer any damage or snags—I'll answer for that.

Leloup nodded acquiescence, but his anguish was visible. It soon gave way to a respectful surprise when he saw Lemoine, who had leapt into the saddle with a single bound, maneuvering the fabulous machine with as much precision and sureness as himself.

When he came back down, without a drop of sweat on his forehead or a shadow of emotion on his face, where a cold resolution was legible, Leloup almost threw his arms around him. Lemoine did not notice; an absorbing preoccupation had taken possession of his mind.

"Your motor is much too heavy," he said to Leloup, incisively.

"Alas, I'm only too well aware of that. But what choice is there? Of all the various motors I've tried, in turn—steam, petroleum, even liquefied gas, it's still his one that gives me the best return for the smallest volume and weight. It's not the dream, to be sure, and I'm far from having, according to the ideal formula, a horse-power in a watch-case—but at the end of the day, it's still the most perfect among existing motors, and I doubt that one can do better in the present state of science."

"I beg your pardon," Lemoine put in. "I already have something much better. Would you care to entrust one of your airships to me? I'll take responsibility for fitting it with a motor of chimerical lightness, not even 500 grams per horse-power, the exclusive right of exploitation of which I'll gladly abandon to you when I've carried out a few experiments dear to me heart."

Skeptical and perplexed at the same time, but shaken by the suggestive confidence of his interlocutor, whose gaze magnetized him, after a fashion, Leloup did not know what reply to make.

"Oh, my God, it's quite simple," Lemoine insisted, "and I can give you all the necessary guarantees. I need a dirigible flying machine like yours for an enterprise to which I attach a capital importance—but I can't make use of it until I've fitted my motor to it. I therefore propose that I only take delivery of your aircraft when you've seen my mechanism in operation. Is that all right with you?"

"Perfectly," Leloup replied, finally having collected himself. "It's a deal! If your motor is as good as you say, my machine is at your disposal, and I'll have it taken to any location you wish." In response to an interrogative gesture from Olivier Martin, he added: "Nothing easier, for it can all be dismantled piece by piece."

"All settled," said Lemoine then, cordially shaking the engineer's extended hand. "No later than the afternoon of the day after tomorrow, you'll be fixed up—ten o'clock sharp at my laboratory."

"All settled!"

The two physicians took their leave of the engineer. They had scarcely climbed back into the electric automobile that had brought them than Oliver Martin, no longer able to restrain himself, abruptly hurled at his master the question that had been burning his tongue for several minutes. "Damn!" he exclaimed, "it seems to me that you've promised a great deal. Five hundred grams per horse-power? How the devil will you realize that miracle?"

"It's as simple as saying hello, my dear friend," Lemoine replied. "With a thermoelectric pile."

"But I thought that the thermoelectric pile, ideal in theory, had never materialized in practice..."[69]

"You were right. Neither Melloni, nor Becquerel, nor Clamond, nor Renault, nor anyone else has ever been able to obtain anything significant from thermoelectricity. They all passed the question by, having approached it from the wrong end—so even the best of their machines have never been anything but laboratory toys. Mine, on the other hand, works on an absolutely new principal.

"I've discovered a chemical substance, a metallic salt, which, treated in a certain fashion, delivers as many watts as you wish with perfect constancy, without friction or deterioration. In brief, with a weight of twenty-three or twenty-four kilograms, which can be stored and transported in a handbag, I can easily produce forty to fifty horse-power."

"Damn! That's wonderful. But how do you heat it?"

"With coal, coke, petroleum or alcohol—anything at all. Believe me, young Martin, it's a revolution. But the funniest thing is that I picked up that first-class idea while idling at table, dining at Saint-Magloire's house."

"Impossible!"

"It's just as I've had the honor of telling you. That old American was there—that Smithson we've mentioned: an eccentric, to be sure, but an eccentric of genius, so distinguished, so majestic, with strange eyes that are simultaneously those of an inspired individual and a lunatic, with a childish candor. We were talking about technology. He told me extraordinary things, with a lucidity, a far-sightedness and a logic that you can hardly imagine...of, he's truly a master, that one: a scientist such as has never been seen.

"In the course of the conversation, Smithson let slip, with regard to Becquerel's experiments with copper sulfate, a few well-chosen words that didn't fall on deaf ears. It seemed that a veil had just been lifted from my eyes, and I glimpsed an entire chain of unsuspected horizons. I had nothing more pressing to do than start experiments, which have succeeded marvelously, beyond my hopes...

---

[69] In fact, a whole series of thermopiles had been produced in the 19th century since Oersted and Fourier constructed the first in 1823, but their output was small; the 1879 coke-fueled thermopile developed by Clamond in 1879 put out 192 watts, but it was a massive device

"That's how I'm able today, to make Leloup's aircraft into something perfect. My battery is all ready; it only has to be set up, as you shall see."

Lemoine was not exaggerating. His modesty was such that, when talking about himself, for fear of overstatement, he always said too little. Is that not the trait that distinguishes men of superior but calm and well-balanced intelligence from certain geniuses whose transcendent egotism and abnormal megalomania confines them to monstrosity?

This time, Lemoine had been more than modest. In fact, his copper sulfate thermoelectric battery was a miracle. With a weight equal to the average weight of a tall man—seventy or eighty kilograms—it easily produced a hundred and fifty horse-power.

Thus, at the first trial, an agreement was quickly concluded with Leloup, whose enthusiasm was boundless. He hastened to dismantle the best of his flying machines and put it at the disposal of the scientist, who had rented for that purpose a large field surrounded by a high fence and equipped with a hangar on the Rue du Docteur-Blanche in Auteuil, in close proximity to the Baron de Saint Magloire's mysterious villa.

Lemoine and Martin set to work forthwith, in order to learn to maneuver the fabulous machine that its inventor called "the Avion" but which Olivier Martin, who liked picturesque descriptions, preferred to baptize "the Bird-Ship."

In three days, the two friends were sure of their mastery. They had their aerostat perfectly under control, and could confront the hazards of the aerial ocean with impunity.

Thanks to a curtain of tall trees that extended all around their improvised aerodrome like a screen of impenetrable verdure, their daily experiments had not attracted much attention in the neighborhood, which was, in any case, rather deserted—not to mention that aerial navigation was very fashionable at that time, causing a literal furore in a certain society. Every day, provided that the weather was propitious and the wind dropped, five or six airships of the most various forms, more or less dirigible, could be seen floating somewhere over Paris.

The blasé public no longer paid any attention to the evolution of such aerial vessels. The avion was not noticed any more or less than other flying machines. Only one scientific columnist for *Le Journal*, struck by the unusual form of the giant bat, made the periodic apparition the theme of a highly fanciful article, the ambiguous conclusions of which, in spite of their far-reaching scientific and philosophical implications, could not teach the most subtle of readers anything new.

Only the head of the Sûreté was in on the secret.

Lemoine even had installed a wireless telegraph apparatus installed in his private apartment, with an automatic recorder, in case he had to communicate interesting information urgently while up in the air.

VIII. Aerial Police

Since he had perfected Leloup's avion, Dr. Lemoine had undertaken a flight every day. He went up high enough to embrace a relatively extensive panorama with his eyes, without exposing himself unduly to the indiscretions of the immediate neighborhood.

In that regard, the location in the Rue du Docteur-Blanche was particularly well-chosen. The curtain of trees encircling the property on all sides formed the idea screen. The avion could only be seen from a distance at which it was impossible to make out the slightest detail and give substance to any suspicion, even admitting that any suspicion could arise. From below, except within the enclosure that the doctor had made into his aerodrome—at the foot of the work, so to speak—no one could discover anything.

In hunting, however, there is no real point in being invisible; it is necessary to be seen. For that, according to the picturesque expression of Olivier Martin—who, in his quality as a pure-blooded native of Montmartre, had a touch of the street-urchin about him—it is necessary to "show one's skin."

Lemoine knew that, but as his innate prudence, further emphasized by a series of disappointments attributable to some extent to haste, forbade him to leave anything to chance, he only wanted run the risk of "emerging from cover" judiciously, with the maximum number of trump cards in his hand.

So, he multiplied his trials so as to become as sure in the saddle as a professional cyclist on his steel horse. Sometimes, Olivier Martin went up in his stead. Then, they resolved to go up together, the thermoelectric motor being powerful enough to lift the weight of two men without difficulty and without fear of a loss of equilibrium. It would even have lifted more.

It was, of course, necessary for that purpose to modify the passenger accommodation—comprised, it will be remembered, by a simple bicycle saddle, less than a bracket-seat. That transformation was, however, child's play for a technologist like Lemoine. It did not take him long to find a mechanism permitting flight through the air in tandem.

The modification had taken a few days, which, in any case, had not been time wasted, because Lemoine had taken advantage of it to install a new model of wireless telegraph transmitter that he could take with him in his aerial excursions without hindering his freedom of movement.

His intention was, in case he discovered from high in the air some incident worth being immediately made known, in order to alert the head of the Sûreté without delay—in whose office, as we have said a receiver sensitive to Hertzian waves had been installed.

Finally, the moment arrived when everything was ready for them to set forth definitively on campaign. Sometimes alone and sometimes with his pupil behind him, Lemoine began to rise above the line of projection of the opaque foliage that had served as a safeguard thus far. Gradually, he even began to describe concentric circles of increasing radius around his point of departure, going so far as to fly directly over the mysterious enclosure whose secret he had sworn to penetrate.

The first experiments were not very successful. Neither in the house in the Rue Jasmin, whose windows remained hermetically sealed, nor in the immense garden, nor even in the vicinity of the building, did they ever see anyone. If torrents of black smoke had not sometimes emerged from the chimneys, whose empyreumatic odor sometimes intrigued the aeronauts lying in ambush in the clouds, and if, in the evening, they had not seen the polychromatic reflections of bizarre gleams filtering through the closed shutters, Lemoine and his pupil might have thought the house abandoned. Those indications, however, which had something akin to the color and reek of alchemy, did not permit the acceptance of such a hypothesis.

Something abnormal had to be happening behind those walls, under that roof, in spite of the apparent absence of any living being.

The reports of the inspectors of the Sûreté charged with watching the neighborhood of the mysterious house, suggested, as before, that it was a love-nest to which Saint-Magloire came surreptitiously to frolic with the diva Germaine Reyval. It was quite possible that these suggestions were correct; the two lovers had, indeed, often been seen in the little hue late at night. The observations made by Lemoine from the height of his aerial observatory, however, convinced him that the house must serve some other purpose than sheltering the amours of the Baron and the cantatrice.

One other person, the American Smithson, ought to be resident there, according to the information the police had; he rarely went out and had the reputation of being an ascetic. Lemoine knew him, by virtue of having met him once or twice at Saint-Magloire's house—and that austere individual had to have a very good reason to tolerate the financier coming to "play his pranks" there. A solid bond had to link the two men, so different in appearance and character.

It was precisely that bond that the doctor hoped to discover.

One day, he saw Smithson coming out of the house in company with Saint-Magloire. The scientist was easily recognizable by virtue of his tall stature and his apostolic head. He was dressed like a workman in knee-length trousers and a smock. He was bare-headed and his rolled-up sleeves allowed his muscular arms to be seen.

What the devil could the man be doing there? His clothing clearing indicated that he must be working, and that observation, combined with the observation previously made of suspicious fumes vomiting from the chimney, demonstrated that the scientist had a laboratory in which he was conducting research—and that research must interest Saint-Magloire, who came to visit him frequently.

The American—that was how Lemoine thought of Sokoloff, of whose identity he was unaware—had to be working for the Baron, but how could he find out exactly what the nature of that work was? Lemoine was frustrated. Far from clarifying the mystery, the observations of the aeronautical detectives were had thickened and complicated it even further.

Nevertheless, one thing was obvious: Saint-Magloire was still coming to the house in Auteuil, but no longer bringing Germaine Revyal. And when the Baron came to visit his friend Smithson he arrived in a cab, sometimes even on foot.

Lemoine attached considerable importance to these observations. He knew that the banker was not a man to put himself out, in order to make secret visits to this remote quarter, without an important reason, in which sentiment could not play the slightest role. The American must be his accomplice. He gave the impression, however, of being an honest man. Lemoine, who was a physiognomist and had trained himself methodically to decipher the most closed faces, would have sworn that he belonged to the species of worthy individuals.

The American might be a madman, a mystic, a bore or a fanatic—the asymmetrical form of his skull, the style of his gestures and his gaze denounced fanaticism—but he did not have the appearance of a rogue. A bandit could not have those limpid eyes, that frank smile and that entire appearance of honesty, almost of chivalry, which commanded esteem.

Don Quixote? Perhaps. Cartouche? Never.

But then, how could that familiarity with Saint-Magloire, and that effusiveness, be explained? The doctor deduced therefrom that Smithson was the Baron's dupe; his imagination, working overtime, began to construct an entire romance. He saw the American as some eccentric millionaire whose confidence had been captured by Saint-Magloire, with an intention that was easy to deduce. He would certainly rob him, perhaps murder him...

And the good doctor, carried away by these generous hypotheses, wondered whether he would not do well to warn the scientist, perhaps by dropping an anonymous note wrapped around a stone into his garden, letting him know that he was in bad company...

Cooler and less overworked, Olivier Martin listened with surprise to these grotesque confidences, and a word from his pupil quickly brought the master back to the reality of the situation—which was that it was necessary to determine the role this Smithson was playing: a very important role, to judge by the extreme respect that Saint-Magloire showed him, which Lemoine had witnessed in the house in the Champs-Élysées.

The question was tormenting: why was that enigmatic American, whom he had seen comporting himself as an impeccable man of the word, an accomplished gentleman at home in a drawing-room, here, dressed as a man of the people, in the costume of a mechanic or zinc-worker?

Lemoine and Martin continued their surveillance. Almost every day, sometimes several times a day, to settle their conscience, one or other of them, if not both, would straddle the mechanical hippogriff and set off to explore the atmosphere. Alas, they always returned empty-handed.

For an entire week, they saw nothing new. The American scarcely showed himself; they only glimpsed him occasionally walking in the garden with a distracted expression, still dressed as a worker. Only once did he appear dressed as a gentleman, wearing a felt hat, with a large silk scarf around his neck, wearing a worn overcoat. That day, an individual that the aeronauts had had no difficulty recognizing as Yu, Saint-Magloire's trusted Chinese servant, had entered the property mysteriously, and Smithson had gone out with him…but they soon lost sight of them in the inextricable maze of the side-streets of Auteuil.

All of that was vague, and only confused matters further. Time passed, and Lemoine was unable to give the head of the Sûreté any significant information. The nocturnal excursions that the war-weary amateur policemen ended up risking, pushing imprudence as far as to skim the chimneys of the villa, taught them no more than their diurnal ascensions. At the very most, they had observed that a strange noise rose up, comparable to the distant hum of a powerful dynamo rotating rapidly in a padded room, with dull and rhythmic pulsations, like the swinging of a gigantic pendulum.

Finally, one day when Lemoine, convinced by an overlong excursion that he had completely his time, was getting ready to come back down to earth, without any thought of returning, Saint-Magloire reappeared in the grounds, as if emerging from nowhere. This time however, he was not alone; he had brought the American another visitor: a short, thickset man, with the waddling gait, simultaneously supple and unsteady, affected by seamen ashore and trapeze-artists, characteristic of true sons of the barrières.

So far as Lemoine could tell, the individual might have been a croupier in a casino or a bookmaker. There was no doubt, however, given the attitudes of the three individuals, that Saint-Magloire and the American were treating the newcomer as a comrade. He took them by the arm in a familiar fashion.

Lemoine was flabbergasted. His thoughts were racing, and in their confusion he could not find the elements of a logical and satisfactory explanation. The doctor maneuvered the avion in such a way as to get a little closer, and gazed at the individual with the aid of his binoculars.

"But it seems to me," he murmured, "that that fellow in none other than Mr. Robertson, Oliva's suitor." Then he uttered a muffled exclamation. "Damn! They've seen me. This is no time to be flying here. Forward! I haven't wasted my time today, and my report will interest Cardec. Smithson, Robertson, Saint-Magloire. Come on! For sure, the Baron's up to something unusual…"

While talking to himself, Lemoine carried out a bold maneuver. His intention was to give the impression a simple experimental flight. He thought that might lull the suspicions of the people who could have spotted him. With a powerful thrust of the wings he took his machine up to an altitude of six hundred meters and, describing an immense circle above the Point-du-Jour viaduct, was soon out of sight of the trio.

Five minutes later, he came back at a tangent, hiding behind the treetops, just in time to see the financier, the American and the bookmaker go into an isolated outbuilding in a corner of the grounds, abruptly closing the door behind them.

Without looking back, he set about returning to his hangar by means of a slow spiral descent.

If, however, his gaze had been able to penetrate the roof of the mysterious building in which he had seen the three suspects take refuge, the doctor would have seen them keeping watch on his slightest movements. His aerial incognito had been compromised. The roles had changed; the hunter had become the hunted.

Let us leave Dr. Lemoine and penetrate, with the three colleagues, into the room in which they had sealed themselves.

Still extremely disturbed by the sight of the aircraft flying overhead, they were talking in low voices.

"Do you know," Sokoloff said to Saint-Magloire, "what that strange flying machine is? I've already glimpsed it from time to time, behind the poplars, describing arabesques in the sky."

"I don't know anything about it," the Baron replied. "One sees all sorts of dirigible balloons and such-like over Paris nowadays. Not a day goes past without someone wanting me to finance a new one. It's a true craze, and the only thing that astonishes me is that here aren't more accidents. There must be a god to protect madmen, I swear!"

"This time, you're mistaken," Sokoloff put in. "That's surely not a product of folly. It's something very interesting, very serious. I haven't been able to make out with sufficient exactitude what it amounts to, having other things to do, but I sense that he man who has constructed and is manning that machine isn't just anyone. Besides which, it's not an ordinary balloon. That bat-like thing is visibly a 'heavier-than-air' machine."

"Oh, I remember!" Rozen declared. "I must have read something about it in a newspaper. Right! But to tell the truth, I didn't pay much attention to it."

"You were wrong," the Russian replied. "That airplane works marvelously, and its pilot seems to be steering it with incredible confidence. You ought to find out who the machine belongs to…you have the means of getting precise information. Believe me, it's very important, firstly because the problem of aerial navigation is, in itself, one of the most exciting scientific questions I know—I'd give a great deal to see it resolved—and secondly, think of the powerful collaboration that such a machine could give Anarchism on the day, which I hope won't be long delayed, of the supreme battle!"

The Baron de Saint-Magloire shrugged his shoulders imperceptibly, while an ironic smile creased his lips. Nevertheless, he promised to make the requested enquiries.

"Understood," said Sokoloff. "I hope that you'll have found out tomorrow. I'll expect you here, at the same time, with Bastien."

The next day, Saint-Magloire interrogated a few journalists, but he only obtained evasive replies. In Paris, at that moment, public opinion as completely absorbed by three sensational events: firstly, by a divorce case whose protagonists belonged to the highest political society, to what is conventionally known as the "Republican nobility," and which promised to be particularly fecund in spicy and scandalous revelations; secondly, by the epic struggle of the director of a subsidized theater and a supremely pretty actress of dubious talent who had been imposed upon him, in return for her favors, by an important person close to the Head of State; and finally, by a murky affair of espionage, rapidly envenomed by political hatreds that had spontaneously seized upon that pretext to explode...there were denunciations flying in every direction, insinuations worse than formal accusations; very important people were caught up in the drama, which had emerged into the judiciary domain to the great harm of the country.

There was enough there to hypnotize boulevardian and faubourgian gossip for a long time, which curiosity the newspapers also undertook to excite with a considerable reinforcement of dramatic or piquant details. No one had the slightest idea of bothering about aeronauts, and the Auteuil avion had not attracted any more attention than the other flying machines competing for the conquest of the air.

So, when Saint-Magloire, accompanied by Bastien, went to his rendezvous with Sokoloff, he did not have anything new to tell him. The Russian, however, was in no mood to insist. He had summoned his two associates to talk to them about a matter of an entirely different sort, which was much dearer to his heart.

At his express request, Saint-Magloire had brought Bastien back from London, where he had sent him to cut short his compromising idyll with Madame Vauclair. The Baron had raised a few objections. He had declared that Macaron was in England undertaking a very special mission, making contact with several exiled comrades—but Sokoloff had held firm and imperiously demanded Bastien's recall.

In all the aggregations of the workers of France, but principally in mining centers, general strikes were the order of the day. They were being organized in the shadows, without noise or declamations, like a vast conspiracy of which the government did not even have a vague indication.

The organizers, among whom the anarchist party had been able to insert the most energetic, albeit the least noisy and the least popular, of lay apostles, had steered their course so well that no precautions had been taken by the public authorities. A few more days and the eruption would take place everywhere at the same time, to the great stupefaction of the ruling classes, in the midst of the tumult of a general panic. There was a formal assurance that the Red Unions,[70] formed by committed revolutionaries would march together to assist in the upheaval.

One can imagine the joy with which Sokoloff had greeted this news, which appeared to him to be the signal for the Great Work, the supreme goal of his life. It seemed to him that he could hear the first blast of the trumpet of the Last Judgment.

Even Saint-Magloire, in spite of the hypocrisy of his pretended convictions, was not indifferent to the movement in question, albeit for other reasons. In fact, after having tipped off the Minister of the Interior and the Minister of War as soon as he heard about it, in order that they could mobilize the gendarmerie and the army in time to nip the proletarian revolt in the bud, even at the price of torrents of blood, he had set himself up to profit from public emotion by mounting a double coup on mining shares and imports of American coal. All his batteries were in position, all his preparations made. The final result could no longer be in the slightest doubt; he would profit to the tune of a good twelve million.

That explained the triumphant and radiant expression on his face, which was normally a trifle irritated when he came to Auteuil. Sokoloff and Macaron respectively, in their naïve candor, took that expression for a reflection of the intimate seething of his revolutionary faith.

The three "comrades," meeting for the second time in order to elaborate a plan of attack, were pacing around the grounds of the property, discussing their dreams of the future in low voices, when a bizarre shadow suddenly appeared on the ground at their feet, as if a geometrically-contoured cloud had just passed over the sun.

Macaron was the first to raise his head, mechanically. "Damn!" he exclaimed. "There's that flying beast again that we saw yesterday." And, pointing his cane into the air, he designated the avion, which was floating at an altitude of scarcely a hundred meters, almost motionless, with a slight flutter of its immense wings.

"It is, indeed, a flying machine," Sokoloff out in. "See, Saint-Magloire, how curious it is and how well it flies!"

"A strange fashion of pedaling, all the same," Macaron added. "It's amazing! But damn it, one might think that the chap was spying on us. Look how he's stretching his neck in our direction. Well, my lad, you've got a nerve!"

---

[70] The French far left, at this time, marched under two opposed flags: the red flag of Socialism and the black flag of Anarchism; it was rare for the two revolutionary parties actually to join forces, although few outsiders could see much difference between their rival brands of egalitarianism, except that Anarchism, by definition, refused all appointed or elected leaders, while Socialism typically envisaged some kind of Republican, and hence Presidential, government.

"It's true," said Saint-Magloire in his turn, astonishment and anger making his voice tremble. And after having looked at the bird-ship through a little pocket telescope, he added: "Macaron's right. The man's watching us. He's a spy."

"If he's a spy, he's terribly dangerous," Sokoloff replied, torn between his hatred of intruders and his passionate admiration for masterpieces of science, "for it's certainly a man of genius who has created that miraculous machine. What a pity you weren't able to find out who the man is…just as long as we don't have cause to regret it! No one must know what is happening here. Woe betide that aeronaut if he takes it into his head to stick his nose in our business, even from up in the sky. We need to clear this up. Let's run to the outhouse at the far end of the garden. I have a collection of powerful marine telescopes there, which will permit us to find out more. Come on—there's not a moment to lose."

"Zut!" exclaimed Macaron, while following Rozen and Sokoloff, who were walking rapidly toward the building in question. "Too late—he's off! He's caught wind of the fact that the sight of him disturbed us, and he won't be back any time soon. He's gone to play with the sylphs for good."

"No, no," said Sokoloff. "It's his habit to veer off to the right and left like that—but he always comes back. He must be based somewhere in the vicinity."

"Come on!" said Saint-Magloire. "Not so much talk. Let's find out who we're dealing with first. We can discuss it afterwards…"

Macaron had guessed correctly. On perceiving them in the garden, Lemoine had allowed himself to descend close enough to study their physiognomies and, in the ambient calm, to catch a few shreds of their conversation. Intent on his observation, he had not noticed that the cloudy sky, which had permitted him to approach without attracting attention, was gradually clearing. A ray of sunlight, filtering through a gap in the clouds, had suddenly projected the shadow of the aircraft over the three strollers.

The doctor had seen Macaron's gesture. This time, there was no doubt. He had been seen—and he had to fly away as quickly as possible. Then he had successfully carried out the same audacious maneuver as the day before.

The adventurers had scarcely taken cover behind the shutters of the attic in the pavilion, each equipped with a powerful telescope, when the avion reappeared, flying swiftly from the direction of the Point-du-Jour. Having reached the curtain of trees that bordered the grounds, but which had a wide gap at that exact point, it slowed down, and spiraled round, preparing to descend. The slightest details of all their faces were distinguishable.

Sokoloff could not suppress a cluck of enthusiasm—but he broke off abruptly at a furious exclamation from Saint-Magloire: "God's thunder! It's that damned Dr. Lemoine again!"

"I recognized him too," said Macaron. "I've often seen him with Madame Vauclair—and I've spotted him a few times at the races with the head of the

Sûreté. He's in the pay of the Tour Pointue. But what's that machine he has in his lap, with copper parts? It's shining like gold coins."

"It's a telegraphic apparatus!" Sokoloff replied. "I've got it—he's sending a wireless telegraphy signal. Yes, yes…I can make out the spools of the resonator, the big coil, the manipulator, everything! I can understand now why he has some sort of cable or chain in tow, like the tail of a kite. Look! Can you see it, at the end of his chain? He has a little windlass between his legs, with which he raises it up whenever he wants to fly upwards, but when he's gliding he lets it hang down to the ground; it serves as a kind of antenna and earth connection. There's no doubt about it; he's carrying out aerial experiments in wireless telegraphy."

"Yes," retorted Saint-Magloire, "and it's at our expense, you can be sure. He's watching us, trying to see what's happening here, in order to telegraph the information instantly. I've suspected the fellow for a long time. I can't guarantee that he doesn't already know something. At the very least, he has his suspicions."

"I've seen him in your house several times," Sokoloff replied, having recovered all his composure. "I've even chatted to him at length about thermoelectricity—and what struck me is that the engine of his aircraft looks like a thermoelectric motor. Only a motor of that type could develop so much force with so little noise and so little trepidation. One might think that he'd taken my idea…"

"That damned Sokoloff," Macaron interjected. "He has no peer for giving things away and letting people get him to talk."

But Sokoloff continued: "He's a first-class mind, a rare scientist. He also struck me as a good man, with a broad mind…I would have sworn that he had the heart of an anarchist."

"With the nose and eye of a policeman," shouted Saint-Magloire, violently—who, sensing the imminence and gravity of the danger better than the others, emphasized each of those vain words. "Anarchist or not, honest man or rogue, we need to have his hide, if we don't want him to have ours. Come on—we won't see any more. He's landed over there, behind that big house that opens, if I'm not mistaken, on to the Rue de l'Yvette. His lair must be over there. Tomorrow, I'll find out what I want to know, and we'll take action. In the meantime—prudence! We must no longer even show the tips of our noses."

"In the meantime," Sokoloff retorted, there are better things to do. Since this Lemoine is amusing himself sending wireless telegraph messages from the air, I'll try to catch his secret messages in flight. I have a receiver in my laboratory with an automatic receiver. I only have to connect it up to a Branly tube. He can telegraph as much as he wants to thereafter; we'll receive his messages at the same time as, if not sooner than, their intended recipient. In a few minutes, everything will be ready.

And at the top speed of his long stride, he went back to the villa, drawing his two companions after him—who, in spite of the tranquil cynicism that normally characterized them, were having difficulty hiding their anxieties. Macaron especially, less self-controlled, uttered a stream of invective, for which the exhausted the rich treasures of the blasphematory vocabularies of French and English—or, rather, of argot and slang.

The marvels of science, over which his uncultivated imagination stumbled, sometimes seemed to him to be rather like sorcery, awakening the old leaven of superstitious terror that lay formant in the depths of his apparently skeptical and mocking street-arab's soul. The man who would not have trembled before any blade—including that, as he loved to repeat in moments of intimate expansiveness, of "the Widow"[71]—was positively fearful this time, afraid of the incomprehensible.

Sokoloff had little to do in the admirably-equipped laboratory that occupied an entire floor of his house to get his apparatus into working order. He had a battery of piles there with a telegraphic relay, linked on one side to the stem of a lightning-conductor, and on the other to a receiving apparatus with an automatically-unwinding ribbon.

He integrated a Branly tube, or radio-conductor, into the circuit—which is to say, one of those little crystal cases half-covered with silver filings, which serve as a key to open the sensitive heart, so to speak, of wireless telegraph installations. In its normal state, such a tube does not allow an electric current to pass through, so the circuit remains open, as if the electrodes were not in contact, and the relays do not work—but if a electric spark of a particular kind is generated in the vicinity, which provokes the quiver of an undulatory field around it, and the radiation thus produced, comparable to luminous waves except that they are invisible, strike the tube, the latter immediately becomes conductive. In other words, the circuit closes, as if the electrodes laced at opposite ends of the crystal case had been brought together; it follows that the current, interrupted until then, flows and the relay functions, so that the receiver, whose ribbon automatically inscribes either a dot or a dash, in accordance with the duration of the passage of the current provoked by the electric wave. Moreover, as soon as the electric wave—the Hertzian wave, according to the accepted terminology—has ceased to act, a small hammer known as a decoherer strikes the tube, and that impact suffices to restore the initial resistance of the filings. The current is no longer transmitted, until a new emission of waves renders it conductive again, and so on.

And as the entire transmission, in matters of wireless telegraphy, consists of producing a flow of Hertzian waves, periodically interrupted by intervals of varying duration, one can see that one can thus exchange at a distance, without any intermediary material, comprehensible appearances in the form of signals encoded in the Morse alphabet, which is composed of dots and dashes.

---

[71] The author inserts a footnote to explain that "*la Veuve*" [the Widow] is the guillotine.

Because the Hertzian waves spread out in all directions concentrically, however—or, rather, spherically—it goes without saying that all receivers placed within range will register the variations at the same time and in the same way, thus collecting the messages transmitted as well as the receiver at the intended destination.

While setting up his apparatus, having begun by checking its continuous communication with the earth—for otherwise, nothing would have happened—Sokoloff tried in vain to get these summary explanations into Macaron's skull, although the latter shook his head stubbornly and sulkily, repeating like a *leitmotiv*: "I don't understand any of this jiggery-pokery."

On the other hand, Saint-Magloire understood it, and even raised an objection. "If the destination receiver," he murmured, "is specifically tuned to the aircraft's transmitter, we won't receive anything at all."

"It's not probable," Sokoloff replied. "I know, of course, that one can synchronize such apparatus, in such a way that the transmitter and receiver are harmonized in order to transmit and receive certain waves to the exclusion of others. In that case, my receiver can only function usefully on condition that it, too, vibrates in unison, and the secret of accursed aeronaut's communication will be protected, but I don't believe that that will be the case. The synchronization of which you speak can, in fact, only be realized by means of special coils that require a particular placement. We didn't notice anything of that sort just now. I conclude, in consequence, that we're dealing with a banal and commonplace indiscreet apparatus."

He had not finished when a sudden series of significant clicks was heard. The receiver had sprung spontaneously into action.

The three men looked at one another, Sokoloff and Saint-Magloire with a triumphant joy that they did not seek to hide, Macaron with a comical bewilderment, of which he took account himself and at which he was the first to laugh.

"I must look like a chicken that's found a knife," he said.

For five minutes the blue paper ribbon continued to unroll, covering itself with small cabalistic signs, which Sokoloff and Saint-Magloire, both familiar with the cryptograms of the Morse alphabet, tried to read as they emerged.

"That's strange," said Sokoloff, suddenly. "I don't understand any of it."

"Neither do I," said the Baron. "It's nothing but incoherent signs, a salad of disjointed letters with neither head nor tail."

Sokoloff pursed his lips, and his straw-colored tresses bristled like a lion's mane. He waited for the tick-tock of the receiver to stop, thus indicating that the transmitter had stopped working and that, in consequence, the message was complete. He severed the printed strip, and began to study it like a puzzle, with a spasmodic contraction of the forehead and eyebrows that revealed his mental tension, while Macaron yawned as if to dislocate his jaw and Saint-Magloire stamped his feet in impatience and annoyance.

"Aha!" the Russian finally exclaimed, brandishing he blue coils. "I have the key to the enigma. The telegram is drafted in accordance with a conventional cipher, in a secret script—but it's not a cipher that a mathematician can't decipher, not a secret script for which he can't find the key. Just give me an hour, and we'll know everything."

And, departing like a bomb, he ran downstairs to shut himself up in a room cluttered with books and papers, to which he referred as his study, and which Macaron called his thinking room.

There is no infallible cryptography—no indecipherable cipher, as Sokoloff had put it.

In the same way that, by means of magnetized wheels, one can eventually separate the iron from the copper in a mass of scrap iron, a skilled cryptologist can, by relying on the particularities of the language, fairly rapidly put each conventional sign back in place, and render the most abstruse and confused of secret scripts in clear. Conspirators and adulterers, the irregulars of politics and love, would do well to take that as read.

Of course, the task is variable in its difficulty, delicacy and slowness. To complete it rapidly and reliably, it is not enough to be experienced, to have spent long days and nights poring over problems of that sort, the solution of which, like games of chess, obsess impassioned amateurs. It is necessary to have the gift—which is to say, a mathematical mind orientated in a particular fashion, with a flair *sui generis*, combined with an uncommon faculty of attention and a patience proof against anything. All these qualities, all these conditions, Sokoloff possessed to the highest degree.

Perhaps, in another milieu than the one into which hazard had thrown him, in other circumstances than those that had dominated is life, he might have become a rival of Viète, Rossignol de Vimbois, Trixandière, Kerckhoffs, Commandant Bazeries and other celebrated codebreakers.[72]

Let us add that during the forced leisure of his exile in Siberia, he had once been constrained, in order to suppress the revolts of his flesh and his soul, equally impatient with servitude, to work on transcendent cryptology, in such a fashion that he had become a veritable master of that kind of game, to which he sometimes went back by way of distraction.

---

[72] The mathematician François Viète (1540-1603) became famous for breaking a cipher used by the Spanish while working for Henri IV, thus greatly favoring French diplomatic maneuvers. Antoine Rossignol (1600-1682) and his sons took over where Viète left off, eventually developing the *"Grand Cipher"* for Louis XIV and ran his *cabinet noir* [Black Chamber], thus making that term a generic name for code-breaking enterprises. The Grand Cipher remained unbreakable until the 1890s, when a method for deciphering it was developed by Étienne Bazeries (1846-1891). Auguste Kerckhoffs (miserendered Kerkhoff in the original text) was a 19th century cryptanalyst who published a classic essay on military cryptography in 1883. The name Trixandière is presumably misrendered; the intended reference might conceivably be to Johannes Trithemius, who developed a famous cipher in the 15th century and published the first book on cryptology.

The cipher employed by Lemoine for his aerial telegrams could have been something exceptionally subtle, but Sokoloff, better than anyone, would have been able to discover the key. That was not the case, however. The cipher in question was one of the simplest imaginable, not to say the most childish.

Dr. Lemoine had never anticipated that correspondence transmitted by that unexpected means might be intercepted in flight, for wireless telegraphy, in spite of its relative perfection, had not yet entered common use. It only had a few applications aboard ships and along the coasts of the civilized countries. He had only thought of forearming himself against possible indiscretions by employees of the Prefecture of Police, in agreeing with the head of the Sûreté to use a cipher, without any malicious intent and without attaching any particular importance to it.

Thus, Sokoloff, who expected to have extreme difficulties to overcome, whose solution might require hours, was quite surprised, after a few minutes of mental concentration, to be able to read the cabalistic code fluently.

That message sent from the sky was not very long. It would not have seemed, in the eyes of an uninformed man, to signify anything much, or to signify anything serious or very precise.

Sokoloff, Saint-Magloire and Macaron shivered when they read it, however, for they sensed the most terrible and imminent of threats looming over them.

Our man is at Auteuil with the Englishman and the American. Send an agent urgently to follow the Englishman when he leaves.

"Well, damn it!" Macaron growled. "All the message tells us is that we're being spied on."

"This is very serious, very serious," said Sokoloff, finally very anxious. "It's incontestably us that the man is watching, and if he's watching us, it's not only the case that he has hostile intentions, which would be bad enough, but precise suspicions, which is worse."

"Let's not exaggerate," Saint-Magloire replied, having recovered all his self-possession after a few seconds of silence. "It's me that they're on to, and only me, that's obvious. 'Our man is at Auteuil'—that's me. You're only mixed up in the affair because you've been seen with me. They don't know who you really are, though, since they call you 'the Englishman' and 'the American.' Now we know that Macaron will be followed, it'll be easy for him to avoid these messieurs by means of the tunnel.

"So, I'm the only one under discussion. In consequence, it's much less serious. I have a great many enemies; I've often been attacked, denounced—I've had to ward off so many blows that I'm blasé about that sort of exercise. What does one more or less matter? We'll see who'll have the last word, especially as we now have a good idea of what we're dealing with. A man forewarned is worth two."

"So, three men forewarned are worth six," Macaron put in, whose incorrigible sense of humor never let up, not even at the most tragic moments.

"Only one point remains obscure in my mind," Saint-Magloire continued, in a lower voice, as if speaking to himself, "and that's the role that Lemoine is playing in this business. What the devil does he have against me, this four-sou physician who has no interest in politics or finance, with whom I've never had the slightest friction? Is it, perhaps, because..."

He did not finish. Involuntarily, the memory of Lemoine on his knees to Eléna's feet, as he had glimpsed him one day through the telectroscope, obsessed him like a night mere. At that moment, the obsession became precise, and took on an atrocious intensity...

Was it, perchance, that the Baronne, vaguely amorous with regard to Lemoine, had talked? Might she not, in the delirium of the illness, so certain and so cleverly induced, from which Lemoine had saved her, against all expectation, have let slip some compromising revelation? Or had the doctor—a cunning fellow, there was no denying, and a diabolically clever one—discovered or deduced something?

A cruel enigma!

In any case, it was necessary, at all costs, to get rid of the hindrance. On that, the three accomplices were in agreement. Even Sokoloff, in spite of his repugnance for violent means, felt it was a matter of self-defense, not to mention the defense of the sacred cause of anarchism, incarnate, until further notice, in the trio.

"The brigand's goose is cooked," Saint-Magloire eventually went on. "I'll take care of him personally. You two, don't make a move. It's my business, and it won't take long. Except that I'll wait for the right time and place. Besides which, it's best to know as much as possible about this jabbering between the balloon and the Prefect of Police...for it's definitely the Prefecture that he's telegraphing, since the dispatch mentions sending agents after us. To find out more, we need to filch more messages. So, tomorrow morning, my old Sokoloff, you know what you have to do."

"Perfectly," the Russian replied. No Hertzian wave will pass within range without my immediately having traced it here."

"Death to spies!" howled Macaron. Then a sudden idea occurred to him. He proposed that he should go the following night to prowl around the property where the flying machine was based, climbing over the wall, if necessary, in order to find out once and for all what they were dealing with.

Every time the opportunity for a fight cropped up, and every time it was necessary to defend against a peril, Bastien felt the stir of his anarchist principles, which an easy life and the pleasures of the tavern had put to sleep. Happy and tranquil, Macaron hardly gave a thought to the renovation of a humankind that he found much to his liking—but when danger burst forth, he was ready to give up the soft life he led under the name of Robertson and quickly became the reckless comrade, the pure anarchist, ready for the most audacious strikes...

"It can't be put in a pocket, a machine like that," he said, "nor in a drawer. I'll bet anything you like that I can sniff it out in less than an hour. After that, there are mates—true anarchists, attack dogs, not talkers—brothers who'll help me take care of it. We'll blow it all up, and set fire to the place into the bargain! Unseen and unknown!"

"Not in this life," replied Saint-Magloire, severely. "That would be the worst of stupidities, and I forbid it. You can take it for granted that the shed must be guarded, and that the police are lying in ambush there. You be certain to get pinched, you and your anarchists. We'd be in a fine mess then."

"All right, Boss, all right," Macaron went on, cooling down. "I'll be good. It's up to Sokoloff, then—he'll get us out of it."

"Yes, it's up to Sokoloff," Rozen concluded. "But for my part, I won't waste my time. In any case, rendezvous here at the same time. We can come back here, since they know that we come—but keep your eyes open on the way, and no imprudence."

With that, the bookmaker and the financier took their leave of the scientist. The latter held the Baron back momentarily, and spoke to him in a low voice.

"Indeed," murmured the banker, replying to the desire expressed by Sokoloff. "That's the idea: To receive their dispatches and stop them receiving them. I'll let you know when the time's ripe."

Macaron had gone on ahead. The Parisian street-arab and the financier each went their own way, hugging the walls, not without checking to see that no one was following them.

The street was absolutely deserted, as is almost always the case in that eccentric quarter, more rural than urban.

Neither Saint-Magloire or Macaron noticed anything suspicious, for the simple reason that no one was following them, and that no one at the Sûreté suspected anything. Lemoine's message had not reached its destination.

At that very moment, the doctor was in the process of acquiring the dolorous certainty of that fact.

As soon as the avion was safe inside its hangar, in fact, into which it had been quietly led, rolling it on the castors that served to support it on the round, and he had inspected its various parts with the fussiness of a locomotive driver arrived at the terminus, he had raced at top speed to the Quai des Orfèvres, without even taking the trouble to wash his hands.

"Well," he exclaimed, going into Monsieur Cardec's office, "What do you think of my tips? Are we on the right track this time?"

"What tips? What track?"

"The dispatch that I just sent you! You didn't find it suggestive enough? My word, you're difficult. That trio's planning something. By following Macaron, we might find out what it's about..."

"I haven't received any dispatch," the head of the Sûreté declared.

"By the wireless telegraph—a coded message?"

"Once again, I repeat that I haven't received anything, either via the wire or the wireless."

Prey to the most violent surprise, Lemoine demanded to see the apparatus that Cardec had had installed in his private apartment, which was directly above his office. As soon as they had gone upstairs, the doctor looked at the apparatus. The radioconductor—the Branly tube—was in its place, as was the traditional blue paper ribbon, wound around its drum. Lemoine unwound the end of the ribbon between his feverishly tremulous fingers. It was blank. No sign had been inscribed there. Obviously, by virtue of a cause that as difficult to discern, the Hertzian waves radiated from the avion had not been received there.

Lemoine's face convulsed. He had such a disappointed expression that Cardec, inclined to see the comical side of men and things, could not help laughing.

"Well, what's up, old chap? Has someone stolen your dispatch?"

Lemoine muttered a curse between his teeth. "Let me be, damnable joker. With the wireless telegraph, one can indeed intercept messages in flight, but that doesn't prevent them reaching their destination. Several people read them, that's all—but they don't evaporate for so little...

"No luck, all the same. An apparatus that works so well, so carefully set up, that hasn't had the slightest breakdown. We had to find it faulty just at the critical moment! Just my luck! Unless, at least, no one's surreptitious cut the end of the strip?"

"Impossible. I stayed here after lunch. I only went downstairs a quarter of a hour ago, and I put an orderly at the door of my apartment so that he could let me know if the bell on the apparatus rang."

"In that case," Lemoine said, "some fortuitous cause must have stopped the propagation of the Hertzian wave, for, in sum, your receiver is in perfect order."

"What do you expect me to do about it?" Cardec replied. "Even precision chronometers have their caprices. It's not such a great misfortune, in the final analysis, since you're here and you can give me your message in person. Instead of weeping over your lost dispatch, you'd do better to tell me about it."

"But it's too late now to do what I asked you to do by telegraph, urgently."

"Come on!" said the head of the Sûreté. It's no use crying over spilt milk. If it's too late, too bad. That doesn't prevent you from bringing me up to date. I'm listening."

The reasoning was sound. Lemoine understood that. He therefore hastened to tell his friend, briefly, everything that he had seen from his aerial observatory. To his profound disappointment, Cardec did not seem to be excited by it.

"If that's the only tip you can report on the basis of your excursions over the chimneys, old chap, it really isn't worth the risk of breaking your neck every day. In truth, the game's not worth the candle. Saint-Magloire meets with suspect characters in a mysterious house in the depths of a remote quarter? Well, so what? What does that prove? What does it tell us that we didn't already know about him? What new weapon does this fine discovery give us against him?

"Besides which, we know the two equivocal companions you've seen with him. You identified the old one yourself—it's the American Smithson that you told me you'd seen in the Champs-Élysées: an old lunatic, as erudite as a Benedictine, but perfectly harmless. He's probably an inventor without a sou, a dreamer whom Saint-Magloire's exploiting..."

"No," Lemoine put in, "he's a man of the world—he has the manners of a true gentleman."

"All right; I'll take your word for it. He's a visionary squandering his money running after chimeras. If Saint-Magloire eats him up and squeezes him like a lemon, that's his business. He's eaten many others.

"As for the other, that's this Robertson, the pseudo-Englishman, an incorrigible drunkard, in whom Saint-Magloire is officially interested, whom he got out of that business when the agents picked him out of the gutter one day. Since then I've learned that Robertson's real name is Bastien, that he escaped from Cayenne...and I beg you to believe that, if I haven't yet sent him back to the colony, it's because I think that the fellow might be useful to us some day in unmasking the Baron. We won't lose sight of him—don't worry. But what do you expect us to make of the observation you've made? Will it deliver us Saint-Magloire?"

"I hear you," said Lemoine, with a hint of irritation, "but I think we're marching on the spot. My opinion is that we ought to search this house in Auteuil from which strange noises emerge."

"By what right? Have you a search warrant to give me? If I took such a step, I'd be accused of acting arbitrarily; there'd be talk of nothing less than sacking me...and people would wonder whether I ought not to be sent to the bagne to replace the vanished Gaston Rozen. Abuses of power aren't treated kindly—and I'd be in big trouble. All I can do is to organize a more active surveillance around the famous house."

"Oh, that won't do any good," said the doctor. "I know all about police surveillance and tailing...they usually end up with the inspectors of the Sûreté catching chills and bronchitis. Do you think people like Saint-Magloire and his associates would take long to give your agents the slip?"

"I can't do anything else, though, until further notice—until you bring me more precise information, something more tangible."

"That's all right," Lemoine replied, getting to his feet with an angry gesture. "You'll have the material indication you want tomorrow, the day after, in six weeks or three months. Every day, I'll resume my aerial ambush. I'll be damned if I don't end up finding out where the prize is buried...or I'll die trying."

"Be careful they don't find out what you're up to," said Cardec, amicably. "You've already told me that they've noticed your presence. Be prudent."

"Bah! My avion causes some sensation wherever it goes. Dishonesty doesn't exclude curiosity…the bandits at Auteuil probably looked at me as they might look at a monster, as they'd look at any dirigible flying overhead, nothing more, and nothing less. In these times of abundant ballooning, it's of no importance. Anyway, too bad—let it not be said that the evildoers will always have the last word."

"Go ahead, then, my dear Lemoine—and good luck!"

"It's enough to make one despair of science," murmured the doctor. "You're scarcely consoling."

"What do you want me to say, my poor friend? You're a great scientist and I'm only a simple policeman, not very well up in science, and I'm wondering whether all this rigmarole of amateur policing—don't take offense—all this wireless telegraph apparatus, this more-or-less dirigible balloon, etc., is worth even one good sleuth, with vulgar means at his disposal, but endowed with a subtle sense of smell and hardened in his profession. In the same was that one doesn't make a physician by following courses at the École des Beaux-Arts, one can't improvise a policeman even out of the most erudite of men. You have a robust faith, but that's not sufficient.

"I've let you go your own way, because you're an apostle, and because, after all, your machinations haven't hindered me and have, on the contrary, interested me. I'm not an enemy of the new, but I'll wager that it's still me, the professional, with my modest baggage, who'll arrive at finding the chink in the armor. Like the hunter lying in wait, I'm watching out for the prey; my patience is inexhaustible and there'll come a day when it passes within firing range. When that day comes, I'll give you the signal, and you can be in on the kill. Adieu, my dear friend. Don't get upset…strong as our man is, we already know quite a lot about him, and the slightest incident might deliver him to us…"

And while Lemoine went away, disappointed, the head of the Sûreté went to sit down at his desk, shaking his head pityingly.

"The poor doctor," he murmured. "He'll hurt himself, and all for nothing!" And he added, by way of conclusion: "The bandits are beginning to call upon the resources of science. Lemoine want to fight them with the same weapons. All that's curious to watch, no doubt…but I persist in thinking that the old means are more reliable. We're not yet ready for the scientific police. It's still in the domain of fiction…"

X. The Fall

While Lemoine valiantly continued his aerial surveillance—which revealed nothing new—Saint-Magloire and Sokoloff tried to find a way of to get rid of the troublesome apparatus that flew over the Auteuil property every day.

"There's certainly one means of putting a stop to that accursed machine and the man flying it…but I'm hesitant…it can't…"

It was with these enigmatic words that Sokoloff greeted Saint-Magloire one morning, when the latter had hurried to Auteuil at dawn, his forehead anxious and his lip curled by the rictus that afflicted it on bad days: ones that were particularly dangerous or put obstacles in his path.

Gaston had resolved, whatever the cost, to get rid of Lemoine, even if he had to do it with his own hand, as he had for Dulac, and send him to a realm where the worst indiscretions are sterile, given that no one ever returns therefrom. Lemoine had been condemned to death by him. It remained to determine how the sentence was to be carried out.

It was not exactly convenient. Paris is not the Grand Chaco and Parisian civilization, so favorable to certain occult villainies, which grow there like mushrooms on a dung-heap, has its restrictions, which Saint-Magloire—for the first time since he had constructed his new identity—was tempted to curse. Certain precautions were imperative, inasmuch as Lemoine was not a Dulac, capable of hurling himself recklessly into the wolf's mouth.

In any case, the mere fact that he was operating in a balloon, at a height of several hundred meters, in almost fabulous conditions, rendered the task even more difficult. How could he be reached? Above all, how could he be reached immediately, that being the essential thing? For it was necessary to act quickly, urgently, without losing a minute, in order not to leave him any longer at the height of his aerial observatory, in order not to give him time to tell the Prefecture of Police everything."

Undoubtedly, he could not have learned very much. His gaze, looking down into the grounds of the villa, obviously could not have pierced the roofs or the walls to the extent of recognizing the forgery equipment and other suspect objects hidden in their shade. But it was already too much for him to have perceived him in that mysterious retreat, in the rather unexpected company of Sokoloff and Macaron. Lemoine had found the meeting unusual, even suspicious, since he had immediately telegraphed to demand a "tail."

Besides which, he was an enemy: a flagrant, undeniable enemy. It needed no more than that for his suppression to be imperative, provided that the suppression did not have troublesome consequences—but that was the snag.

The accursed quack could, of course, easily be caught one day or another in Paris. Already, a man in the Baron's pay, installed in a wine-merchant's facing his domicile, was dogging his footsteps in order never to lose sight of him and keep track of everything he did. It would therefore be possible, sooner or later, to catch up with him in a deserted spot and settle his hash with a sure blow.

Macaron could certainly have done that marvelously. He knew his business, and there was no danger, now that he had a taste for expensive wines and liqueurs, that he would allow himself to be tempted by a basement bartender's rot-gut. So, as he would have said himself, "the job would have been taken care of," all the better if he was nervous about it, that being the best way of preventing him from doing anything stupid or imprudent.

But what a fine move! Macaron must be being tailed himself, and it would have been silly to give him the task of watching Lemoine. In any case, the Baron was only interested in that tailing for reasons of curiosity. It might be necessary to follow the prey for days or weeks in order to find the golden opportunity to kill him without risk. What is the opportunity came too late?

All night, which he had spent pacing around his room like a tiger in a cage, Saint-Magloire had turned his thoughts over and over in his tormented mind, without being able to find a practical solution.

"Only Sokoloff," he said to himself, finally, "can get us out of this. He alone is capable of finding us a trick. Oh, how idiotic I'd have been to smash his skull, as I had a strong desire to do, on the day when he first showed me the secret of the argentaurum. He's sometimes very maddening, but still, he's much more use to me...for he knows everything, that man, and can do everything. Oh, if only I were in his skin, if I knew what he knows, if I could do what he can do!"

In spite of his prodigious vanity, Saint-Magloire was too intelligent not to render justice to Sokoloff's genius. He knew from experience that one never knocked in vain on the door of that marvelous brain, where miracles were permanently simmering, always ready to boil over and translate themselves into tangible realities. So, he was not surprised when Sokoloff, as if responding, like an echo, the tumult of his intimate concerns, addressed the words quoted above to him.

"A means? You have a means? What? Come on, quick, spit it out. We'll discuss your scruples later."

"It's quite simple," the Russian replied, calmly. "Last night, I calculated all the constants of that dirigible aircraft. I know them by heart now; I could construct one like it tomorrow, if necessary..."

"Yes, I know it isn't necessary to show you things twice—but you're not thinking, I imagine, of giving chase to the man through the clouds, or of demolishing him by means of an aerial combat, a battle of eagles..."

"Patience! I'm getting there. The aircraft is a veritable marvel: a marvel of equilibrium—but an unstable equilibrium. Its instability is such—I've established it mathematically—that the slightest disturbance or damage...a broken

416

wire, a spring that extends awkwardly…and bang!" Reclaimed momentarily by the chimera of the impenitent inventor, Sokoloff continued in a lower voice, as if talking to himself: "That's the crucial and fatal flaw of these miraculous machines."

"So what?" the Baron interjected, violently. "It would be necessary to disrupt that unstable equilibrium, to break one of the monster's paws so as to cause and accident—of course! I've already thought of that. But it's the method that escapes me."

"A good rifle, in the hands of a marksman like you, who can put ten bullets out of ten in the black at three hundred meters…"

"Come on, Sokoloff, are you crazy? A rifle shot, with the detonation and the smoke, to rouse the quarter! We'd be pinched five minutes afterwards. Thanks, but I'm not yet ready to commit suicide."

Sokoloff smiled in his long beard, and his green eyes sparkled behind his gold-rimmed spectacles. "I'm not talking about an ordinary rifle," he said, softly.

"An air-rifle, perhaps?" said Saint-Magloire, keenly interested.

"Better than that! A liquefied gas rifle. Come on—I want to show it to you."

And, drawing Saint-Magloire away, he took him into his laboratory, where he put in his hands a strange kind of carbine, with all the appearances of an ordinary precision weapon, except that the firing mechanism, equipped with two knurled triggers, had an abnormal form, and that under the barrel, to which it was solidly attached by soldered and riveted rings, ran a long steel tube sealed by a hood of the same metal.

"In this rifle," Sokoloff explained, "the propulsive force of the projectile is furnished, not by the deflagration of powder, but by the released of a provision of liquefied gas stored in that cylinder. I tried liquid air first, but had to give up on it and give preference to carbon dioxide…"

"Yes, yes," Saint-Magloire interjected, delighted. "It's a Giffard rifle!"[73]

"Much improved, my dear chap. The inferior section of the carbon dioxide magazine is fitted with an automatic valve with a spring. A percussion-pin controls the valve. If you press the trigger, the hammer strikes the percussion-pin, which activates the valve of the reservoir, from which a drop of liquid gas is released. The drop vaporizes immediately, furnishing the force necessary for the projection of the bullet."

---

[73] The French engineer Paul Giffard obtained a patent for a gun design that could be used in association with compressed air or liquefied gas as a propellant. A more practical patent was issued in the late 1880s for a carbon-dioxide gun that actually went into mass-production, awakening great hopes that were soon frustrated, because the weapons could not compete with conventional firearms in terms of power and range.

"How far can the bullet travel?"

"At least five hundred meters; and you have enough in the reservoir—be careful, it's loaded—to fire some fifty shots without lowering the gun. Needless to say, there's no noise or smoke.

"We have our man, then!" exclaimed Saint-Magloire. "I wouldn't give two sous for his skin. It's the solution we need!" And he put out his hand to take possession of the magic weapon.

Sokoloff stepped back. "Stop there," he said, in his grave apostolic voice. "If the balloon crashes, struck by a mysterious bullet, Lemoine is a dead man. We can't do that! Human life is sacred…unless reasons of a superior order…the triumph of anarchism, for instance…"

Saint-Magloire uttered a fearful blasphemy. Momentarily, he was tempted to snatch the rifle from Sokoloff by force and make immediate use of it, first to get rid of the immediate hindrance, the faint-heart…but he got a grip on himself immediately. He knew how to go about defeating Sokoloff's scruples.

"Of course," he said, in his most honeyed voice, "human life is sacred. Consequently, your life is sacred, mine is sacred, and Bastien's to. Now, our three lives are threatened; they're going to be sacrificed if we spare the enemy who is watching us, and won't spare us. It's sometimes necessary to kill one man to save another, whose life is no less sacred. Now, today, it's not merely a matter of saving one life by means of a cruel but necessary action, but a matter of saving three—ours!"

Sokoloff made a vague gesture, in which there was Parisian mockery and Slavic mysticism, indicating that dying, after all, was a matter of indifference to him. A little sooner, a little later…it was the common lot, and revolutionaries, more than anyone, always had to be ready to make the leap.

Saint-Magloire, who had his plan, assumed an inspired expression. "Oh," he continued, "if we were the only ones in play! We've played a good game, we've lot, goodnight all! As the fair-minded gamblers we are, we accept fate bravely, like the soldier who falls on the battlefield. But don't you understand that it's the cause that will perish with us, on the eve of victory? It would put paid to the anarchist movement, so painstakingly prepared.

"Everything would have to begin again, and in unfavorable conditions. We're in charge of the revolution, my friend, let's not forget that. We don't have the right to compromise the interests that we personify, which are far more precious and sacred than the life of a miserable spy, for a vain sentimental scruple. We don't have the right to put international justice in check. You said it just now: the triumph of anarchism excuses the condemnation to death of a man who is a obstacle.

"Remember that, at any moment, from the height of his flying observatory, he might discover the secret exit through which the bombs you've manufactured depart."

Sokoloff hesitated, visibly troubled.

Saint-Magloire persisted: "Have great revolutionaries ever had such weaknesses at critical moments? Have they recoiled before the necessity of bloodshed? Remember Émile Henry, Ravachol, Rysakoff, Jeliaboff, Vera Zasulich."[74]

At that last name, Sokoloff shivered. Saint-Magloire had hit the mark in evoking the memory of the woman who had been the educator, the intimate friend and the sister-in-arms of the woman he adored, hanged before his eyes in a public square, whose cherished image still haunted his dreams, and whose vengeance he had never renounced. He passed his hand over his forehead, as if to chase away a nightmare, and threw back his long straw-colored mane.

"You're right," he said, in a bank voice. "It needed to be ended. Our own conservation, indispensable to the triumph of anarchism and the vengeful concern of justice, commands us to act. Too bad for those who get in the way of the revolutionary work!"

And without any further reluctance, having made his decision energetically, he set about explaining the mechanism and manipulation of his rifle in detail to Saint-Magloire, with his customary admirable lucidity.

Saint-Magloire was a quick learner. In five minutes, he knew as much as the inventor.

He wanted to practice firing it right away, in order to familiarize himself with the weapon completely and definitively.

A target, made from a small piece of wood a decimeter square, was stuck to the enormous wall that separated the grounds from the convent next door, and the Baron started shooting, at first from a hundred meters, then a hundred and fifty, two hundred and two hundred and fifty. That was the maximum distance, beyond which the dimensions of the property forbade him to retreat further.

With the sure eye of a cowboy, he put seven bullets one after another into the same hole, almost in the geometrical center of the target, without anything but a slight hiss—*psschutt!*—giving evidence of the profuse fusillade.

"It's perfect," he said, finally. "Lemoine can come now; I'll bring him down like a partridge with the first shot."

"Be careful!" said Sokoloff then. "It's necessary not to use lead bullets. The projectile might be found after the crash, embedded in some fragment of the debris of the flying machine. That might be sufficient to denounce malevolence and put the police on the track. Let's not leave anything to chance. Instead of

---

[74] Rysakoff and Jeliaboff were Russian nihilists involved in attempts to assassinate Tsar Alexander II, the former being the unsuccessful initial bomb-thrower in the attack whose second missile completed the task. Vera Zasulich was tried for the attempted murder of the repressive governor of St. Petersburg, Theodore Trepov, whom she had shot and injured, but was sensationally acquitted by a jury whose members evidently thought that Trepov deserved to be shot; she subsequently converted to Marxism and translated a number of Marx's works into Russian.

ordinary bullets, I'll give you copper slugs of the same length and caliber, which will produce the same effect, but which might, on the other hand pass for having originated from the materials used in the construction of the aircraft.

And, combining action with speech, he set about cutting a few fragments from a sheet of copper with a metal saw, exactly the same size as the cartridges of the carbon dioxide rifle. He had scarcely finished this operation when a muted hum advertised the approach of the avion.

Rapidly, Saint-Magloire slipped one of the small metal cylinders into the breech of the rifle, and, with his finger on the trigger, hid in a thick clump of giant spindle-trees.

Sokoloff, who had run after him, followed the movements of the Bird-Ship with attentive eyes. The slightest details of the framework were visible, its aluminum fibers shining like silver against the khaki backcloth of the wings.

"Can you see where you need to aim?" he murmured in Gaston Rozen's ear. "It's not the man that it's necessary to hit, for it's indispensable that it's believed to be a accident—it's the articulation for the wing. That's the critical point of equilibrium."

"Yes," Rozen replied, over his shoulder. "I know that."

The avion was gliding smoothly over the waste ground of the Rue Jasmin, at an altitude of about a hundred meters, about a hundred and eight meters away from where they were stationed. An imperceptible rhythmic quivering was agitating its wings. It seemed to be almost motionless in the splendor of the rising sun. Standing up on his pedals, Lemoine was searching the bushes in the grounds and the partly-opened blinds of the villa's first-floor windows with his binoculars.

Suddenly, without any sound being audible, the avion rose up abruptly into the sky, like a bird taking flight. Then it began to spin, one of its wings hanging down lamentably, and fall with increasing speed, describing an irregular parabola, like a kite in the process of "taking a dive," all the way to the height of the curtain of trees, behind which it disappeared.

"There!" said Rozen. "A Hertzian wave that animal didn't expect. There goes the wireless telegraph, all the way! The dispatch hasn't gone to the wrong address."

"Poor fellow," murmured Sokoloff, like an echo. "It's a shame—such a fine intelligence!" Then the scientist got the upper hand again. "Did you see," he asked, "how the aircraft, once damaged, began to rise up in the air instead of falling instantly like a stone? That was the propulsive force of the motor, which, no longer being counterbalanced, suddenly changed direction. It's very curious, all the same!"

"Yes, yes," Saint-Magloire replied, "and it meant that he fell at least an extra fifty meters."

With that, delighted with his work, with his mind tranquil and his heart at ease, he got ready to finish a day so well begun in joyful fashion, while

Sokoloff, the incorrigible mathematician, went back to shut himself in his study, alone with a blackboard, to try to calculate by virtue of what law a dirigible aircraft whose wing had just been broken might rise up to begin with, instead of falling down.

XI. The Resources of Science

Saint-Magloire was not in too much of a hurry to celebrate his enemy's inevitable death. He was not in too much of a hurry to compose, privately, the funeral oration, so penetrating and so heartfelt, by which he would salute, at the Bourse, in the salons, in the wings and in the cabarets—everywhere—the sad news of a foolish accident that had cost the life of a man of Lemoine's value:

"The martyrology of science counts one victim more... Science too has its battlefields, where blood flows and cadavers pile up... Even the earth is insufficient for its ambitions; it is in infinite space that it operates—and kills. Above, as below, it must go: a Minotaur insatiable for human sacrifices...Nature never yields her majestic secrets gratuitously! But what a loss for France, for civilization! The life of a man like Lemoine, one of the most admirable of the contemporary era—which had not yet given its all, it must be said—is too high a price to pay for a progress as fecund as the solution to the irritating problem."

Certainly that sensational occurrence—a man dying in a balloon-crash is fairly rare—would be a good opportunity for "the King of Paris" the strike fine poses and achieve fine oratory effects. Everything was definitely working out for the best, since his prestige would gain from it as well as his security.

But it was necessary for the news of the catastrophe to spread through the city first—and the evening newspapers did not breathe a word and out it, even in the "stop press."

Saint-Magloire was slightly surprised by that silence, but not unduly worried about it. Doubtless Lemoine had come down in some waste ground, or in some deserted worksite, without anyone seeing the crash. Hours might pass, perhaps days, before his body was found in the midst of the debris of his broken machine.

So much the better. In the final analysis, wasn't that delay one more stroke of luck?

The truth, however, was quite different.

The truth was that Dr. Lemoine was not dead. He had not suffered the slightest scratch. A further miracle—a scientific miracle, premeditated and designed—had saved him.

That morning, without knowing why, Lemoine had been full of hope.

Perfectly fit in body and mind, with more courage and resolution than ever, he had set out under the empire of a singular presentiment. A sort of divinatory intuition, with which subtle psychologists accustomed to refined observation are sometimes equipped, informed him very quietly that he was finally approaching the end of his epic struggle against the evil genius, and that the day would not pass without some serious event.

When he took off, with a powerful thrust of wings, into the limpid morning air over is aerodrome, everything in the mysterious villa seemed dead. Only the shutters, slightly open, and a thin plume of smoke emerging from one of the chimneys, attested that the house was not completely uninhabited.

The doctor steered his avion to skim the curtain of trees limiting the grounds and there, in order to be able to observe more comfortably, he began to hover—which is to say, to remain stationary, neither climbing nor descending, without veering to the right or the left, by means of a maneuver that he had perfected after long practice.

He was there, as tranquil as in the armchair in his study, when all of a sudden, above his head, there was a sinister cracking sound, like the impact of a stone vigorously hurled against a wooden partition.

The intrepid airman did not have time to raise his eyes before he felt himself being lifted up—or, rather, projected into the air—with his machine, as if by an irresistible upward pressure. At the same time, the left wing of the avion slumped, dislocated, hiding the horizon behind its inopportune screen.

If the instinct of self-preservation that operates at crucial moments by reflex action, without the cooperation of the will, had not caused him to clench his knees vigorously, he would have been unseated.

He did not, however, lose his self-composure.

One of my wings is broken, he said to himself. *The airplane is no longer offering a sufficient surface to counterbalance the ascensional force of the moving propellers. That's why I'm rising up. That could be dangerous; let's put a stop to it.*

And, turning the commutator placed beneath his hand with a nervous gesture, he cut off the current. When the motor stopped turning, the ascensional movement was transformed for a fraction of a second into a fall—not a vertical fall, but, because of the acquired momentum, an obliquely parabolic fall—and, for the duration of a lightning-flash, Lemoine had the anguishing sensation of a man falling, with accelerating velocity, from the top of the Arc de Triomphe or the Eiffel Tower.

He did not get excited, however, for he knew what he was doing. That precipitation was premeditated, the peril that had to be countered having been anticipated and warded off in advance. What the engineer Leloup, with an inventor's hectic enthusiasm, had forgotten, the possibility of an accident, a rupture of equilibrium or damage to the machine never having entered his head, Lemoine had considered and thought about in advance—and he had made arrangements to reduce the risks to a minimum.

One cannot, of course, prevent an aircraft, especially one that is, by definition, "heavier than air," from obeying the law of gravity, when no ascensional force is counterbalancing the effect of that law—but one can, at least, slow down the fall.

A lead bullet and a tuft of down are equally subject to gravity; however, by virtue of the resistance of the air, the tuft of down takes a great deal longer to descend. Lemoine knew that, like everyone else, but, as no one else would perhaps have thought of doing, he had designed his avion in consequence.

He had therefore begun, before even starting his fall by stopping the motor, by retracting the right wing of the apparatus by means of a trigger controlled by a spring. Remaining extended on its own, it could not have failed to bring about a rupture of equilibrium, probably followed by a disastrous crash.

Once both wings were symmetrically refurled, the first by virtue of the impact of the bullet that had broken its articulation, the second by virtue of a voluntary maneuver, the movement of descent automatically opened, above the avion, an immense parachute in the form of a umbrella, constituted by a system of silk panels extended over a double frame of aluminum wire.

While moving upwards, these panels were maintained almost vertically, but during a descent, especially an abrupt descent, they tended toward the horizontal, and stuck together like the scales of a fish, thus opposing to the pressure of the air a resistant surface great enough to slow down the fall to the point of rendering it almost devoid of danger.

It followed that the avion could never fall vertically, the parachute that deployed *proprio motu* as soon as the need arose also being maneuverable by the pilot, by means of a system of ropes and pulleys placed within arm's reach.

As soon as the parachute opened, Lemoine had nothing more to fear. He had once again become the master of the "Bird-Ship," exactly as if nothing had happened, save that it had become impossible for him to rise up. The descent, however, which he still steered as he wished, was sufficiently slow to offer no particular danger.

He was just in time, though. When the parachute completed opening, with the clicking of wood and silk, the avion was no more than fifty meters above the ground. One second longer, a little stiffness in the bodywork of the suspension panels, or a fault sufficient to cause a rupture...and the machine would have smashed mercilessly into the pavement of a street or the angle of a roof.

Fortunately, the ingenious mechanism functioned as intended, soon enough for Lemoine to be able to choose his landing-spot—but too late, on the other hand, for the deceleration of the fall, interrupted by the unexpected intervention of a paradoxical safety-mechanism, to inform the murderer that his shot had failed.

By multiplying pirouettes and swerves, for which he made the parachute play the role of an improvised rudder, Lemoine succeeded in returning to his base, where the avion finally settled, a trifle heavily, like a huge injured bird, with a grinding of metal.

The impact was a trifle rude, but Lemoine, who took care to jump out of the saddle with a slight rearward leap just as it was about to occur, got away with a slight shock that left him stunned for a few seconds.

Nothing broken, he said to himself, *feeling his limbs and flexing all his joints. Noting broken...except for my poor avion! That's all right! I've been very lucky, and I can tell myself that I've had a narrow escape. It's necessary to believe, all things considered, that I was born under a lucky star!*

To a reflective observer like Lemoine, however, it was not sufficient to have come out of a dramatic adventure safe and sound; he needed to know exactly what had happened, what it's cause had been—in brief, how and why the incomprehensible accident had occurred. At the critical moment, when it was necessary to attend to more pressing matters, he had not even asked himself the question, but now that he felt safe, with his feet solidly on the ground, his instinct as a researcher, always determined to get to the bottom of things—especially mysterious things—was awakened more sharply than ever.

He therefore began examining the damaged carcass of the avion with meticulous attention, and soon discovered the mortal wound.

At the articulation of the left wing, at the point where the aluminum wires were united in a sheaf, there was a clearly-perceptible fracture, apparently made by a blunt instrument such as a hatchet or a powerful hammer.

Not having heard a detonation, Lemoine did not even think of a rifle-shot, even though the damage bore a singular resemblance to a bullet-hole. The bullet had, in any case, disappeared. The copper slug that Saint-Magloire had used by way of a projectile had remained in the hole that it had made in the aluminum armature, but at the moment when the mutilated avion had touché down, it had been dislodged. The bullet had fallen out and was lost in the grass, where the doctor, who did not even think of looking there for it, did not find it.

He noticed at the location of the fracture—on the rim of the wound, so to speak—a few yellowish imprints, easy to distinguish from the silver-grey of the aluminum, which intrigued him. He did not, however, perceive any indication sufficiently precise for him to draw even the slightest hypothetical presumption therefrom.

The devil must be mixed up in it, he said to himself. *Might not a criminal hand have applied the thrust of a file or a saw to the joint of the wing last night, which subsequently caused the break under the effort of mechanical work? It's possible, but scarcely probable...if that had been the case, I wouldn't have been up in the air for three minutes, but I must have been flying or at least a quarter of an hour.*

I give up. I'll come back later to search for the key to the mystery with Olivier Martin and Leloup. Three pairs of eyes are better than one! It's not the most urgent thing, right now. Better to go to the Sûreté to see what's going on.

As soon as he had touched down, he had transmitted news of his accident to Cardec by wireless telegraph. He ought to go there immediately to reassure his friend.

The dispatch had, in addition, been intercepted by Sokoloff, who hastened to let Rozen know the result of the rifle-shot.

The Russian was glad to know that Lemoine was alive. The aircraft would be out of commission for some time. That was already a great deal, and he would have time to get his "munitions" out before the doctor could resume his aerial surveillance.

Without any more excitement than if the accident had happened to someone else and he had only been a witness to it, Lemoine went calmly on foot along the quais, mulling over the events of the tumultuous morning—which, in sum, preoccupied him more than he wanted to admit—without being able to cast any light thereon.

Curiously enough, the thought that Saint-Magloire might be no stranger to the catastrophe that he had so narrowly escaped did not even cross his mind. Just as he was leaving the Quai des Orfèvres, however, in order to go into the corridor that led to the office of the head of the Sûreté, he had a flash of intuition.

What if it were Rozen?

He did not stop there, however.

Telepathy would need to have made singular progress, he said to himself, *for it to possible to kill a mandarin at a distance by simple suggestion, or break metal rods with nothing but metal effort.*

He was still laughing, almost out loud, at his own naivety and the puerile hypothesis when he arrived at the door and asked the office orderly whether Monsieur Cardec was there.

"Yes," the orderly replied. "Monsieur le Commissaire is there—but I don't know whether he'll be able to see you. There's a lady with him, who asked to see him ten minutes ago. It must be a serious matter, because the chief let her in straight away, and even said that he'd no longer be in to anyone."

Damn! Lemoine said to himself. *Our friend the magistrate is being difficult...*

Aloud, he said: "The order doesn't apply to me. You know that Monsieur Cardec never makes me wait. Tell him that it's Dr. Lemoine, and that it's urgent."

The attendant did as he was told and came back a few moments later.

"Monsieur le Chef asks you to wait in his secretary's office or a moment. He'll see you as soon as he can."

XII. Germaine's Friend

Shortly thereafter, Lemoine went into the office of the head of the Sûreté.

"Well, old man, that's a bit stiff—receiving women while your friends kick their heels in the antechamber!"

"You'll forgive me," Cardec replied, "when you know that the person I received and have sent away, at least temporarily, in your favor is none other than Germaine Revyal. Do you think I was flirting?"

"Germaine here! Damn! Are things hotting up? Are there new developments? Is the torch alight?"

"Perhaps, my friend. I don't know what will come of it. It might be that the woman only came to see me about one of the thousand silly things to which people mixed up in Parisian society are prone, but, in any case, I'm ready to take advantage of the circumstance that brought her here in order to get some useful information out of her."

"You're perfectly capable of that, for you have a marvelous understanding of how to get people to talk..."

"With women, it's generally easy, especially when they're angry. Who could ever analyze what goes on in a woman's brain? Here's one, for example, on which Saint-Magloire has lavished love and money—well, it wouldn't be astonishing if, in a burst of fury, a sharp fit of petulance, she started running him down extravagantly."

"Which would be highly desirable."

"We'll see about that this evening, when she comes back. She might know a great deal, and I promise that I'll push her to as complete a confession as possible."

"Once again, old chap, I'll trust to your subtle flair—but since you're doing me a favor, I need to tell you right away what's happened to me. You were close to never seeing me again—alive, at least."

"What?" said Cardec. "Have you been attacked?"

"And in an uncommon fashion. I've taken a dive in my bird-ship. I telegraphed to let you know..."

"I haven't received anything."

"You're joking, my dear Cardec. You're having me on..."

"I swear that I'm not. Since yesterday, my receiver hasn't registered any message."

Lemoine frowned. He reflected momentarily, then said, stressing the words: "Are you sure of all the people who have access to your quarters?"

"Why?"

"You'll understand—but first, show me your apparatus. This time, we need to have an explanation of why it didn't work."

"Willingly."

They both went upstairs to the head of the Sûreté's apartment. The doctor examined all the parts of the instrument attentively, and said, after a moment: "You've touched the radioconductor."

"No. Since you installed it, I swear that neither I nor anyone else has disturbed anything. The only person who's touched it is you, the other day, with regard to the dispatch I didn't receive."

"Well, my dear chap, I can assure you of the contrary—and the proof is that this radioconductor is incapable of functioning, while the one that I put in place was in perfect working order, and should still be..."

"Who the devil do you think...?"

"Oh," said Lemoine, "there's no point arguing about it any longer. Someone has been in here."

"I sometimes let my agents in when they have something urgent to tell me, but none of them is suspect."

"You haven't received anyone else?"

No...except...someone came to repair my electric bells..."

"Well, my friend," said Lemoine, swiftly, "Saint-Magloire has simply taken a peek. One of his acolytes has got in here, in the guise of an electrician. He's repaired your bells, to be sure, and must have done that well, but at the same time, he's replaced a working radioconductor with one that doesn't work. Make all the enquiries you wish, but the fact is obvious and undeniable..."

"You're scaring me."

"Oh, you see, my friend, that we're dealing with a powerful adversary. The Baron is infernal, and it's high time that chance—the god of policemen—helped us to defeat him; otherwise, we'll lose. Anyway, this explains one thing that I didn't understand. Of course—Saint-Magloire, or rather his friend Smithson, who is a peerless scientist, has found a means of receiving my telegrams, instead of you. It's relatively easy, given that we only have standard equipment. As always, the police are behind the times. Don't protest—we're backward, and instead of these instruments, fit for the rubbish bin, we should have synchronized apparatus."

"I admit, frankly, that you've lost me with all this scientific jargon."

"I've we'd had that apparatus, it would taken Smithson some time to find a receiver tuned into ours. Instead of which, we're burned now—well burned. We need to find another means...once again, our science has been vanquished."

"We'll go back to the old means, of course..."

"Why not. You're a resourceful man. You have imagination..."

"Come on, Doctor, don't get carried away," Cardec interjected. "So, you said that the bandit nearly killed you..."

"Yes, but for a providential hazard, I'd have been done for. My machine's fall was caused by a fracture in one of its wing-struts. Now, that fracture seems to have been produced by a violent blow—one might think that it had been hit by a projectile."

"Bah! Where did the projectile come from?"

"That animal Saint-Magloire, of course. He's one step ahead of us again. He's discovered and disposed of the surveillance I'd set up around him, thanks to those telegrams that you didn't receive but that he intercepted, as I've just told you. It's that infernal Baron who caused my bird to fall by means of some other invention, surely believing that he'd kill me..."

"He was mistaken, fortunately."

"Yes, Providence was on the side of good."

"Oh," murmured the head of the Sûreté, "if only we could prove that attempted murder."

"It's impossible, my friend. Who would believe that our bandit has found a means of hitting my aerial machine at a distance of three or four hundred meters, without any detonation advertising the attempt? People would simply laugh in our faces, saying that we were dreaming."

"We'll see it through to the end even so!" the policeman exclaimed. "The day when I get the slightest leverage, I can assure you that it will be all I need..."

"Perhaps. We've already forced him to abandon some of his shady operations, for no one can rid me of the idea that he was the secret chief of the gangs that committed the audacious thefts for which you and the prefect were pilloried."

"Obviously. Saint-Magloire, as a member of several clubs and acquainted with all of high society, could easily discover when anyone was departing to spend the winter in Nice, Menton or Monte Carlo, or the summer in Biarritz, Royan, Paramé, Dieppe or Trouvillle, or the autumn in a châteaux. Without being suspected, he could inform his men, who could thus operate freely..."

"What proves that our suspicions are well-founded is that the series of burglaries came to a stop at the exact moment we began our surveillance, which the villain had to put off the track right away."

"And we also saw the end of the financial misappropriations, for the delivery truck robbery was surely his work."

"Of course. He had to reimburse the bonds he's begun to put into circulation, generously..."

"Generously and promptly," said the head of the Sûreté, smiling.

"His generosity was a clever calculation. It sheltered him from any suspicion, and behind that screen, the bold rogue was able to continue his financial operations at his ease."

"And he's still using them!"

"And abusing them."

"In sum," Cardec concluded, "We're reduced to the old means. This evening, I'll grill Germaine Reyval carefully."

"That's your business. I hope she furnishes you with a useful clue...and that everything will go well."

"I'm confident. Would you like to listen in on the interview?"

"I'd be something of a hindrance."

"Not at all. You can station yourself in my secretary's office, next door to mine. The door's thick, but I'll leave it ajar, masked by a curtain."

"Perfect. I'd be very interested..."

"And you might be useful to me, by listening carefully to the diva's replies."

"As long as I can hear..."

"Don't worry...we'll be talking loudly. For days now, Saint-Magloire's mistress hasn't calmed down; she'll cry if I let her."

"Until this evening, then—what time?"

"I've given her an appointment at ten o'clock. She's not singing today...besides, she says that she's ill."

As Lemoine shook his hand to bid him farewell, Cardec held him back. "Shall we dine together? That would be more practical."

"Casually?"

"Of course—as comrades."

"Agreed."

The head of the Sûreté went down to his office and gave a few orders; then the two men went to the restaurant.

On leaving the office of the head of the Sûreté, Germaine Reyval had gone along the corridor that led to the Quasi des Orfèvres. Her carriage, a coupé with two horses, was waiting for her.

"The house," she instructed.

Germaine's house, a gift from Saint-Magloire, was in the Rue de Prony. It was one of those pretty modern buildings between a courtyard and a garden. A veranda overlooked the street, and the apartments were on the other side, where no indiscreet gaze could intrude.

When her carriage stopped under the entrance arch, Germaine stepped nimbly down and ran up the stairway leading to the first floor. With the same haste, she opened doors and went into a boudoir whose walls were decked with pink satin, adjacent to the drawing-room.

In that restful room, a rather plump man was lying on a divan upholstered in the same fabric as the wall-hangings, smoking a cigarette. He did not get up when the young woman came in, and continued to contemplate the capricious spirals of smoke rising up to the ceiling.

The cantatrice stood still momentary, seemingly awaiting a word or a smile from the man who was installed there as if at home. She coughed lightly.

The individual did not appear to notice Germaine's arrival; the latter finally decided to speak.

"It's me, Auguste," she said, approaching the person timidly.

"I can see that." Auguste replied, in a hoarse voice. "Of course it's you. I didn't think it was the President of the Republic."

"You haven't budged since I came in. I thought you hadn't heard me."

"You don't want me to tire myself out bowing to you. The very idea! And you're very polite, yourself! I've been kicking my heels here for at least two hours."

"It's not my fault, darling," Germaine stammered. "I was delayed. You know that I don't want to annoy you." Imploringly, she added: "Come on, don't grumble...come and kiss me."

Monsieur Auguste stood up. He was a man of about twenty-five, of medium height but broad-shouldered rather massive. Very dark-complexioned, he had short hair and was clean-shaven.

Monsieur Auguste was an artiste. He sang Polin[75] in second- and third-rate music halls. Absolutely devoid of talent, the low comedian only imitated his model very poorly. Although he lacked ability on stage, he had the gift of pleasing a certain category of women...among them, Auguste had a reputation that probably overrated him somewhat, but he was very popular in that milieu. Women tore one another's hair out over him. He had been the hero of numerous adventures, and women went crazy for his physique.

Germaine, who gladly mixed with riff-raff, had wanted to conquer the Don Juan of the cafés and for the sake of ostentation and pride, had stolen him from a dancer of whom the victory had made a mortal enemy.

Lemoine had judged La Reyval accurately. Her beauty concealed a vicious soul. She was, in the full sense of the term, a whore. Only chance and her talent as a singer had saved her from the sidewalk. Incapable of finer sentiments, she had betrayed Dulac for the banker who had provided her with her first luxury. Then she had dropped the banker for Saint-Magloire. Finally, she was deceiving Saint-Magloire with Monsieur Auguste, a "lyric artiste" for the sake of saving appearances, but in reality a pimp.

The fellow made fun of her, exploited her, insulted her and beat her, but Germain had what is conventionally called a "crush" on him. She supported him very comfortably, and Monsieur Auguste, seeing that the strategy was successful, paid her back in increasingly emphatic brutalities.

The amiable fellow had, however, gone too far. He was no longer taking his role as a heartfelt lover seriously, to the extent that the actress, having been mad about him for a few weeks, had gradually wearied of that regime, whose originality had seduced her to begin with but which had eventually become intolerable.

---

[75] "Polin" was the stage name of Pierre Paul Marsales (1863-1927), the leading figure in the French music halls of the period.

Except that when she had tried to get rid of Auguste, the latter, finding his situation lucrative and pleasant, had held firm. He had even done better. He had declared explicitly to Germaine that if she broke with him, he would inform both the banker and Saint-Magloire that she had deceived both of them with him.

"They'll both clear out," he added, with a cynical laugh. "That'll be funny!"

That threat of blackmail plunged Germaine into a continual anxiety, and Auguste had profited from it to redouble his insolence. At the beginning of the liaison he had seemed amorous and thoughtful, initially coming to see her in secret; now he had a key to the service stairway, and installed himself in the house as if it were his home whenever he wished. To the slightest observation he responded with brutal scenes, accompanied by blows, and if Germaine did not cave in, and did not submit to his demands, he threatened to go to see Saint-Magloire and his rival right away and "spill the beans."

The objective of Germaine's visit to Monsieur Cardec had been to ask for help against the blackmailer, who might cause her to lose her situation at any moment. Once she was in the office of the head of the Sûreté, however, she had been gripped by hesitation, and, almost glad not to be seen straight way, she had quickly returned to the house, where Auguste was waiting for her, smoking cigarettes. She hoped to be able to mollify the terrible villain.

"Kiss me," she repeated, with a tender intonation.

"Zut! I'm standing up, since you're here," groaned Auguste, stretching his arms. "I'll kiss you later, when you've told me where you've been."

"I've been for my music lesson."

"I haven't been holding my breath...but I'm bored. You're here, that's the main thing. Am I dining here today?"

"Impossible, darling. I have a rendezvous with the Baron."

"Do you expect me to believe that?"

"Why would I lie?"

"Enough fuss—you've been putting on singular airs for some time now. You must be planning some dirty trick against Bibi. Beware!"

"Of what?"

"Of me. I think you want to get rid of me."

"Me? Do you think...?"

"Yes—and I won't stand for it, you know."

"I swear..."

"You're boring me. I know what I'm talking about. I don't keep my eyes in my pocket—I know what women are like, all more spiteful than one another. But remember one thing, my darling...I like it here with you, and as the maréchal said: 'I'm here, and I'm staying.'"

"You're becoming unbearable," Germaine replied, putting on a show of rebellion. "We're not married."

"It's as good as, and if you have ideas about letting Auguste go, you'd better not count your chickens, as they say. After the bout I'll do what I promised relative to your wretched Baron and your other fancy man…and then what, eh? I don't like scenes. Since we can't have dinner together, offer me an aperitif—I'm thirsty."

"My pleasure, darling. What would you like? Port or Madeira?"

"Absinthe, if you have any…That's still my favorite. I'm not singing tonight. My evening's free. "He added, with a marked emphasis: "I'll go amuse myself in town too."

Contrary to Auguste's hope, however, this insinuation did not have the expected effect. Germaine had not been jealous for a long time. She shrugged her shoulders, rang, and sent for the requested absinthe.

"You don't want a drop?" Auguste asked. "That's right—you're afraid of that perfume, for your Baron. Poor dear—he's so delicate."

The young woman needed all her courage not to explode. The man had never seemed so ignoble.

"Oh," she murmured, "to think that I was able to love that!"

Auguste gulped down his liquor conscientiously. "And now," he said, wiping his lips, "*au revoir*, my pet. Give my good wishes to the dear Baron, and try to get rid of him tomorrow, so that we can spend the evening together. I'm full of pretty things to say to you."

He kissed her. Germaine returned the kiss and hid her anger behind a forced smile. "Adieu," she said.

"Until tomorrow," shouted Auguste from the doorway.

The actress did not reply.

Oh, she said to herself, *when he had gone, I can still play the comedy of love with those who pay me, but with that one, never! He nauseates me. I can't remain in is grip any longer. No, no, no! Whatever he might do, I have to get rid of him.*

She rang again.

"Have dinner served right away, and hitch up the carriage for nine o'clock. I'm going out."

"What if Monsieur le Baron comes?"

"I'm not in to anyone."

The chambermaid bowed and went out, a little surprised.

"Let's go!" Germaine murmured. "The die is cast. I need to rest easy from now on."

XIII. Confidences

At ten o'clock, the exact time of her appointment, Germaine Reyval went into the office of the head of the Sûreté.

She was still under the influence of the scene, that "her Auguste" had just made, and Monsieur Cardec did not fail to notice that the cantatrice was very overexcited.

Good, he said to himself. *With a nervous and angry woman, it will be easier for me to guide the conversation as I intend.* Addressing Germaine, and directing her to a seat next to his desk, he said: "Sit down, my dear Madame. First of all, forgive me for having asked you to come back..."

"Oh, Monsieur," said Germaine, "it's me who ought to apologize to you for taking this step. You have so much to do and you have so little time that, truly, I feel guilty for distracting you with matters that are personal...intimate, I should say."

"Is it not my duty to help everyone?" said Cardec, smiling. "Am I not here, like a sort of confessor, called to render tranquility to persons under threat? I consider that a policeman's role is never more useful than when he can anticipate a drama, prevent an evil deed from being committed. In a word, I prefer the preventive method to the curative. You've come to me, and you've done well. I will do everything possible to save you from annoyance. If I grasped the few rapid explanations you gave me a little while ago correctly, it's a matter of blackmail that you want to avoid?"

"Yes," the diva replied, clenching her delicate fists. "Yes, I'm under the dominion of a wretch I was once unfortunate enough to love. Oh, the bandit!"

"Calm down, calm down! I understand your indignation, but it's necessary not to let yourself get carried away by anger—otherwise we won't get anywhere..."

"I'm so unhappy! The coward maltreats me. He plants himself in my house, robs me, insults me, even beats me...and when, prompted by disgust, I talk about throwing him out, he threatens to make me lose my situation..."

"So what caused you to throw yourself into the arms of the individual?"

"What indeed! But we women, you know, need affection, and he seemed so polite, so attentive..."

"That's always how these things begin..."

"And then...I ought to tell you the whole truth..."

"Certainly."

"When I took Auguste for a lover, I was obedient to a sentiment of vanity..."

"Vanity?" repeated Cardec, pretending not to understand.

434

"Auguste was sought after by so many other women that I wanted to have him all to myself. Oh, I certainly succeeded! Today, he's making me pay for it with my head…and I need to get rid of that M…onsieur…at all costs. But he only has to talk, and I'd be lost…"

"You're panicking, I think…"

"Not at all. I have two lovers to whom I owe all my luxury. Please permit me not to go into detail…"

"On the contrary. As I told you, I'm a confessor…"

"They're both unaware that I've deceived them…"

"Naturally."

"If they found out that I've paid Monsieur Auguste, perhaps that wouldn't cause them any great annoyance…"

"Do you think so?"

"Yes. I could easily convince them that there's a…sentimental side to that infidelity, which they'd forgive me. An actor is of no consequence. A lover is a gentleman that one receives secretly, and who withdraws prudently when the lord and master appears…"

Cardec could not help smiling on hearing that explanation offered so ingenuously.

"However," Germaine continued, "neither of my lovers would forgive me for receiving other subsidies than theirs…"

"I understand. Their vanity would be wounded by that."

"And I sense strongly that, for them, I'm an object of luxury that they want to keep to themselves…they they alone want to be able to buy. It's necessary to play to the gallery. The Baron would never accept that someone else was helping to support me…so you understand how sorry I'd be if that villain Auguste stuck his feet in the dish…"

"In sum," Cardec declared, "you're at the mercy of this Auguste."

"Yes. I sing…and I suffer, because I'm afraid."

"I feel sorry for you," replied the head of the Sûreté, with an admirably feigned expression of commiseration.

"Really? I know how good you are. I didn't doubt that you would save me…"

"Oh! Let's not get ahead of ourselves. It might not be as easy as that. Let's see: do you have any kind of weapon against the person who's tormenting you? Do you know of any incident or affair that would permit me to muzzle him?"

"Alas, no—otherwise I wouldn't have waited so long to take action."

"Damn. You don't know anything about his life?"

"I know that he's a vile person, a filthy individual, a pimp…"

"That's something and nothing. The 1895 law can't touch him. He works…?"

"Oh, not much…"

"He's an artiste…"

"A buffoon..."

"I don't say any different, but he has a profession, and I can't do anything against him. We don't have the right to act arbitrarily..."

"In that case," moaned the cantatrice, "I believe there's only one thing to do—kill Auguste."

"A bad means...it would cost you dearly and wouldn't avoid the scandal. On the contrary..."

"Oh, I'm being punished...severely punished. To think that I have been loved...truly loved...by a man who was selfless, good, honest..."

"And you let that rare bird escape?"

"The poor fellow killed himself..."

"For you?"

"So it's said...so it's believed...because I once left him. It was necessary, though. A dramatic career has its exigencies. We're not mistresses of our own actions..."

"However," the head of the Sûreté put in, "Dulac—for it's him we're talking about, isn't it...?"

Germaine nodded her head.

"Dulac had acquired a brilliant situation, and could have..."

"Kept me? Say it, Monsieur. Yes...but at that moment, I was the mistress of the Baron de Saint-Magloire..."

Cardec was delighted by the turn the conversation was taking, without his having to bring it to the point that interested him.

"You could have left the Baron..."

"He would have killed Dulac, Monsieur..."

"Really? The Baron, it's said, has a broad mind, and he was the first to deplore the death of the unfortunate Dulac, found hanged from your gate..."

"I can assure you that the Baron would never have tolerated my becoming that man's mistress. Oh, many things have been said against me, with regard to that death...I've been held, in a way, responsible. People have even gone so far as to say that I made an advertisement of it..."

"Calumnies, obviously," said Cardec.

"Some advertisement!" exclaimed Germaine, hotly. "It caused me so much trouble. I had to leave that house, where I couldn't stay, after that drama. I had to answer a summons to appear in court..."

"I remember, in fact...it was alleged that Dulac had followed you and the Baron to Auteuil."

"That's true. On the way, Saint-Magloire told me that...and I shivered; I was afraid, because the Baron, at one time, made threats; he wanted to stop the carriage and have it out with the intruder. I got an atrocious headache from that...but when I got out of the carriage when we arrived at Auteuil, no more Dulac. I was reassured. Saint-Magloire came back cheerful."

"You didn't confide these details to the judge..."

"What was the point? It was of no importance, and I tell you, frankly, I was afraid of adding weight to those malevolent rumors that attributed Dulac's death to my coquetry. And if the Baron hadn't begged me so insistently, I wouldn't have shown them the note found in my dressing-room."

"Oh. It was the Baron who..."

"Well, it was necessary to silence certain absurd accusations. It was my duty..."

"Of course."

"And yet, it was impossible to have the slightest doubt about Dulac's suicide..."

"The law is curious," said Cardec.

"And indiscreet. I had to say that the Baron hadn't left me for a single instant that night."

"Which can't have been very pleasant for you..." And, as Germaine Reyval looked at him uncomprehendingly, the head of the Sûreté added: "You had an atrocious headache..."

"That's true, but my lover, who's very expert in chemistry—he's a scientist—had given me some tea to drink, in which he'd put a few drops of a sovereign liquor, and I slept as if miraculously..."

"You slept for a long time?"

"Why do you ask that?"

"Not to embarrass you," riposted the head of the Sûreté, with a singular smile, fixing his eyes on the actress, who was embarrassed by that penetrating gaze.

"No, after all," she replied, hesitantly. "I know that I slept well. How long? I don't know. What I do know is that when I woke up, the Baron was beside me...and that I no longer had the headache."

"It's obvious," Cardec continued, resuming his placid physiognomy, "that all these accusations against the Baron don't stand up. Anyway, he hardly knew Dulac..."

"You're mistaken," Germaine put in. "On the contrary—they'd known one another for long time..."

"Oh!"

"Yes. Saint-Magloire, Sokoloff and Dulac met one another in Buenos Aires, several years ago..."

"Sokoloff?" asked the head of the Sûreté, struck by the name, which he had heard pronounced before. "Who's he?"

"Sokoloff," repeated Germaine, trembling from head to toe. "I said Sokoloff...oh my God!"

"What's the matter?"

"Oh, I beg you...if Saint-Magloire knew that, he'd be capable...of...no, no...you won't betray the secret I let slip, will you? Sokoloff...is hiding in Paris under an assumed name."

"Smithson, perhaps?"

"You know that?"

"And many other things too. I have a good memory. Sokoloff is a Russian prince who as obliged to leave his homeland after a nihilist plot..."

"I don't know...but one day, in the house in Auteuil, Saint-Magloire asked Yu—his Chinese servant—whether Sokoloff was there. Until then, he'd be introduced to me under the name Smithson. And afterwards, the Baron made me swear never to make any allusion to that error on his part..."

"You've broken your word," said Cardec, laughing. "But that's not a problem, Madame. Don't worry. I wish you nothing but good, you know that. And by the way, suppose we get back to Monsieur Auguste, since, after all, it's about him that you came to see me...and we've become somewhat sidetracked. I've caused you to remember things that might be disagreeable to Monsieur le Baron de Saint-Magloire, whom you love..."

"Oh, I *loved* him. Today, I tolerate him, because he's generous..."

"A confession devoid of artifice!"

"Completely."

"The honeymoon's over, then, with the Baron?"

"Yes. People think I'm worse than I am...they say that I'm heartless..."

"Impossible."

"Yes, they say so because I'm royally paid. Why should I do otherwise? But, you see, since I'm making my confession, I can tell you that I no longer love Saint-Magloire. To begin with, he treated me harshly when I expressed my regrets at Dulac's death..."

"That was a delicate sentiment on your part..."

"Wasn't it? The Baron's attitude shocked me...and I was gripped by a kind of worship for the man who had adored me to the point of dying of it. That might seem bizarre in a woman like me—a whore, as right-thinking people say..."

"But no, no...when one has your talent, one can brave certain prejudices. There are two moralities: one for the use of common mortals and a broader one for the use of genius and talent. Many things are permissible to artistes—and you're a great artiste..."

A smile from Germaine thanked Cardec for this small item of calculated flattery.

The head of the Sûreté had just learned some extremely important things, and he did not want the diva to perceive the interest that he had taken in the few revelations that she had let slip.

"Well," said Germaine, "I've begun to love Dulac again now he's dead. His memory is sweet to me...and I'm completely detached from the Baron. He's my money-provider, and that's all. Furthermore, during the Baronne's serious illness, when he was with me I saw him cheerful and sprightly, although people everywhere were praising his grief sand admirable devotion. I even had to remind him about propriety. He wanted to hold a house-warming party at my house in the Rue de Prony when his wife was dying! He understood...and we put off our little celebration... until the day after tomorrow..."

With his chin in his right hand, Cardec reflected. An idea suddenly occurred to him. "Will it be a success, your party?"

"I hope so. There'll be singing, a comedy play, a champagne lunch. We're invited a lot of guests...all the notable people in literature and the arts, all the prettiest women in Paris..."

"People won't get bored," said Monsieur Cardec, laughing.

"No...and if I dared...but you're too serious, too severe...otherwise, I'd invite you...but you'd refuse."

"Why? On the contrary. In life, as the poet says, it's necessary to mingle the serious and the tender, the pleasant and the severe..."

"Then you accept?"

"With pleasure. I'll even ask for two invitations."

"For a lady friend?"

"No...a man...who will interest you greatly."

"What's his name?"

"I'll introduce him to you."

"A mystery?"

"Perhaps."

"It's agreed, then. You have your two invitations—and you'll tell us stories of brigands..." Germaine concluded with a burst of laughter. Then, with the versatility that was characteristic of her nature, she added, with a discomfited grimace. "There's one person I'd like to be far away from there—he'll spoil all my pleasure..."

"Auguste Chiron?"

"What! You know his name?"

"And his life story. Vey edifying, I assure you."

"Unfortunately!" sighed Germaine.

"On the contrary—you'll see." The head of the Sûreté pressed the button of a bell.

The office orderly came in. "Tell my secretary to bring me file 254," Cardec ordered.

"But that's extraordinary!" claimed the cantatrice. "How did you discover all that...so quickly?"

The head of the Sûreté did not reply immediately. Germaine Reyval's astonishment was amusing..

In reality, there was no great difficulty in keeping track of the comings and goings of Monsieur Auguste, who was nothing, in sum, but an old lag. When he had seen Germaine the first time, he had immediately made enquiries that had soon enabled him to retrieve the individual's file.

"You can see," he said, after a brief pause, "that the Paris police are efficient...whatever people say..."

At that moment, one of the head of the Sûreté's secretaries brought in the requested file. Cardec opened it, and took out a piece of card to which two photographs were stuck, side by side, one in profile and the other full face.

"Look," he said to Germaine. "Do you know this handsome fellow?"

The singer hesitated. "Oh," she said, "it's Auguste—but not at his best."

Indeed, the photographs taken by the anthropometric service represented an individual with a surly face, to whom unkempt hair and a bushy moustache gave a wild expression. The shirt, without a collar, left the neck completely bare, and in the middle of the chest, a number attached to the waistcoat by a small pin added to the sinister aspect of the portrait.

"You find him less handsome than in life," said the head of the Sûreté, smiling at Germaine's disconcerted expression.

"The fact is that he's quite ugly like this!"

"And if you had seen him like that, you'd never have opened your arms to him. Our photographers at the Prefecture are terrible people...they don't beautify their clients. They don't go in for retouching, for those advantageous poses the portrait artists know how to take. That's nature.

"Then again, when he was put in front of the objective that day, Monsieur Auguste wasn't exactly in a good moon. He had good reason—the poor thing had just been pinched, for a bit of blackmail exercised against a slightly mature lady who had had the weakness-like you—to be smitten by his charm...at Granville, where he had gone to perform at the Casino...

"And Auguste, who had already come to our notice two or three times, knew pretty much what to expect: a five year holiday at Poissy. I'll wager he never mentioned that charming sojourn..."

"Oh!" said the cantatrice, utterly confused. "A jailbird..."

"My God, yes! But don't be too upset about it; it will make it easier for me to get rid of him for you. The worthy fellow in a Belgian citizen. If he doesn't go quietly, he'll be taken to the frontier between two agents, after having obtained an expulsion order. You can see that you have no further need to worry. He won't be bothering you for a long time..."

Germaine Reyval got to her feet, radiant. "How kind you are. I'll never be grateful enough for what you've done for me, and I don't know how to thank you..."

She had stood up in order to take her leave of Monsieur Cardec; the latter accompanied her to the door.

"One more word," he said, retaining her. "In order that I can act in total security, don't tell anyone what you've done today. Continue to be amiable with Auguste until after your soirée. He'll go away as meekly as a lamb. Keep the conversation we've just had secret. Promise me that."

"I swear."

"Until the day after tomorrow, then."

"At ten o'clock. Understood—and a thousand thanks..."

Cheerful and smiling, she left in a rustle of silk, leaving a heady odor of violets in the somber corridor of the Sûreté.

When he had closed his office door again, the head of the Sûreté went straight to the secretarial office where Dr. Lemoine was. "Well," he said, triumphantly, "did you hear?"

"Everything."

"I believe we're now close to our goal..."

"How's that?"

"Why, old chap, the Baron's a friend of Sokoloff, and the Russian is an anarchist of the most dangerous kind. The conferences you spotted from your aerial observatory must have some connection with the revolutionary movement that's brewing in the provinces. Now I can give the Minister a serious reason for taking action and unmasking Saint-Magloire..."

"That's why you got yourself invited..."

"And why I got you invited too..."

"Me?"

"Yes—you're the mysterious friend. I have a plan, and I guarantee that it will succeed...but it's late. Come to see me tomorrow, and we'll settle the details tomorrow—and the devil may take me, this time, if we don't get our hands on the accursed Rozen..."

"I'm at your disposal—even if it requires the use of force."

"Cunning will suffice," Cardec concluded. "Until tomorrow."

After an energetic handshake, the two friends separated, and, while Dr. Lemoine went away, intrigued, Cardec went back up to his apartment, whistling a popular tune—which was, in him, a mark of the utmost contentment.

XIV. The House-Warming

It was nearing midnight, and there as great activity in the Rue de Prony, at the house of Madame Germaine Reyval.

On the ground floor, entirely devoted to the servants' quarters, the concierge's lodge, the garage, stables and kitchen, an unaccustomed animation reigned. Before the ovens the chef, whose crimson face seemed ready to explode beneath his white hat, was moving back and forth with the imposing bearing of a general on the eve of a great battle. He harassed his two assistants while preparing the main dishes for the meal with the sure hand of a veritable artiste.

In the cellar, Monsieur Jean, the sommelier, assisted by the coachman—recruited for the occasion—was choosing the wines, taking care to set aside a few bottles of each vintage for them and their mates.

At the bottom of the dumb-waiter that connected the kitchens to the servants' parlor, Monsieur Joseph, the valet from the house next door, who had come to lend a hand, was conveying the crockery and cutlery to the butler, Monsieur Pierre and his assistants, busy setting the small tables in the large dining room, whose sideboards and dressers were overloaded with crystal glass and silverware.

Germaine Reyval, in the hands of two chambermaids, was finishing getting dressed.

The artiste was sparkling with beauty, but anxiety was legible in her face.

What was happening at the Sûreté, to which—as Monsieur Cardec had promised, Auguste ought to have been summoned by now?

How would he take it? Might he not seek to take his revenge by coming to cause a scandal in the middle of the party? Then again, the young woman remembered certain details of the visit to the head of the Sûreté. Monsieur Cardec had been very quick to accept that invitation to her soirée. He had talked to her about Saint-Magloire with such persistence, and he had asked her to keep her approach to the Sûreté secret. The Baron, moreover, had been anxious and nervous for several days—and in spite of everything she told herself in order to reassure herself, she had not succeeded in chasing away her apprehensions.

The guests, who were beginning to arrive, gradually caused her to forget her worries. It was necessary for her to show the newcomers around the house. Germaine, very proud to be able to display her luxury to a great number of eyes, had nevertheless been selective in her guest-list: only the most fashionable women, the prettiest and most expensive; as for the men, she and Saint-Magloire had invited those most in view, the cream of those who liked partying, whatever their official or social status.

As they were greeted, the actress's good friends waxed ecstatic over the wealth and god taste of the house, with an admiration strongly seasoned with envy.

The antechamber, in a pure Gothic style, opened over a vast winter garden garnished with rare plants; three ornamental doors gave access to the main hall, the boudoirs and the dining room.

Already, everyone was gathering in that vast room, and taking their places at the small tables for supper.

Saint-Magloire, overflowing with verve and good cheer, was enthroned alongside Germaine. The Baron had never been on better form—but when the footman announced Monsieur Cardec, the head of the Sûreté, and Dr. Lemoine, Germaine's lover started, and suddenly went pale.

"What are they doing here?" he asked his mistress, rapidly.

"I invited them," she replied. "They're friends."

"You could at least have warned me," the banker murmured, his teeth clenched—but he was not a man to let his annoyance show for long. No one other than Germaine had perceived the impression that the entrance of the new-comers had made on him.

The presence of the head of the Sûreté at the house of the cantatrice was no surprise to the people who were there, all Parisians and Parisiennes who had needed at some time to ask Monsieur Cardec for information or advice. In spite of his absolute propriety, the latter never hesitated in his affability, and made himself useful whenever he could. The cares of duty did not prevent the head of the Sûreté from being a cheerful companion and a lover of pleasure. Never, however, had the magistrate neglected his business for that, thinking about it constantly.

Germaine had moved rapidly to Monsieur Cardec's side. Immediately, with a feverish haste, she asked him, in a low voice: "Auguste?"

"Muzzled," the head of the Sûreté replied, smiling. And, introducing her to the doctor, who had remained slightly behind him: "My friend Dr. Lemoine."

"A pleasant surprise," said the cantatrice, joyfully. "I've heard a lot about the doctor, and I'm flattered by the honor..."

Lemoine bowed courteously.

"Come on, Messieurs—I'll introduce you to the Baron."

Saint-Magloire had not waited for them to come to him, however. His face illuminated by a benevolent smile, he was coming forward to met his mistress's guests with his hands extended. "No need for introductions, my dear. I know Monsieur le Chef de la Sûreté, who has never missed an opportunity to be agreeable to me. As for Dr. Lemoine, he's more than a friend—he's a savior." Then, addressing Lemoine in a tone full of warm solicitude, he added: "I'm glad to see that you suffered no repercussions from your unfortunate accident, Doctor. It has deprived us of your visits to the house—but I hope that you'll come back, won't you? Inasmuch as the Baronne has need of your enlightened care..."

Without replying, the doctor bowed and shook the Baron's hand limply.

The latter noticed the doctor's hostile attitude, and his face contracted momentarily, but his swiftly dispelled that impression and said, in a jovial voice: "Welcome, Messieurs. You are in the home of the Queen of Paris, whose motto is: 'Long live pleasure!' Shame upon serious people in the palace of the most beautiful of Parisiennes!"

"God!" said Germaine, worried at first by Dr. Lemoine's attitude. She pointed to a table at which there were two young women, and said: "I'll introduce you to Mademoiselle Anita of the Bouffes-Parisiennes and Mademoiselle Van Hove of the Théâtre Antoine, two of my good friends." When she had made the introductions she added: "I'll leave you now, Messieurs. You know the password: 'Enjoy!'"

The head of the Sûreté and the doctor sat down. Seeing that Saint-Magloire was watching them, they struck up a very animated conversation with their companions. Burst of laughter soon resounded, louder than those of their neighbors.

Might I be mistaken? The Baron wondered. *Is their presence here really fortuitous?* On seeing the doctor drink a glass of champagne, he felt completely reassured.

The meal continued, increasingly lively.

Although the billiard-room was open, in order to serve as a smoking-room, several of the men had lit cigars without getting up from their tables; the women had authorized them to do so. Liberality had been decreed, and no one was any longer standing on ceremony.

The conversation moved from the particular to the general.

"Do you know what we all ought to do?" declared Mademoiselle Anita.

"No."

"Well, you ought to join your pleas with mine for Monsieur le Chef de la Sûreté to initiate us into the mysteries of the Tour Pointue. We were talking just now about the Anthropometric Service—that must be very curious."

"Yes…yes..."

"You should tell us stories of brigands," said Germaine Reyval.

"You shall have them, my dear Madame..."

"Modern ones, especially," said a female guest.

"They shall be served up piping hot," the magistrate replied, darting a glance at the Baron de Saint-Magloire, who was in the first row.

The latter, vaguely anxious, had sensed Cardec's gaze weighing upon him. He wondered what all this police intrigue might have to do with the party give in Germaine's honor. He decided to deflect attention by taking the floor.

"My opinion," he said, "is that a lecture on the Anthropometric Service would be most interesting. For myself, I'd be delighted by it, for I've promised myself to study that important branch of police work."

"Unfortunately," someone said, "Monsieur le Chef de la Sûreté has no apparatus here that would be useful for demonstration..."

"It would indeed be interesting to carry out a few experiments in measurement," Cardec replied, negligently, "and to give you a few examples of recognition by means of the records, but..."

There was a pause. The Baron smiled, delighted with the guests' disappointment. The head of the Sûreté had spoiled his effect; that gave him pleasure. "We'll be obliged to seek another kind of distraction," he said. "Messieurs, the gaming awaits you..."

"One moment!" said Cardec, cutting off the Baron. And, taking on the tone of a street-hawker, he went on: "Mesdames et Messieurs, like the celebrated Robert Houdin, I have the ability to perform miracles..."

"Ha ha!" cried the guests, in chorus.

"It is as I have the honor of telling you...and I shall prove it. Look—I press this button three times..."

Matching action to speech, the head of the Sûreté pressed the button of an electric bell. It was assumed to be a joke, and laughter broke out among the audience.

A footman appeared at the door of the antechamber. "Madame rang?" he asked, in the midst of a general silence.

"No, it was me," Cardec replied. "Go to the fiacre that brought us here...number 883 I think..."

"No," said Lemoine. "It was 963."

"You have a better memory that I do, my dear chap. Thank you." And, continuing to give orders to the domestic, he went on: "Take the two boxes that are under the coachman's seat—he'll give them to you..."

Saint-Magloire frowned. He looked at Cardec anxiously. The number 883, which the head of the Sûreté had pronounced in an indifferent tone had sent a shiver through his body. 883 had been Rozen's number as a convict, and it was not possible that Cardec had been moved to mention it by chance alone.

He understood that a plot was being woven against him—but like a true gambler, he was determined to face up to the storm that he sensed rumbling in the distance. He heard a few whispers in the audience.

"It's prescience," said some.

"No, no," others declared. "It's like a conjuring trick...the obligatory card..."

"No," Cardec declared, "it's hazard alone, the god of the police, that is coming to my aid. I thought that there might perhaps be talk of criminology, and as my friend Lemoine has made a thorough study of Alphonse Bertillon's theory, and as, moreover, the charming lady we are celebrating had told me, when she invited me, about her desire to hear stories of brigands...I took my precautions, that's all, and equipped myself with everything necessary to interest people, if the need arose."

The footman, quite out of breath, brought Cardec the two boxes that he had gone to fetch. The circle around the head of the Sûreté and Lemoine had been enlarged somewhat. The Baron, putting on a brave face, had sat down in the front row next to Germaine Reyval.

The police magistrate opened one of the boxes; it was an elongated flat case in which various instruments resembling those of a draughtsman were maintained by hooks and pegs. There were compasses, graduated rulers and an instrument like the one that shoemakers employ for measuring their clients' feet; a meter rule, a manual, and printed cards completed the contents of the small case.

"This is a portable kit," said Cardec. "We intend to give you something more here than a glimpse of that interesting and complicated branch of police work. Permit me to explain to you how the various instruments that you have before your eyes are used, and to tell you what immense services the patient and savant schemes of Alphonse Bertillon have made to criminal research.

"Suppose, for example, that we arrest a bandit who is carefully dissimulating his identity. This is how we operate. He is taken to the Anthropometric Service, and there, he is measured..."

While speaking, Cardec had drawn closer to Saint-Magloire. "I need a volunteer," he said, "who will lend himself to the experiment. You, for example, Baron..."

The banker shook his head.

"Have no fear," said the head of the Sûreté, laughing.

Visibly annoyed, however, the Baron sought a means to avoid serving as the subject. "It would be more interesting to measure a lady," he said, with a slight tremor in his voice that Lemoine and the magistrate were the only ones to notice.

The guests, on seeing the Amphitryon striving to escape what they believed to be a simple joke, demanded insistently that he lend himself to the demonstration.

"Yes...yes...the Baron!"

"Go on, my friend," Germaine said to him. "Preach by example..."

"The Baron! The Baron! The Baron!" clamored the women in chorus, to the tune of a drinkers' chant.

Saint-Magloire understood that it might be awkward to resist any longer.

"All right, all right!" he laughed. "I yield to the plea of the fair sex. I've never refused anything to ladies..."

"Ever gallant!"

"Oh, very good, very good..."

"Would you like to sit here," the head of the Sûreté continued. "My friend Lemoine will now take my place. As he goes along he'll explain the phases of the measurement, its essential features, the process of swiftly achieving a recognition..."

The doctor went into action.

With the aid of the instruments from the box he took Saint-Magloire's measurements successively.

The banker was making a powerful effort of self-control. Even so, Lemoine felt his trembling.

When he had finished the demonstration of the measurement procedure, skillfully bringing out the essential features in order to help the lay audience to understand, he handed Cardec the printed card on which he had inscribed all the measurements he had taken as he went along.

"Now," the head of the Sûreté added, "this is the means of ascertaining whether the bandit who has just been measured is an old acquaintance of the Prefecture. I beg your pardon, Baron—it's just a manner of speaking..."

"I understand that," said Saint-Magloire, with a constrained laugh.

"Here," Cardec continued, "is a series of authentic records, for which I'm obliged to the Head of Anthropometry..."

At this point, we owe the reader an explanation.

When he had eagerly accepted Germaine's invitation, the head of the Sûreté already had an idea. He had developed it further thereafter in concert with Lemoine, who had thought it superb, and he had gone to refer it to the Prefect of Police.

The pretext for striking at Saint-Magloire had been found. It was known that he often saw the nihilist Sokoloff in the little house at Auteuil. It was also known that Bastien, alias Macaron, an undeniable anarchist, was a party to the conversations in question. These comings and goings of the three mysterious individuals indicated that they were hatching some plot against society, and it was indispensable to nip it in the bud. Did not the famous Article 10 of the Code d'Instruction Criminelle give the Prefect of Police full power to act in such circumstances?

In brief, Monsieur Cardec had been given *carte blanche*. He had been permitted to acquire from the Anthropometric Service everything necessary to the execution of the plan that he had made and which we have seen put into operation. Monsieur Bertillon being away, Lemoine had been deputed to assist the head of the Sûreté.

"Let us suppose," Cardec declaimed, pompously, "that by a series of selections made from the height, the color of the eyes, the color of the hair, etc., etc., we find a particular group that includes the data that will convince us of the gentleman's identity, which he is being carefully concealed..."

While speaking, Cardec never lost sight of the Baron. He saw his gaze fixed, as if hypnotized, on the box containing the authentic records advertised by the head of the Sûreté.

The man in question, who had never trembled in previous circumstances, that bold, audacious and powerful adventurer, felt weak at that moment. He understood that a danger was threatening him, and could not entirely divine its nature.

More than once, he had asked himself whether it would not be better to cut short the scene and use the pretext of a indisposition to absent himself—to escape them mental torture that the policeman was inflicting upon him with his bantering tone...but he told himself that flight would be stupid, if this "experiment," obviously planed in advance—he had no doubt about that—had only been attempted with the objective of pushing him to betray himself...

After a few seconds of suspense, in order to keep his audience breathless, the head of the Sûreté, placing his finger on the lid of the box that contained the records leant to him by Monsieur Bertillon's service, continued, raising his voice slightly.

"I have collected here the descriptions of several famous murderers, a few crooks of genius, numerous cut-throats, fraudulent bankrupts, etc. There are some to satisfy all tastes! But there is one in particular that concerns the most extraordinary individual with whom I have had to occupy myself in the course of my career."

Here, Cardec opened the box, rummaged through the records and extracted one of them.

"Here it is," he said, "here it is! Oh, the fellow whose complete description is inscribed on this little card had given us quite a thread to unravel...he was a man of intelligence—intelligence unfortunately devoted to evil. You're all familiar with the story of that surprising criminal, Mesdames et Messieurs. It filled the columns of Parisian newspapers some years ago; there is probably no need to remind you now..."

"No... No!" exclaimed a few guests, gripped by Cardec's patter. "The story... The story!"

"I repeat that you all know it...at least up to the time that he was sent to Cayenne. In the aristocracy of criminality he was very highly placed...a prince of thieves, a king of fraud...

"Unfortunately, he came to a bad end. So it was believed, at least, for today, we cannot be entirely certain that he died escaping from Cayenne. Who knows? Perhaps he's among us!"

Saint-Magloire started violently—which everyone assumed to be the indignant protest of the master of the house reproached for entertaining a disreputable individual. "That joke oversteps the limits!" he said, in a voice that he strove to render firm.

"I'm not joking, Monsieur le Baron, "and I would not dreams of betraying the charming hospitality that Madame Reyval has accorded to me by doing so. I was asked for a story of brigands; I'm narrating the one that appears to me to be the most interesting. I said that this crook of genius might be among us. I meant that he is in Paris...for here, we all know one another, and I don't quite understand Monsieur de Saint-Magloire's interruption..."

"I beg you to excuse me," the Baron declared, having recovered his self-composure somewhat. "I misinterpreted..."

"It's for me to excuse myself," the head of the Sûreté riposted, darting a malicious glance at Saint-Magloire, who shivered. "I know how carefully the invitations were made that have brought us together in this delightful house. But I'll get back to my story. So, the bandit in question might be alive—and, rightly or wrongly, we suspect that, under a respected name, under a cover of perfect honorability and a brilliant position, he is the author of the crimes and thefts that have made Paris tremble in recent times. I shall not astonish you, Mesdames et Messieurs, when I tell you the name of this modern Cartouche..." He brandished the card he held between his thumb and index-finger. "The name of that emperor of crime was Rozen."

Saint-Magloire went pale, but held firm under Cardec's penetrating gaze, and that of Lemoine, which he felt weighing upon him.

"But we're getting away from our anthropometric experiment," said Cardec, abandoning his declamatory tone. Over to you, Lemoine. Identify Monsieur le Baron de Saint-Magloire..."

Lemoine took the cards that were in the box and, while giving a few explanations on the method adopted to filter the comparative reports, made a semblance of examining a few attentively.

"Oh!" he said. "Here's something curious!"

"What is it?"

"It's enough to make one doubt the Bertillon system!"

"Go on."

"Yes...this summary report that I've just drawn up of Monsieur le Baron's measurements, corresponds point by point with that of Rozen."

A general burst of laughter greeted this remark.

"Yes," Lemoine went on, when silence was reestablished, "it's all there: the length and breadth of the skull...the extension of the medius and the left auricular...the dimensions of the right ear, etc., etc. It's extraordinary! If we weren't certain of being in the presence of the true Baron de Saint-Magloire...if we didn't have the honor of being the guest of his friend, I would say to the man I've just measured: Monsieur, you are Rozen."

"And," said the head of the Sûreté, putting his hand on the Baron's shoulder, I would add: "In the name of the law, I arrest you."

Cardec could feel the Baron trembling like a leaf. His eyes were flashing with fury. He was lived.

But the guests, not forewarned, did not notice those details.

A salvo of applause thanked the head of the Sûreté and his friend for the scene they had just performed...

That created a diversion and permitted Saint-Magloire to pull himself together somewhat. Momentarily, he had thought that it was all over. He looked at the head of the Sûreté anxiously, believing that he was about to flourish an arrest warrant, that inspectors were about to arrive in response an agreed signal, and that he would leave the hotel with his wrists imprisoned in a set of handcuffs...but none of that happened, and hope was reborn. It really had been a comedy...and he supposed that he had not been betrayed.

He stood up, and, while laughing, concluded: "That's funny...very funny..."

"Isn't it?" said Cardec, ironically. And the head of the Sûreté resumed the tone of the salesman, crying in a loud voice; "Come on, Mesdames, whose turn is it? My friend Lemoine and his compasses are at your disposal. Who doesn't have her little card? Take advantage of the opportunity..."

"Me! Me!" clamored several women, enormous amused.

Lemoine set about measuring several pretty guests in succession, who lent themselves to the operation gladly.

While the doctor was occupied in that game, in which everyone was taking a keen interest, Cardec did not lose sight of Saint-Magloire.

Taking advantage of the general inattention, the Baron had gone to the table on which stood the box in which the head of the Sûreté had replaced Rozen's record card. The Baron did not think that Cardec was tracking his movements, but while pretending to assist Lemoine, the magistrate was watching the banker attentively.

The latter, while putting on a semblance of examining the contents of the box curiously, had delicately abstracted Rozen's record and was heading for the large fireplace, where an ardent wood fire was burning.

At that moment, Cardec came toward him. In the most natural fashion in the world, Saint-Magloire put his hands behind his back, and struck the pose of someone warming his legs.

"Are you cold, Baron?" asked the head of the Sûreté, sarcastically.

"Yes," Saint-Magloire replied. "I don't feel well, and I'm going to ask our guests for permission to withdraw...all the more so as Madame Saint-Magloire is ill, and..."

Suddenly, with a flick of his fingers, he threw the card that he was holding into the hearth—but before it had fallen into the fire, Cardec had caught it in mid-air.

Eye to eye, the two men remained silent for a moment. Then the magistrate, handed the card to the petrified Saint-Magloire.

"You dropped this."

"Me."

"Yes. You're stupid, Baron...Rozen. The exemplar isn't unique. Come on, Rozen, you've given yourself away twenty times over. Your mask has been torn away. You're caught."

"I beg you," murmured Saint-Magloire, "don't arrest me here. Avoid the scandal...for Germaine's sake." The banker's face was distraught. He could scarcely stand up. The blow that had struck him full in the chest was rude.

But Cardec had already gone back to resume his place beside Lemoine. The anthropometry session continued. Everyone wanted to have a card...and two operators were not sufficient.

The night was wearing on, however...

It was four o'clock in the morning...

Suddenly, Germane Reyval, anxious at no longer being able to see the Baron, questioned her guests.

Everyone looked for the Baron.

"The Baron!" exclaimed Cardec. "Oh, I forgot; a little while ago, he was suddenly taken ill and was obliged to ask me to excuse him..."

The head of the Sûreté went over to Germaine, shook her hand in a significant fashion, and said to her in a low voice: "Not a word—the Baron has fled..."

"Oh, my God," the young woman murmured. "Fled! Him! It wasn't a joke, then?"

"Keep it quiet, I said. I wanted to avoid an arrest that would cause a scandal in your home." And, raising his voice in such a way as to be heard by the assembly, the magistrate thanked Germaine for her hospitality.

Lemoine added his compliments to his friend's, and they both went out, carrying the boxes that had played such a fantastic role a little while before.

Germaine, ready to weep, accompanied them to the door—but she made an effort to hide her trouble, and it was with a smile on her lips that she returned to the midst of her guests.

In the fiacre that was taking them home, Dr. Lemoine questioned his friend Cardec. "I don't understand. You let him run away."

"Exactly. Believe me, I'm convinced that the big chiefs with be grateful to me for acting that way rather than otherwise."

"But that's insane. He'll run home, collect his money, and tomorrow, he'll have put the frontier between himself and the law. It's crazy..."

"Collect his money?" riposted the head of the Sûreté. "I hope so. The bank and the house are under surveillance."

"Oh!"

"Come on—you don't take me for a novice, I assume. Without a sou, Rozen won't get far—and besides, all my measures have been taken; we'll always know where to find him when we want. In any cases, Paris is free of him—*Deo gratias!* This morning, the bank, his house and the house at Auteuil will be searched. We'll arrest Sokoloff and Bastien there..."

"Be careful at Auteuil. The house is booby-trapped."

"Good, good...that won't make any difference."

"Finally," Lemoine concluded, "we've had the last word...and all the honor for that is yours."

"You've played your part, old man."

"Tomorrow," Lemoine declared, when he separated from his friend, "I must go to Eléna. Poor woman..."

451

"You're wrong to feel sorry for her. The bandit would have killed her some day."

XV. The Debacle

When the head of the Sûreté had left the Baron de Saint-Magloire after the scene we have just described, the latter stood there momentarily, rooted to the spot. He was trembling as if he had suddenly been afflicted with epilepsy. It seemed to him that his shriveled, desiccated brain was swinging in his skull like the clapper of a bell.

Livid, he wanted for the two inspectors who were going to collect him and take him to the Station in handcuffs. A miserable end to a grandiose dream...

The colossus with feet of clay collapsed. The bandit who had planned to dominate toppled from the height of his immeasurable ambition.

This time, it would not be the bagne. The crimes committed since his escape destined him for the guillotine. His head belonged to Monsieur de Paris. Rozen could already feel the ignominious blade descending upon his neck. A sigh, almost a death-rattle, escaped his throat. He was obliged to lean on the marble fireplace in order not to fall over.

When he perceived that he had been left alone, however, and that no one had come in to arrest him; when he saw Cardec and Dr. Lemoine calmly continuing their anthropometric experiments as if nothing had happened, Saint-Magloire gradually recovered his composure. A smile passed over his discolored lips; his gaze resumed its intelligent expression.

Am I mad? he asked himself. *Arrest me, put me on trial? They wouldn't dare. It's simply a warning that they're giving me. It's a demanded that I disappear, that I abdicate. I hold too many people in my hand for them to have the courage to take me to court; it's my silence they're buying...*

Well, yes, I'll go; yes, I'll go and set myself up somewhere else...the game I'm playing isn't conclusively lost yet...

Come on, Rozen, be brave! You'll have the last word.

He had drawn himself up to his full height again and, certain that Germaine's guests, distracted by Lemoine's explanations, could not see him, he headed for the antechamber, rapidly put on his overcoat and left the house.

Down below, the servants were gaily emptying the bottles put aside by the sommelier, and no one paid any attention to Monsieur le Baron.

In the street, the carriages were lined up under the guard of two or three coachmen. The others had gone to a nearby wine-merchant's to play Zanzibar and chat.

Momentarily, Saint-Magloire thought about taking his coupé, which was parked outside Germaine's house, but he abandoned that plan. To what address would he have himself taken? Would his servants not observe his agitation?

In any case, the Baron needed to walk. The night air would do him good.

He increased his pace, and went down toward the Parc Monceau, not without checking to see that he was not being followed. An attentive examination reassured him. No one appeared to be dogging his footsteps.

Rozen was mistaken. Three men had attached themselves to his tail. The first two were moving prudently along the railings of the park, in the shadows projected by its border. They were two of Monsieur Cardec's agents, whom he had posted in the vicinity of Germaine Reyval's house with orders not to lose sight of the Baron. The third person, who had quit the guard of one of the carriages arranged along the Rue de Prony, was following at a distance. He was easily recognizable by his tall stature and exotic costume; it was the Chinaman Yu.

The good servant had been taken by surprise. He found it strange that the Baron did not climb into his coupé. Endowed with great perspicacity, he had noticed the banker's jerky gait. Why was a man ordinarily so calm walking so rapidly?

Yu wanted to know where he was going, and he set off, leaving the footman to guard the vehicle.

After having walked for some time, Saint-Magloire, who had recovered all of his mental lucidity, slowed down in order to collect his thoughts.

For a moment, he thought about going to Auteuil to warn Sokoloff, but he did not persist in that idea. Why warn Sokoloff? The most urgent thing was to take immediate advantage of the facility of flight that had been granted to him. The others were of scant importance to him. They could get themselves out of trouble as best they could—and in the final analysis, Sokoloff and Bastien were somewhat inconvenient. It would not have been disagreeable to see them disappear."

At that moment, a fiacre was going along the Boulevard de Courcelles. It was one of those nocturnal vehicles driven by an aged, wrinkled coachman, one of those countless unpainted vehicles that are falling apart, clinking metallically, seemingly held together by a miracle of equilibrium, such as passengers disembarking in Paris by night at railway stations find at their disposal. The antique rattletrap going past Saint-Magloire was a veritable model of the type. The horse, the coachman and the carriage itself seemed to be a hundred years old. One might have thought it a prodigy that the rig was still moving. The starveling beast could not have been unhitched since time immemorial; the driver seemed riveted to the worm-eaten sets; inside, the worn and greasy cushions reeked of mold. A bizarre odor emerged from the "roller": a mixture of the residues of old pipes, sweat and horse manure.

On seeing Rozen walking at a measured pace along the sidewalk, the coachman scented a client and called out to him in a hoarse voice: "A carriage, my prince? Ordinary rate. Go on, let yourself go…it's no trouble…you'll have a nice ride…"

Saint-Magloire hesitated momentarily; then he thought that he would not find a regular coupé, and leapt into the carriage, which groaned under his weight. He was so preoccupied at that moment that he paid no attention o the repulsive dirtiness of the vehicle. Even his sense of smell was not offended by the reek exhaled by the cushions on which he had sat down, weary and bowed down by the atrocious fear that was still running through him.

"Where to, Bourgeois?" asked the coachman.

"Place Vendôme."

Believing himself to be alone, the Baron had spoken distinctly. One of the policemen—the nearer of the two to the Baron—overheard. He made a sign to his colleague, who came closer.

"No need to follow now," murmured the agent. "We know where he's going. The orders are to let him go."

The rattletrap had already set off, making an infernal racket on the roadway.

"Hang on," said one of the policemen. "Who's that fellow running after the jalopy at top speed?"

"A Chinaman!" said the other, astonished.

"Well, old chap, if he keeps that up all the way to the Place Vendôme, he'll deserve a round of applause.

"We're finished, right?"

"Completely. Now, I think it's time to go to bed."

"That's my opinion. Since Monsieur le Baron permits...don't forget to mention the Chinaman in your report."

"Understood. *Au revoir.*"

While the two men were separating, the carriage sped on, followed by Yu, who was running breathlessly.

The emaciated mare hitched to the fiacre, excited by cracks of the whip delivered by the coachman, glad to have found a client, was galloping like a thoroughbred.

Saint-Magloire, completely in control of himself, was establishing his plan of campaign.

I've got about twelve hundred thousand francs in the safe at the bank, he said to himself. *That's a pretty penny...and I'll be able to recommence the assault...make myself a new identity abroad, while waiting for better days...and come back to Paris in a few years' time. Then again, I don't want to leave them my papers, for the bank will naturally be searched tomorrow. The curiosity-seekers won't find anything. Stupid of them not to have grabbed me straight away...prepared to let me go because they're afraid of my revelations...*

A pitying smile passed over his lips.

I'm definitely stronger than them. I'll roll them over...all the way...

The carriage was about to turn the corner of the Rue des Capucines and the boulevard when the Baron told the coachman to stop. He judged it unnecessary to let the man know exactly where he was going. He put a louis in the dazzled Automedon's hand, and blessings accompanied the client all the way to the corner.

Having reached the Place Vendôme, Saint-Magloire stifled an oath. Men were racing back and forth in front of the bank. At that ungodly hour, they were obviously not strollers.

That was a harsh blow. The bandit's disappointment was bitter.

He understood that the struggle was impossible—and he had an intuition that at present, Cardec was playing with him like a cat with a mouse. Evidently, he was caught in the head of the Sûreté's net. The latter had not wanted to arrest him at Germaine's house; he had been prepared to wait to arrest him in his own time, without causing a scene. It was necessary to run, to shake off the agents of the Prefecture he sensed at his heels. But how could he reach the frontier with the derisory sum he had on him?

The situation was becoming critical.

What could he do without any other money than the few hundred-franc bills contained in his wallet?

That evening, he had not thought it necessary to carry very much money. In Germaine's house, the gambling would not be very expensive.

It was definitely a debacle...wretched flight, life without a sou...an existence of expedients...the small crimes he would be obliged to commit...

If he had only been able to go to his house in the Champs-Élysées! There, in his private safe, he had about two hundred thousand francs in bearer bonds and twenty thousand-franc bills; he could also take Eléna's jewelry...with that it would still be possible to do something serious...

But the house in the Champs-Élysées was bound to be guarded, like the building in the Place Vendôme.

Somber, his fists clenched and his lip trembling, he retreated at a fast pace under the Arcades of the Rue Castiglione.

And he thought once again about Sokoloff. The Russian had money. The house at Auteuil contained the funds that were to aliment the anarchist army on the day when it would be mobilized for the general upheaval. But would Sokoloff let him dip into his war-chest? He would certainly forbid it.

But then, no! Rozen would be able to take possession of it, if only at the price of a crime. Why hesitate to kill Sokoloff?

All these thoughts were floating incoherently in the wretch's mind. In his confusion he had not thought right away that the house in Auteuil must be under surveillance, like the house in the Champs-Élysées—and when that idea occurred to him, he realized that he was encircled by a ring of iron. It really was the end, with no hope of getting up again.

At that early hour, the Rue Castiglione was deserted. Gradually, the Baron felt his self-composure ebbing away. He wandered aimlessly, talking to himself like a drunkard. All those successive emotions had annihilated his physical vigor. His eyes were veiled; he was walking as if in a nightmare, and, in the darkness, fell prey to a kind of nightmare.

He suddenly thought he saw Dulac's corpse looming up before him. His former comrade had the rope around his neck that he had passed over the gate of Germaine's villa…and Dulac was laughing in a sinister fashion.

Rozen thought he was going mad.

Beside Dulac he saw Lavardens, and then the boatman from Cayenne, and then the Maltese killed by Macaron, and also the poor gaucho, the true Saint-Magloire, whose documents he had stolen…

All those phantoms were following him…and soon, the group was swollen by all the anarchist comrades shot down on Île Royale.

Unsteady and bewildered, the Baron stopped.

The strongest and most hardened of men, under the influence of physical fatigue, sometimes loses all his mental energy. Fear and panic took possession of him…and Rozen, who had never been afraid, trembled.

That impression of fear dissipated rapidly, however. Moreover, someone had just arrived by his side, and he stood up, ready to defend himself if it were a policeman.

"Oh, it's you, Yu," he murmured. "I'm doomed, my poor Yu, doomed…for the sacred cause."

Even at that critical moment, the actor in Rozen survived. In a few seconds, he made up an entire story of the discovered plot.

"It's the end, you see," he concluded. "There's nothing I can do. No money accessible…it's the end…the end."

The Chinaman smiled and shook his head.

"No?" said Saint-Magloire. "You're saying no?"

The mute picked up the slate he was never without, and by the light of the street-lamps the Baron as able to read the words that the Celestial scribbled in haste: *Master, tell Yu what he can do to save you, and Yu will do it.*

"If I could just get into my house," the Baron replied, "if only for a quarter of an hour…I could find what I need to go abroad and recommence the struggle…"

There was a flicker of hope in the Chinaman's eyes. The revolutionary could not admit that the man who personified, in his eyes, the great work of social regeneration, his life's dream, the god of his religion, was defeated. He was ready to do anything to help him pick himself up again.

Rapidly, he wrote on the slate: *Come with me. You'll get into the house.* And the physiognomy of the Son of Heaven expressed grim resolution.

Hope returned to Rozen. It was a vague hope, but in his present state of distress, he would have grasped at the slightest straw.

"Let's go," he said.

They both left silently by way of the Rue Rivoli; they went through the Place de la Concorde and up the Avenue des Champs-Élysées.

Level with the Rue de Washington, You took the Baron's arm and showed him the slate. Rozen read: *Go in by the little door to the Rue de Balzac.*

The Chinaman's idea was excellent. Why had he not thought of it sooner? Perhaps that door, opening into the garden of the house, would not be well-guarded. It was possible, after all, that the police did not know about that secret exit, which the inhabitants of the house never used.

However, as they emerged from the Avenue Friedland into the Rue de Balzac, the Baron uttered a muffled exclamation. Two men were stationed on the sidewalk in front of the little hidden door.

Cardec had not neglected anything. He had foreseen everything. It was an impasse into which he had drawn the adventurer. For want of official punishment he had inflicted a penalty upon him that was perhaps harsher for him than those foreseen by the Code: poverty! He, Saint-Magloire, accustomed to throwing money out of the windows, would be reduced to living meagerly—dying of hunger, so to speak...

But Yu took hold of his wrist and, pointing at the two men, made him understand by signs that he would take care of them, and that Rozen only had to concern himself with one thing: getting into the house.

Rozen had a fit of sincere gratitude; he shook the hands of that precious man affectionately. Not for an instant did he think that he was betraying the poor Chinaman, who believed that he was working for the revolutionary cause, but whose devotion was only favoring the interests of a thief and murderer...

Yu responded to his mater's grip with an expressive handshake, and set off, shaving the walls, followed at a distance by the Baron.

Resolutely, he arrived at the little door, and put on a show of going to open it. With one bound, one of the agents of the Sûreté posted in the street was beside the Chinaman.

"You can't go in there," he said.

The policeman's only response was a punch in the head that knocked him down in the roadway. It had happened so rapidly that the second inspector had not had time to lend his colleague a hand. He launched himself at the Chinaman in his turn and a terrible struggle began between the two men.

Hidden in the arch of a coaching-entrance, Saint-Magloire watched the scene, waiting anxiously for the way to be clear.

The first agent had got up again, and Yu was now fighting furiously against two adversaries, but with the vigor of desperation he shook the two inspectors so violently that they were obliged to let go of him. Then the Celestial, gesturing to Saint-Magloire, hurled himself into the Avenue des Chaps-Élysées.

Instinctively, the two inspectors launched themselves in pursuit, and one of them fired a revolver shot into the air to warn his colleagues in the avenue.

Yu's stratagem had succeeded completely.

With a turn of his wrist, Saint-Magloire opened the door, went into the garden of his house and swiftly closed it behind him.

At the corner of the avenue and the Rue de Balzac, Yu ran into a group of four men—an inspector and three guardians of the peace—attracted by the shot, who had run to help their fellows. In the blink of an eye the Chinaman was grabbed and knocked to the ground—but in the struggle, which he sustained with a strength multiplied tenfold by desperation, Yu had succeeded in snatching the bayonet from one of the *sergents de ville*, and he stood up, thrusting off the human cluster that was holding on to him. Somewhat disconcerted by that surprising vigor, the policemen had recoiled and drawn their revolvers.

Yu was frightening. His eyes were bulging; his mouth, twisted in a horrible rictus, allowed the sight of the horrible mutilation of the tongue that he had once suffered. His face had been raked by fingernails during the struggle and blood was running from his bruised features. His clothes were in tatters.

With the naked blade in his hand, he whirled his arms around, trying to get through—but the agents held him at by with their revolvers.

While continuing to threaten the policemen, the Chinaman glanced in the direction of the Rue de Balzac. He saw that Saint-Magloire was no longer there and his face lit up.

At that moment, one of the agents ordered him to drop his weapon. Yu shook his head. The revolvers were aimed at him again, and the Celestial understood that escape was impossible.

He preferred to end it. A mad rage took hold of him. He did not want to fall into the hands of the police.

Then, casting a defiant gaze at all the men who, for him, were enemies of the Revolution, the Chinaman raised his blade, turned the point toward his breast, and ran himself through with a single thrust.

For a moment he remained upright, tragically, his face turned toward the heavens; then he spun round and collapsed, uttering a formidable sigh.

"Well, old chap, it was bound to happen!" exclaimed one of the guardians of the peace.

"We have to tell the boss," said one of the inspectors.

And while the cadaver of the man who had died for him was carried away, Saint-Magloire, completely reassured, went stealthily through the garden of his house and silently went into the building.

XVI. The Flight

Inside the house, everything was silent. With infinite precaution, Saint-Magloire opened the door which gave access to the garden. To facilitate his exit, he avoided closing it.

Turning a commutator, he illuminated the staircase and went up to his study on tiptoe, fearful that every step that some creak or bump might reveal his presence.

Still with a view to a rapid escape, he left the door to the landing ajar.

That doorway was, in any case, lined with a curtain that was sufficient to muffle any slight sound he might make in sorting through the papers that he wanted to carry away.

Once in his study, where no one but himself and his faithful Yu had ever set foot, he felt slightly reassured. His gaze went to the safe, set in a corner of the room, and a glint of joy appeared in his eyes. Finally, he was about to take possession of the two hundred thousand francs it contained, and the compromising documents he had locked up with them, thanks to which he would be able to blackmail many people.

That thought restored a little of the strength that had abandoned him a short while before.

Two hundred thousand francs was obviously a trivial amount by comparison with the colossal sums he had handled, but with such a capital, he told himself, a resourceful man like him would quickly rebuild his fortune.

Eléna's jewels? He left them out for the time being. It would have been dangerous to go into the Baronne's apartment, to brazen out an encounter with her; better to play a discreet part and content himself with what he had to hand.

Rozen was back on his feet now.

On reflection, he no longer believed his situation to be as critical as he had thought a little while ago, in the moment of madness that had overtaken him.

Extradition…he had thought of that, but he would be able to avoid it, if anyone even bothered to request it. The essential thing was to depart as soon as possible, on the first train to Brussels. It was necessary not to allow the police time to get back...

Evidently, all the precautions taken by Cardec proved that the head of the Sûreté did not believe that he should arrest someone as important at the Baron de Saint-Magloire. The police magistrate did not want to be responsible for the scandal that would be the inevitable consequence of such an arrest, and he had spread his agents around to act in the event that an order from the Ministry of the Interior authorized him to do so.

Come on, Rozen, the adventurer said to himself. *You weakened jut now...pull yourself together; a little backbone, and victory is still possible...*

With that private admonition, he set about opening the safe—but no matter how gently he went about it, he could not avoid the slight click produced by the catch.

He shivered. It seemed that he had heard someone move in the next room. He listened.

Nothing. The silence was absolute.

Another hallucination, he thought. You're definitely weakening, Saint-Magloire.

He took various wads from the drawers of the safe, and after having examined them rapidly, he stuck the bonds and banknotes in a wallet, and placed the precious package next to his breast, between his waistcoat and shirt-front.

Then he went through the papers scattered on his desk, kept those that interested him and threw the rest in the fireplace. When that was done, he set fire to the latter pile of papers.

There's no need for them to find the elements of the case for the prosecution when they search, he said to himself. *It's not worth the trouble of brining them up to date with my little operations.*

Crouching in front of the hearth, he was stirring the pieces of paper with a poker in order to make sure that they burned completely, when he heard someone call softly from behind: "Rozen."

With one bound he was upright. Pale, his eyes crazed, his body was agitated by a convulsive tremor...but there was no one in the study.

Suppressing his emotion, he resumed poking the blaze of papers.

A second time he heard his name whispered: "Rozen."

"Damn it," he muttered, through clenched teeth, racked by an atrocious fear. "Am I going mad? Who pronounced my name? What does it mean?"

The curtain masking the door had been raised.

Her eyes sparkling, firm and resolute, a woman was standing there, threatening him with a revolver. "It means, wretch, that you've given yourself away twice over."

"Madame Vauclair," he murmured.

"No—Oliva Lavardens: the widow of the unfortunate man who trusted you, and whom you murdered."

It was indeed Oliva who was standing vengefully before Saint-Magloire.

Madame Lavardens, woken up by the noise of Yu's battle with the police, had heard the door to the garden open. She had, so to speak, followed all of Rozen's movements and for a few moments, hidden behind the curtain in the doorway of the study, had been watching the bandit's movements.

Momentarily, Rozen thought about leaping at Oliva's throat, but he glimpsed the consequences of that action: the house woken up, the servants and Eléna running...

461

He changed his mind, and it was with a perfectly feigned astonishment that he replied: "Madame, I don't understand this comedy. Will you please return to the Baronne and let me work..."

"Oh, you don't understand? It wasn't you, Rozen who killed my poor Charles like the coward you are?"

"Rozen? Charles? Madame Vauclair, you're mad..."

"No, I'm not mad. No, you really are Rozen...for jut now, your name, pronounced in a low voice, threw you into such terror that you were no longer in control of yourself..."

"Once again, I beg you..."

"Shut up," Oliva ordered, imperiously, "and listen to me. The day when I had the bloody and disfigured corpse of the husband I adored before my eyes, I swore that I would find his murderer and deliver him to the law. I devoted my life to that task. Patiently, accepting the most dolorous proofs, I pursued my goal...to avenge the victim of an abominable crime. I've known for some time that the Baron de Saint-Magloire was an escaped convict..."

"Madness..." groaned the banker.

"Truth. Ask your accomplice, that Robertson, whose ignominious society I tolerated, who confessed that he had known you out there. Oh, he had no need to tell me that it was in Cayenne; I understood...and if I have not acted sooner, Rozen, it's because I knew that you were going to be unmasked. Tonight, they were supposed to arrest you.

"You've been able to escape the claws of the police thus far...but Heaven has placed me in your path. You won't escape me. I shall deliver you to the law, and you'll finally answer for your crimes. It doesn't matter to me that others will be compromised by you, or that there will be a scandal. I want the scaffold to avenge my husband's death. It's inevitable that you'll be condemned to death once you're in the hands of the judges. No mercy will stop the punishment."

"This is too much," said Rozen, finally. "I'm going to ring for someone to get rid of you."

"You won't ring; I don't want you to wake the unhappy woman, that you've treacherously brought to the brink of the tomb. She would be dead if Dr. Lemoine hadn't been there to save her. Listen to me carefully, Rozen. I'm going to stay here with you until the police come to take you. If you take one step to leave, I'll kill you like a dog."

"That's good," the bandit murmured. "Wait until you recognize yourself the ridiculous error that you've made. You see, Madame Vauclair, my attitude ought to demonstrate to you that I have nothing but pity for your absurd accusations—but tomorrow...or rather, very soon—you'll leave this house.. I don't want madwomen n my home. You'll permit me, at least, to sit down at my desk. I have important work to finish." With a sarcastic smile, he added: "Oh, you won't disturb me. You can stand guard if you wish."

Sure of herself, Oliva acceded to this desire. She could not suspect what was going through the mind of that man endowed with a diabolical intelligence. While listening to Madame Lavardens, Rozen had thought of a way to get himself out of trouble.

Instead of going to sit down at his desk, as he had requested, he had moved gradually closer to Oliva, and with gesture as rapid as lightning he had seized her wrist, which he squeezed as if to break it.

The pain obliged the widow to drop the weapon she held in her hand. She tried in vain to pick it up. Rozen kicked the revolver under the desk.

"And now, Oliva Lavardens," he said, with a frightful calm, "you won't prevent Rozen from escaping.

Momentarily terrorized, Oliva tried to shout for help, but Gaston Rozen's iron hand stifled the unfortunate woman's cry of distress.

"You asked for it—too bad!" And while he squeezed the young woman's throat, as if in a vice, he took a dagger from his desk, which he used as a paper-knife, and stabbed Oliva with a terrible thrust.

She fell inert, her breast punctured: one more crime marking out 883's route.

"She had it coming," Rozen murmured—and, without looking at the corpse of his victim, he made sure that the wallet next to his own breast had not shifted, calmly picked up the papers he had put to one side before Oliva's arrival from his desk, and went downstairs.

Dawn was just breaking when he arrived in the street. He looked to the right and the left, but did not see anyone. Then he went rapidly along the Rue de Balzac, only slowing his pace when he reached the corner of the Faubourg Saint-Honoré and the Boulevard Haussmann.

At a placid pace he walked to the Gare Saint-Lazare.

Already, a few marauding coachmen were circulating in quest of clients to take aboard. He stopped one of the carriages and installed himself therein, after having said to the coachman: "Gare du Nord…there's a good tip."

Almost at the same time, a man he had not noticed, who had followed him prudently from the Rue Balzac, climbed into another fiacre, having spoken a few rapid words to the Automedon.

The second carriage did not take long to overtake Saint-Magloire's, and arrived at the Gare du Nord a few minutes before his.

The man got down and hurriedly went into the waiting room.

Five minutes later, the Barton de Saint-Magloire bought a first-class ticket to Brussels.

Immediately behind him, two travelers, who looked like provincial *petits bourgeois*, and who gave no sign of recognizing him, asked at the window for second-class tickets to the same destination.

Cardec had arranged things well, and the Baron de Saint-Magloire, in flight, could not, according to the time-honored saying, pass unnoticed.

XVII. The Last Battle

Monsieur Cardec did not go to bed that night.

It was not enough for him to have unmasked Saint-Magloire; certain that the adventurer could not escape the toils of the extended net, and that he could take him into custody whenever he wishes, even if he tried to leave the country, the head of the Sûreté had, in spite of the early hour, alerted his direct superior, the Prefect of Police.

Warmly congratulated for the initiative of which he had given proof and the prudent tact with which he had operated. Cardec rapidly brought the Prefect up to date regarding the situation.

The conspiracy discovered between Saint-Magloire, Macaron and Sokoloff was clear evidence that an anarchist plot, of which he was the mastermind, was being hatched in the villa at Auteuil.

The measures taken by the head of the Sûreté had not permitted the banker to warn his acolytes or to get rid of the important papers held in the premises in the Place Vendôme, where he funds of the anarchist party had to be deposited, which would throw the principal affiliates of that dangerous organization into the hands of the police.

Without wasting a minute, the Prefect of Police alerted the Minister of the Interior, and at dawn, at the very moment when Saint-Magloire was heading for Belgium, closely followed by the two sleuths from the Quasi des Orfèvres, the police forces were on the move.

The court was immediately involved in the affair, and arrest warrants were issued for Sokoloff sand Bastien, alias Macaron. Other blank warrants awaited the names that the searches immediately ordered of the premises in the Place Vendôme, the Avenue des Champs-Élysées and at Auteuil would yield.

The search of the Banque Saint-Magloire was edifying, with regard to the shady operations of the former convict. The examining magistrate, assisted by Cardec and several gents of the Sûreté, placed all the papers seized under seal, as well as the bank's accountant—and the usher Florent, utterly bewildered and very pained by the terrible things that were happening to Monsieur le Baron, tremulously gave all the information he could. As he was, in sum, an honest man, a good servant on whom no suspicion could weigh, he was left at the bank, where two agents were guarding the seals.

The magistrates would have liked to question Monsieur Baker, the principal employee, who was designated as the boss's right arm, but Baker, too subtle to throw himself into the wolf's mouth, had scented, on seeing the bank under guard, that it was no longer a safe place for him, and had simply and phlegmatically turned on his heels and immediately gone to pack his bag for the free country of England, where he knew that no one would come looking for him.

Another individual had similarly come to prowl around the vicinity of the bank. On perceiving the curious crowds in the square in front of the bank, he felt that he had been kicked in the stomach. It was Bastien, who had come to "tap" Saint-Magloire for a few banknotes. Following the Baron's strict orders, he no longer set foot in the house in the Champs-Élysées, and when he wanted to see the boss he asked for him at his office.

In order to find out exactly what was happening, Macaron joined the gawkers. From the right and the left he collected a few items of information, and learned that the Baron de Saint-Magloire had fled, and that the bank was being searched. There was already talk of a plot.

In the blink of an eye, Rozen's accomplice glimpsed the danger. He understood that the "balloon man," as he called Lemoine, must have denounced the meetings in the house at Auteuil to the "cops."

One thing astonished him, however. Why had Rozen not warned him?

It did not take him long to find an answer to that question, which he asked himself mentally.

Why? Because he's not a brother, of course. Others are of no consequence to him. He's taken a hike…get out of it if you can, the rest of you. Me, I'll get out! Damn it, if I catch up with him, that Rozen…I'll spit in his eye. But that's not all…must warn Sokoloff…save the comrades. A pity, if the searchers in there get their hands, as is all too probable, on the association's money…that will do for us good and proper…

Bastien, as we have said, felt his sentiments of anarchist brotherhood revive in moments of peril. He was a bandit, capable of the most criminal acts, a dilettante murderer, but he was not a traitor, and rather than run away like Rozen, leaving his friends in the lurch, he preferred to be arrested trying to save the fervent adherents of the revolutionary cause. Moreover, he had an admiration for Sokoloff bordering on worship; for Bastien, the Russian was a god…and it was necessary to warn him about the danger at all costs. He was surely strong enough to ward off the gathering storm.

While making these reflections, Macaron had quit the group of curiosity-seekers that was swelling in the Place Vendôme and arrived in the Rue Rivoli. Several times, he had looked back mechanically and had noticed, some distance behind him, two men who seemed to be following the same route as him.

Damn! he said to himself. *I think they're two* flics*, who are rather inconvenient, and if there's a way to shake them off, that would be a great help to my cause…*

Of course, the moment that Rozen was rumbled, I was bound to be as well…

He walked rapidly, and made sure that the two men adjusted their pace similarly. There was no more doubt; they were inspectors—and they had orders not to lose sight of him. They probably thought that he would go to his friends, the anarchists, to give them the warning…it was as clear as crystal.

465

At the Place de la Concorde he saw an empty coupé going past. He still had two louis in his pocket. He ran to the coachman. "Hey, old man—two louis for you if you can take me in the direction of the Cours La Reine, flat out. Urgent business."

"Fine," said the coachman. "Pay up front."

"Here's one louis. You'll get the other in due course."

Bastien dived into the coupé, which moved off at a rapid pace.

Raising the cloth screen that masked the small window set in the rear of the vehicle, the anarchist saw the two agents desperately searching for another cab, but he was already in the Cours La Reine and was going away a hellish speed, while the inspectors had not yet found a fiacre.

Good, he said to himself. *Now I've got time to get ahead of the cops. So far, so good.*

Leaning out of the window, he gave the coachman an address quite different from that of Sokoloff's villa.

Having arrived at the destination, he gave the second louis to the Automedon, who, glad to have earned his daily wage so easily, dissolved in expressions of thanks, to which Bastien was in no mood to listen.

Once alone, he walked through the side-streets of Auteuil and went into an isolated house to which he had a key

They didn't put a guard on that door, he said to himself. *One can't think of everything.*

He closed the door carefully behind him, put the key back in his pocket, and swiftly went down to the house's cellar. The small house, bought by Sokoloff shortly after the acquisition of the villa in Auteuil, backed on to the wall that enclosed the property. A subterranean tunnel connected the cellars of the two houses. Sokoloff had taken his precautions, not with a view to eventual flight, but in order to be able to export from his laboratory, without awakening suspicion, the explosive devices that he manufactured for the comrades working for social renovation and simultaneously sowing terror in the four corners of Europe.

The Russian's plan was to be able to blow up entire quarters of capital cities. The man, naturally so gentle, became more ferocious than the worst murderers when, in his hallucinated dreams, he believed that he was acting for the future good of humankind. That was why Dr. Lemoine's aerial surveillance had alarmed him. Had that surveillance persisted, the aeronaut might, at any moment, have discovered the secret exit by which the bombs manufactured in the villa had to be shipped out—and it was for that reason that he had lent his hand to a crime…for the success of the sacred cause.

Let us return to Bastien.

Once in the tunnel, he pressed a button set near the door, and the vault lit up. He went rapidly to two large panels equipped with commutators, whose copper sparkled in the rays of electric lamps.

"The heavy artillery," he said. "A turn of the wrist and *boom!* Everything blown sky high. All the same, that damned Sokoloff has the most delightful inventions."

Having arrived at the end of the tunnel he found a small iron spiral staircase, a few steps of which he climbed. He learned on a bell-push. The bell started ringing, and almost immediately, a panel was raised. Bastien saw Sokoloff, cold and resolute, waiting at the entrance to the tunnel.

"Why did you come that way? What's happening?" the Russian demanded, calmly.

"What's happening, Master," said Macaron, closing the trap-door, "is quite simple. We're stuffed! Within half an hour, the police, the law and the whole caboodle will be here."

"What about Rosen?"

"Rozen's taken off. I don't know what happened last night, but this morning, as I was going to the Place Vendôme to see him before our rendezvous here, I found out that he's made himself scarce—without warning his friends. He's a traitor."

"You might be right, Bastien," the scientist declared. "Yesterday, I received various letters, which reached me by roundabout ways because I'm afraid of the *chambre noire*, as you know…and I was expecting to get some serious explanations from Rozen today. Certain large sums of money, which I had instructed him to distribute for our propaganda in the strikebound regions haven't reached their destination.

"For a long time, I've reproached our associate for his frivolous lifestyle and his laxity in serving our cause, but I thought he was faithful, if not fervent…"

"Well, Master," Bastien groaned, "if you want explanations from the Baron, you'll have to take the train. Would you like some advice?"

"Speak."

"Do the same. Get away. There's still time."

"No," Sokoloff replied. "I don't want to go without collecting all our documents and putting them in a safe place—buried in the cellars of the small house at the end of the tunnel."

"But you haven't understood," said Bastien, bewildered. "The police will be here soon—you don't have time. Get away. Let's go, quickly—quickly!"

"The doors are solid," the scientist retorted, "and before our enemies have got in…"

There was no time to say any more. Repeated blows hammered on the coaching entrance in the Rue Jasmin.

"You can hear," Macaron murmured, pale with fear. "It's them."

They both listened. A loud voice outside shouted: "Open up, in the name of the law!"

"It's them," Macaron repeated, trembling from head to toe. "Let's go, Master, let's go…please…and we'll blow up the house…"

"People will be killed," Sokoloff replied, sadly.

"So what? And afterwards? I don't suppose your bombs are made for dogs. A great misfortune, when we'll have killed cops and detectives…"

"Shut up," said the Russian, "and listen hard to what I'm going to tell you. At this moment, I need to be obeyed…like a leader."

These words were pronounced in such a tone of authority that Bastien murmured: "Go on. I'll do whatever you want, and if it's necessary to die…well, I'm in it with you…"

"No, you're going to go. I'll stay here, alone…"

While they were arguing, noises from outside were clearly audible. There was a redoubled hammering at the coaching entrance; they were obviously trying to break it down. But those sounds, which made the Parisian shiver, did not frighten the scientist at all. Calmly and thoughtfully, he picked up a packet of letters that were on his workbench and threw them into the fire.

"They won't find that…and we'll spare our friends from arrest…"

"But what about the papers in the room next door?" Bastien observed. "Your archives.. the whole party organization, by sections, with special instructions for each post…"

"Listen carefully," said Sokoloff. "I'm approaching the supreme moment. I'm old. Then again, I don't know why, but doubt is taking hold of me. Might we not be mistaken? Is it really the right path that we've followed? I sense that I no longer have the faith! I'm old, tired…disgusted by life. For me, death will be a relief. For the others, it will be an example…

"The blood of martyrs is like a benevolent dew for the roots of the revolutionary tree…"

"You're crazy! Kill yourself! That's stupid! I don't want that, damn it!"

"Shut up. And do as I command…

"They're going to break down the door, and I'll let them come in. I won't use any of the powerful means I have to hand in order to stop them. I don't want to make use of the defenses I've organized in the villa. So, they'll come in, and it's me who'll receive them."

"They'll take you away, and you'll go to the bagne—you, master! Too bad! I'll stay and let myself be captured with you, since that's the way it is…"

"They won't capture me. I want to die, and my death will serve our cause. It will prove to the party that the man who was at its head was able to sacrifice his life…

"You'll search for Rozen. You'll make certain whether he betrayed us— and if you acquire that conviction, your arm will avenge us. That example will also serve the cause of Anarchism. There must be no traitors in our ranks. Swear to me that you will deliver justice…"

"For sure—you can count on that. There'll be no shirking, I guarantee..." A sinister gleam passed through Macaron's gaze.

"Good," said Sokoloff. "Now, take this money." The Russian handed him a wallet stuffed with banknotes.

"A fair bit of cash!" murmured the Parisian, excited by the thought of having a fortune on him.

"There are two hundred and fifty thousand francs there. Two hundred thousand I want to you take to Saint Petersburg. You'll find all the instructions in the wallet. I've only kept that here. The rest was on deposit in the Place Vendôme..."

Well placed, Bastien thought.

"The other fifty thousand francs are for you...to employ for the good of our cause. Go everywhere in France, tell the comrades that my last adieu was for them."

"No, no..."

A violent blow, followed by a loud crack, cut off Macaron's words. The coaching entrance had just caved in. The sound of voices could be heard in the garden.

Sokoloff went to the window and saw men advancing cautiously, revolvers in hand. "Go—run," he ordered the Parisian. Stop at the electric panel in the tunnel and in twenty minutes, watch in hand, turn the commutators marked A and Z. Adieu—and long live Anarchism!"

At that moment, someone knocked on the entrance door to the villa.

Sokoloff held out his arms to Bastien. The latter, although usually not very sensitive, had tears in his eyes. For a moment, they two men remained thus.

"Adieu, Brother..."

"Adieu, Master..."

Then, resolutely, Sokoloff lifted the trap-door, through which Bastien disappeared.

"In twenty minutes," the scientist repeated. "That's understood. Rozen...the companions...Saint Petersburg..."

"Don't worry, damn it! One doesn't have a Prix Monthyon, but one is pure...and one has courage..."

The trap-door fell back.

Left alone, Sokoloff closed all the doors giving access to the room where he was, which served as his study. It was the antechamber to his laboratory. It was necessary to go through it to get into the rooms where the secret documents of the Anarchist organization were, and the bombs ready to receive the explosives buried in a small underground store at the far end of the building.

All the doors that the Russian had just closed were lined with iron and the locks could only be opened by someone who knew their secret.

When that was done he took a minuscule phial with a ground-glass stopper from a cupboard, which he kept in his hand, and then went to open the door on which the public prosecutor, accompanied by an examining magistrate and the head of the Sûreté were still knocking and shouting: "Open up, in the name of the law!"

Behind the magistrates, agents and guardians of the peace were standing, ready to attempts an assault on the mysterious villa.

When the door opened, Sokoloff appeared to the gaze of the magistrates and the policemen, majestic and imposing. He drew himself up to his full height; his masculine and intelligent face seemed to be surrounded by a luminous aureole.

The newcomers stopped momentarily, immobilized, struck by admiration before that Titan of the Anarchist cause.

Sokoloff was famous. They remembered his past, the sacrifices he had made for the revolutionary ideal. The men in front of him—the prosecutor, the examining magistrate and Cardec, knew that the erudite man had given up his position and he wealth in order to serve Anarchism—and, while doing their duty, which was to arrest a man who was dangerous to the social order, they could not help feeling a sort of respect for him.

The Russian thought they were afraid.

"Have no fear, Messieurs," he said, with a smile. "I have no homicidal intention toward you. Dutiful soldiers, you are acting in the name of a society that I execrate, whose foundations I would like to undermine in order to rebuild it on the bases of justice and fraternity...

"You are the instruments of the egotistical bourgeoisie, which proclaims the rights of man but which today, belying its oaths, crushes all who are weak. You are the executors of the laws and barbaric desires of the powerful and cowardly hypocrites who consider the people as a vile herd only good for feeding their appetites...

"It isn't you that I shall strike. You're not here by virtue of your own will; you're obedient slaves of an order..."

"Arrest that man," ordered the prosecutor, cutting short the scientist's inflamed harangue.

"One moment!" shouted Sokoloff. "In the interest of your lives...

"There are papers in this house that your mission is to seize, machines that you ought to destroy. I could have let you in, and with a gesture without warning, annihilated you all.

"That, I repeat, is no longer my intention. I don't strike servants. It's the masters that I want to attain. In circumstances in which the denunciation of a coward has caused the work to fail at the very moment when everything was ready...when general terror would have give us Power...I have lost the game. I condemn myself, leaving others the care of continuing..."

Before anyone could interrupt him, he rapidly unsealed the little bottle that he had in his hand and swallowed its contents.

"In a minute," he went on, "I shall be dead...but don't try to search the house. Flee, if you don't want to perish..."

Visibly, he went pale, and tottered, leaning against the door...

Hesitant, momentarily nonplussed by the tragic scene, which they had not expected, the magistrates and the head of the Sûreté ran toward Sokoloff. The scientist's eyes were already clouding over, however, and his violet-tinted lips could scarcely articulate a sound.

Death was coming rapidly.

"Go...go...for the sake of your families...the explosion...the expl..."

He collapsed, and in a last surge of his entire being, as if life had suddenly returned to him, he cried in a loud voice: "Long live Anarchism!"

Then a violent spasm ran through him, and he expired.

While this drama was unfolding, agents and guardians of the peace had climbed up to the windows, and, standing on the sills, they were trying to open them with pliers they had found in a workshop situated in one of the corners of the garden.

The prosecutor, the examining magistrate and he head of the Sûreté conferred. Was it not all mere bravado of the vanquished man attempting to terrorize his vanquishers in exhaling his last breath?

The impetuous examining magistrate wanted to go on right away—but Cardec stopped him.

"Better to wait, Monsieur," the policeman said, "in case some infernal machine is hidden in the villa; prudence commands us to withdraw our men. I observed the unfortunate while he was speaking—he could have been sincere..."

"You're right, Monsieur," the prosecutor declared. "It's better..."

The magistrate did not finish. A mighty explosion lifted up the ground.

A cloud of dust surrounded the three men, at the same time as debris of stones and wood, hurled in all directions, rained back down on the property. Cries of agony rang out.

The inspectors of the Sûreté and the guardians of the peace fled in panic toward the exit—and as they ran they tripped over the iron wires distributed throughout the lawns, and bells rang furiously on all sides.

There was a moment of indescribable confusion—but Cardec and the magistrates quickly pulled themselves together. They had got away with a violent shock, and a thick layer of dust covering their clothing.

The head of the Sûreté swiftly brought all his men back to their posts. In a few words, setting them an example with his own composure, he reassured them, and they set about taking account of the damage done by the explosion.

The entire left hand side of the villa had collapsed. Fire was beginning to destroy what still remained standing. Unfortunately, there were casualties. One Sûreté inspector was lying on the ground, his limbs lacerated. Two guardians of the peace, only recognizable by their half-burned uniforms were no longer anything but a frightful pulp of mingled flesh and rubble.

While firemen arrived in haste to fight the fire, Sokoloff's corpse and those of the soldiers of the police, victims of their duty, were taken away.

Once again, Anarchism had immolated the humble. They were three threads of the people, struck down by the blind utopia.

Monsieur Cardec, the magistrates and all those close to the dwelling had had a narrow escape. If Bastien had followed Sokoloff's instructions punctiliously, not one of those who were there would have escaped the disaster, but the nuclei of the explosion were commanded by the combination of commutators A and Z, which it was necessary to operate in that order, and Macaron had turned the commutator marked Z first, with the result that the explosion had only been produced in the room where the archives were, and had not extended to the storage bunker where the explosive materials were that Sokoloff had prepared to arm the bombs destined to be transported by affiliates to the provincial comrades.

Nevertheless, the Russian scientist's objective had been attained. It was impossible for the magistrates, in spite of a minute search, to discover any paper able to assist them in putting their hands on the principal members of the formidable association of which Sokoloff was the soul.

XVIII. The Hunt for the Traitor

Although Monsieur Cardec had done all kinds of things since the previous day, he had not thought of taking a rest. Very active and highly strung, it often happened that, when he was preoccupied with important business, he went without sleep for several successive nights—and no affair had ever been closer to his heart than putting a stop to the bandit who had been mocking the police and terrorizing Paris for years.

The name of Sokoloff, carelessly and unconsciously let slip by Germaine Reyval, had been a flash of light for the head of the Sûreté. He had finally found the weak point, the chink in the armor. Sokoloff, a Russian anarchist, lost to sight for a long time, Bastien, alias Macaron, a propagandist by action, and Saint-Magloire were evidently putting together some formidable plot—and thanks to that discovery, Cardec was certain that his superiors would give him *carte blanche* to act.

We have seen how he had executed the first part of the plan that he had contrived for Rozen's ruin. The banker was in flight, unmasked and irremediably fallen...but he had been able, by eluding some of the head of the Sûreté's provisions, to take away enough money to attempt a comeback.

It was, however, necessary not to stop the bandit, whose crimes—the murder of Lavardens, the attempted murder of Eléna—it would have been difficult, if not impossible, to prove. The redoubtable adventurer would escape the scaffold. He would certainly be sent back to the penitentiary, but after what scandal, and what sensational revelations? How many unfortunates who had trusted him would have been splashed with mud by the pseudo-Baron's revelations?

Thus, it had been necessary to find another way to make the vile being disappear—and Monsieur Cardec had found that means.

Immediately after the dramatic operation in Auteuil, the police magistrate had gone to the office of the Minister of the Interior, who been had already been brought up to date by the Prefect of Police with all the serious events that had just taken place.

The supreme master of the police had seen the head of the Sûreté immediately, and when the latter had emerged from the building in the Place Beauvau he was radiant.

It was not the compliments that had been lavished upon him that had given Cardec that joy; he was especially happy to have received authorization from the Minister to carry the war against the criminal that could not be delivered to Monsieur de Paris all the way to the end.

From the Ministry of the Interior the head of the Sûreté had himself taken to the Ministry of the Colonies in the Pavillon de Flore, and went up to see the

Director of Penitentiary Services. There, he was immediately handed a voluminous file concerning the convict Rozenkruz.

On consulting this dossier, Cardec uttered an exclamation of triumph. The entire story of the anarchist revolt on Île Royale fomented by Rozen and denounced by him was recounted there. A report compiled by the directory of the penitentiary related "the service rendered to the colony by number 883" and mentioned the anarchist "eliminations" carried out thanks to the Levantine's treachery.

On arrival at the Quai des Orfèvres, the policeman found Dr. Lemoine waiting for him, who immediately reassured him at to the fate of Madame Lavardens.

The blow inflicted by Saint-Magloire on the courageous woman had been less terrible that had initially been supposed when, shortly after the Baron's flight, people had come running on hearing the injured woman's moans. Olivier Martin, hastily summoned, had lavished his intelligent care on the widow, and had dressed the wound, having become less anxious after a serious examination thereof. The patient had no fever, and there was every reason to hope that she would be on her feet in a matter of days.

Lemoine, continuing to inform his friend, also told him how Eléna had learned, stoically, of the tragic adventure that had separated her forever from the wretch she had loved. The doctor was unable to keep quiet about his admiration for that energetic woman, a worthy descendant of the heroic man who had died in defense of Cuban liberty. He spoke abundantly, the good doctor, with an eloquence that came from the heart—and Cardec listened, smiling, while scribbling notes on a pad.

"Oh," said Lemoine, concluding his story, "it's truly unfortunate that the man is still alive—for, in sum, you've unmasked him, ruined him, destroyed him…but with a fellow of his stripe, can one ever know what might happen? He's capable of getting back on his feet one day, and resuming the exploits that you've so skillfully interrupted elsewhere, under another name…"

"No," Cardec riposted, "he won't recover…I'll guarantee that. I promised that you'd be in on the kill and I'll keep my promise…or very nearly, as I don't know exactly where the wild beast will be brought down." As the doctor looked at him in astonishment, not grasping the meaning of his words, the head of the Sûreté added: "You'll understand in time. I'm only asking for a little patience." He pressed a bell-push set within arm's reach.

The office orderly appeared in response to the summons.

"Tell my secretaries to come in right away."

"Yes, sir."

A few moments later, Monsieur Cardec was striding back and forth in his office, dictating a rather long note to his secretaries, in which he brought to light the role played by Rozenkruz in the drama on Île Royale.

"Make copies of that urgently," he ordered. "Bring them to me as soon as they're ready."

"What are you going to do with that story?" asked Lemoine, as soon as the secretaries had gone out.

"It will appear this evening in all the Paris newspapers, and tomorrow in all those in the provinces and abroad." Cardec's eyes were shining. "And I hope it won't fall on deaf ears...now do you understand?"

"No—I confess that you've got ahead of me since yesterday."

"Well, my friend, that story is the equivalent of a jury's verdict without attenuating circumstances. If I'm not mistaken, it's the death-warrant of the man that I regret not having sent to Monsieur Deibler."[76]

"But he's run away."

"Don't worry. I'll be informed telegraphically by the inspectors who are on his heels with special instructions, and I'll have the extreme generosity to give his address to any comrades who might, by chance, have the desire to catch up with him..."

"Damn!" cried the doctor. "That's Machiavellian. It's ferocious...but very clever."

"Ferocious!" Cardec replied. "My word, one might think that you felt pity for a bandit of that sort. Count the bodies that he's left along his route. The comrades on Île Royale, Lavardens, Dulac. Is it his fault that Eléna Ruiz is still alive? Do you think that he failed to kill Oliva Lavardens deliberately? And what about you—your fall from the balloon? And many other 'good deeds' of which we're unaware. If you think that he doesn't deserve the death penalty..."

"Twenty times over," said the doctor. "Yes, you're right. It's necessary to kill the bandit."

"I'll do my best," Cardec went on, "and I hope it won't take long. I assure you, my dear friend, that is spite of my usual repugnance for the death penalty, I'll utter a sigh of relief on the day when a 'fatal accident' has scythed down the Baron de Saint-Magloire..."

"And you won't be alone," Lemoine concluded. "All honest folk will be with you."

"Honest folk," said the head of the Sûreté, smiling, "and many others too, for at this moment, there are quite a few people more or less in view who aren't celebrating, I can assure you—and they'll be glad to escape the scandal, and the blackmail to which, at a time perhaps not very far in the future, the villain would not fail to have recourse to try and get himself afloat again."

That same evening, extraordinary articles appeared in all the Paris newspapers:

---

[76] Anatole Deibler was the French executioner from 1890 until well into the 20th century.

The End of an adventurer.
From Cayenne to the Place Vendôme.
The house-warming in the Rue de Prony.
In flight.
The death of a prince.
Terrible explosion.
The Anarchist Plot.
Etc.

No one in Paris was talking about anything other than the affair in question. In every newspaper, entire columns were devoted to the story of the Baron de Saint-Magloire—and clearly in view, in the adventurer's antecedents, was the note drafted by Monsieur Cardec, who had obligingly allowed himself to be interviewed, informing the "Comrades" of the treason of the man they had always considered, thanks of the intermediary of Sokoloff, as a brother.

The man who was the most flabbergasted of all was Bastien, alias Macaron.

"Shit!" he growled, his fist clenched. "I'll have his hide, the swine..." Saint-Magloire's accomplice was sincere in his hatred. The death of Sokoloff, whom he had liked a great deal, and for whom he had a profound admiration, whom he considered as the god of the revolutionary ideal, had already set him against Rozen—and the story of the ex-883's treason laid bare, brought his rage to a paroxysm.

For sure, he would kill the traitor. Was it not necessary to prove to the comrades that he was not involved in the filthy plot on Île Royale?

Macaron forgot that he had not had as many scruples out there, and that he had accepted Rozen's help to flee the penitentiary, with his eyes closed. That was one of the curious aspects of the Parisian *gamin*'s versatile nature.

And without any concern for his own safety, Bastien—who had prudently hidden after leaving the house in Auteuil after the explosion that he believed to have been complete—took a fiacre and had himself taken to the Montagne Sainte-Geneviève, to the home of one of the most fervent disciples of Anarchism, Comrade Duloup.

Several adepts of propaganda by action were meeting in Duloup's house at that moment, and Macaron had a veritable success when he announced his intention of "skinning the hide of the false brother."

Duloup and another comrade, the anarchist Sanclair—a colossus who seemed to have been hewn by blows of a billhook from a knotty tree-trunk—offered enthusiastically to help Bastien in his work of vengeance.

An exemplary punishment was required.

The Baron de Saint-Magloire as help responsible for the irremediable check to which the revolution had just been subjected. It was because of him that Sokoloff had died heroically, destroying all the documents that might have delivered the leaders of the party to the police. It was that wretched banker, that sybarite, that traitor, who had obviously given up the secret of the house in Auteuil, just as he had given up the brothers who had died in Guiana under the rifle-fire of the soldiers, armed slaves of the infamous bourgeoisie...

And Duloup, in a few inflammatory declarations, swore not to rest until the traitor had paid for his treason.

There was no shortage of money; Bastien had enough on him to organize a serious manhunt.

That same evening, Bastien and his two aides took the train to Brussels—where, according to the newspapers, Saint-Magloire must have taken refuge.

In the Belgian capital, the three comrades divided up the search. They went to the principal hotels, and the homes of the anarchists they knew and with whom they were in communication—but they could not lay their hands on the Baron.

The latter, having noticed on arrival in Brussels that he was being followed, had not felt safe, and had only stayed in the city for a matter of hours. He had taken the first train to Rotterdam.

His plan was simple. He intended to embark on the first steamship leaving for America, and he hoped to give the slip to the two agents of the Sûreté on his heels.

In fact, when he disembarked on the platform at Rotterdam station, he could no longer see the sleuths from the Quai des Orfèvres. Entirely reassured, he went to one of the city's best hotels and dined with a healthy appetite.

The next morning, he went to the harbor to obtain information about the ships that were getting ready to depart in the near future. The departure of a steamship was advertised for the day after next. Rozen reserved a berth and returned to his hotel, not without checking carefully to see that he was not being followed—but he did not see anything suspicious.

Already, he was beginning to get his breath back.

The shock he had received had shaken him severely, and since his flight from the Champs-Élysées he had lived in a terrible fear. He still did not entirely understand why he had not been arrested.

Reading the newspapers, however, informed him in that regard. He had time to read them now that he believed himself to be safe. He had not been arrested because they feared his revelations; they thought that he was gone forever, and they were no longer afraid of him.

They were wrong! For he promised himself that he would have his revenge.

He left aside all the details that were given regarding Sokoloff's death and his own past; that was not what interested him. He wanted to know whether the police intended to arrest him; that was the most important thing to him.

Suddenly, he went pale. A nervous tremor took possession of him.

No!" he murmured.

He reread the lines that had frightened him.

We are assured, said the newspaper that he held in his hand, *that Rozen, alias the Baron de Saint-Magloire, has taken refuge in Rotterdam, and that a request for extradition has been made to the Dutch government. The adventurer's arrest is now only a matter of hours.*

"In that case," the fugitive said to himself, "have I been followed this far? What does the article mean…in evident contradiction to what I've read so far?"

He crumpled the newspaper angrily, got to his feet, and strode feverishly back and forth in his room, with his fists clenched and his eyes flashing.

"Let them arrest me, then! We'll see who has the last laugh! If I go under, I'll take a great many others down with me."

At that moment, there was a knock on his door.

His hair prickled; his hand clasped the dagger that he was carrying in his trouser pocket, and he immediately drew the weapon from its leather sheath.

Someone knocked a second time.

He did not answer…and stood there anxiously, ready to sell his skin dearly if it was agents who had come to arrest him. He intended to leap upon them, weapon raised, when they broke down the door, and he thought that the advantage of surprise might give him the means to escape the grip of the police.

Ears pricked, he listened—but no suspicious sound could be heard.

A slight shiver suddenly ran through him as he saw a white envelope that had just been passed under the door.

Rapidly, he picked it up and opened it.

He trembled as if he had been struck by any icy blast. He was obliged to sit down and wait for a few seconds before he was able to read the note that he had unfolded.

Terror had scarcely any purchase on that man; he quickly suppressed the most violent emotions.

"Why," he said, both surprised and satisfied. "It's from Bastien."

And he read: *Old man, after all the dirty tricks of recent days, I too have taken to my heels. As I've found your address—I'll explain how—and as I think it dangerous to see you, I'm writing. Be at the harbor at midnight; I'll wait for you. I have cash to give you on behalf of our poor friend Sokoloff, and I've hired a boat that will take us both to England.*

Robertson.

Rozen's nerves relaxed. He uttered a sigh of relief.

"Come on," he said to himself. "All's not lost. Sokoloff has thought about me."

Not for a moment did the idea occur to him that a trap might have been set for him. He believed absolutely in Bastien's loyalty. The moment Sokoloff ordered something, Macaron carried out the order punctiliously.

That was how thing worked…

What made him smile most of all, apart from the matter of the money sent by the Russian before his death, was the idea that Macaron had had of hiring the boat to go to England.

Obviously, they would only be watching the steamships.

And, completely set at ease, the Baron ordered dinner to be served in his room.

A brief explanation is necessary here. Imperturbably following his plan, Cardec, kept up to date by his agents regarding Rozen's movements, had immediately passed the information on to the newspapers.

As he assumed that the bandit would seek passage on a ship, he had added the little note about the extradition request. That was sufficient to warn Saint-Magloire that he ought not to attempt to embark if he did not want to be immediately arrested.

Informed by the special commissaire at the Gare du Nord, who have observed the departure of Bastien and his two companions, Duloup and Sanclair, for Brussels, the head of the Sûreté, knowing that they would read the papers, had put them on the track of the quarry they were hunting.

In Rotterdam, following Rozen's trail, Bastien had soon discovered his hotel.

Initially, on arriving in Rotterdam, comrades Duloup and Sanclair had proposed going to the hotel that evening to deal with the traitor, but Bastien had claimed that honor, and "knowing the fellow," as he put it, had thought of luring him to a deserted spot by night.

At the appointed hour, the three anarchists were waiting in the harbor. Only Bastien was visible; the other two were hidden, ready to come to his aid if necessary.

The night was dark and foggy, and the docks were ill-lit.

Midnight had just chimed on the nearby clocks when Macaron saw Saint-Magloire's silhouette outlined in the fog a few meters away; he recognized him immediately.

When the Baron approached him, he took him by the arm and drew him into a corner, next to a path of waste ground where the harbor employees discarded their household wastes, which night-soil collectors took away at dawn.

In his right hand, Bastien clutched his flick-knife, which he had taken care to open.

The Parisian felt sure of himself. He knew that one thrust of his "*eustache*," well-placed in the middle of the torso, would sent his man *ad patres*, so he wanted to enjoy Rozen's terror first.

"Let's go," Saint-Magloire said, immediately. "Where's the boat you've hired? We'll chat later..."

"Just a minute, Colonel. I have something to tell you first."

"You're sure you weren't followed?"

"Listen," Macaron retorted. "There's a matter we have to settle." A surge of anger swept over in the anarchist's brain, and, incapable of restraining himself, in a hoarse voice, he said to his old friend, whose arm he was gripping forcefully: "Just the two of us, Gaston Rozen—us two, false brother. The comrades you betrayed on Île Royale are crying out for vengeance…for you to pay for your treason. I'm going to kill you, you swine!"

"You're crazy," Gaston murmured. "If it's to tell me such stupid things that you disturbed me…"

"No, it's to stick this in your skin!" Matching the action to the words, Bastien raised is knife.

Saint-Magloire had seen the movement. With a violent thrust, he pulled away from Macaron's grip. The Parisian fell to the ground.

"Damn it!" growled Rozen. "You're the one who'll die."

And before Bastien had time to get up, the Levantine, his strength multiplied tenfold by the danger he was in, hurled himself upon his former accomplice.

There was a brief, atrocious fight.

While struggling to free himself from Rozen's hands, which were around his throat, Macaron lashed out—but the knife slid over Saint-Magloire's shoulder, and, tearing through his garment, the blade only grazed him.

One of the Baron's hands released the anarchist's neck and grabbed his wrist, as if to break it. Under that vigorous pressure, the hand opened, and the weapon fell.

Then, with a desperate effort, Rozen lifted his adversary up and slammed him down again, head first.

"Help!" yelped Macaron.

Rapidly as Duloup and Sanclair responded to that appeal, they did not have time to save their comrade.

Saint-Magloire, drunk with fury, had seized the Parisian by the throat again, and with two curt blows he smashed his skull on the stones of the dock.

"You asked for it," he growled. And he set about searching his former associate's pockets conscientiously.

The place was utterly deserted; he had plenty of time to take possession of the cash given to Bastien by that imbecile Sokoloff.

Suddenly, however, Rozen felt himself pulled backwards and laid down o the ground—and without him even being able to make a gesture to defend himself, he was gagged, held down by the Herculean wrist of Sanclair. And while the latter held the wretch down, Duloup tied him up securely with a length of twine.

When that was done, the two comrades examined Bastien. They had no difficulty in establishing that he was dead. His skull had been split by the violent impact, and brain-tissue was leaking out.

"Poor chap," murmured Sanclair, gripped by pity. "He's croaked."

"He'll be avenged too," growled Duloup.

They picked Rozen up then, and placed him upright beneath a street-lamp.

"Do you know," said the anarchist, with a frightful calmness, "the fate reserved for those who betray us? We accepted responsibility, along with the comrade you've just killed, for avenging our brothers, who you sold in a cowardly manner on Île Royale. You also have to account to us for Sokoloff's death...and we want you to suffer enough to expiate your infamy.

"It's me, Comrade Duloup, who will make you see how we punish traitors. It's with your blood that I'm going to write your sentence..."

His eyes crazed with fear, Rozen writhed in his bonds. He tried to rip the gag that was stifling him with his teeth.

He wanted to shout for help, to escape his executioners. The danger of being recognized and arrested did not matter now. It was his life that he wanted to preserve—the life that would permit him to fight another day, perhaps advantageously...

But Duloup had opened his large knife, coldly, and with a curt thrust, he sliced Rozen's right wrist, from which blood flowed.

Sanclair handed his comrade a blank piece of paper, which he unfolded—and the latter, dipping his finger in Rozen's blood, wrote in capital letters:

TRAITOR TO ANARCHISM

"You see," he said to Saint-Magloire. "People will know why we have executed you. It's written in this newspaper, which we're going to pin to your breast."

Carefully, the anarchist placed on the torso of the Levantine, whose body was writhing frightfully, a newspaper in which the article about the slaughter on Île Royale was circled in black. He placed the implacable sentence on top of it and maintained the papers in position with his right hand. Then he handed the knife to Sanclair.

"Over to you," he said. "Strike the heart..."

Sanclair obeyed, and with a single thrust, sank the blade into the breast of the condemned man.

Rozen was agitated by a spasm. His eyes grew immeasurably wide, and a hoarse croak escaped his throat behind the gag. Then he fell heavily, face forward.

"He's had his reckoning," said Duloup. "Come on, help me—we have to take him to his final resting-place—the only one he deserves."

And they carried the cadaver to the waste-depository.

"Carrion on the dung-heap!" pronounced Sanclair. That was the entire funeral oration for the man who had been the King of Paris.

And at daybreak, when the night-soil collectors of Rotterdam came to take away the detritus, they perceived, half-buried in the filth, stained with mud and blood, the cadaver of the man whose dream had been to live in the apotheosis of power and luxury.

"You didn't dream of so complete a vengeance," said Lemoine to Cardec when they learned about the bandit's demise.

"Those officious executioners," the head of the Sûreté replied, "do indeed have a heavier hand than their official counterpart, but I had no choice in the matter of means. At any rate, Rozen is dead, and Bastien too. Two fine rogues fewer! *De profundis!* Dead the beast, dead the venom, the proverb says—an eternal truth, especially in Paris, where people soon forget, in the whirlwind of feverish life in which some new event chases away those of the eve on a daily basis."

Three months after the tragic adventure in Rotterdam, there was hardly any mention of the late Baron de Saint-Magloire. Already, the odyssey of that extraordinary bandit was no longer in the realm of reality. Henceforth, it belonged to those popular historians we call novelists, whose talent strives to show us life through a magic lantern with magnifying lenses.

It is necessary to say, in truth, that, especially among those who got closest to the Baron and who grew fat on the crumbs of the prodigious crook, no one wanted to have known him. They had all repudiated the villain who had come to such a miserable end.

There was perhaps only one man who retained a little gratitude toward Rozen, and that was Monsieur Cardec, who owed the most interesting case of his career to him.

The day after the disappearance of the man with whom she had lived as a spouse, Eléna Ruiz left the house in the Champs-Élysées and took up residence in a modest family boarding-house.

Before leaving for Havana she waited for Madame Lavardens to make a complete recovery. Oliva was to go with Eléna on that voyage.

The Cuban woman hoped that the air of her birthplace would purify her, and that, in the midst of memories of her childhood, she might gradually forget the years spent with the adventurer whose unwitting accomplice she had been.

While regretting the separation, Lemoine, on the advice of Monsieur Cardec, had encouraged the young woman in her plan. And on the day when the physicians declared that Madame Lavardens could tolerate the fatigue of a long voyage, the two women, escorted by Olivier Martin and Lemoine, took the train to Bordeaux from the Gare d'Austerlitz.

As the staff were closing the carriage doors, shouting the traditional "All aboard!" there were emotional embraces on both sides.

They were parting with the hope of seeing one another again soon.

Love knows no obstacles!

As for Germaine Reyval, whom the emotion experienced on the night of her opulent protector's fall had rendered voiceless, she abandoned her theatrical career. In the world of finance—banks had an irresistible attraction for the ex-diva—she sought out Saint-Magloire's successors. She was often seen in the Bois, always beautiful, always provocative, but the gentleman accompanying her was rarely the same one.

"The fact is," she said, "that one doesn't find twice in one lifetime a lover like Saint-Magloire, between whose fingers other people's money flowed so easily."

SF & FANTASY

Henri Allorge. *The Great Cataclysm*
Guy d'Armen. *Doc Ardan: The City of Gold and Lepers*
G.-J. Arnaud. *The Ice Company*
Charles Asselineau. *The Double Life*
Cyprien Bérard. *The Vampire Lord Ruthwen*
Aloysius Bertrand. *Gaspard de la Nuit*
Richard Bessière. *The Gardens of the Apocalypse*
Albert Bleunard. *Ever Smaller*
Félix Bodin. *The Novel of the Future*
Alphonse Brown. *City of Glass*
André Caroff. *The Terror of Madame Atomos; Miss Atomos; The Return of Madame Atomos; The Mistake of Madame Atomos; The Monsters of Madame Atomos; The Revenge of Madame Atomos*
Félicien Champsaur. *The Human Arrow; Ouha*
Didier de Chousy. *Ignis*
Captain Danrit. *Undersea Odyssey*
C. I. Defontenay. *Star (Psi Cassiopeia)*
Charles Derennes. *The People of the Pole*
Georges Dodds (anthologist). *The Missing Link*
Harry Dickson. *The Heir of Dracula*
Jules Dornay. *Lord Ruthven Begins*
Alfred Driou. *The Adventures of a Parisian Aeronaut*
Sâr Dubnotal *vs. Jack the Ripper*
Alexandre Dumas. *The Return of Lord Ruthven*
Renée Dunan. *Baal*
J.-C. Dunyach. *The Night Orchid; The Thieves of Silence*
Henri Duvernois. *The Man Who Found Himself*
Achille Eyraud. *Voyage to Venus*
Henri Falk. *The Age of Lead*
Paul Féval. *Anne of the Isles; Knightshade; Revenants; Vampire City; The Vampire Countess; The Wandering Jew's Daughter*
Paul Féval, *fils. Felifax, the Tiger-Man*
Charles de Fieux. *Lamékis*
Arnould Galopin. *Doctor Omega; Doctor Omega & The Shadowmen*
Léon Gozlan. *The Vampire of the Val-de-Grâce*
G.L. Gick. *Harry Dickson and the Werewolf of Rutherford Grange*
Edmond Haraucourt. *Illusions of Immortality*
Nathalie Henneberg. *The Green Gods*
V. Hugo, P. Foucher & P. Meurice. *The Hunchback of Notre-Dame*
Michel Jeury. *Chronolysis*
Gustave Kahn. *The Tale of Gold and Silence*
Gérard Klein. *The Mote in Time's Eye*
Louis-Guillaume de La Follie. *The Unpretentious Philosopher*
Jean de La Hire. *Enter the Nyctalope; The Nyctalope on Mars; The Nyctalope vs. Lucifer; The Nyctalope Steps In; Night of the Nyctalope*

Etienne-Léon de Lamothe-Langon. *The Virgin Vampire*
André Laurie. *Spiridon*
Gabriel de Lautrec. *The Vengeance of the Oval Portrait*
Alain le Drimeur. *The Future City*
Georges Le Faure & Henri de Graffigny. *The Extraordinary Adventures of a Russian Scientist Across the Solar System* (2 vols.)
Gustave Le Rouge. *The Vampires of Mars The Dominion of the World* (w/Gustave Guitton) (4 vols.)
Jules Lermina. *Mysteryville; Panic in Paris; To-Ho and the Gold Destroyers; The Secret of Zippelius*
Jean-Marc & Randy Lofficier. *Edgar Allan Poe on Mars; The Katrina Protocol; Pacifica; Robonocchio; Tales of the Shadowmen 1-9*
Xavier Mauméjean. *The League of Heroes*
Joseph Méry. *The Tower of Destiny*
Hippolyte Mettais. *The Year 5865*
Louise Michel. *The Human Microbes; The New World*
José Moselli. *Illa's End*
John-Antoine Nau. *Enemy Force*
Marie Nizet. *Captain Vampire*
C. Nodier, A. Beraud & Toussaint-Merle. *Frankenstein*
Henri de Parville. *An Inhabitant of the Planet Mars*
Gaston de Pawlowski. *Journey to the Land of the 4th Dimension*
Georges Pellerin. *The World in 2000 Years*
Ernest Pérochon. *The Frenetic People*
Pierre Pelot. *The Child Who Walked on the Sky*
J. Polidori, C. Nodier, E. Scribe. *Lord Ruthven the Vampire*
P.-A. Ponson du Terrail. *The Vampire and the Devil's Son*
Henri de Régnier. *A Surfeit of Mirrors*
Maurice Renard. *The Blue Peril; Doctor Lerne; The Doctored Man; A Man Among the Microbes; The Master of Light*
Jean Richepin. *The Wing; The Crazy Corner*
Albert Robida. *The Adventures of Saturnin Farandoul; The Clock of the Centuries; Chalet in the Sky*
J.-H. Rosny Aîné. *Helgvor of the Blue River; The Givreuse Enigma; The Mysterious Force; The Navigators of Space; Vamireh; The World of the Variants; The Young Vampire*
Marcel Rouff. *Journey to the Inverted World*
Han Ryner. *The Superhumans*
Brian Stableford. *The New Faust at the Tragicomique; The Empire of the Necromancers (The Shadow of Frankenstein; Frankenstein and the Vampire Countess; Frankenstein in London); Sherlock Holmes & The Vampires of Eternity; The Stones of Camelot; The Wayward Muse.* (anthologist) *The Germans on Venus; News from the Moon; The Supreme Progress; The World Above the World; Nemoville; Investigations of the Future*
Jacques Spitz. *The Eye of Purgatory*
Kurt Steiner. *Ortog*
Eugène Thébault. *Radio-Terror*
C.-F. Tiphaigne de La Roche. *Amilec*

Théo Varlet. *The Golden Rock. The Xenobiotic Invasion; Timeslip Troopers* (w/André Blandin); *The Martian Epic* (w/Octave Joncquel)
Paul Vibert. *The Mysterious Fluid*
Villiers de l'Isle-Adam. *The Scaffold; The Vampire Soul*
Philippe Ward. *Artahe*
Philippe Ward & Sylvie Miller. *The Song of Montségur*

MYSTERIES & THRILLERS

M. Allain & P. Souvestre. *The Daughter of Fantômas*
A. Anicet-Bourgeois, Lucien Dabril. *Rocambole*
A. Bernède. *Belphegor; Judex* (w/Louis Feuillade)
A. Bisson & G. Livet. *Nick Carter vs. Fantômas*
V. Darlay & H. de Gorsse. *Lupin vs. Holmes: The Stage Play*
Paul Féval. *Gentlemen of the Night; John Devil; The Black Coats ('Salem Street; The Invisible Weapon; The Parisian Jungle; The Companions of the Treasure; Heart of Steel; The Cadet Gang; The Sword-Swallower)*
Emile Gaboriau. *Monsieur Lecoq*
Goron & Emile Gautier. *Spawn of the Penitentiary*
Steve Leadley. *Sherlock Holmes: The Circle of Blood*
Maurice Leblanc. *Arsène Lupin vs. Countess Cagliostro; Lupin vs. Holmes (The Blonde Phantom; The Hollow Needle); The Many Faces of Arsène Lupin*
Gaston Leroux. *Chéri-Bibi; The Phantom of the Opera; Rouletabille & the Mystery of the Yellow Room Rouletabille at Krupp's*
Richard Marsh. *The Complete Adventures of Judith Lee*
William Patrick Maynard. *The Terror of Fu Manchu; The Destiny of Fu Manchu*
Frank J. Morlock. *Sherlock Holmes: The Grand Horizontals; Sherlock Holmes vs Jack the Ripper*
Antonin Reschal. *The Adventures of Miss Boston*
P. de Wattyne & Y. Walter. *Sherlock Holmes vs. Fantômas*
David White. *Fantômas in America*

SCREENPLAYS

Mike Baron. *The Iron Triangle*
Emma Bull & Will Shetterly. *Nightspeeder; War for the Oaks*
Gerry Conway & Roy Thomas. *Doc Dynamo*
Steve Englehart. *Majorca*
James Hudnall. *The Devastator*
Jean-Marc & Randy Lofficier. *Royal Flush*
J.-M. & R. Lofficier & Marc Agapit. *Despair*
J.-M. & R. Lofficier & Joël Houssin. *City*
Andrew Paquette. *Peripheral Vision*
Robert L. Robinson, Jr. *Judex*
R. Thomas, J. Hendler & L. Sprague de Camp. *Rivers of Time*

NON-FICTION

Stephen R. Bissette. *Blur 1-5. Green Mountain Cinema 1; Teen Angels*
Win Scott Eckert. *Crossovers* (2 vols.)
Jean-Marc & Randy Lofficier. *Shadowmen* (2 vols.)
Randy Lofficier. *Over Here*

HEXAGON COMICS

Franco Frescura & Luciano Bernasconi. *Wampus*
Franco Frescura & Giorgio Trevisan. *CLASH*
L. Bernasconi, J.-M. Lofficier & Juan Roncagliolo Berger. *Phenix*
Claude Legrand, J.-M. Lofficier & L. Bernasconi. *Kabur*
Franco Oneta. *Zembla*
L. Buffolente, Lofficier & J.-J. Dzialowski. *Strangers: Homicron*
Danilo Grossi. *Strangers: Jaydee*
Claude Legrand & Luciano Bernasconi. *Strangers: Starlock*

ART BOOKS

Jean-Pierre Normand. *Science Fiction Illustrations*
Raven Okeefe. *Raven's L'il Critters; Rave's Faves*
Randy Lofficier & Raven Okeefe. *If Your Possum Go Daylight...*
Daniele Serra. *Illusions*

www.ingramcontent.com/pod-product-compliance
Lightning Source LLC
Chambersburg PA
CBHW030925020726
47498CB00001B/113